BETWEEN
TWO WORLDS

BETWEEN

TWO WORLDS

BETWEEN
TWO WORLDS

Upton Sinclair

The Viking Press · New York
1945

COPYRIGHT 1941 BY UPTON SINCLAIR

FIRST PUBLISHED IN MARCH 1941
SECOND PRINTING MARCH 1941
THIRD PRINTING MAY 1943
FOURTH PRINTING JULY 1944
FIFTH PRINTING MARCH 1945

PRINTED IN U. S. A. BY AMERICAN BOOK—STRATFORD PRESS

"Wandering between two worlds, one dead,
The other powerless to be born."

—MATTHEW ARNOLD

TO

my friends in England,

Mr. Werner Laurie,

Contents

BOOK ONE

We Are the Music-Makers

1

Peace Be within Thy Walls

I

WHEN one has been away from home for more than two years, and has seen Paris and London and New York, one's house may be found to have grown strangely smaller, its glamour turned to dinginess. Lanny Budd walked around the outside, noting how the sky-blue paint on the shutters had faded and what the malicious sea air had done to the hinges. Inside, the upholstery was soiled, the curtains drooped drearily, the piano was out of tune—in short, the place would have to be done over. Only van Gogh's sunrise and Monet's lilypond had their glories undiminished—*ars* instead of *aes perennis*.

Lanny, still in his twentieth year, had full authority and a bank account replenished; so as he strolled he meditated upon the various styles he had observed in his travels. Would he care to dwell in the presence of French splendor, such as he had grown used to in the Hotel Crillon and the Foreign Office on the Quai d'Orsay: huge gilded chandeliers, heavy tapestries, stucco cupids on the ceiling, silk upholstery on spindly chairs? Or would he prefer the austere fashion of his father's home in Connecticut, the woodwork painted white and the old furniture cut in straight lines without ornament? Would van Gogh and Monet look well against a paneling of dark wood in the dignified English fashion? Or should he be jolly and modern, and turn the drawing-room into a child's nursery with primary colors, a frieze of wild animals chasing one another, and draperies of eccentric designs put on by batik? His thoughts moved from one to another of the villas along this Côte d'Azur; he had been in scores of them—but mostly when he was younger, and his mind wasn't on interior decoration.

3

Midsummer of the year 1919, and Lanny had just witnessed the closing of the Peace Conference of Paris. He had cherished a dream to help remake Europe, and for six months had worked hard, and had made a mess of it—so he believed, and his friends agreed. Now he had taken on a simpler job—to fix up his mother's home and add a studio for a new member of their family. That, at least, one ought to be able to do without bungling! Lanny's mind, in sharp reaction from world politics, was set upon mastering the techniques of architecture, carpentry, masonry, interior decoration, and landscape gardening.

II

In one corner of this estate was a small building of stone. It stood on the edge of a grove of trees, facing the west, looking out over the blue and gold Mediterranean. It had only a couple of windows and got most of its light from a skylight on the north side. The building was less than five years old, but already it was haunted, and Lanny after two years' absence had waited a while before summoning the courage to go near it. When he unlocked and opened the door he stood for a few moments looking in, as if he thought the very dust on the floor ought not to be disturbed.

Nothing had been touched since that tragic day, a little more than a year ago, when Marcel Detaze had laid down his palette and brush, written a note to his wife, and stolen away to throw himself into the hell of war. Lanny hadn't been here, and hadn't thought it wise to question his mother about it; better if she forgot it quickly. But Lanny himself wasn't going to forget his stepfather.

He came slowly into the room, looking about. The easel had something on it, covered with a cloth. The palette was on the table, face up, the colors hard and dry. The painter's little blue cap, worn and faded, lay near; also a newspaper, with headlines telling of the last German rush on Paris. A ghostly voice was saying to Lanny: "You see—I had to go." A quiet voice, for Marcel had never had to argue with his stepson.

He was gone, France was saved, and here was the studio, the

shutters closed and fastened, the shade pulled over the skylight, and a year's drifting of dust which the mistral had forced through cracks of windows and doors. Lanny opened one of the shutters, creaking on its rusty hinges, and let in the bright sunlight of the Midi. He saw that Marcel had been reading a book on military strategy—an odd subject for a painter, but of course he had been trying to understand what was happening to *la patrie* and whether she needed the life of one of her sons, already crippled in her service.

Lanny raised the cloth from the easel. There was a crayon sketch which clutched him like a hand. It was the face of a peasant, and the youth knew him at once—an old truckman for one of the flower-growers here on the Cap d'Antibes; he had taught Lanny to drive a car. Marcel had the gift of line: the slightest stroke of his pencil, and something lived and moved. In these crayon lines you saw what weather had done to the face of a man. In the wrinkles around the eyes was sly humor, in the bristling mustaches the spirit of those forefathers who had marched all the way to Paris, dragging their cannon and singing: "To arms, to arms, ye brave!" Lanny took the sketch to the light to study its fine points. Again he heard the ghostly voice: "You see—I have left something of myself!"

In back of the studio was a storeroom, and the youth unlocked the door. Along the walls were racks which Beauty, his mother, had had built, sparing no expense in her futile effort to keep a French husband at home when *la patrie* was in danger. On these racks were canvases, each tacked on its wooden frame and overlaid with dust. The work of Marcel Detaze was not bid for in auction rooms, its prices were not the subject of gossip in the newspapers, so it hadn't been worth anyone's while to break into the place.

Lanny didn't need to take any of the canvases down. He knew which shelves held the war paintings, and which the landscapes of the Cap, which the fiords of Norway, which the Isles of Greece and the shores of Africa. Standing in that dim and dusty room, he experienced a return of the strange feeling which had stolen over him amid the ruins of ancient temples, with his stepfather telling about the lives of those long-vanished lovers of beauty. Now Marcel had gone to join them: were they meeting in some Greek limbo,

sharing the secrets of their techniques of painting—or perhaps fighting their battles over again? Marcel, who had stood at the second
battle of the Marne, could meet the heroes of Thermopylae on
equal terms. In Lanny's mind were many sentences from the book
of Greek epigrams which they had read amid the ruins. "In peace
sons bury their fathers; in war fathers bury their sons." Twenty-two
centuries had passed, and Lanny had seen it happening in France,
England, and America.

III

Over at the villa was another souvenir of Marcel, one which
Lanny was inspecting for the first time. Baby Marceline had about
as many months as Lanny had years, and like him she was a child
of the Midi; playing about in the patio, rolling on the grass in the
hot sunshine, with only a breechclout, and the rest of her brown
as a hazelnut. The old family dog had presented the household with
a litter of puppies, and Marceline toddled, and these raced after her,
falling over themselves and she falling over them. It made a charming picture, and how the father would have loved to sit and make
sketches of it! Once more Lanny thought, what a strange thing is
life—and how wasteful. Marcel had learned so much, and now he
was gone, and his daughter had to begin at the beginning and learn
to walk, picking herself up and starting again when she failed.

She had her mother's sweet and gentle features, and her mother's
natural gaiety; also, apparently, her mother's impulse wherever she
was to want to be somewhere else. Lanny found it interesting to
have a half-sister and to engage in child study. Quickly he realized
that Marceline perceived what he was doing, and enjoyed being
the center of attention. Did she get that from her mother? Lanny
decided to read a book and find out what was known about heredity.
Marceline had her father's odd combination of blond eyebrows and
darker hair; was she developing traces of his gentle melancholy?
When the puppies fell asleep and the child sat gazing before her,
what mysterious processes were going on in the budding soul?

Apparently she had no memory of the lovely blond being who

had brought her into the world and performed the feat, almost forgotten among fashionable ladies, of nourishing her at the breast. Six months had passed since Beauty had gone away, and what Baby Marceline depended on was a rosy peasant woman who was growing larger week by week and developing a soft brown mustache. It was Leese's firm faith that to be fat was the proper destiny of all female creatures. She fed the darling *petite* at all hours, and rocked her to sleep, and fondled and kissed her, and brought many relatives to do the same—all in violation of basic rules laid down by pediatricians. But it didn't worry Lanny, because he had had the same kind of upbringing, and the soft Provençal dialect had been as you might say his foster-mother tongue.

One thing troubled him, the fishpond with a little fountain which graced the center of the patio. Marceline would lie and watch the goldfish and try to catch them, and Leese insisted that she knew enough not to fall in—and, anyhow, the water wasn't deep. But Lanny would take no chance, and got a carpenter to make a little picket fence in sections hooked together; so the baby could watch the fish but not join them. The youth wrote his mother that all was well, and she might enjoy her third honeymoon with a good conscience. He smiled as he penned the words, for he had sojourned in New England and learned that people differed in matters of conscience; but he and Beauty had their private understandings.

IV

The mother wrote long letters. She and her lover had found a cottage on the rugged shore of the Bay of Biscay; a Basque woman came in to clean up for them, and they were living *la vie simple*, a charming adventure for complicated persons. For the first time, the mother had no interest in meeting the fashionable and important of the earth; there were reasons which were never mentioned in her carefully guarded letters. The war censorship of mail was supposed to be at an end, but you could never be sure.

For the third time in her life Mabel Blackless, alias Beauty Budd, alias Madame Detaze, *veuve*, had taken the difficult role of everything in the world to a man. She was trying to be family, friends, country—plus the whole German army. She had to make her lover forget defeat and shame, poverty and ruin. In this role she was one among millions; for Europe was full of men whose lives had been shattered and disorganized, and of women trying to comfort them and help them back to normality. Don't scold them, don't nag them; don't be shocked by anything they do or say! Understand that they have been living in hell, their lungs are impregnated with fumes of that region—only be glad it isn't mustard or chlorine gas. Let them do anything they please with you and pretend that you like it; tell them anything they want to believe; sing them to sleep, and when they have nightmares wake them and soothe them like sick children. Feed them, play with them, and count it a triumph if now and then you get them to laugh.

Spain had got rich out of the war, and her leisure classes were flocking to their northern coast; it was like winter on the Riviera in old days. There were many Germans, both traders and officials, and any one of them might recognize Kurt Meissner. Beauty referred to this possibility, using her code which Lanny understood. Kurt was "our friend," and the Germans were "his old associates." A censor would have thought it was a burglar she was trying to reform, or at least a drunkard. "I want our friend to break off permanently. Help me to persuade him that he has done his full duty, and should forget the past."

Lanny, eager to oblige, would compose joyous letters about the life of art, and his friend's genius, and the happiness they were all going to enjoy. Originally it had been the younger man's idea to build a new studio as a surprise for both his mother and her lover; some day they would drive up to the gate of Bienvenu, and Lanny would take them to the new building, and hear their cries of pleasure. But now he decided that this was risky. Kurt might make up his mind to return to his own land, to help rebuild it, or to get ready for another war—who could guess what impulse might seize a Prussian artillery officer, one month after the treaty of Versailles had been rammed down his country's throat?

So the subtle Lanny Budd revealed what he was doing; a delightful adventure, constructing a studio for the composing of music that was to bring back the days of Bach and Brahms and restore the prestige of the Teutonic race in the noblest field of human activity. The masons were laying the firm foundation, and Lanny gave a sketch of the groundplan. The work was being done by those relatives of Leese who hadn't been killed or crippled in the war, and Lanny told whimsical stories about workingmen of the Midi, class-conscious and inclined to be suspicious, but opening up like flowers when you chatted with them, and especially when you tried to help on the job and let them laugh at your blunders. The artist in them was touched when it was revealed that a musician was to live here and compose; a Swiss gentleman, he was being called.

Lanny knew that Kurt was among the millions of unemployed men; for the German army had been cut to almost nothing, and Kurt's family couldn't have saved much from the ruins of war. So Lanny expounded his dream of being a young Lorenzo dei Medici and gathering around him a noble company of worthy artists. "My father gives me some money," he wrote. "I haven't earned it—and maybe he hasn't either!" Since Lanny had been meeting Socialists and other unorthodox persons at the Peace Conference, his mind was full of their dangerous phrases. "What better use can I make of money than to help men who have the gifts that I lack? My father wants me to spend it to make myself happy, and if it makes me happy to help my friends, and my mother's friends, why shouldn't I have that pleasure?"

Be careful of every word, Lanny! Kurt Meissner, in spite of his notion that he is a modern man and artist, has the instincts of a German aristocrat, and how can he face the thought of being supported by a woman, especially by the one he loves? The English have a name for a man like that, and Kurt has no mind to carry it. When Kurt writes this, Lanny has to be deeply hurt, and to argue for his mother's right to be happy too. Lanny's money is his, not his mother's, and it may be a loan if Kurt insists—every franc of it carefully recorded, so that a great musician can repay it out of the proceeds of future performances, or royalties, or salary as a conductor, whatever it may be. There is precedent enough in the lives of musicians—for the borrowing if not for the repaying!

V

The painters came and started on the outside trim of the villa. The paperhangers were working inside the drawing-room. The upholsterers took away the furniture, to do it over with soft brown cloth that would wear. The background was to be a wallpaper of cream color with an unobtrusive pattern, Lanny having decided that this would be in keeping with the austere spirit of his friend and the domestic intentions of his reformed mother.

A man came and tuned the piano; and Lanny lived again in that music to which his fancy had turned during the past couple of years, whenever life had become too complicated. A translator-secretary at a peace conference had been powerless to restrain Italians from seizing Yugoslav territory, or Turks from slaughtering Armenians; but when he sat down at the piano he was his own master, and if he didn't like the way a composer achieved his modulations he could change them. Lanny's fingers had lost some of their speed while preparing reports on the distribution of Europe's populations; but when fingers are not yet twenty years old they limber up quickly, and Lanny soon had the freedom of that garden of delights in which he planned to spend the rest of his days.

At the driveway entrance of Bienvenu were a pair of heavy gates which you could lock if you wished. At the entrance to the footpath was a light wooden door with a tall aloe, now in blossom, on either side, and a bell which you had to ring. Inside were palms and bananas, a cascade of purple bougainvillaea, the scent of narcissus and the murmur of bees; there were beauty and peace, and Lanny meant that there should be friendship and love. Good-by, proud world, I'm going home! So he had said, the day the unsatisfactory treaty had been signed. Every month Robbie Budd sent Beauty a check for a thousand dollars, and from now on Lanny was to have three hundred. Besides that, he had a thousand which he had earned his very self, and of which he was unduly proud. It was mixed up with the rest in his bank account at Cannes, but in his mind he saw it separately, a series of checks signed by the disbursing officer of the State Department of the United States.

He wanted to spend these sums to make a little happiness and order in the world. He would get a few friends around him, persons who loved the arts and were content to live with them. The fact that his mother had fallen in love with one of his best friends was an odd circumstance which would help to close the little circle. It would solve the problem of a German army officer's broken life, and at the same time would keep Beauty out of the clutches of those many fashionable persons who abused her hospitality and won her money at bridge. While Lanny wrestled with the intricacies of a Bach fugue he told himself that Kurt's serious disposition would reform him as well as his mother, and keep him from futile love affairs and other escapades that he wanted to put behind him.

VI

The carpenters were working on the new studio. The framework had magically arisen—one large room with a small bedroom and bath in the rear. Lanny would watch the work and amuse himself trying to help; then he would go and practice sight-reading for a while. When he felt the need of companionship, he would phone to Jerry Pendleton to come over for a swim, or perhaps go torch-fishing at night. They would sit in the boat on the still water and recall the Austrian submarine that had risen in the sea close beside them. The ex-tutor and veteran of the Meuse-Argonne was in much the same mood as his former pupil; he too had wanted to get away from it all—and what an unusual sort of refuge he had found for himself in the Pension Flavin in Cannes!

He had married the French nation, so he told Lanny: the sweet and gentle Cerise, the mother who owned half the pension, the aunt who owned the other half and helped to run it, and the boarders, who in this hot midsummer season were not tourists but respectable French permanents employed in banks or other offices, and who considered themselves as members of the family, entitled to be concerned with its affairs. Jerry had to have some American to whom he could unbosom himself, and as Lanny had lived most of his life in France, he was able to explain matters and clear up misunderstandings. Another peace conference!

French women of the middle class are apt to be frugal, and when they are in business they have to be if they are to survive. And here was a son-in-law who presented them with a complicated problem. An upstanding, capable young American, he had plunged into a fiery furnace and helped to rescue *la patrie*. American soldiers enjoyed enormous prestige among the French in those days; they had come as semi-divine beings, several inches taller than the average *poilu*, accoutered and equipped like no troops ever seen in Europe, and laughing, insolent, ready to make a lark even out of a plunge into a furnace. "*Ah, comme ils sont beaux!*" the mademoiselles had cried with one voice.

Lieutenant Jerry Pendleton, handsome and red-headed, was now a husband with responsibilities; but what was he to do about them? He had no money, and there was no work to be had in Cannes. Thousands of Frenchmen coming back from the war, all looking for jobs; and no tourists in summertime, no certainty that there would be any in winter. Jerry was willing to go to work with his hands, *à l'américaine*, but that was unthinkable in France; he must have a white-collar job, and uphold the dignity and prestige of a pension which catered to the most respectable bourgeois. The two anxious ladies fed him, and withheld any word that would remind him of his humiliating position. His father owned a couple of drug-stores in a far-off region of cyclones called Kansas, and if Jerry's dignity was affronted, he might order his wife to pack up and follow him across the seas—thus depriving the two ladies of their hopes, one for a grandson and the other for a grandnephew.

A happy solution *ad interim*—Jerry would go fishing, taking a basket and bringing back specimens of the many strange creatures that swarm along the rocky Mediterranean shore: *mérou*, and *mostele*, the long green moray, the gray *langouste* in his hard shell, cuttlefish large or small, each with his own ink to be cooked in. This pleased the palates of all the guests, and at the same time was entirely respectable, being *le sport*. The son-in-law went with a friend who owned a sailboat, and lived in an elegant villa on the Cap, and associated with the wealthiest and most distinguished persons. While Jerry entertained his friend with stories about the boarders, the widow ladies fed the boarders upon details of a new studio at Bienvenu, the redecorating of the villa, and the sad case of Madame Detaze, whose husband had given his life for *la patrie*, and who was now spending her period of mourning in Spain.

VII

In a corner of the garage at Bienvenu were piled some forty wooden cases which had come by steamer from Connecticut to Marseille, containing the library willed by Great-Great-Uncle Eli Budd to Lanny. The youth summoned his courage and took a carpenter to Marcel's studio and set him to lining the walls with shelves. Lanny was taking this place for his own, being certain that if anywhere in the limbo of good souls Marcel was watching, he would approve that course. The studio meant more to Lanny than to anybody else, not even excepting Beauty. She had loved Marcel's paintings because they were his, but Lanny had loved them because they were works of art, and Marcel had understood this difference and made jokes about it in his fashion half gay and half sad.

After the shelves were stained and dried, Lanny had the cases brought down a few at a time, and Jerry came to help him unpack. The ex-lieutenant was no scholar, in spite of having been nearly through college; but he was impressed by the physical bulk of two thousand volumes and by Lanny's firm declaration that he intended to read them all. The old Unitarian minister had been even more learned than his heir had realized, for here was a pretty complete collection of the best books of the world in half a dozen languages: not much theology, but a great deal of philosophy, history, and biography, and a little of every sort of *belles-lettres*. Only the Latin and Greek were hopeless, Lanny decided. He had French and German, and could brush up his Italian, and soon learn Spanish, which Beauty and Kurt were now studying.

The classifying of so many books was quite a job. They moved armloads to one shelf, and then decided they had made a mistake and moved them to another. Presently there came another assistant —M. Rochambeau, the elderly Swiss diplomat who was spending his declining years in this village of Juan-les-Pins. He lived in a little apartment with a niece, and found it lonely during the summer season. He had known Marcel and admired his paintings before the war, and had stood by him in those dreadful days when the painter had been brought back from battle with his mutilated face covered by a silk mask. A man of reading and taste, M. Rochambeau could tell about these books, and where the doubtful ones should be placed. He would become excited by the contents of this one or that, and Lanny would tell him to take it home and read it.

The friends would leave, and evening fall; Lanny would stroll down to the studio and sit inside, with the pale moonlight streaming in at the door. The place now had two ghosts to haunt it. Lanny would introduce the ghost of Marcel to the ghost of his great-great-uncle and please himself with the fancy that this introduction was taking effect in the limbo where they now resided. Lanny listened to their cultured conversation, which began, naturally, with Greek art and civilization; for the youth had told Eli how the yacht *Blue-bird* had taken him and Marcel to the Isles of Greece, and how they had stood among the ruined temples and Marcel had read aloud out of the anthology. Lanny had written Marcel about Eli's comments; so the two ghosts were no strangers, but exchanged freely their deepest sentiments. The young ghost, who had arrived first in this limbo, made the old ghost welcome. "Upon that far shore I wait for thee, O Callimachus, and prepare for thee a banquet worthy of thy noble deeds."

VIII

So passed the rest of the summer. The workingmen labored steadily, and the villa shone like new, and the studio approached completion. Lanny had written Kurt to inquire what sort of interior decoration might be appropriate to the music of Bach and Brahms; Kurt had tactfully expressed approval of Lanny's taste, so the studio was being done uniform with the villa. Step by step Lanny sought to lure his friend on. "That thousand dollars which I earned trying to make a just peace I want to spend for the best piano that can be found in Paris, and I want you to select it so I can be sure it really is the best."

But seducing Kurt was no simple task. Beauty's letters would reveal that the haughty one was brooding over his country's fate, and thinking of Brazil or the Argentine, where Germans were still able to earn a living without British or American permission. Lanny would have to go deeply into the psychology of vanquished artillery officers, aspiring musical geniuses, and lovers dependent upon their ladies. The money of Beauty and her son had come out of guns and ammunition used to blast the hopes of the Fatherland; how now could Kurt endure to live upon it? Lanny would make tactful references to the moral problems of a munitions manufacturer and his son. "My father refuses to let his own conscience be troubled, but he can't help knowing that mine is. It pleases him when he can give me money, because then he doesn't have to think of me as sitting aloof and condemning him in my mind. You and I can't change what has happened, Kurt; but if you believe in music and in your own gifts, why shouldn't you turn some of our money into beauty and kindness?"

Kurt of course would share these letters with his companion, and she would report to Lanny what effect they were producing. Having spent more than half her thirty-eight years managing recalcitrant men, Beauty possessed a store of wisdom. She wouldn't plead too much, and never find fault, but just make love the loveliest thing in Spain. She would reveal her own weakness and the need of a man's moral strength. She would gently refer to Lanny's needs; he was a good boy, but so easily influenced, and with a tendency to wander from one art to the next. He needed some older and steadier person to help him concentrate. For such a service many a rich man would be glad to pay, but couldn't buy it at any price. So many tutors Lanny had had, of German and Italian, of piano and dancing and the study of the encyclopedia. The least competent of them had received more than it would cost for Kurt to stay at Bienvenu.

What Kurt did for Lanny's mother would be purely incidental—and surely the dullest person who came to the home would know that!

So at last the young officer's scruples were broken down, and he wrote his parents in Schloss Stubendorf—now a part of Poland, thanks to the evil treaty—to ship him the music and the instruments which he had collected. Kurt told them that he was to be the teacher of that American boy who had been the family's guest nearly six years ago. Since the boy's mother hadn't been a guest, it was not necessary to tell about her. Kurt hoped that his parents would forgive him for living in France; he would have nothing to do with that hateful people, but would live a retired life inside the Budd estate and go on with his serious labors as at home before the war.

IX

Lanny's twentieth birthday came, and the adoring mother was sad because she wasn't with him; her conscience pricked her, and she wrote a letter full of apologies and of advice which she herself had not always put to use. Not for the first time, nor for the last, her pen turned to the subject of love, and the women who would be after her precious one, and his need of caution in such matters. So many cunning creatures hunting him with deadly arts, impossible to resist!

It went without saying that no woman could really be worthy of Lanny Budd in the estimation of his mother; least of all these modern chits, these shallow ones, bold and froward products of the war, which Beauty thought of as a universal plague that had poisoned the world. She had watched them in Paris during the Peace Conference, and reported them ravenous for pleasure, for sensation; knowing no restraint, no loyalty; greedy for attention, for worldly success— "golddiggers" was the new name for them, and a woman of the old days contemplated them with a horror which was rather comical when you recalled how far she herself had been from a model of discretion.

Perhaps it was Beauty Budd's sins returning to torment her—a not uncommon phenomenon of the moral life. While Kurt worked at his music, Beauty would sit upon the shore of the Bay of Biscay, and before her mind's eye would arise an image of a youth slender, graceful, with brown eyes forever a-shine with the expectation of new delights; with wavy brown hair worn long according to the fashion, and having a tendency to drop over into his eyes; a smile quick yet gentle, a heart kind as a girl's. Lanny, back there in Bienvenu, was nearing the age at which his father, traveling in Paris, had met an artists' model even younger than himself. Beauty knew exactly what had befallen that youth, for she had planned it; even in the moments when her heart had seemed to be hitting hard blows under her throat, she had known what she was doing, and why, and how. Women always know, and whatever happens is their fault—so Beauty insisted!

But she had really loved Robbie Budd; not merely his money or his position as the son of an old and proud New England family. She had proved it when the cruel test came, when by a little effort she might have married him and caused him to break with his stern old father. Where would you find a woman today who would make such a sacrifice? Was Lanny going to meet one on that Coast of Pleasure, where already the roulette wheels were beginning to spin and the colored bands to thump and screech? When Lanny in his letters mentioned the sloe-eyed demoiselle in the pension, the jeweler's daughter who wore too many of her father's wares; when he referred to the American females who had come down from Paris to lie in the sand and forget the war that had been won and the peace that had been lost—and how they drank too much and drove motor-cars crazily—yes, Beauty knew them, she had attended the after-midnight parties and knew what the pleasure-hungry creatures might be doing to her darling, her precocious, her incomparable son! "Remember, Lanny," warned the birthday letter, "the more attractive you make Bienvenu, the more eager some woman will be to get in there before I do." Lanny chuckled; he could have named a woman, several in fact; but he couldn't fail to be amused when his flighty mother turned Puritan—a joke which he and his father had shared on many an occasion.

X

Lanny would go back to his music. He had learned a lot of Bach by heart, thus paying tribute to Kurt's taste. Also he derived pleasure from the swiftly falling notes of Debussy's *Gardens in the Rain*, but wasn't sure if Kurt would permit himself to approve any French music. He enjoyed the strange fantasies of Moussorgsky's *Pictures at an Exposition;* having visited one exposition with Kurt, and others with his English friend Rick and with his stepfather, Lanny took all these friends with him to this odd Russian exposition. Ordinarily he didn't care for "program music," but when it was humorous and full of quaint turns, his curiosity was aroused and he wished that the pictures had come with the score.

Baby Marceline had solved the problems of equipoise, and was able to walk and even to run without stumbling. She would stand in the doorway while Lanny played, and presently, watching her, he saw that she was swaying to the rhythm. He played a simple tune with a strong accent, and her steps began to move to it; he decided then that she should discover the art of the dance all by herself. A new department of child study; it went on for weeks, while the tiny feet tottered here and there and the laughing brown eyes shone with the delight of adventure. Suddenly she began to display marvelous improvement, and Lanny was about to write his mother that they had a terpsichorean prodigy, when he learned that Leese had unwittingly spoiled a scientific experiment by taking the little one's two hands and dancing with her out in the patio. After that Lanny would put a record on the phonograph, and Baby Marceline began a full course in the eurythmics of Jaques-Dalcroze, with variations according to the free expressionism of Isadora Duncan.

There was hardly a spot in or about Bienvenu where Lanny hadn't danced. The loggia in front of the home was smooth, and Beauty had had *al fresco* parties here, and musicians had come from Cannes, and the fashionable ladies and gentlemen had taken the good the gods provided them. First it had been the waltz, and later the Argentine tango, and then crazy inventions from New York. To that loggia had come M. Pinjon, the gigolo with whom Lanny had struck up an acquaintance in Nice; he had brought his piccolo flute, and played it while he danced the farandole. That poor fellow had lost one leg in the war, and was now back with his peasant father, and on the table in the drawing-room was a little dancing man carved in wood which he had sent to his friend in the *grand monde*.

By that old piano in the drawing-room Lanny had learned old dances such as the minuet and the polonaise, and had teased his mother and some of her friends to practice with him. Here too he had danced "Dalcroze" with Kurt when the two boys had come from Hellerau. In the sad days after the outbreak of the war, when Marcel had been called to the army, Lanny had made dancing with his mother a part of their day's regimen, to keep up her spirits and keep down her *embonpoint*. There were few of those phonograph records which hadn't such memories bound up in them.

Now Lanny was beginning a new dancing life with this half-sister, this tiny mite of budding fun, this box of stored miracles. Her laughter was like bubbles from champagne when you pull the cork. Her feet were all motion, whether they were on the ground or waving in the air. Her large brown eyes watched Lanny, and her arms and legs tried to imitate what he did. If he moved slowly and repeated the motion often, she would follow him, and he was proud when he had taught her the Dalcroze motions for three-part time and four-part time. He wrote Beauty, who had learned all this from him, and was learning more of it from Kurt—for the monster of *embonpoint* was stalking her in Spain!

The Dalcroze school in Germany had been closed during the war, and the tall white temple on the bright meadow had been turned into a factory for the manufacturing of poison gas. But the seeds of joy and beauty had been scattered widely, and here were two households, one on the Riviera and the other on the Bay of Biscay, where the lovely art of eurythmics was being kept alive. There was another on the River Thames, because Lanny wrote to Rick, the English friend who had been with him and Kurt at the school. Poor Rick was a cripple and would never dance again, but he and Nina had a little boy, not much older than Marceline, and Lanny wrote about his experiments in child training and Nina promised to repeat them.

XI

Lanny thought continually about those two boyhood friends who had fought each other in the war, and whom he was resolved to bring together again. He didn't mention this to Kurt; he just forwarded Rick's letters to Beauty, knowing that she would read them aloud. Lanny's idea was to get Kurt settled in the new studio, with the new piano and all his other instruments and his music scores; then, after things were going well, Rick and his little family would come for a visit and perhaps find a villa or bungalow near by. The three musketeers of the arts would talk about the really important things of life, carefully avoiding world politics and other forms of rascality.

Such was Lanny's plan. He remembered Newcastle, Connecticut, and his stern old Puritan grandfather who manufactured machine guns and ammunition and conducted a Sunday morning Bible class. On the Sunday after the Armistice he had expounded a text from the hundred and twenty-second Psalm: "Peace be within thy walls, and prosperity within thy palaces." The grandson learned that one of the carpenters working on the place was a skilled wood-carver, and he brought this man into the drawing-room and had him cut the first half of this text in old English letters on the thick edge of the heavy mantel.

After the work was done, Lanny happened to read one of his great-great-uncle's books on ancient Greece, and learned that the poet Aristophanes had said "Euphemia 'sto," which is "Peace be here," or "Peace to this house." It was one point on which the Greek and the Hebrew spirits had met; it was a longing in the hearts of all decent people the world over. But Lanny had derived from his six months' adventure in diplomacy the conviction that the decent people were still a long way from getting what they wanted. The best that anyone could do for the present was to build him a not too costly home in some part of the earth where there was no gold, oil, coal, or other mineral treasure, and which was not near a disputed boundary or strategic configuration of land or water. There with reasonable luck he might have peace within his own walls, and perhaps think some thoughts which might be helpful to a hate-tormented world.

2

Kennst Du das Land?

I

THE "season" was coming once more to the Riviera; and all over Europe and the Americas individuals and families were realizing that it was possible once again to get passports and to travel freely, *en prince* if you had the price. Swedish lumber merchants and Norwegian operators of whaling fleets, Dutch traders in coffee and rubber and tin, Swiss holders of electrical shares, British owners of coal and iron mines, French masters of munitions plants which had magically escaped bombing through a devastating war—such lucky persons now heard at the family breakfast table laments about damp fogs and icy gales, and were reminded of a land where the lemon trees bloom, in the dark arbors the golden oranges glow, a soft wind is wafted from the blue heaven, the myrtle stands still and the laurel high—*kennst du es wohl?*

So once more the white yachts began to appear off the little harbors of Cannes and Nice, and the long blue express trains from Paris were crowded with passengers. Perhaps half of them were Americans, who for five years and more had been reading about Europe twice every day, but had been denied their customary cultural holidays. Now again there were luxurious steamers, and no submarines to challenge their crossing. Tourists took sight-seeing busses to the war zones, visiting those towns whose names had become historic, even though they were mispronounced. Sight-seers roamed over battle-fields whose dreadful smells had not yet been washed away. They peered into blasted trenches with human hands and booted feet sticking out of the debris. They gathered trench helmets and shell cases to be taken home and used as book-ends or umbrella-stands.

21

And when these thrills began to pall, there was the Côte d'Azur, the beautiful, the romantic, unscarred by war; its rocky shores and cliffs and winding valleys, its ever-blue sea and ever-shining sun. Here you wore sport clothes and strolled on fashionable promenades, staring at great personages about whom you had read in the news-papers: kings and their mistresses, Asiatic potentates and their boys, Russian grand dukes escaped from the Bolsheviks, and a miscellany of statesmen and prizefighters, journalists and jockeys, masters of industry and stars of stage and screen. In the evening you could put on your finery and rub elbows with these celebrated ones in the gambling casinos, and even hope to pick up acquaintance with them in the so-called American bars.

This latter institution had moved into what promised to be per-manent exile; for at home a strange new phenomenon had developed out of the war, a throw-back to old-time Puritanism. It had begun as a war measure, to save foodstuffs, and now was being riveted upon the country by means of a constitutional amendment that could never be repealed, so everybody said. As the awful reality of Pro-hibition dawned upon the pleasure-seeking classes, they had but one impulse, to purchase steamer tickets for the land of wine, women, and song. When the steamer had passed the three-mile limit off Sandy Hook the corks began to pop and the joy to flow, and first-class passengers swore solemn oaths that never, never would they return to the land of the Pilgrims' pride. How often they said it made little difference, because they had forgotten it all next morning.

II

Of course not all the visitors to the Riviera were like that. People of cultivated taste came to enjoy the warm climate and lovely scen-ery. Up in the hills behind Cannes were villas belonging to English and Americans who came regularly each winter and lived decorous lives. Among these was Mrs. Emily Chattersworth, who had turned her estate into a home for the re-education of French *mutilés*. Mar-cel had gone up there and entertained them by making sketches on a blackboard, and after Lanny's return to Bienvenu one of his first duties had been to pay these poor fellows a call. He was interested in their progress, and also he wanted to see the portrait which Marcel had made of Mrs. Emily.

It had a central position in the drawing-room of Sept Chênes, and showed a tall and stately lady, with entirely white hair, standing by a small table which you could see in this room. So she had stood in the early days of the war, when she had called the American residents together and urged them to active succor of the refugees and the wounded. The face in the portrait was grave, not to say stern, and the pose and feeling of the picture were so real that the lips seemed about to open and say, as Lanny had heard them say more than once: "My friends, we have accepted the hospitality of France, and if there is such a thing as gratitude in the world, we owe it now to her people." To Lanny it was as if he heard also the voice of Marcel declaring the debt that *la patrie* was paying to the chatelaine by the agency of his fine portrait.

A year had passed since victory had been secured, and the hostess could feel that she had done her duty. The crippled men who had learned new trades were sent back to their homes, and those whose cases were hopeless were placed in government care. Sept Chênes, like Bienvenu, was done over, and the owner came to spend the winter. When Lanny heard of it he went to call, and told the great lady how much he thought of the portrait, and she in turn told him how the reputation of Marcel Detaze was spreading among art lovers. "What are you going to do with all those beautiful paintings, Lanny?"

He answered that his mother was intending to arrange for an exhibition as soon as she returned; and this brought up a subject by which their friend's mind was deeply intrigued. "What on earth is Beauty doing in Spain?"

The young man hadn't been a budding diplomat for six months to no purpose. He was prepared for the question, and smiled lightly. "She'll be home soon, and will tell you about it."

"You mean you're *not* going to tell me?"

Lanny kept on smiling. "I think she wants to have the fun."

"But what on earth? Is it something sensational?"

"Why should you think that?"

He had learned a lot about the feminine soul, and one thing was its intense preoccupation with matters of the heart. Here was this stately lady, almost sixty—he knew it to the day because her mother had once told him she had been born in Baltimore to the tramping of the Sixth Massachusetts Regiment, marching to the American Civil War. In fifty-eight and three-quarter years the infant Emily Sibley had become what the French call a *grande dame;* presiding over a *salon* and matching wits with the keenest minds in France. She had cultivated an impressive manner, she dressed with studied care, and provided for herself a semi-royal background; but here she was possessed by an itch of curiosity, revealing to Lanny the soul of a child who simply couldn't endure to be kept in the dark about what had happened to her intimate friend Mabel Blackless, alias Beauty Budd, alias Madame Detaze, *veuve.*

Lanny told her about Baby Marceline and his own researches into the development of the musical sense in infants. He told about Robbie Budd, and the progress of his oil venture in southern Arabia. This involved the fate of Emir Feisal, that dark-skinned replica of Christ whom Lanny had met at Mrs. Emily's town house during the Peace Conference. The young Emir was again in Paris, pleading to be allowed to rule his native land; his friend Lawrence had gone into hiding, for shame at the breach of trust. Mrs. Emily ought to have been deeply interested in them both; but instead she broke in: "Tell me the truth, Lanny—has Beauty married again?"

He had to resume his gay smile. "There's a reason why she wants to tell you herself, and when you hear it you'll understand."

"Such a woman! Such a woman! I never know what to expect of her."

"Well, at least she doesn't bore you," replied Lanny, his smile widening to a grin. Many others did, he knew.

III

With the coming of cold weather, Beauty and Kurt had motored to the Mediterranean coast of Spain. Beauty had been away from her baby and her home a full year, and couldn't stand it much longer. She was still afraid to bring Kurt into France; but she got him comfortably settled in another cottage, this time with a Catalan woman to do his cooking and cleaning up. Then she sent a wire to Lanny and took a train for Cannes.

Stepping from that train she looked just as lovely as on the first day that Lanny could remember. In the sunshine her hair still had glints of gold, and it wasn't gilt. She wore a light gray traveling dress and a little hat like a flower-basket turned upside down. When the youth had seen her last she had grown slender because she was too badly frightened to eat; but now her natural gaiety had come back, and all her colors—also that torment of womankind which you politely called "plumpness." Lanny would have to start scolding her again, and keep the cream pitcher on his own side of the table.

Beauty saw that both her offspring were brown and well; the baby shy, and not pleased to have a stranger seize her and cover her with kisses. To call her "*Maman*" awakened no memories and gave no pleasure. The mother was anxious; had she lost the affection of her darling forever? Lanny told her to chase the puppies around the patio, and she and the baby would be friends in half an hour; and so it proved.

Beauty inspected the new architecture and interior decoration and gave it her approval. A lovelier home could not be desired: when would she be able to live in it? She hadn't been able to write about her anxieties, and now she poured them out. Should she risk bringing Kurt here? Or should she take him to New York or some other remote place until his record had been forgotten?

They shut themselves up in her boudoir for a long conference. Lanny, manlike, was disposed to minimize the danger. The war was over; the intelligence department of the French army must have been demobilized along with the rest; there wouldn't be so many agents seeking for men who traveled on false passports, and if one were caught it would be a matter for criminal, not military, law. Officials could be reached by influence, or, in the last extreme, by money.

"But what about Leese?" argued the mother. "She's bound to recognize Kurt, and she knows that he's German."

"I've fixed that all up," said the worldly-wise youth. "I told her I was building the new studio for my friend the Swiss boy who had visited us before the war. Did she remember Kurt? She said she had thought he was a German. I explained that he came from the German part of Switzerland. *La Suisse* and *la Silésie* don't sound very different to her, and she has got the new idea well fixed in her mind."

Lanny went on to tell about Emily Chattersworth and the curiosity that was troubling her so greatly. She also had met Kurt, so it would be necessary to make a confidante of her. Lanny drove his mother to Sept Chênes, and left the pair together, while he sat out in the sunshine on the piazza, reading a novel he had chosen from his new library, Hawthorne's *Blithedale Romance,* which his great-great-uncle had talked about. A fervor for social perfection had seized upon the young idealists of New England before the Civil War, and they had tried living in a colony. It hadn't worked, but it was fun, at any rate in a book. Lanny would read for a while, and then stop and wonder how Mrs. Emily was taking the still stranger romance which she was hearing from the lips of its heroine.

IV

"This much I have guessed," the mistress of Sept Chênes was saying. "It's a man!"

"I seem to be built that way," replied Beauty, sorrowfully. "Honestly, Emily, I hadn't the remotest idea it could happen to me again. I thought I was going to spend the rest of my life grieving for Marcel. But men have suffered so dreadfully in this war——"

"And you met one who couldn't live without you?" There was mischief in the eyes of the *salonnière*.

"Don't tease me, Emily. It's a tragic story, and you'll see how helpless I was. But first you have to swear on your knees that you won't breathe a word of it to anyone; you must really mean that, because it might be a matter of life and death—to say nothing of a perfectly frightful scandal. The man was a German agent."

"Oh, *mon dieu!*" exclaimed the other.

"I need your friendship as I never did before. Maybe you will decide not to have anything to do with me, but at least you will keep my secret until I release you."

"You have my word," said the older woman.

"You remember the summer that Lanny was in Hellerau, before the war. One of the boys he met there was a German named Kurt Meissner; his father is what they call the comptroller-general of a great estate, Schloss Stubendorf, in Upper Silesia, which is now a part of Poland. I don't know if you will recall that Lanny went to spend Christmas with that family."

"I believe I do," replied Emily, and added: "You've been robbing the cradle?"

"No—you may say I've been robbing the grave."

"Well, I knew it would be something unusual. Go on."

"This boy was older than Lanny, and had a great influence over him. He was serious and hard-working, in the German fashion. He was studying to become a composer of music, and he had all the different instruments and was learning to play them. He was a moral boy, and Lanny looked up to him as being a sort of inspired character, and always talked about trying to be as good as Kurt, and so on. They kept exchanging letters, and Lanny let me read them, so I knew him quite well."

"And you were falling in love with him?"

"I never thought of any man but Marcel. Kurt was Lanny's friend and I thought he was helping Lanny to be a good boy, and I used to hold him up as an example. Then the war came, and Kurt became an officer in the German army. He and Lanny kept in touch, because Lanny had a friend in Holland and Kurt had one in Switzerland who forwarded letters for them. After the Armistice, when Lanny and I met in Paris, he was unhappy because he hadn't got word from Kurt, and thought he must have been killed in the last fighting, like Marcel. Lanny wrote to Kurt's father in Stubendorf, but no answer came. He went on worrying half-way through the Peace Conference; and then one day, walking on the Rue de la Paix, he saw his friend riding in a taxi."

"A German officer?"

"In civilian clothes. Lanny knew he must be there on a forged passport. He followed him and made himself known. Kurt tried not to recognize him, but finally admitted what he was doing. Of course it would have meant shooting if he had been caught. Lanny didn't tell me, he didn't tell anyone; he just went on doing his work at the Crillon, and keeping that secret locked in his heart."

"How perfectly awful, Beauty!"

"That went on until late one night Kurt got word to Lanny that the French police had raided the headquarters of the group for which Kurt was working. The poor fellow had been walking the streets for twenty-four hours before he called Lanny; and they went on walking on a rainy winter night while Lanny tried to think of some place to take him. He thought of you—but you had so many servants, they decided you couldn't hide anyone. They thought of my brother Jesse, who is some sort of Red, as you know; but the police were watching Jesse—this was right after Clemenceau had been shot. When Kurt was about exhausted, Lanny decided there was nothing to do but bring him to my hotel. After midnight I heard a tap on my door, and there were the pair of them, and what could I do?"

"You mean you kept that man in your apartment?"

"If I had sent him out on the street, it would have been to certain death; and I had seen so much killing. I thought the war was over, and we were supposed to be making peace."

"What was he doing in Paris, Beauty?"

"He was trying to influence French and Allied opinion for the lifting of the blockade against Germany. You remember how it was —we were so indignant about the starving of German women and children."

"But what could a German agent do along that line?"

"He had large sums of money at his disposal. He won't talk about it, but from hints I have picked up I gather that he accomplished a good deal. He managed to meet some influential people. Don't you begin to guess anything, Emily?"

Mrs. Chattersworth had been listening to the troubles of a harum-scarum friend; it hadn't dawned on her that they might have anything to do with herself. But now suddenly a bolt of lightning flashed in her mind. "Beauty Budd! That Swiss musician?"

"Yes, Emily," said the anxious culprit. "That Swiss musician was Kurt Meissner."

V

The time had come to which Lanny's mother had been looking forward over a period of six months. Sooner or later she was going to have to make a clean breast of these matters to Emily, and with forebodings in her heart she had rehearsed the scene. Now, when it actually confronted her and she saw the look of horror on Emily's face, she couldn't bear to let her speak, but rushed on desperately:

"For God's sake, Emily, don't think that I meant to do this to you! Nothing on earth could have made me do it. I hadn't an idea of it until I walked into your drawing-room and saw Kurt standing at your side. I never had such a shock in my life. I came near to fainting, and can't imagine how I managed to carry it off."

"How did this man know about me?"

"As I told you, Lanny had discussed you along with others. He mentioned a list of his friends. What Kurt did was write to Switzerland and get in touch with his superiors, and with their help he went to work on the names he had got."

"But he wrote me that he was a cousin of an old friend of mine who had died in Switzerland. How could he have known about that?"

"He tells me the German intelligence service can find out anything. That's all I know. His lips are sealed, and not even love can open them."

"But what could he have been expecting to accomplish in my home, Beauty?"

"He wanted to meet influential persons, and he did. Presumably he got what he wanted from one of them—so he didn't come back to you any more."

"How perfectly appalling, Beauty!"

"I assure you I haven't got over the shock of it yet. I tremble every time I see a French uniform."

"And you never gave me an idea what was happening to me!"

"Lanny and I debated that problem in great distress of mind. We figured that you wouldn't want to give him up to be shot; that didn't seem according to your nature. On the other hand, if you didn't report him, you'd become responsible for what he might do. So long as you didn't know, you couldn't be blamed. After you came and told me that the police had questioned you about Kurt, I never slept a wink. How we got him out of the country is a long story that I won't bore you with now."

"I can't think when I was ever less bored," replied the other. She looked into those lovely, gentle features, now so strained and anxious, and added: "I used to think of you as a sort of cross between a gazelle and a butterfly; now I'll have to call you one of the world's great actresses. I have never been so completely taken in."

"You have to find it in your heart to forgive me. I was caught up by a whirlwind. You see, I had fallen in love with the man. It sounds disgraceful, but let me tell you how it was."

"I'm not so surprised by that part. How long were you shut up in the apartment with him?"

"A whole week; but it wasn't only that, it was the tragedy of his position. You know, Emily, how I felt about the war at the outset. I hated it, and only as I watched Marcel's frightful sufferings did I begin to hate the Germans. Before the war was over, I had learned to hate them heartily. And there were Kurt and I all day and all night—he couldn't leave—at least, I wouldn't let him. Everything I believed about the war was a challenge to him. We argued and quarreled, we fought the whole war over, until at last Kurt made me see the German side. They really have a side, Emily."

"I suppose they think so." Mrs. Chattersworth's voice was cold.

"Kurt was wounded twice; the last time he had pieces of his ribs shot away, and while he was in the hospital he was nursed by a young woman who had been a schoolteacher. They fell in love and were married, and she was expecting a baby. That was the time toward the end of the dreadful food shortage caused by the blockade. The baby was born dead, and the mother contracted T.B., but she went on working; Kurt was at the front, and didn't know about it until she had died of a hemorrhage. That's the story he told me; and there he was—having lost everything, even his home—he swears he will never live in Poland. The Germans are a proud and bitter people, Emily, and they're not going to take their defeat gracefully. It's not merely the territory they've lost, the ships and all the material things; it's the humiliation, the insult of having been made to admit a guilt they don't feel. I really thought that when the Versailles treaty was signed Kurt might take his own life. And you know, I wasn't so happy myself: the world after the war didn't look lovely to me; the way people were behaving made me sick. I thought: Here's Lanny's friend whom I might help. And I did that; I've managed to get him back to something at least half-way normal. I know it seems a ridiculous love affair, but if only the world will let us alone and not have any more wars, Lanny and I between us can keep Kurt at his music. I've come to beg your forgiveness—and for your help in this task."

VI

The stately Mrs. Emily Chattersworth had not always enjoyed the secure position which was hers in France. Far back in the past, but still vivid in memory, were the days when she had been the wife of a great New York banker, whose institutions had been under investigation by a legislative committee. Then she had known what it was to read scare headlines about her husband's business and even his private life; to have her telephone wires tapped, her servants bribed, her home burglarized and papers stolen. She said nothing about it now, but remembered that she too was an exile!

Nor was the *salonnière* in position to throw stones on account of the younger woman's sexual irregularity. Emily had had an unhappy married life, and after her husband's death in France she had taken a well-known French art authority as her *ami*, gently putting aside his offers of marriage because she wouldn't trust any man's attitude toward a great fortune. Now her hair had turned white, and the band of black velvet which she wore about her throat was no longer wide enough to conceal the wrinkles; her heart was sad, because she was losing the man she loved, and, fearing that, was ceasing to love him. Now she faced the problem: was she going to give up another friend?

Emily had met Beauty at the time of the latter's unmatched loveliness, and when she was generally accepted as the wife of the wealthy and handsome Robbie Budd. Americans came to France to do as they pleased, and it wasn't the fashion to ask to see marriage certificates. It was only later that Emily Chattersworth had learned about the stern old Puritan father in Connecticut who threatened to disown his son—and meant it—if he should wed an artists' model in Paris. By that time Emily had come to know Beauty and to appreciate her natural sweetness of disposition. Also, the childless Mrs. Chattersworth had grown fond of an eager and precocious lad whom she would have been glad to have as a son.

With one-half of her mind she listened to the details of a strange love entanglement, while with the other half she debated what course she was going to take. The voice of prudence said: "A German agent will always be a German agent, no matter what he may pretend. At any rate, you can never have any peace of mind about him. The possibilities of embarrassment are endless, and will last as long as Germany and France last. While you were being deceived, you could be excused; but now that you know, what excuse can you give?"

But the voice of the heart said: "This woman is in trouble, and it isn't of her making. Am I to say to her: 'I will have nothing more to do with you or your son'?"

Aloud, the mistress of Sept Chênes remarked: "What on earth do you expect of me, Beauty? I introduced your friend to a large company in my home as M. Dalcroze. Now how can I tell them that he is Herr Meissner?"

"At present he travels as my chauffeur, and his passport reads 'D. Armand.' We will let the D stand for Dalcroze, and call him Kurt Dalcroze-Armand. If anyone remembers meeting him in Paris, you can say that he came to you as a stranger and that you introduced him by the wrong name."

"You seem to have thought of everything, Beauty."

"I spent weeks shut up in that dreadful hotel suite with nothing to do but plan and scheme ways to make some sort of future for Kurt and myself."

What Emily said at the end of the session was that she would stand by her friends so long as Kurt devoted himself strictly to music. Let the Swiss gentleman with the unusual name of Dalcroze-Armand arrive in Bienvenu as Lanny's friend and music-teacher, and stay inside the estate and work at his art. "Frenchmen will soon be doing business with Germans again," said Emily, "and I doubt if anyone will concern himself with your visitors or employees. If the police should happen to trace him, we'll have to see some of our friends in the government."

Beauty sat with her hands clasped and the tears starting on her cheeks. "Oh, thank you, thank you, Emily! You will see how hard I shall work to repay your kindness!"

VII

Fortified by this powerful support, Beauty went back to Spain, and her tall chauffeur with the bright blue eyes and abundant straw-colored hair donned his uniform and motored his mistress to the French border. That was the point of peril, and in preparation for it Beauty had donned the gayest costume ever worn by an American lady of fashion on a motor-tour. Not too *outré*, no jewels, and only a little make-up and perfume, but an effect of springtime, most agreeable in December; a jardiniere hat sprouting golden poppies, a pink crape dress hinting at hidden charms, and a full-length silver-fox coat spread on the seat at her back, ready for use when the sun dropped low and the chill of the Riviera night descended. Border guards and customs officials would know that this must be the favored one of some fabulous American magnate; and when she presented her passports and descended from the car to fill out her declaration, she enveloped them in gracious smiles, costly perfumes, and fluent French. Each one imagined himself a master of multi-millions, embracing that vision of joy, and no one had more than a glance for a chauffeur standing by a car, keeping guard over a silver-fox coat and other treasures.

When they were safe in France and darkness covered them, the chauffeur slipped out of his uniform and donned a well-tailored costume appropriate to a Swiss piano virtuoso. They spent the night in an inn at Cette, and drove all the next day and night, arriving at Bienvenu in the small hours. The gates were swung open and then locked behind the car, and Beauty's protégé was safe in a love-nest from which he was not going to emerge for many a month if his *amie* could have her way.

There was that new studio, all pink stucco with sky-blue shutters; and a new grand piano—or should one say a grand new piano? Lanny had had to give up the idea of having Kurt choose it, and had found it himself in Cannes. Those two boys—so they still thought of each other—exchanged embraces with ardor born of anxiety on the one side and of gratitude on the other. Tired and stiff as Kurt was after a grueling journey, he seated himself at the sonorous instrument and poured out the tumult of Schumann's *Widmung. Ich liebe dich in Zeit und Ewigkeit*—and Beauty and Lanny and the piano each might take it as applying to her or him or it!

VIII

That pink and white motherly hen had her three chicks under her warm wings—and how she would guard them! She had seen so much of cruelty and suffering, she had felt so much of grief and terror, that all she asked of a harsh world was to be let alone in her quiet nest; she could get along without any more glory, or whatever it was that a "professional beauty" had craved. Her smart clothes were hung in closets, where they would grow quickly out of date; but never mind, she said, fashions move in spirals, and they'd be good ten years from now. When her smart friends invited her to dances, she told them that she was still in mourning for Marcel. Naturally they would wonder about that severe and dignified-looking music-teacher of whom they caught glimpses; but if they suspected a scandal it would be sexual, not military.

Two children and a lover were three children in Beauty's eyes, and she would do everything in her power to spoil them. If they wanted anything they should have it, and if they did anything it was marvelous. She wanted them to take that attitude to one another; she would sing the praises of each to the others, and watch them all with anxious eyes. Fortunately no sign of disharmony appeared. Kurt found Baby Marceline a charming creature, and joined Lanny in his course of child study. Kurt hadn't thought that one so young could perceive musical rhythm, and when she would toddle over to his studio he did not resent the interruption, but played little German folk tunes for her to dance to, and then carried her home and laid her in her crib. Beauty understood that he was thinking of the child he had hoped for and lost.

When Kurt had visited Bienvenu in the year 1913 there had been two women servants. Rosine was now married, and had a family of her own; Leese had brought one of her nieces as maid-of-all-work, and a brother as handyman. Of course these servants gossiped about the family, as did the servants of all the other families on the Cap d'Antibes. Very soon the peasants and fisherfolk knew that the young music-master was also the lover of Madame; but nobody objected to that—"*C'est la nature.*" They took it for granted that he was Swiss, and knew that he spent his time causing thunderous volumes of sound to echo through the pine woods and over the *golfe.* Passing on the road they would stop to listen, and between hauls of their nets the fishermen would look at one another and exclaim: "*Sapristi!*"

Kurt had got all his instruments and his large stock of music. Lanny also had a supply, and they carried armfuls back and forth and soon got them hopelessly mixed. Lanny was relieved to find that Kurt did not carry the late international unhappiness into the realm of art; he was willing to listen to English and French and even to Italian music. But he had severe standards; he liked music that was structurally sound and hated that which was showy. Presently Lanny began to note that it was the great German composers who had the desired qualities and the foreign ones who lacked them. Lanny said nothing about this, because he was trying so hard to please his friend.

IX

Lanny was only a little more than a year younger than Kurt, but this had made a great difference when they were boys, and his attitude of deference still continued. It was Lanny's nature to admire other people and find them wonderful. His mother had often objected to that attitude, but in the case of Kurt she didn't; so all things worked together to make Kurt the master of this household. It was his genius which was being cultivated; it was his taste which set the standards. Beauty didn't really know anything about music, except for dancing. She liked pretty tunes, but didn't know why everything had to become so complicated and so noisy. But that was the way Kurt liked it, and that was the way he had it.

Beauty's first man had wanted her to be the most admired woman in a ballroom, and so she had spent his money upon clothes; he had liked to sit up most of the night playing poker, and so she had lost a lot of his money for him. Beauty's second man had liked to sit out on the rocks and observe the colors of sunsets and breaking waves; he had raved about the way certain men put upon canvas little dabs of lead dissolved in oil. All right, Beauty had given tea-parties for painters, and had listened to their patter, and learned to tell Manet from Monet, Redon from Rodin, and Pissarro from Picasso. Now here was another kind of genius, another strange and bewildering art; Beauty listened, and it seemed to her a chaos of sound, going on without any discoverable reason for either starting or stopping. But Lanny would cry out that it was magnificent, he had always known Kurt had it in him; Beauty decided that she had known it too.

There was a thing called a "concerto" which Kurt had been working on all his sojourn in Spain. Every now and then a new passage would be completed, and then the whole thing would be played through, up to and including that. Beauty had heard it while reading the popular magazines, while putting supper on the table, while sitting on the rocky shore of the Bay of Biscay, O. If her fingers had been physically capable of the task she could have played every note of it. It meant to her: "Thank God, Kurt is busy! Kurt is keeping out of danger! Kurt is not killing other men, or being killed by them!"

They had been able to get only a small upright piano in Spain, but still he had been able to extract a tremendous racket from it. From watching him rather than from listening, Beauty had come to understand that he was trying to find something to take the place of the war; trying to vent his rage and despair, his love for his own people, his grief at their humiliation and defeat. Watching his face while he played, Beauty lived through her agonies with Marcel, and then those with Kurt, shifting back and forth between the German soul and the French.

Now Kurt had got a man-sized piano, and could really hear his concerto, and Lanny could clasp him and hug him, behaving the way music lovers did at concerts, and which Beauty considered extravagant. The composition was supposed to have an orchestral accompaniment; Lanny could read this with his swiftly flying eyes, and would sit with the score and imagine it while Kurt played the piano part. Then Lanny proceeded to learn Kurt's part, and while he played it Kurt would sit with several instruments about him and pick them up one after another and play snatches on the violin, the oboe, or the flute. The next thing, Lanny was learning to play the orchestral part on his piano, and at the final stage the gardener came with three sturdy sons of the Midi and picked up the old piano in the drawing-room; puffing and grunting, with sweat streaming from their faces, they lugged it over to Kurt's studio and set it down beside the new instrument. So the two maestri could play both parts, and then indeed the passers-by on the road heard something; the rumble of it shook the bedrock of the Cap. But it was all right with Beauty; if they had asked her, she would have consented to build a railroad so that they might transport pianos all over the estate. Anything to keep one's male creatures at home!

X

One of the first things Lanny did was to take Kurt down to Marcel's studio. He had placed the heavy easel in the middle of the floor, so that the right amount of north light fell upon it. There was a large painting on it covered with a cloth, and Lanny put Kurt in front of it, saying: "This is going to knock you over."

It pretty nearly did. When Lanny took off the cover, Kurt found himself facing a half-sized portrait of his mistress at the age of seventeen, when she had been a famed artists' model in Paris. The painter had portrayed her in the nude, sitting upon a silken couch, leaning slightly upon one arm and with a light blue veil half crossing her lap. A shower of golden hair fell over one shoulder, and bright sunlight streamed upon it and upon the creamy white skin delicately tinged with pink. The painter had been a lover of the flesh, and had studied all the curves and shadows, making something luxurious and seductive, causing every male creature to catch his breath. "Oh, Lanny!" exclaimed his friend. "What a gorgeous thing!"

"I found it so," said Lanny.

"Is that Marcel's?"

"Marcel wasn't painting then. It's an Oscar Deroulé. He was a fashionable painter of the *fin de siècle*. Robbie says it is the sort of thing they put in high-class American bars."

"You can put it in a bar or in a church, according to how you look at life," said Kurt.

After he had studied this work, Lanny said: "I'll show you Beauty dressed for church." He took the cloth into the storeroom and put it over another painting and brought it forth; he set it on the easel, and with a proper sense of drama lifted the cover. This was the *Sister of Mercy*, which Marcel had made of his wife during the long agony of the battle of Verdun. Beauty wore a nurse's costume, and in her face was all the anguish and pity that Marcel had seen while she was bringing him back to life. Kurt, who had had the same experience, rejoiced that a painter had immortalized the soul of this woman they both had loved.

One by one Lanny brought out the best of his stepfather's works: his war painting of the *poilu*, and the dreadful one he had called *Fear*. Nobody was to see that, Marcel had said, until the Germans could see it also. Now a German saw it, and knew that what he had suffered in his secret soul was the same as a Frenchman had suffered.

Why should either have wished to inflict it upon the other? So Marcel seemed to say, and Kurt felt himself at one with his late antagonist.

Lanny brought out samples of the earlier work: the scenes of the Cap, which Kurt could check in various weathers and at various hours of the day; those of Norway, and the Isles of Greece and the shores of Africa, fruit of the *Bluebird* cruises. After Kurt had seen a dozen or so of these, he felt he knew Marcel both as painter and as man, and was not ashamed to be his successor in love.

XI

Once every twenty-four hours a glow stole up behind the Cap and spread over the sky, and dazzling sunlight descended upon the flowers and foliage and red-roofed houses of Bienvenu. The great orb moved its appointed way over the blue Mediterranean, and sank in a blaze of color behind the dim Estérels. Then the dark half of the sky-wheel moved through its unvarying course, and streams of twinkling stars dropped into the abyss behind the mountains. Every four weeks the moon appeared as a gleaming crescent above the same mountains, and night by night grew larger until it was a great silver ball, by whose light the woods and gardens took on a new and mystical beauty, troubling to the soul. The flowers poured out their tiny jets of perfume upon the still night air, and two young musicians would sit upon the shore, watching the lights of the city across the bay and listening to the sounds of distant music, experiencing a strange awe which they sought vainly to express in their art.

Here was everything that a lover of nature could ask, and more than any philosopher could understand in the longest lifetime. The flowers in the crannied walls held all the secrets of God and man; like sun and moon and stars, they too had their appointed courses, they budded, blossomed, died, and were renewed according to age-old patterns. There was an insect world living upon the plants and upon itself, and a bird world living upon both. If you looked below the surface of the sea, you found a myriad of fantastic forms, each following unceasingly its predatory role. Who or what had been interested to contrive these complicated structures and inspire them with a determination to struggle and seek through millions of centuries? And those more powerful creatures which had a brain, and were able to study and comprehend the others, and use them for their purposes—yet knew no more why they did it, or thought they ought to! "So hot, little sir?" the stars had said to Emerson; and Lanny gave this great man's essays to Kurt, introducing him to New England transcendentalism, stepdaughter of Kurt's German idealism.

The two budding philosophers would take long walks at night, when no one paid any attention to them. They would wander over the shore-paths which had delighted them in boyhood; they would visit by moonlight the ruins of long-dead civilizations, and speculate as to what had brought them down and whether the same forces were at work in their own heedless world—but not quite so sure of itself as it had been a few years before! Kurt would be moved to tell what he had experienced during the war, and Lanny during peace-making. Across the bay lay the île Sainte-Marguerite, where Kurt's aunt, the Frau Doktor Hofrat von und zu Nebenaltenberg, had been interned as an enemy alien for five years. Now she was home again, hating the French. Kurt told about her and other members of his family, all greatly reduced in circumstances but not in pride.

As time passed, Beauty's fears diminished, and she was willing for them to take walks by day, provided they kept out of the towns and never spoke German. Tourists were numerous, and the sight of a tall man with blond hair and blue eyes no longer attracted attention. The two friends dived off the rocks, they sailed in the golfe and outside it, they climbed into the distant hills covered with thyme and lavender, and looked upon orange and olive vineyards and the marble palaces of fashionable folk. Once again they sat in front of that ancient monastery of Notre-Dame-de-Bon-Port and gazed at the lovely prospect of blue and green water, the shining towns of the Riviera, and the Italian Alps with their snowy tops. From here the Estérels were dark red porphyry, and the horizon was a blur of blue mountains where it was not a ring of blue sea.

Here six years earlier two boys had sat, talking with preternatural solemnity about their lives and what they were going to make of them. Lanny had been the more deeply impressed, and recalled what his older friend had said about the mission of art and their duty as carriers of the torch of culture. Kurt remembered it, and declared that he still held to that faith. It was profoundly true that movements of the human spirit came first, and that the events of history were consequences thereof. Very tactfully Lanny sought to encourage this mood in his friend; for history had been hard upon Kurt and his people, and it was much desired by the rest of the world that they should draw back into themselves and experience a new birth of the spirit.

In the earlier, boyhood conversation Lanny had enlisted himself as a disciple of German idealism, and now he told his friend that he was waiting to be justified in his faith. All three of the great B's of German music, Bach, Beethoven, and Brahms, were calling to Kurt Meissner to carry on their tradition. Lanny talked about them with such intensity of feeling that the German was deeply touched. The new Kurt of political bitterness seemed to fade and dissolve, and the old Kurt of moral fervor and devotion came back to life. When in the twilight they descended the slope, it seemed to Lanny that the war was really over and the soul life of Europe beginning again.

3

Double, Double Toil and Trouble

I

ERIC VIVIAN POMEROY-NIELSON had planned to devote his life to the study of what he called "theater." He had chosen that career after seeing his first children's play at the age of six, and from then on he had set out to learn all he could about playwriting and acting, stage- and scene-painting, music, poetry, and dancing. The practice of these combined arts would, of course, call for a lot of activity; one would have to go about, and stand up and show other people what to do, and stick at it through all-night rehearsals; and here was Rick, at the age of twenty-two, a war cripple with essential parts of one knee missing and a steel brace on his leg. Also with a wife and baby, and his father having to sell parts of the family estate on account of war taxes. But still, Rick wasn't going to give up his career!

"It's dogged as does it," is the English saying, and Rick had figured out a long campaign, beginning with those activities which were easiest. He didn't need his knee to work a typewriter, so he would acquire that art, and at the same time practice writing. He would make some money, and, if possible, a reputation; then he would do a play, and his father would help him to find a producer, and he could go in his own right and sit in a chair and watch rehearsals, and if his play was a success, a whole chain of mountains would come to Mahomet.

All this Rick wrote to his friend Lanny Budd, with many typographical errors; it was his first job on a machine, he said, and Lanny put the letter away in his desk, certain that it would find a place in a museum some day. Just as Lanny knew that Marcel Detaze was going to be recognized as a painter, and Kurt as a composer, so he knew that Eric Vivian Pomeroy-Nielson would become a famous name of the English theater. Almost at once Lanny's judgment began to be vindicated, for as soon as Rick had learned to do a manuscript without errors he wrote a sketch drawn from his war adventures, the simple story of a flier who started out at dawn and what thoughts went through his mind as he headed for Germany. It was authentic and moving, and was accepted and paid for by the first newspaper to which Rick offered it. Lanny was so pleased, he bought every copy of the paper he could find in Cannes, and sent one to his father in Connecticut and others to friends who had met Rick.

The baronet's son, brilliant and versatile, was also trying his hand at poetry. His own severest critic, he wouldn't send any of it to Lanny. Nobody could possibly publish it, he declared, because it was so bitter. He was one of those many heroes who were not satisfied with what they had accomplished by their sacrifices and were questioning the whole universe to know who was to blame. Was it the stupid old men who had sat in the council chambers and sent the young men out to be drowned in mud and blood? Was it all mankind, which was able to invent and build machines but not to control them? Was it God, who had made men wrong—and why? Rick quoted four lines from a poem he called *After War:*

> Are nations like the men they make?
> Or was it God who fashioned men?
> O God, who willed the clay awake,
> Will now to sleeping clay again!

Lanny was impressed by these lines and begged for the rest, and Rick with a sudden impulse sent him a large batch of verses, saying that they were hopelessly crude but couldn't do any worse than bore him. However, Lanny refused to be bored; he thought that Rick was voicing what was in the hearts of millions of people, himself included. It happened that in London, at the home of Lady Eversham-Watson, Lanny had met a magazine editor, and, without telling Rick, he sent the poem *After War* and was delighted when the editor offered to publish it and pay two guineas.

Kurt agreed that the verses were good; and Jerry Pendleton, sarcastic fellow, remarked—not in the presence of Kurt—that any German would be glad to hear that an Englishman regretted having licked him. Jerry was one doughboy who had no sorrows over the Versailles treaty, and declared that "Old Whiskers," as he irreverently called Kaiser Wilhelm, was a lot better off sawing cordwood at Doorn. Lanny's former tutor had heard a lot about Kurt Meissner, so it had been necessary to take him into the secret; but of course he didn't know about Kurt's having been a secret agent. If he guessed the situation between Kurt and Beauty, he was discreet enough never to refer to it.

II

The fact that Rick had come so near to Kurt's point of view concerning the late unpleasantness made easier Lanny's project for reconciling England and Germany. Kurt said that Rick had evidently matured into a man of judgment, and that it would be a pleasure to meet him again. So Lanny's letters to Rick and Nina began to be full of the wonders of the Côte d'Azur: the lovely flowers in their garden, the soft white sand of the beach at Juan, the delights of sailing in the bay, the health-giving qualities of ozone and sunshine. When Rick developed a cold, the pressure became intensified. More people had died of the flu than had been killed in the war—and England had lost too much of its young manhood already!

Lanny repeated the arguments which had succeeded with Kurt. What was the use of a fellow's having money if he couldn't spend it on his friends? Robbie Budd knew Rick and admired him, and had cabled offers of help when he had learned about Rick's crash. Now that kind father was sitting at home, unhappy because Lanny wouldn't spend his money; it could only mean that Lanny had been seduced by the propaganda of the Reds and was offended by the smell of munitions profits! But if Lanny should cable that he wanted to rent a villa for Rick and his family, Robbie would cheer up at once. Lanny wrote this, and then, fearing that it might not be the best argument for an anti-war poet, he tore up the letter and wrote another of somewhat doubtful ethical quality—he offered to spend for Rick that thousand dollars which he had got from the State Department of the United States, and which he had already spent for Kurt's piano! A genial device: Lanny would keep that thousand dollars in mind, and spend it over and over on anybody who had conscientious scruples against munitions profits!

Sophie, Baroness de la Tourette, had a pleasant little villa on the other side of the Cap, near Antibes, where she had stayed off and on for years. Now she had gone to visit her people in Cincinnati, and wrote Beauty that she was remaining in order to get a divorce. "The hardware business has been shot to pieces," she explained, "and I find I can't afford the upkeep of a title." Lanny sent her a cable, offering to rent the house for Rick, and she said all right, and after he had done it Rick had to come.

Lanny met the little family at the station. He saw that Rick was thinner; he was working hard, and forcing himself to take exercise. His keen features had more of the old fire in them, and Lanny realized that it was one thing to weep for the world's wrong, and another to write verses about it. Rick had always been mature beyond his years. He made jokes in his old fashion, and spoke with his customary contempt of those whose artistic standards were beneath his own. There were touches of gray in his wavy black hair; this appeared to be one of the effects of shellfire upon the human organism.

Nina was her pretty, birdlike self, only she was a mother-bird, and both husband and son were her babies. Little Alfy, as they called him, had been named after his grandfather, but was a miniature of Rick; he didn't take kindly to railroad trains and automobiles, but was trying to get loose and start to explore the wonderful new world. He had been born in the midst of war and horror, but didn't know anything about it. Was this a blessing of nature or a betrayal? His father asked the question in a sonnet.

They drove first to Bienvenu to have lunch, and on the way Lanny told about Kurt's state of mind, and asked his friends to go easy on the subject of the past five years. He told about the concerto, now finished. Incidentally he remarked, quite casually: "Kurt has become Beauty's lover." Such was the correct tone among the young sophisticates. You said it *en passant*, as if it were: "Beauty and Kurt have gone sailing this morning." Your friends said: "Oh, jolly!" or "Ripping!" and that was that.

III

Rick hadn't seen Beauty or Kurt since the outbreak of the war, and Nina had never met either of them. So there were greetings to be exchanged and curiosities to be satisfied. Little Alfy was set down in front of Baby Marceline, who gazed at him with wide brown eyes and one finger in her mouth; he took command, as he would throughout life: seeing the dogs, he toddled after them, and Marceline followed. He was going to be a baronet and a member of the English ruling classes, and Marceline was going to have a half-share of Bienvenu, a valuable property; also of whatever her father's paintings might bring. As soon as they were born Lanny had written the two mothers, bidding them start matchmaking, and in their minds they had done so; now when their eyes met there was appraisal, not merely of each other, but of the future of two families.

Lanny and Rick and Kurt at Hellerau had dubbed themselves the three musketeers of the arts. "When shall we three meet again In thunder, lightning, or in rain?" So they had asked, and here was the answer. There had been plenty of thunder and lightning, but now the uproar had died away, there was a rainbow in the sky, and a heavenly melody floating in the air, as you hear in the *William Tell* overture—or preferably in Beethoven's *Pastoral Symphony*, since Kurt Meissner will tell you that Rossini's music is somewhat meretricious. It will be to music of the highest quality that these three musketeers march forward into life, resolutely, in spite of defeats and disappointments. When Rick hears fate knocking at the door in four thundering notes it will not tell him that he is growing deaf, but that he is a cripple for life; and with the help of art he will learn to take these blows of fate and make a *scherzo* out of them, and in the end perhaps a triumphal march.

After lunch Lanny drove the new family over to their temporary home, which he had stocked up with tinned goods enough for an African safari. There was one of Leese's able-bodied relatives to act as maid-of-all-work; one of her orders would be to carry Rick's typing machine out to a rustic table every morning when the weather was fair. There he would sit alone, and his rage against human stupidity would fan itself white hot, and molten words would pour from the typewriter, all but burning the pages. Strange as it might seem, the more he lashed the damned human race the better they liked it; such was the mood of the time—all thinking men agreed that the peoples of Europe had made fools of themselves, and it was proof of advanced views to abuse the "old men," the "brass hats," the "patrioteers," the "merchants of death."

It was as if you had been on a terrible "bat" the night before, and had got into a row with your best friend and blacked both his eyes. Next morning you were apologetic, and willing to let him have the best of all the arguments. So it was that both Lanny and Rick dealt with their German friend; the Englishman talked as if it was really quite embarrassing to have won a war, and of course what he wrote about British bungling pleased Kurt entirely—only he found it difficult to understand how British editors were willing to pay money for it!

IV

One of the consequences of Rick's coming was that the subject of world politics was brought back into the family conversation. Lanny had deliberately put the subject out of his mind, and tried tactfully to have Kurt do the same. Kurt got no newspapers from home, and when members of his family wrote to him, they put the envelope in a second envelope addressed to Lanny Budd, so as to avoid attracting attention. But now came Rick, bringing with him the custom which prevailed in his father's home of discussing public affairs at all hours of the day and night. Rick took a couple of newspapers and half a dozen weeklies, and would lie propped up in bed reading and making notes. The war, however many bad things it had done, had brought it about that British politics were French politics and German politics and Russian politics and American politics. All the nations of the earth had been thrown into one stew-pot, there to simmer slowly. Double, double toil and trouble; Fire burn and cauldron bubble!

So Lanning Prescott Budd descended the steps of his ivory tower and pushed open its gold-embossed doors and thrust out his delicately chiseled nose. Instantly it was assailed by the odors of a colossal charnel-pit, a shell-hole as big as the crater of a volcano, filled with the mangled flesh and bones of millions of human beings. His ears, carefully schooled to the appreciation of exquisite music, were stunned by the screams of dying populations, the wails of starving children, the imprecations of the frustrated, the moans of the hopeless. Before his eyes stretched a prospect of desolation; shell-blasted fields, skeleton trees without a leaf, buildings that were smoke-blackened walls, their empty windows like human faces with eyes picked out by birds of prey.

The Turks were still slaughtering Armenian peasants. Civil war was still raging in Russia, the Whites now being driven in rout to all points of the compass. In Siberia a freight-train loaded with Reds was wandering aimlessly upon an eight-thousand-mile track, the locked-in prisoners perishing of starvation and disease. The Polish armies, invading Russia, were still dreaming of world empire. The White Finns were killing tens of thousands of Red Finns. The Rumanians were killing Red Hungarians. There were insurrections and mass strikes in Germany, a plague of labor revolts in France and Britain, millions unemployed in every great nation, famine everywhere in Europe, flu in the western half and typhus in the eastern.

When, in the middle of 1919, President Wilson and his staff had left the Peace Conference, that body had stayed on to settle the destinies of Austria and Hungary and Bulgaria and Turkey. It was still holding sessions, with despairing peoples waiting upon its decisions; when these were announced they were generally out of date, because events had moved beyond them. The British and French statesmen were agreed that Italy should not have Fiume, but an Italian poet with a glory complex had raised a revolt and seized the city. All statesmen agreed that the Bolshevik madness must be put down, but meanwhile it throve and spread, and mountains of supplies which the Allies had furnished to the White generals were being captured and used by the Reds. The statesmen decided that Turkey should lose most of her empire, but the Turks dissented and retired into their mountains, and who had an army to go after them? The French had seized the land of poor Emir Feisal—all but those parts which had oil; the British had these, and there was a bitter wrangle, and it looked as if the alliance which had won the war would break up before it finished dividing the spoils.

British statesmen had promised to make a world fit for heroes to live in, and now Rick's version was that they had made one it needed heroes to live in. Lying on the table in Lanny's study was one of Eli Budd's volumes, the poetry of an old-time New Englander who had been one of the patron saints of Rick's grandmothers, but to

Rick himself was no more than a name. Rick was moved by curiosity to dip into the volume, and he happened upon *A Psalm of Life*, which was to be found in all school readers. The crippled aviator declared that it "griped his guts"; anybody could write "doggerel" like that, and to prove it he composed on the spot a revised version:

> Tell me not, ye wishful thinkers,
> That the spirit reigns supreme,
> And man's hoping is a token
> Of the mortal's valid dream.

The modern psalmist went on to tell the world how he had "seen the Brute in action," and his conclusion was:

> I have wakened from a nightmare
> To a living death by day;
> All my dreams a tabulation
> Of the price my hope must pay.

V

On the first day of every month, unless it was Sunday, the businesslike Robert Budd dictated a letter to his son—a good, satisfying letter telling about the family and the business, and never failing to include some advice to the boy about taking care of himself, and learning to spend money wisely, and not letting women get too much hold on him. Lanny had saved these communications over a period of years, and if he had published them, judiciously expurgated, they might have made a New England equivalent of the letters of Lord Chesterfield.

The family in Connecticut was thriving, as it always had, and meant to; they were solid people. Lanny's two half-brothers were in St. Thomas's; they could enter younger than Lanny, because they had been trained according to a system. Lanny's half-sister Bess, who adored his memory, was reading a book he had recommended and struggling to play a piano piece he had mentioned. Esther Budd, his stepmother, was marshaling the ladies of Newcastle for the relief of war victims in Armenia and Poland. The president of Budd Gunmakers Corporation was showing his age, but could by no means be induced to relax his grip upon affairs; he had inherited a great institution and was determined to pass it on to his heirs in better condition than he had received it.

They were going to save the business, Robbie assured his son; they were making the dangerous transformation of their activities, and instead of machine guns and carbines and automatic revolvers, cartridges and hand grenades and time fuses, were producing a great variety of implements of peace. No easy task finding markets for new products, but they would do better in the boom which was surely on the way. But what a tragedy for America, and how it would some day regret the dismantling of its vitally important munitions industry! Lanny understood that to his father there was a loss of dignity and prestige, even a personal humiliation, in having to turn from the fashioning of beautiful, shining, deadly machine guns to the monotonous multiplication of frying pans, tack hammers, and freight elevators. It was possible to feel romantic about the Budd gun, which was the best in the world and had proved it in the rock-strewn thickets of the Meuse-Argonne; but who the hell wanted to hear about hardware?

However, the great plant had to go on; wages had to be earned, and taxes and upkeep, and dividends if possible. The world had munitions enough to last a decade, and the pacifists were in the saddle in America; the hallelujah shouters were proclaiming that the war to end war had been won and the world made safe for democracy. There was no philanthropist to subsidize and save an American munitions industry, built at breakneck speed by heroic labors. Far from appreciating this service, the nation had turned upon its benefactors and was calling them profiteers and merchants of death. Robbie Budd was a deeply offended munitions salesman, and the more so because his oldest and best-loved son had taken up with these critics and no longer desired to follow in his father's footsteps. Robbie never referred to this, but Lanny knew what was in his heart.

However, Robbie was a businessman, and the customer is always right. The customer didn't want machine guns, he wanted automobile parts and bicycles and gadgets of a thousand sorts, and Budd's would oblige him at mass-production prices. Also the customer would want oil, and Robbie, having many connections in Europe, had picked up a good thing in that line, and had let his friends and innumerable cousins in on it, and now was concerned to prove himself a business-man in his own right, not merely a son of Budd's. He had come to London twice during the fall and winter, and had been too busy to go down to Juan; Lanny had protested and pleaded, and so in the month of March Robbie cabled that he was on his way to Paris, and that nothing should interfere with a holiday. This sort of cablegram always marked a red-letter day in Lanny's young life. Moralists might scold about blood and profits, but none of them could deny that Robbie Budd was good company.

VI

The foreign representative of Budd Gunmakers had known for some time that he had got himself an odd sort of extra family, and he was curious to see what had been happening to it of late. Impossible to imagine a more unlikely tie-up than the butterfly Beauty and the grave and punctilious artillery officer turned spy! Add to it Lanny, product of a sexual irregularity, who didn't mind his fate, but seemed to have decided that the moralists were out of step with him. So many families were breaking up and recombining, wasn't it more sensible to leave everyone free to move without notice?

Father and son went for a long walk, as was their custom. Robbie was in his middle forties and had been leading a sedentary life all winter; for the first time in Lanny's experience he puffed a bit on the hills, but he didn't like to admit it and went on talking. He was a hearty, solid man, with brown eyes and hair—when he went swimming you saw the hair growing all over his chest. He liked having a good time, but underneath he was greatly worried about the world, which was in what he called a god-awful mess. People in Europe had been fighting for so long, they seemed to have forgotten what productive labor was. Lanny knew that his father's mind had water-tight compartments in it, and there was no use mentioning the difficulty of combining peaceful industry with the mass production and marketing of instruments of slaughter. What Lanny had to do was to let his father talk, and when he couldn't agree, say nothing. All through the war, both in France and in New England, Lanny had had to practice the art of keeping his thoughts to himself, and at the Peace Conference he had perfected his technique.

He described the life of Beauty and Kurt, who were getting along surprisingly well. Beauty was much in love with her man, and had got over being embarrassed about it; Kurt was a good influence because he kept her at home—he wouldn't let her spend money on him, so she didn't spend it on herself. You could see Kurt's musical stature growing, Lanny said; and Robbie listened politely, but without much enthusiasm. Robbie had been to Yale, and had got vaccinated with culture, but it hadn't "taken"; he knew a lot of college songs and popular stuff, but left highbrow music to those who pretended to understand it. Maybe Lanny did; in any case, his father was satisfied if it kept him happy and out of mischief.

One important question: Was Kurt having much to do with Germans? Lanny answered: "No. What could he do, anyhow?" The father didn't know, but he said there would be war of one sort or another between France and Germany so long as those two nations existed. And certainly Bienvenu must not become a secret headquarters of the Germans.

They went back and had a swim with the family. There was a boat-landing with steps, and on the bottom step Lanny had had two iron handles fastened for Rick. If there were no strangers present to embarrass him he would unstrap his leg brace, and with his two arms and one good leg would help himself down into the water, where he could float around and swim with his hands. Nobody must offer to help him, or take any notice of his troubles, just let him alone and in his own way he would work them out. Meanwhile, observe the blue sky and the varicolored houses, the gray rocks and green hills of the Golfe Juan. Robbie, who had seen Rick in Paris just before he went out to his near-death, had admired his grit then and admired it now. He told Lanny that was one fellow who must have help whenever he needed it.

Also Robbie saw Beauty in her tight bathing suit, and had a good time describing in exaggerated language the ravages of *embon-*

point upon her charms. Beauty and the cream pitcher were a standing joke in that family. You might have thought it in dubious taste while millions of babies were perishing of slow malnutrition. If Beauty had had one of those little ones before her, she would have starved herself to feed it; but the little ones were in the newspapers, while the cream pitcher was on the table four times a day, including teatime. Also there was Leese, whose arts were a perpetual conspiracy against the figures of ladies who came to Bienvenu. *Bouillabaisse* with butter floating on top, *rissoles* fried in olive oil, sugary fruit *pâtés* with curlicues of whipped cream—so it went, and Beauty would tell herself she was just tasting this or that, and would go on until there was no more taste on her plate.

VII

In the evening the family sat in front of a log fire, for the nights were chilly. Mrs. Emily had been invited to join them, and they talked about the state of the world, concerning which various members of the group had special information.

Robbie told about America. President Wilson had come home from his peacemaking to find the country wholly indisposed to ratify the commitments he had made. He had spent his last reserves of health upon a tour of the nation; then a paralytic stroke had laid him low and he was a helpless invalid. If you were willing to believe Robbie Budd, the executive branch of the United States government now consisted of an elegant lady who owned a jewelry business, and whom Lanny had seen in Paris wearing a gorgeous purple gown and a purple hat with plumes; a navy doctor whom the President had raised to the rank of admiral; and a secretary whom Robbie described by a term of depreciation common among the ruling classes of New England—"Irish Catholic." The President saw no one, and this triumvirate of amateurs decided what papers he was permitted to read and sign. The Constitution of the United States might be the most perfect instrument which had ever emanated from the brain of man, but it had its oversights, and one was a failure to provide what was to happen when a president had a paralytic stroke.

However, it was an election year. In three months the Republican party would name its candidate; no college president, but someone who understood American business and its needs. The money to elect him would be forthcoming—Robbie knew where it was coming from—and in a little less than a year America would confront the world as a new-born nation, no longer to be trifled with in international affairs. Robbie didn't think that, Robbie *told* it, and the others listened respectfully.

The talk turned to the state of France, and here they heard a *salonnière* who numbered men of affairs among her friends. Clemenceau, the Tiger, had won the war but lost the peace—at least in the estimation of the Robbie Budds of France—and he had been ousted. There was a new premier, Millerand, and now it appeared that he too was yielding to the blandishments of Lloyd George. They were likely soon to have Poincaré, which meant simply that the war with Germany would be resumed in one form or another. Nobody in Europe was in a mood to think of mercy—save only the Germans! It was a very sad picture that Emily Chattersworth drew.

The mention of Lloyd George brought Rick into the conversation. Rick's father knew the key men of his country, and reported what they were saying in the clubs. Lloyd George was the only one of the war chiefs who still held power, and he did it because he had no principles, but was able to say, with the most passionate fervor, the opposite of what he said the day before. The "little squirt of a Welsh lawyer" had wrecked his own party getting power, and now was the prisoner of the Conservatives; useful to them because he could talk Liberal, and that was necessary with a bitterly discontented electorate.

Lanny told a story about his English friend Fessenden, one of the secretaries attached to the British staff at the Peace Conference. Fessenden had noticed that through a long and tedious discussion Lloyd George was "doodling" on a sheet of paper, and at the end crumpled it up and threw it onto the floor. Young Fessenden rescued it, thinking it might be something that would be of advantage to his country's opponents. He found that the British Prime Minister had covered an entire sheet with repetitions of one single word: "Votes. Votes. Votes."

VIII

Here sat these seven friends in soft-cushioned chairs, seeing one another's faces by the light of shaded lamps and the red and gold flames of burning cypress logs. Convenient little tables held ashtrays for their cigarettes and glasses for their drinks. On the walls around them were fine pictures, and shelves full of books for every taste. In one corner of the room was a piano, and when they asked him to play, Kurt produced soft music which turned time into beauty and glorified the processes of the human spirit.

Everything in the world appeared to be theirs, and yet their talk was troubled; it was as if the ground upon which this lovely home was built had turned to sand and might slide into the sea. On the center table lay newspapers telling with shocked headlines that the French and British armies had occupied Constantinople, which was threatened with revolution and might plunge the world into another war. When one said "another war" one didn't count the dozen or so small wars which were going on all the time, and which one had come to take for granted; one meant another war involving one's own land; one meant—horror of horrors—a war in which the late Allies might be fighting against each other!

Robbie Budd, newly hatched oil man, could tell them what the day's news meant. The old Turkish Empire had collapsed, and a new Turkey was going to be born, with all the benefits of modern civilization, such as oil wells and tanks and pipelines, not to mention copper mines in Armenia and potash works on the Dead Sea. The only question was, which benevolent nation was going to have the pleasure of conferring these blessings upon the Turks? (This wasn't Robbie's phrase; it was Rick's rephrasing.) The British had got hold of all the oil, but the French had got Syria and the Hejaz and were trying to control the routes of the pipelines; behind the scenes there was a furious quarrel going on, with screaming and calling of names in the nasal French language.

Now suddenly came this *coup d'état* in Constantinople. The benighted Turks didn't want to accept benefits from either Britain or France, but wanted to dig their own oil wells and keep the oil; so the quarreling friends were obliged to act together in spite of their wishes. Lloyd George was talking about a holy war, in which the Christian Greeks would put down the heathen Turks; but what effect would that have upon the several hundred millions of Moslems who lived under the Union Jack or near it?

Robbie pointed out that a certain Greek trader by the name of Basil Zaharoff had just been made Knight Commander of the Bath in England, a high honor rarely extended to aliens; Zaharoff controlled Vickers, the great munitions industry of Britain, and had saved the Empire at a net profit which people said was a quarter of a billion dollars—though Robbie Budd considered the figure exaggerated. Zaharoff was a friend of Lloyd George, and was reported to be one of his financial backers, which was only natural, considering how much money a politician had to have and how much governmental backing an international financier had to have. Zaharoff's hatred of the Turks was one passion of his life that he didn't have to hide.

"So," said Robbie, "you can see why British troops have been put ashore in Constantinople, and why French troops had to follow, even though the French government is supporting the Turks behind the scenes. Added to this is the fact that Constantinople until eighteen months ago was a German city, and German agents have been left behind there, to make all the trouble they can for both British and French. Naturally that would include a revolution by young Turkish patriots."

Robbie said this much and then stopped, realizing that he was in the presence of an agent whom the Germans had left behind in Paris. Kurt made no comment; of all persons in this room, he had had the best practice in keeping his thoughts to himself. But Lanny could imagine those thoughts without trouble, for only a couple of days earlier Kurt had received a letter from the comptroller-general of Schloss Stubendorf and had read passages to his friend. There, too, the British and French troops had found it necessary to intervene— not in Stubendorf itself, but in districts near by, known as "plebiscitary," whose inhabitants were going to have the right to decide whether they wished to be German or Polish. A bitter campaign of propaganda was going on, and a fanatical Polish patriot was organizing the young Poles to intimidate the Germans and try to drive them out before the voting took place. At any rate, that was the way Kurt's father described the events. Lanny remembered the name of Korfanty, which he was to hear frequently during the next year or two.

IX

When a fellow hasn't seen his father for eight or nine months and can't be sure when he will see him again, he naturally wants to make the most of his opportunity; so Lanny was pleased next morning when Robbie said: "I have some business to attend to that will interest you. Would you like to drive me?"

"Would I!" said the youth. He knew it was important because Robbie didn't say anything about it in the presence of the others. What Beauty didn't know she wouldn't tell!

When the car had passed the gates and headed toward the village, Lanny said: "Which way?" The father answered: "To Monty," and the son got a thrill.

"One guess!" he laughed. "Zaharoff?"

"You win," was the reply.

As a method of education, Robbie had made it a practice to tell his son about his affairs. Always he would say gravely that nobody else was to know about the matter, and never in his life had the boy let anything slip. He must be especially careful now, the father warned, since one of his pals was a budding journalist and the other a German.

Robbie revealed that he had taken the munitions king of Europe into his "New England-Arabian Oil Company." The old Greek devil had learned about it—he learned about everything in his various lines—and had sent for the American and made a proposal which it seemed the part of discretion to accept. "We're in British mandated territory, and we can't expect to operate without their protection; so we have to give a slice to some British insiders."

"Who sups with the devil must have a long spoon," quoted the youth, sagely.

"We have measured the spoon," smiled the father. "He has a twenty-five percent interest."

"But mayn't he buy up some of the other stockholders?"

"I have the pledges of our American investors, and I think they'll stick. More than thirty percent are Budds."

Robbie told about the oil business as it was carried on in southern Arabia, a wild and desolate land, the home of fanatical tribesmen, mostly nomads. You paid one chieftain for a concession, but you couldn't know what day he might be driven out. However, they had made a strike, and the clean-up would be rapid. Robbie portrayed khaki-clad young American engineers and leather-skinned drillers from Texas, sweating on a sun-scorched coast lined with sand and rocks, and living in a stockade with a watch tower and machine guns mounted on the walls. "Would you like to see it?" asked the father, and Lanny said: "Some time when you go."

The youth understood quite well that his father was trying to make the oil business sound romantic. Robbie Budd could not give up hope for the response he used to get in years past, when an eager lad had drunk in every word about the selling of machine guns and had leaped at every chance to believe that he was helping. But now, alas, Lanny's mind had suffered a sea-change; it was full of ideas about oil as a cause of war. When he learned that his father had let Zaharoff in "on the ground floor" so that he might have a British gunboat lying in the little bay near his oil wells, Lanny wasn't surprised, and didn't blame anybody, but just preferred to stay at Juan and play the piano.

"You are happy in what you are doing?" asked the father, later in their drive.

"Really I am, Robbie. You've no idea how many fine books there are in that library. It seems every time I open one I get a new view of life. I hope you don't think I'm wasting my time."

"Not at all. You know what you want, and if you're getting it, all right."

"I want you to understand I'm not going to live on you the rest of my life, Robbie. I'll find some way to put to use what I've learned."

"Forget it," was the reply. "So long as I have money, you're welcome to a share." Robbie said it and meant it, but Lanny knew that it involved giving up a long-cherished dream that these two might work together and that the son would take over what the father was building.

X

Eighteen months hadn't been time enough to replace all the motorvehicles of France, and the Route Nationale had less traffic than they remembered in old days. They sped past famous vistas of hills and valleys, blue sea and rocky shore, and came to Monte Carlo on its high promontory. Zaharoff was still staying at the hotel where a small boy had been able to steal his correspondence; he had a large suite there, suitable to his station as Grand Officer of the Légion d'Honneur and Knight Commander of the Bath. Robbie said he owned the hotel and was a heavy stockholder in the gambling casino at "Monty," well known to be one of the gold mines of Europe.

The munitions king looked paler and even more tired than when Lanny had seen him last, in his palace on the Avenue Hoche in Paris. That had been a social occasion, but this was a business one, and the gentle duquesa and her two daughters did not put in an appearance. Robbie had come with a portfolio of documents, to give information and get advice from a one-time fireman of Constantinople who had entrusted a couple of million dollars to his care.

No manners could have been more polite than Zaharoff's, no voice more soft and persuasive; yet it seemed to the youth that there was a subtle change in the relationship of the two men: his father was now the subordinate and the other the master. Perhaps this was just because Lanny remembered so vividly the occasions when the Levantine trader had suggested the idea that Vickers might buy out Budd's, and Robbie had answered suavely that Budd's might prefer to consider buying out Vickers. Time had passed, and Zaharoff's judgment had been vindicated; Robbie's wonderful dream of the world's greatest munitions industry up the Newcastle River seemed dead forever. Budd's was having to abandon that field to a great extent, while Vickers—it was having one hell of a time, as Robbie said and as the old man admitted, but Britain and France were going to keep their munitions industries, both under the control of this big-bodied Greek with the hawk's nose, the white imperial that bobbed while he talked, and the steely-blue eyes that never smiled even when the lips pretended to.

Lanny had nothing to do but listen while his father produced documents and explained them. If Lanny ever wanted to drill a couple of dozen oil wells he would know what it cost; also he would understand that Arab sheiks, so romantic on the motion-picture screen, were rapacious and incendiary in their attitude toward petroleum companies. Zaharoff knew that he was dealing with a capable businessman, and what he had to say was put in the form of suggestions. He revealed his distrust of all Moslem peoples, so entirely lacking in modern business sense and in respect for vested capital. With that frankness which had always surprised Robbie Budd's son, he discussed the attempted revolution in Constantinople, the scene of his youthful struggles. He defended the right of the Greek peoples to recover the lands taken long ago by the Turks, and said that he was insisting that the Allies should put the Turks out of Europe for good and all. Once more Lanny sat behind the scenes of the world puppet-show and saw where the strings led and who pulled them.

He learned that the strings reached even to that far-off land of liberty which he had been taught to consider his own. The munitions king wanted to know about the prospects of the election of a Republican president of the United States; he knew the names of the prominent aspirants, and listened attentively while Robbie described their personalities and connections. When Zaharoff heard that the Budd clan expected to have a voice in selecting a dependable man, he remarked: "You will be needing funds and may call on me for my share." Robbie hadn't expected that, and said so, whereupon the master of Europe replied: "When I invest my money in an American company, I become an American, don't I?" It was a remark that Lanny would never forget.

4

A Young Man's Fancy

I

ROBBIE sailed for home by way of Marseille, and Lanny motored him to the steamer, so they had a chance for another heart-to-heart talk. Robbie wanted to know what his son was doing about the problem which was the torment of great numbers of men—a woman. Lanny said he was getting along all right; there were so many interesting things in the world, and he was holding to the suggestion of the idealistic young master at St. Thomas's Academy, that it was wiser to live a celibate life until he had met the woman who was to be his permanent mate. Robbie agreed that that was all right if you could do it. Lanny revealed that he sometimes found himself with shivers running over him at the thought of a woman, but he would look at those who offered themselves openly in public places on the Riviera and decide that he wouldn't be satisfied with them; then he would come home and play sweet sentimental music on the piano until he had tears in his eyes, and after that he would feel all right. Father and son laughed together.

Robbie had been discussing this also with Lanny's mother, and he talked a little about her attitude. To Beauty social life now presented itself as a conspiracy of mothers and daughters to trap her too eligible darling. Everywhere he went were simpering misses making eyes at him, and hawk-eyed, hawk-faced old women watching from the sidelines. Beauty knew, for she had heard them plotting against other victims. Budding females were trained for the marriage market, they were dressed for it, they learned to walk and talk and dance and flirt for it. In the presence of their highly developed arts the unhappy male creature was as helpless as a moth in a candle-flame.

"You're going to have a hard time finding one who will please Beauty," said Robbie, with a smile; "but all the same, don't fail to have her advice, because that's her department."

"What I want," said Lanny, "is to learn something worth while, and meet some woman who is interested in the same things."

"It can happen," said Robbie. "But most of the time what the woman is thinking about is making you think she's interested. And if you're fooled it can play the devil with your life."

"I know," said the youth; "I've been keeping my eyes open." He didn't feel as young as his years.

"I don't mean for you to worry," added Robbie. "When the time comes, ask yourself what you really want and if you're getting it."

There the matter rested. Lanny saw his father on board the steamer, and gave him messages for the many Budds, and hugged him hard, and then stood on the quay and watched the steamer warped out into the harbor. Waving to the receding figure on the deck he thought: What a wonderful world, what a blessed state, when one can see one's father off on a comfortable sea-hotel, and know that neither in the Mediterranean nor in the outside ocean will there be any submarines watching for a chance to send it to the bottom!

II

Three months had passed since Beauty and Kurt had returned from Spain, and nobody had manifested the least suspicion of or hostility toward a Swiss music-teacher; so gradually peace settled in the woman's heart, and there began the burgeoning of new impulses toward her fellow-creatures. What was the use of being beautiful unless once in a while you allowed others to enjoy the sight? What was the use of having a handsome, eager, and eligible son if you kept him shut up in a garden? Afraid of fire as Beauty was, it appeared that she had to play with it.

The Duchesse de Meuse-Montigny was giving a very grand garden-party; and since Beauty's costumes were all hopelessly out of date she went in to Nice and had M. Claire fit her with something worthy of the occasion. Lanny was supplied with a light worsted suit of that spring's cut. Kurt couldn't go to parties, of course, and didn't want to—he was working on a Spanish suite for strings. So there was Lanny on a smooth green lawn with a Japanese peach tree for a background, and all around him predatory creatures flaunting costumes bright with freshly discovered hydrocarbon dyes, and cheeks and hair with the same; smiling coyly or wantonly, and doing their best to say something original and brilliant to please a youth reputed aloof and unattainable. It was just after a devastating war, when young males were scarce and young females ravenous. Inside the white marble palace a colored band was thumping, and Lanny would take the would-be brides in his arms one by one, sampling their charms symbolically, and Beauty would watch out of the corner of her eye and ask questions about the one in pink organdy or the one in white tulle with yellow shoulder-bows, and seldom be satisfied with what she learned.

What did she expect? Well, obviously, any woman who aspired to marry Lanny Budd had to be beautiful. How could he endure to have her about the house otherwise? She had to be rich—not just comfortably, but something super and solid, no fly-by-night fortune based on speculation. There were heiresses all over the place, and why not cultivate them? Lanny had told Beauty of Tennyson's *Northern Farmer*, and she endorsed his formula: "Doänt thou marry for munny, but goä wheer munny is!" Also, it would be safer if the chosen one belonged to an established family, and could prove it by Debrett. Finally, she would have to be clever, almost a blue-stocking, otherwise how could she keep from boring Lanny? Even his own mother couldn't do that!

To find all this in one package was no easy matter; Beauty had been to many social affairs, and had inspected the best that Paris and London and the Riviera had to offer, but she was still looking. Her friend Emily was in the conspiracy, and at this garden-party the pair inspected new candidates and discussed them *sotto voce*. The daughter of the California shipping magnate was overgrown and flavorless, like the fruit of her native state. The French girl was real Saint-Germain, but looked anemic; moreover, the family estate was mortgaged. The one whose father was a cabinet minister used her eyes like a screen actress and, anyhow, French politicians were mostly riffraff. The English girl doubtless had more sense and better breeding than any of them, but look at that gawky figure! The inevitable Russian princess, escaped from the Bolsheviks—her title sounded so impressive, but it meant merely a country squire's daughter in Russia, and even if she had once been rich she probably had nothing now except the jewels she had been able to hide in her garters or the heels of her shoes. Also, she might be promiscuous.

Such were a mother's thoughts at a garden-party; but meanwhile Lanny was having a very good time. He loved to dance, and if delicately gowned and perfumed young things were available for the purpose, he would take them in his arms, and carry home memories which would last him many a day. He would try to set these thrills to music like Kurt, or put them into verses like Rick, and when he wasn't satisfied with his own attempts, he would turn to the masters. A *thé dansant*, a flower show, or a dinner dance would lend wings to the music of Chopin and illuminate the pages of Shelley. The sunlight clasped the earth and the moonbeams kissed the sea, and all these kissings were worth something to Lanny, even though they kissed not him.

III

A large white yacht slid into the harbor of Cannes. Its flag showed that the owner was aboard, and presently it showed that he was not. His name was Jeremiah Wagstaffe and he was a Philadelphia banker who had been involved in the scandal with Emily's husband, but since he had operated through dummies, he hadn't had to move to France. His fortune was of the third generation, and in America you can build a tremendous tower of pride in that time. Mr. Wagstaffe's tower was his wife, who held herself like a drill sergeant and looked at the rest of mankind through a lorgnette.

They were just completing a Mediterranean cruise, and with them was their niece, Miss Nellie Wagstaffe. She was a year older than Lanny, which wasn't so good, but she was an orphan and had a large fortune in her own right. She had pale blue eyes and lovely white skin, a quiet manner, a mild disposition—just the thing that a rather talkative and confident young man might prefer. She didn't carry her money with her and sit on top of it as her aunt did. Emily Chattersworth phoned over to Bienvenu and told Beauty that these old friends were to be at Sept Chênes for lunch, and that Lanny should come alone, since romance blossoms better in the absence of mothers. Lanny guessed what it was about—it had happened before.

Mr. Wagstaffe was a short, rotund gentleman in a white yachting costume, and had a white mustache decorating a fiery-red face; Lanny knew from his own experience that people dined well on yachts and that the sun of Africa was hot in April. Also he knew what it was to be inspected through a gold lorgnette, and it didn't cow him. He knew that when you sat next to a young lady who had several millions of dollars in traction and bank stocks in her own name, you were supposed to perk up and think of striking things to say. The trouble was with Mr. Wagstaffe's stories. He had a stock of them, and they weren't bad stories, but everything reminded him of one and the telling left little room for other conversation at a small luncheon table.

It happened that another guest had been previously invited for this day. Her name was Madame de Bruyne, and the hostess called her Marie. Lanny remembered having met her more than once at Mrs. Emily's country place, Les Forêts, near Paris; but that had been before the war, when Lanny was a youngster, and he couldn't recall that he had ever talked with her. She was a Frenchwoman, slender, with dark brown eyes and hair; she had delicate, pale features, and what Lanny thought the saddest face he had ever seen upon a woman; he had seen his mother in great grief, but this was a kind of permanent, settled sorrow. She smiled faintly at the stories, whether she understood them or not. She said little—but then she had no chance, except when Mr. Wagstaffe had his mouth full of asparagus and mayonnaise. She was placed across the table from Lanny, and of course their eyes had to meet now and then. There was understanding in the woman's, as if she knew that he had lived most of his life in France, and would be thinking: "*Que les Américains sont drôles!*"

After the meal it was up to Lanny to invite the heiress to view the gardens and the scenery. He did so, and they chatted. She had been to the places which the *Bluebird* had visited; Lanny told about his trip and she proved a good listener. To try her out he described how the ancient ruins had made him feel melancholy; her comment was that there were so many troubles in the world nowadays, she didn't see the use of bothering about any that were so far off. Then they talked about the war; she had a brother who had been in the French ambulance service, and Lanny told her about Eddie Patterson, who had been killed in that service, and she said she would ask her brother if he had met him.

She was a pleasant enough girl, and Lanny could imagine himself pitching in and making himself agreeable and perhaps winning her; then he would be fixed for life, he wouldn't ever have to work. But it didn't seem to him like much fun, and the girl was entitled to better luck, though she would probably not have it. How many men were there who could come that close to several million dollars in one lump and not think it was cheap at the price? Such things subjected human nature to too great a strain!

The pair strolled in, and the aunt said they must be going, they had other friends to call on. Emily, who didn't know how the conspiracy had progressed, asked Nellie if she wouldn't like to stay a while; Emily would be glad to deliver her to the yacht. It was a bid; but the heiress said that she had better go with her aunt. This was the moment for Lanny to ask: "May I have the pleasure of seeing you again before you sail?" But he just wasn't interested enough to face that gold lorgnette swinging upon him. What he did was to bid the travelers a polite *bon voyage*, and thank Mrs. Emily for a pleasant occasion.

Madame de Bruyne said that she was sorry to have to bother her friend to send her home. So of course it was Lanny's duty to offer to drive her. "Oh, but I live far to the west of Cannes," said the French lady with the sad brown eyes.

"I like to drive," Lanny replied. It was kind of him, and Mrs. Emily knew that he was always kind—it explained why she was taking the trouble to find him a rich wife.

IV

On the way Lanny chuckled over the bouncing old gentleman who had left no time for conversation, also the heiress who had looked at the ruins of the Parthenon without feeling sad. Madame de Bruyne said that she was very young, and would learn more about sorrow as she went on. One needed suffering in order to appreciate any form of art. "But not too much," she added; "that dulls the sensibilities."

They were speaking French, and Lanny translated the words of Goethe about eating one's bread with tears. "Yes," said the woman, "and Heine gives the same testimony about his verses."

"So she reads!" thought Lanny, and added, out of his own reading: "The people who are sensitive to beauty expect too much of life, and it doesn't fulfill their hopes."

"I wonder about that problem with my own children. If I tell them what lies ahead, I may fill them with fears and spoil their childhood. On the other hand, would I let them walk into a burning house without warning them?"

"I think it depends on the children," said Lanny. "I had plenty of warnings of all sorts, but I don't know that they worried me. Generally they weren't real to me. We have to feel the heat before we know what fire is."

They continued exchanging ideas about life, and when they came to the little villa where Madame de Bruyne lived, she asked: "Wouldn't you like to come in for a while?"

Lanny thought he would, and sat in a modest drawing-room—it was the home of her aunt, she explained. She offered him something to drink, but he said he didn't take it, and she asked with a smile: "Did somebody warn you?" He explained that his father had done that; also he had watched people who drank. He didn't need stimulants, because he was happy anyhow.

"I've always remarked that about you," said the woman.

"I'm surprised to hear you ever noticed me," he replied.

"Oh, women notice personal details. I thought I'd like my two boys to have natures as sunny as yours. How have you managed to stay so, all through six dreadful years?"

He told her various things about his life. He mentioned the two friends he had met learning to dance "Dalcroze," one an English boy and the other a Swiss. "You are fortunate to have kept your friends," she said. "My brother was killed, and two cousins, my childhood playmates."

He spoke of Marcel. She knew that story; she knew Beauty and had seen the painting, *Sister of Mercy*, in the Paris *salon*. It was as if she had been sitting up on a cloud somewhere watching Lanny's life. He told her about his strange experience in his father's home in Connecticut, when a ghost or something of Rick had appeared in his bedroom at dawn, just as Rick crashed and lay near death in Picardy. The story affected her greatly; her lips trembled and she said: "I had the same sort of experience with my brother; but he died. I have never told about it, because it was so frightening, and I didn't know what to make of it."

Said Lanny: "My great-great-uncle in Connecticut, a Unitarian minister, believed that there is a universal consciousness, and that we are part of it, in some way that we do not understand yet."

They were talking about the deepest problems of the soul. Did Lanny believe that the dead still live? He told her that he didn't know what he believed; he had never been taught anything about religion, and hadn't been able to work it out for himself.

"I was brought up a Catholic," said Madame de Bruyne. "I was devout when I was a girl, but for several years the conviction has been coming over me that I don't really believe the things I have been taught. At first I was frightened by this realization: it seemed wicked, and I thought that God would punish me—but now I seem to have grown hardened to the idea. I cannot believe what seems to me unreasonable, even if I am damned for it."

"Whatever it is that gave us our reason doubtless intended us to use it," said Lanny.

"I've never had anybody say that to me," declared the woman. It sounded naïve, and Lanny was flattered to be taken as a spiritual adviser to so mature a person. He told her about Emerson, who had helped to give him the concept of spiritual freedom. She answered that Emerson was a mere name to her, and this pleased Lanny. He had met society ladies who would pretend to have read any book you mentioned; but when this one didn't know something she asked about it and listened to what you said.

Lanny saw that there was a piano in the room, and asked if she played. He had told her how hard he worked at it, and she invited him to play for her. He played several things, and she knew what they were; her comments pleased him. It seemed that he had never met anyone with whom he shared such quick understandings; their ideas fitted together like mortised joints in a well-built house. When he played happy music she forgot her grief, and their spirits danced together over flower-strewn meadows. When he played Mac-Dowell's *An Old Trysting Place,* her eyes were misty, and she did not have to talk. Lanny thought: "I have found a friend!"

V

They forgot all about time, and he was still playing when her aunt came in. Lanny was introduced to a wizened but agreeable old lady, who insisted upon serving tea for them. Over the ceremony Madame de Bruyne told about the capitalist from Philadelphia and his stories. "What was so funny about the horse-race?" she asked, and Lanny tried to explain American humor. He didn't mention that he had been expected to marry the pale-eyed heiress, but doubtless Madame de Bruyne guessed that. Before he left, he asked: "May I come again?" She replied: "We two old women are often lonely."

When Lanny got home, there was another "old woman" waiting eagerly to know what had happened, and sure that he must have made a conquest, having stayed so long. Beauty in her fancy had been dwelling in marble halls across the sea, and she clamored for the full story. Men are frequently unsatisfactory under such circumstances: they neglect to tell the things that women want to know, and they have to be plied with questions that bore them— "What was she like?" and "What did she say?" and "Was that all you could find to talk about? What have you been doing all afternoon?"

"I talked with Mrs. Emily for a while," he said, and, strictly speaking, this was true, though the "while" had been short.

"Was anybody else there?" persisted Beauty.

"A Madame de Bruyne."

"Marie de Bruyne? What on earth did Emily want her for?"

"I think she had been invited previously."

"And what did she have to say?"

"She doesn't talk much. She's one of the saddest-looking women I ever saw. She's grieving over a brother that she lost in the war."

"She has more than that to worry about," remarked Beauty.

"What else?"

"Emily says her husband is one of those elderly men who have to have virgins."

"Oh!" exclaimed Lanny, shocked.

"And she isn't a virgin," added Beauty, with unnecessary emphasis.

"She told me she has two boys in school."

"You had a talk with her?"

"I drove her home, and played the piano for her. I met her aunt, Madame Scelles."

"She's the widow of a professor at the Sorbonne."

"I knew they were cultivated people," said Lanny. "They have very refined manners."

"For heaven's sake be careful!" exclaimed the mother. "There's nothing more dangerous than an unhappily married woman. Remember, she's as old as your mother."

Lanny chuckled. "As old as my mother admits!"

VI

Lanny had said that young people don't take advice; and right away he set out to prove it. He inquired in the bookstores and found a copy of his much-loved Emerson and sent it to Madame de Bruyne by messenger. A couple of days later he called at teatime, and found his new friend at home; also he found that she had read the book. There are doubtless many women of the world who, when you make them a present of a book, sit down and read it straight through; but this was the first time Lanny had had that experience, and it seemed extraordinary to him. They discussed the Concord philosopher's abstruse and elevated ideas; they reason'd high of providence, foreknowledge, will, and fate, fix'd fate, free-will, foreknowledge absolute; and found no end, in wand'ring mazes lost.

Lanny played music, and the widow of the Sorbonne professor came in and listened, and her comments indicated that she also had a cultivated taste. They invited him to supper, a frugal and unfashionable meal which the old lady herself put on the table; they had a maid only in the morning, it appeared. Gradually Lanny began to discover the situation in this household; Madame de Bruyne had left the rich husband who had to have virgins, and was staying with the sister of her mother long since deceased. They were interested in a school where the orphans of French soldiers were cared for, and went there sometimes to help. Madame de Bruyne was avoiding social life, and spent most of her time at home; but she would always be glad to see Lanny, and very soon he came to feel at home in this household, and would stay for lunch or supper, as they called their informal meals.

A worrisome situation for Beauty Budd! Her darling, her supereligible offspring, was missing at odd hours, and contented himself with saying: "I was over at Madame de Bruyne's." If she asked: "What were you doing?" he would say: "Playing Debussy"; or maybe it would be Chabrier, or César Franck, or de Falla—they were all a blur to Beauty. Or perhaps he would say: "We were reading Racine"—or it might be Rolland or Maeterlinck. She was sure that this couldn't go on—sooner or later there would be an explosion, dreadful to think of. But what could she say—she who kept a young lover on the place, and in a house which Lanny had constructed for the purpose! Was this a most ingenious form of punishment, devised by some angry god or devil who spied upon the sex-life of the social élite? How different our own actions appear when we see them committed by others—and especially by one for whom we have been planning the great wedding of the season, with half a dozen bridesmaids in pink duchesse satin and white hats, and carrying armfuls of roses to match the satin!

VII

She couldn't refrain from speaking. She came to his room, and shut the door portentously, and sat by him and gazed into his eyes. "Lanny, tell me honestly!"

"What, dear?"

"Are you falling in love with Marie de Bruyne?"

"Oh, for heaven's sake!" he exclaimed. "She's a good sport, and a most intelligent woman. I like to talk to her."

"But, Lanny—it's playing with fire! A man and a woman can't——"

"Forget it," he said. "She's a second mother to me."

"But isn't one enough?"

"You're the dearest that ever was in the world; but you haven't read the books that I'm reading, and you don't play the music I play——"

"I could, Lanny, if you really wanted me to."

"Bless your heart! It would be hard work, and it would make you nervous and maybe spoil your complexion. Let me have an auxiliary mother, and don't be jealous."

"It's not jealousy, Lanny! I'm thinking about your whole future."

"I assure you there's nothing to worry about," he insisted. "She's a really honest woman—and they're scarce, as you know."

"But, Lanny, it's not natural. You'll find you're getting involved with her."

"I hadn't thought about it, old girl; but if you insist, I'll ask her about it." There was a grin on his face.

But Beauty couldn't see any fun. "For God's sake, no!" she exclaimed.

She dropped the subject; but, oh, how she hated that creature, that shrewd, designing bundle of tricks! "Honest," indeed! The devil had made all women! This one knew that Lanny was naïve and sympathetic, so she pretended to be full of "sorrow"! "Hell!" thought Beauty. "As if I haven't had sorrow enough! But I smile, I make myself agreeable; I don't go around mooning and sighing, reading poetry books and quoting them while I make my eyelids tremble! My God, what fools men are!"

VIII

The anxious mother, meaning so well, had struck a spark in a tinder-box. Lanny went off and thought it over. Could it really be true that he was falling in love with Marie de Bruyne? What would it be like to love her? Right away, of course, nature began to tell him: a warm feeling stole over him, a delicious feeling, of which she was part and parcel—her goodness and kindness, as well as her beauty, which he hadn't noticed at first, but which had grown on him. He decided that if he didn't love her, he could easily learn to; and why not?

It was such an intriguing idea that he couldn't resist talking it over with her. Her reaction to it would be fascinating; he would know her better for it. He waited until the hour when the old lady usually was at the school; Marie didn't go so often—perhaps because she preferred the company of Lanny to that of orphan children.

They sat alone in the small drawing-room; Lanny in a large soft chair, leaning forward on his elbows. "See here, Marie," he said. "I've an interesting idea. I am wondering if you and I mightn't be falling in love."

"Oh, Lanny!" she cried; he saw that she was shocked.

"Hadn't you thought of it?"

Her eyes dropped. "Yes," she whispered. "I thought of it, but I hoped you wouldn't."

"Why?"

"We have such a pleasant friendship."

"Of course. But mightn't we be friends and lovers too? That might be twice as pleasant."

"It wouldn't, Lanny—it would ruin it all."

"For heaven's sake, why?"

"You can't understand——"

"I'd like to try. Will you answer me a few questions, fairly and squarely?"

"All right." Her voice was faint, as if she knew the questions would be painful.

"Are you the least bit in love with your husband?"

"No."

"Have you been living with him as his wife?"

"Not for a long time."

"Do you feel that you owe him any moral obligation?"

"It's not that, Lanny."

"Then what can it be?"

"It's hard to explain."

"Do the best you can."

"I gave my trust to a man, and I bore him two sons; then gradually I discovered that he was horrible in his habits."

"So you decided that all love is horrible?"

"No, not that. I decided I wouldn't stoop to his level. I would do my duty, even though he might fail in his."

"Of course you want to do your duty; you're that sort of person. The question is, what *is* your duty? Because one man isn't what he ought to be doesn't mean that all men are. Are my habits horrible?"

"No, Lanny, of course not."

"Because one love fails, does that mean that all love must be stifled? Are you a Hindu woman, who has to give herself to the flames with her husband's corpse?"

She said "No" again, but her voice was faint. His analogy was a rather violent one.

"What else?" he persisted; and as she hesitated, he went on: "You were brought up a Catholic, and you've been realizing that you don't believe all that. What about their ideas on the subject of the sex-life? Have you some of those superstitions still in your mind? They separate the love of the body from the love of the soul, and so they degrade both. The love of the body alone is a shame, and the love of the soul alone is a neurosis. Do you get what I mean?"

"I suppose so, Lanny." She generally did.

He had thought very carefully what he wished to say to her. He didn't wish to rush her off her feet, but to appeal to her judgment. Now he spoke slowly and precisely, as if it were a speech that he had learned. "If I should love you, I would love you all the ways there are. It would be a clean love, and an honest one, that you wouldn't have to be ashamed of. I would be kind and gentle; you wouldn't have to make any painful discoveries. I've had opportunities with women, but it's been a year and a half since I've taken one in my arms. That's not such a bad record for this part of the world—and for these post-war days. I have learned to control myself, and to know what I am doing; so I have a right to ask a woman to trust me. Doesn't that seem reasonable?"

"Yes, Lanny." Her voice had grown fainter still.

IX

For one of his age, Lanny Budd had acquired a considerable store of knowledge as to the structure and functioning of the feminine heart. At the age of thirteen he had discovered that his mother was the *amie* of a French painter, and had talked this situation out with her. As a result of the discretion thus acquired, he had become eligible for the pleasure cruise of the *Bluebird*, and had heard the conversation and observed the conduct of a group of ladies and gentlemen who might have come out of the *Decameron* of Boccaccio. Immediately afterward he had had the responsibility of helping his mother decide whether she was going to stick by her poor painter or be respectably married to a plate-glass millionaire from Pittsburgh. The war having come, Lanny and Beauty had read the romances of Stendhal and Anatole France together and discussed the opinions of these two authorities on love. After Marcel had been brought home with his face burned off, Lanny had helped his mother to nurse him back to life, and there wasn't much he didn't find out about those two in the process.

His own experiences, both on the Côte d'Azur and on the shore of Long Island, had taught him much, and in between his labors at the Peace Conference he had learned about his mother and his boyhood friend. He had built a love-nest, and watched two turtles pair who never meant to part. Furthermore, his head was full of phrases from the love-poets of England, France, and Germany, plus translations from the ancient Greeks. All that lore he was now putting at the service of Marie de Bruyne, who had told herself that her heart was a desert where no flowers could bloom or bird-songs be heard.

She said something obvious but painful: "Lanny, I am much too old a woman for you!"

He answered: "There are a few things you can leave to me, and that's one. I've met no end of young girls, and they're fun to dance with, and even to get thrills from; but when they try to make intellectual conversation it just doesn't come off. All my life I've spent time with older people, my mother and father and their friends; maybe that was a mistake, but, anyhow, it's made me so that I like to talk to you. When I say something about a book, you know what I mean, and if you answer, I learn something new, and that makes conversation a pleasure. Don't you think that's a part of love worth considering?"

"Yes, dear; but it mightn't be like that always."

"Always is a word too big for everyday use. None of us knows what he's going to be ten years from now; but if we have sense we can know what we are now, and what we need. I'm pretty sure you could make me happy, and I'd stand a chance to make you happy. The more I think about it the better I know that it would be lovely to take you in my arms. I could take you out of those dreadful memories that torment you; I could make love something different, so that you wouldn't go around looking like a mask of grief."

"Is that the way I appear?" she asked, as if shocked.

"That's the phrase I used to myself the day I saw you at Mrs. Emily's. But already the magic of love has been at work. You do love me a little, don't you?"

"Yes, Lanny," she whispered.

"Well, then, you have to choose—a great happiness or a great torment. Prudery, or monkery, or whatever you call it, says renunciation and loneliness; common sense says companionship and peace. Which do you want?"

"If it were only as simple as that, dear! But we live in the world!"

"Oh, yes; we have laws and conventions, and relatives and friends, and gossip and scandal, and superstitions that poison life and strangle happiness. What else?"

"You really think we have a right to do what we please?"

"I think that what you and I do in the privacy of our life would concern us very deeply, and concern no one else on this earth."

"I have two children."

"I don't begrudge you your children, and I don't want to take your love from them. There's plenty and to spare in your heart, I am sure."

"But they would find out about us, Lanny!"

"When I was thirteen and discovered that my mother was in love with Marcel Detaze, I told her that I wouldn't stand in the way of her happiness. Marcel became an extra father to me, and we never had one moment's difference in our lives."

"But that's extraordinary, Lanny."

"It may seem so to one who has been brought up to believe that love is sin; but I was brought up to believe in my reason. I take it as a matter of course that I should love you, and be kind to you, and do everything I could to make you happy—provided only you didn't let some black-robed priest tell you that I've lured you into mortal sin."

"No, Lanny, it's not that. But your mother would hate me dreadfully!"

"My mother has a dream for me to marry some divinely beautiful and fabulously rich daughter of the aristocracy, preferably English. When I was sixteen I had my first love affair with the granddaughter of an earl, but she turned me down for the grandson of another earl, and since then I have been more modest in my aspirations. You would suit me perfectly, and when my mother realizes that the matter is settled, she will adjust herself to it and perhaps bore you with her excess of kindness."

"But you ought to marry and have children!"

"I haven't any money to marry, and I don't seem to have any desire to reproduce myself. I have a delightful little half-sister at home, and Beauty insists upon spoiling her, so I have to take Marcel's place many a time. I know what he would say and I say it, and so my paternal impulses get satisfied. What I need right now is not a child, but friendship and happiness, and those are a part of love's gifts worth having and cherishing."

Her eyelids had dropped and he saw that her lips were trembling. He moved over to the sofa beside her and said: "I would like to kiss you." When she did not say no, he put his arms about her and gently touched his lips to her cheek. After a while he drew back his head and looked at her. "What do you say?"

"Lanny," she whispered, "I ought not decide such a thing in a hurry. I ought to think about it."

"That is fair," he answered; he released her and took one of her hands instead. "If you are going to be happy, you mustn't do anything that your reason and conscience don't approve."

"Oh, thank you!" she exclaimed. "That's the way to be kind!"

"How long do you want?"

"I don't know. I'll send for you. It's all so startling to me, so different from what I've been taught to feel. Play me something gentle and tender—like yourself." He played the Brahms *Cradle Song*, slowly and softly, and while he played he imagined that she was in his arms.

X

The young prodigal went home, and there was his mother, waiting in great anxiety. It would have been hard for him to conceal the shine in his eyes; he had never lied to her about matters of love, or indeed about anything except world diplomacy when that had been his job. Now he said: "Well, old girl, I followed your suggestion and had a talk with Marie about being in love with her."

"Oh, my God!" cried the mother. As he smiled teasingly, she clamored: "Well? What happened?"

"She wanted time to think it over, and I gave it to her. But I'm not sure that was wise. What do you think?"

Beauty thought a lot, and said it. He let her pour out her feelings, and ruin several handkerchiefs.

"See here," he said, at last. "You know what I did for you and Marcel, and what I'm doing now for you and Kurt. You owe me a debt, and you have to repay it. That's all there is to it, and you might as well pay up like a good sport."

"Oh, Lanny!" she sobbed. "I tried so hard to find you the right woman!"

"I know, dear; but you remember what Dr. Bauer-Siemans told me when I was a kid, that I couldn't expect to know what sort of man my mother needed. Now it's the other way around. You presented me to various young ladies who ought to have made me happy, but they didn't. I went out and found one for myself, and, believe me, I haven't any idea of letting her get away from me."

"A woman old enough to be your mother. Lanny!"

He had expected that from Marie, but not from Beauty. "Old goose!" he laughed. "Don't talk too loud or Kurt may hear you!"

"Yes, Lanny, but——"

"But that was you, while this is some other woman! What is sauce for one goose is sauce for any other."

Argument was so hopeless that she had to share his laughter, even while she went on sobbing. He went to the drawer of her dressing-table and brought her a handful of the tiny, delicate *mouchoirs* that ladies use; he dropped them into her lap, and said: "Cheer up, old dear. It isn't as if I'd gone out and picked up a tart on the boulevard. I've got one of the sweetest women you ever knew, and when you make up your mind to appreciate her you'll have a sister. It'll make our household hopelessly queer, I know——"

"Oh, Lanny!" she gasped. "Are you expecting to bring her here?"

"I couldn't on account of her husband; we mustn't take any chances of attracting attention to Kurt. Marie and I will work matters out by ourselves."

"Oh, dear, oh, dear!" lamented Beauty. "I was hoping to make our lives more respectable!"

Poor soul, he knew that this was the deepest longing of her heart; but there was nothing he could do except to go on laughing. "You began it!" he said.

"I know! I never really blame anybody else."

"Your chickens have come home to roost!" Lanny was young, and it seemed to him best to enjoy life as he went along. "They are roosting all over this baby-blue boudoir, and you and Kurt can hear them chirping on the headboard of your bed!"

5

Weep for the World's Wrong

I

ERIC VIVIAN POMEROY-NIELSON was sticking with
his British tenacity at the job of learning to write. He had got several editors interested in his efforts, and every now and then would
get a new idea and work furiously at it. When it was done, Lanny
would find it "swell," but Rick would frequently declare it "putrid"
and want to tear it up. Between the litter of manuscripts and the
litter of a baby it was hard to keep the little villa in order, but Nina
worked cheerfully, declaring that after what they had been through,
it was happiness just to be alive. From time to time Beauty would
decide that they were lonely, and would get up a picnic or sailing
party, which really they didn't care about very much; but Beauty
did.

One morning near the end of April Rick telephoned to Lanny and
read a telegram from the editor of a liberal weekly in London. There
was a conference of the Allied premiers opening at San Remo, a
town on the Italian Riviera, and the editor suggested that Rick
might like to try his luck with an article about it. The editor couldn't
promise to take what he wrote, but he said there was a story in this
conference, and it was up to a youngster to get the facts and present
them acceptably. Rick considered this a great chance, and he was
proposing to take a train that afternoon. Would Lanny like to go
along?

Lanny didn't hesitate. "I'll drive you," he said. "Maybe I can help
you get in on the inside."

Less than a year had passed since Lanny had registered a vow that
he was through with international politics and the pompous bigwigs

80

and solemn stuffed shirts who made the headlines at conferences. But time heals all wounds, and the war-horse resting in the pasture smelleth the battle afar off, the thunder of the captains and the shouting. Lanny wouldn't have admitted to himself that he wanted to gaze once more upon the cherubic countenance of David Lloyd George, or to see what the Frenchman Millerand or the Italian Nitti looked like; but when it was a question of helping Rick to get a story and perhaps make a reputation for himself, the devoted friend went into his dressing-room and started chucking his things into a couple of bags.

Meanwhile, of course, he was thinking about Marie. If only she would be sensible, what a delightful holiday they might make of it! Really an education for her! He'd not fail to give her the chance. He put his bags into the car, and gave Beauty a couple of hugs, and promised to drive carefully—there had been a dreadful accident to one of her friends the previous week. "All right—yes—I'll keep my eyes open." He shook hands with Kurt and told him to get that *fiesta* part of the Spanish suite into shape. Lanny couldn't say how long he'd be gone—one could never tell about those talk-fests of politicians—he'd stick by Rick and help him get about—good-by and good luck——

"Lanny, tell me!" exclaimed Beauty. "Are you going to take that woman?"

"Ask me no questions and I'll tell you no lies!" he chuckled.

II

Marie was alone in the house, except for the servant. He led her into the garden, where there couldn't be any eavesdropping. Three days had passed since he had left her, and he hoped that was time enough for thinking. He looked into her eyes to find an answer, but instead there seemed to be anxiety.

"Something exciting has happened," he said.

"What, Lanny?"

"There's an old town about ten miles inside Italy called San Remo. It looks out over our sea but it's older, and has a grand old Romanesque cathedral." (Lanny was grinning, for he didn't really think she'd want to see cathedrals.) "There are good hotels, and I've no doubt nice respectable *pensioni* where you get ravioli when you don't get spaghetti."

"I have been to San Remo, Lanny."

"A charming place for a holiday, don't you agree? Rick and I are leaving as soon as you can get your things packed. There's to be an international conference—a whopping big one—all the diplomatic world. Rick has an assignment to write it up and it may be the making of him."

"What an idea, Lanny—to take me to a conspicuous place like that! I couldn't fail to meet people who know me."

"Make it a brother-and-sister party. Stay at the most respectable place in the town. Arrive by train if you like, and meet me by accident."

"But nobody would believe that."

"Surely you have a right to be interested in international affairs! Aren't you curious to see the master minds who are making the world safe for democracy? You can stay in some near-by town if you prefer, and if you and I should disappear now and then—*così fan tutti!*"

"Lanny, it is sweet of you; but I've just had a letter with troubling news. My little Charlot is down with that dreadful flu, and I may have to take him out of school."

"Oh, I'm sorry!" he exclaimed.

"You see, dear, I just don't belong to myself. You can't think of me as you would of a debutante."

"I wouldn't think of a debutante. Where will you take the boy?"

"To our country place in Seine-et-Oise."

"Does that mean going back to your husband?"

"Not as his wife—never, Lanny. We can live in the same house and be polite to each other, as we have done in the past. He has a right to see the children, and I don't want to divorce him and make a scandal that would hurt them. These matters are different with us from what they are with you Americans."

"What is going to be your husband's attitude to our affair? Will he be jealous, or will he be glad to be let alone?"

"I don't know, Lanny. I've tried hard to think what to do. There are many painful possibilities. I am afraid of marring my children's life, and yours, too."

"Listen, darling," he said. "It's all right to worry about your children, but please don't take me on. There's no harm that you can do me, I assure you. I know what I want, and I mean to get it—the cost is no obstacle. I'll gladly tell the world that I love you. I'll put an advertisement in the papers for all the scandal-mongers to read. I'll put a sign on my back and parade up and down in front of your house: '*J'aime Marie de Bruyne!*'"

She couldn't keep from laughing. "Please, dear," she pleaded, "give me time. Take Rick and let him do his story. I'm waiting for a telegram about my son, and I'll write you later."

"That's all very well," replied Lanny. "But you overlook the fact that I'm in love. A man doesn't enjoy going off and leaving his woman without knowing how he stands."

"You can be sure there's nobody in my heart but you, Lanny."

"I wish I could accept your word, but I know there are a lot of other bodies in your heart. There's a large body called 'the world,' which you are afraid to expel. Why it should be malicious and hateful is something I've never been able to figure out, but it is. It likes to destroy other people's happiness. Look at what it did in the war—it has made a wreck of half Europe, just because some people couldn't bear to see other people free and happy! And now it wants to take charge of your life and mine; to say: '*Verboten!* Taboo! Keep off the grass! *Défense d'aimer!*' It has words in every language."

"I have given it hostages, Lanny. It will punish my two sons."

"Think about those sons, and how you mean to bring them up. Do you want to make them into time-servers and conformists? Are they going to have their loves in slum bedrooms and behind haystacks? If not, you'd better tell them the truth about love, and begin early, before the other boys have debauched them. One way to begin is to say: 'I have a lover, and you can see that he is honest and decent and kind, and nothing for you or me to be ashamed of.' "

They went into the house, and he closed the door of the drawing-room and took her in his arms, a long, long embrace. She clung to him, so that he knew she wasn't going to hold out forever.

"Marie, I love you," he declared, "and I'm not going to give you up—not for the Pope and all the hierarchy, the saints in heaven and the devils in hell. I'm coming for you, and I want to know I'll have you."

"All right, Lanny," she answered. "I'll work out a way."

III

The little town of San Remo lies in a sheltered bay, with a crescent breakwater forming its harbor and range upon range of mountains sheltering it from the northern blasts. The narrow streets of the Old Town climb the hills wherever they can, and the houses have triple buttresses against earthquakes; on the main streets they have arched loggias running together, not one daring to stand apart. When Rick saw this he said it was a lesson for the peoples of Europe—let them learn to build their states as they had built their homes!

High up on one of the slopes, with a walled road approaching it, stood a pretentious two-story villa having in front a semi-circular portico with tall narrow columns; Villa Devachan was its name. It had been the "Second Paradise" of the Theosophists, and now it was the council place of the Allied premiers and their advisers. Lanny Budd had seen so much of European splendor that he knew what he would find inside, even before he had an opportunity to enter. Large rooms with huge chandeliers dangling from the ceiling—how he would hate to be under one of them when the next earthquake hit! Heavy plush curtains protecting the inmates from the deadly possibility of a change of air. Gilt chairs with silk or satin upholstery, of colors which would quickly reveal the stains of human contact. Tables with inlaid tops and hand-carved legs, their curves as standardized as the beards of Egyptian pharaohs. Lanny had guessed that

Theosophical interior decoration would be no different from pseudo-Christian, and he found that he was right.

Each premier brought his elaborate staff, which had its own hotel or palace. From each nation came also a swarm of journalists, fending for themselves and grumbling bitterly over the sparsity of official "hand-outs." Also came delegations from the little nations and oppressed minorities; Estonians, Letts, and Lithuanians; Ukrainians, Hungarians, and Caucasians; Armenians, Arabs, and Assyro-Chaldeans. They had been told that this was "the New Freedom," this was "self-determination for all peoples," and they believed it, or said they did as a matter of policy. Some brought credentials, and others only moral powers; they put up in pensions or poor lodgings, and labored earnestly but for the most part vainly to get somebody to listen to them. When their funds ran out they borrowed from one another, or from anyone who looked as if he might believe in the brotherhood of man.

It was all so familiar to Lanny Budd, it was as if he had had an elaborate nightmare and now was starting it all over again. When he made this remark to a journalist from America, the man advised him to get used to this nightmare, because he would be riding it several times every year for how long nobody could say. The nations would be wrangling and arguing over the Versailles treaty until they were at war again. Newspaper men are notoriously cynical.

The Senate of the United States having refused to ratify the treaty or to join the League of Nations, Lanny's country had no representative at San Remo, not even an unofficial observer. But of course the American press had a large delegation, and among these were men whom Lanny had come to know in Paris, where he had served as a sort of secret pipeline through which news was permitted to leak. These men were under obligations to him, and greeted him cordially and took him and his aviator friend into their confidence. Lanny had advised Rick to say nothing about his proposed article, but to make his way with Americans on his war record, and with his compatriots on the basis of being the son of Sir Alfred Pomeroy-Nielson, Bart. Rick wouldn't be violating any confidences, because these correspondents were cabling "spot news" for various deadlines, and by the time a magazine article could appear they would be off on some other assignment.

IV

The Englishman, endeavoring to save his money, wanted to live *en pension*, but Lanny was used to living *en prince* and insisted that Rick should be his guest; it would be fatal to stop anywhere but at the most expensive hotel, for only there would you meet the people who were on the inside of affairs. On account of the crowds the pair had to bunk in one small room and bathe in a hand-basin; but they put on their "smokings" and went down into the dining-room, and the first person the American laid eyes on was the tall, sandy-haired young Fessenden who had been a member of the British secretariat in Paris. The last time they had met, this chap had been decidedly cool, because Lanny had resigned in protest against the concessions made by the American Commission, and Fessenden, a "career man," had been afraid for his future. But that had been nearly a year ago, and the world had changed greatly.

Now the secretary jumped up and greeted Lanny. He was introduced to Rick, and when he heard his accent and saw that he was "right," he invited the pair to his table, where two other young members of the staff were sitting. All three had been in war service, and they and Rick appeared to have secret passwords or insignia, for they fell to talking about one another's families and friends, old school ties, boat-races, cricket-matches, and other esoteric matters. Lanny, being an American, was not expected to produce credentials or to understand this conversation.

Before long they began talking about the task on which they were engaged, and it was better than listening to journalists who were being deliberately kept in the dark. These chaps had handled confidential memoranda, and one had just had a session with a department head in his portable bathtub. Rick remarked what a pleasant place the statesmen had picked out for themselves; whereupon Fessenden chimed in: "Did you hear what Lloyd George said to the premiers? A red-hot one! 'Well, gentlemen, we are in the Garden of Eden, and I wonder who will play the snake!'"

The San Remo conference had assembled amid direful forebodings. Many bitter disputes had arisen among the former Allies: over the remains of the Turkish Empire—Constantinople and Armenia, Syria and Palestine, the Hejaz, and especially Mesopotamia with its treasure of oil, vital alike to British, French, and Italian navies; over Russia and its Bolshevik government, and the war against it which had collapsed; over the *cordon sanitaire*, and Poland invading Russia and most of her neighbors at the same time; over German reparations and how they were to be shared; above all, over the new French invasion of the Rhineland, and the risk that France was taking of dragging Europe into another war.

There had recently been an attempted revolt of German reactionaries, known as the "Kapp Putsch." It had been put down by a general strike of the German workers, and there had followed a Communist revolt in the Ruhr, and the Socialist government of Germany had sent in troops to put that down. The move was a technical violation of the treaty of Versailles, and the French army had promptly seized a couple of German towns on the far side of the Rhine. Were they going to conquer their ancient enemy all over again, and were they expecting to get British sanction? This was the question these budding diplomats discussed with solemn faces. They told of the firm resolve of their chiefs that the French must be made to back down, and allow trade to be resumed and the German people to be saved from starvation and chaos.

To Lanny it seemed an odd thing to hear these official persons saying the very things for which the liberals on the American staff had been called "Pinkos" and troublemakers. So rapidly had opinion changed under the pressure of events! The British were now giving all their efforts to trying to get blockades lifted and trade started. But the French still lived under the shadow of a dreadful fear. Was German militarism to be allowed to come back? And if it did, would France again have Britain's help? With the French it was dominate or be dominated—and the moment they took to dominating, the British would begin giving help to the Germans, raising them up as a counter-force to France. As Robbie Budd had told his son repeatedly, it was dog eat dog all over Europe; and when Lanny had watched it for a while, he wanted to go back to Bienvenu and play the piano!

V

Fessenden said: "You must meet Mrs. Plumer; that's where everybody goes." This was a member of the English colony who had a beautiful villa up on the Berigo Road. Wherever the English live they have places like that, to which you can go if you have a proper introduction. Also there is always an English club, where the men drink whiskies and soda, and play billiards, and talk about the stock market, trade, and politics, in a language that you have to be brought up on to understand. Lanny and Rick were invited to tea by Mrs. Plumer, and received guest-cards at the club, and so they heard what had been said that day in the council chamber at the Villa Devachan. Rick exclaimed to his friend: "If it hadn't been for you, Lanny, I'd have been a fish tossed up on dry land!"

"I'm getting my share of fun," replied Lanny. "Only don't try to do too much in one day." There was a ceaseless round of activities, all day and most of the night, and it was hard for a man with a steel leg to get in and out of cars and up flights of stairs. Lanny would persuade him to come back to the hotel in the afternoon for a siesta. Even at the end of April it was hot in this sun-bowl of San Remo.

While Rick lay propped up on the bed making notes of what he had heard, Lanny would go out and wander through the narrow streets where old pirates from Africa had charged up the hills, slaughtering the inhabitants or dragging them off in chains. He strolled on paths shaded by palm trees, or by pepper trees loaded with white blossoms. He climbed to the heights where the wild flowers spread sheets of purple, gold, and pink. He gazed down onto red-roofed houses, and the blue and green sea which each and every Mediterranean people claims as its own. *Mare nostrum*—how many had made the boast through the ages, and their blood had been drained into the sea and their dust blown over the hills, and the very names of their tribes were lost to history!

Lanny always had the fancy to know what the plain people were thinking and saying, as well as the great and important ones who made the headlines. He and Rick would attend a session of the journalists in which the new Italian Premier would expatiate on the dire need of his people for coal and wheat, and the necessity of reopening trade with the Russians through their Black Sea ports. From there Lanny would drive his friend to a *trattoria* on an obscure street where most of the conversation was in the Ligurian dialect. Lanny knew some of it, just as he knew Provençal, because in his childhood he had played with the fisherfolk, many of whom had dwelt on the Côte d'Azur since it had been a part of Italy. For a couple of lire you could have a good meal in this *trattoria*—though served on a plain board table set on a floor strewn with sawdust. Lanny would start jabbering away, half in French, half in Italian, with a dark-skinned workingman in a sweaty shirt, and would report to Rick how the declarations of the liberal Francesco Nitti sounded to the dwellers in musty old tenements with cracked walls and the darkness of caves inside.

What they learned was that the workers of Italy were in a dangerous ferment. They despised and distrusted their political leaders, calling them cheats and liars, hired agents of the capitalist class. These *cattivi* had dragged their country into a war to no purpose, and now they left the people to starve while they stuffed themselves with rich foods and fine wines. Here in San Remo the workers had elected a Socialist mayor, and what was he? A banker! And what did he do? The gesture of the angry dock-laborer imperiled the glassware on the table.

It might have been difficult for a stiff young Englishman, brought up in the public school tradition, to get into the confidence of such a person; but Lanny made it easy for him. He bought an extra bottle, and when others perceived that free wine and free conversation were available, they moved over to listen and take part. Horny dark fists were clenched and raucous voices proclaimed that a change was coming in Italy, and soon; what the workers had done in Russia was not so bad as *le gazzette capitaliste* had made it seem. Already many of the factories in Milan and Turin and other cities were in the hands of the workers, who would be running them for themselves and not for the *padroni*.

VI

When this piece of research had been completed and Lanny and Rick were on their way to the hotel, Rick said: "I've an idea there's another story in Italy: the spread of Socialism."

"Let's go after it," said his friend.

"It's wonderful the way you can understand these people, Lanny."

"When I was a kid I used to haul the seine with fisherboys who talked this dialect, and one would take me to his cabin where his mother would feed us on dandelion salad and shrimp fried in oil. They always thought it was funny if anybody didn't know their words."

"It would be difficult to do anything like that in Berkshire," commented Rick. "But if I'm going to be a journalist I'll have to learn. After I get the San Remo article off I want to do one on the state of mind of Italian labor. Let's eat in places like that from now on."

"The food agrees with me," said Lanny.

They dined in a somewhat better place, frequented by intellectuals as well as workers. They watched the various types and Lanny speculated: this one might be a teacher at the *accademia*, and that one a musician in the orchestra of the Teatro Principe Umberto; a third might be the editor of the local labor paper. Rick asked: Could that large gentleman with the black beard and pince-nez be the Socialist mayor? "No," said Lanny, "he'd have come here when he was campaigning, but he'd be too important now. Which one would you like to talk to?"

"Can you just go up and talk to anybody in the place?"

"Italians are always ready for conversation. They will take us for tourists."

"But they're angry with Americans right now." Rick had been informed that on the previous day the city council of San Remo had voted to change the name of the Corso Wilson to the Corso Fiume —which was certainly a pointed gesture.

"They will tell us their grievances, of course," replied Lanny; "but they will talk."

Their attention was attracted to the table across the aisle, where several men were lingering over their coffee. Evidently it was a political discussion, and now and then a voice would be raised; they heard the word *Americani* more than once, and fell silent, listening.

At the head of the table, facing them, sat a dark-eyed Italian with a little black mustache; a smallish man with a pale, almost pasty face and melancholy expression when it was in repose. But now he was becoming excited, and waving his hands as he orated in a shrill, tense voice. "*Porca Madonna!*" Rick heard, and whispered to his friend: "What is *Porca Madonna?*"

"It is an oath," Lanny explained. "It is meant to be very offensive. It means that the Holy Virgin is a sow." He listened again and added: "They are talking about Italy, and the way it has been robbed by the Allies. That dark fellow is telling the filthy English bastards that the Italians are going to stay in Fiume, and if Nitti dares to yield it, they will cut his throat on the steps of the Villa Devachan."

"There's nothing for us in that lot," said Rick, hastily.

VII

The door of the *trattoria* opened and two persons came in, a man and a woman. It happened that Lanny was facing the door, and as the woman came up the aisle between the tables he had a good look at her. She was frail and gray-haired, with fine, ascetic features, and it struck him instantly that he had seen the face before. He tried to think where.

The pair were close to him when the woman's escort noticed the orator seated at the table. He stopped, turned toward the man, raised his clenched hand, and cried in a fury: "*Eh via, puh! Furfante! Traditore dei lavoratori!*"

Instantly the place was in an uproar. The insulted one leaped to his feet—whether it was to fight or to run Lanny couldn't know, for others on each side sprang up to restrain him. He began to yell curses at the invader, and the latter shouted back. The woman, greatly troubled, seized her escort's arm and began pleading with him: "*No, no, compagno!* Restrain yourself. The wretch is not worth it!"

"I will not eat with that *porco!*" exclaimed the man.

"*Su! Via!*" cried the woman. "Let us go." Amid jeers from those at the table the disturber let himself be persuaded to the door and outside.

The excitement was slow in subsiding. The diners talked volubly about what had been said and by whom. The dark-eyed man with the little black mustache considered that he had played the hero; he shook his fist and became inspired, telling what he would have done to the accursed one, the enemy of *la patria*. Working himself into a warlike mood, he challenged the enemies of Italy to come from all quarters of the earth and he would deal with them single-handed. It is the nature of Italians to say a lot about what they intend to do, and it is the nature of Englishmen to look upon them with an aloof expression which seems to say: "What unpleasant insects!" Lanny was amused by both types.

He explained to his friend that it was a political dispute; the new arrival had called the orator a traitor and betrayer of the working class. Probably this orator had belonged to the extreme left, but had become patriotic during the war; it was a common happening.

"I've been trying to remember where I've seen that woman," Lanny remarked; "and now it comes to me. You remember I told you I had an uncle who is a Red; and once when I was young he took me on a slumming trip—we called on a friend of his in a tenement in Cannes, and it was this woman. Her name is Barbara—I have forgotten the second name. My father was angry and made a fuss, and I had to promise that I would have nothing more to do with my Uncle Jesse."

"Would your father feel that way now?" asked Rick.

"Indeed he would; the day the treaty was signed my father and my uncle had a frightful row. Robbie has a regular phobia on the subject of the Reds and what they might do to me. You know they have a lot of facts on their side, and they are damned clever at making use of them."

"Listen, Lanny; I don't want you to do anything you shouldn't, but it might be a rare good thing for me to have a talk with that woman. She could tell me everything I need; and there's what you call local color, human interest—I'd get the feel of the people from her."

Lanny was taken aback. "I suppose—if it's a professional matter—" He stopped, and a grin came on his face. "That's exactly the way it happened at the Peace Conference. I had to go and see my uncle, because Colonel House wanted to get in touch with the Bolshevik agents!"

Rick laughed in turn. "But after all, Lanny, you're going to live in a different world from your father. You'll have to believe what you believe and not what he tells you."

Lanny saw that his friend was in earnest about the woman, so he said: "I wonder if we could find her."

"They'll be looking for a place to get a meal. They probably won't go far."

"All right. You sit here and finish your dinner, and I'll scout around and see if I can spot them."

VIII

It proved an easy assignment. In the third place Lanny looked he saw the pair seated at a table. As they were eating, he did not disturb them, but went back and fetched Rick, and the two of them approached the table together. "I wonder if you remember me, Signora," said Lanny, in French, which he knew the woman spoke. "You are, I believe, a friend of my uncle, Jesse Blackless."

"Oh, of course!" she exclaimed. She rose up and looked at Lanny's smiling features, and remembered. "You are that little boy who came to see me in Cannes!"

"No longer so little," he replied. "I have never forgotten you. Your name is Barbara—" He had expected to stop, but at exactly the right instant the other name popped into his mind. "Pugliese," he said—pronouncing it in the Italian manner, "Pool-yay-say."

"You have a remarkable memory!" she testified.

"You were sick when I saw you. I am glad that you appear to be better."

"We poor are hard to kill. We have to be."

"You made a great impression upon me, Signora. I thought you had the most saintly face I had ever seen. But perhaps you would not like to be described in that way."

The woman was amused, and translated the remark to her friend, whose French was apparently not so good.

"My name is Lanny Budd, and this is my friend, an English flier who was wounded in the war. He has a long English name which is hard to spell or to remember, so pretend that he is another little boy and call him Rick."

"I will do that if you will call me Barbara. Your uncle is a man for whom I have a high regard. He stands by his convictions. Where is he now?"

"I believe at his home, near Saint-Tropez. You know that he paints pictures when he is not rebelling."

Barbara smiled. Her face was sad and could be very stern, but it was lighted by intelligence and kindness, and Lanny the young man confirmed what Lanny the lad had judged, that she was a rare and good person in spite of her evil reputation.

She introduced her companion by the name of Giulio, and all four seated themselves. Rick ordered coffee, and Lanny ordered the tail end of a dinner. Now and then the two would exchange a glance, and Lanny knew that a member of the English ruling classes was getting a thrill out of addressing two dangerous Italian Reds by their first names. Now indeed he was a journalist, getting local color in great splashes!

Lanny mentioned that they had been witnesses of the recent fracas, and Barbara's face lost all its gentleness. "That is the most abominable little wretch that I have met upon this earth!" she told them. "When I first knew him in Milan, where I was an official of the party, he was a poor waif who came to meetings, a sick beggar who haunted our headquarters to sponge upon the kindness of members. Now and then someone would give him food—just because it is impossible to eat with any satisfaction while a starving dog is cringing by the table. You cannot imagine the misery of this ragged and homeless one, lamenting the hopelessness of his fate, the worthlessness of himself, the pains he suffered from syphilis—this, I imagine, would not be considered quite good taste in England?"

"Rather not," said Rick, to whom the question was addressed.

"We of the party of course have to allow for the degradation of the workers. It is our duty to lift them up and teach them, and so we aided this poor Benito—the name is Spanish and means 'Blessed One' and is freely bestowed by pious mothers. So we taught the favorite of heaven the philosophy of brotherhood and solidarity, and he proved to be quick at learning phrases and using them in speeches. It was not long before he was addressing the workers, denouncing all capitalists and clamoring that their throats should be cut. There was only one person in the world to whom he could not give courage, and that was his mournful self. There is a pun I used to make upon his name, which is Mussolini. I would leave out one of the *s*'s. The Italian word *muso* means—I cannot recall the French word, but it is when a child has his feelings hurt, and he will not play, but makes a face very ugly——"

"*Boudant*," supplied Lanny, and added for Rick's benefit: "Pouting."

"That is it," said Barbara. "And so Benito Musolini means Blessed Little Pouter. In that way I would try to tease him out of his self-pity—and you see how in the end I succeeded. His poor thin cheeks have filled out, he wears well-tailored clothes and orates in the *trattorie*."

"How does he manage this?" inquired Rick, thinking of his "human interest."

"He became the editor of the Socialist paper in Milan; and when the British agents or French came to him he took their gold. The paper changed its tone overnight; and when the party kicked him out, he got more gold to start a paper of his own and to denounce his former comrades as traitors to *la patria*. Now he is here getting material for articles about the conference. He is all for the *sacro egoismo*; he preaches to the starving workers the glory of holding

Fiume and seizing the Dalmatian coast, and that it is their sublime destiny to help fill a sea of blood upon which the Italian navy may sail to world empire. Never has there been such a transformation in a man—you should see him on the platform, how he has learned to thrust out his chin and swell up his chest—our Blessed Little Pouter."

"You are making a better pun than you know," put in Lanny. "There is a kind of pigeon which swells up its chest in such a way, and by a strange chance is called a pouter."

The woman was delighted, and told her friend about it—*uno colombo!* He laughed with glee, and learned to say it in English—Benito Musolini—Blessed Little Pouter Pigeon!

IX

Rick questioned his new acquaintance about the state of mind of the Italian workers, and she described the tragic years of slaughter and semi-famine. For her the war had been a struggle of rival imperialisms, and as always the people had paid for it with their blood and tears. But now they had learned their lesson, and soon were going to take affairs into their own hands.

"You don't think the war-mongers can mislead them?" asked Rick, by way of drawing her out.

"*Mai più!*" exclaimed Barbara. "Our people are disciplined; they have their labor unions, their great co-operatives, their presses, their schools for the children. They are class-conscious and mentally armed."

"Yes, but are they armed with weapons?"

"The soldiers are of the people; would they turn their guns upon their own? You see that already the workers have seized many factories and are holding them."

"But can they run them?"

"Our great weakness in Italy is that we have no coal; we are dependent upon your British capitalists, who will not give credit to revolutionary workers. But the Russian workers are digging coal, and soon it will be coming to us. That is why trade through the Black Sea is so vital to us."

"I see that Nitti has come out for the lifting of the blockade."

"Nitti is a politician, a twin brother to your Lloyd George. He makes bold speeches, but what he is doing behind the locked doors of the council chamber is another matter."

"You don't think he means it, then?"

"The Socialists have just shown him that they have the votes. If he does not wish to retire to private life, he must force the French to let us trade with our Russian comrades."

"You really believe," persisted the interviewer, "that labor unions can manage to run factories and produce goods?"

"Why can they not? Who is it that does the work today?"

"They do the manual work; but the directing——"

"Is done by technicians, hired by the capitalists. Why can they not be hired by the workers?"

They discussed the theories of syndicalism, or labor-union control of industry. Barbara hated every form of government; she would trust no politicians, whatever label they gave themselves. Rick pointed out that in Russia the workers had a strong government; syndicalism appeared to have merged with Bolshevism, which put everything into the hands of the state. Barbara attributed this to the civil war, which was really an invasion of Russia by the capitalist nations. Government control of industry might be a temporary necessity, but she didn't like it. Rick ventured the guess that if she were to go to Russia she mightn't find what she expected.

The woman rebel had one argument to which she would return. Could the workers make a worse mess of the world than their masters had done? Look at what they had made of Europe! One more such holocaust and the Continent would be a wilderness inhabited by savages wearing skins and hiding in caves. "Capitalism is war," declared Barbara Pugliese; "its peace is nothing but a truce. If once the workers own the tools of production, they do not produce for profit, but for their own use, and trade becomes free exchange and not a war for markets."

"I have to admit," said the interviewer, "that our British labor movement seems to have the sanest program at present." Lanny found that a startling opinion to come from a baronet's son. Was

Eric Vivian Pomeroy-Nielson turning into a Pink? And if he did, what would Robbie make of it?

X

The San Remo conference broke up at the end of ten days, and Rick had his article ready by that time. He had shut himself up in the stuffy hotel room while Lanny was out playing tennis with Fessenden and his friends, or inspecting a sixteenth-century palace and a votive chapel having wax images of portions of the human body which had been healed—including some not customarily exposed to public gaze. When Rick worked, he worked like one possessed, and Lanny read the manuscript page by page and kept his friend cheered by extravagant praises.

Really it was a first-class article, written by a man who had been behind the scenes and hadn't been fooled by official propaganda. Rick described the loveliness of the background of the conference; was it the region referred to by the hymn-writer, where "every prospect pleases, and only man is vile"? Here were flower-covered hills, roads lined with palm trees, hedges of roses and oleanders, cactus gardens and towering aloes; and here were elderly politicians whose minds were labyrinths full of snares for the feet of even their friends and allies. Rick cited official statements which had gone all over the earth and which were at a variance with facts. He showed how the old men used words to take the place of realities, until for their peace of mind they had to force themselves to believe their own propaganda.

The French wanted to weaken Germany, while the British wanted to raise Germany so that they could trade with her: that in one sentence was what all the conferring was about. They had effected a compromise by which they were going to do both at the same time. Privately they admitted that the Versailles treaty was unenforceable, but they solemnly told the world that it was not to be revised; they would "interpret" it—which was another word. They would bluff, and overlook the fact that no one heeded their bluffs. They had announced that they would not discuss the question of Russia, and the next day they proceeded to discuss it. They denounced Germany for not having delivered coal to France, but at the same time they pledged France to take no action about it. The French were helping to drive the Turks from Constantinople, but at the same time they were arming the Turks against the British; gun-running and smuggling were going on all along the Arabian coasts, and wherever else any traders saw a chance for profit.

The world had been told that it had a League of Nations, which was going to deal with all these problems. But what power had this League, asked Rick, and who cared to give it power? Instead of taking these issues before the League, the three premiers met in a locked chamber and settled them according to the interests of their three political parties. Such, it appeared, was to be the new government of Europe. They were to meet again at Spa, in Belgium, and the Germans were to be summoned to attend; the "Big Three" would again become the "Big Four." "*Absit omen!*" wrote Rick—for readers who had been educated in English public schools and therefore carried various tags of Latin in their heads.

Lanny couldn't find enough praise for this outspoken article, but it was hard indeed for him to believe that any editor would publish it. Rick said that was a chance he had to take; he would tell the truth, and if the editors couldn't face it, that was their readers' hard luck. "I suppose some leftist sheet would print it," he added; "but they probably can't pay."

The precious document was entrusted to the post, and after saying good-by to the friends they had made, Lanny and Rick motored back to Juan. A couple of days later they read in their newspaper that Lloyd George had returned to England and made a speech in Parliament reporting the outcome of the conference. Rick read it aloud, punctuating it with such words as "tommyrot," "bilge," and "hot air." Everything was lovely, harmony ruled in the hearts of all the Allies, and the British public might rest assured that nothing could weaken the solidarity of the victors in the late conflict. Germany was being disarmed and, in spite of all her subterfuges, this necessary work would be continued. "Airplanes we will get," declared the rosy-faced cherub with the snow-white mop of hair. "We cannot allow these terrific weapons of war to be left lying about in Germany, with nobody in authority to see to them."

"I can tell him he had jolly well better not!" commented the young Englishman, who had been up in the air so many times and had looked down upon the puny works of man from a height of ten thousand feet.

BOOK TWO

Someone Whom I Could Court

6

A Sweet Unrest

I

LANNY came home somewhat bored with statesmen, and resolved to devote his attention to a strictly private matter. He found a letter which he opened with great eagerness. It said:

DEAR LANNY:

I have to be with my little son. I hope that you and Rick have been having a pleasant holiday, and that his effort will succeed. I have given a good deal of thought to your project of marketing the pictures. I approve of it, and hope that later on I may be able to give you assistance. In the meantime, believe me, with all good wishes,

MARIE.

Lanny didn't have to puzzle over that. He had told her that some day he had planned to have Marcel's paintings put on the market; he hadn't asked for her help, of course, but she had thought of this as a camouflage which he would not fail to understand. Her fears were very real to her; he wondered if they would ever permit her to be happy.

She had given her address, and he wrote a note like her own, carefully guarded. The project for marketing the pictures was in his thoughts continually, he said. He looked forward to having her advice, for he trusted her judgment about art more than that of any other person. He hoped that her patient was improving. He posted this, and tried to put his mind on piano practice, but found it far from easy. All music now turned into Marie; when it danced he was dancing with her, when it was sad he was sad about her, and when it ceased, he was alone, and restless and discontented.

103

He took to wandering about at night, brooding over the problem of their love and what they were going to do with it. Beauty, watching her darling anxiously, sought to break into his confidence, and he could not very well exclude her. As usual, it was a relief to share his troubles, and he told what little his friend had imparted about herself and her husband. Under Beauty's relentless questioning he repeated talks with Marie, and from these his mother was able to comprehend the basis of this unfortunate entanglement. Lanny had always been a precocious child; he had always had ideas beyond his age—and so now he was bored by young girls and wanted a mature woman. Love to him didn't mean moonlight and roses, it meant what he called "conversation."

It was hard to gain understanding of a woman through the mind of a youth who didn't understand her very well himself. But Beauty kept on trying, for love was her field, and her curiosity was inexhaustible. It was hard for her to accept the simple explanation that Marie de Bruyne was virtuous; it was easier for Beauty to believe that every woman had some carefully concealed purpose. Did it please her vanity to keep a handsome and attractive youth dancing attendance? Or was she perhaps trying to control her husband by giving him cause for jealousy? Or could it be that she was an intriguer, and already had another lover? Such surmises the mother kept to herself, but she tried tactfully to convey the fact that women of the world are rarely simple and straightforward; even the best of them have more than one purpose, more than one facet to their characters.

Meanwhile Beauty took her friend Emily Chattersworth into the secret. Emily carried a share of the responsibility, she being the one who had introduced a susceptible youth to this *femme fatale*. Emily knew Monsieur de Bruyne, having once been the object of his attentions, so she could throw light upon the problem; she described him as a man of sixty or more, sturdily built, decidedly good-looking, and strongly attractive to women. He had, she reported, "a roving eye": he picked out the best-looking woman in a company and you felt that he was undressing her in his fancy. It was a form of mental disease, and ought to have treatment by a psychiatrist; but it was diffi-

cult to suggest that to a gray-haired man of good family and standing. The marriage, Emily said, had been one of those French affairs,
arranged by the family; sometimes they turned out well and sometimes badly—but of what marriage system could one say more?

II

There was a day of excitement in the Pomeroy-Nielson family
when a letter came from the editor in London saying that he was
publishing Rick's article in his next issue. "It is convincing and in-
formative," he wrote, "and I believe will make an impression. If you
can continue to write on international affairs with such insight, you
should be able to make a reputation."

Rick insisted upon giving Lanny more than half the credit for
this happy issue. He did the same for the second article, which he
now had ready to post to the editor; that was made out of Compagna
Barbara, and the dock-laborer, and others whose minds Lanny had
pumped for his friend. Rick had made skillful use of his data, so that
you would have thought he had been living for a long time among
the laboring masses of Italy, sharing their political secrets. The
writer didn't reveal his own convictions, but left his readers with
the idea that statesmen and others in authority had better get food
into the country without delay, unless they wished to see what they
had already seen in Russia, Hungary, and Bavaria. In due course the
editor wrote that he liked this article also. He paid ten pounds for
each, and Rick was as proud of these checks as Lanny had been of
his first earnings.

This happy outcome gave the American a fresh understanding of
the English people and their peculiar ways. It just hadn't seemed
possible to him that an English magazine would publish such an indictment of English policy and procedure. That they paid for it,
and held out the promise of a career to the man who wrote it, was
something to be graven in one's memory. You might paint the crimes
of the British Empire as black as you pleased, but you would never
say anything worse than Britons themselves would be printing and
proclaiming in public meetings; and little by little the opinions of

that "saving remnant," the agitation which they maintained, would penetrate the case-hardened minds of elder statesmen, and British policy would be brought into line with the conscience of humanity. Watching Rick's budding career and helping him in various ways, Lanny once more began to take an interest in world affairs, and to descend more frequently from his ivory tower.

Hot weather came, and Rick and his little family were planning to return to their home. Rick wrote to his editor suggesting that on the way he might take in the conference at Spa, in Belgium, near the German border. The gathering would be of importance, because it represented the beginning of consultation between the Allies and their former foes. The editor agreed to reserve this topic for Rick, and again Lanny volunteered to act as chauffeur and cicerone. It fitted in very well with certain purposes of his own, he said. They got out their maps and planned a motor-tour, in the course of which Nina and the baby would be delivered to the Channel ferry at Calais, and then Rick would be set down in Spa and introduced to diplomats and journalists. After that Lanny would take the wings of a dove and fly away to be at rest in Seine-et-Oise, a district immediately west of Paris which happily had escaped the ravages of war. He wrote to his lady-love to say that he was going to be in her neighborhood, and would bring in his car some of the art-works concerning which he hoped to have her sage counsel.

III

The little town of Spa is in the Belgian Ardennes, and has mineral springs from which seven centuries of invalids have believed that they derived mysterious benefits. It is a forest and hill resort which has horse-racing and pigeon-shooting, and a casino with plenty of gambling; also a number of hotels suitable for three elderly gentlemen who had constituted themselves the government of Europe. Comfort is important to persons of advancing years, so in the winter season their assemblies would be scheduled for the Riviera, and in the summer's heat at some agreeable retreat in the north. Hopeful crowds would cheer their progress from one land to another, and a swarm of newspaper men would follow and gather up such crumbs of news as fell from their council tables.

A new stage of world reconstruction was beginning at this ancient center of healing, for here came representatives of the new Socialist government of Germany. It must be admitted that they looked much like the old-time Prussians, and from their buccal cavities emerged the same guttural sounds; but they were speaking for a republic, and declaring their desire to serve the whole German people, not just a military caste. They expected no cordiality, and their expectations were fulfilled; but at least they were not penned up behind barbed wire as the German peace delegation in Paris had been. Liberal-minded persons hoped that by tactful conduct they might succeed in appeasing their former foes and so gradually bring back the days of the "good Europeans." The meetings of the conference took place in the large white villa which had been the Kaiser's headquarters during the war.

Lanny and Rick found most of the American reporters whom they had met in San Remo. Several had read Rick's articles, so he was now a personality, a member of the fraternity. They talked to him freely, because his deadline came so long after theirs. Fessenden and his friends were here, and also there was an English colony and an English club; so Rick's way was made smooth. He and his friend discovered that the healing springs which bubbled forth from those Belgian hills found no counterpart in the hearts of the conferring diplomats; from them came poisonous fumes of greed and hate and fear. Lanny made this remark, and straightway his friend reached for the wad of copy paper which he kept in his pocket. Lanny in turn made note of the psychology of the professional writer, a man with a split personality; one half of his mind thinks clearly and feels keenly, while the other half keeps watch for "copy."

The most urgent question which troubled the gathering was the delayed deliveries of coal from the Ruhr. The Germans having wantonly destroyed the French mines, somebody had to go without coal; and was it going to be the innocent French or the guilty Germans? In vain the delegates from the new republic pleaded that if they could not get their factories going they could not meet the

reparations demands. The French wanted to start their own industries, so that they could regain their share of world trade, and they
were embarrassed by the idea of having German goods coming into
France, even though it might be to pay war-debts. There was a
peculiar quirk in this situation, which was explained to Rick by an
English economist on his country's staff. Germany couldn't pay
with gold because there wasn't enough in the world, and she couldn't
pay with goods without ruining French industry and throwing
French workers onto the scrap-heap. Yet the political lives of both
French and British statesmen rested upon their willingness to go on
repeating day and night: "The Germans shall pay to the last sou!"—
or "to the last farthing!" as the case might be.

Rick, in his capacity of "liberal," wanted to hear what the Germans had to say; and this was not difficult, as there was a large
delegation on hand, all eager to talk to journalists. A large and
florid member of the Berlin city council talked vehemently to the
two young men about the effects of the starvation blockade, but unfortunately he was not a convincing illustration of his own argument.
The main grievance was that the Allies could not be persuaded to
fix the amount of the indemnities, and thus the Germans could not
know where they stood in any business affairs. Rick was prepared
to concede that, but the official answerer of questions went on to
contend that the treaty of Versailles was so bad that it justified the
Germans in refusing to comply with any of the terms that did not
seem fair to them. The young Englishman's patience gave out, and
he asked: "What do you want the Allies to do—fight the war over
again?" It seemed to Lanny that the method of "conference" didn't
always work as the liberals expected!

IV

Another subject which was causing embittered controversy was
the failure of the Germans to surrender war materials to the Allies
as the treaty had provided. Concerning this there could be no argument—at least from the Allies' point of view. Unless the war was to
be fought over again, for what did Germany need heavy guns and

bombing planes? In vain would suave confidential agents whisper into the ears of Allied staff members that German armies might be needed to put down the subhuman Bolshevist conspiracy that was establishing itself in eastern Europe. The French wanted this done, but by their own allies, the Poles and other border peoples; they wouldn't let any Russian territories be occupied by Germans—their *cordon sanitaire* was double-fronted, to keep Germans from going east as well as to keep Russians from coming west.

Lanny and Rick got an inside view of this special problem of German disarmament when they ran into a British officer, that Captain Finchley who had been Rick's superior in training-camp, and whom Lanny had met at the War Planes Review on Salisbury Plain a few days before the outbreak of war. He was glad to see them both, and interested to talk about the strange duty which had been his for the past year and a half—going into a hostile land to supervise the exportation of surrendered implements of slaughter. Captain Finchley was here to report to the Allied staffs concerning the progress of his labors; to tell them, among other things, that he had counted four hundred and seventy-three million cartridges and thirty-eight million seven hundred and fifty thousand shrapnel shells!

Such astronomical figures gave Lanny a depressing sense of the hopelessness of his father's future as a salesman of arms in Europe. How long would it take to shoot off that much ammunition? he asked, and the captain, who had had dealings with Robbie Budd and knew him well, replied cheerfully: "Don't worry! They'll be used in the end. They're for sale cheap, and some poor blighters will kill some other poor blighters with them."

"Who, for example?" inquired the youth.

"Chinese war lords are buying them to fight their rivals. South American revolutionists are using them against their governments. Traders are smuggling them in to the Bolsheviks, while the French are supplying them to the Poles to fight the Bolsheviks. The French are selling them to the Turks to fight us with, and I suppose our traders are selling them to the Arabs to fight the French with."

It all sounded rather shocking, but you couldn't blame a British army officer. He had his hands full unearthing secret hiding-places of the wily Germans and forcing them to load their own weapons into freight-cars; it was no good expecting him to travel over the earth and follow those arms to their final destinations. The British Empire was run under an ancient and honorable system known as "free trade," and anybody who had money had the right to buy arms and load them onto a ship and disappear from the ken of governments.

V

After several days of research Rick said: "I'm all right now, Lanny; and I can see that you are 'r'arin' to go.'" One read American slang in the movie "subtitles," and one adopted it.

"But how will you manage to get about, Rick?"

"I'll take a *fiacre* if it's far. I'll work it out."

So Lanny put his bags into his car and set out for Paris. The route took him through the very heart of the war zone, about which he had been reading and hearing countless times; but nothing could equal the actual sight—and the smell, which now, twenty months after the Armistice, still hung over those regions of horror. Forests were represented by a few shattered treetrunks thrusting to the sky, often with a raven or a buzzard on top. Villages once populous were represented by a smoke-blackened wall with a gaping hole that had been a window. Trenches were slowly collapsing, and with them the empty tins and the rags and bones that had once been soldiers wearing uniforms and eating meals. Shell craters still made one think of a land that had had smallpox; also, it seemed now to have vermin in the shape of parties of tourists parked by the roadside and poking among the ruins.

One crossed the vast series of trenches and entanglements which had been the Hindenburg line, and from there on the signs of damage grew fewer, the work of repair less hopeless. So he came to the Château Les Forêts, the summer home of Emily Chattersworth, where the "Huns" had had only a few days, and American money had put great numbers of men to work removing the evidence of their ravages. The dead bodies of a German division had been buried in the beech forests which Lanny had explored as a lad, and patient care was restoring the beautiful green lawns on which he had listened to Anatole France relating the sins of old-time kings and queens.

He spent the night here, and, sitting in the spacious drawing-room from which the valuable paintings and tapestries had been stolen, his good friend revealed to him that she was a sharer in the secret of this motor-tour. She was a wise woman, and in the course of more than twenty years had learned a lot about the ways of Europe; she told Lanny about Frenchwomen, the intense passions which animate them and the rigid conventions which bind them. Do not expect them to depart too far from those conventions and retain any happiness, for we are what social forces have made us, and we are not able to shed our skins like snakes and lizards. *Garde à vous*, Lanny Budd!—for when you venture into a woman's heart you are taking a long journey, and if you think you can retrace your steps, you may find that thorny barricades have sprung up behind you.

However, the experienced Mrs. Emily did not try to dissuade him from his enterprise. She understood his liking for older women, and it was not to be supposed that he would lead a celibate life on the Riviera, or anywhere else on the continent of Europe, unless he was in a monastery with heavy stone walls and iron gates. She told him what she knew about the woman of his choice, and about the man who was to become his associate in *la vie à trois*. Denis de Bruyne, owner of a large fleet of taxicabs and other business enterprises, would probably accept the situation when he learned about it, but that was a matter concerning which you could never be sure. The male animal under the influence of sexual jealousy is dangerous and unpredictable, whether he be the laboring brute in the slums or the master of money accustomed to commanding what he wants. Emily Chattersworth, who had lived among the masters in Newport and New York as well as in Paris and on the Coast of Pleasure, could tell strange tales of things she had seen and heard; she told them to her young friend, not sparing him, because he was stepping out on an uncharted path, and treasons, stratagems, and spoils might be his portion from the next day on.

VI

Lanny Budd was motoring on one of the smooth straight highways of France, in the pleasant mildness of a July morning, with a light haze tempering the glare of the sun and lending the landscape shades of pastel. Making a circle to the north of Paris to avoid the traffic, he was presently in the Seine-et-Oise country, a kind of rarefied suburb of a great city, with small fruit and vegetable farms mixed with villas and country residences of the well-to-do and medium classes. A gentle, pleasant land, which had known peace for generations; a land in which the old and the new are oddly mixed—an old church with dwellings huddled against it, as if seeking protection from a modern motor-road which has cut off one corner; a land of comfort and leisure, where even the rivers have time to meander, to make playful eddies and ripples as they slide past gardens with willow trees bending down to the water, and villas and summer cottages with tiny landing-piers for rowboats, and here and there a man or a boy sitting with a fishing-pole. A tantalizing dream haunts the souls of men and boys in rural France, and apparently they never lose it, but will sit for hours in a gentle glow of expectancy; if once the dream should happen to come true, they would rush home in excitement and mark a red circle around the date on a calendar: *Un poisson!*

Lanny had a different kind of hope, no less important to him. His heart was high, and each feature of the ever-varying landscape would suggest lines out of the poetry books he had learned pretty nearly by heart. Each stream might flow past her door, each villa might resemble hers, each walled garden—surely she would have a walled garden, with old pear and apricot trees trained against it, their fruits in the hot sunshine performing their quiet miracle. Now she would be walking in the garden, waiting for his call; his thoughts reached out to her in happy songs. There had fallen a splendid tear from the passion-flower at the gate; she was coming, his dove, his dear; she was coming, his life, his fate!

He arrived at the village which she had given as her postoffice address. Not wishing to attract attention he did not stop, but drove about slowly, observing the landscape, the direction of the roads, the names of inns and other landmarks. He couldn't expect to have the good fortune to meet her on the highway, nor could he recognize her home by some telepathic sense; but he had a plan, and it seemed romantic to him. *L'Enlèvement au Sérail*—he thought of Mozart's opera by its French title, and the gay music came tripping through his head. He would sing her some of it—he would be Belmonte, the dare-devil rescuer.

When he had the map of the region in mind he drove to a neighboring village and found a telephone. He called her number, and when a servant answered he asked for "Madame"—no name for any listening ears! When he heard her voice he spoke in a businesslike tone: "Madame, I have come to show you those pictures of which I wrote you."

She was not one to make any blunder. In a tone as matter-of-fact as his own she replied: "I shall be interested to see them. Where can we arrange it?"

"I am at your service, Madame. I have them in my car."

"I was about to go for a walk," she said—a very quick mind! "You might pick me up and take me to the village."

"Be so kind as to indicate the place, Madame."

"You know where the Quatre Chats is?" It was a little inn with a gay sign in the modern fashion; he had marked it, and she said: "A road runs west from there. I shall be on it shortly."

VII

He saw her coming, wearing a dark blue summer dress, and a sun-hat, as if she had been working in the garden. Blue dresses would have magic from that day on! Every motion of her slender figure pleased him; her whole personality radiated those qualities which he most esteemed. When she was nearer, he saw that excitement—or was it the walk?—had brought a glow to her cheeks; her step had a spring—the magic was working in her also. *Glücklich allein ist die Seele die liebt!*

He started his engine and turned the car about, and when she came to him, in she stepped and away they went. *L'Enlèvement au Sérail!*

He made no move to embrace her, or even to touch her hand. He whispered: "Darling!" It was enough.

"Where are you going, Lanny?" she asked.

"Whichever way there will be least chance of your being noticed."

"The first turn to the right," she said. He took it and found himself on a country road, following the bank of a small stream. Trees shaded it, and houses were few.

"Now, dear," he said, "listen to me. I have waited three months, and it seems as many years. I have had time to think it over, and to know that I love you. I love you with body, mind, and soul. I have no doubt about it, and no fears of anybody or anything. I have come to tell you that, and to claim you. It all depends on one answer to one question. Do you love *me*?"

"Yes, Lanny."

"Do you love as I have just told you I love you?"

"Yes, Lanny; but——"

"Answer me some more questions. Are the boys reasonably well?"

"Yes."

"Who is in charge of them?"

"A governess."

"Where are they now?"

"They have gone fishing with her."

"Delightful!" he said. "Perhaps I saw them. Where is your husband?"

"In Paris."

"When do you expect him home?"

"He has no regular times."

"Then you need have none. This is what I propose: we drive over the roads of *la belle France*. When the time comes so that mademoiselle the governess will have returned to the house, you telephone her and inform her that you have received word of a woman friend who is ill, and that you have gone to her; you will write or telephone later. Then we continue to drive over the long roads of *la belle France* and see the country of which it is never possible to see too much. We will avoid all resorts and places where you might meet anyone you know; we will stay in country inns. We will have a week of happiness, and at the end there will be no possible way for anyone to find out where you have been."

"But, Lanny, that is mad!"

"I am mad, love is mad, and very soon you will be mad. But it will be a calculated madness, supervised by your wise mind and your honorable conscience. You have had time to think it over. You have a right to the joy I can give you, and I have a right to the joy you can give me."

"But, Lanny, I have no things!" Her phrase was the French one, *articles de voyage*.

"*Articles?*" he repeated, laughing. "*Articles* are for sale in *boutiques* and *boutiques* are to be found in *villes*, large or small. I have taken the precaution to bring a little money with me, and some time before long we will prove that there exist in France a *robe de nuit*, and a *peigne* and a *brosse* and some *mouchoirs*, and a *portemanteau* to carry them in, and possibly even a small bottle of *rouge vinaigre*— though I think from the present appearance of your cheeks that you will not need it!"

VIII

She began a long expostulation, and he let her go through with it. He had a formula of ancient and well-established power: "*Je vous aime.*" He had learned that it is not wise to let an hour pass without saying it to a woman, and in times of stress such as this its spell is more effective if it is repeated every two minutes. He drove very slowly, following the curves of the road with one hand, while he laid the other upon hers and poured out his heart.

"Chérie, sooner or later we have to take the first step." He was speaking in French—*c'est le premier pas qui coûte*. "I do not believe that you have ever known what it is to be happy in love. I really believe that you have borne two children without knowing what love is. That happens to many women, and they have to be taught. Then everything becomes simple, all problems become solvable, because you are determined to solve them, whereas now you are not sure."

She brought up one problem after another, but he persisted in laying them aside. "All that will be simple, when you know what love is. This is our honeymoon, and it is our time for happiness; let yourself be happy, I entreat you. Tell me that you love me, and tell me nothing else."

"You are trying to sweep me off my feet, Lanny!" Her voice had grown faint.

"Of course, dear! That is exactly what I am doing. If I were trying to teach you to swim, I would have to get you into the water. You surely know that I am no seducer; I do not find my pleasure in deflowering virgins, or in breaking marital vows. I am offering you my faith; I am pledging everything that I have. I am carrying you away because I know there is no other way to do it, and because I know that before this night is over you will thank me. You will no longer have any doubts, but will set to work with me in a firm and sensible way to face our problem and remove the barriers from the path of our love."

"Oh, Lanny! Lanny darling!" She began to sob softly to herself, and he knew that that was all right, for love is frequently born amid tears.

The car rolled on, mile after mile, past the summer landscapes of France, and she did not demand that it turn back. Late in the afternoon she telephoned to her home and told mademoiselle what Lanny had suggested, adding many injunctions which he had not thought of. Another drive, and they stopped in a small town, where they found it possible to purchase all the *articles de voyage*. She wouldn't let him come into the shop with her, because she feared she couldn't hide her tumult of emotion, and was ashamed to appear as the lover of one who was young enough to be her son.

"Almost, but not quite!" smiled Lanny. "Perhaps in the South Seas, or some of those warm places where they begin unusually early!"

IX

They continued westward, into a land of flat plains and ditches lined with poplars, and under the shelter of darkness halted at a little tavern. A waiter in a red-and-white-striped coat escorted them with candles to two connecting chambers provided with a superfluity of curtains, and ancient carved oak beds in which at least ten generations of sturdy Normans had been begotten. The man brought them a well-cooked supper, and manifested no curiosity as to their affairs; tourists of all kinds motored through this land in summer, and his concern was to get the largest possible tip from each.

In this safe retreat Lanny carried out his promise to make Marie happy, and she left him no doubt that he had done so; she accepted him as her fate, and there would be no further need of persuasion. In the morning the waiter appeared as a *valet de chambre* to open the shutters and let in the morning sun and tell them the weather prospects; he brought their *déjeuner* while they were still in bed, and this carried a comforting reassurance of domesticity. God was in His heaven and all was right with the world. Perpetual blushes suffused the cheeks of Lanny's *amie*, and laughter bubbled forth from her so that he was reminded of the healing springs which he had recently left.

They headed west into Brittany; a land of granite rocks of all sizes, of which walls and pavements and houses are built; a land of oak forests which the people carve into balustrades, and huge *armoires*, and *sabots* which clatter on the pavements; a land of wind and fog and gray skies, pleasant enough in July. The peasant women wear stiff white caps and bulging skirts with white aprons; from their apple orchards they derive a bitter and deadly cider; and over the door of every home they put a little niche for their saint. Since the sea winds do not respect sanctity, the people cover the niches with a pane of glass, from which they have frequently to rub the salt. It is a sternly royalist land and has a lady patron in heaven.

The fugitives from the seraglio drove to Saint-Malo, which neither had ever visited before. They climbed streets like long stairways, so narrow that you could almost touch the house-walls on both sides; they walked on a broad city wall, and gazed down on crowded tall buildings and a harbor enclosed by craggy rocks and speckled white by little boats having the oddest mainsails divided horizontally into several sections. They were followed everywhere by urchins begging ceaselessly for a "paynee," and if you gave them one you did not get rid of them. Lanny said this was a feature of all Catholic countries. Marie said: "Of others also!"

They spent the night, or rather part of it, in an old inn, built lopsided in the ancient fashion, and having beds in enclosed shelves. They cut short their stay because of the painful discovery that a tiny round flat insect is the world's most aggressive enemy of romance. Lanny said this too was to be expected in Catholic lands. Evidently Sainte Anne did not approve of what they were doing, so they left her domain in the small hours of the morning, brushed off their troubles with laughter, and saw the dawn come up like thunder on the broad estuary of the river Rance.

X

They headed south toward the region of the lower Loire; and while they watched the landscapes they talked about each other. Their minds were opened as well as their hearts, and they had all things in common. She told him about her girlhood, which had been a happy one. Her father had been an *avocat* in the city of Reims; the Germans had swept over the place, and the mother had died during the war; the father was now living with an older daughter in Paris. Marie had been educated in a convent; it had not been altogether successful, she remarked ruefully. Lanny expatiated upon the evils of superstition, which he thought of as a black cloud shutting off the sunlight of knowledge from the mind and the sunlight of joy from the heart.

She plied him with questions about his own life. She could never hear enough about this youth who had come, clad in shining armor, to lead her out of her state of resignation. How did it happen that one who had not yet attained his majority should think and speak so like a mature man? He explained the unusual opportunities he had enjoyed; his father had brought important people to their home, his mother had cultivated them, and an only child had listened and learned how the *grand monde* was run. Before him fashionable ladies had talked freely—never dreaming that he was understanding the dreadful things they said. Also there had been books; he had begun learning about the world from pictures before he could read. There had been travel all over Europe; he had visited country homes —he had been on a yacht cruise——

"Yes, Lanny," she said, "but other children of the rich are dragged about Europe, and it doesn't mean much to them. You learn everything, forget nothing, and yet contrive not to become conceited about your mind!"

"I've enjoyed thrills when older people marveled over some precocious remark of mine—something which I had heard one of them say a short time previously. But I have always found it more interesting to be learning new things; about you, for example, and about love, and whether I am going to be able to keep you happy, and not let you slide back into that slough of resignation."

"Darling!" she exclaimed. "I have moved on a thousand years— out of the old night of the race, the Dark Ages!"

"You won't go home and start remembering some of the prayers you learned, and worrying about your immortal soul on its way to hell?"

"If I say any prayers, Lanny, they will be to you. I think about our love and a warm glow spreads over my being; little bells start ringing, little shivers pass over me like moonlight on water. I'm afraid to go home, because I look so happy; I don't see how it will be possible to hide my secret."

"You will have to watch your diet like my mother," he told her. "One consequence of this happiness is that your metabolic rate will be increased."

"Now that is what I mean about your mind!" she exclaimed. "Where on earth did you obtain that item of information?"

"That is too easy!" he laughed. "Rick writes for an English weekly, and in the last issue I read an article by an English surgeon on the subject of the female organism. He says that woman is 'an appendage to the uterus.' "

"*Mon dieu!*" exclaimed Marie. "So that is what is the matter with me!"

XI

They were in the "château country." They rambled at will, and between embraces they inspected tremendous castles from three to ten centuries old. They were escorted through vaulted halls where mighty lords had feasted, and into underground dungeons where luckless wretches had been tortured with diabolical contrivances. They shuddered at the realization of what cruelty had been and might still be in the hearts of men. The woman exclaimed: "Oh, Lanny! Do you suppose there will ever be a time when love will prevail in the world? When shall we be able to trust one another?"

"I'm afraid it's still a long way off," he said. "The best we can do is to make for ourselves a little island of safety." He recited some lines from Matthew Arnold which had struck deep into his soul during the dreadful years of the war:

> Ah, love, let us be true
> To one another! for the world, which seems
> To lie before us like a land of dreams,
> So various, so beautiful, so new,
> Hath really neither joy, nor love, nor light,
> Nor certitude, nor peace, nor help for pain;
> And we are here as on a darkling plain
> Swept with confus'd alarms of struggle and flight,
> Where ignorant armies clash by night.

XII

In between these grave reflections they discussed the problem of Denis de Bruyne, involuntary participant in their intimacy. Marie said that as soon as she returned to her home she would tell him, as an alternative to a divorce, she must have an understanding that she was free to live her own life. He would, of course, know this meant a lover; but she would refuse to discuss the matter, taking the position that her affairs were her own.

"Suppose he declines to agree?" asked Lanny.

"He won't, dear!"

"While we are by ourselves, and have time to talk frankly, we dare not fail to consider all possibilities. When we part, will you be writing me about the marketing of pictures?"

"No, Lanny; I am going to be free!"

"All right; but suppose your husband says a flat no?" Lanny had already discussed this practical question with Mrs. Emily. "He may have you watched, and get evidence against you, and so be in position to divorce you and take your children from you. What will your answer be?"

"I cannot face such a thought, Lanny!"

"I am trying to protect your happiness. My father has a competent lawyer in Paris. If I go to him, tell him the situation, and put up the necessary costs, we can get our evidence first and you will have something definite to reply to your husband."

"Oh, no, Lanny! That would not be according to my code. Denis is the father of my children, and I cannot believe that he would be capable of baseness! He has his weaknesses, but he has virtues too. I could not make the first move in such a conflict."

He made certain that her scruples were deeply based. She would have to be attacked before she would think of fighting back. "It will become a contest in continence," he said. "If he opposes you, you will have to prove that you can live a celibate life longer than he can."

"I believe that with your help I should win."

They left the matter there. He would go back to Juan at once, and she would write as soon as she had news. In September the boys would be going to school, and then she would come to stay with her aunt in Cannes.

"Will that proper old lady sanction our love?" he inquired.

"I believe she will when I explain it to her. Anyhow, I will come to you in September. Will you be able to wait that long?"

"I can wait as long as I have to; but that doesn't mean that I shall enjoy it."

"You will have to take what I can give, dear. I believe that everything will be easier when my husband has adjusted himself to the idea that women too have their needs. You know that I myself required some time to adjust myself to the idea."

"I have not forgotten that waiting," he smiled. "Tell me again—have I kept my promises?"

"You have filled the cup of my happiness brim-full. You have given me a new life, and the courage to live it."

More landscapes and old châteaux, as they worked their way eastward in the direction of her home. She wouldn't let him take her near it, but had him set her down on the outskirts of a town from which a public conveyance ran to her neighborhood. When the time had come for parting, she said:

"One thing I want you to have in mind, darling—and never forget it. The time will come when you will want to marry, and it would be wicked for you not to marry—some woman who can give you children, and be in your life to its end. I want you to know that when the time comes, I will step out of your way."

"Forget it, dear!" he commanded. "My bump of philoprogenitiveness seems to be poorly developed." He didn't know the French for this long word, but said it in English, and added: "You may be astonished once more by the extent of my learning, so let me explain. In that wonderful library accumulated by my great-great-uncle I stumbled upon a work on the science of phrenology, containing a chart of all the bumps on the human skull. I examined my own with great interest, and was pained to discover that I have flat surfaces and even hollows at those places where the most desirable qualities are to be found."

"I shall never give any credence to that so-called science," declared Marie de Bruyne, with emphasis.

7
Sweet, Sweet, O Pan!

I

SAFE at home in his ivory tower, Lanny waited, and in due course the promised letter arrived:

CHÉRI:

I have had the talk with my friend as planned, and I am happy to report that all is well. It is a strange story, which I shall have the pleasure of telling you some day. As you know, I have been bitter, and have kept my feelings locked in my heart. This, it seems, has not been without effect upon my friend. He has been remorseful, and was deeply affected by the news I brought him. It was a strange and touching scene. There are worlds within worlds inside the human heart, and one could spend a lifetime studying a single one. May I live to have that pleasure! Suffice it to say now that the future gives us no occasion for anxiety. My friend concedes my right to be happy. I concede his, but doubt if that will help him. This is a story of only indirect interest to you, so I will not go into details. Everything is as you would wish it to be, and the schedule agreed upon will be followed.

Your devoted Marie.

Lanny read this letter many times and studied its phrases. It told him what he needed to know, but with much reserve, and he saw that caution was deeply rooted in her nature. Was she afraid that her letters might be opened by some other person? He had told her of his frank talks with his mother; but all the same Marie would keep their love as something for the privacy of their chamber, and would never spread it on paper. Leave that for the poets and writers of romance!

123

He told Beauty the events of their honeymoon, and answered her long string of questions. She had something to do with their future happiness, and Lanny was determined to have a clear understanding with her. Marie de Bruyne was his choice, and was worthy of all honor; she was going to be received precisely as if there had been that fashionable wedding with flower-laden bridesmaids. What he said was: "I ask you to treat her as I treated Marcel." A difficult stroke to parry! The mother could only answer, feebly: "If she is as good to you as Marcel was to me, Lanny."

"I let you be the judge in the case of Marcel, and now it is my turn to be the judge. So long as she makes me happy, my mother has to be grateful to her and receive her as a daughter."

"Or as a sister, Lanny?" Beauty couldn't resist the temptation. Claws have been given to cats for use, and they retract them only with reluctance. Lanny decided right then that the main headquarters of his romance had best be located in the home of the Sorbonne professor's widow.

With Marie's permission he went over to call on the old lady, who occupied her cottage the year round, as persons in modest circumstances have to do. Lanny sat down with her and told the story of his heart; he made love to Marie *in absentia*, by proxy, and the desert sprang into bloom, the birds sang in the garden of an elderly widow's heart. Madame Scelles was a most respectable old lady, but she was a French old lady and knew the customs of her country; she agreed that she would chaperon this romance and adopt Lanny as her son.

Also the dutiful youth wrote to his father in Connecticut. He named no names, but revealed that he had fallen in love with an unhappily married French lady, and had just had a delightful motor-trip with her. Knowing his father, Lanny added that his *innamorata* enjoyed his piano playing, and that they read classic French literature together; she wore few jewels, and those few were family heirlooms; her idea of an acceptable gift was one of Great-Great-Uncle Eli's books. A cautious father might rest secure in the knowledge that his son had found for the gravest of a young man's problems a solution which would not involve him in any scandals, extravagances, or dissipations. "But tear up this letter and don't tell anybody in Newcastle!"

II

Strange as it might have seemed to an outsider, Kurt Meissner also appeared to have found a solution of his sex-problem. He stayed right there inside the walls of Bienvenu, rarely going out except for a long walk. Whatever discontent he may have felt he sublimated and poured into his compositions. The world outside might be a madhouse, beyond any man's power to control, but a piece of unfrozen architecture could be reshaped until one had got it right; that was art, and it was also science. If the world didn't like it, so much the worse for the world.

Beauty was not a little in awe of this tall erect young soldier with the smooth straw-colored hair and the pale blue eyes that could so easily turn to steel. Lanny watched their relationship and was amused by the developments. Beauty would take things from Kurt that she had never taken from any other man. The gay daughter of pleasure who had been willing to stake her whole future upon a whim had quarreled often with Marcel over his efforts to keep her from playing poker all night; but no one ever heard anything like that now. Kurt would make it plain that he expected Beauty's company at night, and he had it. Kurt would look at her across the breakfast table and say, quietly: "I thought you said you weren't going to have any more cream with your fruit." And Beauty would eat plain fruit. Kurt would say: "Do you really need to keep up with the fashions while half the children in Europe are crying with hunger?" So Beauty would wear a last season's costume, and send a check to the American relief, which now was helping to feed the children of Germany.

The pair had been living together for more than a year, and the first year is the hardest for the ill-assorted, who have much adjusting to do. Lanny, always curious about love, learned many things that might be useful to him in his own *affaire*. His mother was much enamored, and also had been cowed by grief and fear. She was almost forty, which is known as "the dangerous age." It is supposed to be a woman's last chance; if she doesn't get a man then and manage to hold him, she will have a lonely old age. Beauty was trying her best to hold Kurt; she would hide her weaknesses, she would starve her vanities in the effort to keep his respect. Both the men of her household were leagued against the poor soul; for Lanny told her that Kurt was a great man and had more brains than she would ever be able to share.

The result was to cut her off more and more from what is called "social life." If she could have worn Kurt as a decoration, a shining jewel in a tiara, she would have had a grand time in Cannes and Nice and Paris; she would have intrigued to have her protégé invited into the most elegant homes, and would have lured the musical élite to hear him perform his compositions. But Kurt had to be hidden; he had to be Lanny's music-teacher—and how could one confer distinction upon a hired person? So Beauty stayed at home, wore the dresses that Kurt considered becoming, and instead of repeating the chatter of the fashionable she listened while Kurt and Lanny discussed the Brahms *Variations on a Theme by Haydn.*

Kurt had become devoted to Baby Marceline, who no longer stumbled and groped, but danced to music with spontaneous grace; she no longer stammered a few childish words, but prattled all day, and was a little fairy in the household. Her mother's one idea of bringing up a child was to give it everything it asked for; and here again she ran head on into German ideas of *Zucht.* Beauty would say no, and the little one would start to wheedle, and Beauty would be on the point of giving way, when Kurt would remark: "You said no," and Beauty would decide that she had meant no. Nor did she dare to cheat and give way in secret, for when Kurt found that out, he became very angry. There could, he said, be nothing worse for a child than to discover a division in a household; to be able to play one of its elders against another, and to get its way by intrigue. Kurt called Lanny into conference, and of course Lanny agreed with him, as he always did. So Beauty had to give up the pleasure of spoiling her darling, and these two aggressive young males assumed still further command of the ménage.

III

A good part of Lanny's allowance was going for music scores new and old. He always pretended that he wanted them for himself; he and Kurt would practice them, Kurt using any one of his various instruments. Lanny had read somewhere that Liszt had performed the prodigious feat of taking a new opera score and rendering it so far as possible on the piano at first sight; to a star such as that Lanny had hitched his wagon. But just as in his father's business there was a race between the makers of armorplate and the makers of guns, so in the music world there appeared to be a race between performers and composers; as fast as the former have achieved some prodigy of technique, the latter proceed to set a new standard of digital agility.

Lanny didn't have to buy books, for there was that library, and Kurt stuck to the conviction that old books are the best. Kurt discovered America in an odd way, through the literature of New England transcendentalism. It was, he said, a pale copy of German philosophical idealism, but it was interesting to see a provincial people groping their way in a field of speculative thought and coloring it with their peculiar pioneer qualities. Kurt said that Americans pursued metaphysical activities in the same way that they hunted wild Indians in their forests, each man picking out his own tree or rock and aiming his own gun. Said Lanny: "I suppose the German philosophers march in well-ordered ranks, thinking in unison and armed with government subsidies." Kurt laughed, but all the same he thought that was the way to set about any undertaking, military or metaphysical.

Kurt read Herndon's life of Abraham Lincoln, and was greatly impressed by the spectacle of a railsplitter out of a pioneer cabin rising to become the leader of a nation in a crisis. But he was repelled by the details of democratic political manipulation, the things a man had to do in order to become "the people's choice" in a land which had no traditions and no discipline as Kurt understood them. "Such a career would be inconceivable anywhere in Europe," he declared.

"Are you sure?" Lanny asked. "Aren't you forgetting that you have a saddlemaker running your own country now?"

It had never occurred to the fastidious German aesthete to think of Fritz Ebert in that way; he had seen only the seamy side of German Social-Democracy and his prejudices against it were intense. But he had to admit that the movement had saved Germany from Bolshevism in the course of the past few months, and from his point of view that was a most important service. Also Kurt had been impressed by Rick's statement that the program of British labor was the most constructive now before the country. In these desperate times one had to be prepared to revise one's thinking, and Kurt was reading English magazines which were full of strange and disturbing ideas.

He received letters from his family that would leave him in a state of depression for days. The situation in Germany was appalling; there appeared to be an almost complete absence of necessities, and no way to get industry or trade started. The government could exist only by printing paper money, and as a result retail prices were six or eight times what they had been before the war. In Stubendorf it wasn't so bad, because this was an agricultural district, and crops were in the ground, and some harvested; so the Meissners had food. But the workers in the towns were starving, and there was chaos in most of Upper Silesia, which didn't know whether it was Polish or German, so people who should have been at work were arguing and fighting over the forthcoming plebiscite. There were "polling police," half German and half Polish, supposed to be keeping order, but much of the time they were fighting among themselves. There was that terrible Korfanty, half patriot and half gangster, who was inciting the Poles; in August he tried to seize the whole of Upper Silesia by force, and there was a state of disorder for several weeks. To Herr Meissner, comptroller-general of Schloss Stubendorf, order was the breath of life, and to Herr Meissner's son it was gall in the mouth to read of indignities which his father and family were suffering at the hands of a people whom they regarded as sub-human.

IV

One morning Lanny was called from his music practice to the telephone, and heard a man's voice, speaking English with a foreign accent. "Do you know me this time?" This time Lanny did, and cried: "Mr. Robin! Where are you?"

"At the station in Cannes. I have been to Milan on business and am on my way to Paris. I promised the boys I would not pass by without seeing you, if you would permit."

"Of course I will! Shall I drive over for you?"

"I will be taking a taxi."

"Be prepared to stay for lunch and tell me all the news."

Lanny went to his mother; she had never met Johannes Robin, but understood that he was in various business deals with Robbie Budd, and she took it as a law of nature that Robbie's friends had to be entertained. Lanny had told Kurt about the Jewish salesman of electrical gadgets who had served all through the war as a channel for Lanny's letters to Kurt, receiving them in Holland and remailing them into Germany. Kurt knew how the small Lanny Budd had picked up Robin on a train, and how the man had since become very rich by selling magnetos and other war materials to Germany. Kurt said he had no prejudice against Jews when they were great moral philosophers like Spinoza or joyous musicians like Mendelssohn, but he didn't care for those who coined money out of the needs of his people. However, it was necessary to take the visitor into the secret of Kurt's identity, for of course he would remember the name, and could hardly fail to penetrate the disguise of a Swiss music-teacher.

When the taxi arrived at the gate, Lanny was waiting to greet his guest. The dark-eyed and handsome Jewish gentleman became more expansive and self-assured with every year, but he would never fail to be humble with the Budd family, eager for their approval and grateful when he got it. Lanny explained how he was giving shelter to his old German friend, whose home had been turned over to the enemy and whose family had been all but ruined. Mr. Robin replied that both as a businessman and as a Jew he was without national prejudices; many of his best friends were Germans. Also he was a lover of the arts, and would be proud to meet a composer who, he felt certain, was destined to a great future. "Tell him that!" said Lanny, with a smile.

They sat down to a lunch upon which Leese had expended her talents, and the guest started in right away to say what happiness his elder son had derived from a short violin composition of Kurt's which Lanny had taken the trouble to copy out and send to Rotterdam. Hansi had played it at a recital at the conservatory, where many had inquired concerning its author. Then Kurt knew that he was dealing with no ordinary money-grubber, and he listened while Mr. Robin told about his wonderful first-born, who was now sixteen, and possessed such fire and temperament that he was able to draw out of pieces of dead wood and strips of pig's intestines the intensest expressions of the soul of man.

That darling Hansi, about whom Lanny had been hearing for seven years, had grown tall but very thin, because he worked so hard that it was difficult to bring him to meals; he had large soulful eyes and wavy black hair, in short, the very picture of an inspired young musician. "Oh, M. Dalcroze"—so Kurt was addressed in the household—"I wish that you might hear him and play with him! And you, Lanny—he talks about nothing so often as when shall he meet Lanny Budd, and do I think that Lanny Budd will like him, even though he is Jewish and so many people have prejudices against his race."

"Listen, Mr. Robin," the long-talked-of Lanny Budd remarked, on the impulse of the moment, "why don't you let those two boys come to see us?"

"Oh, but I would be delighted!" replied the father.

"What are they doing now?"

"Now they are in the country, where we have a lovely place. But Hansi will practice every day. In September they go back to school."

"In September I have an engagement too," said Lanny. "But why not let them come now and spend a week or two with us?"

"Would you really like to have them?" The Jewish gentleman

looked from Lanny to Lanny's mother, and each could see the gratification in his dark eyes.

"I am sure it would give us all great pleasure," said Beauty, to
whom "company" was as a summer shower to a thirsty garden.

"We have a lot of violin music that we should like to know better," put in Kurt. "I make a stab at it, but it is not like really
hearing it."

"If I would telegraph to them, they would be starting tomorrow."

"The sooner the better," said Lanny. "Tell them to fly."

The father turned pale at the thought. "Never would I take such
a chance with the two most precious of beings to me! I cannot tell
you, Madame Budd, what those two lads mean to me and my wife.
For whatever I do in this world I make the excuse that Hansi and
Freddi will make it worth while that I have lived." Beauty smiled
gently and told him that she knew the feeling well. He was a very
nice man, she decided, in spite of that one trouble for which he
couldn't be blamed.

V

Kurt went back to his work, and Lanny took the visitor to his
studio for a quiet talk. Now and then Robbie had mentioned in
his letters how well Johannes was doing, and Lanny was always
proud of this, because the Jewish partner was his discovery. The
firm of Robbie and Robin was engaged in a series of complicated
transactions, for which the New England aristocrat put up the
money and the refugee from a ghetto in Russian Poland furnished
the judgment and hard work. They were an active pair of traders,
and nothing gave Johannes more pleasure than to talk about their
successes.

He told the outcome of their first venture, the hundreds of thousands of hand grenades which had been turned into children's
savings-banks for the Christmas trade; those which had not been
sold last year were now in the hands of dealers, awaiting that season
of joy and brotherhood which comes but once a year and unfortunately does not last until the next one. They had bought an amazing

assortment of products which the American Expeditionary Force had brought to France and had to get rid of at any price: canned tuna-fish, wooden legs, and alarm clocks; thirty-seven thousand padlocks with two keys each, fourteen thousand gross of lead-pencils with erasers attached——

"You cannot imagine how many unlikely things are required by an army," explained Johannes Robin. "Can you suggest to me any patriotic organization which might be wishing to purchase an edition of twenty-five thousand lives of the one-time President, William McKinley?"

"I regret that I cannot think of one at the moment," replied Lanny, gravely.

"He was the most handsome statesman that could be imagined, but confidentially I admit that my efforts to read his speeches have been failures. I fear it will prove the least profitable of all my speculations, even though I bid only a quarter of a cent per copy for the books. It will be necessary to take off the covers, or 'cases,' as they are called, and turn the paper to pulp, and I must find out if it will be possible to restamp the cases and put some other books inside them, perhaps a life of Pope Benedict XV or else of Tovarish Lenin."

Mr. Robin went on to explain that he had been planning to move into Germany, but was waiting until matters settled down so that it would be easier to come and go. He was buying up properties of all sorts in the Fatherland. "Do not think that I am being vainglorious if I say that I am going to become an extremely rich man, for I have information as to coming events, and it would be foolish not to make use of my opportunities. If one is in business, one buys what one believes will increase in value and sells what one believes will lose in value."

Lanny agreed that this was according to his understanding of the game.

"Tell your father to trust me a little more, Lanny," urged the other. "I failed to see him the last time he came over, and I am sorry, because one cannot judge events from far away. Your father is troubled that I persist in selling German marks; in America he gets the propaganda which the Germans are putting out—you understand the situation?"

"I haven't been watching the money-market, Mr. Robin."

"You would not, being an art lover, and for that I honor you. But I explain that all over the world are people of German race who have money, and love the Fatherland, and the Fatherland needs help, but how can the help be given? If these Germans can be persuaded to invest in the Fatherland's paper money, life may continue at home. So the government gives out news to the effect that prosperity is beginning, that Germany is coming back with a rush, that there will be no more paper marks, that the mark has reached its lowest point—and so they sell plenty more marks. But they do not sell them to Johannes Robin—on the contrary, I sell millions and millions to Germans for delivery in three months, and when the time comes I buy them for half what I am due to receive. This troubles your father, because he considers it a risk. Tell him to trust me and I will make him a really rich man. not just one of the medium fellows!"

"I'll tell him what you say, Mr. Robin," said Lanny; "but I know that my father always prefers to invest in real things."

"He is wise in that he keeps his money in dollars, and when the mark is really down we will go into Germany and buy great manufacturing concerns for a few thousands each. I will take you, Lanny, and we will buy old masterpieces of painting for the price of a good dinner."

"I wouldn't know what to do with them," said Lanny. "I have a storeroom full of the paintings of Marcel Detaze which we ought to sell."

"Oh, take my advice and do nothing yet!" exclaimed the shrewd man of business. "Now everything is in a slump, but in a short time things will get started again, and there will be such a boom as no man has ever dreamed of. Then your father and I will be riding on top of the wave."

VI

Lanny went to the train to meet the young travelers from Rotterdam. He would have known them anywhere, having had so many snapshots of two dark-eyed, dream-smitten children of ancient Judea, whose shoulders some prophet had covered with his mantle, whose heads he had anointed with holy oil. Lanny Budd, in the Sunday school class of the stern old Puritan manufacturer, his grandfather, had learned about a shepherd boy named David, who had played the harp, listened to the voice of Jehovah, and entered into communion with the Almighty One, the Lord God of Hosts. If you counted up the number of man's descendants in a hundred generations, you could be sure that every Jew in the world shared the blood of that minstrel and future king; and here were two of them, stepping from the Blue Express, one carrying a suitcase and a violin case, the other a suitcase and a clarinet case.

Both of them eager, both with dark eyes shining and red lips smiling; a dream of seven years coming true for them—they were meeting the wonderful Lanny Budd! It is a pleasure to be able to make anybody so happy, and Lanny would do his best by kindness and gaiety to come up to their expectations. He understood the situation, because long ago Mr. Robin had revealed how Lanny Budd was the model of all things excellent to those boys; he was cultured, he had traveled, and he belonged to the ruling caste of the modern world, for whom the arts were created and before whom the artists performed.

Lanny remembered how thrilled he had been, how the whole earth had taken on hues of enchantment, when he had traveled to Kurt Meissner's home and seen a great castle with its snow-covered turrets gleaming in the early morning sun. Now came little Freddi Robin, at that same age of fourteen. He and his brother were seeing the Côte d'Azur for the first time, and semi-tropical landscapes were as magical to them as snow had been to Lanny. Trees laden with oranges and lemons, bowers of roses and cascades of purple bougainvillaea, rocky shores with blue water turning green in the shallows— all these sights brought cries of wonder, and then anxiety as to whether one was being too demonstrative in the presence of Anglo-Saxon reticence. Everybody at Bienvenu liked them at once; impossible not to, they were so gentle, so sweet-tempered and anxious to please. They spoke acceptable English, French, and German, as well as their native Dutch. Their eager conscientiousness was evident, and persons who knew the harsh world were touched by the thought of what these boys might be made to suffer.

VII

For so long Hansi Robin had been looking forward to the day when he would play a duet with Lanny Budd; and now in the generously proportioned drawing-room of the villa he got out his fiddle and tuned it to Lanny's piano. From his portfolio he took the score of the César Franck *Sonata in A Major*, made popular by Ysaye. He laid the piano part on the rack in front of his friend, and waited to give him time to note the key and the tempo, and to bend up the corner of the first page so that he could turn it quickly. He put his fiddle in position and raised his bow; then he put it down again, and said, in a low voice: "I am sorry to be so nervous. I have wanted so much to do this. Now I am afraid I may stumble."

"You are less likely to stumble than I," said Lanny, comfortingly. "I have heard this sonata, but I have never seen the score. Let us agree to pardon each other."

Little Freddi had his hands clenched tightly and also his lips, and could give no comfort to anybody. But Kurt and Beauty, who were sitting by, said reassuring things, and presently Hansi got himself together; he raised his bow and nodded, and Lanny began. When the violin came in, a tender and questioning melody floated onto the air, and Kurt, the real musician of the family, started inwardly, for he knew tone when he heard it, he knew feeling and *élan*. This music was restless and swiftly changing, it pleased and then became vehement; its fleeting forms were the perpetual miracle of life, something new unfolding itself, discoveries being made, vistas of experience being opened. The frail lad forgot his anxieties and played as if he and his violin were one being. When the sonata came to its climax in a long and well-executed trill, Kurt exclaimed: "Oh, good!" which meant a tremendous lot, coming from him. Lanny, who had been raised in France, jumped up and grabbed Hansi and gave him a hug. The lad had tears in his eyes; it was such a moment as doesn't come often, even to the emotional tribe of the music-makers.

Kurt asked for something else, and Hansi brought out a violin and piano arrangement of Wieniawski's *Second Concerto*. Lanny knew that Kurt disliked the Poles above all the other tribes of men; but the artist is above prejudice, and Hansi executed these fireworks with great éclat. The *Romance* wept and wailed, and when they came to the *allegro con fuoco* and the *molto appassionato*, then indeed Lanny had to get a hump on him, as the saying is. He missed some of the notes, but never failed to get the first in every bar, and he was there at the finish. An exhilarating race, and they wound up with a grand flourish, red in the face and proud of themselves.

Politeness required that they should hear Freddi also. He insisted that he wasn't anything compared to his brother, but they wanted him to play his clarinet, and Hansi produced the score of Haydn's *Gypsy Rondo*, part of a trio. Kurt took the piano this time, and Lanny listened to gaily tripping music out of the eighteenth century, when it seemed easier to be contented with one's lot in life. Lanny was proud of these two charming lads, and certain that they would be loved by all good people. He saw that his mother was pleased with them. Some day she would be taking them to play for Mrs. Emily, and they would be invited to give a recital at Sept Chênes, where all the rich and famous persons on the Riviera would hear them. Such is the pathway to fame.

VIII

From then on what a tootling and a tinkling, a blaring and a banging, in the studio behind the high garden wall! Lanny thumping valiantly the new grand piano, afraid of nothing; Hansi with his fiddle and a head full of millions of notes; little Freddi with his sweetly wailing clarinet; Kurt sometimes with a cello, sometimes a flute, sometimes a French horn—he could have played the kettle-drums if he had had a couple of them. Food was forgotten, sleep forgotten—time was so short and art so long! Now indeed would the passers-by on the highway stop and sit in the shade of the wall for a free concert. Sweet, sweet, O Pan! The sun on the hills forgot to die, the lilies revived, and the dragon-fly—there was no river for him to dream on, but the fishpond in the patio served the purpose, and everything in Bienvenu was happy, and wished that the two minstrels out of ancient Judea might stay with them and help to banish sorrow.

Beauty would send the maid and summon them to meals. Also she would insist that growing lads had to have exercise. "Exercise, my eye!" exclaimed Lanny, dripping with perspiration from the ferocious labor of trying to play orchestral accompaniments on the piano. However, she would make them go sailing and swimming; and surely Lanny ought to take them torch-fishing, and let them have at least one motor-ride along this world-famous coast!

One afternoon, while they were in the midst of their musical riots, the maid come over to report that there was somebody at the telephone, asking for "Monsieur Rick." A lady who said that her name was "Barbara." Lanny went to the phone, for he owed a debt of courtesy to this woman who had given his friend such great assistance. Rick had taken her address and sent her a copy of his published article, and had received a friendly letter, congratulating him upon the intelligence it displayed.

Now Lanny explained over the phone that Rick had gone back to England. Barbara told him that she was visiting in Cannes, and he didn't like to say an abrupt good-by and hang up; he always had the impulse to be friendly to people, and he told her that he and some musician friends were enjoying themselves, and wouldn't she like to come over for tea and hear them? Only after she had accepted the invitation did the thought occur to him that maybe an Italian syndicalist agitator might not seem so acceptable an acquaintance to his mother as she had to an English journalist on the hunt for copy!

He decided to exercise discretion, and tell Beauty no more than he had to. It was an Italian lady he had met in San Remo, unusually well informed as to the international situation; she had given Rick a lot of data, so Lanny had thought he ought to be polite. "You don't have to bother with her," he added. "Send the tea over to the studio and we'll take care of her." It was a blazing hot afternoon, and company meant dressing up; Beauty voted to have her siesta, and Lanny was relieved.

IX

It was the assumption that persons coming to Bienvenu would step into a conveyance; Lanny just forgot that some people were poor—it is so easy to forget that when you live in an ivory tower! Barbara Pugliese walked from the village, and arrived dust-stained and sweaty, in which condition she did not look attractive. Lanny was inclined to be embarrassed before his friends; but she sat quietly and listened to the music, and expressed her appreciation in well-chosen words. He decided that he was being a snob, and that two Jewish boys whose father had been born in a hut with a mud floor had no call to look down upon a woman of culture who had given up her social position to help the downtrodden.

As it turned out, nothing could have been further from the thoughts of the two musical Robins; they were glad to chirp for anyone who cared to listen; and when the tea was brought, they fixed their solemn dark eyes upon the strange Italian woman with the sad thin face, and kept them there for the rest of the afternoon. Lanny told them how his uncle had once taken him on a visit to the "cabbage patch" of Cannes, and how he had there met a sick lady who was living not for herself, but for the poor and oppressed whom she had taken as her friends.

This was an invitation to Barbara to explain how she had come to adopt this unusual way of life. She told about her girlhood in a small Italian village, where her father had been a physician, and thus she had grown up in daily contact with the bitter poverty of the peasants. Her father had been one of the soldiers of Garibaldi, a Free Mason and a rebel, so that early in life Barbara had been made aware of the power of landlords and monopolists over the people. She told dreadful stories of suffering and oppression, and how, when she had tried to enlighten the victims, the priests had denounced her and stirred up mobs against her. But she had persisted, and her fame had spread among the peasants, until when she traveled to their villages the black-shawled women would come with torches to lead her to the place where she was to speak.

She told also about the crowded cities of Italy to which the tourists flocked, and about which the poets imagined romantic things. Rarely did it occur to these persons to visit the moldering slums, where the lace-makers sat on the balconies, not to enjoy the sunsets, but to catch the last gleams of light and toil for the last moment possible in order to earn a crust of bread for the children. Lanny thought it was just as well that his mother was not present, for she was fond of lace, and wouldn't like to have these distressing thoughts about it. Also she smoked cigarettes and favored an Italian brand, and would not have enjoyed knowing that they were made by tiny children, who contracted nicotine poisoning and crawled home to die. But Barbara Pugliese hadn't run away from such things—she had made these people her friends and helped them to form co-operatives, workers' schools and libraries, people's houses, all the means of their education and organization.

Perhaps it was not tactful of her to talk so long. After tea she should have said: "You will wish to go on with the music." But before her sat two heirs of the ancient Hebrew exaltation, drinking in her words as the thirsty multitudes on the desert had drunk the water that gushed forth when Moses smote the rock. "As the hart panteth after the water-brooks, so panteth my soul after Thee, O God!" Barbara was a propagandist, and here were two empty vessels to be filled, two dry sponges ready to absorb her doctrine.

Lanny could understand what was going on, for he himself had had the same experience nearly seven years ago. Now he was disillusioned and world-weary, or so it pleased him to think; he had been behind the scenes and learned the futility of efforts to save mankind from the consequences of its own follies and greeds. But to these naïve children with the blood of the prophets in their veins, this was the very voice of the Almighty One speaking from Mount Sinai; the woman who delivered it was holy, her aspect noble, her face beautiful—even though the wind had made her hair straggly, and dried perspiration gave her a shiny nose!

"Then you don't think the Bolsheviks are wicked?" exclaimed Hansi Robin.

"The Bolsheviks are trying to end poverty and war, the two greatest curses of mankind. Can that be wicked?"

"But they kill so many people!"

"Always through history you find slaves revolting, and they are put down with dreadful slaughter. You find that any killing done by the slaves is small compared with what the masters do. The capitalist system, which is the cause of modern war, has destroyed thirty million people by battle, starvation, and disease; what moral claims can it have after that?"

"But can't people be persuaded to be kind to one another?" This from the gentle Freddi.

"No one can say that we of the working people haven't tried. We have pleaded and explained, we have tried to educate the whole people; we have built a great system of co-operatives and workers' schools, paid for with our very lifeblood. But the masters, who fear us and hate us, are doing their best to destroy all these things."

So it went, until Lanny thought: "Mr. Robin wouldn't like this any better than my father!" He saw that he ought to break it up, so he said: "Hansi, won't you play something for Compagna Barbara before she leaves?"

Hansi started as it were from a dream. "Surely!" he responded; and to the woman: "We Jews have been an oppressed race for a long time. I will play you something from our modern music." He took his fiddle, and his brother, who also played the piano, accompanied him. Two shepherd boys took their stand by the Wailing Wall of their Holy City, and played music new to their friends, Ravel's *Kaddisch*: music of sorrow, music of tumultuous grief, anger, despair; music of a people once chosen by their Lord but forgotten through long centuries, and who cried out to Him in torment of body and bewilderment of soul. Barbara Pugliese was deeply moved, and exclaimed: "Oh, you must come and play music like that for our workers' groups!"

"Indeed we will," declared the pair.

X

As she was leaving, the revolutionist remarked to Lanny: "We have been having a sort of conference in Cannes. Your Uncle Jesse is there."

"Indeed?" said Lanny, politely. "How is he?"

"He looks run down, I think."

"I thought Uncle Jesse was made of leather," he smiled.

"You were much mistaken," was the reply. "He has suffered agonies of mind over the war on Russia."

"I will tell my mother," said Lanny. He didn't care to add that he himself was not permitted to see this painter-revolutionist. Of course it was possible that Uncle Jesse had told this to Barbara— he not being the sort to keep family secrets.

Lanny mentioned the matter to Beauty, who said: "Yes, I had a note from him. I suppose I ought to look him up." She had some shopping to do, and Lanny wanted to pick up some music which his friends had talked about, so he offered to drive her to town next morning.

As fate would have it, Jesse Blackless chose the same time to call upon his sister. He walked, because he liked to walk; he came by a short cut, so he missed them driving. When he rang the bell at the gate, the maid told him that the family had gone to Cannes, so he said: "I'll wait." As he walked up the drive he heard loud music from a newly erected building, and asked: "Who is that?" The maid told him: "Monsieur Kurt" and two young gentlemen who were visiting the family.

"Monsieur Kurt?" asked Jesse. "Who is he?"

"A Swiss gentleman, M. Kurt Armand-Dalcroze, who is M. Lanny's music-teacher."

"Oh," said Jesse. "I'll go over and hear them." He strolled over and sat on the steps of the studio, while Kurt and Hansi were playing the Mendelssohn violin concerto, an impassioned work receiving what Jesse judged to be a fine performance.

The relationship between Jesse Blackless and Kurt Meissner was of the strangest. Each had heard much about the other from Lanny, but the only times they had met had been in the darkness outside Jesse's tenement room, on two occasions when Kurt had appeared and put into the painter's hands a very large sum of money to be used in promoting working-class uprisings in Paris during the Peace Conference. On those two occasions Kurt had known to whom he was giving the money, but Jesse had not known from whom he was receiving it. Subsequently Jesse had been told who it was, but Kurt had never been told that Jesse had been told; a tangle of complications.

The painter had known that his sister was having a long sojourn in Spain and had taken it for granted that it meant a man; but he hadn't been concerned to know what man. Now he sat on the steps of the new studio, watching a tall and handsome blond Nordic playing an expensive new piano, and it didn't take him more than a minute to penetrate the camouflage of a false name and nationality. Of course this was Lanny's boyhood friend from Silesia; he must have met Beauty in Paris and become her lover, and now was being hidden in Bienvenu! The pieces fitted together.

XI

Jesse Blackless had been attending a secret gathering of a dozen or so left-wing labor leaders of Italy and France. He had been hearing stories of mass starvation and repression, of the arrest and jailing of workers, the organizing and arming of forces of reaction intended to stamp out the people's movements of both countries. It was a life-and-death struggle, most of it underground. The left-wing press was full of it, but the general public didn't read the left-wing press and the regular papers never mentioned it, so the events might as well have been happening in Mars.

So far as the leaders were concerned, their most desperate need was for money. Unemployed and half-starved workingmen couldn't even pay their union dues, to say nothing of supporting newspapers. And here in front of Jesse Blackless was a man who had played the role of Aladdin with his wonderful lamp, rubbing it and producing thick packages of fresh new banknotes! Jesse Blackless had not yet got over the shock of this experience, and never could get over the hope that it might happen again. So when the movement of the concerto was completed, he strolled in, introduced himself, and was introduced to the two guests.

He had never heard of the Robin family of Rotterdam, and took but the briefest glance at the lads. Not being a romantic or sentimental person, he saw them not as shepherd boys out of ancient Judea, but merely as youngsters who were in the way of an important conversation. At first he tried to figure out how to get rid of them, but then he decided to make use of them; instead of making a direct approach to the German agent, he would tell these children what was happening in Europe and let Kurt hear it by accident.

The pair seemed to have some idea of it already, and wanted to ask questions. All right, let them ask, and Jesse would answer. Thus for two solid hours the embittered revolutionist poured out his soul to the two sensitive lads. Nobody knew more about intrigue and villainy in the ruling-class world, and nobody saw with clearer insight the wellspring from which all these evils flowed, the greed of high finance and big business, their determination to crush the movement of the class-conscious workers, to tie it, cripple it, break its neck. Hansi and Freddi sat gazing in open-eyed wonder at this strange-looking gentleman, bald, lean, and with wrinkled leathery skin, saying dreadful things in a somewhat harsh voice, with a twisted smile that left you uncertain how much he really meant and how much was a cruel kind of jesting.

Jesse wasn't sure what Kurt's political views were, but to look at him he was a German aristocrat. So the painter explained that Germany was now listed among the down-and-outs; the British and French empires had her there and meant to keep her there. For a long time to come, the international workers would be the natural allies of the Fatherland; in left-wing labor throughout Europe lay the one hope of freedom for the German people. Jesse explained to the lads what the Versailles peace treaty meant to its victims, and why the Reparations Commission was still refusing to fix the amount of the indemnities. That must mean, and was meant to mean, bankruptcy for Germany, loss of her foreign trade, and slow, inevitable starvation for the masses.

At the outset of the talk Kurt had the belief that Jesse didn't know who had brought him the money. But everything the painter said was so directly to the point that finally Kurt decided he must have made a clever guess. Kurt had heard a lot about this Red sheep of his lady-love's family, and was glad to hear what he had to say. It wasn't even necessary to ask questions to help the conversation along; the two eager lads provided all the cues. They drank in the speaker's every word, and what he was doing to them was a matter he had no time to consider. Jesse set forth the grim facts which were making revolutions in many parts of Europe, and he explained them according to the system of thought which he called "dialectical materialism."

XII

The session continued until Lanny got back from town and came over to the studio. He was polite to his uncle, as always; but, keeping his promise to his father, he said no more than a how-dy-do. Kurt informed Jesse that he was now entirely out of politics, and devoting his time to music; whereupon Jesse, somewhat crestfallen, went over to the villa to meet his sister.

At once the two lads fell upon their host. "Oh, Lanny, what a time we had listening to your uncle! What a marvelous man!"

They poured out a chorus of excited praise; and Lanny, of course, had to make some response. "He is very well informed."

"I have never met anybody like him!" Hansi declared. "He explains everything that is going on in Europe. He makes it all so clear—it is like seeing a map for the first time."

"He has his very definite point of view," replied Lanny. He didn't want to throw cold water on their fervors, but at the same time he ought to provide some antidote for the double dose of Red medicine they had swallowed. "You must realize that there are other points of view, Hansi. The truth is never all on one side."

The retired artillery officer came to his friend's support. Two blasé, world-weary dwellers in the ivory tower, trying to keep two neophytes from venturing down onto that darkling plain where the ignorant armies clashed by night! Said Kurt: "Never let anybody make you forget that you are artists. It is your function to provide spiritual illumination for mankind and not to waste your faculties in the clamor and strife of politics. If you are good artists, that is all the world has any right to expect of you."

"But," argued Hansi, "how can our music have any real vitality if we harden our hearts to the cries of suffering people?"

"Poor Mr. Robin!" thought Lanny. What anguish in the home of a war profiteer and his wife, if those darlings returned to Rotterdam spouting the formulas of the Reds! And the worst of it was, there was so much truth in what these fanatics had to say; you could never answer them completely, and so your conscience was always being kept in a ferment. You wished the pests in Hades; and then right away you were ashamed of the wish!

8

With No Great Change of Manner

I

In that summer of 1920 a fresh calamity fell upon an afflicted world. It started in the United States of America, that most fortunate of all lands; a severe spell of "hard times," a mysterious phenomenon which came every few years, and for which nobody seemed to have a clear explanation. Robbie wrote his own view, that the farmers, under pressure of war needs, had plowed up millions of acres of new land and greatly increased the crop yields of the country. Now there was no longer a market for so much food; the fact that people were starving made no difference, so long as they didn't have the price. The farmers, who had gone heavily into debt to buy high-priced lands, were now stuck, and half of them would lose their farms to the banks.

And of course when the farmers couldn't buy, the manufacturers couldn't sell. Budd's, which was so busy turning its swords into plowshares, now discovered that nobody had the price of a shovel. And over in Arabia, where Robbie's new company had struck a pool of oil, the wells had to be capped and shut down, because factory wheels were still and farmers were staying at home instead of driving motor-cars. A time of suffering and strain for everybody, and Robbie wouldn't be taking any trips to Europe, but would "stick around" and help his father and brothers to stand the financial siege. Lanny became anxious, and wrote offering to get along without his allowance for a while; but Robbie said that that was just chicken-feed—anyhow, it came out of the earnings of "R and R." That smart trader in Rotterdam was the only one who was making real money, because he kept betting on calamity and getting it.

However, Robbie was sure that everything would be "hunkydory" very soon, because he had had his way in the political affairs of his country. The Republican convention had met and nominated just the right sort of fellow: a certain Senator Harding of Ohio, who was known to all the businessmen and could be trusted. They were going to put him over with a bang, and from then on America would mind its own business and prosperity would come back and stay. So Lanny needn't worry his head about finances or any other problems; just go on with his piano practice and leave the rest of the world to his old man! Lanny didn't mention how two Red serpents had recently crept into his Eden and persuaded him once more to take a nibble at the forbidden fruit of the tree of knowledge.

It was something Lanny didn't mention even to Kurt Meissner, that all three times in his life when he had listened to Barbara Pugliese his mind had become confused and his conscience troubled.

Could it really be true that poverty was caused by the profit system? By the fact that owners of land and capital held their products for a profit, and that no more goods could be produced until the owners had got their price? Of course Lanny knew what his father would reply to such an argument. "Look at the producers now—bankrupt, and having to sell below cost! If they take their present losses, aren't they entitled to their future gains?" It was very complicated, and whenever Lanny tried to think about it he found himself stuck in a maze and not knowing which way to turn. Earlier in his life he had been content to say: "My father wishes me to believe such and so." But now he realized that this didn't satisfy anybody, and he was ashamed to say it. Did he have the moral right to believe what his father wished him to believe, rather than what seemed to be true?

II

Gather ye rosebuds while ye may, Old time is still a-flying! Marie de Bruyne had set a date, and the thought of her drove all others out of his mind. He visioned her by day and dreamed of her by night; he counted the days and then the hours. His music danced with her—or it came walking down a country road, clad in a sunhat and a blue summer dress. He wrote to her: "Wear that dress!"

On the fateful morning he went and got the old lady and drove her to meet the train; sure enough, when Marie stepped from it she was wearing the honeymoon dress! In the interest of propriety he gave her a friendly handshake, and when her bags were safely stowed he drove Mme. Scelles to the establishment where she took care of her orphans; she said they would need a lot of care, so she wouldn't be coming home for lunch. She had tactfully seen to it that there was no servant in the house; and Lanny had told his mother to expect him when she saw him.

So there were at least two happy people in war-wrecked France that day. It wasn't so much that they asked of the world, just to be left alone in a room together. There was between them that perfect understanding which is the warrant and seal of love. His was gentle and kind, and hers was a blissful acquiescence. They shared, and would continue to share, everything they had. They could lie in each other's arms for hours in bliss, and it was hardly any less happiness just to hold each other's hands. That extended to all their activities; if an idea occurred to him, his greatest pleasure was to share it with her; if an adventure befell him, his first thought was to tell her about it. They could be silent for long periods; just to be together was enough. They did not have to make any apologies for wasted time, or feel any qualms or doubts concerning excess of passion. She was for him the reality of the poet's dream of

> Some one whom I could court
>   With no great change of manner,
> Still holding reason's fort
>   Though waving fancy's banner.

When their first transports had passed, Marie told him the strange story of what had been happening to her during the past few weeks. After sixteen years of married life, she had imagined that she knew her husband, but had discovered that she knew only the surface, and that deep below were caverns inhabited by strange creatures. The man had been shocked by her revelations; as a result of it they had talked frankly for the first time in their lives, and she had got a new understanding of the complexity of the human personality. Denis de Bruyne, vigorous and active businessman, was a victim of cravings which he did not understand and which since youth he had been unable to control. He was one of those sex-tormented beings which the Catholic religion produces in great number. He had been taught that sex was something forbidden and repulsive, and so he made it that; he wanted from it what he dared not permit himself to get, and thus what might have been the basis of ecstasy became a cause of shame and fear.

Now had come this sudden and to him distressing revelation that his wife, whom he had imagined aloof and "pure," had fallen into the same cesspool as himself. "He has several reactions all tangled together," she explained. "He has a certain amount of relief, because a weight of condemnation is lifted from his soul. My one transgression excuses his many, and he feels that we are partners in sin. On that basis we can talk plainly—while before it was almost as if I were a virgin."

"I suppose it's all right," commented Lanny, "provided he doesn't try to get you to repent!"

"But that's just what he did! I think he would have been glad to come back into the paths of virtue with me."

"Oh, my God!" exclaimed the youth.

"I tried to get him to understand that I am really in love, but that is difficult for him. One does not easily get over these attitudes that are stamped into one's soul in childhood. Denis can forgive me for sinning; he knows that I can go to confession and have the slate wiped clean; but that I should believe in my sin, and call it virtue, that is an act of defiance, a rebellion against the very throne of God."

"Did you tell him about me?"

"He asked me to, but I told him I had no right to do so without your consent. I promised to try to get it."

"What good will that do him?"

"He is genuinely concerned about my happiness. His basic idea is that it is the woman who is seduced and betrayed. He cannot believe that any man means well by a woman—I mean when he wants her sexually."

"Does he expect to reform me, too?"

"Don't laugh, dear! This is a Catholic land, and I am telling you what goes on in the souls of men and women here."

"Bless your heart," he said; "one has to laugh so that one need not weep. Nature has made life simple, and happiness easy. What devil is it that creeps into our hearts and creates taboos and superstitions? My mother told me that when she was a girl her mother put off a long-planned excursion because it was suddenly discovered that the date was Friday, the thirteenth of the month."

"Yes, dear; but this is different, this is his religion."

"What does it matter what name you give it, if it is crazy? The Catholic won't eat beefsteak on Friday, the Hindu won't eat it any day, the Jew won't eat it from the same plate with butter; and each one says: 'That is my religion; that is what God told me.'

But I say it's a notion that got stuck in the addled brain of some poor savage sitting in a cave gnawing the bone of an aurochs, or maybe the bone of an enemy he had just killed in battle."

They smiled together, and she said: "Don't let it worry you, dear. It will never make any difference in our love."

"Tell your husband that your lover is a faun; that he has no morals."

"What I have told him," she answered, gravely, "is that you have the best morals of any man I have ever known. I have told him that you believe in love, and that you grant me all my rights in love, and think about my happiness equally with your own." He took her in his arms again and kissed her many times, to prove to her that this was true, and that love is lovely and not mortal sin.

III

So began for these two a long period of untarnished happiness. A warm glow diffused itself through all the activities of their lives; love became music, it became poetry and art, dancing and swimming, walking and driving, eating and sleeping, and, above all, that "conversation" which Lanny, as a denizen of France, had learned to esteem so highly. Everything they did was touched with the hues of romance, doubly delightful because they could find more pleasure in each other's pleasure than in their own.

Seeing her son thus walking in the clouds, Beauty had to give up. After all, Marie was a lady, and she wasn't exploiting Lanny or getting his money for jewels and furs and expensive entertainments. He brought her to Bienvenu, and Beauty looked her over and couldn't deny that she was beautiful, with the golden light of the honeymoon upon her. The two women declared a truce; if they couldn't be mother and daughter, or sisters, they could at least be co-operators in the difficult task of keeping men satisfied at home. The cat's claws would be retracted, the serpent's fangs laid flat, the wasp's sting drawn out of sight; they would make no hurtful allusions to each other's weaknesses or defects, but would help each other by giving hints as to the whims and eccentricities of the dangerous male creature. More could not be expected of women in a highly competitive world.

They did not make the mistake of letting each other see the signs of their infatuation, for these are rarely pleasing to any but the infatuated ones. Lanny would take Marie to his studio; there was a library there, providing decorous excuse for long absences; also there were Marcel's paintings, and a story about each which Lanny knew and which Marie was interested to hear. She was impressed by these works, and that was one way to win the friendship of Beauty; for to praise them was not merely to endorse her taste in art and in husbands, it was also to promote the worldly aspects of her widowhood. Beauty was certain, and all her friends agreed, that some day she would make a lot of money out of that inheritance.

Another factor in the situation was Baby Marceline. As a boy Lanny had always observed that he could win the heart of any peasant woman by showing interest in her children, and Marie didn't need to have this ancient technique pointed out to her. Marceline was an easy child to love; affectionate and eager, she came at once to Marie as to an old friend. Also Marie appreciated Kurt, who was dignified and reserved in his attitude toward her; so all was well in the household. There was no end of joking among Beauty's fashionable friends when they came to realize the odd situation. But love outweighs gossip, and those two "cradle-snatchers," as they were called, told themselves that not one of the witty worldlings but would have snatched their happiness if she could.

IV

The elections in the United States were held in November, and resulted in a landslide for Robbie's candidate. This was such an important event that he wrote a special letter to his son, a sort of war-dance over the body of the stricken idealist in the White House. Never had there been a more complete repudiation of a personality and a set of ideas; the invalid Woodrow Wilson was still President, but no one paid the least attention to him—except that the Senate took delight in rejecting everything that he had done, and every request coming from the "nursery junta," as someone called it. On March 4 next the businessmen of the United States would take charge and show how a modern and up-to-date nation should be run. "Watch our smoke!" said Robbie Budd.

The man of business didn't ask what his son thought about these matters; he told him, and took it for granted that the son would agree—and for the most part Lanny did, for he didn't keep very well informed as to affairs in the land where his fathers had died. Robbie sent him the *Literary Digest*, a dull weekly which gave various points of view of what was going on, but as a rule Lanny found it more agreeable to play a new musical work with Kurt. Most of his ideas about world events came from the English weeklies in which Rick had contributions and which he never failed to send.

Rick wasn't coming to the Riviera that winter, for a number of reasons. For one, Lanny didn't feel free to invite him, on account of the hard times; for another, Nina had her second baby, according to plan, and she needed the care which she received in the home of Rick's family; for a third, Rick's health was growing better. Perhaps it was because he was happier; his work was succeeding, and his courage was triumphing over his pain. He still raged over his discovery as to the little intelligence with which the world was governed, but now he was able to get more pleasure out of the raging. Again Lanny observed the peculiar duality of the artistic temperament, which is bowed down with grief, horror, or other tragic emotion, then finds a phrase to express it, and slaps its knee, exclaiming: "By God, a masterstroke!"

Rick's eyes were still upon the theater. He would go up to London, attend a play, and then go home to write an article about it and offer it to the various weeklies. It was a difficult field to break into, but Rick had advantages in that his father was one of those amateurs who haunt the green-rooms and know everybody, and so was a mine of the sort of information a journalist requires. Sir Alfred could introduce his son to important persons, and everybody would be kind to Rick because of his having been a flier for king and country. Rick claimed no credit, but wrote to Lanny: "There are hundreds of fellows with as much talent as I have who are now peddling matches in Regent Street." Such remarks gave the letters of the baronet's son a decidedly pinkish tinge. All Lanny's friends appeared to be moving toward the "left." Was the whole world doing that? If so, it was going to be a lonesome place for the son of a munitions salesman!

There came a letter from Hansi and Freddi Robin, telling about their studies. The older brother said: "One of my teachers gave me an article from a Socialist paper telling about the progress of the labor movement in Italy, and it mentions Barbara Pugliese as one of the leaders. My teacher also gave me a book about co-operatives, and it is a wonderful movement that I am happy to know about. I shall never cease to be grateful to you for having put me in touch with it."

So, the Red plague had spread to Rotterdam! Lanny wondered: Was Mr. Robin going to be distressed and make a fuss like Robbie? And how was the devoted Hansi going to react when in some of those Red publications he came upon denunciations of war profiteers and speculators? Lanny would never forget what ferocious things they had said in the *affiches* announcing the meeting for which Kurt had put up the money and at which Jesse Blackless had delivered a fiery address.

V

Marie went home to her family for Christmas, and left Lanny in a sort of polar night. His mother sought to brighten it by a tree covered with tinsel and illuminated with a string of tiny colored electric lights. This was a present from Robbie Budd, who was a great fellow for discovering new gadgets and singing their praises. He said the lights would make a fireproof Christmas, which was important in Juan, whose fire-department fell short of Robbie's standard of competence. The lights gave pleasure to Baby Marceline, and to Leese and the maid, and to various children, relatives of the servants and of peasants and fisherfolk, their neighbors, who came in to receive candy and toys. They all noticed how deeply these scenes touched Kurt Meissner, and Lanny sympathized, because all his memories of Schloss Stubendorf had to do with Christmas. He knew that Kurt was still getting sad and painful letters from his family. It was the third Christmas since the Armistice—but how far the world was from the spirit of peace on earth, good will toward men!

Marie returned to Cannes, and the intimacy was resumed. She reported that her children were well, and that her relations with her husband were becoming stabilized. With Lanny's consent she had described the exemplary young man to whom her future was committed: a musician, a student, a person of experience and discretion far beyond his years. Denis had been relieved at the tidings, and had expressed the hope that he might have the pleasure of meeting this worthy one and assuring him of his esteem. Good form required that Lanny should express his appreciation of this considerate attitude.

It was all a matter of custom. If Lanny and Marie had lived in the sweet land of liberty, she would have proceeded to Reno, Nevada, and sworn to some more or less false charges against her polite husband; then she would have married Lanny Budd, and their friends would have thought it a queer match but moral. Marie, however, was a Frenchwoman, and a mother, and if she had taken such a course she would have been considered cruel and irresponsible; she would have broken up a home and shamed two old and respectable families, her husband's and her father's. She would never have been forgiven by either family, and her children would have been handicapped in their opportunities of marriage according to the custom prevailing.

The French way suited the French; it was discreet and kept the affairs of important persons a secret, save for those who had the right to know about them. Lanny had been a guest in more than one such household, both in France and in England. He knew, for example, that the greatest of living French writers had as his *amie* a highly respected lady, Mme. de Caillavet, and spent much of his time in the home of that lady and her husband, a wealthy banker. Lanny had met both Anatole France and his friend at Emily Chattersworth's, and knew that everybody considered Mme. de Caillavet the force which had driven a lazy writer to his best work and had made his fame in the world of letters. Incidentally, they considered that the now aged gentleman wasn't treating her very well. Lanny meant to treat the wife of Denis de Bruyne in a way which no one would criticize.

VI

The "crisis" had spread over the whole world, and statesmen were at their wit's end. Those of the victorious nations had told their peoples that times would soon be all right, because the Germans were going to pay for everything; so now, when times were all wrong, the obvious explanation was that the Germans were refusing to pay. A cheap and easy way out; politically easy, emotionally easy, because everybody was used to blaming the Germans for troubles.

In Paris there was another conference between the heads of the various governments, for whom life had now become a perpetual quarrel over reparations. Ever since Spa their experts had been meeting the German experts and discussing what Germany could pay; they had arrived at an agreement, but the Allied governments were not satisfied with the amounts and insisted upon more. The Germans said they couldn't pay the increases; the Allies insisted they could but didn't want to.

The perpetual conference was transferred to London, where Rick had the inside "dope" and passed it on to his friend. Rick sent newspapers and magazine articles which Lanny read with care. He had lived with these problems for the six most exciting months of his life; he had worried over them and argued about them. Now there was a melancholy satisfaction in finding that he had been right, and that the world was going to the devil exactly as he had foretold.

There just wasn't enough intelligence on the poor tormented planet; not enough statesmanship, not enough ordinary decency. The people weren't able to control the forces which modern industrialism had created; they didn't even have the means of getting the facts. There were a few honest papers, but they reached only a small public; the big press was in the hands of the big interests, and told the people whatever suited the purposes of the masters of steel and munitions and oil.

For example, that question of Turkey and Greece, one of the problems about which the statesmen were wrangling in London at the outset of the year 1921. Robbie Budd knew about it—he had to, for his own business was at stake, and in his sudden way he stepped onto a steamer and arrived in London, wiring Lanny to join him if he cared to. Lanny didn't go, because he was so happy with Marie, and there was nothing he could do in the oil business. Robbie wrote him a few sentences typed on his little portable machine—the sort of thing one wouldn't trust to a stenographer. "Z is here, keeping out of sight as usual, but pulling all the strings." Lanny knew who "Z" was, and he knew who "LG" was. "LG is in pawn to him, and he is directing policy. You would be amused to hear Z telling me about his sentimental interest in his homeland, when I know about the concessions he has been promised; he has already formed the companies. Don't say anything about this, of course."

Lanny felt embarrassed, because he had told Rick some time back about the relationship between the munitions king of Europe and the British Prime Minister, and right now Rick was on the trail of a story about the intrigues over Greece and her seizure of Turkish territory. Lanny told his father what Rick was doing, so that he could stop him if he thought it necessary; but Robbie answered that Rick couldn't get the real facts, and if he did they were so startling that nobody would dare to publish them.

And that was the way it worked out. Rick got what he thought was a story, and his magazine editors said their printers would refuse to put it on the presses. The libel laws were strict in England, and it was no defense to prove that what you said was true. "Yet they say they have free speech!" wrote Robbie. "They put on a show in Hyde Park every Sunday—anybody can get up on a stand and say anything he pleases—curse the King and the royal family in the presence of a few hundred poor devils and one or two American visitors—and that serves to convince the world that it's a free country!" Robbie Budd wasn't ever going to like the British ruling class—not even while he was shipping out Arabian oil under the protection of one of their warships!

VII

Easter holidays are important in France. The boys would be home from school, and it was their mother's duty to be with them. Would not Lanny take this occasion to make their acquaintance? Lanny perceived that, just as he himself wanted to share all his experiences and ideas with Marie, so she desired to have him love her darling boys, and at least to understand the gratitude and sympathy which she felt for her husband. A year had passed since she and Lanny had declared their love, and it might now be considered as established.

Lanny said all right, fine; they would motor up and back again. The best makes of French cars were famous over the world, and Robbie's generosity enabled Lanny to have one. Any time the whim seized him, he could command the great scenes of history to roll past him while he sat in comfort and security. He could stop in whatever inn he judged suitable, and servants would hasten to provide for his wants; he could stand by with clean hands and watch mechanics with greasy hands attend to the wants of his car.

Enjoying these privileges, he would never find it difficult to persuade some woman to travel with him and entertain him with gay conversation. Lanny had quoted to his father the verse of the poet Clough: "How pleasant it is to have money, heigh-ho!" What was the defect in Lanny's mind or temperament which caused him to be always a little uneasy about his pleasures, a little hesitant and apologetic? It puzzled his mother and father and some of his friends. Was it because he had read too many books, and got his mind full of images of skeletons at ancient feasts, of handwritings on the walls of palaces? Thus conscience doth make cowards of us all!

But Lanny had no troubles of conscience concerning Marie de Bruyne, and motoring with her would be a repetition of their happy first week. They followed the varied Riviera coast, past Toulon, where the French fleet kept guard over the Mediterranean, and the great harbor of Marseille, where Lanny had traveled since childhood to meet his father or friends who came by the southern route. Past the wide delta of the great river Rhône the pair came to Arles, and Lanny told the strange story of the half-crazed painter who had cut off his ear and sent it to a prostitute. Farther north was Avignon, seat of the popes in their days of exile; the travelers stopped to inspect the great palace which these potentates had been thirty years a-building. Then came the industrial city of Lyon, and then Chalon-sur-Saône, where their guidebook told them they might see the tomb of Abelard, but they didn't; it sufficed to talk about that old story of unhappy love, and thank whatever gods might be that they had been born in a day when love was free for the taking.

They crossed a ridge, and following the Burgundy canal and the valley of the river Yonne they came to Paris. Delightful for Lanny to drive about those splendid boulevards in the warm sunshine of early spring and tell his sweetheart about his adventures in the stirring war days. Some of them were still under seal—he couldn't say that Kurt had been a German agent, and that he and his mother had lived in terror of their friend's being caught and shot; but Lanny could tell how the police had seized him for the offense of possessing some of his Red uncle's incendiary literature. Lanny had never read Cicero, and didn't know that elder statesman's remark that we find pleasure in recalling past troubles; but sitting at a table in a sidewalk café, partaking of a delicious luncheon, he knew that he enjoyed telling the sweetest woman in the world how it felt to hear the clang of a cell-door upon you, and to wonder when it was opened if you were going to be led out and shot!

VIII

The Château de Bruyne bore that imposing title because for a couple of centuries it had belonged to the gentle family of the neighborhood; but really it was no more than a modest villa. Just as Lanny had imagined, it had a lovely garden, including a wall with a southern front and pear and apricot trees trained like vines against it. They were in bloom now, and so were the tulips and the fleurs-de-lis, the hyacinths and crocuses and narcissi. Everything was dressed up for the lovers, and they had the place to themselves for two or three blessed hours, the master of the house being in the city and the boys not expected until the morrow.

The old house was built of a reddish stone, and had some modern improvements. Marie explained that her husband's family had been ruined in the days of the Panama Canal fiasco, and the family had lost this home. Denis had made his own fortune and bought it back and had it fixed up for his bride. Better not think too much about that; better go upstairs and see the chamber assigned to Lanny, which had a door connecting with Marie's. A table would be kept in front of the door when it was not in use. This was supposed to fool the servants, but of course it wouldn't; they would tell the other servants of the neighborhood, and these would tell their mistresses in the regular way. But that did no harm, for an *affaire* remained a secret so long as you pretended it was; it didn't become a scandal unless you let it get into the courts or the newspapers.

All this suited Lanny; but he had to admit to some trepidation when the car of Denis de Bruyne rolled up to the door. It is one thing to read about *la vie à trois* in romances, but it is something else to be formally inducted into it. M. de Bruyne was in his early sixties—so Lanny could comfort himself with the reflection that if he was twenty years too young for Marie, her husband was twenty years too old for her. He was a solidly built, good-looking man, gray-haired, with dark, melancholy eyes and rather pale, aristocratic features. He was scrupulously polite to Lanny, treating him as an honored guest and not as a punishment for Denis's sins.

The pair practiced the French art of conversation, which meant that neither tried to force his ideas, but each brought forward such wit or wisdom as he possessed, and the other listened and in return received an equal share of attention. They talked about the state of the world, and the position of France in relation to her friends and her foes. They talked about the precarious condition of business, and also about the new *salon*, the opera, and the current drama—the fact that Denis de Bruyne was managing a large fleet of taxicabs did not keep him from being informed about these matters. If Lanny knew anything to the point he said it, and if he didn't he listened, and so the host was able to satisfy himself that the lady who bore his name had chosen a youth of discretion and taste.

Also, Lanny had the further task of winning the regard of two lads with whom he was to stand *in loco parentis*. This proved to be in no way difficult, for they were friendly and well brought up. Denis *fils* was fifteen and Charlot a year younger; they were dark-eyed and handsome like their father, and had their mother's sweet disposition. After the fashion of French boys they wore stockings which stopped far below their knees, and pants which stopped far above them, so there was a long bare stretch upon which the mosquitoes fed voraciously.

Most young Americans whom Lanny had met in Europe had seemed to him undisciplined and vacant-minded. These two French lads were serious, and accepted hard work as their destiny. Even during their holidays each practiced the piano for an hour a day, and gave another hour to reading some worthwhile book. So they had something to talk about; and when Lanny showed them Dalcroze dancing they found him a delightful companion. They played tennis with him, and on one occasion took him fishing, and his ideas concerning one aspect of French life were completely revolutionized—they caught no less than five small fishes.

Marie had repudiated Lanny's horrid idea of telling these children the truth about her lover; they took him as a family friend, and on that basis he passed a week of agreeable domesticity. Then Marie told him that her husband had received word that a widowed sister was arriving in Paris next day, and it would be necessary to invite her to the home. Denis was not yet prepared to share their secret with this lady, who was "devout" and at the same time observant; so Lanny was asked to spend a few days in Paris, after which the boys would be going back to school and Marie would be returning to Cannes. Of course one could always have a pleasant time in La Ville Lumière, especially in the delightful month of April; there was the *salon* to be visited, and plays about which Lanny could tell Rick. The world of art was reviving, and the art lovers of Europe were resuming their cosmopolitan attitude, flocking from one great capital to another to see what new wonders were on display.

9

Consider the Lilies

I

IMAGINE that one could walk freely into the Hotel Crillon, no longer sacred territory, guarded by American naval yeomen in white caps! Lanny strolled in, just for the fun of it, but he didn't put up there, because he told himself that one must economize in these hard times. He went to the smaller hotel where his mother had stopped, and where they knew him and were glad to see him. Again he didn't need any Cicero to tell him that it was pleasant to sit in the *foyer* and not shiver at the thought of the Sûreté Générale lurking behind the pillars.

Paris hadn't been able to afford a new coat of paint, but the ladies on the boulevards had. The tourists were returning, and everybody was trying to look cheerful and receptive. It was only if you went out into the suburbs that you would find war wreckage which had not yet been cleared away; only there would you be apt to notice the great numbers of young women in black, and the undue proportion of elderly men and cripples. Everybody agreed that victory was glorious, that fashions were daring, and the *salons* more brilliant than ever; the cafés and theaters were crowded every night, and if the ladies on the stage were not more naked, it was only because it is the nature of nakedness to be neither more nor less.

Fortunately intellectual entertainment had not been entirely overlooked. All the smart people were talking about the *Chauve Souris*, a refugee group of the Moscow Art Theater; a kind of "highbrow" vaudeville, clever and well acted. You sat in a hall of green-painted wood decorated with bunches of pink-painted roses, and having yellow-painted columns with white-painted teapots around them. A waiter in white overdress brought you iced drinks and preserves, while a droll little man by the name of Balieff introduced the scenes on the stage. First you saw a Russian episode with dancing, and then you saw Voltaire, and then the German Kaiser.

Between the acts Lanny looked about, and recognized a young attaché of the French Foreign Office whom he had come to know during the conference. Lanny joined him and they talked about times old and new. Lanny's attention was directed to the fashions, which were *très snob*—a word of praise in French. Some ladies were wearing a sort of elaborately embroidered apron—only they wore it behind instead of in front! They wore red hats of the most glaring shades—or else they wore black ones made of monkey-fur. Extraordinary the ravenous craving for monkey-fur which had seized upon women in the season of 1921; capes, collars, muffs, sleeves, handbags —the monkey tribes of all tropic lands were near to extermination, and still there wasn't enough, so the goat tribes were being sacrificed. Lanny said that some of the furs looked as if they were the trimmings from beards in the Quartier Latin; but his companion denied that any beards had been trimmed there.

Lanny was invited to spend the night in a place where they would find *très chic* ladies; but he explained that he had an engagement with a particular one, and returned to his hotel. Next day he went to the Grand Palais to inspect the newly opened Salon des Indépendants, and spent many hours remarking the hard, bright colors in which French painters were seeing the world. Oddities of many sorts provided topics for conversation. A nude woman being carried between the horns of a large brown bull against a green background was called *The Abduction of Europa*. A pink triangle set against an orange background and covered with spots of green and red—that was *An Expression of Simple Happiness*.

II

After Lanny had enjoyed his fill of such happiness he wanted to tell someone about it, so he telephoned to his friend Emily Chattersworth, who had just returned to Les Forêts. When he explained why he was in town, this hospitable soul replied: "Why don't you come out and stay with me? Isadora will be here tomorrow."

"Oh, gosh!" he exclaimed. "Are you sure I wouldn't be in the way?"

"Not in the least. You can play for her and she'll be delighted."

"You won't have to say it twice!"

Next morning when he arrived at the château, there was the divine one already installed, and saying very kindly that she remembered him from the days before the war. Possibly she did, but she had had a swarm of children on her hands, and he had been one more. Isadora Duncan at this time was forty-three, and her loveliness had become maternal; her gentle features showed the ravages of grief and pain. "The poor soul is terribly *distraite*," said Emily Chattersworth. "Try to keep her from drinking."

"I surely won't lead her into temptation," replied Lanny, and his friend said: "That's one reason I wanted you."

Isadora had just come back from a sojourn in Greece, and wore the costume of that land in its days of glory. Her art was based on the Greek spirit, and so was her life; in a long white stola, caught up and draped at the waist, she looked like a noble and gentle caryatid. She had regular and sweet features, with lovely brown eyes, and brown hair coiled into a loose knot at the nape of her neck.

She told about her adventures under the government of Venizelos, which had made her into a national institution. She had brought with her a few of the children whom Lanny had watched her training just a few days before the outbreak of war; she had taken this troupe to the United States, and then back to France, and so to Greece. They had danced among the splendid ruins which Lanny would never forget; he told how he and Marcel Detaze had stood among them and watched the dying of the sun and speculated about the dying of worlds. Isadora perceived that here was a kindred soul, and she talked glowingly about her life and labors.

She was the frankest-spoken person Lanny had ever met; she hid nothing from anybody, and said what she thought about everything. She had never really got over the tragic death of her two lovely children, followed by the loss of a newly born baby on the day the

French troops were called to war; all this heaping up of calamities had come near to unhinging the reason of a sensitive *artiste*. The world was a dreadful and cruel place! The hotel at Bellevue which she had planned to make the temple of a new art had served as a hospital for broken bodies and was now being made into a factory for poison gases. Greece, to which she had hoped to restore its ancient glories, had fallen prey to the pro-German King Constantine, who had driven Isadora's patron into exile and turned her and her school adrift. Now she had come to Paris and about ruined herself with all patrons by hailing Soviet Russia as the last remaining hope of mankind. She had waved a flaming red scarf during some of her dances, and so wasn't invited to dance very often.

III

She desired that this agreeable young man should play for her. He did so, and she was pleased. She took off her Greek sandals and put on one of her light dancing tunics. A servant set the furniture of the drawing-room back against the walls, so that the hostess could enjoy a treat—but not a free one, no, for Isadora was the most impecunious person who ever lived; all her life she had spent all her earnings on her school, and now somebody, man or woman, had to put up the funds for her and her art and her pupils, wherever on earth they might be. Consider the lilies of the field, how they grow; they toil not, neither do they spin!

The dancer was no sylph, and seemed better equipped to represent *Les Feuilles d'Automne* than the *Spring Song* of Mendelssohn or of Grieg. But life which had battered and bruised her cruelly had not tamed her ardor; she danced everything, and when the spirit possessed her she rose above the limitations of the flesh. Lanny had never seen her dance, and didn't see much of it now, for he had to sit at the piano and work hard. She was an exacting taskmistress; the best wasn't good enough for her, and she never stooped to flattery. Over his shoulder he got glimpses of the most graceful motions he had ever seen made by a human body; and when the dance was over and the dream had fled, there was a well-fleshed middle-aged woman, puffing audibly, lying down and covering herself with a robe, but still trying to communicate her vision, telling Lanny what the music meant and what the motions meant, and how the two were blended into something entirely new in the world. Isadora Duncan wasn't modest about her genius, and didn't need to be, for she had proved it in every great capital of the world. Starting as an unknown girl from San Francisco, she had created her art, and enormous audiences had accepted it with acclaim rarely seen in the theater.

Freedom was her watchword; freedom in her thinking, in her personal life, in her representations. She hated all chains upon the human mind and spirit; she hated injustice and stupidity, and when these things were brought to her attention she raged at them. She despised the conventional ballet; toe-dancing was to her simpering idiocy, and such forms as the minuet were expressions of conventionality based upon class dominance. The Anglo-Saxon peoples were long-limbed and free, and she gave them a long-limbed and free art form.

Lanny was startled to meet another defender of the revolutionary upheaval in Russia. He questioned her about this, and found that she didn't really know much about what was going on there—not as much as he himself had learned from Lincoln Steffens and Bill Bullitt and his uncle Jesse. Isadora took it on faith, because she had to have something to believe in, and because the so-called "capitalist world" had horrified her by its blind and bloody slaughters. She described to Lanny one of the great moments of her life, her first visit to St. Petersburg in the year 1905. Her train had been late and she had arrived alone in arctic cold and darkness, and while being driven to a hotel had seen a long procession of dark figures staggering under heavy burdens—it was the funeral of the workers who had been slaughtered by the Tsar's troops on the previous day. Against that age-old oppression her heart had registered a vow of hatred, and that same heart had leaped with joy when the peasants and workers had thrown off their shackles. "Peace, Land, and Bread"—how could any free spirit fail to acclaim that slogan? Surely not Isadora, who, before the revolution, had put on a scarlet tunic and danced the *Marseillaise* in the Metropolitan Opera House, to the great dismay of the wealthy patrons of that great New York institution.

IV

"Oh, Lanny," she said, "do stay for a while! You understand my work so well; and I must practice to keep my condition."

"I'll stay as long as I can," he promised. He played everything he knew and everything Mrs Emily had, and Isadora became possessed of her daimons, or muses, or both. She gave him glimpses of her Omar Khayyám dances, the first creation of her youth. To his infinite delight she showed him the dance she had made on her first visit to Greece, the chorus of the *Suppliants of Aeschylus*. She danced a Chopin prelude and a polonaise, and Schubert's *Marche Militaire*. She danced snatches of Beethoven's *Seventh*, and of Tschaikowsky's *Pathétique*. Both of them toiled and sweated—it was no unusual thing for her to lose four or five pounds in one morning's practice. Lanny had been working for years to acquire speed in reading, and now he knew what he had done it for.

The hostess had to go to the city, and they gave her a list of music scores which she promised to bring back. They were alone in the wide-spaced drawing-room, Lanny playing the *Second Hungarian Rhapsody* of Liszt. Here was a great musician and a great soul, Isadora said; the world didn't rate him highly enough. She rated him a tumultuous dance, ending in a wild climax; when she finished, she fled to Lanny and fell upon her knees, clasped her arms about him and clung to him, breathing as if all the air in the large drawing-room were not enough for her needs. She was a genius, and physically a colossal engine, the most thrilling that Lanny had ever encountered. He knew that artists and theatrical people were demonstrative in their manners, so he rested his hands upon her shoulders and waited for her to recover from her tremendous exertions.

Gradually he realized that she was going to stay right there. After her breathing had become normal, she still held him tightly, and her head lay against him. "Lanny," she whispered, "wouldn't you like to take me driving?"

"Why, surely, if you wish," he said.

"I am crazy about motoring. Nothing gives me such a thrill as to drive fast—very fast—ninety miles an hour!"

When this youth had received a present of a car, he had made promises to his father on the subject of speed. But he didn't think it necessary to go into details now. If Isadora wanted a ride he would provide it, and fast enough would be enough. "Where do you want to go?"

"Anywhere; I don't care, so long as it is far. Let us drive and drive, and not come back for a while, perhaps not ever. It has been a long time since I have met a man who might mean as much to me as you."

Lanny was startled, and not a little disturbed. He was made of flesh and blood, and here was a woman who had been one of the loveliest in the world, and still was one of its greatest artists. He knew that she proclaimed "free love" as a part of her religion; but he had had the idea that Emily would have told her about Marie, and so he would be able to play the piano and treat her as the Muse Terpsichore.

His hands trembled as they rested upon her; but that wasn't enough. "What's the matter, Lanny?" she whispered. "Don't you want to love me?"

"Listen, dear," he said—one must be as kind as possible—"I must tell you——"

He felt her recoil. "Oh, you are going to refuse me!"

"Please——"

But she didn't please in the least. She didn't want to hear arguments. "Oh, Lanny!" she exclaimed. "We could be so happy! Really, we are made for each other!"

"But I am already in love!" he blurted out.

"Oh, I know, but it can't be like this. I am Isadora!" She said it in a tone of awe, as he ought to have said it; as if it had been: "I am the goddess Diana!"—or possibly Venus, *pro tem.*

"I know, dear——"

"Lanny, it would be so wonderful! I had given up hope that I could ever be so happy with a man as I have been with you. You have thrilled me to my deepest recesses!"

"I am honored, of course; but I am really very much in love, and I'm bound in honor."

"Who is this woman?"

"I am afraid I oughtn't to tell."

"A married woman?"

"Yes."

"Oh, dear, oh, dear, how very annoying! Is she the type that would be jealous?"

"I have never tried her; and I mustn't."

"Oh, but this is humiliating! No man has ever turned me down—excepting only Stanislavsky!" There was a story there, he guessed, but she didn't stop to tell it. "Think what you are doing, Lanny! I have so much to offer you!"

"I know, Isadora; don't think I am ungrateful——"

"Am I not attractive to you?"

"You are one of the loveliest beings I have ever known."

"Oh, I am losing my charm!" There was a look of woe in the lovely brown eyes. "I am becoming an old woman!"

"You are an angel—and they are ageless and deathless, I believe."

"You are trying to make it easy for me—but you are refusing to love me!"

Tears were coming into her eyes, and he knew that pity moves the soul to love. "Listen, dear," he said, quickly. "You have known real love, I am sure. Haven't you been in love so that you just couldn't think of anybody else—not even a greater and perhaps more desirable person? Love isn't altogether rational, you know." He was doing his very best in a ticklish situation.

"I know, I know," she said. Perhaps he had stirred some memory in her soul. "Love is blind, love is crazy, often."

"Yes, that is it! That is the way with me."

"But, oh, Lanny, it is such a pity! I thought we were going to have a delightful time together! You understand me marvelously—and while your playing is far from perfect, it serves for practice."

"Thank you," he said, humbly. "Let me go on and play for you now."

"Oh, it isn't the same thing, it can't be! When you play and I dance, our souls flow together, they become one; yours gives me inspiration, and mine does the same for you. But when I have to think: 'He does not love me; he will not love me; he loves somebody else,' then all the fire goes out of me, and I think: 'I am an old and tired and discouraged woman, and the time has come that I have dreaded—when no man will be interested in me, and I am alone for the rest of my days.' "

V

Carrying the burden of that heavy sorrow, Isadora Duncan put her embroidered Chinese robe about her shoulders and led him out to the loggia from which you looked over the gardens and park in the rear of the gray stone château. There was an artificial lake, and steps leading down an embankment which resembled a dock for ships and had two towers like lighthouses from which the lake could be illumined at night. On both sides were gardens, and behind them a background of beech trees, the extensive forests for which the place was named. It was melancholy to think of all the unknown soldiers who were buried among those trees; and Isadora was in a melancholy mood.

She wanted this sympathetic youth to understand the soul need which had caused her to try to kidnap him—and was still causing it, for she couldn't believe that he wasn't going to change his mind and cry suddenly: "Let us go for that motor-ride!" She told him about the musician—"much better than you, Lanny!"—who had been her accompanist for many years. He was tall and slender, with a high forehead topped with hair like burnished copper; she had met him in Paris during the war, and amid the booming of the Big Berthas he had played Liszt's *Thoughts of God in the Wilderness*, St. Francis speaking to the birds. "I composed new dances, made all of prayer and sweetness and light. My spirit came back to life, and we became lovers, intense and passionate lovers—" She told Lanny about it, hoping to attract him by her vivid images, but only making him think about Marie.

Isadora always had to have romantic names for her lovers. The sewing-machine man who had financed her school for many years and had bought the Bellevue hotel for her—he had been "Lohengrin"; now this pianist became "the Archangel." They had moved to Cap Ferrat, not far from Lanny's home, and during the days when Lanny had been visiting the Budd family in Connecticut, Isadora had been dancing before the war-wounded or for their benefit.

After the war she had brought her pupils from their refuge in New York. "Perhaps I made a mistake," she said. "They had been children when I sent them there, and I forgot that they would come back young women. I took them with me to Athens, and the government gave us the Zeppeion for our school, and the Archangel played and I taught them new dances. All day we worked hard, and in the evening we would wreathe our brows with circlets of white jasmine flowers and stroll down to have supper by the sea."

But then had come the dreadful serpent crawling into that Eden. Isadora began to notice significant glances being exchanged between her Archangel and one of her lovely pupils. She had thought that intellect and soul had been dominant in his love for her, but now she learned that this was not so, and had the painful experience of watching the development of his intimacy with the young girl. A fury of jealousy seized her, and she wandered over the hills for a whole night.

"A frightful situation!" she exclaimed. "I could not turn this girl away from the school which had been her home. I had to go on teaching her, and pretend to be serene, devoted to the spirit of harmony, when it was as if I had some fierce creature gnawing at my vitals."

The episode was ended by a strange accident, the young King of Greece being bitten by a pet monkey and dying of infection; at least, that was the story, but everyone wondered, had he been poisoned? The country was thrown into political turmoil, Venizelos fell, and Isadora's school came to an end. She returned to Paris, and fell into a quarrel with her pupil, who took the Archangel away and blamed the teacher for having failed to live up to the doctrine she had taught.

"Maybe she was right," said Isadora, sadly. "We are not always strong enough to follow our own ideals. Anyhow, here I am, desolate, with an empty heart. Many women will say it is my folly to dream of holding a man's love at my age, but I cannot see it that way. There are spring flowers and there are autumnal flowers, and both have their beauties. I know that I have much to give—but, oh, Lanny, why is it that I have never been able to find a love that will last? What is the curse that rests upon me, that I can give happiness to millions of other people but cannot find it for myself?"

A profound question to put to one who had spent such a short time on earth—half Isadora's time. Lanny could only say what he had observed, that artists didn't seem a happy tribe; perhaps it was that they were meant to suffer so that they might turn it into beauty. Maybe the right thing to say was, not that artists suffered, but that people suffered, and thus became artists. Only desperate need of some sort would drive anyone to try as hard as they had to in order to excel. "That's what's the matter with me," said the young philosopher. "I've never really had to do anything, so I remain an amateur."

"Oh, don't let anybody change you!" exclaimed the daughter of the Muses. "Go on and be happy! Somebody has to, if we are not to forget the possibility!"

VI

Their hostess came back with a load of newly purchased music, and Lanny played and Isadora danced; but it was as she had said: the fire had gone out of her, and what had been play was now hard work. They all felt it, and Lanny was relieved when a cablegram came and changed the atmosphere at Les Forêts. The most marvelous cablegram that anyone had ever received, declared the *artiste* with the broken heart. It was from Moscow, signed by the name of Lunacharsky, Commissar of Education in the Soviet government. It said: "The Russian government alone can understand you. Come to us; we will make your school."

It took Isadora about two minutes to write a reply to that message: "Yes, I will come to Russia, and I will teach your children, on one condition, that you will give me a studio and the wherewithal to work." *

Lanny had never seen so quick a transformation in a human being. It was the rolling away of storm-clouds and the breaking of rainbows and bird-songs in the *Pastoral Symphony*. She began to dance; she danced all the spring songs that Lanny knew; all the bird music and the wind music and the fire music. She was sure what the answer would be, and she was going to Russia and make over the life of a hundred and forty million people—or whatever part of them were left after war and revolution.

She wanted Lanny to play revolutionary music, but he didn't know much of it, and there wasn't much in the Château les Forêts. Lanny didn't even know the *Internationale*—oh, shame, shame, not to know the *Internationale!* Isadora sang it, and he followed her, and learned it quickly; he played it with crashing chords, and their hostess, the formal and proper *salonnière*, watched, fascinated and perhaps a little horrified, while Isadora with her flaming red scarf rehearsed the tramping of the awakened and triumphant proletariat. She would produce it with ten thousand boys and girls wearing red tunics in the great square in front of the Kremlin; so she declared, while Lanny pounded out the prophecy that the international army would be the human race. "Oh, Lanny, don't you want to come to Russia with me?"

Fortunately the phone rang just then. It was Marie de Bruyne, telling him that she was leaving for Paris with her husband and would meet him at his hotel in a couple of hours. He said that he would be there, and hung up. Wishing to leave no uncertainty in the mind of his friend Emily, he remarked in the presence of both ladies: "That was a call from the woman I love, so I must go."

He kissed the warm perspiring hand of the new Terpsichore, and assured her that the memory of their revels would shine like a precious jewel in his heart forever. He told her that she was first among all women geniuses of this or any other time, and that he

---

* Details of these episodes have been taken from Isadora Duncan's *My Life*, and a few of her words have been quoted by permission of the publishers, Liveright Publishing Corporation.

was sure she would be happy in the workers' republic, building a new culture untarnished by the evils of capitalism. And so "*Au revoir.*"

VII

After that eagle flight, the lady of Lanny's heart seemed like a plain little domestic brown wren. But she was restful, and he was ready to rest! On the long drive south he told how it felt to be so high in the clouds, and moving so fast. He told the whole story— this was no disloyalty to Isadora, for she would tell Emily all about it, just as she had told Lanny about heartaches and ecstasies with her Archangel. She would find a romantic name for the son of an American munitions manufacturer: "Sir Galahad" or maybe "Young Joseph" or "my Anchorite." According to the laws of her being she would see it under some poetical aspect; it would become a sad little love that had died before it was born, and she would dance it to Ravel's *Pavane pour une Infante Défunte.*

The youth was surprised at Marie's reaction to the narrative. "Oh, Lanny, what a dreadful woman! If anything like that ever happens to you again, don't tell me, because it makes me ashamed for my sex!"

"But it isn't as bad as that, dear!"

"It seems to me as bad as it can be. A woman like that talks about love, but what does she know about it? What did she really know about you—your character, your soul, even your mind?"

He saw that he was treading on dangerous ground, and became cautious. "Mayn't she have intuitions? She's a genius, you know."

"She's a woman who changes her loves as she does her shoes; and no high-sounding names can make that any the less repugnant to me. Do you really think that great art can come out of such behavior?"

He wanted to say: "But it has!" Instead he asked: "Have you ever seen her dance?"

"Some years ago, and I thought she was lovely. But what I have heard about her wildness repelled me, and I haven't cared to see her again."

"It doesn't seem to have changed her art," argued Lanny; "at least so everyone agrees. She dances springtime and nature, grief and revolt, but no one ever saw her do a sex-dance of any sort."

It was plain that he wouldn't get anywhere with a defense of free-love *artistes*. It was the first tiny rift between Marie and himself, and he hastened to close it. He laid his hand upon hers and said: "Don't forget, darling, it is you I am driving, and not Isadora!"

She responded to his smile. "I thank you for that. But I don't thank *her!*"

They were silent for a long while, and when she began speaking again, her voice was trembling. "Lanny, that was a woman older than I; but some day there will be a woman younger!"

"That won't make any difference, dear."

"Some day I shall have to see what Isadora saw in Greece."

"Don't be silly, dear!"

"Let me say what I'm trying to say. I want you to know, whatever happens, all my life I am going to think about what is best for you, not for myself. No matter how much it may hurt, that is what I shall act on."

"All right, dear heart," he replied. "You think what is best for me, and I'll think what is best for you, and all will be well." Because it isn't safe to kiss while driving, he drew up by the side of the road for a few minutes.

VIII

When he got home he told both these stories to his mother; the story of the artist-soul whose cravings would never be satisfied, and the story of the mother-soul who thought about what she could give to a man instead of what she could get. Beauty said yes, there were those two kinds of women, and there was eternal deadly war between them. Beauty didn't give any fancy names to them; what she said was that a woman who really loves a man merges her life with his and tries to help him make something of himself; she chooses to express herself through him and through their children; she gives her youth and perhaps her health and her good looks, everything she has, to wifehood and motherhood; and then, when she has reached middle age and has nothing but that man and that family, and no chance of getting any other, then along comes some fresh little chit, thinking about nothing but the gratifying of her vanity, amusing herself by carrying a man off and breaking up a home——

Lanny couldn't keep from laughing. "Isadora isn't exactly a chit!"

"There are two periods when they do their raiding," answered the woman of the world; "when they're young fillies, first feeling their oats, and when their racing days are over and they're ready to be retired to the pasture. It's hard to say which is the more dangerous, but every wife hates them both and would like nothing better than to turn them over to the Apache Indians and have them roasted over a slow fire."

"You're mixing your metaphors," grinned the youth. "The Apaches didn't torture horses!"

"I'm not mixing my women!" declared Beauty, grimly. "Take my advice and don't let anybody fool you with toplofty words—soul-mates and affinities, ecstasies and yearnings and romantic raptures. Burglary is burglary, and a woman suffers torment even to think about it; and when she tells you that she won't or don't, she's already doing it. The misery in her life is that she can never be sure what is going to happen to her man the next time he goes out of the house."

Beauty seemed unusually vehement on the subject of unmanageable men, and Lanny began to wonder about it. She explained herself very soon; her voice sank, and she said: "There doesn't seem to be any place for love in this world of ours—mine any more than the others'."

"What's the matter?" For a moment he thought she meant that Kurt was interested in some other woman, and he was shocked.

"It's the old, old story; I don't believe I'm going to be able to keep Kurt out of mischief. He gets letters from his family, and then he has fits of depression. He tries to hide them from me, but of course he can't."

"But what's wrong now? I thought he was so happy because Germany won the plebiscite."

"He doesn't think the Poles will obey; and he doesn't think the Allies will make them. You talk to him, Lanny. I can't, without making myself a scold and a shrew!"

IX

The elections in Upper Silesia had been held in the month of March, with the result that a majority of the districts had voted to remain with Germany. That didn't include Stubendorf, which had been given to Poland by the treaty; but it would save most of the industrial regions, and the coal and iron mines desperately needed by Germany if it was to resume as an industrial nation. Kurt had felt a great burden lifted from his spirit; but now had come that terrible Korfanty, organizing the young Polish patriots, arming them and drilling them all over Poland and even in Stubendorf. It was plain that they meant to seize the plebiscitary provinces.

Lanny went to Kurt, who showed him the letters he had received, and extracts from newspapers with accounts of the turmoil prevailing. It was undeniably terrible, with organized gangs raiding the homes of German patriots at night, carrying people away and beating them dreadfully. Poles and Germans just couldn't and wouldn't mix. Kurt drew harrowing pictures of the superstition and filth in which the Polish peasants lived; so of course they fell prey to demagogues and agitators—especially when these were secretly provided with arms and money by the Polish government. What was supposed to be an uprising of the Silesian peasants was clearly a raid by Warsaw, and a challenge to the fumbling and hesitant Allies.

Lanny couldn't say: "Kurt, you are under obligations to my mother, and you haven't the right to go off and leave her." No; but he could say: "Kurt, you always insisted that art comes before politics, the Idea before the Thing. In fact, it was you who taught me that, and I have shaped my life on it. I too have seen cruelty and wrong, and have impulses to leap in and stop it; but I've thought: No, Kurt is right; I am going to help to make beauty in the world, and prepare the minds of people for something wiser than fighting and robbing."

Kurt couldn't deny any of that. He remembered their talks in Hellerau, and on the height in front of the church of Notre-Dame-de-Bon-Port. Yes, he had said it, and he believed it still, at least with half his mind, the better half; but the other half hated the Polish usurpers and invaders, the preachers of militant nationalism—of the wrong nation. That half of Kurt was a trained artillery officer and wanted to go and serve a battery of field-guns to protect his home-land.

Lanny poured out his soul to his friend. "Perhaps you think I am just a playboy, and that it comes natural to me to be happy and to live in music. But let me tell you that I too am having moral struggles, I too wonder if I have a right to be happy while so many children are starving and half of Europe is in chaos. I don't know just what I could do about it, but I have crazy impulses to drop everything and try. I think maybe I'll do like Barbara Pugliese—go and live in the slums, and meet the poor, and help them to climb out of the pit. I know how dreadfully unhappy I'd make Robbie, but, after all, Robbie belongs to an earlier generation and he won't have to live in the world he's making. Then I think about you, Kurt; I say that you are wise and self-contained—at least that's the way you've appeared to me. Now I ask, if you can't survive as an artist, who in all Europe can?"

So they argued; and the disciple of Bach was convinced against his will. They renewed their pledges, and went back to their music—while Korfanty went on organizing the nationalist youth of Poland!

X

Happiness inside the safe retreat of Bienvenu, happiness for all the creatures which made it their home. The birds built nests in the vines and the high bushes, and raised and fed their young, and if these fell out they were replaced by friendly humans. The dogs barked at the birds, but it was merely an expression of the joy of living. Baby Marceline ran a little faster every day, chattered a little more freely, picked up some new ideas. Beauty, the loving mother, kept watch over all her pets and babies of various sorts and sizes; studied them, and within the limits of her understanding did what she could to fill their needs.

Lanny had brought from Paris the good tidings that the German ambassador had at last been formally received by the French government, so Germany was again a friendly nation and its citizens were free to come into France. They would sell the products of their country, or study at the Sorbonne or the Conservatoire, or sun their large fat backs on the beach at Juan—and while people might look askance at them, no one would call for the police. This meant that Kurt might emerge from his hiding-place and have himself fitted with a suit of clothes; also visit the music-store and make his own selection of compositions. Next winter it might be possible for Mrs. Emily to have him give a recital at Sept Chênes; something which Beauty looked forward to as a child toward Christmas.

The happy solution of Marie's marital problem made it possible for her to come and stay at Bienvenu. She took one of the guest-rooms, and combined forces with the mistress of the villa. It is hard enough for a mature woman to hold a young man, and if there are two such women, it is certainly the part of wisdom to make a co-operative enterprise of it. So Marie shared all the secrets that her man's mother knew about him, and Beauty had the advantage of the opinions that her man's best friend's sweetheart had formed about her man. This sounds complicated—but then Herbert Spencer taught that progress is a development from the simple to the complex.

So Lanny Budd enjoyed the most expert attention and service that the heart of youth could have desired. Marie de Bruyne laughed and sang with him, she danced and played with him, she climbed the hills and swam in the sea with him, she went sailing and fishing with him, she played his music and read his books, she adored him and praised everything he did, and at the same time spurred him to new efforts; she gave him sound ideas—in short, she was sweetheart, wife, mother, guide, and friend, and nowhere on the horizon of their life was there the tiniest trace of a cloud. Could you blame him for thinking that French arrangements for marriage and afterward are not so bad as they are represented in those Anglo-Saxon countries where pre-marital chastity and postmarital fidelity so generally prevail?

XI

Marie and Lanny in the goodness of their hearts had a guilty feeling as to Mme. Scelles, who had helped them so loyally and who now saw less of them. They decided to devote a day to her entertainment; so they loaded up the car and packed the old lady into the seat between them, and drove up one of the valleys where the cork trees grow, and had a delightful time. In the afternoon they called on friends of hers in a place called Cimiez, and played tennis and had tea; then, since the old lady was still game, they drove to "Monty" and had a sumptuous dinner at Ciro's, and gave their guest a twenty-franc note to lose in the Casino and feel devilish.

So it was after midnight when Lanny got home; and there he encountered a distressing scene—his mother, pacing the floor of her boudoir, her eyes red with long weeping, her face set in grim and bitter anger. "It's all over," she said. "Kurt is gone."

"*Gone?* Where?"

"To fight the Poles."

"Oh, my God! What happened?"

"There's a letter—he left it for you to read. From his father."

She indicated the escritoire and Lanny looked, but did not take the letter at once. "What is it about?"

"One of Kurt's friends has been killed in some of their rows. There's a long account of how Korfanty is overthrowing the plebiscite. He has declared himself dictator."

"And the Allies are allowing it?"

"So Kurt's father says; and the Germans are defending themselves. Kurt is wild about it, and I couldn't do anything with him. We spent hours wrangling."

"Couldn't you get him to wait until I came home?"

"I didn't try. If he doesn't care enough for me to stay on my account, I might as well know it now as later."

"Poor dear!" exclaimed Lanny. His mother's face was gray with anguish, and he saw that she had been through a siege. He put his arm around her and led her to the bed and sat beside her. "Don't take it too desperately. This Silesian question is bound to be settled before long, and he will come back."

"Never! I told him if he went it would be the end. It's the very same thing that I went through with Marcel, and I will not live such a life."

"Many women have to, Beauty."

"I am one who won't. If the men can find nothing to do but kill one another, I am through with them for the rest of my days."

"Let me stay, anyhow," said Lanny. "I don't want to kill anybody."

He judged it best not to argue with her. There was nothing very good he could say about the men, except that they loved their native land and their families, but didn't have enough collective intelligence to handle the new industrial forces they had created. Perhaps later on they might; but Beauty had chosen a bad time to be born on earth, and there was no way to save her from the consequences of that mistake. He said what he could to comfort her; they were as they had been before Kurt had come into their home—except that Beauty now had Baby Marceline, very good company and improving all the time. They would get along somehow.

XII

He got her into bed and gave her something to make her sleep. He himself had had practice in not worrying about what he couldn't help, so he didn't need drugs. In the morning he was awakened by the maid tapping on his door—M. Kurt on the telephone, she reported. Lanny threw on his dressing-gown and answered.

"*Allo,*" said the voice of his friend. "I am at the railroad station in Nice. I want to tell you that I have changed my mind, and will come back."

"Oh, thank God, Kurt!"

"Do you want me?"

"What a question! Of course!"

"Does Beauty want me?"

"I gave her a sleeping-powder, so she doesn't want anything right now. But when she wakes up she will kill the fatted calf for you. Where have you been?"

"I spent hours walking up and down on the station platform at Cannes, waiting for the morning train. Here at Nice I saw a newspaper and read that the British government has sent six battalions to Silesia to enforce order. So I guess the torment of my people will end."

"I hope so, Kurt. But you ought to make up your mind to something and stick by it. You haven't the right to keep Beauty on tenterhooks all the time." Lanny, the young moralist, exhibiting firmness!

"You are right," said the other. "I have had it out with myself, and I will give you my word."

"Hurrah!" cried Lanny. "The death warrant of the fatted calf."

When Beauty awakened, she said that she herself was the calf, and she was dead, and had no interest in the news he gave her. He set to work to tempt her back to life—the first step being to ring for a pot of coffee. "You have won, old dear. He has tied himself down."

"I don't care, Lanny. I can't stand any more. I never want to see another man."

"There are a lot of us around, and you can't wear blinders; so cheer up and don't be a goose. It's no crime for Kurt to love his Fatherland, and if he finds it hard to choose between two duties, remember what a time you had making up your mind whether you were going to stick by Marcel or run off to be the plateglass queen of Pittsburgh!"

He began to cajole her, and reawaken her interest in making a career for a musical artist. After his recent encounter with Isadora, he was in position to explain these unstable creatures. Kurt had had a tremendous brain-storm, and as soon as he had got settled down he would proceed to see it *sub specie artis*, and make it the basis of a sublime tone poem or at least a piano sonata. A stormy first movement, *allegro molto*, in which the world breaks in upon the artist soul and a powerful war theme conflicts with and tramples down the lovely-woman theme! Second movement, *andante*, the woman mourns the departed man! Third movement, *scherzo*, the soul of the artist triumphs over the world! Finale, *alla marcia*, the themes of the first movement blend in a triumphant choral hymn, the victory of love over all the other forces of the world! "Can't you hear it, Beauty?"

He offered to go and play it for her, and so got her to laughing. Then he led her to her dressing-table and let her see what a perfect fright she looked. To start to improve herself was automatic; and he persuaded her that when Kurt appeared she would be her loveliest, she would kiss him and make him happy, and not say a word about the quarrel.

"I'll attend to the rest," said the determined youth, and he did; for when Kurt heard that outline of a piano sonata he said: "But, Lanny, that's very interesting! Would you mind if I took it up some day?"

"I'd brag about it for the rest of my life," said the faithful friend. "But I thought you didn't like program music."

"I wouldn't go into details," said the disciple of Bach, "but a hint doesn't hurt."

"So knocks fate upon the door!" said Lanny, smiling.

10

From Precedent to Precedent

I

IN THE middle of June the boys were to come home from school, and Denis de Bruyne very politely invited Lanny to spend the summer; the home didn't seem the same without Marie in it, he said, and Lanny was able to believe him. While the pair of lovers were discussing their plans there came a letter from Rick, saying that he had a commission from his editor to visit Geneva and report on the unfolding activities of the new League of Nations, upon which many liberals were now centering their hopes. "Big things may be happening soon," wrote the baronet's son. "I must get at the men who count. You know many of them, and I'm relying on you."

Lanny recalled that members of the American staff in Paris had transferred their services to the League. Also there was Dr. Herron, whose home was in Geneva and with whom Lanny had exchanged a couple of letters. It would be interesting to talk to him after two years. "Marie," he said, on the spur of the moment, "how would you like a trip to Switzerland?"

The idea took her breath away. She had missed the San Remo conference because she didn't dare risk a scandal; but now, being duly established as Lanny's *amie*, she could travel with him and be received with honors. "We could drive there in a couple of days," he said, "and spend a week or so, and get to your home in time to meet the boys. You'd enjoy knowing Rick, I'm sure."

"Oh, Lanny, I'd love it!"

"All right, chuck your things into your bags!"

That was how it was with the delightful leisure classes; a whim seized you, and you "chucked," and away you went. No need to bother about money, you bought a bunch of traveler's checks and cashed them one by one. No need to think about the car, for that was kept in order all the time. Just "hop in" and "step on the gas." These lively American phrases were coming into use all over Europe, largely because the movies had made that country so popular. You practiced *le sport* and *le flirt*, you offered *le handshake*, you drank *le coqtail*, you danced *le jazz*, and you aimed to be and were *très snob*.

Now Lanny "shot a wire" to Rick, and told Beauty and Kurt of their plans, and drove to Mme. Scelles's and told her; then, their last duty done, they drove once more up the wide valley of the Rhône. But this time they didn't turn off toward the west; they followed the upper reaches of the stream, winding through hills and climbing steadily into country where tall pine trees grew and the air was fresh and chilly in June. The stream became narrower and its course more rapid, until they were among high mountains with snow-capped peaks in the distance. In front of them was a great dam over which the river flowed in torrents of green foam; and when their car had got above the level of this dam, there was a long blue lake, on the far side of it the mighty peak of Mont Blanc, and along both shores the tall houses of a shining white city of watch-makers and money-changers and tourists.

The broad avenue along the lake front was lined with hotels having green shutters, terraced lawns shaded by horse-chestnuts, and dining-rooms with glass walls and roofs. In summertime the cafés moved out to the sidewalks and the kursaal was crowded with guests; the lake was gay with swans and ducks and gulls, two-decked steamers painted white and gold, and tiny sailboats with red lateen sails sliding over sun-sparkled water. But do not trust any Alpine lake, for a sudden storm called the bise swoops down from the mountains and throws things into confusion—all music lovers know it from the *William Tell* overture!

It was an aged city, and somewhat faded; a Protestant city, still protesting the same things as four centuries ago. It had many memorials to John Calvin, and Lanny might stand and gaze at them and learn where the religion of his stern old grandfather had come from. There were a great many churches, and in most of them Lanny might have listened to a pastor resembling the Rev. Mr. Saddleback of the First Congregational Church of Newcastle, Connecticut—but Lanny didn't. He learned about the town from American newspapermen who were assigned here and who called it a narrow and musty place, ruled by businessmen and bankers who professed pious orthodoxy but permitted a normal amount of old-world corruption for the benefit of the tourists. Geneva looked askance at the League, considering that it brought undesirable characters to town—including American journalists who put un-orthodox ideas on the wires and padded their expense accounts for the benefit of the *boîtes de nuit*.

II

Eric Vivian Pomeroy-Nielson was already on the job, and welcomed them with dignity. Marie had heard so much about him, and here he was, a tall fellow with thin features and a keen expression, and wavy dark hair which resented efforts to control it. Marie's heart warmed to him at once, for she sensed a proud spirit struggling with physical handicaps; she wanted to help him, but Lanny had told her to do nothing, just talk about the job, in which the budding journalist was all wrapped up. He had met a couple of colleagues who had been at Spa, so he was already in touch with affairs. He was impressed by what he had found here; the League appeared to be really coming to life, and far too little attention had been given to it by the press.

Rick had put up at a modest-priced hotel, and Lanny and Marie decided to go where he was. The hotel gave them connecting rooms and asked no questions—in spite of the statues of very stern Calvinists all over the city. The first thing Lanny did was to make inquiries concerning a young member of the Crillon staff who had become a minor functionary of the League; Lanny's friends had been bitter against this chap Armstrong, being of the opinion that he had sold out his convictions for a soft berth; but he had taken the imputation mildly, saying there was work to be done and it interested him.

Sidney Armstrong had pale sandy hair and a round amiable face with horn-rimmed spectacles; he looked like a good "Y" secretary, and was doing much that sort of work, having to do with international problems of child welfare. He came to dinner, and was glad to tell about what was going on, and to meet an English journalist who had written an article dealing with the results of San Remo and Spa. There was a quiet tug-of-war going on between the officials of this infant League of Nations and those more important persons who attended the conferences of the Allied premiers and of the Supreme Economic Council. The League people thought they ought to replace these two bodies, and meant to do so in the end.

A number of different problems had been assigned to the League by the treaty of Versailles: the Saar district, Danzig, and all the "mandates"—a new name for a method of ruling the primitive races of the earth which it was hoped wouldn't be so bad as the old colonial method of missionaries with Bibles and traders with rum and syphilis. Other problems had been assigned by the Supreme Allied Council—those in which the Allies had no overwhelming interest, and which were found to be difficult and dangerous. There were Lithuania and Armenia to be protected; there were famines to be relieved, refugees to be fed, and all the prisoners in Russia, Turkey, and other countries to be repatriated; there were questions of health and transit, intellectual intercourse and child welfare, and traffic in drugs and in women.

Lanny brought up the subject of Upper Silesia, and Armstrong said this was an illustration of the mistake the Allied powers made in trying to settle problems which properly belonged to the League. People would believe in the disinterestedness of a world body, but who could believe in the disinterestedness of France with regard to Poland? The latter country had a bad, reactionary government, hard to handle; they had grabbed Vilna from Lithuania—another question the League was trying to settle. In Silesia the Poles were demanding all the wealthier districts, and it was a complicated situation, because, however you did the dividing, you gave a lot of Germans to Poles and Poles to Germans; also the economic interests —wherever you drew a boundary line you broke up industries and brought ruin to great numbers of people. Too bad they couldn't be moved across borders, like chessmen; all the Germans into Germany and all the Poles into Poland!

"What do you think will be the outcome?" asked Lanny.

"If the Allies can be induced to turn the question over to us, we'll appoint a commission, and it will work out the best settlement it can. We have, of course, no means of enforcing decisions, except as the great powers are willing to back us."

"Then," asked Rick, "one can say that the League will work only so long as it serves the purposes of Britain and France?"

The young functionary wouldn't answer that blunt question. "We'll just try to show what we can do, and the nations will support us if we make it worth while."

III

This serious and hard-working fellow introduced them to others of the same sort, and soon they were living *en famille*, as it were, with the League of Nations; an odd sort of colony of diplomats and secretaries gathered from a score of nations, inhabiting this ancient city with its stiff bourgeoisie for the most part devoted to money-making and the saving of their own souls by the method of doctrinal conformity. The League had purchased one of Geneva's biggest hotels, the National, with its quota of lawns and horse-chestnuts, and a statue of a Negro girl thrown in. The beds and dressing-tables had been moved out and the rooms filled with filing-cabinets, typewriters, and multigraphing-machines. The officials and secretaries dined in the city's restaurants and took their constitutionals on the avenues shaded with plane trees, but they were rarely invited to the homes of the citizens. Said Armstrong: "From what I hear we don't miss much."

The head nurse of this ugly duckling was a Scotch gentleman named Sir Eric Drummond, a caricaturist's dream of a British bureaucrat; tall, thin, with fair hair, a long neck and prominent Adam's apple; wearing, of course, a short black coat, a watch-chain, and dark-striped trousers, and carrying a black umbrella neatly rolled. He had had a dreadful time getting started, because nobody would send him any money; but he had gone patiently ahead, selecting with extraordinary discernment exactly the right sort of men to run what might some day become the biggest enterprise in the history of mankind.

Impossible not to sympathize with such efforts, and to respect the men who were making them. Lanny thought of that pitiful invalid, now a private citizen in Washington, from whose soul this League had sprung. Lanny had seen a picture of him, riding to the inaugural ceremony with his bland and well-fed successor; Wilson's face drawn and haggard, the mask of a man suffering, not his own martyrdom, but that of his hopes and dreams. Here in Geneva he had planted a little acorn which had become a vigorous sprout. Would it live to be a great oak? If it did, the name of

Woodrow Wilson would live on, while the names of his antagonists would be buried in the encyclopedias.

Such were the questions which Lanny and his friends debated in between their inquiries and interviews. Lanny had in mind the bitter scorn of his father and his uncle. Robbie Budd and Jesse Blackless were at one in their certainty that the League must collapse, and that it would be the struggle for markets and raw materials, the commercial rivalries of great states which would bring it down. Jesse hated that blind greed and the men who embodied it; Robbie, one of those men himself, took it as a basic law of nature, the condition upon which life was lived. Might it be that neither of them was entirely right, but that the greed of men might be gradually tamed and brought under the rule of law; that freedom might slowly broaden down from precedent to precedent?

Lanny had been reading a history of his own country, selected from several in the Eli Budd library. He had freshly in mind the loose Confederation which the thirteen colonies had formed while they were struggling for their freedom. It had served a temporary purpose, keeping them together until public opinion had time to form in favor of an enduring union. Might it not be that something of the same sort was happening here? Let the nations recover from their war psychosis and realize how much better it was to reason together than to fight, how much easier to produce goods with modern machinery than to take one another's goods by force—then you might see a real Federation of the World such as Tennyson and other poets had sung.

IV

Lanny called up George D. Herron and was invited to bring his friends to tea. The Socialist exile lived in a beautiful villa called Le Retour, but he was one of the unhappiest men alive, and a very sick one, as Lanny well knew. His face was like marble, and his black beard and mustache were turning gray; he seldom had an hour without pain, but what troubled him most was the agony of civilization. Herron was literally dying of grief over the mass tragedy which he had witnessed in Paris. He had poured his anguish into a book called *The Defeat in the Victory*, which was soon to appear through an English publishing-house. Impossible to get it published in his native land, where everybody was done with Europe, forever and ever, amen.

Herron was a gracious and charming host. He had conceived a sort of fatherly affection for Lanny, doubtless still thinking of him as a possible convert. Because he had lived in Geneva since the beginning of the war, he was a mine of information about the place and its doings. He had read the world's best literature in half a dozen languages, and so his conversation was that of a scholar as well as of a prophet.

Lanny told what his English friend had come for, so Herron talked about the League; it was a League of governments, not of peoples, and from none of the existing governments was any good thing to be expected. He said that the hope of the world now lay in its youth, which had the task of forging a new spiritual and intellectual sword for the overcoming of those greedy powers which ruled our society. While he said this the Socialist prophet looked into the eyes of two representatives of that youth, and seemed to be asking: "How well are you prepared for your task?"

Lanny mentioned the problem of Upper Silesia, and how it weighed upon him because of his German friend. That led Herron to talk about the experiences he had had with the Germans all through the war. It had been known that he was in touch with President Wilson, and was sending reports through the State Department, so the Germans assumed that he was authorized to negotiate with them—which wasn't so. First the Socialists and the pacifists, and later on, as Germany's situation became worse, the representatives of the government, came to Le Retour in an unceasing stream.

"They constituted," said Herron, "a veritable clinic for the observation of the German mind; and my conclusion was that there is something inherently amiss in its make-up. The German, in his present stage of development, cannot think directly and therefore morally. He still moves, he still has his psychic being, collectively speaking, in what seems like prehuman nature. The German commonly reasons that whatever accomplishes his ends as an agent or citizen of the State is both mystically and scientifically justifiable. No matter how reprehensible the means, there is no responsibility higher than these ends that can claim his confidence."

"Do you mean that this is the creed that every German has thought out?" It was Rick questioning.

"I mean it is the mental stuff of his motivation, whether conscious or unconscious. The sheer might that achieves the thing in view becomes his supreme good. You understand that I am speaking of a stream of visitors continuing over a period of three or four years. Each discussion, without regard to the messenger's intellectual repute, or his high or low official degree, began with his assumption that Germany was misunderstood and wronged, even to the extent of a piteous martyrdom. If ever there was any grudging admission that Germany might have been remiss, it was because of deception practiced by jealous neighbors upon this too trustful, too childlike people. And always Germany must be preserved from discovering that the responsibility was hers. As an instance, an eminent and official German of high intellectual quality—a German whom I had long held in affectionate admiration—continually sought to show me that the war must be so ended as to save Germany from the humiliation of a confession. The preservation of Germany's national pride, rather than the revelation of righteousness to her people, was basic in all this good man's quest for a better German future. Well aware as he was of the historical abnormality of his race, admitting it candidly enough in our discussions, yet so thoroughly German was he that he could conceive no peace except one that would save Germany from self-accusation."

V

All the time that Lanny Budd was listening to this pain-driven man, he had in the back of his mind a question which his father had asked after meeting him, at lunch in the Hotel Crillon: "For God's sake, who is that nut?" Now Lanny tried to make up his own mind. "What is a 'nut'? And why is he?" Certainly Herron had a mass of information, and had co-ordinated it into a definite system of thought. He was an absolutist; he formed certain standards of justice and truth-telling which he had derived from the prophets and saints of old, especially Jesus, and he tried to apply those standards to a world ruled by force and guile. Perhaps they didn't apply to that world, and couldn't ever be made to apply; Robbie avowed that they couldn't—and perhaps that was the way to get along. But Herron refused to give up; he said, as Jesus had said: "Be ye therefore perfect, even as your Father which is in heaven is perfect." Nobody paid much attention to this modern prophet, any more than to the old-time one. Manifestly, theirs was not the way to get along and be happy in this world.

Nothing had been done or was going to be done according to this prophet's standards of righteousness. He said it himself, in words which had the ring of Isaiah and Jeremiah. When he learned that Lanny and Rick had attended the San Remo conference, he read from the proofs of his book about the doings there: "The Supreme Council, gambling in last chances, tosses Armenia to the Kurdish dogs and gaily stakes the destinies of three continents on the capture of new supplies of oil. The starving Poles, typhus-stricken and at risk of national extinction, march to the blackmailer's music, stabbing Soviet Russia in the back while the British Prime Minister negotiates with that same Russia for a trader's truce."

A terrible thing to hear such words and not be able to contradict them! How pathetic seemed the labors of earnest and patient functionaries, putting a patch of plaster here and a bandage there on the body of the suffering world, when you listened to Herron's fateful statement upon the four treaties which had ended the World War: "These are not peace, they are rather a pitiless provision for a military and predatory government of the world. They are pregnant with wars more destructive, both physically and spiritually, than history has yet registered, with the resultant prospect of a generation if not a century of tartarean tortures for the whole family of man."

VI

The three friends came out from that interview in a sober mood, and discussed the various points Herron had raised. Rick, with his practical English sense, said that it was easy enough to condemn what the Peace Conference had done, but that didn't get you very far; what you had to do was to have a shot at what could be done next and what forces you could make use of. Marie, with her logical French mind, detected what she said were inconsistencies in the prophet's fervors. No one had ever presented a clearer indictment of those German qualities which made the race a menace to the peace of Europe, and Herron himself had called for the military defeat of Germanism; but he overlooked the plain fact that to achieve such a defeat you had to generate anger and determination in other peoples, and such feelings just cannot be turned off by a stopcock the day an armistice is signed.

"For fifty years," said Marie, "we French have had the fear of German invasion, and who is going to rid us of it? How shall we be protected? Dr. Herron wants us to forgive, and let everything be as if there hadn't been any war; but how can we be sure how that will work? Suppose the Germans take it as a sign of weakness? Suppose they see it as credulity? There are things for which they went to war, and which they'd still like to have. Suppose they take them?"

Difficult questions indeed; not to be answered that day, or for many days to come! Lanny drove Rick to another appointment, and the two lovers went for a walk on the lake front. They looked across the darkling water to the peak of Mont Blanc, changing from snow-white to pale pink and then to purple. They went on talking about George D. Herron, and when Lanny expressed sympathy for him, his friend asked with some anxiety: "Are you going to let yourself be drawn into that sort of extremism?"

He smiled and reassured her. "Pretty soon I'll meet somebody who will argue the opposite, and I'll find myself agreeing with him—at least part of the way. I suppose that to be a man of action one has to be able to see only one side, and be absolutely certain that it's the whole truth."

Inside himself Lanny was amused to see his *amie* mounting guard over him, keeping him out of trouble, just as Beauty did with Kurt. Were all women always trying to keep their men for themselves? His mind went back over the histories which he had read. How many married heroes could he recall?

VII

The day came when they had to leave. Rick said he had got stuff for more than one article, so they put him on the evening train, and then by the light of a large golden moon they set out along the river Rhône. They spent the night at Bourg, and by steady driving they reached the Château de Bruyne the following evening. There Lanny resumed that agreeable life into which he had already been initiated. The boys returned the next day, and were pleased to find that they were to have the companionship of this friendly young man, who would make music come alive for them, teach them various kinds of dancing, and tell them entertaining stories about Germany and England and Greece, and also a family of Puritan munitions makers who had helped to deliver *la belle France*.

Lanny still urged that Marie should tell the boys the truth about their relationship, or let him tell it; but Denis had been shocked by the suggestion, and he had a right to say no. These must be good Catholic boys; that is, they had to be taught to look upon sex as something inherently shameful and unclean; but also it would be something irresistibly fascinating—nature would see to that—and so they would find out about it in secret ways. Sooner or later, from the gossip of servants or other boys, they would learn about Lanny and their mother, and would be forced to choose between thinking less of their mother and thinking less of the religion they had been taught. At that time Marie would have to fight for herself; but she couldn't do it now, and Lanny couldn't urge it without causing a rift in the lute which was producing such pleasant music for him.

They lived, externally, a most proper life. They made a rule that they would never so much as touch hands except when they were in their own rooms with the doors locked. Everywhere else Lanny was a friend of the family, and when visitors came he met them if he wished, or stayed in a corner of the garden and read his books. He acquired a stack of music and played for hours, and Marie never tired of listening. They went in to Paris for the various art shows, for theaters and opera, and occasionally Denis would join them; he was unobtrusive and they did their best to make him feel that he was not *de trop*.

Robbie Budd went to London again, and Lanny offered to pay him a visit, but Robbie wired that he would be in Paris in a couple of days; Lanny was glad, for of course he wanted his father to meet his *amie*. The *amie* looked forward to the occasion with feelings in which curiosity and trepidation were about equally balanced. Denis, most perfect of gentlemen, said that he had heard about M. Budd, a very solid businessman, and would like nothing better than to welcome him as a week-end guest at the château.

"By heck," exclaimed Robbie, when he heard the proposal, "that's a new one on me!" But he was game. If he had been among the Turkomans and had been invited to eat boiling-hot lamb and rice with his fingers, he would have done so. Lanny was living in France, and if he had found a French lady to make him happy, it was all right with his father, who had given him an unorthodox start and could hardly blame him for following his stars.

Lanny came in and met the morning train, and drove his progenitor around while he attended to various business matters, and then in the cool of the evening drove him out to the château. Robbie had everything carefully explained to him in advance, and if he felt the least bit queasy he certainly didn't let it show. He could see at one glance that Lanny had found a woman of charm, and he didn't have to talk with her long to see that she had both culture and character. "I wouldn't mind having a woman like that myself!" he said, and meant it as a compliment. As for Denis, he was the sort of man that Robbie enjoyed being with; a sensible fellow who had made his own way in the world, and knew what was going on and could exchange ideas about it. In short, an agreeable family, and a delightfully original way for a youth to spend a summer vacation.

"But don't say anything about it in Newcastle," advised Lanny. The father replied: "God Almighty!"

VIII

Listening to the conversation of two men of affairs, Lanny got an insight into the realities of French politics. Denis was a "Nationalist," which meant that he thought it was the business of the French government to look after the interests of France, and especially of French businessmen, the persons who would give employment to French workers if they were to get any. That was exactly the idea of Robbie's Republican party as to the United States, so these two understood each other perfectly; when Denis denounced the present French Premier, it might have been Robbie expressing his opinion of a certain scholar in politics who had departed from the White House five months previously.

The Premier of France was a man named Aristide Briand, and he was what the French call "a son of the people." His father had been an innkeeper in that Loire country where Lanny and Marie had spent their honeymoon—perhaps they had stayed in that very inn. Like most French politicians, Briand had begun as an extreme Socialist, but when he got power he smashed a strike of the railwaymen by the device of ordering them all on military duty. However, that wasn't enough to cause Denis de Bruyne to trust him, for he was called a "man of peace," which meant, in effect, that he was one more Frenchman succumbing to the blandishments of David Lloyd George, that master of the arts of political seduction.

Denis explained the situation. Britain had her vast overseas empire and her world trade; she would soon grow rich again, and that was what she was thinking about. But France lay with her most productive provinces in ruins, her people unemployed, and her hereditary enemy refusing to give up her arms, saying, in effect: "Come and get them!" Refusing to meet the reparations bill, deliberately destroying her financial system in order to ruin her rival, and repeating that offer which drove French businessmen frantic—to pay in goods, while French workers stayed idle and French businessmen got no profits!

Time after time, France would be invited to conferences, where the "Welsh wizard" would turn loose his oratorical blandishments; he would take the side of the Germans and persuade the French to give up this and give up that; to let history's greatest robber get away unscathed, with most of his loot safely stowed away in his fastnesses. "*Honteux!*" exclaimed Denis de Bruyne, and pounded his fist on the arm of his chair as he called the roll of these conferences of dishonor—San Remo, Hythe, Spa, Brussels, Paris, London. "*Il faut en finir!*" cried the "Nationalist."

While Robbie was there, early in August, another conference was called in Paris; an emergency one, as they were all coming to be. Imagine, if you could, the rosy little cherub with the lion's mane ensconced with all his staff in the Hotel Crillon, wining and dining the innkeeper's son, treating him as a social equal—and persuading him that the only way to settle the question of Upper Silesia was to refer it to the League of Nations! Playing upon those sentiments politely called "humanitarian," though to Denis de Bruyne they were the cheapest and most disgusting of a demagogue's stocks in trade. Talking about German "rights" to territory which every historian knew had been seized by the Prussian Frederick and which now was absolutely vital to Poland—and to France, if she was to have an ally on the eastern front to hold the ruthless Prussians in check. But of course England didn't want France to be strong on the Continent; she was setting Germany up as a rival—the "balance of power" policy!

Lanny listened to all this and kept his thoughts to himself. He had not told his host that he had a close friend from Upper Silesia, and how different these matters appeared from that friend's point of view. Lanny had come to the reluctant conclusion that his father's political beliefs were conditioned by his business interests, and he now decided that this French gentleman was in the same case. But Lanny wasn't there to educate him; all that Lanny cared about was a remark which his father reported—a remark which Denis had made *à propos de bottes*, as the French say, meaning *à propos* of nothing in particular:

"You know, M. Budd, the arrangement is excellent for all parties. When a woman is not satisfied she is liable to wander off, and I'd hate to have the mother of my children fall into the clutches of some adventurer."

To which Robbie replied with cordiality: "It seems to me, too, the arrangement is an excellent one for all parties, and I hope it may continue."

IX

Robbie Budd was in Paris because of another oil venture he was going in for; yes, in spite of the hard times, or rather because of them. Somebody else was in trouble, while Robbie, far-sighted fellow, had cash in several banks—and not those which had been closed! Robbie didn't tell much about it. Was he afraid that a youngster very much in love might talk too freely to a French lady? Or was it just that he had come to the realization that his son didn't like the smell of oil?

What he did tell about was Johannes Robin. It beat the Dutch the way that fellow was coining money! He had moved to Berlin, to be nearer his sources of information, and had just taken a trip to London to meet his associate. Six months ago he had dragged Robbie into selling the German mark short; he wasn't taking any commission, it was pure friendship, or gratitude—"and I suppose pride to be associated with us," added the father. "He wants you to play duets with Hansi!"

"He surely doesn't have to pay us for that," replied Lanny.

"Well, I agreed to go in with him, and every now and then I get a cablegram telling me that I have another deposit in a New York bank. We have a code, and he'll say: 'Methuselah seventieth birthday November'—that means that the mark will be seventy to the dollar in three months. You see, he predicted a long time ago that some day one dollar would buy as many marks as the years of Methuselah! Have you been watching the quotations?"

"I look now and then, because I know you're betting on it."

"It seems that Robin really has the inside dope. The mark was four to the dollar before the war, and today it's quoted at sixty-three. He insists it can't come back."

"I suppose there's nothing the Germans can do but go on printing money."

"What they are doing," said Robbie, "is reducing the public debt; an easy 'out' for a Socialist government."

"I had a letter from the boys," remarked Lanny. "They are happy about being in Berlin, it's such a wonderful city, and Hansi will have great teachers at the Conservatory."

"If things work out the way that doggone Jew says, he's going to own half the town before he's through."

"I'm afraid the Germans won't like him for it," remarked Lanny, dubiously. "They call such people *Schieber*."

"Well, if properties are for sale, he surely has a right to buy them. And of course if things get too hot, he can move back to Holland."

X

Lanny told about his visit to Geneva and what he had learned there. Robbie said he had no quarrel with the League as an attempt of Europe to solve its own problems; he didn't think it would last long, because, as soon as some major issue arose, the nations would fight it out; they would never surrender their right to do that. Robbie's concern was to keep the United States out of it; and on this point he was in a mood of extreme vexation, because the new President, upon whom he had based such high hopes, had already capitulated to the meddlers and the pacifists—he had just issued a call for an international conference for limitation of navies to meet in Washington on next Armistice Day.

To the head salesman of Budd's, who had put up campaign funds so generously, that was indeed a betrayal. Robbie Budd was too tactful a man to say to anybody, even his son: "This will knock out my chance for profits for many years." No, what he said was: "This will knock out **America's chance** to get an adequate armament industry. Britain and France will diddle us, they will fix up an agreement to leave us weak where we need to be strong; we will keep our part of the bargain, and then when it is too late find out that they have been wriggling out of their part."

"What do you suppose put Harding up to that?" asked the son.

"The proposal came from London. It's popular because so many people are sick of war, and insisting that something be tried. You hear it in the most unexpected places. The Reverend Saddleback preached what was almost a pacifist sermon. I didn't hear it, but that's what everybody said."

"That must have given Grandfather quite a jolt!"

"We have lived through so many earthquakes that we don't notice jolts any more. You can't imagine how things are at home. That nightmare in Russia has driven our agitators crazy; in New York you hear them shouting on every other street corner."

"And in Newcastle?"

"We don't let them get that far; but they're working underground, hundreds of them, Father says. Some day we may have a strike to deal with, but hardly while jobs are so scarce."

Lanny didn't say how he himself had been consorting with such enemies of the public welfare. He wondered: Had Johannes Robin noted his sons' interest in Red ideas, and perhaps mentioned to Robbie how the boys had met Beauty's Red brother? Apparently he hadn't, and Lanny didn't bring up the subject, for he knew exactly what his father would say, and when you have heard one line of discourse a certain number of times, you lose interest in hearing it again—especially when it has to do with your not doing something that you might want to do!

XI

Dropping the ticklish topic of politics, Lanny asked the news about that large and eccentric family at home. Old ones on the way out and new ones on the way in—but not so rapidly as in old days. Robbie's oldest brother, Lawford, continuing to be a "sorehead" and to quarrel with Robbie whenever possible. Grandfather Samuel showing his age, but still set in determination to run the business

and the family. Esther, Lanny's stepmother, helping to raise funds
for the needy, whom she no longer had to seek in Europe—there
was an abundance of them right in Newcastle. Robbie gave her a
large allowance to be spent on the former employees of Budd Gunmakers and their families. "You know," he explained, "people say
that when you give a hand-out to a tramp he makes a sign on your
gate to let the other tramps know that you're an easy mark. It's
about the same with your ex-employees, I find—they write to their
relatives and the whole gang comes hitch-hiking into town!"

Lanny asked about the children. The two boys were well, and
were going to be sturdy fellows. Bess, now thirteen, was a dynamo
of energy, and had commissioned her father to scold Lanny because
he didn't write often enough. "I ought to send her a present," said
the half-brother, and Robbie replied: "Send something to all of
them."

It was hard to think what to give to persons whose every want
was so carefully met. Lanny asked: "Do you think they might like
a painting?" He would have offered one of Marcel's, but he knew
that Esther would find it embarrassing to explain the stepfather of
her stepson—it sounded queer, and suggestive of a double im-
propriety. "I'll look in the shops and see if I can find something
French that will be different from what they are used to."

"Nothing sexy," warned Robbie.

"Oh, of course not. I mean something gay; something with a little
esprit."

XII

When he took his father into Paris to consult with oil tycoons,
Lanny went for a stroll on the Boulevard Montparnasse. You would
have thought that every other person in France aspired to be a
painter; not merely were there innumerable art dealers, but little
shops like grocers' and cobblers' would have paintings in the windows. Lanny's eyes were quick, and he didn't mind walking, so he
must have seen a thousand paintings that morning before he found
what he wanted, some very lively little wash drawings of Parisian
street scenes, full of character.

Having lived in France most of his life, he knew how to buy things. He knew that there was one price if you were French, a higher one if you were Spanish, a still higher one if you were German, and a triple or quadruple one if you bore the faintest sign of Americanism. It was a game, and the proper way to play it was to price other things first and say that all the prices were too high. You took only a casual glance at the thing you really wanted, and you asked its price indifferently, and then started out, remarking with a laugh that half that would be about right; as a rule your suggestion would be accepted before you got to the door.

Lanny offered a hundred francs for four of those drawings, with the right to make his choice. He picked out a jolly little Pierrot for Bess, and two street urchins for the boys, and for his stepmother a sturdy market-woman standing by her little handcart full of fruit, with her arms akimbo and an expression that told you how she would storm at you if you attempted to pinch one of her precious pears to see if it was ripe. The drawings were the work of an unknown artist, and when you made a purchase like that you were taking a chance in a lottery; the chance that your great-grandchildren might discover them in some dust-covered trunk, and recognize a famous signature, and sell them to a collector for several thousand dollars apiece.

To the Budd family the drawings would be a friendly reminder of one who had been a dangerous and disturbing guest, but was romantic while he dwelt overseas. Robbie promised to have them framed, and not to forget which one was for which. Then he made the suggestion that Lanny should take another walk, this time along the Rue de la Paix, and look into the windows of the jewelry shops and find a present for his *amie*. But Lanny thought it over and said no, he didn't think Marie would desire that; he was making her happy day by day, and that was enough.

Robbie thought it over in turn, and said: "Maybe you are right. If you start making presents you can't be sure where it will stop." The cautious man of business added: "Better not tell Beauty that I'm making so much money. Hard times are good for her!"

BOOK THREE

The Staircase of History

11

Woe to the Conquered

I

FOR a long time to come Lanny's life was destined to be governed by the calendar of a French boarding-school for boys. When the school closed, he would come to Seine-et-Oise, and when it opened again he was free to go to the Midi, or to any other parts of the world which appealed to him and his *amie*. In September the lovers returned to Bienvenu, and Lanny set to work upon a task which he had discussed with his father, the erection of another villa on the estate. The Riviera was becoming crowded, and in the "season" it was difficult to find anything to rent. Lanny hoped to invite Rick and Nina the coming winter, and, anyhow, it seemed sensible to have a guest-house. Robbie, who believed in buildings, was pleased to invest some of the money he was getting from Johannes Robin. He advised putting the house in one corner of the estate, so that it could be sold separately if ever they wanted to.

Lanny talked things over with his mother and engaged a contractor. Of course he wrote to Rick about it, and told him that the family's feelings would be hurt if he and Nina didn't make their plans to come for a housewarming during the winter.

In the midst of these operations who should show up but their old friend, the former Baroness de la Tourette, who had shed her title by means of an American divorce, and was now plain Sophie Timmons of Cincinnati, Ohio—and if you didn't like it you could lump it, said the daughter of a hardware manufacturer. Sophie was done both with the aristocracy and with men, she declared; she would be willing for the Bolshies to wipe out all the former, while the scientists rendered the latter superfluous by means of artificial parthenogenesis. Beauty had never heard that jawbreaker, but when Sophie explained the idea she approved it heartily. Men were mostly unreliable, and when you had two of them about the house all the time they were intolerable. Having said this, Beauty began running over in her mind all the eligible men she knew, to decide which was the best for Sophie Timmons.

Of course the retired baroness had heard about the queer extra-marital arrangements of this family, and was "dying with curiosity." Lanny had been her pet as a boy, and she had known Marie in society; it seemed to her the oddest prank that Cupid had ever played—and that was saying a lot. She had never met the fourth member of the family, and found herself a little in awe of a serious blue-eyed artillery officer, who, for all Sophie could ever know, might have fired the shell which killed her own *ami*, poor Eddie Patterson, driving an ambulance on the Marne front in the last days of the war.

Sophie settled down in her villa with a maid and a couple of servants, saying that she needed to recuperate from living with her family in Ohio. She liked to play bridge, so in the evenings she would drive to Bienvenu, picking up old M. Rochambeau and his niece; they would play for small stakes, because the elderly ex-diplomat couldn't afford to lose much. If this pair were not available, they would phone for Jerry Pendleton and press Marie into service. It was all right for Lanny to prefer to read, but it was considered "sniffy" if a woman took such a pose.

Lanny's ex-tutor was on call for any goings-on—a picnic, a sail, a swim. He had held a position in a tourist office during the winter, and Lanny now arranged for him to oversee the building job, as a pretext for helping him out. Jerry had two babies at home, and his little French wife was busy with these; if she had social aspirations, they could be satisfied by inviting her to a lawn party or something of a not too intimate nature. Women were a drug on the market in post-war France, but desirable men were scarce, and especially in this obscure village of Juan-les-Pins in the "off season."

II

In November Lanny had his twenty-second birthday, and his mother decided to give him a party. For two years and a half she had been hiding as it were in a cave on account of Kurt; now, under the guise of a celebration for Lanny, she was going to present his "music-teacher" to the world. It would be a tennis party and an *al fresco* supper, with music and dancing in the evening. Kurt Meissner would play, and he would be introduced under his own name. The few friends who had met him as M. Dalcroze would be told that that was his middle name, which he used for professional purposes.

One of the reasons for all this was that Kurt wished to go back and visit his people during the coming Christmas. Three years had passed since the Armistice, and that was surely enough for safety. As the treaty of Versailles had fixed matters, Kurt was a citizen of Poland, and that country being an ally of France, it would be easy for him to return. This was a way to get rid of the forged passport upon which he had been traveling as a German agent.

Affairs had settled down in Silesia, because the League of Nations had effected a compromise, dividing the industrial districts between Germany and Poland, but providing that for fifteen years there should be no customs barriers between the parts. A joint Polish-German commission was working out the details, so there would be no more fighting. Beauty was worried, but she couldn't deny the rightness of Kurt's desire to see his people after so long a time, and she was wise enough not to let him feel that she was putting chains upon him. Lanny was going along—to keep him in order, so he said with a smile. It would be eight years since Lanny had seen Schloss Stubendorf—and what an eight years in the history of mankind!

Lanny mentioned the proposed trip in a letter to the two young Robins, and right away came a telegram—oh, please, please, please—they paid for three extra words—come to Berlin and stay with them, and hear Hansi play the Bruch concerto! Kurt and Lanny talked it over. Kurt's oldest brother, an army officer, was stationed in Potsdam, and might not be able to get off for Christmas—most of them had to be on duty all the time, holding down the Reds. Kurt hadn't planned to see him, because he couldn't afford the extra journey; but Lanny said nonsense, he was going to pay for the whole trip. They would go to Berlin before Christmas, and Kurt would stay with his brother. He would never say anything to hurt the feelings of the Robins, he said, but he wouldn't bring himself to condone the doings of a *Schieber* by entering his home.

Lanny knew better than to argue about the matter. He hadn't told Kurt that Robbie was a *Schieber*, too, and that the money for the trip would come out of his ill-gotten gains! In the month of Lanny's birthday Methuselah had reached the age of two hundred; that is to say, with one American copper cent you could buy two marks' worth of anything in Germany—and you would be humbly thanked for doing it.

III

Lanny and Kurt descending from the *wagon-lit* in the Potsdamer Bahnhof, and being welcomed by Kurt's eldest brother, Emil, whom Lanny had never met before; an elegant tall fellow with yellow mustaches waxed to points, a monocle, and a long gray military cloak nearly to his ankles; clicking his heels, bowing from the waist, doing all the honors for Kurt's friend, who was also his employer—so the family had been told. A long thin face, this Prussian officer's, difficult to relax, and his pale steely eyes made Lanny think of an eagle's. Not that Lanny had ever seen an eagle's eyes, but he imagined what they would be like. The Prussian eagle had a double head, and Kurt was the other head of this one.

Emil did everything possible to maintain his pride, but Lanny noticed that his cloak was badly worn and faded, and had a telltale patch near the bottom—perhaps a bullet had carried some of it away. The truth was that Emil was lucky to have a job at all, for there were close to a million officers of all ranks who had been turned out of work by the Versailles treaty. The three walked along the platform, and Lanny noted many signs of poverty; a well-nourished face was rare, and the crowds looked as if they had got their clothes in second-hand shops. Germans would always be clean, even if they had to wash themselves with soda instead of soap; but they had no way to repair or paint their houses, or to mend things broken in civil war. Ragged beggars were everywhere, and women with pinched faces and pitiful finery—not even in Paris did you see so many prostitutes. Bodies of suicides were being found every day in the river and the canals of Berlin, and never did one of them have on underwear. Lanny and Kurt were ashamed to be dressed so well— and glad they had not let Beauty equip them with fresh outfits.

There was a military automobile with a uniformed chauffeur waiting for Kurt's brother. More heel-clicking and bowing, and Lanny saw them off, and took a taxi to the Robins' nest. The taxi looked as if it had been through several wars; it had a ragged seat and a bullet-hole through the window; but the apartment house where the *Schieber* lived was most elegant and had a functionary in a bright-colored uniform to open the door. The best of everything was yours if you had foreign money; keep it safe in the bank, and change it every day as you needed it, because it multiplied itself faster than rabbits.

One of the first things Lanny noted about the Robin apartment was that it had been specially provided with a steel door having heavy hinges and bolts. This had been put in by the previous tenants during the period of the Communist uprisings. A strange, precarious life in this world of runaway inflation! The owner of the fashionable apartment house had just called upon his tenants and informed them that he was no longer able to purchase coal, and that they would have to get together and work out some co-operative way of keeping themselves warm.

Never had Lanny received such a welcome as that Jewish family gave him. When the steel door swung open they all cried out with delight and came swarming around him. Freddi took his hat and bags and Hansi his overcoat. Mama Robin, whom Lanny met for the first time, was a hearty, active little woman whose German had a strong Yiddish accent; kindness exuded from every pore of her, and she was so eager to make her guest comfortable that she made him the opposite. He was used to the English form of hospitality, which took it for granted that everything in the house was yours and let you help yourself without comment. But when you sat down to dinner with Mama Robin, she insisted that you eat this and enjoy that and have more of the other thing; she would clamor until Hansi would say, gently: "Mama, you are bothering Lanny." Then there would be a discussion as to whether she was or not, and Lanny would have to eat more than he wanted, in order to avoid hurting the feelings of this Jewish mother whose hospitality lacked a sense of security.

But all the discomfort vanished when Lanny sat at the piano and Hansi took up his violin. Then everybody fell silent, and mysterious presences entered the garishly furnished room. Beauty came, not Lanny's mother, but a goddess, white-robed, broad-browed, with stardust in her hair; Joy came, the daughter of Elysium; Pity came, with tear-dimmed eyes, and Grief with head bowed and dark robes trailing. Life became transfigured, and human insects stirring in primeval slime suddenly discovered themselves to be seers of visions, members of a mystical brotherhood, allies of a godhead. Genius had made its appearance upon earth, and its wonders were the heritage of all worshipers in the temple of Art.

IV

But one couldn't play or listen to music all the time in this world. Johannes Robin had to go out and make money for his family and satisfy the ambitions which drove him. The mother had to attend to her household duties, and three young fellows had to eat and sleep, and see something of the great city of Berlin, it being Lanny's first visit. Snow was on the ground, and bitter winds blew part of the time, but there came one sunny day, and they hired a coach with a bony nag, and inspected the Reichstag building, and drove down the Siegesallee, which celebrated the war before the last with a double row of enormous Teutonic heroes in white marble. It was not permitted to laugh at them, because these were dangerous times, and the shivering old coachman might have been one of the Kaiser's own guards. Berlin was orderly now, but street-fighting had been going on for a couple of years and no one could say when it might break out again. Well-dressed people didn't dare go into the working-class districts, but they scolded because the workers were getting more of the depreciated marks than the people who had incomes. The hungry poor formed breadlines, while the speculators danced and drank in the night-clubs.

When Lanny got back from the drive he found "Mama"—so she told him to call her—in a great fuss because there had come a telephone call from the American Embassy, which of course sounded tremendous to her. Lanny didn't know anybody there and couldn't imagine what it might be, but he called and was put through to the chargé d'affaires—no ambassador had been named yet. The chargé, it appeared, was a fraternity brother of Robbie Budd, and had a cablegram telling him that Lanny was to be visiting the Robins.

The official wanted to show him the town, and would he come and have lunch at the Kaiserliche Automobil Klub the following day? Lanny accepted, and an embassy car called for him and brought him to a quite palatial building with lackeys in pink knee-breeches and white silk stockings and gloves. Lanny couldn't help thinking that he was in a movie—except that a modern American career man, his host, didn't fit therein. "Do you always do your guests as proud as this?" inquired the youth, and the chargé said: "They presented our staff with membership cards. We are the most important people in the world right now—we have all the wheat and the pork!"

Evidently Germany still had venison and grouse, and the velvet-footed servitors brought them enormous portions. Lanny wondered what thoughts would be in the heads of these lackeys. They might be Junkers or they might be Socialists, but in either case they wouldn't have any use for American bourgeois. Lanny told his father's old friend the news about Robbie and his business, and about the family in Connecticut. They talked about the European situation in guarded terms, for of course every waiter might be a spy, and a diplomatic official must neither betray secrets nor give offense.

V

The chargé said he had brought Lanny here thinking he might like to see some of the important men of Berlin. Into this stately dining-room came members of the ruling classes—not the politicians, the Socialist and popular party upstarts who might be kicked out any day, but the financial men and businessmen whose power would endure. They were large men with bull necks, red faces, and bristly mustaches or beards; the blockade had affected their bulk no more than that of the white marble statues on the Siegesallee. They wore the short black coats called "mornings," which had come to replace the longer frock-coats of old days. Those passing bowed to the American official, and several stopped and were introduced to his guest.

The chargé indicated a short but broad and bulky fellow, swarthy as a Mediterranean, with a thick black beard and dingy clothes that fitted him, so Lanny said, "like socks on a rooster." It was Hugo Stinnes, the coal magnate, and the youth mentioned: "I saw him at Spa. He laid down the law, I was told, and made the German delegation accept the coal agreement. The French are to pay the pithead cost and freight, plus five marks per ton to feed the miners."

"You can be sure Stinnes will get his share," commented the official. "He has bought up most of the newspapers in Germany, so the politicians have to dance to his piping."

There entered a handsome, elegantly dressed man with a small gray mustache and goatee and a nearly bald head. Passing their table, he stopped for a greeting. "Dr. Rathenau," said the chargé, introducing him. Lanny knew the name, for his father had praised him as a symbol of German organizing ability; he was the head of the country's great electrical trust, and during the war had been in charge of the supply of raw materials. It was owing to him that the Fatherland had been able to hold out so long, and now he was Minister of Reconstruction, with a still heavier task.

"A son of Robert Budd of Budd Gunmakers," said the chargé, and as the minister expressed his pleasure, the American added: "Won't you join us?"

Rathenau explained that he was waiting for a friend, but he sat down until this man should arrive. Lanny had a chance to study him, and decided that his face was both kind and thoughtful. His manner was suave, and his English flawless; he spoke long and polished sentences like a classical orator—but at the same time with the positiveness of one born to command.

Walther Rathenau had just come back from London, where he had been trying to persuade the British that it was impossible for Germany to meet the payment on reparations which was to fall due in a few days. With what could they meet it? They could sell only marks, and the results of that all the world's money-markets saw. The City men of London had already expressed their opinion on that subject by refusing to extend any credit to Germany, and giving as their reason the exorbitant reparations burden!

"They have decided to call another conference," said Rathenau. "It will be early next month, and I think at Cannes."

"Indeed?" said the chargé. "Then you will be right at Budd's back door. His home is Juan-les-Pins."

"I hope I may have the pleasure of seeing you there," added the youth, and the minister agreed courteously to renew the acquaintance.

"An extraordinary personality," said the American, after Rathenau had left the table. "He really understands the present situation, and it would be well if his advice were taken. The propertied classes of Germany are called upon to make sacrifices which hurt, and the fact that Rathenau is a Jew makes them even less willing to be ruled by him."

"He doesn't look like a Jew," commented Lanny.

"That happens with many of that race. But the Junkers know him, and will never forgive him because he is working with the Social-Democrats—even though it's in an effort to save them and their country."

VI

Lanny and Kurt took the night train for Upper Silesia, and in the morning were at the Polish border. A humiliating thing for Kurt to have to be examined by foreign customs officials and border police in order to get to his own home. The customs men were careless, but the passports were studied minutely; Lanny suspected that the officials didn't know how to read very well. They spoke a bad German when they were compelled to. Afterward Kurt quoted to his friend a saying that when you went east from Germany you were in half-Asia. The signs of it were rutted roads, dilapidated houses, vermin, and superstition.

Stubendorf was a predominantly German district, and the war hadn't reached here, so everything was in order, and the snow made the countryside look fresh and clean; only the worn and patched clothing told cf extreme poverty. The little train which wound up the branch line had evidently been a troop train and was pretty much of a wreck, the seats cut to pieces and the broken windows boarded over. A farmer of the Schloss estate recognized Kurt and touched his hat and gave them a seat by a sound window, so they could look out upon the landscape which stirred them both deeply—Lanny because his previous visit to the "Christmas-card castle" shone in his memory like snow crystals in sunlight.

A sleigh met them and was pulled up the slopes by two rather feeble horses—for the war had left few good ones. On a high ridge the tiny town was clustered about the feet of the main building, the front part of which was modern, six stories high and built of gray stone. The Meissner home was one of the separate houses, and some-one must have been watching at the window, for they all came trooping to the door before the two travelers had alighted from the sleigh. There were cries of delight, and the women had tears in their eyes.

Lanny had wondered what was going to be the attitude of Germans to an American, who had been an enemy only three years ago. Of course the members of this family knew that he personally had taken no part in the war, but still, his people had snatched victory out of the grasp of their people. Already in Berlin Lanny had discovered a peculiar fact, and here he found it confirmed—the Germans didn't seem to blame the Americans, they liked and admired them, and were sure that they had come into the war through a misunderstanding due to the subtlety of British propaganda. Now the Americans realized their mistake and were trying to atone for it, and the Germans would help them by explaining how right they had been.

But that would come later. It was Christmas eve, and every good German was sentimental about it, and if he hated anybody he stowed the feeling away on a back shelf for a week. Here was Herr Meissner, no longer stout and rosy, with partly bald head and pouches under chin and cheeks and eyes. And *die gute verständige Mutter*—Lanny always thought of Goethe's poem in connection with Frau Meissner; her brood had been reduced, for one son was in a hospital for incurables—nobody said what was wrong, but Lanny guessed it was a case of shell shock; another son buried in East Prussia, and in his place a young widow with three children. Also there was the Meissner daughter, whom Lanny remembered as singing Christmas carols and having a long golden plait hanging over each shoulder. Now she too was a widow with two children, and the little ones made the home gay, for they had no knowledge of war and no shadows over their lives. After they had been put to bed Kurt played for the elders the compositions upon which he had been working for so long. They listened enraptured, and could never get enough during his stay.

There were only a few lights on the Christmas tree, and the presents were simple, consisting either of food or of old things from pre-war days. The game in the forests had been greatly depleted, and now was being carefully guarded, but you had a little for Christmas; also you had an abundance of wheat and turnips from your fields, but sugar was among the precious metals and coffee a decoction from unnamed materials. You washed your remaining underwear with the care you would have given to the sheerest silk, for if you tore it you would have difficulty in getting a piece of thread with which to mend it. Lanny and Kurt had brought from France a priceless box of raisins, figs, and chocolates, and they helped to make a miraculous Christmas.

In this era of runaway inflation there were two kinds of rich people, the speculators and the peasants. The latter produced what everybody had to have, and for which everybody paid a higher price every day; so they hoarded their products, and now and then brought home a large wad of paper money. The Polish mark had taken its tumble in advance of the German, and there was a story about a Polish peasant in a near-by district whose hut had burned down during his absence, and he had torn his hair and cried that his whole fortune had been destroyed. When they asked him what it was, he answered: "Forty million marks!"

VII

The Graf Stubendorf whom Lanny had seen had died since the war, and his oldest son ruled in his stead: a stiff Prussian general, of whom everybody said that he had a very high sense of duty, but nobody said he loved him. As his father had done, he greeted and shook hands with all the tenants and retainers gathered in the great hall of the Schloss; he was lacking in his father's geniality, but perhaps that could be excused because the times were so dangerous and the need of discipline so obvious. It was hard indeed for an army officer whose home had been turned over to despised enemies to talk about loving them for even one week.

As before, Herr Meissner spoke freely in the bosom of his family about the affairs of Stubendorf and what the Graf had imparted to him about political affairs. Lanny thought it could do no harm after so many years, so he narrated how on his way home from his previous visit he had been accosted in the railroad station by the editor of a Social-Democratic newspaper, who had lured him into talking indiscreetly about what he had heard at the Schloss. Lanny said that he had often wondered whether the man had published anything, and the Comptroller-General replied that he did remember an article published in the *Arbeiterzeitung* which had puzzled them all greatly, though it had never occurred to them to connect their American visitor with it. Lanny assured his host that he had now attained to years of discretion, so there was no possibility of such a blunder being repeated.

Herr Meissner had somewhat altered his views. The Socialists were now comparatively respectable people with whom one was compelled, however reluctantly, to do business. Their place as public enemies had been taken by the Communists, who were plotting a revolution on the Russian model and therefore had to be regarded as wild beasts. The Socialists, no matter how unsound their ideas, at least believed in law and order and were willing to wait until they had converted a majority of the people to vote their way; meanwhile their help was urgently needed against the Bolshevik menace.

Eight years before, Lanny had sat and listened in silence to what the Comptroller-General told his family; but now he knew much that was of interest to all of them, and Herr Meissner asked him about the Peace Conference and the decisions it had taken concerning their homeland. Lanny outlined some of the discussions to which he had been an auditor. In return the host explained the attitude of the people here and made no effort to conceal the fact that no German had any idea of accepting the settlement as more than a breathing-space.

"The French won the war," said Meissner, "and we are willing to accept that, and to forgive and forget. It has happened before, and can happen again. But what has never happened is that a nation should be loaded down with a debt so out of all reason that every child knows it is not a real claim, but an effort to make it impossible for us to regain our trade and prosperity. To resist that is a fight for survival, and the people who do it to us choose to be our permanent enemies."

Lanny was there to learn and not to argue. He did not tell his host what he had heard Denis de Bruyne saying to his father, nor did he quote George D. Herron's analysis of the German mind. He listened to a detailed story of how the French had plotted to defeat the purposes of the Supreme Allied Council in Upper Silesia. Their army had not merely failed to play fair in the carrying out of the plebiscite decision; they had openly encouraged Korfanty and his *sokols*, the Polish patriot bands. They had allowed some four hundred Polish officers to come in and join these bands and they had permitted gun-running everywhere throughout the land. Here in Stubendorf Polish peasants had been freely recruited, and if information about this was turned over to the French army authorities they did nothing whatever. Said Meissner: "They had the same idea as in the Rhineland, that if a revolution could be accomplished, the Supreme Council would be compelled to recognize it."

The Comptroller-General went on to explain that since the British troops had come in things had been more tolerable. "We have the land, and the Poles can't do us much harm with their taxes, because their money goes down so fast that by the time the taxes are due they aren't so big as they were meant to be. They are still less when the government spends them!" The speaker smiled rather slyly, and added that the Berlin government had accepted the settlement because it had to, but no German in Stubendorf would rest until he and his property were back under the sheltering wings of the Fatherland. "Life means nothing to us otherwise," he said, and authorized Lanny to tell that to all the French and British people he met.

VIII

Kurt had a duty to perform, to visit his sick brother, who was in a private hospital. He said he wouldn't invite Lanny, because it would probably be a painful experience. The brother was in the care of a physician, an old friend of the family; when Lanny learned that the place was in Poland proper, he suggested going along and seeing a bit of the town while Kurt paid his visit. Kurt replied that there wouldn't be much to see, but he'd be glad to have company on a tiresome trip.

They rode on the branch line to the junction and then on another line, in another dilapidated day-coach. The town was in the war zone, and many of its ruins had not yet been touched. The hospital had one wing demolished, and rebuilding was going on. Lanny left his friend at the gate and set out to see Poland. Very few of the streets had any paving whatever; a few had board sidewalks, but many of the boards were missing. Though everything was covered by a blanket of fresh snow, deep ruts and hollows were visible, and one could imagine that travel would become difficult in springtime.

The center of the town was a market-square, with shops and drinking-places around it. Lanny looked in the windows and perceived that there was little merchandise on sale. Two sides of the square were lined with peasant carts. Country produce was set out, and ragged, hungry-looking people wandered by, stopping now and then to haggle. Many of these people were what are called "Water Poles"; of Slovak descent, they are accustomed to go into Germany as laborers, so they speak a mixture of German and Polish, and Lanny could understand a part of what they said. The peasants wore ragged sheepskin coats and heavy caps that could be pulled over the ears; they stamped their feet and beat their arms to keep warm. Lanny judged that in the matter of underwear they resembled the suicides of the Berlin canals. You could smell a single peasant several yards away in still air, and when you had a crowd of them the mucous membranes of your nose were assailed by a steady bombardment of the molecules of ammonia, so highly volatile.

Lanny wandered for a while, looking and listening, trying to imagine what it might be like to be a Polish peasant exchanging cabbages and turnips for greasy pieces of paper with Polish eagles and Arabic numerals on them. Everybody was polite to a magnificent *Fremder* in an elegant woolen overcoat, but few stared at him; they were too miserable and chilled for curiosity. Now and then a beggar followed, whining, but Lanny feared that if he gave to one he would be besieged. No doubt the peasants had the same fear, for they gave to nobody. Altogether Lanny's impressions of the new Polish republic were unfavorable, and it seemed to him that Paderewski would have done better to stick to the concert stage, and he himself to stay at the Meissner home and play accompaniments to old German *Lieder* for two gentle young blond Nordic widows.

IX

Two or three times Lanny passed the hotel where he was to be met by Kurt. It was an unpromising-looking place, so he made up his mind to suggest that they go hungry for a while. Kurt was staying longer than he planned, and Lanny sought in vain for something that could be called picturesque; there was nothing like that in sight, and he wished he had brought a book along.

He had started to walk around the square to keep warm when he saw three soldiers, wearing faded and worn uniforms and carrying bayoneted rifles, enter from one of the streets, leading before them a man with hands tied behind his back. Lanny stopped to watch, and saw one of the soldiers go into a shop, while the other two led their prisoner under a large bare-limbed tree which grew in the square. They stood there, waiting, and presently the third man came out of the shop carrying a long and quite heavy rope; he rejoined the others and proceeded to toss one end of the rope up over a limb of the tree. "My God!" thought Lanny. "They are going to hang him!"

The son of Budd Gunmakers had had many odd experiences during his twenty-two years in a bewildering world, but this was the first time he had ever attended an execution. He looked about him and observed that peasants and townspeople made note of what was going on, but made it quickly, and then turned back to their own affairs. Could it be that they had seen so many people hanged that it was less important than the sale of cabbages and turnips? Or were they for some reason afraid to show any interest or feeling?

It didn't occur to Lanny to be afraid. He was sure that Polish soldiers were not hanging anybody from the sweet land of liberty; and he had yet to meet any people in the world with whom he couldn't get along. Perceiving that the job was going to be a quick one, he started to walk in that direction. As he neared the group he noted that the prisoner was a mere youth, and that he was ragged, pale, and depressed-looking, just like hundreds of others whom Lanny had been watching and smelling. The soldiers also appeared to have missed bathing and shaving for many days.

By the time Lanny reached the scene there was a noose about the neck of the prisoner, and the three men had hold of the other end. "*Guten Tag*," said Lanny, with a pleasant smile, and added a magical word: "*Amerikaner*." The Polish form happens to be "*Amerykanin*," which was near enough.

The faces of the soldiers showed interest, and the leader, who might have been a corporal, said: "*Guten Tag, Herrschaft.*"

That was promising; he was a "Water Pole." Possibly he might have labored in America, so Lanny inquired: "*Sprechen Sie Englisch?*"

"*Nein, nein,*" was the reply.

Lanny had never learned to smoke, but he had discovered that the practice offered a passport to friendship all over this war-torn continent, so while traveling he kept a package of cigarettes in his pocket. Now he drew it forth, tore it open, and held it out. The three soldiers, who had laid their guns against the tree, now hung the rope over their arms and reached out dirty fingers for the lovely little white cylinders which the *Amerykanin* tendered. Grins of pleasure wreathed their faces, and when Lanny produced matches and proceeded to light each in turn, they were sure that he was a royal personage.

It seemed a reasonable guess that no military regulations would be violated if a prisoner lived long enough to watch his captors smoke a cigarette. But the *Herrschaft* had even more original ideas than that. "*Er, auch,*" he said, and pointed a cigarette toward the prisoner. Then he indicated the bonds. "*Los machen? Soll rauchen.*"

Delightful humanity of the noble lord from the land of unlimited possibilities! It was the sort of thing to be expected from people who sent over mountains of food and kind lovely ladies to distribute it among starving women and children. The American millionaire desired that the poor devil should smoke a cigarette in order to give him courage to be hanged! The soldiers grinned with amusement. Why not?

X

So far the youthful captive had manifested no interest in what was going on; he had stood staring sullenly before him. Lanny saw that he had dark eyes and hollow cheeks, and that he was shivering, whether from cold or fright could not be guessed. Certainly a most miserable human specimen, and perhaps to put an end to him would be the greatest kindness. But seeing the doglike eyes turned upon him, Lanny paid tribute to their common humanity by inquiring: "*Wollen Sie rauchen?*"

Apparently the man didn't know German; but what happened was plain in any language—the soldiers untied his hands, though keeping the rope on one wrist. Lanny extended a cigarette, and the prisoner took it and put it into his mouth. Lanny struck a match and lighted the cigarette. So there were four smokers, which meant four contented men for the time being. They smoked and inhaled deeply, giving every sign that it had been long since they had had such a chance.

The occasion called for conversation, and Lanny said: "*Was hat der Kerl getan?*" He pointed to the prisoner, and tried again: "*Was ist los?*"

"*Kommunist,*" explained the corporal.

"*Ach, so!*" Lanny was duly shocked.

"*Ja, Bolschewist,*" said the other.

"*Aber,*" said Lanny, "*was hat er getan?*" He repeated this in several variations, but it was too much for the soldier's vocabulary, or possibly for his mind. Why ask what a Bolshevik had done? In order to be hanged, he didn't have to "do" anything, he just had to be. Surely any *Herrschaft* in the world would understand that!

"*Aber!*" persisted the stubborn American. He wanted to find out if the man had had a trial; but this too was hard to put across. Lanny tried all the German words he could think of: *Gericht, Richter, Untersuchung.* Again he couldn't be sure whether it was that Poles who went into Germany to labor for a few pfennigs a day never heard of such things, or whether the corporal couldn't conceive of applying them to a Communist. Apparently if you met one of these you simply tied his hands behind his back and borrowed or rented a rope and strung him up to the nearest tree for a lesson to the others. From the movies Lanny had learned that this was the practice with horse-thieves in the wild and woolly West, and it appeared that he was now in the wild and woolly East.

He hit upon one word which apparently was well known: "*Polizeiamt.*" That seemed to worry the soldiers; their authority was being questioned, and by one who might himself have to do with the police. Lanny didn't want to worry them too much, so he distributed four more cigarettes, and the badly handicapped talk continued.

For the first time the prisoner took part. Maybe it was the smoke that waked him up, or maybe it was hope at work in his soul. He spoke rapidly in Polish, and Lanny listened closely, for in border lands foreign words creep in and often one word tells the subject of a conversation. Lanny was sure that he heard the word "America"; and then, more than once, a familiar but unexpected pair of syllables: "Brooklyn!"

The corporal turned to Lanny, and in his broken German made plain what was in question. "He says he knows the *Herrschaft*. In America. A city, Broukleen."

Lanny looked at the youth. Indubitably, there was the light of hope in his eyes; and for a moment it was obscured in one of them by the faintest trace of a wink. Lanny, who wasn't slow on the intake, turned to the corporal. "*Ja, gewiss. Ich kenn' ihn.*"

This threw the soldiers into obvious confusion. They began talking rapidly among themselves, and the prisoner joined them. The head man turned to Lanny again. "He says he is no Communist. He says the *Herrschaft* knows he is no Communist."

"*Ja, gewiss!*" repeated Lanny. "I knew him in Brooklyn, America. *Guter Kerl.* Good fellow. *Kein Kommunist. Kein Bolschewist.*"

Why did Lanny say all that? If he had been asked the question then, he couldn't have answered. Something welled up in him, quickly, unexplainably. Was it that he couldn't bear to see a poor devil hanged? Was it that he didn't believe in hanging anybody without a trial? Or was there some secret sympathy in his heart for the Communists? Had he come to the belief that, however they might be mistaken in their tactics, there was a share of justice in their cause? Since human motives are rarely simple, there may have been a bit of all these reasons in Lanny's mind.

Anyhow, he still had two cigarettes in his precious package, and he offered these, wrapper and all, to the corporal. "*Guter Kerl,*" he repeated. Still keeping his amiable smile upon his face, he reached into his pocket and produced some talismans of still more potent magic; objects the existence of which had almost been forgotten in "half-Asia"—four silver coins, German marks about the size of a United States quarter, and having the double-headed Prussian eagle upon one face. With these miraculous little disks one could buy most anything in the land! Lanny handed one to each of the soldiers and was about to give the fourth to the prisoner, but reflected that they might hang him to get it, so he doubled the fee of the head man. "*Guter Kerl! Mach' los!*" he said.

There could be no further argument. The rope was taken off the other hand and the prisoner was free. The prince of the American plutocracy shook the cold grimy hands of his three friends and said: "*Danke schön,*" "*Leben Sie wohl,*" "*Adieu,*" and all the other pleasant words he could think of.

"*Die Herrschaft nehm' mit?*" said the corporal, indicating the prisoner; and Lanny said *Ja*, he would "take with," but where he would take he had no idea—perhaps to Brooklyn, America!

That problem was quickly solved, however. Lanny strolled across the square with his prisoner, followed by many curious eyes. When they got into a side street, the still shivering youth exclaimed: "*Dzieki tobie, panie,*" which is Polish for "Thank you, sir," and, without waiting for a silver coin or even for a handshake, darted behind a house and disappeared. Lanny wasn't surprised or displeased, for he understood that the Brooklyn alibi mightn't last very long, and he had no more cigarettes.

XI

When Lanny told his friend about that adventure Kurt couldn't help being amused, but at the same time he was shocked to the deeps of his Prussian soul. "How could you have thought of such a thing?" he exclaimed.

"But I didn't think of it," chuckled the American. "The prisoner thought of it."

"You didn't know a thing about that fellow! He may have been a criminal, a most dangerous one."

"It may be. On the other hand, he may be a poor devil who told some peasant that the landlords were robbers—which they doubtless are."

"You imagine they would sentence a man to be hanged for that?"

"I don't think anybody sentenced him. I think those soldiers just picked him up and started to hang him because they didn't like what he was saying."

"But that's absurd, Lanny! Governments aren't run on that basis!"

"I gathered that you didn't think so much of the Polish government."

No answering that argument; nothing to do but say that Americans were an irresponsible people, sometimes outright crazy. Kurt looked about him anxiously, thinking that a company of soldiers might arrive at any moment to apprehend them both. "We ought to get out of this town," he said; but it wasn't easy, for there was no train for a couple of hours. They found a sleigh which could be rented, and they had a cold and uncomfortable ride to the next town on the railroad. There again, Kurt was anxious; he even thought the Polish police or army might trace them to Stubendorf, whose Polish authorities would enjoy nothing more than having a serious offense to charge against the family of the Comptroller-General of the Schloss.

No, Kurt couldn't take the Red menace with the gay insouciance of an American playboy. To Germans of the upper classes *Bolschewismus* was real—the newest-born child of Satan. The Reds had seized Bavaria, and had come very near to getting Berlin; they had plundered and killed, and were still boring like termites inside the foundations and walls of the German state structure. Here in Upper Silesia, the moment the French and German troops were withdrawn, there would be an attempted uprising of the miners and factory workers. The German Reds hated the German government and the Polish Reds hated the Polish government, and at any time they were ready to combine against both governments; that was their idea of how to end war—but to Kurt it would be worse than all the wars that had ever been fought in the world.

In short, Lanny was made to realize that what he had done was no joke, but something very serious, that must under no circumstances be mentioned to anyone in Stubendorf. Suppose there should come a revolution in Poland, and he should pick up a newspaper and see a picture of the Polish Trotsky or the Polish Bela Kun, and recognize it as the man for whom he had lighted two cigarettes!

"It might be convenient for you," said the incorrigible American. "It might enable me to save your life!"

12

The Best-Laid Schemes

I

LANNY had written to his mother an account of his meeting with Walther Rathenau, and, as a result of this, when he and Kurt returned to Juan they found Beauty in a state of delightful excitement. She had taken the letter to Emily Chattersworth, who had pointed out the duty as well as opportunity which this circumstance held out to them. The world is supposed to be run by majestic statesmen who strut upon the stage and deliver resounding orations amid the explosion of flashlight bulbs; but everybody knows it is really run by clever women, who stay behind the wings and pull wires. The statesmen-puppets do what is subtly suggested to them, most of the time without knowing that they are being guided.

For three years now the rulers of Britain, France, and Germany had been locked in a tug-of-war, in which all three countries were exhausting themselves without any gains whatever. And now through some prank of fate they were coming to Cannes, right on Emily's front doorstep, just over Beauty's garden wall! The French Foreign Minister had been an habitué of Emily's *salon* for many years; Beauty knew Lloyd George's secretary, Philip Kerr—pronounce it Carr—soon to be the Marquess of Lothian—pronounce it as if you loathed him. And now Lanny had met Rathenau, who was to head the German delegation! Surely the hand of Providence was indicating to two American-French ladies that they should take charge of the Cannes conference and bring the affairs of Europe into some order!

The sessions were scheduled to be held in the Cercle Nautique, a one-story clubhouse of stucco with a magnificent façade and very elegant lofty rooms. There the resounding speeches would be made, the men with black boxes would gather to snap pictures, the journalists would peer and pry and beg for crumbs of news. But if you thought the real work would be done in that place, you would indeed be ignorant of the *haut monde.* After the uproar had died and the crowds had dispersed, the statesmen would slip away to some quiet nook, where a gracious hostess would serve tea and minuscule sandwiches, and by her presence would soothe their ruffled feelings. Presently they would be talking amiably to one another about the opposition at home and the impossibility of retaining office if they made too many concessions—so be a good fellow, now, and let us have this patch of desert, or that extra thousand million off the reparations account!

Beauty and Emily had spent their lives equipping themselves for this special service. They knew the vanities and foibles of each of the elderly gentlemen. They had heard the problems endlessly discussed, and if they didn't understand them, at least they could talk as if they did. Each was complementary to the other, for Emily could handle the cultured ones, the highbrows, while Beauty understood the men of oil and guns and money. Kurt and Lanny had just been to Germany, and could explain that rather terrifying race, and help in the supreme achievement, which would be to induce the British and the French—especially the latter—to enter into social relations with their former foes.

Marie de Bruyne rejoined the household and was offered a share in the conspiracy. Marie wasn't nearly so keen about meeting Germans as the American ladies were, but she saw that they were launched upon this adventure, and that the compliant Lanny was going to be dragged into it; she was shrewd enough, and in love enough, not to throw cold water upon his mother's dreams. And then came Rick and Nina, according to the promise they had made some time earlier. A most fortunate circumstance for Rick, to be right in the center of a big story without any traveling expenses! Nina wasn't much on politics, but she had two babies that she surely didn't want to raise to be soldiers, and whatever prestige might belong to the wife of a future baronet she would use in helping persuade British diplomats to persuade French diplomats to attend tea parties with German diplomats.

II

The new villa, called "The Lodge," wasn't ready on time. What contractor ever did keep his word? When the Pomeroy-Nielsons arrived—crippled husband, lively little wife, two babies, and a maid— they had to be put up in a hotel for a couple of days, until the paint inside the house stopped smelling. Then the curtains had to be hung, and the furniture brought over from Cannes and put in place. Jolly fun fixing up a house—only two women never can agree where any piece of furniture ought to go, and there are some women who can't agree with themselves and are forever deciding that the center table ought to be against the wall or vice versa. If the husband is a writer, he doesn't care where you put the damn thing, if only it can be in the same place the next time he enters the room, and he wants the servants to understand that if they put his papers in order the only thing they have done is to make it impossible for him to find them.

Beauty left all those matters to Lanny, for she was at Sept Chênes most of the time, helping Emily to plan the pacification of Europe; sending the right letters and telegrams to key persons, calling in Sophie Timmons and other trusted friends and outlining to them the parts they were to play in the great world settlement. Lanny had to send a carefully worded telegram to the German Minister of Recon- struction, reminding him of their meeting and telling him that the home of Lanny's mother on the Cap d'Antibes would be at all times open to him as a quiet and safe retreat.

It really was a critical occasion; the fashionable ladies weren't exaggerating that. The German government was practically bankrupt, having no way to get foreign credit with which to meet the overdue reparations payments; and what action was France going to take? Poincaré and his Nationalists were clamoring for the occupation of Rhineland cities, while the British were making a supreme effort to persuade the French government that this course would bring ruin to them all. Britain had two million unemployed, and hardly any trade, and to risk another war might throw a large section of Europe into Bolshevism.

Such were the issues at stake when the great private trains came rolling into the Cannes station, discharging their loads of statesmen and experts. They came from cities of fog and snow turned black by discharges from millions of chimney-pots; they stepped out into dazzling sunshine and balmy air, and were driven along avenues lined with palm trees, past houses of white or pink stucco with shutters painted a bright blue; they gazed over rocky shores on which the blue and green Mediterranean broke in long white lines of foam. A delightful place to spend a holiday: elegant hotels and easy-going, carefree people; theaters, operas, and casinos in which music resounded and dancing and gambling went on all night. The half-starved, half-frozen populations of the northern cities read about it in the papers and took it none too amiably. Why couldn't these politicians do their conferencing at home, and save the cost of junkets to the playgrounds of the parasites?

A member of the British staff explained to Lanny that desire for a holiday had nothing to do with it; the statesmen got very little pleasure out of it. But their police and military authorities were afraid to have them gather in large cities in desperate times like these. Impossible to keep track of anarchists and troublemakers; to know at what moment a machine gun might be turned loose from a window, or a bomb be thrown from a housetop. But in small places like San Remo and Spa and Cannes the police could know who was in town, and stood some chance of protecting their important charges. France wanted no foreign statesmen to be assassinated within her borders. One could hardly say which would be the more awkward, for some Red fanatic to shoot a conservative statesman or for some misguided patriot to bomb a German.

III

Lanny got an inside view of this problem and the methods of handling it. He happened to walk into the village of Juan to make some trifling purchase, and who should be sitting on a bench by the edge of the strip of sand but his crimson Saint Barbara! He saw her first and stopped; she didn't fit the holiday crowd at a seaside resort, but sat staring out over the water as if she were quite alone. In the too bright sunlight her complexion had a jaundiced appearance, but nothing ever changed the sad dignity of her features; once more the romantic Lanny decided that he saw all the sorrows of mankind in that face, and wished that Marcel could come back to life and paint it.

Being now arrived at years of discretion, Lanny should have gone on about his business; but Barbara happened to turn and see him, and of course he had to greet her. It was natural for him to inquire: "What are you doing in this village?"

"I was staying in Cannes," she replied, "but the police have just put me out."

"What?" he exclaimed.

"They are afraid I will plant an infernal machine under their thieves' conference."

"You really mean they ordered you out of town?"

"They gave me just about ten minutes in which to pack my things. Worse than that, they drove out the working-class family with which I was staying; the man, who had a job, now has to go and look for one elsewhere."

"Well, I'll be damned!" said Lanny.

"You may, if you stay and talk to me," replied the woman, grimly.

It made Lanny a bit hot under his collar of gray Oxford cloth.

He would have liked to say: "Won't you come and stay for a while at Bienvenu?" but he knew of course that this would knock Beauty's plans higher than a kite. Instead he sat down by the woman, and said, a trifle embarrassed: "Look here, you may be a bit short of funds. Are you?"

The other flushed with embarrassment. "Oh, I couldn't let you do that!"

"Why not? You are working for your cause, are you not?"

"But you don't believe in my cause!"

"Don't be too sure about that. I believe in your honesty at least; and, as you know, I don't have to work very hard for my money."

A dangerous thing for Lanny to say, and a dangerous course for him to embark upon. If once you start subsidizing a saint, how can you know where you are going to stop? Saints rarely have means of support and, worse yet, they are apt to have friends in the same plight; their biographies are one series of hard-luck stories. The job of taking care of them should be left to the Lord, who has created locusts and wild honey for that purpose, and in extreme cases will send ravens, or manna, or miracles of loaves and fishes.

But Lanny was young, and in this respect would never grow up. He took out his purse and put three hundred-franc notes into Barbara Pugliese's hand. The franc had lost two-thirds of the purchasing-power it had had before the war, so this wasn't such a sumptuous gift as it seemed; but to the poor woman it was a fortune, and she stammered gratitude and embarrassment, which Lanny told her to forget.

"Have you any idea where to go?" he asked.

"I haven't made any plans, because, frankly, I was stranded. I want to go back to Italy and continue my work, but my friends beg me to delay, on account of the great danger."

"What danger?" he asked.

"Have you not heard what is going on in Italy? The employers are hiring gangs of ruffians to beat the friends of the people's cause, and often to murder them. Hundreds of our devoted workers have fallen victims to these *bravi*."

"How terrible!" exclaimed Lanny.

"It is a consequence of the tragic division in the ranks of the workers. When they were in possession of the steel foundries, and it was a question of holding and operating them, the Socialist leaders hesitated and refused their support."

"But how could they operate foundries without large capital?"

"The whole credit of the co-operative movement should have been put behind them, and they could have started to work at full capacity. But no, our Socialists are slaves to the idea of 'legality'; they hope to get possession of industry through the state, by electing politicians. Our workers have seen, time after time, that politicians lose all their working-class ardor as soon as they are elected, and begin putting the bribes of the bourgeois into their pockets. You see how much the masters care about 'legality'; they do not stop at organized assassination of those who dare to oppose their will. They have a new device now: their hirelings force the victims to swallow great quantities of castor oil mixed with benzine or iodine, which causes atrocious sufferings and leaves them physical wrecks for the rest of their lives. That is what is now going on all over Italy. I judge that your capitalist newspapers have not told you much about it."

"Very little," the young man admitted.

"These gangsters call themselves '*Fascisti*'; they have taken the ancient Roman lictors' symbol, of the rods and the ax. They are patriots, you must understand, and it is in the name of the *sacro egoismo* of Italy that they incite the youth to wage street-wars and wreck the offices of co-operatives and workers' newspapers. Do you remember that dark little wretch whom you watched in the *trattoria* in San Remo?"

"The Blessed Little Pouter Pigeon?" said Lanny, with a smile.

"The same. Well, he is now a member of the Chamber of Deputies, and one of these noble patriots that will restore the ancient glories of *la patria*. He calls his vile newspaper *Il Popolo d'Italia*, and every issue of it is smeared with the blood of martyrs. But that does not keep him from being *persona grata* to the police authorities of Cannes."

"You mean he is here?"

"He comes as a journalist, to observe and report the conference; but he brings with him a band of his ruffians, each with a revolver on his hip. That of course is to protect him against Italians. The French police know that he is their man, he serves the same capitalist *infamia* as themselves. You see, my friend, the class struggle grows more desperate every hour, and one is forced to take sides even against one's will. That is why you should ask yourself whether it is wise for you, a member of the privileged classes, to sit on a public bench in the company of a notorious agitator. If you decide that you have been making a mistake, rest assured that I will understand and not blame you."

IV

The conferees opened their sessions in the reception hall of the Cercle Nautique, and Walther Rathenau, master administrator, delivered an address full of figures, explaining the impossibilities under which the infant German republic was laboring. It was so convincing that the Allied representatives were annoyed, and in the middle of the address Lloyd George broke in: "If we listen to you much longer, we shall come to the conclusion that it is we who owe money!" That, of course, was for the record; it would be passed on to the newspapermen outside, and members of the Tory clubs in London would know that their Prime Minister was using the right sort of language to the recalcitrant foe.

The Allies were offering to accept 720,000,000 gold marks during the year, and 1,450,000,000 gold marks' worth of goods of one sort or another, mostly to the French. The British were whispering to the Germans, begging them to take this offer at once, because of the great danger in which the Briand government stood from its enemies; but the stubborn Rathenau was insisting upon making his speech, and trying to get the cash payments reduced to a round 500,000,000 gold marks. There was the usual deadlock of wills.

Meanwhile, behind the scenes, the appeasers were working busily. Mr. Kerr, pronounced Carr, had made a hurried trip to Sept Chênes with a couple of his staff to talk matters over with a widely famed

Riviera hostess. There was a large English colony in Cannes—in fact it was an English nobleman who had put his *cachet* upon the place and established it as the right one for the right people. There were many hostesses eager to serve their country, and ready to be vexed if preference was given an American; but this was an occasion when patriotic sacrifices would have to be made, and it seemed obvious that the French would come more freely to an American tea party, and meetings with Britons could thus be made to seem casual.

The arrangements amounted to a conspiracy against that son of the people, that orator with the silver tongue, the ragged black mustache, and the roomy paunch, Aristide Briand. They were going to surround him, flatter him, play upon his humanitarian sentiments, and persuade him to agree to a temporary moratorium, and not send his armies into the bankrupt German republic. The climax of their scheming was revealed by Emily Chattersworth with delighted chuckles; they were going to lure a French Premier into playing a game of golf with a British Prime Minister! That is the way they keep the political peace in the green and pleasant land across the Channel; the orators tear into one another across the long table which separates the rival front benches, and then they go off and play a foursome together, and afterward have a drink, and thus compromises are arranged and civil wars averted.

After his oratorical effort the German Minister of Reconstruction was in need of respite; and two of his aides put him into a car and drove him to a place where he might have his tired brow smoothed, metaphorically speaking, by an experienced smoother. He came to Bienvenu, where he met a charming hostess and her intelligent and sympathetic son, also a young German musician who had been twice wounded in the war, and was thus in position to put a seal of security upon these Americans and their ménage. Nobody else to bother a visitor, no stupid attempt to make a lion out of him and show him off to idle chatterers. If only all traveling diplomats, authors, lecturers, and other easily bored persons could find a place of refuge like that in every town!

The minister sipped his tea and nibbled his sandwiches, and then Kurt played the first movement of Beethoven's *Moonlight Sonata*, which has nothing to do with moonlight, but is an utterance of profound and poignant sorrow, suited to the mood of German cabinet members in these trying days. The weary man rested his nearly bald head in a soft chair and listened; when he asked for more, and said that he really meant it, Kurt played a couple of the tender little *Songs without Words* of Mendelssohn. Was he saying that the Jews had their place in German culture, and that their many kinds of services were appreciated by the Fatherland? Anyhow, it was a sign of understanding that an overburdened man of affairs was not asked to listen to noisy and disturbing music.

The minister and his friends were invited to come again, and said they would gladly do so. Their lovely hostess explained that she and her son did not like war, and had kept out of it, and had friends here who were supporting them in their efforts to bring the former foes together. If Dr. Rathenau or any of his staff would care to use Bienvenu as a place for inconspicuous meetings, the villa was at their service. Naturally this interested them, and Beauty told them about Mrs. Chattersworth and her other friends, and about the various British and French whom they knew and could invite to this place if requested. The German minister, who knew how the world was run, understood what all this meant. It was something beyond price in this crisis, and no price would be asked; but later, when the German republic had got on its feet, he might receive a note on perfumed stationery bearing the embossed initials or crest of this gracious lady, reminding him of their pleasant meetings at Cannes and inviting him to confer with her old friend and her son's father, the European salesman of Budd Gunmakers Corporation.

V

Lanny told Rick about his talk with Barbara, and everything that she had told him; whereupon Rick, the newshound, pricked up his ears and said: "If that movement in Italy is spreading as fast as she says, there ought to be a story in it."

"A horrible thing!" exclaimed Lanny.

"I know, but important. It's the employers' answer to Communism; and if one spreads, the other is bound to spread too. I ought to look into it."

"Want me to take you to Italy after the conference?"

"Why bother, if the movement has come to us? Do you suppose we could find that fellow Mussolini?"

"I should think the Italians in Cannes would know about him. A pretty ugly customer, Rick."

"We don't have to worry about that. If he's starting a movement, he'll welcome publicity, you may be sure."

Next morning Lanny drove his friend into the Old Town of Cannes, where there was a considerable Italian colony, and told the proprietor of a *trattoria* that he was trying to find a man named Benito Mussolini. The proprietor looked uneasy, and didn't know whether to talk or not; but Lanny explained that an English newspaperman wished to interview him, and the other loosened up sufficiently to say that he was staying at a certain Casa della Rosa not far away.

The place didn't deserve its name; it was dingy and decidedly third-class. When Lanny descended from his expensive car and went in, the neighborhood took note of it. When Lanny asked the woman in charge for Signor Mussolini, she looked him over carefully, went away, and came back with a sinister young fellow wearing a black shirt and having a bulge on his hip at exactly the spot where Lanny expected to find it. In his halting Italian Lanny explained that his friend wished to write an article about Signor Mussolini's movement for a leading English magazine.

"Where is your friend?" asked the other, suspiciously, and Lanny explained that an aviator crippled in the war had trouble getting in and out of cars, and was waiting to make sure that the signor would see him. The young fellow went to the door and took a good look at the car and its occupant; then he said: "I will see."

Presently the blackshirt returned and bade the two visitors follow him. They went down a hall and into a rear room which had only one window. The man they had come to meet had placed himself in an armchair in a corner at one side of the window; he had placed the chairs in which his visitors were to sit in the light of the window.

so that they could be watched while he remained in shadow. An armed blackshirt stood near the window, and another by the wall in such a position that he was behind the two strangers. The one who escorted them remained on guard by the door. Evidently trust in one's fellow-men was no part of the creed of the new movement called *Fascismo!*

VI

Benito Mussolini was at this time just under forty. He was a medium-small man who did everything in his power to look large. He had a high-domed forehead, partly bald, and melancholy black pop-eyes, suggestive of goiter to a physician. When he wanted to look stern and impressive, he would sit very stiff and erect, and make his lower jaw stick out; but sometimes he would forget and relax, and then you would discover that he had a weak face. He did not rise to greet visitors, but kept his pose of being on a throne.

"*Eh b'en, mousseurs?*" he said. His French was bad, but he did not seem to know it, or perhaps held himself above such concerns.

The English journalist, speaking slow and careful French, explained that, like the editor of *Il Popolo d'Italia*, he was covering the Cannes conference. He named the papers for which he wrote, and produced his credentials; one of the guards carried them to the great man.

"Where have you heard about my movement?" he asked.

"It has been attracting a great deal of attention in my country," said Rick, tactfully. "Many people think it may offer a solution to the problem of the Reds."

"You will do well to study it from that point of view."

"I am here in the hope that you will make that possible, Signor Mussolini."

Lanny planned to take no part in the conversation, but to devote himself to studying the Italian as well as the shadows permitted. It appeared as if his ego had expanded at the idea that his fame had spread so far; but then he decided that this was beneath the dignity of a man of destiny. An upper-class Englishman was trying to flatter the founder of *Fascismo* in the effort to get an interview! He remarked in a cold voice: "It is to be doubted if you English can learn the lessons of our movement, because your democratic capitalism represents a stage of social degeneration."

"That may be," said Rick, politely. "Of course if it were so, I should hardly know it."

"That is true," admitted the other. "But what can I do about that?"

To one who had nothing to do but listen and watch, it became clear that the man was playing a part which was difficult for him; a person with a strong sense of inferiority, he was lifting himself by the straps of his boots. His rudeness betrayed self-distrust; his violence was a product of fear. "He's a bounder!" thought Lanny.

Rick went on unruffled. "I hear contradictory statements about your movement, Signor. They tell me that it is anti-capitalist, and yet I find many of the capitalist class who support it ardently. Will you explain that to me?"

"They have perceived that the future is in our hands, because we represent the vital elements of the new, awakening Italy. We are the youth—or those among them who are not satisfied with stale words and formulas, but believe in action and in new fortunes to be won."

The founder of *Fascismo* was launched upon one of his orations. He had been delivering them once a week in his paper, ever since the war. He had been delivering them to his *squadristi*, the young men of Italy who had been trained in war and had been promised wealth and glory but had not got them, and were now organizing to help themselves. Their leader's ideas were a strange mixture of the revolutionary syndicalist anarchism whose formulas had been the mental pabulum of his youth, and the new nationalism which he had learned from the poet-aviator d'Annunzio and his Fiume raiders. If you could believe Barbara, the blacksmith's son had collected large sums of money for the support of the poet and had used them for his own movement. The ego of Benito Mussolini would bear no rival near the throne.

VII

The leader's French was inadequate to the explaining of these complex ideas, and he would use Italian words, and then forget and break into Italian. Lanny ventured to stop him, saying: "Pardon, Signor, my friend does not understand your language, and my own is unfortunately bad. However, if you will speak slowly, I will endeavor to translate."

The orator could not admit that his French was defective, and resumed speaking it. He explained his belief that violence is a sign of virility, and that any society in which it does not have its way is bound to degenerate. "I see that you have been reading Sorel," ventured Rick.

"I do not have to go to Sorel for knowledge," replied Mussolini, with a thrust of his jaw. "I was a pupil of Pareto, in Lausanne."

Rick asked him about the application of violence in the daily affairs of the Italian workers, and the leader made no bones about admitting that he and his *fasci di combattimento* were using it in abundance. "Italy has been kept in chaos by the Reds for three years, and we are giving them doses of their own medicine."

"And when you have put them down, what then?"

"Ours is no mere movement of repression, but an awakening of those elements which alone are capable of reconstructing *la patria*."

"Just what is to be the nature of your construction?"

"A state in which all the various social groups have their proper places and perform their assigned functions under the direction of their leader."

"That being yourself?"

"Who else could it be?" This with another thrust of the jaw and a straightening of the shoulders. "You do not believe that I can do these things?"

Said Rick: "You would hardly be interested in the opinion of a representative of a degenerating society."

It was the sort of reply the editor had been wont to exchange in the days when he was a Socialist intellectual, sipping his red wine in the *trattorie*. For a few minutes he forgot that he was a man of destiny, being interviewed for posterity; he relaxed on his throne and crossed his legs, arguing with two bright young fellows who might be turned into disciples. "You will have to learn from us," he announced. "Our *Fascismo* is not for export; but you will have to devise some remedy of your own for the contradictions which bourgeois democracy is developing."

"*Sì, Signor*," said Rick. "But what if the ambitions of your Italian Fascism happen to clash with those of French imperialism, or German, for example?"

"There is enough and plenty to go round."

"Enough of what, exactly?" It was a trap question. Could it be that what this blacksmith's son from the Romagna had in mind was to divide the colonial possessions of the degenerating British Empire?

"The world is large," said the leader, smiling, "and the future is not easy to foresee. Tell me, are you going back to lie about me, as so many other journalists have done?"

This was meant for a diversion, and it served. "I am not that sort of journalist, Signor. I shall report exactly what I have seen and heard."

"Do you express no opinions of your own?"

"... ometimes—but always making plain that it is opinion and ... ng else."

"... nd what will you say is your opinion of *Fascismo?*"

"... was a condescension. The ego of the one-time proletarian starveling could not repress a desire for applause from a son of the effete British aristocracy! "May I speak frankly?" inquired Rick.

"What else would be of interest to me?"

"Well, I am struck by the resemblance of your technique to that of Bolshevism, which you so despise. In many ways you speak like a pupil of Lenin rather than Pareto."

"You are a shrewd young man. But why should I not learn from Lenin how to fight Lenin? If I capture a gun from a foe, shall I refrain from using it because it is the foe's invention?"

"I see," said Rick. "Would it be correct to say that your move-

this agreement—and now they wanted to strip the nation of her last means of security!

So said a member of Briand's delegation in the drawing-room of Bienvenu; sitting in the same chair that Rathenau had occupied—though he didn't know it. He was talking to M. Rochambeau, the kindly and well-informed diplomat; and Marie was listening, deeply impressed by what her country's statesman was saying. For several days Lanny had been realizing that she was less and less pleased with what the other ladies were doing; that what they considered triumphs seemed like defeats to her. After this talk she came to him and said: "I think it would be better if I went and stayed a few days with my aunt. I am sure you will understand."

"Is it that bad, dear?"

"I just can't go on pretending that I agree with your mother and her friends; and when I keep silent, I wonder if I am shutting my lips too tightly and making myself look disagreeable. I'm not a skilled actress, and I can't be happy pretending what I don't feel. Let me say that Aunt Juliette is not well."

A little cloud, no bigger than a man's hand; and Lanny brushed it away quickly. Of course, it would be perfectly all right; the darned conference would be over and they could all forget politics and be happy again; they would live in art, which was the same to English and French and Germans and Americans, a garden of delight with none of its delicious fruits forbidden.

So Marie made her excuse—and of course didn't fool the mistress of Bienvenu for a single moment. "She's a French patriot," thought Beauty; "a Nationalist, like her husband."

When Lanny came back she said this to him, and he answered: "Oh, surely not that bad!"

"As bad as Poincaré!" insisted the mother. "They're all getting ready to invade Germany. You'll see!"

IX

The conspiracy was marching hour by hour. Rathenau's associates came to Bienvenu, and it happened that the majestic Lord Curzon, that very superior purzon, dropped in, purely by accident. Also came the American ambassador to London, Colonel Harvey; another "Kentucky" title, like that of Colonel House, but the new ambassador took it seriously and could equal any British viscount in self-importance. He had been a New York editor, and boasted of having been the first to suggest the president of Princeton University for President of the United States; but when the campaign had got under way, Wilson had become worried as to Harvey's connections with the unpopular House of Morgan, and had asked him to withdraw from the limelight. So now the Wall Street colonel was a Republican, and Harding had given him the most highly valued of all diplomatic prizes. He was supposed to be in Cannes only as an "observer," but he was doing what he could to get trade with Europe started up again.

Meanwhile the French statesmen were repairing to Sept Chênes, and there too the British were dropping in, purely by accident, and Lloyd George was explaining that he didn't really mean all the harsh things he had said, but it was necessary to satisfy the *Times*. It was while Emily Chattersworth was giving a luncheon for Briand and Lloyd George that the latter sprang his invitation to a game of golf, and it was hard for her to keep her face straight when the French Premier accepted—yes, for that very afternoon! It actually came off, and was the joke of the Riviera for several hours—that is, until Paris was heard from! One can readily believe that the innkeeper's son cut no graceful figure with a golf club in his hands; he had no idea how to hold it, and this showed plainly in the pictures of which the papers were full.

But Briand enjoyed it; he was something of a gay dog, and liked to be conspicuous, and his lack of subtlety kept him from being sure whether people were laughing with him or at him. He was overworked, and glad to get out into the sunshine; he was followed by a crowd of curious spectators, kept at a respectful distance by detectives but making the scene pleasant with their bright costumes.

When he and the genial Prime Minister sat down to rest between holes, Lloyd George said that he had just had a chat with Rathenau, who was really a decent fellow and an author of some distinction—

why couldn't he and Briand have a private meeting and at least try to understand each other's point of view? Was it the sunshine, or the personal charm of the Welsh wizard, or perhaps the ineffable prestige of the British ruling class? Anyhow, in a burst of good nature Briand said all right, but where on the Riviera could they meet without a scandal? Lloyd George said he would undertake to arrange that, and a tentative date was made for five o'clock on the following afternoon.

Whereupon Bienvenu was thrown into the greatest turmoil of its twenty years' history. British emissaries arriving, French and German secretaries, police agents, secret-service men, all whispering together, and conferring with the hostess and her intelligent son—whom none of them had happened to observe in conference with an Italian syndicalist-anarchist on the beach at Juan-les-Pins! Lanny took them for a tour of the estate, and showed them the rear gate, which was on another road; it was his suggestion that the German minister and his aides should drive along this road and stop in front of the gate and slip in quietly while the car went on. They would have quite a walk to the house, but Dr. Rathenau was an active man, his secretary said. The French Premier would be driven in at the front gate and then it would be locked, and the walls patrolled from the inside, and neither anarchists nor newspapermen would get over.

Lanny had never seen his mother in such a flutter. Emily and Sophie Timmons had to come and advise her what to wear, and what kind of sandwiches to serve, and what color flowers for the drawing-room. She couldn't invite them to be present—the agreement was that nobody but herself and her son and her servants should be in the house. No, not even Kurt, there wouldn't be any opportunity for music this time; the destinies of Europe were going to be decided, and peace, real peace, would at last be worked out between France and Germany. Beauty had always wanted peace, even while she wanted also to sell guns! "Why, Lanny," she exclaimed, in the small hours of the morning, "Bienvenu will have a place in the history books!"

Yes, it was true! They would have a brass plaque made and set up beside the front door: "In this house, January 11, 1922, the Premier of France, Aristide Briand, met with Walther Rathenau, German Minister of Reconstruction, and arranged the terms of reconciliation between the two countries." "How's that?" asked Lanny; and his excited mother kissed him and cried: "Oh, you darling!"

X

But alas for the best-laid schemes o' mice an' men! Just when the last of the sandwiches had been made and wrapped in oil paper to keep them fresh; when the wine had been packed in ice and the flower arrangements in the various rooms completed; when the hairdresser had started on Beauty's coiffure, and the maid was laying the proper dress on the bed—right at that instant came the most desolating of messages ever heard over a telephone wire: M. Briand's secretary, grief-stricken to announce that the Premier was compelled to leave immediately for Paris, there being a Cabinet crisis which required his presence without a moment's delay.

All on account of that wretched game of golf—or at any rate that is what Beauty Budd would believe until her dying day. When the pictures had reached Paris a howl of rage had arisen. Young and old, rich and poor, male and female, all admitted with humiliation and shame that the British were making a monkey out of their national leader. Golf is not a French game; there was no French game at a time like this, with widows mourning by the millions and tragedy hanging over the land. Was that the way the destinies of *la patrie* were being decided?—between two games of golf—or between a game of golf and a cup of tea—the journalists didn't seem to agree which way it had been.

The guilty statesman was summoned home—for the Riviera wasn't really France, it was a playground rented or sold to the international idlers. The guilty statesman stood up in the Chamber and defended himself in a long speech, which seemed to everybody a defense of Germany rather than of France; it was full of unpleasant figures, which meant that the people had been cheated ever since the war, that their foes had got away with everything, and there was no way *la patrie* could be recouped or saved. They had won the war but lost the peace, and now they had to decide whether to do it all over again!

Like a thunderbolt hitting one of the chimneys on top of Bienvenu came the news that Briand was out. Resigned, either in a fit of pique or because he saw that his foes had him! And all those intrigues and all those appeasements which had been arranged by Beauty and Emily and Sophie and Nina—all scattered like a house of cards in a hurricane!

The news reached the Cannes conference just as Walther Rathenau was in the midst of another of his elegantly polished speeches. It was hardly worth while finishing; everything was ended now, Poincaré was going to be the next Premier of France, and there would be no more conferences—so he had said, he wouldn't attend 'em! The Germans could go home and find some way to raise the money, or else there would be "sanctions," French troops marching into German cities, and we'll see who won the peace! And no brass plaque by the door of Bienvenu, and nobody to admire the flower arrangements, nobody to eat the sandwiches except the children of Mme. Scelles's school for French orphans—sandwiches don't keep, as everyone knows, and Beauty was sick at heart and done with hospitality forever, so she swore!

For the second time in his young life Lanny Budd had made an attempt to improve the nations, and they had stubbornly remained what they were. Once more he had to retire into his ivory tower, where he could have things as he wanted them; once more he reminded himself that the great masters of the arts were his servants always on call. His German friend had the same reaction; having had brief glimpses of the men who were running the world, he had decided that he preferred the three B's of music. Lanny's French *amie* was humble and apologetic; glad that the Cannes conspiracy had failed, but trying to hide the fact, and by sympathy and kindness to make up for her political intransigence.

Rick was the only one who got anything real out of Cannes. He wrote a coldly ironical article about the conference, and it was published. He wrote also an account of *Fascismo* and the interview with its founder, but this Rick's editor rejected; the article was well written, he reported, but that Italian bounder didn't seem of enough importance to justify the space.

13

The World's Mine Oyster

I

IN THE month of February the Washington Disarmament Conference concluded its labors. Robbie sent information about it, including a letter which he had written to one of the New York newspapers. Said the spokesman of Budd Gunmakers: "It is hard for a sane man to realize that there are people in the world who believe that a nation can keep out of war by being unprepared for war." He was so wrought up about the destruction of the American fleet—so it seemed to him—that he spent a week in Washington, pleading with senators against the ratification of the agreement, but all in vain. "The fools have the votes," he said; "they generally do."

This conference was the achievement of a Wall Street lawyer named Hughes, who had become a Supreme Court justice and was now Harding's Secretary of State. He was the stubborn Baptist type of mind—"Ask Beauty about them," wrote Robbie; "her father is one." Hughes was putting the job through to his own satisfaction, and even the powerful Budd family was helpless. He cut the major navies of the world about in half, and in his closing speech he did not hesitate to make the flat declaration: "This conference absolutely ends the race in competition in naval armament."

Robbie marked that in a newspaper clipping, and wrote on the margin the word: "Jackass." His letter accompanying it was a lamentation in the tone of the Old Testament prophets. "We make claims, such as the Monroe Doctrine, which require arms to back them up, and then we deprive ourselves of the arms. If that is not the way to invite challenge and calamity, put me down for a madman." Lanny read this, and returned to the study of Beethoven's pianoforte sonatas, which he did not find up to the great master's standard.

II

Baby Marceline was four, and the grandson and namesake of Sir Alfred was a month or two older; this is the age when they ask questions, and there was not much peace for the adults of either family, except at siesta time and in the evenings. It became the practice to lend them out, each to the other family, so that Alfy could answer Marceline's questions and vice versa. Lanny would play the piano for them, or put on phonograph records and dance with them, so by now he had a miniature Isadora school. He would listen to their prattle, and start life all over again, marveling at the strangeness of it; these little centers of expanding consciousness, like buds in spring sunshine, bursting with eagerness, with determination; so full of trust in life, so unaware of tragedies which might lie before them! A voyage in the dark, over an invisible sea, from one unknown port to another!

The young philosopher had observed that the children of the rich at this age appeared to be perfect. From their first hour they had expert guidance and the best of food and care; nature and art had combined to do all things possible for them. But from this age on there would begin a change; the needs of the mind were less easy to meet than those of the body. Being waited upon by servants didn't seem to be good for children; having their own way wasn't good; seeing their parents' self-indulgence wasn't good. By the age of fifteen many of them had become intolerable. Lanny looked back and decided that he himself hadn't done so well; he knew that his life had been too easy, and it still was—but how could he make it hard? He read stories of the Great Lord Buddha, and of St. Francis d'Assisi and others who had been born to riches and had cast them away; he decided that he might dare to do it, if only it wouldn't hurt his parents and his friends so deeply!

Marceline Detaze wasn't going to be spoiled so long as that stern German taskmaster lived in the house. Since the dreadful night when he had rushed away, Beauty had been more afraid of him than ever. She no longer had the idea that he would leave her for some other woman, but she was sure that he would go in a moment if his conscience so directed; if she failed to conform to his standards, to live what he considered a worthy life. That was one reason why she had worked so hard during the conference; if she could render a real service to Germany, Kurt would remember it all his days. He didn't blame her for the failure, but it was hard on her because he shut himself up in his music and was more than ever indifferent to the fashionable world.

Beauty could stand being a housekeeper and a mother for just so long, and then she had to be a butterfly and have a flutter over the social garden. She had to do something that would bring a crowd of people to Bienvenu and provide an excuse to buy a pretty new frock and call in a hairdresser and a caterer. She would invite people to listen to Kurt's playing, and some of them would prefer their own chatter, and Kurt's reaction would be the same as that of his idol Beethoven: "*Ich spiele nicht für solche Schweinen!*"

There was Emily Chattersworth with that beautful estate of Sept Chênes; willing to put it and all her social power at the disposal of a musician whom she admired. She would be going north before long, so it was now or never, and Beauty started agitating with Kurt to let them arrange a recital. Kurt said, what good would it do? The French weren't ever going to appreciate his music, nor would the sort of Americans who came to a casino town to gamble and play tennis and golf. What he was interested in was the fact that a publishing-house in Leipzig might bring out his *Spanish Suite;* that was a sign of hope reviving in Germany—but how in God's name could anybody know what price to print on a piece of sheet music, with the mark standing lower every afternoon than it had in the morning?

Beauty wouldn't give up. Suppose that just one person enjoyed

Kurt's playing? Suppose that one critic came and went out and wrote about him—wouldn't that be worth while? It was the same argument that she had had with Marcel, over and over, year after year. What was the matter with artists, that they wanted to paint pictures for storerooms and compose music for the bottom of an old trunk? Kurt said: "Why don't you start promoting Marcel?"—which was rather cruel of him, for her hesitations were caused in part by the fear that it might not be pleasing to Kurt himself. Marcel was France, and Kurt was Germany, and the war was still going on—even though it was called "reparations."

III

In the matter of the recital, Lanny took his mother's side, and finally Kurt said all right, he would come and play whenever he was asked to play, and give them the best he had. It meant that he had to go into Cannes and have himself fitted with heavy black evening clothes of the latest cut, with black silk braid down the trousers. That's the way they dressed a piano virtuoso, having not the remotest conception of the gymnastic feats he was going to perform, and the lather of perspiration into which he would be thrown. But never mind, he was young, and when he got home he could have a bath, and if the suit was damaged, Beauty would gladly pay the price for so much glory.

Mrs. Emily sent out her invitations—and never had she spent so much time upon the compiling of a list. There were all sorts of distinguished persons wintering on the Côte d'Azur that season. The lanky King of Sweden played tennis every afternoon, and Aga Khan, one of the richest men in India, rode polo ponies. There were several Russian grand dukes in exile, who would go wherever there were pretty women. There was the English Lord Derby, who looked like a caricature of John Bull, and King Alfonso of Spain, who looked like a caricature of his Habsburg ancestors. There were fabulously wealthy Argentinians and North Americans, Rumanian boyars and Turkish pashas, and even the King of Dahomey, whose black troops had helped to make the world safe for democracy.

Beauty knew a whole raft of such persons, having cultivated them for Robbie's business; but it was hard to be sure how they would behave at a musicale—they might come thinking it was a cocktail party and be bored and show it. What Kurt desired was a gathering of music lovers, and the problem was to find celebrities who could qualify in that field. Dear old Anatole France would come, of course, and sit and nod his long horse's head surmounted with one of his hundred brightly colored silk skullcaps. Maeterlinck was in Nice, but he was rather *passé*, wasn't he? Besides, a Belgian might not yet have forgiven the Germans. Blasco Ibáñez, the Spaniard, lived at Menton in exile, and his war novels were having amazing success in the United States, but Emily had sworn that she would never invite him again, because he had spat on one of her carpets.

Invitations to Sept Chênes were usually accepted, so there were a hundred or so of Europe's most eminent, and Kurt played his own compositions—not too long ones, his friends had cautioned him. It was music in the old tradition, yet its content was new; if there were any in position to understand what an ex-artillery officer was trying to say, they learned that life had given him chaos and grief, and that he had wrestled with them in agony of soul and tried to make some order and beauty out of them. What most of those present got was that he made a tremendous racket and gave them very few tunes that they could carry off and whistle. However, it was plain that a man had to work hard to bring all that out of a piano, to say nothing of composing it. It might be that he was really a genius, and it wouldn't do to guess wrong, so they applauded cordially and the evening was a success.

Beauty Budd—who was said to be his mistress—was never more lovely or more happy. After all the honors had been done she wrapped him in a warm overcoat and blanket and took him home in a closed car, and there he stripped off his cold clammy things and got into a hot bath, and while he lay there, she rattled away about all the famous persons who had been present, and what this one and that one had said to her, and to Emily and Nina and Marie and Sophie. It would take Kurt's *amoureuse* a full week to collect all the gossip and retail it to the family.

IV

Before the Cannes conference had broken up it had called another to be held at Genoa early in April; and Rick said that he would have to attend this. As it happened to be Easter time, Marie was planning to go north to be with her boys. She had decided that she didn't care for conferences, she didn't like the sort of people she met there or the things they said about France. But she knew that Lanny enjoyed them, and felt that it was his duty to help his friend, so she told him that he was not to miss it on her account. Lanny was in something of a quandary; but the matter was settled by a cablegram from Robbie, saying that he was on his way to Genoa and would be in Juan in a few days. Dates with Robbie took precedence over everything else because they were so scarce.

Robbie Budd was putting on weight. He had passed mid-forty, and no longer played polo or any such violent game; he said that during the winter he had got most of his exercise by letting a masseur knead and punch him. When he arrived at Juan he was as eager as a boy to get into the water, and Lanny saw once more that sturdy hairy frame which had so delighted him all through his childhood and youth. The post-war bathing-suits were getting scantier every season, and you could see a lot of Beauty, who was proud of her slimness; Lanny teased her by telling Robbie that all the credit for it belonged to Kurt. A piano virtuoso also cut a good figure in a bathing-suit, but Kurt would never leave off the upper part because of the caved-in place in his side where the pieces of ribs had been shot away.

Lanny was curious as to why his father was troubling to attend one of these international diplomatic affairs. They went for a long sail together and, thus protected from prying ears, Robbie revealed a curious situation: he was going Bolshevik! Of course in a strictly proper, business way, but even so it represented a tremendous condescension for him and his "syndicate," those friends who had put money into oil with him and were now making a good thing of it in spite of the depression. One feature which distinguished this Genoa conference from the preceding ones was that the Germans and Russians had been invited to attend on equal terms with the Allies. It was Lloyd George's dream of a general and complete pacification of Europe, a conference to end conferences; the Russians were going to be taken back into the family of business nations, and it would mean rich pickings for whoever was first on the ground and had the energy to break through the barriers.

"So," said the man of guns and oil, "your Red friends may be of some use to themselves, if they know which side their bread is buttered on. Do you know whether Lincoln Steffens will be at Genoa?"

"I had a note from him," admitted Lanny; "but he didn't say. He was in the States."

"I saw him at the Washington conference; a queer-looking duck. If he should come to Genoa I'd like to meet him."

Lanny was embarrassed. He was quite sure that "Stef" wouldn't want to be used in an oil game; but it would be difficult to explain this to Robbie, who would probably think it was just naïveté on his son's part. Lanny devoted himself to asking questions, and trying to get the inside of this startling development.

According to Robbie's information, the Russians were in a desperate plight; their industry had been destroyed in the civil war, and how were they ever to get it started again? Millions of people had died of outright starvation during the past winter, and how were peasants without plows or horses going to get grain planted this spring? There was that huge oil-field in the Caucasus, one of the richest in the world; it was pretty much a wreck, and obviously the Bolsheviks couldn't get drilling-tools and pipes and tank-cars except from those industrial nations which made them. There was some kind of big deal being planned—the field was to be turned over to an international consortium, the Russians getting a share of the oil. Robbie didn't know the details—it was Standard Oil which had the inside track and had got the State Department behind it—but he was going to get the whole story before he had been very long in Genoa, and he had the idea that he'd find some back door that he could jimmy open, or some hole big enough for a little fellow to crawl through.

These phrases were Robbie's own, and indicated to his son that they were going to the ancient Italian city on a burglary expedition, and that the son was to have an opportunity to serve as a "finger-man" or something of that sort. The United States was now under a regime of Prohibition, which meant that gentlemen like Robbie Budd had to buy their liquor from bootleggers, and these latter were becoming wealthy and powerful, and developing a culture and language of their own. Lanny had never met any of them, but there existed a machinery whereby their slang was spread throughout the civilized world with extraordinary speed. There was a cinema in Cannes which showed American movies, and any evening that Lanny felt the need of recreation he could enter for a couple of francs, and acquire from the "titles" the very latest up-to-the-minute phrases of Broadway and Forty-Second Street. So now he understood that his father was going to Genoa to get the "right dope" and to "muscle in" on the "racket" of the "big shot"—who in this particular melodrama went by the name of "Standard."

V

The expedition set out, Lanny driving his father in the front seat and Rick in the rear with the luggage. They were going to stop off in "Monty" for a conference with Zaharoff, and Lanny was seeking in his mind for a tactful way to convey to Rick the fact that Robbie couldn't invite him in. But the most punctilious of Englishmen volunteered: "I hope you don't mind if I don't go in, because some day I may want to write about Zaharoff, and if I met him through you my hands would be tied." So Rick sat in the car and read an English magazine; when he was tired of that he strolled to the edge of the embankment, and looked down upon the tiers of house-roofs and the bay, and listened to the sounds of the pigeon-shooting below.

In the previous year the old Greek trader had put on a white satin undercoat and trunk-hose, a plumed hat and white boots with red tops, and a crimson velvet robe lined with white, and had been formally inducted as a Knight Commander of the Bath; so now you addressed him as "Sir Basil." They were going to find a badly worried old bathing-master, Robbie said, for the Washington conference had knocked the props from under armament shares, and Vickers had suffered worst of all. They had turned to the making of elevators and freight-cars and oil-pipe and a thousand things, like Budd's; but where could you find anybody with money to buy them? The world's masters had come to such a desperate pass that they were even thinking of lending money to Bolsheviks—of course on their promise to forget their evil doctrines!

The ex-army officer secretary ushered them into Sir Basil's study, which had a window-box where some of the duquesa's tulips were performing their annual duty, each according to the laws of its being and heedless of all the others. Their master, of whose existence they knew nothing, was performing according to the laws of his being, which required him to plot and scheme day and night, spreading vast networks of intrigue in order to acquire pieces of engraved paper certifying to his ownership of properties in many parts of the world. A strange and mystifying thing called "power," which caused hundreds of thousands, perhaps millions, of men to obey his will, even though few of them had ever seen him and most had never heard his name.

Did it make him happy? Did it make a *bybloem* happy to select certain chemicals from rich garden soil and construct a blossom of pure white with great purple streaks? The young philosopher decided that there must be something in the tulip which brought satisfaction when it achieved exactly the right shade, and there must be something in an old Greek trader that stirred with pleasure when he put one more engraved certificate into a security box. But certainly this did not affect his features, which showed heavy strain, or his voice, which, though always gentle, was full of complaint about what was happening to his interests throughout the world. He was glad to see Robbie Budd and also his son, in whom he still saw the bright little boy who had stolen his letter and then apologized so gamely; but he had no sooner got them seated and served with drinks than he began lamenting the awful plight of the people of his homeland, who had got themselves launched upon a military adventure in the heart of the Anatolian hills, and no man alive could tell what the outcome was to be.

You could take whatever view you pleased of that Greco-Turkish war, which had now been going on for nearly two years. You could call the Turks semi-savages, and point to their hideous slaughters of Armenians and of Greeks wherever they got them in their power; thus you could think of the Greeks as emissaries of civilization—and if you happened to be one of them, and to be the richest man in Europe, with great arms plants in scores of different places, you could pour out tens of millions of dollars and keep their armies fed and supplied in the heart of Turkey, even after they had lost a great battle. But Robbie professed to know about the concessions which Zaharoff had been promised in return for all the Greek bonds he was buying, so to the American this was just one more business venture —and one that had gone sour. Hadn't the old devil begun his career as a salesman of armaments by going to his Greek government and persuading it to buy a Nordenfeldt submarine, and then going to the Turkish government and persuading it to acquire two submarines in order to be safe from the Greeks?

But of course Robbie didn't give any hint of all this in a business conference. He listened with sympathy while Zaharoff lamented the split between the British and the French over the Greco-Turkish issue. Zaharoff was a Grand Officer of the Légion d'Honneur as well as a Knight Commander of the Bath, and he desired amity between the two great Allies, the pillars of Christian civilization, as he called them; but the Poincaré government was persisting in arming the Turks, and in spite of Lloyd George's promises the British government took only a half-hearted interest—in short, they left the conquest of Turkey to their Knight Commander, who had spent a good half of his fortune on a private war and, if it weren't for his oil interests, would now actually be hard pressed for cash.

VI

All this, presumably, to explain why Zaharoff was intent on getting more oil as quickly as possible. Robbie had his own reasons for wanting some, and so the two men of affairs got down to business. Zaharoff didn't mention, as he had on previous occasions, that Robbie's son must be careful and not talk about his father's affairs; that went without saying, Lanny having now attained his full majority and being here presumably as his father's lieutenant. Zaharoff talked about the various interests which would be represented at Genoa—you'd have thought it was going to be an oil conference instead of a political one. Deterding's men would be there, and Zaharoff named them, and explained his relationship with Deterding, who was Royal Dutch Shell and could be trusted a certain distance, but no farther. Anglo-Persian would be there, and Deterding was trying to get hold of its shares which the British government held, but Zaharoff had a clear understanding with both Lloyd George and Curzon, the British Foreign Minister, that the Dutchman wasn't going to get them. Standard would be there, in the person of an A. C. Bedford, and Robbie probably knew their crowd better than Zaharoff did—but it turned out that Zaharoff was the one who knew everybody better.

In short, the old Greek trader had all the data and had saved Robbie the need of taking notes by having the data typed out. He showed papers which he couldn't possibly have come by honestly, and this was taken for granted between the two as they talked; there would be more acquiring of papers and bribing of servants and so on at Genoa. Lanny learned something that his father had neglected to mention, that among those present would be the ex-cowboy Bub Smith, whom Robbie had used to demonstrate the Budd guns, and who had been his secret man watching Zaharoff's companies during the war. Whether Zaharoff knew that wasn't mentioned, and apparently it wouldn't have mattered—Bub was a dependable man, and was going to watch some very tricky ones in Genoa.

Among them, Lanny gathered, was the American ambassador to Italy; his name was Child, and he was a novelist—Lanny recalled having read several of his short stories in magazines. Why had President Harding appointed a flighty literary fellow to this high diplomatic post? There must be some reason, and Robbie would find it out, for he had letters to him. "But don't let him get any hint about me," said Sir Basil, and Robbie said: "Of course not." The ambassador, going officially as an "observer," would doubtless have a staff, and Robbie would find a way to get next to some of them.

Lanny became somewhat uncomfortable as this long interview proceeded; he perceived that his father had become Zaharoff's "man," and that the latter was making no bones about giving him orders. Quite a difference from the time, eight or nine years ago, when the armaments king had suggested Vickers' buying out Budd's, and Robbie had graciously replied that Budd's might prefer to consider buying out Vickers! What had happened to make the difference? Was it the hard times, which had hit Budd's so hard and made profits scarcer? Had Zaharoff held out such rewards that Robbie and his associates couldn't refuse them? Had Robbie got in deeper than he intended, and was he now caught in the spider's web? He seemed quite at ease and satisfied with what he was doing, but Lanny knew that he was proud and wouldn't reveal his troubles if he had any. Whatever happened, Robbie must think that Lanny thought his father a great businessman and master of everything he touched!

Zaharoff was making plain the supreme importance of what was to be done at Genoa. Two years previously, at San Remo, Britain and France had agreed to the dividing of the Mosul oil, and Zaharoff had been in on both portions; but later on, after President Harding had come in, America, in the shape of Standard, had "muscled in" and grabbed a share. That must surely not be allowed to happen again! Zaharoff and Deterding and their associates—which included Robbie Budd's syndicate—were going to get whatever was obtainable of the oil of Baku and Batum, and Zaharoff was going to be sitting right here, pulling the strings and making sure that nothing was overlooked. He was going to have a courier coming every day to bring him news, and there was to be a code which Robbie was to keep on his person—apparently the old spider had sat and devised that code looking at the duquesa's flower-box, for Deterding the Dutchman was to be "Bybloem," and Lloyd George was to be "Bizarre," which is another variety of tulip. The old rascal had a sense of humor, too, for Viscount Curzon of Kedleston was to be "Ineffable," and Richard Washburn Child, United States Envoy Extraordinary and Minister Plenipotentiary to the Kingdom of Italy, was "Cradle!"

VII

The gossips told a story about how this conference had come to be called in a city of Italy. Someone had suggested it under the French name of Gênes, and Lloyd George had understood this to mean Geneva, and had consented accordingly: a neutral city, the home of the League of Nations. Only after arrangements had been made did he discover that Geneva is Genève, and that his conference was to be held under the auspices of a people which was far from international in its mind, and in a city crowded and far from comfortable for elder statesmen!

Genoa is a really old Mediterranean city. It has a fine harbor, which was used before the memory of mankind, but it has very little land, because the Ligurian Alps come crowding down to the sea, and the streets and alleys of the town have to go scrambling up them on steep stairways, and over bridges where there are ravines. So the buildings are tall, even the old ones, and crowded together, and there are many parts of the city where vehicles cannot go. Fortunately for Rick, the Palazzo di San Giorgio, where the conference met, was down near the harbor; a dark, melancholy Gothic building six or seven centuries old, which had long been the home of the Bankers' Guild of the city.

Twenty-nine nations of Europe had been invited to the gathering. The Italian government had taken charge of the occasion and commandeered all the hotels, but Robbie had brought a secretary and sent him on ahead to make arrangements, so everything was comfortable for the little party. There was Bub, the funny-looking fellow with the broken nose that he had never bothered to have fixed; he was full of important news, and went into a huddle with his boss while Lanny drove Rick to the Casa della Stampa, the club set apart for journalists. Rick had only to present his credentials, and he and his friend were admitted, and there were all the old gang and a lot of newcomers; greetings and introductions being exchanged, and gossip going at full blast.

International conferences had by now become an institution; this was number seven on Lanny's list, if you counted two in Paris and one in Geneva. For him they were a delightful spectacle, a refined sort of Roman holiday in which you were spared the sight and smell of blood, though you knew it was being shed freely. For the journalist it was hard work, but also sport, a hunting expedition in which each dreamed of bagging a creature with a priceless pelt known as a "scoop." Each news-hunter tried to get as much as he could from the others and give as little; but since the only way to get was to give, there was a torrent of talk.

The fashion was to be "hard-boiled." The world could not be worse than these men thought it, conferences couldn't be more futile, conferees more stupid or tricky. The newsmen always predicted the worst—and so far their prophecies had been justified. Lanny and Rick preferred the Americans, because their point of view was more aloof, they were freer to say what they thought, both in conversation and in cabling. Now and then, however, Rick would decide that it was too easy to be cynical about the problems of Europe, and he would seek the company of some reserved and careful Englishman. The French and Italians one met less freely, because their points of view were apt to be official.

Lloyd George and Poincaré had had a meeting at Boulogne prior to this conference, and the former had been forced to agree that the question of reparations was not to be raised. That, everybody said, was like playing *Hamlet* without the ghost. The French Premier was refusing to attend, but had sent his Foreign Minister, and was so afraid that this Barthou might fall under the spell of the Welsh wizard that he was sending him a dozen telegrams of instructions every day—actually he sent more than a thousand during the course of the affair!

When Lanny had had his fill of international intrigues he would go out for a walk on the funny cobbled streets of this half-medieval city. The principal ones were beflagged for the occasion, and the cab-drivers wore ribbons dangling from their hats—Lanny didn't know whether that was a general custom or a special honor. At night everything was brilliantly illuminated, and the streets crowded with a holiday throng; girls and soldiers and carabinieri everywhere. There was opera every night, and dancing until morning in the cafés and the *boîtes de nuit*. Lanny looked at sixteenth-century churches with façades in stripes of black and white marble; he went through palaces in which the gentlemen of Shakespeare's plays might have lived their tangled plots. Now the stage was bigger and the plots much harder to follow. How would a playwright manage to put twenty-nine nations into a drama? All the world was a stage in a sense that no sixteenth-century playwright could have dreamed!

VIII

Three years had passed since Lanny had seen Lincoln Steffens, but he didn't look any older; his little gray mustache and goatee appeared to have been trimmed by the same barber, and his quiet business suit to have been cut by the same tailor. He was still the quizzical-kind philosopher, amusing himself with other people's intellectual confusion. They ran into each other in the Casa della Stampa, and Stef took him off to lunch, because he had been drawn to this amiable playboy and wanted to find out what life had been doing to him. "Have you made up your mind to anything yet?" he asked, and Lanny, knowing the game, countered: "Have you?" The other said: "I don't have to. I'm a philosopher." Lanny replied: "I've decided that that's what I am."

In the inexhaustible library of his great-great-uncle, Lanny had come upon the *Dialogues* of Plato, and it seemed to him that Stef must have taken these as the model of his conversation. You'd have thought it was Socrates asking you questions, always friendly but searching your mind, leading you to the point where you realized that you didn't know what you were talking about. But never would he tell you that; you would see it. Never would he say: "Don't you perceive that inconsistency?" The time would come when you would begin to stammer and apologize for your own confusion of mind.

Lanny was in a trying position here in Genoa, having to keep one large part of his thoughts from Robbie and another large part from Rick. He wanted very much to be honest, and suddenly he blurted out: "See here, Stef, will you let me tell you something frankly?"

"Of course," said the other. Looking at this handsome youth with all the signs of wealth on him, he asked: "Are you in love?"

"Indeed I am," said Lanny, "but I don't make any problem of that. It's my father, and our business here in Genoa. Will you keep it to yourself, please?"

"Shoot!" said Stef.

"Well, you know about Budd's; and now my father has gone in for oil, and he's here on business."

"The town is full of them. What is it the Bible says: 'Wheresoever the carcase is, there will the eagles be gathered together'?"

"You know, Robbie has always taught me to hate the Reds. He raised merry hell with me in Paris because I met you and my Uncle Jesse. I got into a scrape with the Paris police that I never had a chance to tell you about. The result was that I had to swear off on meeting any more Bolsheviks."

"And you're breaking the rule now?"

"No, it's just the other way. The Bolsheviks have oil."

'Oh, I see!" exclaimed the muckraker, much amused.

'Now my father wants to meet them. He even wants to meet you."

"Well, why not, Lanny? I'd be glad to meet him."

"But you see, he won't be interested in your ideas the least bit."

"How can you be sure?"

"Because—I know Robbie. He's here on business."

"Listen," said the muckraker. "You never read any of my books, did you?"

"I'm ashamed to say I haven't."

"They're not easy to find any more. But see if you can get a copy of *The Shame of the Cities*. You'll see how, twenty years ago, I used to travel round and interview the toughest guys—the political bosses, and the businessmen who paid them and used them. There were some cases where they wouldn't let me quote them, but I can't recall a single case where they refused to talk to me frankly and tell me what they were doing—some of the very worst things. The System, I called it, and they had been following it all their lives, but they didn't know it, and when I pointed it out to them, they were thunder-struck and thought I was some sort of wizard."

"I don't think you'll find Robbie as naïve as that; he knows what he is doing and he believes in it."

"Maybe so; but this is what I've discovered—honest confession is one of the greatest luxuries the human soul can enjoy. There are few of even the richest men in the world who feel they can afford it."

"All I can say is," said Lanny, "if you can break through my father's coat of chain mail, I'll give you a certificate as a real wizard."

"You arrange for me to have lunch with him—just us two. You keep away; for of course it would be something different if you were there, he has to play a part before you."

"What he really wants, Stef, is for you to introduce him to some of the Soviet representatives."

"Well, why not? He won't shoot them, will he?"

"He wants to get oil concessions."

"They have oil to sell, perhaps. Why shouldn't they meet him?"

"It's all right, only I wanted you to know what we are up to."

The muckraker took this with good humor. "Bless your heart, I wasn't born yesterday, and neither were the Russians. All I need say is 'American oil man,' and wink one eye, and they'll buckle on their chain mail. They can take care of themselves, believe me!"

IX

The luncheon took place next day, in a private room of that particular "grand hotel" in which the Budds were staying; and just what happened was a secret which those two so different warriors would carry to their graves. What Robbie said was: "That's a remarkable mind."

"You bet!" said Lanny.

"Of course," the other hastened to qualify, "it's easy for a man who sits aloof and criticizes, and won't take any stand one way or the other. If he had to act, he'd find he had to make up his mind what he really believes."

"I don't know," said Lanny. "It seems to me he has some very firm convictions."

"What, for example?"

"He believes in facing facts and not being fooled, by yourself or anybody else. It seems to me that's fundamental."

"Well, it's like a gun, or a typewriter, or any other instrument; it depends on what use you make of it after you get it."

Robbie didn't say anything about having made any confessions. Instead, he remarked, with quiet satisfaction: "I got what I was after. He has given me a letter to one of those Soviet people, a man named Krassin, who he says is their expert on foreign trade. Do you know anything about him?"

"He's just a name to me; but I'll see if I can find out. A lot of the newspapermen have been meeting them, and they talk freely."

Lanny, of course, made haste to see Stef again to inquire what happened. It was rather disappointing, for the muckraker said: "He's just like all the others: a man who is unhappy about the way the world is going, but can't bring himself to face the idea that he has any responsibility for it."

"Are you free to tell me about it?"

"I'm afraid not all of it. Your father is a very proud man, I would almost say arrogant; and of course he can't have his own way, so he's going to suffer like the devil."

"I know that," agreed Lanny. "I've known it since the war began. He hated that mess, yet he couldn't help knowing in his heart that he had had a share in bringing it on."

"I told him about elephant-hunting in Siam. He made me think of a powerful bull elephant that has just discovered that he's inside a stockade, and he runs here and there and hurls himself against the barriers until he almost breaks his neck."

"And Robbie took that?"

"I suppose he took it because he never expects to see me again. He probably wouldn't take it from you."

"I guess not!"

"I'll tell you one thing that's important to you," said Stef. "I brought him to admit that he has no right to dominate your thinking. I pointed out to him that it wasn't respecting your personality. I backed him down on that."

"Oh, Stef, I can't tell you what that would mean to me! I've been living in a sort of jail. Do you think he really means it?"

"He meant it when he said it. Whether he'll be able to live up to it is another question, of course."

X

On one of the decorated streets of festive Genoa Lanny ran into three of those Caucasian gentry in high black boots and large black astrakhan bonnets who, at the Paris Peace Conference, had put their excited faces close to his and enveloped him in a fine salivary spray, while telling him in atrocious French the sufferings of their country under the heel of Bolshevism. Now they were here, no longer as official representatives, but as exiles and outcasts; they had been sold out, and whoever got the oil of their native land would pay no royalties to them. Again they surrounded the amiable Lanny Budd and poured out their woes, and he had a hard time making clear to them that he no longer had an official position, was no longer any sort of pipeline for either news or propaganda.

All the little nations were here; they had been officially invited and their coming had been trumpeted; but now who was to pay any attention to them? Their broken and bankrupt peoples needed steel rails and freight-cars, plows and seeds, oil for their lamps and needles to mend their breeches—in short, money, money, money, and who was going to give or lend it? They were besieging the hotels and villas of statesmen, and making life miserable for secretaries; they were sitting in the cafés, drinking themselves melancholy, and ready to weep on the shoulder of any stranger who would listen. Especially they wanted to get hold of Americans, because America had all the money there was left in the world. Lloyd George had a marvelous new scheme for an international loan of two billion dollars for the reconstruction of Europe. America was to put up half;

and a dozen times Lanny was asked: What did he know about it? When would it be available? How would it be divided? Where did you go to get your share?

Painful to an idealistic youth to have to confess that he wasn't trying to help the world out of all these troubles! Painful to have to hear his own voice, speaking inside him: "I am one of the wolves, roaming the edges of the pack, looking for a stray or a weakling, a young one or an old that I can pick up! I am the son of a wolf; and no use telling myself that I don't like what my father wolf is doing, because I live on what he kills."

In short, there was a moral crisis in the soul of Lanny Budd. The Genoa conference was for him no holiday, but a time of inner strife and deep-seated unhappiness. Except for his brief talk with Stef he never mentioned it; and certainly his father did nothing to make it easier for him—for Robbie's mind was on the kill, and he had no time for foolishness. If he was aware that his son was disturbed over helping him to get an oil concession, he must have brushed it aside as something fanciful that a youngster would have to get over quickly. Time enough by and by to sit around and listen to radical chatter called "ideas"; but right now there was big money to be won or lost, and if Robbie needed an introduction he asked for it, if he needed information he asked Lanny to go and get it, and he didn't stop to say: "If you wouldn't mind," or: "If it would be consistent with your notions of delicacy and good taste."

So Lanny roamed the streets of this ancient city with a smoky fire of discontent inside him. Did he need so much money? Did anybody need it? Even granting that you needed it, did you have a right to wreck the world to get it? And after you had wrecked the world, did you have the right to call yourself a "practical man" and everybody else a "dreamer"? These questions had been shaping themselves in Lanny's mind for a matter of eight years—ever since July 31, 1914, to be exact.

Yes, it was a crisis. Hitherto Lanny had been ordered to think what he didn't want to think, and that had been trying enough; now he was ordered to say what he didn't want to say and to do what he didn't want to do, and that was far worse. He suddenly found himself thinking that this wonderful father who had been the ideal of his childhood and youth was somewhat of a bull-headed and insensitive person. Lanny still loved him, of course; that was what made it so miserable, so destructive of peace; it was possible to love your father, and still think such treasonable thoughts about him!

The thoughts took the form of imaginary dialogues, in which Lanny would say: "Look, Robbie, have you forgotten what your father did to you? He wrecked your whole life—so you told me many times—he made it impossible for you to be happy. And now are you going to do it to me?"

14

Blood of the Martyrs

I

LLOYD GEORGE set off the Genoa conference with one of his eloquent and most persuasive speeches. Where everybody else was worried and frightened, he was witty and gay. In his verbal flights he manifested both determination and generosity; this was the greatest gathering in Europe's history, he said, and the Continent was going to be restored. It was such good news that the delegates from twenty-nine nations arose and cheered him to the echo. Then, the ceremony over, the British delegation retired to their Villa d'Albertis and began wrangling with the French and Belgians over the conditions upon which a loan might be made to Russia; they continued this procedure for a matter of six weeks, when the conference came to an end with nothing accomplished.

At the first meeting with the Russians Lloyd George put in the

British claim against the country for British property damaged or confiscated; the amount was two thousand six hundred million pounds—quite a tidy sum which the Russians would kindly acknowledge as a debt. Chicherin, the Soviet Foreign Commissar and head of their delegation, replied courteously that they would be pleased to balance the claims against the Russian claims on the British government for damage done to Russia by British armies at Archangel and Murmansk, and by British-financed armies of Wrangel, Kolchak, and Yudenich, the total of which amounted to five thousand million pounds. After this exchange of bills due, the British retired for tea and the subject was dropped.

The French, of course, had a huge claim against Russia, the money which their bankers had lent to the Tsar. The Soviet's argument was that this money had been used to arm Russia for the benefit of France, and the debt had been paid by ten million lives. Also they advanced against the French a claim similar to that against Britain: Denikin's White Russian armies had been munitioned by France and guided by French officers, and they had ravaged the Ukraine for three dreadful years. Thus Bolshevik Russia *versus* bourgeois France, and on what basis could they settle such a quarrel?

Lloyd George, the practical fellow, said: "Let's forget the old claims, which the Russians are obviously in no position to meet. Let's get something real. Oil, for example! The Russians have it, and we can drill and pump it. Let's lease the district for a matter of ninety years, and pay with a part of the oil." But the stubborn Poincaré sat in his Paris office, poring day and night over his documents—he was a pasty-faced, pragmatical lawyer, and words were sacred to him, ancient bargains must be kept and ancient precedents followed. He made it a point of honor that the Bolsheviks should acknowledge the debt. Said the sarcastic Robbie Budd: "They should do what the French are doing to us—acknowledge, and then not pay!"

II

The Russians had been segregated at a little place called Santa Margherita, some twenty miles down the coast; they were in a comfortable hotel, but to reach it you had to travel by a slow train or motor on a dusty road. Robbie sent his letters of introduction to delegate Krassin, an appointment was made, and Lanny drove his father; they were escorted into the Russian's office, and Robbie got a jolt, for he had expected to meet a proletarian roughneck, and instead here was a tall, old-world aristocrat with fine features, coldly polite and reserved, speaking better English than Robbie did French. Leonid Krassin was an engineer who had managed the great Putilov arms plant in St. Petersburg before the war; he knew all there was to know about the Baku oil-field, because in earlier days he had been in that city as manager for the A.E.G., the German electrical trust of which Walther Rathenau was head.

This Red foreign-trade expert conducted a sort of kindergarten class for the benefit of a businessman from far-off New England. He explained the viewpoint of his government as to the difference between Tsarist obligations and those which the Bolsheviks themselves might incur for the rebuilding of their country. The oil of the Caucasus they considered a heritage to be preserved and worked for the national benefit. If foreign concerns were willing to help in getting out this oil, concessions would be granted for reasonable periods, and all agreements would be strictly kept. Foreign engineers and skilled workers would be welcomed, but insofar as Russian labor was employed, the labor laws of the Soviet Union would have to be conformed to. The Soviets desperately needed oil, but they also needed the contentment and enlightenment of their long-oppressed people.

Robbie brought into play those arts which he had spent so many years in acquiring. He explained that he was an "independent," not controlled by any of the great oil trusts. He took it for granted that this would count in his favor; but the Russian suavely explained that this was a misconception of the Soviet attitude—they did not object to big organizations, but rather preferred dealing with them because they were generally more responsible. "What you Americans call independence, Mr. Budd, we Communists call anarchy; we think that the more quickly industry is integrated and rationalized, the more quickly will it be ready for social ownership."

So Robbie had to hustle and think up a new line of sales talk. He assured Mr. Krassin that he represented responsible people with large amounts of capital. The Russian asked how long a lease they would expect, and intimated that Lloyd George's idea of ninety years would hardly be pleasing to Moscow; twenty years would be better. When Robbie said that was hardly time enough to get the full benefit of development work, the Russian suggested that the government should pay the value of the investment, or part of it, at the end of the lease. They had a discussion as to whether they would pay the value of the field, or only of the money put in. Robbie said that, according to American ideas, one acquired the ownership of the oil that was in the ground; but the Russian idea was that this oil belonged to the people, and that lessors could expect payment only for the value of wells and machinery.

To Robbie Budd life hardly seemed worth living on terms such as those. As he and his son were driving home he said: "That gives me a pain in the neck—about the people owning the oil. The people will never touch it—a bunch of politicians have got control and mean to hold onto it."

Lanny had an impulse to say: "You believe in a government, Robbie; and what can any government be but politicians?" But that was the kind of remark the younger man had learned not to make; it would only mean a tiresome argument and do no good. Say some polite nothing, and let Robbie have it his way.

III

Through Steffens Lanny met a number of left-wing intellectuals. They too were here as "observers"; they wrote stories about international affairs for newspapers and magazines of the various warring Communist and Socialist and labor groups. They sat around in the cafés and argued till all hours, and exchanged ideas and information with sympathetic journalists of the various nations. Some had been to Russia, and regarded this experiment as the one really important thing in the world. The first whom Lanny met was a big, amiable ex-minister, Albert Rhys Williams, who had had adventures which do not often fall to the lot of a man of God. He had summed them up in the titles of two books, *In the Claws of the German Eagle* and *Through the Russian Revolution.* He was friendly with the Soviet delegates and their staff, gave them advice, and tried to explain them to those "bourgeois" journalists who would listen.

There was a tall, extremely handsome, fawnlike man with a soft, caressing voice and prematurely gray hair: Max Eastman, editor of a New York magazine, the *Liberator.* It had been the *Masses,* but the government had suppressed it during the war and indicted and tried its editors. Max had fallen very much in love with a gay young woman on the Russian staff, and was threatening to follow her back home. There was a liberal and pacifist editor named Villard, not able to find much encouragement in anything that was going on here. There was an English editor, Frank Harris—at least, Lanny thought he was English, but learned that he was a Central European who claimed to have been born in Ireland, and had worked as a cowboy in the Far West of America. A fiery-looking man with a heavy black mustache, he was the possessor of a golden tongue, and when he talked about Shakespeare or Jesus you would have thought you were listening to the great one in person; but then the talk would turn to someone against whom Harris had a grudge, and he would pour out such malignancy that you shrank in dismay.

Present also was an American-Jewish sculptor by the name of Jo Davidson; a short, broad fellow with a spreading black beard, quick dark eyes, and deft fingers. He journeyed where the great were to be found and made portrait busts of them. The Russians were preoccupied, much worried men, and Davidson had to get them at whatever they were doing, receiving visitors, eating their lunch, shaving themselves. They didn't know that he understood Russian, and talked intimately among themselves; Jo went ahead and modeled their features and kept their secrets.

Lanny made the discovery that "celebrities" had highly developed egos. They had fought their way up in the world, and hadn't done it by being polite; they had sharp and well-developed spines, claws, and stingers. They were convinced of their own importance, and expected and received deference from plain nobodies whom they met. There was no one of whose unimportance they were more certain than a rich man's son, and for the honor of their acquaintance they permitted him to pay for the food and drinks. Frank Harris even tried to borrow a large sum of money from him, which fortunately Lanny didn't have; he was asked if he couldn't get it from his father, and took refuge in the statement that his father disapproved of the company he was keeping.

There were few things these intellectual battlers agreed about, but one was everywhere taken for granted, and that was the evilness of oil as an influence in international affairs. Wherever you smelled it there were treachery, corruption, and violence. Nor in discussing this matter did any of the left-wingers consider it necessary to spare the feelings of the son of Robbie Budd. If he didn't agree with them, what was he doing in their crowd? If he couldn't bear the truth, let him stay with his own! Lanny tried to do so, but made the discovery that he preferred the harsh and ugly truth to the polite evasions he met with among the "respectable" people.

IV

Walther Rathenau had become the Foreign Minister of the German republic. He had a difficult problem in Genoa, for a huge reparations payment was falling due at the end of May, and no moratorium had been granted; on the contrary, Poincaré was declaring that "sanctions" were going to be applied without fail. The Germans were trying to induce the British to intercede, but couldn't even get at them, everybody being occupied with the squabble over Baku and Batum. The Russians couldn't accomplish anything either, so of course it was natural that the two outcasts of the conference should combine forces. On the sixth day a bombshell was exploded under all Genoa, and the report of it was heard wherever cables or wireless reached. The Germans and Russians had got together at the near-by town of Rapallo and signed a treaty of amity; they agreed to drop all reparations claims against each other, and to settle all future disputes by arbitration.

This treaty seemed harmless enough on its face, but then nobody at Genoa took anything as meaning what it was said to mean. The general belief was that there must be secret military clauses to the agreement, and this enraged the Allied diplomats. Russia had the natural resources and Germany the manufacturing power, and if these two were combined they could dominate Europe. It was the thing the German diplomats were always dropping hints about, and the German general staff was believed to be plotting it. Hadn't the German government brought Lenin and the rest of the Red agents into Russia in a sealed train, and turned them loose to wreck the Tsar's government and take Russia out of the war? By that maneuver the Kaiser had almost won, and here was another trick of the same sort!

The reactionaries hardened their hearts, and the liberals were unhappy, seeing the failure of all efforts at reconciliation. What a tragedy! lamented Villard. The German autocracy was dead, and here was a republic, an oppressed people trying to learn self-government, but nobody would help them, give them any chance to survive! To this the left-wingers replied by mockery. What did capitalism care about a republic? Capitalism was autocracy in industry; that was its essence; it didn't want to help anybody to survive, it wanted to make profits out of human need. The oil men were running this conference, and to them republic or kingdom was all the same—so long as they could get concessions and protect their monopolies throughout the world.

Cynical and cruel-sounding, but there was Lanny Budd's father coming to him to prove that the cynics had it right. "Between you and me," said Robbie, "I think there's a lot more to this Rapallo deal than anyone admits. It means that the Germans are going to get the oil."

"But, Robbie, the Germans haven't capital enough to run their own industry!"

"Don't you fool yourself, the big fellows have money. Do you imagine that Rathenau hasn't got it?"

Lanny couldn't say. He could only wonder, while his father went on to spill what was in his mind. He wanted Lanny to go to the German minister at once, and explain to him that his father was representing a big American syndicate, and might be able to make some useful suggestions to the German delegation.

Lanny didn't want to do it the least bit. He had been trying to be a young idealist, and now Rathenau would think he was just one more schemer. But Lanny coudn't say that—it would be making his father another schemer. He tried feebly to explain that Rathenau was a hard-pressed and exhausted man. Lanny had seen him and knew that it was so.

Said the father: "Don't be childish! One of the things he's exhausted by is trying to get oil for Germany. Now he has the inside track with these Russians, and nothing ought to please him more than to fix up a deal by which American capital would be made available to them both."

So Lanny phoned one of the secretaries whom he had come to know at Bienvenu, and an appointment was arranged. He met that much-harassed statesman again—and, oh, such a tragic face! It seemed that the Jews were born to suffer, and it became their features; at any rate it made them look more like Jews. This man whom the Prussian aristocrats scorned was carrying all their burdens for them, expiating their sins, pleading for mercy with the foes they had so wantonly affronted. He was the scapegoat for another people —the Jews not being allowed even that luxury for themselves!

But it appeared that Robbie was right. Rathenau was a businessman, used to talking to businessmen. He said that he would be very glad to hear what Mr. Budd had to say; he made an appointment for that very day, and he and Robbie spent an hour in conference. It must have been important, because Robbie didn't tell his son much about it, but had his secretary, who had hired another car, drive him at once to "Monty." Lanny was left behind, because he had a date to take Rick to a press conference at the Palazzo di San Giorgio, where Lloyd George was going to answer the questions of newsmen concerning Rapallo, and what it meant, and what would be the attitude of the British government to a *rapprochement* between German Socialists and Russian Communists.

V

It became Lanny's singular duty to drive his father several times to the Soviet hotel at Santa Margherita. Elaborate negotiations were under way, and before they were over, Lanny had met all the heads of the delegation and many of the subordinates; he heard stories of the revolution they had made, and had their hopes and their fears explained to him. He watched with amusement his father's growing surprise at the qualities he kept discovering in Bolshevik leaders. Remarkable men, Robbie was forced to admit; their wits had been sharpened in a school of bitter struggle and suffering. The American hadn't expected to find genuine idealism combined with worldly cunning—in fact he hadn't considered it possible for such a combination to exist in human beings. Least of all had he expected to meet scholarly persons, with whom he was interested to engage in theoretical discussions.

Chicherin, Soviet Foreign Commissar, was a former aristocrat who had been trained for diplomacy in the Tsar's school. He had many of the characteristics which one found in Englishmen of that class; he was tall and stoop-shouldered, sensitive and shy, careless in his dress and absent-minded like some funny old college professor. He lived in his work, hating to trouble anybody, and trying to do all the work, even to the sharpening of his lead-pencils. He turned night into day, and appointments with him were apt to be for two or three o'clock in the morning; even so, he would be unavoidably late and would apologize profusely.

In the meantime Robbie and his son would chat with Rakovsky, Bulgarian-born revolutionist, and his wife, who had been a Russian princess and was now a Communist who used a lorgnette! Both of these were clever talkers, and Robbie said he didn't see how Russia could ever be industrialized while she had so many of these. Rakovsky, discovering the fog of ignorance concerning the Soviet Union which enshrouded Genoa, went to the university and obtained the use of a large lecture hall, and there every afternoon he explained Bolshevik ideas of history to whoever might wish to come. He spoke perfect French, being a graduate of a Paris medical school and having written a book on French culture. The journalists of that country were annoyed to hear him discuss their history, and they would rise and heckle him, but quickly discovered that he knew things about the French Revolution which they hadn't heard before. It was one of those European halls in which the lecturer is down in a pit, and the seats for the audience are in tiers in front and on both sides of him; it wasn't long before the place was packed to the doors—the journalists of all nations were deserting the conference and coming to listen to Rakovsky.

All this was a liberal education for Lanny, and he hoped it might be for his father; but these hopes were not realized. Robbie's mind was on his expected concession, and on the long reports he was sending to Zaharoff, and his code messages to interested parties in Paris and London and New York. What Robbie wanted to know about these Bolsheviks was, would they keep their word and, no less important, would they keep power? That was what the businessmen had such a hell of a time making up their minds about. For four years and a half they had been betting that these fanatics, half idealists and half criminals, would be swept away; but somehow, unaccountably, they were managing to hang on. This imposed upon an American businessman an annoying task, that of understanding a new philosophy, a new economic system, a new code of ethics. In this Robbie's son was helpful to him, and might have been more so if only the son could have kept his head and drawn the line at the proper point; but the young idiot kept taking these fellows seriously, and this upset Robbie and made it hard for him to keep his mind on his work.

There was in the group a rolypoly Jew known as "Papa" Litvinov; round-faced, florid, fond of good living, a hearty, rough-and-ready sort of fellow who might have been boss of a construction camp in the Far West. Robbie employed men like that, and knew how to laugh and jolly them along; if he could have had Litvinov to run the Caucasus oil-field, he would have felt certain of getting out the stuff. It was this man's duty to explain to the would-be concessionaire the labor code of the Soviet Union; that was very important to Robbie, so he listened closely and asked many questions, all from the point of view of a businessman, thinking: "Shall I be able to get any work out of them on that basis?" But there was Lanny, thinking: "How fine for the workers! They can be self-respecting men under such a code!" He would say something like that to the Russian, and the latter would beam with pleasure and start off on a long discourse that had to do with labor psychology instead of production costs of crude oil at the pipeline terminus. Robbie would feel himself in the position of Alice through the Looking-Glass.

VI

Lanny was present at a luncheon which his father gave to the American ambassador, Mr. Child, whom between themselves they always called "Cradle." He was a smooth-faced, boyish-looking man, talkative, and greatly impressed with the service he was rendering his country by seeing that its businessmen got their share of whatever was being distributed at Genoa. The luncheon took place in a *cabinet particulier* of Robbie's hotel, and present also was an admiral of the navy who had been assigned to assist Mr. Child as "observer." This elderly gentleman was doubtless well trained to observe enemy ships upon the sea, but he knew nothing at all about the oil business, and was certainly not a competent observer of the machinations of Robbie Budd.

The father had warned Lanny under no circumstances to drop any hint as to Robbie's connections; he was an "independent," representing an American syndicate, and that was all. The author of popular fiction, to whom words came easily, told what he knew about the conference, what it was doing about oil, and what the Americans wanted it to do; this included a great deal which A. C. Bedford, the big Standard man, would certainly not have wished to have communicated to a Grand Officer of the Legion of Honor and Knight Commander of the Bath.

Again Lanny was being disillusioned. He had always had business put before him as a matter of patriotism; all his young life, when Robbie had talked about his activities, he had been increasing the wealth of America and providing jobs for American workingmen.

Budd's was an American munitions plant, and in building it Robbie was providing for American security. Now America must have oil for its ships abroad wherever they were traveling; and so on. But here was this "independent," in secret alliance with Deterding, the Dutch-Englishman, and with Zaharoff, the Greek citizen of all countries in which he owned munitions plants; and Robbie Budd was intriguing as hard as he could to thwart the efforts of the American ambassador and the companies he was backing! However much you might dislike Standard Oil, it was an American concern, no less so because it was privately owned. Neither the American people nor the government was going to own Robbie's concession; Robbie's associates and backers were going to own it, and Robbie himself was going to run it.

So really it appeared that patriotism was just a screen, behind which selfish interests were operating; old Dr. Samuel Johnson had been right in his bitter saying that patriotism is the last refuge of a scoundrel. Lanny didn't want to think such thoughts about his father, and tried with all his might to keep them from sneaking into his mind. He sat there with nothing to do but listen, and of course he couldn't help seeing how Robbie was deftly leading a man who was a good deal of a nincompoop into telling exactly what instructions he had received from the State Department regarding the support he was to give to Standard Oil and its agents in Genoa.

The ambassador was a bitter hater of the Bolsheviks, and spoke contemptuously of statesmen such as Lloyd George, who were willing to compromise with them; "shaking hands with murder," was the phrase. Of course Mr. Child didn't know what a lot of such handshaking Robbie had been doing, and Robbie didn't mention the matter. He listened, and learned how Mr. Child was working with Barthou, French Foreign Minister, against the British in their efforts for a compromise. The French wanted to suspend all the trade treaties with the Bolsheviks and go back to the policy of the blockade, the *cordon sanitaire;* that was Secretary Hughes's idea of statesmanship, and how should "Cradle," his agent, guess that Robbie Budd would be on the British side in a struggle for the rights of property against Red revolution?

VII

The ambassador told what he had seen in Italy during the year since his appointment. He considered that the country was in a deplorable plight, in imminent danger of a revolution on the Bolshevik model. The cost of living was ten times what it had been before the war, and everywhere you went were beggars asking for a soldo. The people were hungry, the factories idle, the steel mills working on half-time. Already there were regular soviets in the factories, and the police and army were utterly unreliable; the government was so benevolent that it took everybody on its payroll, and it was so liberal that it couldn't enforce order.

"You can't imagine how it is unless you live here," said Mr. Child. "You wish to ride on a street car, but there is a strike; you are told that a carabiniere has struck a street-car worker, so they are all insulted. Next day—*ecco!*—the carabiniere has apologized to the worker, and the cars are running again!"

The ambassador went on to tell a story which he thought would amuse Mr. Budd, who came from New England. A couple of Italian anarchists in Massachusetts had recently been convicted of a payroll hold-up and murder, and sentenced to death. Mr. Child searched his memory and recalled the names, Sacco and Vanzetti. Had Mr. Budd ever heard of them? Robbie said he hadn't. Well, it appeared that the anarchists in Rome had heard of them, and a deputation of five young fellows had come to the American Embassy to demand justice for their comrades and fellow-countrymen. Mr. Child had had an agreeable chat with them, and sent them away satisfied with his promise to have the matter investigated. Subsequently one of these young men had come back and asked for a job! So matters went in this nation which had had sixty-eight governments in the course of sixty years.

The ambassador had been able to find only one hopeful thing in Italy, and that was a new movement called *Fascismo*, about which he talked a great deal. Here was a spirit of unity and resolution. Perhaps that always happens in human societies, he said; when the need grows desperate enough, the organism evolves a remedy. The

Fascisti were organizing the young men of Italy and teaching them a program of action. Their leader was a former soldier named Mussolini; Mr. Child had never met him, but had heard a lot about him, had read some of his articles and admired him greatly.

Lanny spoke up, saying that he had met him. The other was interested to hear about the interview, and asked Lanny's impressions of the man. Mr. Child confirmed Mussolini's claims as to the character of the movement. "Everywhere I see these young blackshirts marching I get the feeling of clean-cut, vigorous youth, conscious of its reforming mission."

"Aren't they sometimes rather violent?" asked Lanny.

"Well, but you have to consider the provocation. It seems to me we're going to need a movement like that at home, if the Reds go on extending their activities as they are doing. Don't you think so, Mr. Budd?"

"I do indeed," said Robbie, cordially. So they were better friends than ever, and Mr. Child told delightful stories about his adventures in the strange role of ambassador. He was much taken with the King of Italy, an energetic little pint-sized man—really a liberal, and quite democratic in his tastes. He had been standing on the piazza, talking with Child, and it was a cold day; the King had bidden the ambassador put his hat on his head. Could anything have been more considerate? Robbie agreed again, but Lanny couldn't help his rebellious thoughts. If you were going to have your king democratic, why have one at all? And why should an ambassador from a republic be so very keen about kings?

VIII

Lanny told Rick about this conversation—the parts having to do with Mussolini—and Rick agreed that the American envoy was a poor judge of Italian character and social forces. They saw Benito Mussolini now and then in the Casa della Stampa, and thought less of him each time. Being now in his homeland, he was even more the braggart and *poseur*. He made a bid for Rick to write about the progress of his *Fascismo* during the past two years; he insisted that he now had four hundred thousand youth of Italy enrolled under his banner. Rick wanted to say: "In your eye!" but remembered that he was a gentleman, even if Mussolini wasn't.

Talking about the Blessed Little Pouter Pigeon and his movement made Lanny remember Barbara Pugliese. He had received a letter from her, thanking him for his kindness and giving him an address in Turin. Since her work of speaking and organizing caused her to do considerable traveling, it occurred to Lanny that she might be coming to the conference, so he wrote a note to the Turin address, giving the name of his hotel. Then he forgot about the matter, because at this moment another bombshell exploded under the conference—the publication of a report that the Soviet government had made a deal with Standard Oil, giving them an exclusive lease upon the Baku field.

An anti-Bolshevik delegate had handed to a New York newspaperman a typewritten sheet containing the substance of the alleged agreement. The newsman tried to verify it, and only got laughed at; for two or three days he went about with that possible great "scoop" burning a hole in his pocket. His newspaper, the *World*, was anti-Standard as well as anti-Bolshevik, so he took a chance and put the story on the wire; it was published, and in an hour or two was back in Genoa, where nobody but the Russians and the Standard people could know whether it was true or not, and nobody would believe anything that either of these groups might say. There was a great uproar, and Robbie had to jump into his car and hurry off to Monty to reassure the frantic Sir Basil. Robbie was quite sure it was a *canard*, because his man Bub was on intimate terms with the young lady secretary of one of the Standard agents.

The fuss died down in two or three days, but it had the disagreeable effect of concentrating the attention of the entire world upon the subject of oil at Genoa and causing the newspapermen to ask prying questions. The Bolsheviks referred to themselves as "proletarians," a fancy word that the American newspapers always put in quotes; now their reporters began writing about "petroletarians" at Genoa, and that wasn't so funny as it sounded. The plain people were sick of war and famine, and didn't care to risk any more of it to help private interests grab some Russian oil.

IX

One evening Lanny went to the opera and, finding a poor performance, came home early. Rick was at a reception in one of the English villas, and Robbie was in conference with some of Zaharoff's men. Lanny had just begun to undress and have a quiet read in his pajamas when a "buttons" tapped on his door and informed him that down in the lobby was *uno ragazzo* asking to see him. Lanny hadn't met any of these in Genoa, nor was he enlightened when the other kept insisting that the *ragazzo* was *molto stracciato;* Lanny had never had occasion to use or hear the word "ragged" in Italy, though he had seen the condition in abundance. He went down into the lobby, and met a street urchin with large dark eyes and peaked face, having in his hand an envelope which he held out to the well-dressed American. Lanny saw at a glance that it was the letter he had written to Barbara Pugliese in Turin.

"*La signora ammalata,*" said the boy, and Lanny knew what that meant; he had seen her ill before. The boy was clearly in a state of fright, and having once got started he talked with rapidity. Lanny didn't know all the words, but made out that *la signora* had been beaten, that she was badly injured, perhaps dying, they had found her in the street, she had had this letter with her. The name of the hotel was upon it, and Lanny's name as the sender, so the boy had come in haste to him.

Perhaps it wasn't altogether wise for Lanny to set out for an unknown destination with a stranger, especially since he had in his pocket a purse containing a considerable sum of money. But he thought of only one thing, that this woman who had so captured his admiration had fallen victim to the ruffians of the Blessed Little Pouter Pigeon; she was in need of help, and Lanny had no idea but to hurry to the garage where his car was stored, and set out to drive under the lad's direction. They came to one of those slum neighborhoods which constitute a horror in every Mediterranean city; winding streets through which a car could hardly be driven, the remains of last week's garbage polluting the air. They got out in front of a tall tenement, and Lanny locked the car and followed the lad through a pitch-dark hall, into a room lighted by one smoky kerosene lamp. There must have been a dozen people crowded into it, all chattering excitedly; but they fell silent when the stranger appeared, and moved back to give him access to a bed on which lay a dark form.

Lanny couldn't see very well, so he took the lamp, and then had a hard time not to drop it, for the sight was the most dreadful that had come under his eyes since that day when he and his mother and Jerry Pendleton had taken Marcel to Paris with his crushed body and burned face. The face of Barbara Pugliese, about which Lanny had imagined so many romantic things, had been beaten until it looked like a piece of butcher's meat; one eye was closed and the socket such a mass of blood that there was no way to know if there was any eye left. The ragged coverlet of the bed was soaked in blood, and so was Barbara's dress.

"Is she alive?" Lanny asked; and that started everybody to talking. They didn't seem to be sure, so Lanny put his hand over her heart, and found that it was beating faintly.

He managed to make out that the people in this tenement didn't know Barbara, hadn't ever heard of her. They had heard screams, they had rushed out and seen a group of youths pounding a woman with blackjacks. The reputation of the *Fascisti* was such that the bystanders didn't dare make a move; they just stood and waited until the assailants had finished their job, and marched off singing their hymn of glory, *Giovinezza*. Then the people had carried her inside. They hadn't dared to notify the police, for fear of being implicated with what they knew must be a Red; this was by now a familiar story in the slums of Italian cities. They had looked in the woman's purse and found the letter; none of them had been able to read the contents, which were in French, but one had been able to read the name of the hotel on the envelope, and Lanny's name above it.

Now they had but one idea, which was to get the *povera signora* off their hands, before the blackshirts came back to finish their job and perhaps to include her supposed friends in the lesson. The people were in a panic about it, and made plain their intention that if the *signor* wouldn't take charge of his friend, they would carry her out in the street and leave her in front of some other house. So Lanny said all right, but they must help him; he took the woman's feet, and two of the men took her by the shoulders, and they carried her to the car and laid her in the back seat. She was unconscious, and did not even groan. There was no time to think about protecting the car cushions; they just laid her down, blood and all. Lanny, afraid of getting lost in these tangled streets, promised the boy a lira to ride beside him and show him the way to one of the main thoroughfares.

As he drove, he tried to think what to do next. To appeal to the police would be futile, for had he not heard Mussolini boast how the police were in league with his blackshirts, or at any rate afraid to interfere with them? To take the victim to a hospital would be risky, for those in charge might themselves be Fascists; the same was true of any doctor to whom he might appeal. The Italians were making an omelet, and now Lanny had one of the eggs on his hands. He decided that he was going to get Barbara out of Italy; he would do it with only enough delay to let his father know what he was up to.

X

The good Samaritan parked his car and hurried into the hotel. Nothing else to do; he was no doctor, and knew very little about first aid to the injured. Robbie was still at his conference in the reception room of their suite, but Lanny interrupted, and took him into another room, where he told the distressing news.

"My God, son!" exclaimed the horrified man. "What is this woman to you?"

"It will be hard to explain, Robbie. You'll just have to take my word that she has impressed me as a noble personality, perhaps the greatest I have ever met. I'll tell you all about her some day, but not while she's lying there perhaps dying. I have to save her if I can, and I don't know anybody in Italy to trust."

"Can't you find any of her friends?"

"I can't go driving around with a half-dead woman in the car, asking for the headquarters of the Socialist party—which have probably been smashed up or burned long ago."

"Have you thought that these blackshirts may attack you yourself?"

"That's a chance I have to take. If I didn't take it, I'd never respect myself again as long as I live."

"What do you plan to do with her when you get her into France?"

"Put her in a *maison de santé* and get proper care for her. After that I'll wire Uncle Jesse. I've no doubt he'll come, or give me the address of some of her friends. She has them everywhere, because she's a speaker, a well-known person in her movement."

"Suppose the woman dies before you get her to a hospital?"

"That's another chance I have to take. All I can do is to tell the truth about what happened."

"But don't you see that you'll be branding yourself as a Red sympathizer? The newspapers will be full of it."

"I know, Robbie, and I'm sorry; but what can I do?"

"You can let me phone to a hospital here, and have them come and take the woman off your hands."

"Even so, won't the police want to know how I got hold of her? Won't I have to show the letter I wrote her? I'll be here in Genoa, in the hands of the gang—and what will Mr. Child's great hero Mussolini do about it?"

"It's hell!" exclaimed Robbie. "I've been warning you from the beginning about associating with these people, and writing them letters. God knows I tried hard enough to keep you out of the hands of Jesse Blackless and all his crew."

"You did, Robbie, and it's damned unfair that I may drag you into such a mess."

"Well, what do you propose to do about that?" The father was greatly provoked, and made no effort to conceal it.

"I've thought about it a lot, Robbie. I don't agree with your ideas, and I want to be free to think what I have to, so perhaps I ought to drop the name of Budd—I'm not really entitled to it, it's just a sham. I ought to carry my mother's name, and I'm perfectly willing to take it and set you free from this continual discomfort. I'm of age now, and ought to be responsible for myself, and not drag your family into scandals."

Lanny meant it, and his father saw that he meant it, so he changed his tone quickly. "I'm not asking you to do anything like that, Lanny. I'll excuse myself from my guests, and drive with you to France."

"That's not necessary, really. I'm not in any serious danger—no police are going to stop my car, once I get started. I'll drive carefully, and the woman can just lie there. When I get to the border and tell the French officials—well, it's no crime to have found a wounded person, and to be trying to help her."

Robbie said: "I'll send Bub Smith with you. He can return on the train. I don't think you ought to come back into Italy."

"All right," assented Lanny. "I've seen enough of this conference, God knows."

"And one thing more, son. If you feel this urge to try to change the world, can't you for Christ's sake manage to work out some peaceable and orderly program?"

"Indeed I want to, Robbie!" Lanny said it with deep feeling. "Come and help me. Nothing would please me so well!"

XI

The good Samaritan didn't stop for his things; they could be forwarded later. He grabbed the astonished Bub Smith, who was getting ready for bed. "Come on—right away. You're driving with me to France. Bring your passport and your gun. Don't stop for anything else—it's an emergency." When they were getting into the car: "There's a woman in the back seat. I'll tell you about her when we get started. She may be dead." The ex-cowboy had had his share of adventure, and was not too easily jolted. He hoped his employer's son hadn't committed any serious crime; but if he had, it was all in a day's work.

Lanny had known of persons being injured in automobile wrecks, and had learned that when one suffers from concussion of the brain and shock, the important thing is to keep him quiet. So he drove carefully, avoiding jolts and sudden turns; now and then Bub would look behind, to be sure that the body was safe on the seat. Just before they reached the border the ex-cowboy got into the rear seat and lifted the woman to a sitting position and held her in his arms. Not very pleasant, but part of the job.

To the border guard Lanny said: "I have a sick lady. I am taking her to a *maison de santé*. Where shall I find the nearest?"

He was an American, driving an expensive car; his papers were in order, and he had no luggage, so there was no reason for delay. They told him where to go, so in a short while Barbara was in a French private hospital with a doctor in attendance. This man had heard of the terrible blackshirts across the border, and fortunately was not a sympathizer of theirs. He examined the woman and made his report; evidently the *squadristi* had taken their time and made a thorough job of disciplining her; they had pounded the whole front of her body, and then rolled her over and worked on the back; hardly a square inch that was not bruised. There were several fractures of the skull, one of them basal, so there was no possibility of operating, nothing to do but leave it to nature. There was a little spark of life in her, and it might survive; they would give stimulants to keep the heart going.

Lanny phoned his father as soon as possible in the morning and sent a telegram to his Uncle Jesse at his home. Bub took the morning train back to Genoa, promising to send Lanny's clothes. The youth wrote to his mother and to Marie, telling what had happened, and then settled down to wait—there was nothing else to do. He slept, and then walked for a while, thinking about his life and what this new crisis meant to him. He had made certain that there were forces in the world which he hated with all his heart and wanted to fight; but just what they were, and how he could recognize them— that would take a bit of study.

He decided that he wanted to talk to Rick, and telephoned his friend, who said that he had had all he needed of Genoa, and came by train and joined Lanny that evening. Uncle Jesse arrived from the other direction, so there were three social philosophers, with nothing to do but argue—for the poor gray-haired old woman still lay unconscious, and it would do no good to her or them to sit and look at her smashed face.

Uncle Jesse had the whole problem laid out in his mind, as if it were a map. He said that Fascism was the answer of capitalism to the workers' attempt at freedom; Mussolini was right in saying that it would spread to other lands, for capitalism was the same in all lands, and would defend itself by the same methods—that is, by subsidizing gangsters, to operate under the label of patriotism, that being the cheapest and easiest of all labels.

Rick, on the other hand, insisted that Fascism was a reaction of the middle classes caught between the two millstones of capitalism and Communism; the white-collar workers suffered all the effects of social breakdown, unemployment, the high cost of living, loss of hope—and they turned for help to any demagogue who promised relief. These two arguers went at each other hammer and tongs, while Lanny sat and listened, and tried to figure out which he believed. He decided, in his usual uncomfortable way, that he believed both at the same time.

It was the best chance he had ever had to understand the ideas of his forbidden uncle. He made up his mind once more that he didn't like him, but also that that had nothing to do with the matter. Bald and wrinkled and harsh, Jesse Blackless was like some old bear of the forest that has fought his enemies until his hide is ragged, his ears missing, and his teeth broken—but still goes on fighting. Jesse Blackless had a cause that he believed in, and Lanny knew few such persons, and couldn't help admiring his grit. Also, once the uncle's bitter sarcasms had got into his mind, he found that it was hard to get them out. They stuck like burrs in wool.

Lanny mentioned his father's suggestion that he should find some peaceable and orderly way to change the world. Jesse said that was a pleasant phrase with which to evade an issue; Robbie had doubtless forgotten it already. When Lanny said he'd remind him, and try to convert him, the uncle said: "Then there'll be two disillusioned idealists instead of one!" When Lanny pointed out that several of the Bolsheviks in Genoa had been members of the capitalist class, Jesse said: "Oh, sure; some individuals go over to the workers, but does that abolish the class struggle? When one rich man turns traitor, the rest of the rich men don't follow him—they hate him."

XII

Two days passed, and they were in the midst of an argument in Lanny's hotel room when a message came from the hospital: Barbara Pugliese was dead. They had to arrange for a funeral; a conspicuous and public one, as a matter of propaganda, a demonstration of working-class protest. The news of Barbara's fate had been published in labor papers, and several journalists and labor leaders came; they took the body to Nice, and the coffin was placed on a truck draped with flowers, and thousands of workingmen and women marched behind it, carrying banners and signs denouncing the vicious *Fascismo*. Uncle Jesse had managed to keep his nephew's name out of the affair, and nobody paid any attention to a well-dressed young American and an English journalist, the latter limping painfully with the procession.

At the grave the throng stood with bared heads and listened to eloquent tributes. A bald-headed American painter told the story of a life consecrated to the cause of the humble and oppressed. Never had this heroic woman flinched from any duty or sacrifice; she had the courage of a lion with the sweetness of a child. Tears came into the orator's eyes as he told of their long friendship, and then rage shook his voice as he denounced the Italian blackshirts. His nephew listened, and agreed with every word he said—and at the same time was ill at ease to find himself in such a company and in such a mood. He looked at these dark, somber people, unfashionably dressed, their faces distorted by violent passions; they were not his kind of people, and he was afraid of them—yet something drew him to them!

"Labor has one more martyr to add to its roll, which is as long as human history." So the speaker declared, and quoted the saying about the early Christians: "The blood of the martyrs was the seed of the Church." It sounded strange from one who hated religion as Jesse Blackless did, but Lanny realized that these Reds were founding another kind. They disliked to hear that, but so it was, and the more you persecuted them, the more you spread their faith over the earth. It was a hard way for truth to be taught, but maybe Uncle Jesse was right in his belief that human beings were ready for no other. An uncomfortable and irrational world that Lanny Budd had been born into! Once again it had dragged a young artist out of his ivory tower, and was buffeting him about in a fashion that interfered greatly with his convenience and his sense of dignity.

15

Roman Holiday

I

LANNY and Rick came back to Juan, and Marie came to join her friend. She knew that he was troubled in spirit, and she was gentle and sweet to him; listened sympathetically to the story of Barbara Pugliese, never tried to argue with him, dropped no hint that he had done anything wrong. But among themselves the ladies consulted anxiously; Marie and Beauty and Nina, and Sophie and Emily when they happened to drop in. How was an impressionable youth to be kept from falling into the hands of agitators, fanatics, and enemies of the public welfare? They were at one in the conviction that they had had a narrow escape from disagreeable publicity. Beauty trembled when she heard what Lanny had said to his father about changing his name; she knew out of what intense emotion such words must have come. She had buried the name of Blackless deep in the past, and got no pleasure out of the thought of its resurrection.

Robbie, having failed to get what he wanted in Genoa, went back home to consult his associates. He stayed only a few days and then returned, for the conference had referred the problem of Russia and its oil to the Supreme Economic Council, summoned to The Hague in June. Rick, his reputation now established, had got an assignment from a daily newspaper to report this affair, and the natural thing would have been for Lanny to take him there, as he had to Geneva. But Marie said: "Oh, Lanny, no more conferences! I missed you so!"—and it was easy for her lover to give up the idea of going, because he was sick of the smell of oil. "Let's stay at home and read some good books," pleaded the woman, not realizing that there might be a difference between them as to what books were "good."

Before they went north for their summer, Lanny made a search of Eli Budd's library. The old gentleman hadn't gone in heavily for economics, and what he had was of the old school. But there were two books by a writer named Bellamy, of whom Lanny had never heard. He read *Looking Backward*, and it seemed surprising to him that this book wasn't more talked about. He tried to find any of his friends who had read it, but there wasn't one. He couldn't see how anybody could fail to want to live in a world like that, a world in which human beings helped one another instead of wasting their efforts trying to keep others from succeeding. Lanny read *Equality*, a still less-known work, which gave him a scientific statement of how a co-operative economy might be organized and run. It seemed to him that this was the best thing that had come out of America, the genius of a practical people applied to the most important problem which confronted mankind.

But, alas, how few Americans were heeding their great social prophet! There was another America, not so different from the Europe in which Lanny lived; a land of poverty and unemployment, of desperate strikes and labor revolts—all the phenomena of that "class struggle" about which Jesse Blackless talked incessantly, which he made the core of all of his social thinking. While Robbie was trying to get the oil of the Russians, other "petroletarians" at home were engaged in appropriating the reserves of their country's navy—with the help of purchased members of President Harding's Cabinet. That was Robbie's own administration, which he had helped to choose and elect. He defended it stubbornly, refusing to believe the story until it was forced into the newspapers by a Senate investigation. Then Robbie belittled it, talking about it sourly as the work of agitators, Red sympathizers, enemies of private business. Lanny didn't argue, but he saw clearly that the oil game was the same, whether it was played in Washington and California or in Italy and Holland.

II

Lanny motored his *amie* to Seine-et-Oise, and Rick took his family by train to Flushing, put them on a packet-boat, and then went to The Hague. Lanny subscribed to the paper for which Rick was writing, so it was the same as receiving long letters from his friend. Also he got news from Robbie, who came to Paris to consult with Zaharoff at his home on the Avenue Hoche. Robbie told about the swarms of oil men at The Hague, and the struggle going on among them, and with the Russians, and with the Supreme Economic Council. The building of the Tower of Babel was the only thing with which you could compare the effort to allot the world's petroleum supply.

The Russians wanted a loan for the reconstruction of their country, and they were using the oil as a bait, saying that without the loan they would prefer to struggle along and repair their own fields as best they could. The British wanted to make the loan, but the French and Belgians and many of the Americans insisted that Bolshevism must be starved out and made to fail. What would become of the intellectual defenses of private property if every street-corner orator could claim that the Communists were rebuilding their country? The oil men would get together and pledge themselves to negotiate as a whole and make no separate offers; then they would wait to see who would be first to break the agreement, and each would be afraid of being the last.

Johannes Robin was at The Hague. He had to know what was going to be decided, not only about oil, but about Germany. The mark's future depended upon the outcome of these negotiations; and of course a speculator had to be on the spot and keep his "pipe-lines" in repair. The statesmen who had the decision in their hands had secretaries and clerks who got inside information, and would pass out tips to a dependable person. The statesmen themselves had powerful friends who knew how to make use of their opportunities, and were generous and discreet in seeing to it that public servants were not left to suffer destitution in their old age.

So Lanny, reading imaginative tales of a perfect world, lived in contact with one which was tragically different. Settled in the comfortable ménage of the Château de Bruyne, reading, practicing the piano, playing tennis with two happy youths, enjoying the society of a lovely and devoted woman, Lanny knew that he was among the most fortunate of men. He tried to keep himself in a mood of gratitude, but on the twenty-fifth of June of that year 1922 he picked up a morning newspaper and read that Walther Rathenau, Foreign Minister of the German Republic, being driven to his office in a large open car, had been startled by a smaller car rushing up beside him, with two men in it wearing leather jackets and helmets; one of them had produced a repeating-gun and fired five bullets into the minister's body, and immediately afterward the other had thrown a hand-grenade into the car.

They had done that because he was a Jew, and was presuming to manage the affairs of Germany and to seek appeasement with both France and Russia. They had done it because it was a violent and cruel world, in which men would rather hate than understand one another, would rather do murder than fail to have their own way. To Lanny it seemed the most dreadful thing that had happened yet, and he bowed his face in his arms to hide his tears. He would never forget his memories of that kind and gentle man, the wisest he had found among the statesmen, the best heart and the best brain that Germany had had in this crisis. To Lanny it was as if he heard the tolling of a bell of doom; the best were going down and the worst were coming to the top in this corrupt and unhappy civilization.

III

Jesse Blackless had taken up his painting again, perhaps in despair concerning the human race. He had come to Paris and set up housekeeping with a young woman who worked on the Communist newspaper *L'Humanité*. He seemed happier that way, and it was pleasanter for his friends, for there were now chairs for them to sit on, and no longer a frying-pan decorating the center table. In fact, the painter and his *amie* set up a sort of *salon* for Reds, who would come at all hours and drink his wine and smoke his cigarettes and tell him the news of the underground movement in the various parts of Europe.

Lanny had declared his independence, and the form it took was to visit his Communist uncle and meet some of these dangerous and yet fascinating personalities. It was Lanny's form of a "spree"; vicious or not, according to your point of view—but he told himself that he wanted to understand the world he lived in, and to hear all opinions about it. Maybe he was fooling himself, and it was just a seeking of sensation, a playing with fire, with what the Japanese police authorities call "dangerous thoughts." Certainly it was a mistake if he wished to remain an ivory-tower dweller, for a bull in a china shop can do no greater damage than one idea inside a human psyche.

There were bookstores in Paris in which Red literature was sold; Lanny visited one of these and got several pamphlets, including an English translation of Lenin's *The State and Revolution*. He took these home and smuggled them into his room, keeping them out of sight and reading them surreptitiously, as if they had been pornography; he knew that both Marie and Denis would have been shocked by it, and that it would have been polluting the minds of two innocent lads to let them know that such printed material existed.

The Soviet leader was another victim of the practice, so widespread in Europe, of shooting bullets into the body of anyone with whose political beliefs you disagreed; he had been an invalid ever since the shooting, and was soon to die. But here was his powerful mind, beyond the reach of any assassin's bullet; he gave what seemed to Lanny a mathematical demonstration of the forces which were destroying the capitalist system and making it necessary for the organized workers to take control of society. The Russian thesis was that there was no way this change could be brought about except by the overthrow and destruction of that bourgeois state which was the policeman of the exploiting classes. This thesis apparently applied to a land like Russia, whose people had never known free institutions; but did it apply equally to France and Britain and America, which had enjoyed the use of the ballot for long periods? This was an important question, because if you were applying the Russian technique to countries where it didn't fit, you might be making a costly blunder.

When Lanny suggested this to Uncle Jesse's friends, they laughed at him and said he had a bourgeois mind; but he wanted to hear all sides, and took to reading *Le Populaire*, the organ of the Socialists. These disagreed violently with the Communists, and each called the other bad names, which seemed to Lanny the great tragedy of the workers' movement; he thought they had enemies enough among the capitalist class, without dividing among themselves. Yet he was forced to realize that if you believed revolutionary violence to be necessary, you were apt to be violent in advocating it; while if you believed in peaceable methods—well, apparently the men of violence would force you to be violent against them!

IV

Robbie Budd didn't get the concessions upon which he had expended such efforts. All the oil men were vexed, and all the governments; the dream of the bourgeois world, to solve its problems at the expense of Russia, wasn't working out. The Bolsheviks were in danger of losing their temporary status of genial conversationalists and resuming that of diabolical monsters. Robbie went back home without seeing his son again, and without giving him any further warning about his conduct. Could it be that the father had thought it over, and was really going to try to let him have his freedom, as Lincoln Steffens had suggested?

In the month of August the Greek army in the heart of the Anatolian hills sustained a terrible defeat, and fled in rout to Smyrna on the coast, where the Turkish cavalry followed them, driving them into the sea and slaughtering tens of thousands. "Our friend on the Avenue Hoche has lost his concessions," wrote Robbie, and explained that Standard would probably get them from the Turks. "Also the stock of his Banque de la Seine has fallen from 500 to 225." Rick, at home in England, reported an underground convulsion in politics. For the first time it was being asked publicly what was the connection between the Prime Minister and the mysterious Greek trader who had become Europe's armament king. Presently it was asked in the House of Commons—which meant that the newspapers could repeat it. This was like taking Sir Basil by the scruff of his crimson velvet robe and dragging him into the glare of a spotlight, something which Lanny knew would cause him intense distress.

This Turkish victory was a grave blow to British prestige. The weakest of the Central Powers, overwhelmingly defeated less than four years earlier, was now publicly tearing up the treaty which had been forced upon it. The triumphant Turkish armies, having captured great quantities of Vickers motorized artillery and tanks, all made by Zaharoff, came to the gates of Constantinople and were kept out only by fear of British naval guns—also made by Zaharoff. It looked for a while as if Britain had another war on its hands, and without any help from the French; it was poor consolation to see France apparently headed for another war with Germany, without any help from the British. The outcome was that in October Lloyd George was forced to resign—the last of the Versailles statesmen, the "Big Four" who had set out with so much authority to settle the problems of the world!

Lanny and Marie were back in Bienvenu when that happened. They were happy, because Lanny was "behaving," according to the standards of the ladies of his family and their friends. He kept the worst of his Red literature buried among the respectable books of a New England clergyman, who was not in position to protest against such treatment. He kept his Red ideas buried in his own head, and did nothing about them except to make cynical remarks concerning statesmen. That shocked nobody, it being the fashion in the smart world to accuse political persons of venality as well as stupidity. There was even a fringe of the well-to-do, those who went in for advanced ideas, who were beginning to find good things to say for the Reds. They had been able to survive for five years, in spite of civil wars and famines, and that seemed a miracle. Also, they had the support of popular writers such as Barbusse and Rolland and Anatole France. The last-named came to a hotel on the Cap, and Lanny went to call on him. The old man was showing his many years, but his brain was as clear as ever and his tongue as incisive; the things he said about the situation in Europe differed but little from what Lanny had heard in the establishment of his Red uncle.

Lanny was as happy as one could have expected a sensitive person to be in those troubled days. His *amie* was all that he needed, and he never looked a second time at any of the fashionable ladies, married or unmarried, who spread their charms before him. He dutifully put on the proper clothes and attended the social functions which his mother gave, and some of those of Emily and Sophie when they made a special point of inviting him. He was proud of the success of his two best friends. Rick was working that autumn on a play about the war, and the scenes which Lanny read interested him, and he made suggestions, and thought well of himself when some of them were accepted. Kurt had completed another suite, this time having to do with a soldier's life, and Lanny watched the parturition and birth of an art-work, having all the pleasures of the event and none of the pains. Also there was Marceline, five years old and growing fast; she was by now the liveliest little dancer you ever saw, and knew most everything that Lanny had to teach her along that line. She was a little duck in the water, and a little enchantress everywhere. Very amusing to watch her use her eyes, and practice her arts on every new person who came along. Kurt might be ever so stern a stepfather, but this was a fundamental instinct of the female organism, and he might as well have tried to stop the bougainvillaea in the patio from putting the purple color into its blossoms.

V

In this autumn there came an event whose importance in the history of Europe was realized only gradually. The workers of Italy called a general strike in protest against the permitted cruelties of the blackshirts; the strike failed because the workers had no arms and were powerless against unlimited violence. In this hour of confusion the *Fascisti* took their opportunity and began to assemble; their editor, that Blessed Little Pouter Pigeon at whom Lanny and Rick had laughed, sounded his slogans of glory and summoned his youth to the building of a new Roman Empire.

The American ambassador, "Cradle," played an important part in these events, and was so proud of it that he came home and boasted about it in print. Mussolini came to the embassy and had tea with him, and charmed him so greatly that he defended the dictator and everything he did from that time on. A new government, to have any success, has to have funds, and the editor was seeking support for a movement to restore law and order to his strike-ridden land. Surely an Italy without labor unions, without the co-operatives which deprived businessmen of their profits, ought to be a sound investment! The ambassador thought so, and persuaded the great House of Morgan to promise a loan of two hundred million dollars to the government which Mussolini was planning. Let no one say that America wasn't doing its part in building defenses against the Reds!

There were said to be a hundred and sixty thousand former army officers in Italy, most of them out of jobs and in need of funds. Many had joined the *Fascisti*, and they now led the "March on Rome" which skilled propaganda would make into a heroic episode. Their founder did not walk with them, but traveled more quickly and safely in a sleeping-car. Eight thousand dusty and bedraggled youths could, of course, have accomplished nothing without the acquiescence of police and army. The pint-sized king with the democratic sympathies was told that his cousin had joined the *Fascisti* and was ready to take his throne unless he obeyed orders; therefore he refused to sign the order declaring a state of siege, and the black-shirts entered the capital unopposed.

That "cheap actor" whom Lanny and Rick had interviewed in Cannes now made his appearance before his sovereign, wearing a black shirt, a Sam Browne belt, and a sash of the Fiume colors, and was invited to form a government; later he appeared before the Parlamento and told them that he was the master. No longer was it difficult for him to play the pouter pigeon, for he had had several years' practice in thrusting out his jaw and expanding his chest. The name of Benito Mussolini was flashed around the world, and that interview which Rick had peddled in vain among British editors now suddenly became "spot news." Rick dug it out and rewrote it with fresh trimmings, and his editor paid for it gladly.

VI

The founder of *Fascismo* had proved his thesis of the beneficence of violence. The Americans had a phrase, "climbing onto the band-wagon," and Lanny could imagine all the time-servers, the petty officials and bourgeois "intellectuals," who would hasten to pay homage to the new Roman emperor and make him drunk upon his own glory. A master actor by now, he had served first the left and then the right, and had carefully selected the best phrases of both. Every day he would produce new stunts to delight the Roman mob; he would jump over hurdles to show how lively he was, and be photographed in a cage with a toothless lion cub to show how brave he was.

But woe to those who had fought him, and taught him to hate them! There is no one who hates with such bitterness as a renegade, who has to keep the flame hot that its roaring may be louder than the voice of his conscience. The Socialists, the pacifists, and even the harmless co-operators were shot in their beds or hunted in the mountains; and meanwhile the new ruler in whose honor this Roman holiday was celebrated would stand before the Chamber of Deputies and solemnly ordain: "There shall be no reprisals." That was the pattern of this new society, as Lanny came to know it; boundless cruelty combined with bland and pious lying. The *Fascisti* would develop falsehood into a new science and a new art; they would teach it to one dictator after another, until half the human race would no longer have any means of telling truth from falsehood.

Lanny knew what was happening in Italy, because he was continually meeting victims of it. That was the heritage which his friend Barbara Pugliese had left him; she had told some of her friends about this generous-hearted American youth, and now they had his address. Lanny remembered what his father had said about the practice of hobos in the United States; he had got a mark on his gatepost, and there would be no way ever to get it rubbed out!

The first who came was that young Giulio who had been with Barbara in San Remo and had shouted his contempt at Mussolini in the *trattoria*. The *squadristi* wouldn't overlook a person like that; they gave him his dose of castor oil, and Lanny could hardly recognize the wreck of a human being who appeared at the gate of Bienvenu one morning. He was put into a hospital for a few weeks, but nothing could help him very much, for his digestive tract had been ruined; Giulio was a medical student, so he knew about his own case. He was the first of many who came, each with a more harrowing story; and of course this wasn't pleasant to the ladies of a villa on the Cap d'Antibes. They were sorry of these unfortunates, but also afraid of them, for who would have wanted to treat them that way unless they had done something very terrible? Anyhow, it kept the place in an uproar, and they couldn't see what Lanny had to do with it, or how he expected to set himself single-handed against the new Roman Empire.

Lanny had been able to hide his Red literature, but he tried in vain to hide his Red refugees. It got so that Beauty and Marie worried every time he went to Cannes, for fear that he was meeting some evil companions; it could hardly have been worse if he had been suspected of having another mistress! The people in the village were talking about it, and Beauty was afraid the police authorities might take cognizance. France was a free republic, and proud of its reputation as a home for the oppressed of other lands; all the same, no police like to have swarms of Reds pouring into a country over all the mountain passes and even in rowboats. Beauty could never forget that she herself was a suspected person, living with a German whose past would not bear investigation.

VII

There was another conference, this time at Lausanne, on the other side of the beautiful Lake Geneva. The British had to make a new treaty with the Turks; and of course the French had to be there to get their share. The new Italian Premier had to be there, because the day of glory had arrived, and never again would anybody decide any question about the Mediterranean without consulting him. The new emperor revived the phrase of the old ones—it was *Mare Nostrum*, "Our Sea." To make sure that the world didn't miss the point he kept a long-nosed British nobleman, the "ineffable" Earl Curzon, and with him a Premier of France, waiting like a couple of office boys for a chance to see him and find out what he wanted. A revolution in conferences!

The Turkish treasures were at stake, and that included Mosul, an even more magical name than Baku; so Robbie Budd came again, and all the other oil men. In order to punish the French for having aided the Turks, the British had recognized the Emir Feisal as ruler of Syria; at long last a promise was partly kept, and that dark brown replica of Christ whom Lanny had met and admired during the Peace Conference would come into a part of his own—but not the part with the oil! Tom Lawrence, the blue-eyed, sandy-haired young British agent, had changed his name and was Aircraftsman Shaw, blacking the boots of some minor officer at home. Would he now go back to the desert and resume his place as companion of one who scorned to be called king because he was a descendant of the Prophet? This world that Lanny Budd had been born into was full of strange stories, and travelers from the Mediterranean lands were listened to with interest in his home.

Lanny hadn't planned to go to Lausanne; but the conference adjourned for the Christmas holidays, and there were Robbie and Rick available. The former had business in Berlin; also, Kurt was planning to spend another Christmas at Stubendorf, and Marie was going north to be with her boys. So Lanny, with the Fortunatus purse of his father, laid out a journey for himself and his friends. He and Kurt would escort Marie to Paris, and then go to Lausanne and pick up Robbie and Rick and take them to Berlin, where Lanny and Rick would visit the Robins, and Kurt his brother; then Kurt and Lanny and Rick would go to Stubendorf—Rick's first visit to that place. They would come back to Lausanne and leave Rick for the second stage of the conference, while Lanny and Kurt proceeded to Paris to pick up Marie again.

A jolly thing to plan journeys with the help of a self-renewing purse! You and your friends would be transported from country to country, would talk to the people, gather the news, visit operas and theaters and art-shows; ride on fast and comfortable trains, stop at *de luxe* hotels, eat food novelties in the most elegant restaurants, have all your burdens carried for you, and by the magic of a pocketful of paper money see everybody smiling, obsequious, and delighted. But pay no attention to the signs of bitter poverty on the way; half-starved children begging for bread, women selling their bodies for it—and now and then a Red being hanged or beaten into insensibility!

VIII

Another of those great international gatherings, with diplomats from a score of countries and publicists and journalists from twice as many. Lanny knew so many of them that it was like a larger, outside family, a fluid periphery of friendship. You didn't know who was coming, but there they were; then presently they were gone and others had come. Life consisted of talking and listening to talk; there was a modern, perfected method whereby you hammered out your talk on little typewriter keys, and "filed it," and next morning it would be on a million breakfast tables, or maybe ten million. Moving in that world you were close to the seats of power, and something you said or did might help to "make history."

Mr. Child was there, with a large staff. America had come back into the affairs of Europe, after three years of vowing "Never again!" Mr. Child announced America's policy regarding the Near East; it was "the open door," and who could deny that this was a delicate and tactful way of asserting Standard's claim to twenty-five percent of Mosul oil? The Russians were there, still trying for their loan, and dangling an empty oilcan in front of the noses of Robbie Budd and others. Deterding and the rest of the big fellows had agreed upon a boycott; they had formed an organization called the Groupement, pledging themselves to buy no Russian oil, and now they were waiting to see who would break it first. Robbie predicted that it would be Deterding himself; and sure enough, within two or three months he had bought seventy thousand tons of kerosene and taken an option for another hundred thousand. He had thought, so naïvely, that the agreement applied only to crude!

Berlin would have a poor Christmas this year. The mark stood at nearly one thousand to the dollar, and all but the very rich were poor. Everybody was fear-stricken, for the quarrel with France had come to a crisis; the reparations payments were long since overdue, the coal deliveries in arrears, and there was that round, pasty-faced Poincaré with his jaws clenched, determined to move in and seize the Ruhr, industrial heart of the Reich, without which half the Germans would starve. Rick, eager journalist, wanted to interview people of all classes and write an article after he came out; he found them glad to talk to him, for the hymn of hate had been forgotten and they thought of Britons as friends and protectors against French avarice.

Lanny and Rick went to stay with the Robins. Comfort and safety in that warm nest, and Papa Robin a mine of information about everything that was going on, political and economic. Trust a *Schieber* to know! The hard-working man of affairs was troubled by the bad name which people gave him, and defended himself with vigor. It wasn't he who was going to invade the Ruhr and drive the mark still lower; all he did was to know it was going to happen. People who believed that it wouldn't happen were eager to buy marks for future delivery; if Johannes didn't sell them, others would, and what difference would it make?

But the Robins didn't spend all their time talking about money. Far from it; there were Hansi's fiddle and Freddi's clarinet, and a great stack of accompaniments which Lanny would play or make a stab at. Hansi had had a year of drill by the best teacher in Germany, and it was astonishing how he had grown; he played with authority, and Lanny was greatly delighted, and the others were delighted with his delight. Touching to see how they all praised one another, adored one another, forming a solid family phalanx. The father would conquer the world of finance and the son that of art, and there would be two ways to reduce the handicap under which the Jews labored in this part of the world.

IX

Lanny had written to the boys about Barbara, and now he told them details of that dreadful story, and saw horror in their faces and the tears in their eyes. Their abhorrence of the blackshirts was instinctive, and their sympathy with the rebel refugees complete; they had none of that inner conflict which Lanny perceived in himself. Was it because they were members of a persecuted race, with ancient memories of exile deeply buried in their souls? Or was it that they were more completely artists than Lanny? The artist is by nature, one might say by definition, an anarchist. He lives in the freedom of his own imagination, and represents the experimental element of life. If "authority" should intervene and tell him what to think or to feel, the experiment would not be tried, the brain-child would be born dead.

To the sons of Johannes Robin it seemed the most natural thing in the world to accept those ideas which so greatly troubled the son of Robbie Budd. Of course it was wrong that some should be born to privilege while others did not have enough to eat. Of course it was right that the disinherited should protest and try to change the ancient evils of the world. Who would not demand food when he was starving? Who would not fight for liberty when he was oppressed? Who could fail to hate cruelty and injustice, and cry out for it to be ended? So asked Hansi, and Freddi knew that his adored elder brother must be right.

They asked what Lanny thought, and he was ashamed to tell them of his hesitations and bewilderments. It seemed cowardly not to believe what was so obviously true; it seemed weakness to consider such questions as what would offend your father or imperil your mother's social position. Having met Lanny's Red uncle, the Jewish lads didn't think of him as a dangerous man, but as an amazingly understanding one, and they wanted to know where he was and what he was doing and what he had said about the present state of Germany and France and Russia. Lanny mentioned books that he had read, and Hansi declared that when the summer came and he had free time, he was going to learn the difference between Communists and Socialists, and try really to understand the tormented world in which he lived.

Lanny wondered, what was Papa Robin going to make of that? He asked the question tactfully, and learned that it had never been raised in the family. Both Hansi and Freddi took it for granted that their father would want them to believe what was right. Lanny didn't say it aloud, but he thought: "Suppose you take to associating with Reds, like me? Suppose you start rescuing them from the Fascists, and having refugees come to this home with the heavily barred steel door—how will it be then?"

X

Lanny hadn't had much talk with Kurt's older brother Emil on his previous visit, but this time Emil had leave for Christmas, and the four of them traveled to Stubendorf together. Lanny sat and listened, as he liked to do, while the serious Prussian officer discussed the state of his country, and the English journalist plied him with questions. Rather easy-going himself, Lanny liked to watch Rick work efficiently; he would jack himself up and resolve to do likewise, but he didn't always keep the pledge. However, when Rick had a few pages of the article done, Lanny would read them, and make comments and suggestions which Rick found useful. Perhaps that was work, even though others got the credit for it.

Emil might have been described as Kurt without those elements of sympathy and imagination which made Kurt an artist. The elder brother was wrapped up in his professional duties, and when he thought about politics and world events it was as part of the problem of the defense of Germany. He was disturbed, not to say tormented, over the present situation, because Germany was without defense, and the French armies were assembled at the border, ready to move at any moment. From the point of view of a military man that was the worst of all possible situations; Emil's fear of what the French would do was conditioned by what he himself had been taught to do under similar circumstances.

They talked about Italy, and the Prussian officer's viewpoint of events there provoked a lively argument. Emil spoke of the Fascist "revolution," and when Rick objected to that term he said: "Call it a 'counter-revolution' if you choose, but names don't alter the fact that it's a natural reaction against the futilities of so-called democracy. The people attempt a task which is beyond their powers, the governing of a modern state, and they are brought to a plight where they are glad to have a strong man get them out of it. The strong man studies the people, understands them better than they understand themselves, and promises them everything they want; he constructs a program with an appeal which they are powerless to resist. Say that he's 'fooling them,' if you wish, but even so, he gets control, and having once got it, he keeps it—because modern weapons are so efficient that those who have them are masters, provided they are not afraid to use them. The machine gun and the airplane bomb with poison gas promise mankind a long era of firm government."

Such was Emil Meissner's interpretation of Fascism; and he revealed the interesting fact that a movement not unlike it had been under way in Germany ever since the end of the war. It was a native product—never would you hear a Prussian staff officer admit that virile and scientific Germans might learn anything from de-

generate and soft Italians! The movement called itself the National
Socialist German Workingmen's Party, and its center was in Munich; one of its leaders was General Ludendorff, who next to Hindenburg was regarded as the nation's greatest war leader. This new
party promised the German people deliverance from humiliation,
and it was spreading with great rapidity. If it took the form of fresh
opposition to France and Britain, these nations would have only the
stupidity of their own statesmen to blame. So declared this stiff yet
passionate Prussian officer.

XI

Christmas at Schloss Stubendorf was even more pinched and
straitened than it had been the previous year. With the mark so low,
it was impossible to import anything, so in a country district like
this you lived as in primitive times, upon what you got from the
soil or made with your hands. But you could still have courage and
loyalty, *deutsche Treu und Werde;* also the tender sentiments of
the *Weihnachtsfest* were unaffected by inflation of the currency.
The Meissners played a great deal of music and sang all the old
Christmas songs; everybody was gracious to the visiting strangers,
and the two young war widows experienced hot and cold flushes
in the presence of the eligible young American. He had no way to
let them know that he had an *amie,* so he never offered to play accompaniments for one without also inviting the other.

Rick, of course, was deeply interested in everything he saw here,
and in everyone he met. "Upper Silesia after the Settlement" was
the form the data were taking in his professional mind. A joint
Polish-German commission had worked out an elaborate protocol,
having six hundred and six sections, and it seemed to be working
pretty well; but if France invaded the Ruhr, would Korfanty the
troublemaker get busy again? Herr Meissner and his sons discussed
these questions at length; of course nothing pleased them more than
the idea of having a sympathetic English journalist report their point
of view to the outside world.

Among Kurt's friends in the village was a lad named Heinrich

Jung, son of that *Oberförster* who provided them with an escort whenever they wished to go hunting. Heinrich, it appeared, was studying forestry in Munich, and had joined the National Socialist German Workingmen's Party about which Emil had told. Since Rick was so interested, Kurt brought the lad up to the house and had him talk—something that was not difficult, for his movement was a proselytizing one, and he knew its formulas by heart. He was nineteen, and sturdily built; war and famine hadn't hurt him, for he had got both food and schooling in Stubendorf. He had extraordinarily bright blue eyes, rosy cheeks, and pale hair over which the barber ran the clippers once a month. Heinrich performed conscientiously all his duties to the Fatherland, which included explaining the new creed to two visitors of Aryan blood like himself. He and his partisans were known as "Nazis," because that was the German pronunciation of the first two syllables of the word "National."

Lanny had decided that Communism was a new religion; and here was another, this time German instead of Russian. It inspired its youth with the idea that they were destined to redeem the Fatherland and make it over into something new and more wonderful. It filled them with a fervor of faith; it taught them to march and drill for the cause, to sing songs about it, to be ready to die for it. The program of these "Nazis" sounded so completely Red that at first it was hard to understand how any army officer could be sympathetic to it. It held out all imaginable promises to lure the poor and unhappy. All German citizens were to have equal rights; all were to work, and unearned incomes were to be abolished; the bonds of "interest slavery" were to be broken, war gains confiscated, trusts nationalized, department stores communalized, speculation in land prevented, and land for common purposes confiscated without compensation. Usurers and profiteers were to suffer the death penalty, a paid army was to be abolished, and lying newspapers suppressed; on the other hand, there was to be higher education for all good Germans, and for youth every benefit and advantage they could imagine. The blue eyes of Heinrich Jung shone like those of a young archangel as he invited the two Aryan strangers to give their support to this redemptive enterprise.

"This looks like the seed of a new revolution," said the impressionable Lanny to his English friend, when they were alone in their room.

"Maybe so," replied the more critical journalist, "but to me it sounds like the old Pan-Germanism dressed up in a new stage costume."

"But, Rick, can they get the young people wrought up as Heinrich is, and then not do any of the things they have promised?"

"Political slogans are like grain scattered to draw birds into a snare. Find out who's putting up the money for a political party, and then you know what it will do."

Lanny, enthusiastic himself, couldn't take a cynical view of the enthusiasms of other young persons. "They really have inspired that lad with a lot of high ideals, Rick; I mean loyalty, self-sacrifice, devotion to duty."

"But isn't that what every master wants of his servants? The Kaiser preached it long before the war. What you have to do, Lanny, is to look into Pan-Germanism. They talk about the superiority of the Aryan race, the making over of the world, and all that, but at bottom it's no more than the Berlin-to-Baghdad railroad, so that Germany can get the oil of Mosul; it means colonies in Africa, which aren't of any economic use to Germany, but have harbors which can be fortified and serve as hiding-places for submarines to cut the life-lines of Britain."

"Maybe you're right," admitted Lanny, "but don't say any of that before Kurt, for he wouldn't take it very well." Lanny, still working at his self-appointed task of keeping Britain and Germany reconciled!

XII

On their way to Switzerland the three friends had to pass through Munich, so Heinrich, returning to school, traveled with them. They talked with him further, and Rick probed his mind. Once you knew his formulas, he could do nothing but repeat, and that soon became monotonous. They discovered that the lad knew little about the outside world, and didn't seem interested to learn; he was going to make it so different that what it now was didn't really matter. If you told him something about England or France or America that didn't fit in with the National Socialist formula, he was too polite to say that he doubted, but he let it slip off the outside of his mind without penetrating.

Rick, the efficient journalist, was just the opposite of this. Much as he was repelled by Pan-Germanism, whether in its new or old stage costume, he considered it his business to know about it. He remembered the bad guess he had made about Mussolini, and he didn't want to repeat it with General Ludendorff, or whoever might be the coming savior of the Fatherland. "Let's stop off for a day in Munich, and let me get the smell of this movement." Lanny, who had the curiosity of a deer concerning any new phenomenon of the forest, said: "O.K." Heinrich, of course, was overjoyed, and offered to take them to headquarters and see them properly introduced.

The place had been a *Kaffeehaus*, in the Korneliusstrasse, a working-class district. There was a large room with a few tables and chairs, and pamphlets in the windows. There was a counter where the members paid their dues, and a couple of small private rooms in back. The place was called the Braunhaus, for everything of the Nazis had to be brown, as that of the Fascists was black; let no one say the Germans were imitating anyone! Instead of the lictors' fasces, Nazis wore the Oriental swastika, or hooked cross, on an armband, and carried it on their banners; but they didn't have many, for cloth was scarce. Practically all the Nazis were young ex-soldiers, and many wore their old uniforms turned inside out.

A young party official answered the questions of the visitors, and told them about conditions throughout Bavaria, where fighting among the Reds and the Catholics went on almost daily; the members of the new party were accumulating arms and drilling in the near-by forests, for the purpose of putting an end to all that. It was their declared purpose to seize the government, first of Bavaria and then of the republic. They were a peculiar combination of conspirators and propagandists; they told you exactly what they were going to do, and indeed everything but the date of the uprising.

"And that," said the young party official, "is because we don't know it ourselves."

The visitors were fortunate in having arrived in Munich on the day of a great meeting in the Bürgerbräukeller, and if they would attend they would learn all about the movement, and would hear a speech by "Adi." This was short for Adolf, the great orator of the party; his last name was Schicklgruber, but this was rarely mentioned, it not being considered a very dignified name.

Lanny took Rick and Kurt to the Aden Hotel and, after the fashion which Robbie had taught him, put them up in proper style. They spent the rest of the day looking at pictures in the Schack Gallery. After supper they took a taxi to the beer hall in the Rosenheimerstrasse. The term "beer hall" in Munich means something really big; this was one of the biggest, with tables and seats for a couple of thousand people. The Munichers sit in these seats and by slow sipping can make one stein last all evening. Of course if they can afford it they take much more, and the practice seems to agree with them, for the fortunate ones acquire large round bodies and great wads of fat on cheeks and necks.

The place was crowded; but a piece of paper money obtained front seats for three strangers, and they looked about the smoke-filled room and were sorry for the German people—for not even in Poland had Lanny seen more pitiful clothing. Evidently what in Rick's country were known as "the lower orders" had turned out to hear their favorite orator. At the table with Lanny and his friends sat a man who told them he was a party journalist; a little lame fellow with twisted features and a shrill voice. When he had become acquainted with the visitors he told them a lot about Adi, not all of it favorable, by any means.

There was a large band blaring loudly, and when it played *Deutschland über Alles*, everybody stood up and gave the Nazi salute, the right arm extended upward and in front; then they sat down again, and the shrill voice of the party journalist told them of the unhappy childhood of Adolf Hitler Schicklgruber, how he had left home, struggled in vain to be an artist, and had become a pitiful bum living in flophouses, earning a few pfennigs painting postcards, or sometimes houses. In the war he had been a lance corporal, and had been gassed. After the war his army superiors had sent him to a secret meeting of Munich workingmen, to spy upon them and report what they were doing and planning. Adi had found out, and the next time he came it was not as a spy but as a convert to the cause. Now he was one of the leaders of that movement which was inspiring the German people and preparing to make over the world.

The band struck up, and Charlie Chaplin came upon the stage. At least Lanny and Rick thought it was an imitation of that little comedian, whose pictures were the rage all over America and Europe at that time—even the highbrow critics raved over him and called him a genius. The features by which you knew him were baggy pants and big shoes, tousled hair and a tiny dark mustache, a pasty face and a simper. The man who hurried onto the stage had all of these, and also a very soiled old trench-coat. Lanny and Rick really thought he was going to do a comic "turn" in imitation of the little Hollywood comedian. But then they realized that this was the man they had come to hear make a speech.

XIII

The music and the applause ceased, and the orator began. He spoke the dialect of the district of Austria where he had been born, and at first it was hard for Lanny to understand him. He spoke with violent gesticulations, which caused his much too big clothing to flap about him. He had a bellowing voice, and when he became excited it reminded Lanny of a turkey gobbler he had listened to in Connecticut. Presently he worked himself into a frenzy, and then it seemed that what he was saying no longer made sense; but the crowd seemed to find something in it, for when the orator's voice gave out and the sentence died in a gabble, they drowned it out in thunders of applause.

The substance of the discourse was the wrongs which Germany had suffered during the lifetime of Adolf Hitler Schicklgruber. Having heard the story of his frustrated life, one didn't have to be more of a psychologist than Lanny Budd to understand how he had come to identify himself with his Fatherland and its woes. Germany's lack of resources before the war had caused Adolf Hitler Schicklgruber to have to sleep in flophouses; the Versailles peace was Adolf Hitler Schicklgruber's failure to reap glory and wealth from the war; the shouting of the excited audience in the Bürgerbräukeller was Adolf Hitler Schicklgruber's determination to rise in the world in spite of all the efforts of his enemies to hold him down.

These enemies were many, and the orator hated and cursed them in turn and in combination. They were Britain and France and Poland; they were the Reds inside and outside of Germany; they were the international bankers; they were the Jews, that accursed race which was poisoning the blood of all Aryan peoples, infecting the German soul with pessimism, cynicism, and unfaith in its own destiny. Adi seemed to have got his enemies all mixed up together, for the Reds were Jews and the international bankers were Jews, and it was the Jews who controlled Wall Street and the London City and the Paris bourse; apparently he thought that the same Jews had brought Bolshevism to Russia; they were in control of the world's finances and at the same time were starving the German people for the purpose of forcing them into the clutches of the Reds!

This tirade lasted for more than two hours, going back again and again over the same grievances and the same threats. Lanny thought he had never heard anything so fantastic in all his life. But there was something terrifying about it, especially the effect it had upon this packed throng. It was like seeing the war break out again, as Lanny had seen it in Paris in the dreadful summer of 1914; like hearing the trampling of the troops, the guns clattering on the roadways, the crowds roaring for blood.

When they came out, and were safe in their taxi, Lanny said: "Well, is that the German Mussolini?"

Rick replied: "No; I don't think I'll ever have to write about Herr Schicklgruber!"

He talked along that line, but when he finished, Kurt said, quietly:

"You are making a mistake. You could write a very important article about that man and that speech. He is confused, but so are the German people. Also he is desperate—and they are that, too. Believe me, he is not to be overlooked."

BOOK FOUR

Money Grows on Trees

16

Contend for Homer Dead

I

MORE than once Lanny had said to his mother: "I think we ought to do something about Marcel's paintings." He would say: "I don't want to live on Robbie the rest of my life, and I think he'd respect me more if I showed him I could make some money." It had been agreed between them that when any of the works were sold the proceeds would be divided into three parts, the third to be kept for Marceline's *dot*.

One day Emily Chattersworth phoned and invited Lanny over to lunch at Sept Chênes. "There's a man coming I think you'll like to meet. He's an art expert, and he's heard about Marcel's work. I won't invite anybody else, so you can have a chance to get acquainted."

Thus came Zoltan Kertezsi, a middle-aged Hungarian who had been taken to New York as a child and since then had lived all over the world. His father was an engraver and the family was musical, so Kertezsi had grown up with art; he was an excellent violinist, and when Lanny told him about Kurt and his work he was so much interested that he forgot about Marcel for a while. He was a man with a kind and gentle face, and fair hair and mustache; his graciousness was somewhat airy; he moved with a kind of lightness so that at first you might think he was affected, but you discovered that it was the expression of a personality. He loved delicate and refined things, and had spent his life seeking them, studying and savoring them.

The profession of art expert was a new one to Lanny, and he listened with interest while this rapid and eager talker explained

319

it with humor and the opposite of pretense. He described himself as a sort of upper servant to the rich, new or old, a culture-tutor to grown-up children, a guide and bodyguard to amateur explorers of a field where more snares were laid for their feet than had ever existed in the defenses of the Meuse-Argonne. This was a new view of the art world to Lanny; he had thought of a painting as something to look at and enjoy, but Kertezsi said that was very naïve—a painting was something to be sold to a pork merchant or the dowager empress of a chain-store system, persons who had acquired huge sums of money in a short time and were seeking some way to distinguish themselves. The crimes committed in the course of selling art-works to them were more numerous than would ever be listed by the Sûreté Générale. Kertezsi didn't say that he was one of the few honest experts in Europe, but that was the impression his conversation gave. He was simple, swift, and precise in his judgments, and Lanny was delighted to follow wherever his conversation led.

It led to Guatemala, Tibet, and Central Africa, where Kertezsi had traveled seeking native works for museums. He had climbed to monasteries in high mountains, and discovered long-buried palaces in jungles and deserts. He had had strange adventures, and liked to tell about them. He loved every beautiful thing that he had ever bought or sold, and would describe each with ecstatic words and airily gesticulating hands. He would become so absorbed in telling how he had found a great David or Rossetti's *Blessed Damozel*, and by what extraordinary luck he had been able to purchase it, that he would forget all about his *mostele à l'anglaise*, and Mrs. Emily's considerate butler would leave his plate to the last moment, hoping he would remember what he was there for.

II

Lanny decided that this was a man he wanted to know; so after luncheon he took him over to Bienvenu and introduced him to Beauty and to Kurt, and took him down to the studio and opened the storeroom of paintings. This, too, was an adventure, for by the magic of art Marcel Detaze, burned up in the fires of battle, came back, sat with them, and told them the intimate secrets of his soul; he made a new friend, and to Lanny it was more exciting to see this happen than it was to make one for himself.

The introduction was carried on chronologically. First, those lovely paintings of the Cap, in which a son of the cold north had expressed his delight in sunshine and color; the blue and green sea lifting itself heavily, breaking into curves of white foam or showers of sapphire flame. "How he loves it!" exclaimed Kertezsi. "You see how passionately he paints; he is trying to say something that he cannot say; perhaps he will never be able to. But the man has talent, extraordinary talent. The whole Riviera is here. How could people fail to know this work?"

"He was a very shy man," replied Lanny; "he didn't know how to advertise his stuff, and was always more interested in trying to do something better."

"We must find a way to make him known," said the other. "You have a treasure here."

Lanny brought out the scenes of Norway. Now the painter had gone into a strange world, and was awed by it; these waters were cold, these rocks were dark, and these people lived hard; it was a feat just to be alive on a Norwegian fiord. "They are all summer scenes," said Kertezsi. "But you feel that he is thinking about winter."

"He painted many of them in the winter, after he had come back."

"His brushwork has become different. He is groping for a new technique. This isn't the same water that he watched from the Cap, or the same paint that represents it."

Then Greece and Africa. Lanny told about the cruise of the *Bluebird*, and how he and Marcel had felt, and what they had talked about. The other man knew all these places, and got the intense feeling that had been poured into the work: the melancholy of Greece and the hard, stern cruelty of the lands from which the corsairs had sailed, from which the slavers had raided across the deserts into the jungles since time more distant than the eye of history could reach. Marcel had lived alone in his little cottage on the Cap, painting these pictures while he waited for his beautiful blond mistress to come back to him, and perhaps the fear of a great sorrow had hung over him during this time.

Then the war, and the painter's dreadful mutilation; so there was a new man to know. The art buyer had heard something of the story —perhaps Emily Chattersworth had told him. Lanny brought out the sketches which he had managed to keep his stepfather from destroying; and then one by one he set on the easel those war works into which Marcel had poured his horror, grief, and love of *la patrie*. That *Soldier in Pain*, tormented by the little Hun devils, which the painter had insisted was only a cartoon, but which Kertezsi now said was worthy of Daumier. That *Fear*, which the critic said could have been done by no one but William Blake at his best; that portrait of Beauty called *Sister of Mercy*, which Lanny said she would never sell and which Kertezsi predicted would be borrowed for exhibition all over the world if they knew about it.

"Really, Mr. Budd," said the visitor, "it is a mistake not to let the public have this work. I don't suppose you need the money, but I point out that, from the purely business point of view, if you let part of these treasures go, they will work for the rest. If you sell all but a small part, what you have left will in course of years become worth more than the whole thing if you keep it hidden."

"We have often talked about putting some of them on the market," assented Lanny. "How would you suggest going about it?"

"Suppose you begin with a test. Take one of these Riviera seascapes, just an average one, and put it up at a London auction room, say Christie's, at one of their really good miscellaneous sales—a little later, when the foreigners are crowding into the hotels. I'll do a little boosting in a quiet way—I mean, I'll get some worthwhile people to look at it, and perhaps I can find some rich American friend to bid for it. You never can tell what may happen; the dealers get to whispering among themselves: 'Zoltan Kertezsi is interested in that Detaze, he says he's a coming man,' and so on—that's the way the game is played, and there's no harm in it, because I really will be interested. You can put a minimum price on the picture if you wish, and if it fails to bring that, I'll bid it in, and in that case you will only be out the commission of the auction room."

"What do you charge for such a service, Mr. Kertezsi?"

"A flat ten percent, whether I am acting for the buyer or the seller. Many dealers will charge both parties, but that I have never done. If you wish me to represent you and try to interest buyers, you may pay me; or if you prefer that I take a chance and try to find some one of my customers who will commission me to buy the picture at a certain price, I will do that."

Said Lanny: "It will seem strange to be making a lot of money out of Marcel's work, when he was able to make so little during his whole life."

To which the other answered by quoting the couplet on the disputed birthplace of an ancient poet:

"Seven wealthy towns contend for Homer dead,
Through which the living Homer begged his bread."

III

Rick hadn't brought his family to the Riviera that winter, because his play had been accepted by one of the stage societies and he had to be on hand to assist in the production. That was something exciting, and Lanny wanted to see it; now he had a double excuse, because of this offer of Zoltan Kertezsi, which Beauty decided to accept. They picked out what they considered a good specimen of Marcel's seascapes—*Sea and Rocks*, they named it—and the arrangement was made for it to be put up at auction just after Easter. That being the period when Marie went north, Lanny drove her, and then went on to London—the obliging ferry took your car across, so you spoke of motoring to London as if the Channel wasn't there.

Rick's play was just going into rehearsal, so he was in town and much occupied. Lanny went to the theater with him, and lived again those days in Connecticut when he had acted in one play and helped to stage another; memories swept over him—and they were intensified manifold when he chanced to looked over the list of plays showing in London and saw the announcement: "Phyllis Gracyn in the sensational New York success, *All Things for Love*."

"Well, well!" he thought. "She's made good!" Indeed, that was the heights for an American actress, to be starred in a London production!

Lanny decided that he wanted to see her act, and persuaded Rick to go with him. Of course he had told his friend about the old love affair, and Rick was curious to have a look at the lady; as for Lanny —well, if you are going to be jilted and have your heart broken, let it be by somebody who is somebody!

The play wasn't much, they agreed; a society drama, the conventional "triangle," with Gracyn playing the part of a young music student who becomes involved with a married man and gives him up when she realizes that he cares more about his family's reputation and social position than he does about love. The "star" herself was the life of the play; the same delicate boyish figure, seeming not a day older than when Lanny had held her in his arms nearly five years earlier. She had acquired poise and skill in putting her personality across; nothing could be more spontaneous than her gaiety, and her charm was controlled like water from a tap.

"I don't wonder you fell for that," said Rick. "Does she still cause you melancholy feelings?"

"I like what I have much better," declared Lanny. "What sort of life would I have chasing about in the entourage of a stage queen?"

"Count yourself well out of it," agreed the other. "I'm having troubles with a stage queen myself just now."

A few days later Lanny saw his old sweetheart having luncheon in the hotel where he was staying. She was with a fashionably dressed man and Lanny had no mind to interrupt, but she saw him and sent the waiter for him, so he went over to her table. The man to whom she introduced him was her producer, and Lanny wondered, was she playing the same old game? Not *All Things for Love*, but *A Part for Love!* She was showing her old friend off to her new, as Lanny had shown her off to Rick. She seemed delighted to see him— but he wondered, can you ever trust an actress? They learn to do these things on the stage, and can they keep from practicing offstage? It was a case of once bit, twice shy.

He paid the customary compliments to her performance, and was prepared to go, but she wouldn't have it so; she made him sit down —one didn't give up old friends so lightly. She wanted him to know that success hadn't gone to her head; she told the other man how Lanny had helped her in her struggling days, that bitter, lonely time when she had been a high school student, pining to get onto the stage but having no more idea how to set about it than if it was the pearly gates of heaven she wished to crash.

"How are you, Lanny, and what are you doing in London?" He told her that he had a friend with a new play; also a painting of his stepfather's was to be sold at auction. "Oh, do they have auctions of paintings? Could I come and see it? I might buy one, just to show that I'm getting culture!"

"A lot of people buy them for that reason," smiled the young man-about-town. "Naturally I'd be pleased to have you attend." Zoltan Kertezsi had explained that it was important to have people looking at the picture and asking questions about it, especially prominent persons—and who could serve better than the star of a current stage hit?

IV

One thing Robbie Budd had always insisted upon in his travels: you must stop at the most expensive hotel in town, because that way you meet the people you need in your business. Now, being in business, Lanny learned how wise this precept was. Walking through the lobby, with its elaborate display of marble and brass and ormolu and plush, who should be passing but Harry Murchison, that plate-glass manufacturer who had come so close to kidnaping Beauty Budd and her son and carrying them away to his valley of smoke and steel! Nearly nine years had passed since that had happened, or rather failed to happen, and the young businessman from Pittsburgh had grown stouter and more serious than ever; but Lanny knew him at once, and the other had to stare for only a moment or two. He greeted his almost-stepson cordially, and asked the polite questions, how was his mother, and was she with him, and what was he doing. When Lanny told him, he said, in much the same spirit as Gracyn: "I'd be interested to see your stepfather's painting. Could

I come, and bring my wife?" Of course Lanny said he'd be delighted to meet Mrs. Murchison.

He wasn't clear in his mind just how much Harry knew about Marcel Detaze. He had known that Beauty had a lover down on the Cap, but did he realize that this was the man? Had he told his wife about his adventure, or misadventure, in the far-off days before the war? That was one of their family secrets, into which Lanny was not expected to pry.

Adella Murchison was a tall, good-looking, youngish brunette who had been her husband's secretary and still took that attitude, doing for him many of the things that secretaries do. They had three children at home, and Lanny knew that they had been married soon after Harry's return to the States; he made a story out of it in his imagination: the heir of a fortune had lost his great love, and was lonely, and a woman employee had "caught him on the rebound," as they say. Lanny liked her because she was straightforward and unpretentious; she said that she didn't know much about painting, but would like to learn, and he gave her such instruction as time permitted.

The rooms of Christie's are in a very old building on King Street, near St. James's Palace. They are extraordinarily shabby, which tells you that they are so aristocratic that they don't have to bother about looks; they are intended for persons so important that their clothes look as if they had been slept in, and who carry rolled umbrellas that have begun to turn green with age. There is a man at the door who is prepared to receive royalty. You go upstairs and find four or five rooms where the paintings are on exhibition, and a salesroom with backless benches on which you sit if you come early. (Proceedings begin at one o'clock, which keeps you from getting any lunch.) The most fashionable people crowd in, those who love expensive art, the critics who write about it, and the dealers who buy and resell it; also the inquisitive public that likes to observe celebrities in action.

The tone of the place is very English, that is to say, dignified, solemn, even pompous. You stroll through the rooms and inspect what is offered. If you are "anybody," you are known to "everybody," and they watch you, and try to guess what you are there for. The cash value of a work of art is one of the most highly speculative things in the world—Zoltan Kertezsi said, almost as much so as the cash value of a woman. It can be changed for better or for worse by a casual phrase, the lifting of an eyebrow, a depreciatory smile. There are some whose word is taken, and others whose money is taken, and of these two forces there can be an infinitude of subtle combinations and shadings.

Lanny had explained to his agent that he was bringing a multi-millionaire from Pittsburgh, a place that sounded like money. Both Harry and his wife looked like money—vulgar, American money that had to be manifested by new clothes. There also was the adorable Phyllis Gracyn, even more elaborately dressed, and it was soon known that the handsome young man who was showing her the Detaze—number 37 in the catalogue—was the scion of Budd's, the American munitions works; he was the owner of the painting and stepson of the painter. Such items cause polite murmurs among visitors at art-sales.

When the important Zoltan Kertezsi came along with a German chemicals man who was in the financial pages of the newspapers, that, too, was something to whisper about; the Germans were said to be putting their money into paintings and diamonds, because they couldn't trust the mark any more. The newspapers have reporters at these sales, to note who bids and what prices are paid, and that is one of the ways that reputations are made for artists both living and dead. The *Sunday Times* had singled out *Sea and Rocks* for praise, and the French dealers who were present had of course made note of that. Now they saw Zoltan Kertezsi leading his man in front of that picture and pointing out its merits. Everybody began suddenly talking Detaze. Oh, yes, that French painter who had had his face burned off in the war and had worn a mask for years. A work of art about which you can tell such a story to your friends is obviously much more interesting than one by a painter of whom you can say only that he was born on such a day and died on such another day.

V

The room was packed to the doors when the sale began. Those who expected to bid sat close under the auctioneer's pulpit; he knew most of them and their ways, and required only the faintest sign from them. An attendant would set a painting upon a high easel; the auctioneer would give its catalogue number and say a few words about it; reserved English words, no circus-poster adjectives, no motion-picture language. This is the right little, tight little island, where we know our own minds and tolerate no nonsense. Give us the facts, name of the artist, his nationality and date, and perhaps what collection the work has come from; we know the fellow, and if we want the thing, we nod our head one-quarter of an inch, enough for the auctioneer and not enough for the chap alongside, for it's none of his business whether we have bid or not.

But the dealers, of course, are different. Those fellows are out to make money; rather vulgar chaps, you know, full of gossip and gabble; they want to know whether Detaze is going to go, and they watch for the signs, and try to find out who is bidding, and whom he represents. They are all playing a game, each against the others, and they run here and there like a herd of stampeded animals—not physically, of course, but emotionally, in their judgments of art, and what will increase in value and what will not. They are playing a thousand little tricks upon one another; each having his favorite that he has stocked up on, or got options on, and is trying to promote. He can't do it alone, of course; he has to persuade some of the others that here is the coming man; has to get him into the newspapers, and lure rich clients into thinking that he is tops, not merely for the moment but for the future. Buying a painting is one of civilization's most fascinating lotteries.

Zoltan Kertezsi had done an excellent job with that Detaze. Somebody started off at twenty guineas, and then the bidding became picturesque: the American actress, the Pittsburgh plateglass man, the German chemicals man all mixing in. They bid it up to five hundred and seventy-five guineas, which was a terrific sum for a small work, the first of its creator's ever to come on public sale. The wind-up was striking too, for an entirely unknown person stepped in at the last moment and said five hundred and eighty, and all the others quit. He was a quietly determined old gentleman with a neatly trimmed white beard and gold pince-nez; he gave the name of John Smith, which must have been a pseudonym; he counted out a stack of fresh crisp banknotes, got his bill of sale, tucked the painting under his arm and walked out to a taxicab, and that was the end of that particular Detaze. It just disappeared off the face of the earth and nobody ever heard of it again.

There were other consequences of this sensational sale. The German chemicals man decided that he wanted a Detaze, and would pay the price he had bid at the sale, five hundred and sixty guineas, if Kertezsi could find him one as good as the *Sea and Rocks*. Then Harry Murchison called up Lanny and swore him to secrecy, and said he wanted to have such a seascape hanging in his home when his wife entered it again. He too would pay what he had bid, five hundred and fifty guineas, and would trust Lanny to pick him out a good one. Lanny was embarrassed to sell to a friend, but Harry said nonsense, the paintings were for sale, weren't they, and he wouldn't have a fit of shyness if Lanny were trying to buy some plateglass.

Lanny wrote his mother about this good outcome; but before the letter arrived she sent him a telegram, saying that a man unknown to her had come to Bienvenu and asked to see samples of Marcel's work; after seeing them, he had offered to buy everything they had, two hundred and seventeen paintings, for a flat price of two million francs, and he would have the money wired to Beauty's bank in Cannes within a couple of hours if she accepted the offer. Lanny was in a panic for fear Beauty might be tempted and he sent her back a red-hot telegram: "For heaven's sake no, we'll get several times that before we are through. Answer immediately assurance."

Lanny said that at Zoltan Kertezsi's direction, and Beauty wired that she would comply, but it was the awfullest temptation. A few hours later she wired that the mysterious visitor was now offering three hundred thousand francs for the privilege of selecting twelve land- and seascapes. Kertezsi said that was more like it, and he advised taking the offer. "Obviously some dealer thinks he can do business with them, and that means he'll be getting publicity for Detaze and building him up. He'll be working for us, and it's all right to pay him for it."

So Lanny wired: "Accept offer but specify in writing no wartime pictures included." At the same time he wired Jerry Pendleton to go at once to Bienvenu and see to the handling of the transaction. That redhead was a good fighting man, and wouldn't be too polite to inspect what the mysterious stranger was carrying off the premises.

VI

Things went on happening. Next morning Mrs. Murchison telephoned, saying that her husband was lunching with a business associate, and wouldn't Lanny come and lunch with her; she had something confidential to tell him. Lanny said: "Of course," and hoped it wasn't a flirtation; he had had that happen more than once, but he thought of the former secretary as a frank and sensible woman, and he himself was not available for an affair.

When they were settled in the hotel dining-room, she asked if she might tell him a little about life in Pittsburgh, and he was tempted to reply: "I once thought I was going to live there." Instead, he answered discreetly that he'd be interested to know all about it.

She talked for a while about a city that had worked very hard, and now had more money than it knew what to do with; especially the women who had both time and money on their hands. She talked about a social set whose members were selected on the basis of their having about the same financial means. Adella Murchison's dark eyes sparkled with mischief as she described "young matrons" who played golf and bridge, and gossiped about one another, and discussed their children and their servants and their ailments.

"It doesn't sound so different from home," said Lanny, and wondered what was coming out of this.

"I can't afford to be upstage with my husband's friends," continued the woman. "They had him when I was just an employee. So I said to him: 'We're getting into a rut, Harry. Let's break away for a while and see something of the world; let's get some fun out of our money.' So I got him over here, and I want to accomplish something before we go back—already I know he's getting restless."

"What is it you want?" asked the young man, trying to be businesslike.

"I want some culture! I listened to you and Mr. Kertezsi talking, and it was like moving into a different world. Of course I know he was talking partly for my benefit—I've been in business offices and I know a line of sales talk when I hear it—but at the same time he does love beautiful things."

"No doubt about that."

"Do you remember his telling about the big sausage man from Kansas City who bought a Greco and took it home with him, and right away he became famous, and all the people who had never come near him now wanted to see his Greco? It isn't that bad with us, but I thought, if we had something really first class of our own, interesting people might ask to see it, and they would talk about it, and that would be better than playing bridge, or dancing to jazz music over the radio—you know how 'smart' people pass their time."

"I live on the Riviera," said Lanny.

"I suppose that's where the bored people in Europe go. Anyhow, I've decided to take Mr. Kertezsi's suggestion and get a Greco. I'll tell you frankly, I didn't know what it was—if it hadn't been that an art expert was talking I'd have thought it was a kind of lizard."

"A gecko, I believe it is," ventured the other, and they laughed.

"I've acquired a book on art," continued the "young matron." "I looked in the index, and now I know enough about El Greco for conversation. In the book there's a painting of an old man, supposed to be El Greco himself."

"I'm afraid you can't get that. I saw it in the Metropolitan in New York."

"There are others, I suppose?"

"One might be found. But it would cost a lot."

"About what do you think?"

"One or two million francs, for a really fine one."

"I never can get this currency business straight."

"Fifty or a hundred thousand dollars—maybe less, with the franc dropping as it is."

"I think I could get Harry to spend that. He's been impressed by the idea that paintings are an investment."

"No doubt about that," Lanny assured her. "Tell him about Yussupoff, the young cousin of the Tsar, the one who killed Rasputin. He barely escaped from the Bolsheviks with his life, but he managed to bring out his two Rembrandts, rolled up. He can live in luxury for the rest of his life on the sum that Joseph Widener paid him for them. If you should have a revolution in Pittsburgh, now—!" They laughed, as the rich always do at revolutions—beforehand.

VII

Adella Murchison talked some more about her culture aspirations, and then came to a part of the matter that she said was a bit delicate. "What does Mr. Kertezsi charge to buy a painting, or to advise in the buying?"

"Ten percent."

"That's a lot of money for what may be very little work."

"What you pay for is his expert knowledge, which it took a long time to acquire. You have to be sure what you are buying."

"What is on my mind is that he might be persuaded to divide the commission with you; because we should want your advice also."

"Oh, but I'm not an expert, Mrs. Murchison!"

"I have listened to you two talking; and I said to myself: 'There's a young man who really loves art as I should like to love it.' I want the painting I get to be one that you think is worth while. I want to hear you tell me why. I want you to show me the fine points—in short, give me a sales talk about that picture, so I can take it back to a smoky city where I have to change my window curtains twice every week and my husband has to keep a supply of clean shirts at the office."

"You are paying me a compliment, Mrs. Murchison, and of course

I'll be glad to help you and Harry, and tell you everything I can. But you don't need to pay me for it."

"I knew you'd say that. But in Pittsburgh we think a young fellow ought to earn some money; indeed, we don't think well of him if he doesn't. I'm sure Harry feels that way. How is it with your father?"

She was smiling, and Lanny smiled at her. He understood that she was being extremely kind.

"Both Harry and I would feel badly if we had to pay Mr. Kertezsi five or ten thousand dollars while we knew that a friend of ours was doing half the work for nothing. I'd rather take a chance on your expertness, and employ you to find us a painting. There must be ways to find out if a Greco is really a Greco, without paying quite such a big fee."

"As a matter of fact," said Lanny, "I know where there's an undoubtedly genuine one on the Riviera; it belongs to the Duquesa de San Angelo, who is a relation of King Alfonso, and it's been in her family since it was painted."

"Well, that makes it easy; I mean, if you know that she really is what she claims to be."

"There's no question about that; the family is well known."

"Do you suppose she would sell it?"

"It wouldn't do any harm to ask."

"Have you seen it?"

"No, but I could see it, because our friend, Mrs. Emily Chattersworth, knows her."

"Well, there you are. What do we need of an expert?"

"For one thing, you'll pretty certainly get it cheaper if you call Kertezsi in. He knows how to buy, and I don't."

"Maybe so; but certainly he ought to divide the fee with you."

"I'll talk it over with him if you insist."

"The main thing with Harry will be that the picture is genuine beyond question. As for me, I hope it will look like something I can recognize."

"It will be a portrait, probably of one of the duquesa's ancestors."

"And I'll be able to know it's a human being? Some of the new art I've seen, it's hard to tell!"

Lanny laughed. "El Greco was a representational painter, though he was one of the strangest. Tell me, are you absolutely set on one of his?"

"I may change, after I've read some more in that book. But El Greco sounds romantic. If anybody said: 'The Greek,' I'd think it was a bootlegger, or maybe a fish-and-oyster stand across the way from our glass plant. But El Greco is a name one can imagine things about, and if I have an old master at the head of my staircase, I'll find out all about the man it portrays, and I'll read about his time, and the first thing you know, I'll be an authority, and professors at the university will be asking to bring their classes to look at it and hear me tell about it."

"If that's what you want," chuckled the other, "you can be sure a Greco would fetch them in swarms!"

VIII

Lanny Budd and Zoltan Kertezsi had become very friendly; they had played a lot of music together, and Lanny had listened for hours to Kertezsi's stories of "old masters," where they were, and how he had caused them to be in that place. Whatever Lanny knew about the art business he had got from his new friend, so he took the problem of Mrs. Murchison to him. Kertezsi listened, and said that the lady was right about the splitting of the commission; this was a common practice of dealers when somebody brought them a customer, or helped them to find or obtain a work which met some customer's demands.

"But in this case," added the Hungarian, "you have found both the customer and the work, so why do you need me at all?"

"But I'm not competent to handle it, Zoltan."

"Listen," said the other. "Don't you ever expect to earn any money in your life?"

"I want to very much, but I'm not an art expert."

"Why not consider becoming one? It's along the line of your interest, and there's plenty of easy money in it."

"But I don't know enough!"

"Why not learn? Adopt the modern educational method and learn by doing. I'll be delighted to help you."

"Well, that's awfully kind, but I couldn't let you do it without your having a share."

"Listen, my dear boy; I have made all the money I need if I live to be a hundred. I have made it by hard work, and close attention to the whims of the wealthy. Some time ago I said to myself that I could now afford to do what I please—which is in my opinion the greatest luxury a man can enjoy on this earth. I said to myself: 'From now on the art lover is first and the art dealer is second. From now on I will say only what I think.' To one of the richest men in America I recently said: 'Your taste in art is very bad, and if you are determined to buy a thing like that, you will have to get someone else to do it for you. I am interested in helping your collection only provided that you permit me to point out to you the difference between great art and rubbish.' It was a revolutionary uprising, akin to that of the Bolsheviks."

"Has it succeeded?"

"So far, yes; but of course one cannot tell when counter-revolution may arrive."

Lanny was amused, and thought it might be fun to deal in art on that basis. But Zoltan told him that he couldn't expect to take such an attitude until his reputation was established. Moreover, he would find that some of the rich had real taste, and were making extraordinary collections which they intended to bequeath to posterity. Each person was an individual problem, and you had to study your patron, as well as those from whom you expected to buy. Whatever you did would be hard work if you wished to do it well. Zoltan narrated anecdotes, illustrating the patient siege which must be laid to collectors and would-be collectors, first to meet them and then to meet their desires.

What the dealer wanted out of this proposed transaction, he said, was a friend; he liked to meet the sort of people who appreciated what you did for them, and would make a return because they were built that way. He wouldn't bother about the money, because that was so easy when you knew the right people. The important thing was to have access to them, and this was equally true whether you wished to sell a picture to the wife of a Pittsburgh millionaire or to find out whether a Spanish duchess living in exile was in need of funds and might be persuaded to part with one of her family treasures.

"Perhaps," said Zoltan, "you never stopped to figure out the effect of the war upon this business. Europe has had to turn over most of its gold to America, and still owes it God only knows how many billions. One way that debt is being paid is with old masters. American millionaires are coming over here in droves to buy art, and there are literally thousands of rascals and parasites working day and night to persuade them to accept trash. Don't you see that here is a useful career for a man who has instinctive taste, and also the tact, or social prestige, or whatever you wish to call it, so that he knows how to convince others that he is honest?"

So Lanny paid another secret visit to the lady from Pittsburgh and told her that he would make an attempt to find her a Greco, or something as good. Zoltan Kertezsi was going to advise and guide him, and the two would spend a lot of time, each trying to persuade the other to receive the commission. Mrs. Murchison referred to this as an "Alphonse and Gaston act," and then, discovering that Lanny had never read the American "funnies," she explained that there were two Frenchmen who were always getting into trouble because in emergencies they stopped to bow to each other and say: "After you, my dear Alphonse. . . . No, after you, my dear Gaston." Lanny promised that they would do their bowing alone, and not bother Mrs. Murchison with it.

IX

Rick's play had its opening performance; and Lanny, on the strength of all the money he was going to make in his new profession, invited his friends to a dinner party *de luxe* before the show. It was a painful play, not made for the entertainment of the idle rich; it had to do with the psychology of a British flight officer at an air base who had to send mere boys out to their death, knowing that they had received only scant training. He was an unhappy offi-cer, and all of them drank a great deal, and war appeared a hideous and filthy business, which everybody in England was solemnly resolved never to touch again. This play of Rick's was the sort which stood no chance with the general public, but would have a critical success and be a very good start for so young a writer.

Lanny drove Rick back to The Reaches, as the Pomeroy-Nielson home was called, and saw that green and pleasant land once more, and met that friendly and agreeable family. Four years had passed since he had been there, but it was as if he were returning after four days in town. They made no fuss over you, but put the house at your disposal, and well-trained servants ministered to your wants. You punted and played tennis, and played music for those who cared to listen; then in the twilight you sat outside, or if the spring evening was chilly you sat before a fireplace, and heard talk about the problems of the world by persons who had a share in gov-erning it.

A very disturbed and unhappy world just then, and if you had wisdom or knowledge to contribute it was welcomed. The French had moved into the Ruhr and a new war had begun, a strange and puzzling kind, never before tried; blockade and slow strangulation applied to one of the greatest industrial districts in the world. The Germans, helpless as regards military force, were trying a policy of non-co-operation. The workers simply laid down their tools and did nothing; and what could the enemy do? They couldn't bring in French labor and work the coal mines, because the ma-chinery was complicated, and, moreover, the mines were among the most dangerous, the control of firedamp being a special technique which the Germans had been learning for centuries.

So everything just remained in a state of paralysis; the Germans shipped in food, barely enough to keep their workers alive, and printed mountains of paper money to pay for it. Robbie Budd had learned from his partner in Berlin that the government was permit-ting Stinnes and the other Ruhr magnates to print money to pay their own workers, an absolutely unprecedented action. Of course it could have only one effect: the mark was now tumbling in an avalanche; the firm of "R and R," which had foreseen this, was making money faster than if they owned the printing-presses themselves.

British statesmanship, the most conservative in the world, looked upon all this with horror. Downing Street had explicitly disapproved the French invasion, and the alliance seemed about at its last gasp. France was isolated on the Continent—unless you chose to count Poland, which Sir Alfred Pomeroy-Nielson and his friends mostly didn't. They thought that Poincaré was leading the country straight to ruin. France simply didn't have the numbers or the resources to dominate Europe; the old trouble against which Clemenceau had railed—the fact that there were twenty million too many Germans —was still unremedied, and the seizure of the Ruhr wasn't going to alter that. Not even the most rabid French patriot would propose to starve all those workers to death, and putting Krupp and his directors into jail, as the French had done, wasn't going to kill even one German.

X

A strange thing for Lanny to leave this realm, this England, where everything was so serene and rational, and arrive a few hours later in Seine-et-Oise and spend an evening listening to one of Poincaré's supporters, one of the pillars of the Nationalist party. Denis de Bruyne was quite exultant, because he believed that Germany was going to be brought to her knees at last; the peace which had been lost by the Allies was to be won by *la patrie* alone. The hereditary foe was to be disarmed, the indemnities to be paid, the treaty of Versailles to be enforced. Lanny found that this treaty was taken as a sort of holy writ by a French businessman; a text like the law of the Medes and Persians, which altereth not.

Knowing how futile it would be to argue, Lanny held his peace to the best of his ability. But Denis knew that his young visitor had recently been in Germany, and couldn't resist questioning him. Wasn't it true that the Germans had hidden great quantities of arms, and that they were insulting and sometimes even abusing the Allied commissioners who were supposed to find and destroy them? Yes, Lanny had to admit that this was true; he had heard about thousands of rifles walled up in vaults in the monasteries of Catholic Munich; but he was forced to add that he didn't see how the French could ever get these except by invading the country, and did forty million people have the military force to garrison and hold down sixty million? If they tried it, could they stand the expense, or would they bankrupt themselves? Was it possible to run modern industry by force, in the Ruhr or anywhere else?

These were questions to trouble any capitalist; and it is only human to be annoyed by a person who forces such unwelcome facts upon your attention. Lanny was glad that he was spending only one night in the Château de Bruyne; and perhaps his host had the same gladness. How did he feel about having this arrogant and self-confident young man carry away with him the chief treasure of the château? Denis was paying for his sins; but rarely does it happen that we love the rod which scourges us, however much we may have deserved it.

XI

Lanny, motoring his sweetheart to Juan, carried with him the uncomfortable certainty that she too was a Nationalist; she believed all those things which her husband had told her about France and the outside world. She considered Kurt Meissner one of the few good members of a cruel race which was bent upon the subjection of *la patrie;* she considered Eric Vivian Pomeroy-Nielson one of the few cultured members of a nation of shopkeepers which was willing to set the Prussian monster on its feet again as a counterforce to keep France from becoming prosperous and powerful. She believed these things because they had been taught to her from childhood, and because they were in all the newspapers she saw.

There was no use trying to change her mind about any such matters; Lanny had tried it and discovered that he caused her distress. She considered that her lover was credulous, because of his generous temperament, his impulse to believe that other people were as good as himself. She considered that he was being misled by German and British propaganda, and by his faith in his friends. Worse yet, his sympathy for the poor and afflicted led him into the trap of the

Reds, and that was something which filled Marie with terror. She tried not to voice it, but kept it locked in her heart; she would watch her lover, and note the little signs of what he was feeling and thinking, and often the image of him which she constructed in her mind was more alarming than the reality. Nothing could ever change that, for she was a cautious Frenchwoman of middle age, and he was an imaginative youth, descended from ancestors who had crossed a stormy ocean in order to have their own way in a land where no white man had ever lived before.

Lanny told her about his adventures in London; and here again his enthusiasm encountered her fears. What sort of woman was that who invited a handsome young man to meet her secretly, and pretended to wish to buy a picture at an unthinkable price? In vain Lanny assured his *amie* that Adella Murchison was a straightforward American type; Marie had never met such a type, and was not to be fooled. The woman was a subtle schemer, and the longer she delayed to reveal her true purpose, the more dangerous she was. Though Marie had declared her willingness to give up her lover when he was ready for marriage, here was a married woman, a mother of children as Marie was, and toward such a one she had no impulse of self-sacrifice, but on the contrary the feeling of a tigress on guard.

However, the desire for money is a powerful force in the French; and Lanny was firmly convinced that these Americans might actually send him a million francs to buy a picture, and pay him a hundred thousand additional for the service. Of course it is well known that rich Americans are fantastic, and the bare chance of such a thing was not to be thrown away. Marie didn't want the money for herself, but she wanted Lanny to want it—it would be a way to tone him down and make him into a careful conservative citizen. So she informed him that she had met the Duquesa de San Angelo, and thought she could arrange for Lanny to see the painting. In her secret soul Marie resolved to keep a day-and-night watch over that strange female from the valley of steel and smoke—and, oh, how the Frenchwoman was prepared to hate her if she ventured to move so much as an eyelash in the direction of Lanny Budd!

17

Merchants of Beauty

I

THE war of the Ruhr continued; a war of starvation, of slow decay; a war carried on within the countless cells of millions of human bodies. How long could they endure the steady weakening, the fading away of their powers? There comes a time when an underfed man can no longer labor, a time when he can no longer walk, no longer stand up, no longer move his arms, his tongue. The women bear their children dead, and those already born acquire distended stomachs and crooked bones; they cease to run and play, but sit listlessly staring ahead, or crawl away into some dark corner where their wailing will not be punished. Nature, more merciful than statesmen, usually steps in at one of these stages, and sends the victim some germs of pneumonia or of flu, and puts an end to his misery.

It was a war also of ideas, of propaganda; cries of anguish mixed with those of hate. To the fastidious Lanny Budd it seemed like a fight between two fishwives in the marketplace, screaming, cursing, tearing each other's hair. It was something hardly to be dignified by the name of politics; just a squabble over great sums of money and the means of making more. Lanny, by right of birth, was privileged to know about it, and his father explained that on the one side were Stinnes and Thyssen and Krupp, the great Ruhr magnates, and on the other side the de Wendels and other French steel men, who had got the iron ore of Lorraine and now wanted the coal and coke of the Ruhr so as to work it cheaply.

Robbie Budd was in Lausanne again; or back and forth between there and London and New York. The great conference was still going on—and that was another squabble over property, the oil and other natural resources hidden in the Turkish land. Robbie, with the help of Zaharoff and his new associates, was "horning in" on Mosul and getting a big concession; he was elated about it, also not a little harassed, and to his son rather pathetic. Why he wanted so much more money was something he couldn't answer, and it was better not to embarrass him by repeating the question.

The Turks were getting back Constantinople and much of what they had lost in the World War. The French were on top, and the British humiliated—but they were holding onto the oil and to Palestine, through which the pipeline was bringing the precious fluid to the sea. The Russians were attending the conference, for they had rights to defend in the Black Sea, and were still hoping for loans. One of their delegates was Vorovsky, with whom Lanny and his father had talked at Genoa, and whom Lanny remembered vividly: a thin, ascetic intellectual with wistful gray eyes, a soft brown beard, and the delicate, sensitive hands of a lover of art like Lanny himself. Now an assassin shot him dead in a café; and in due course a jury of moral businessmen would acquit the killer, thus informing the other Whites in Switzerland that it was open season for Bolshevik diplomats.

II

It was in the midst of such world events that Lanny Budd, having learned that there was money in art-works, set about the task of learning how to get it out. Marie phoned to the duquesa, who graciously agreed to permit a young American connoisseur to inspect her family treasures. She proved to be a little, wizened, dark old lady whose dental plates didn't seem to fit her very well; in appearance she was as far from aristocratic as you could have imagined, but Lanny had learned that that was frequently so, and he did not fail in any of the courtesies which a highborn lady would expect. The duquesa was dressed in black for a husband who had been killed in the Moroccan wars two decades or more ago.

She showed him the paintings herself, and told him their histories;

he listened attentively to everything she said, and remembered it, and praised the paintings—for it was no part of his technique to conceal his love of great art. The Greco proved to be a portrait of a clerical member of the duquesa's family: a strange figure of a man, distorted like so many of this painter's representations; abnormally tall and lean, and having fingers longer and thinner than nature has ever seen fit to lend to man. A dark picture, rather sinister, and Lanny couldn't imagine that Adella Murchison would want it in her house.

But there was a Goya; and, oh, what a Goya for a valley of steel and smoke! A figure of a soldier, splendid, yet decadent, and with a touch of the painter's satire; a costume with all the colors that a man of arms must have put on when he went to report a victory to King Charles IV. It was a grand piece of composition, with everything arranged to lead your eye to the tall figure with the face of a warrior and the eyes of a bird of prey. Yes, if a plateglass man's wife wanted something to stir her imagination, and that of the professors of her university, here it was!

Also there was a Velásquez, a double portrait. Lanny had read that many pictures attributed to Velásquez had really been painted by his son-in-law; but superficially they could hardly be distinguished from the real ones, and fetched very high prices on the chance that the master might have put his brush upon them. Being now in the process of learning, Lanny asked the duquesa about this, and saw right away that he had hurt her feelings. He was sorry—but he knew all the same that he had brought down the price, if price there was to be.

Only when he was ready to leave did he venture to ask timidly whether his hostess had ever considered the possibility of parting with any of these treasures. She answered proudly that she never had; and this was in accordance with what Zoltan Kertezsi had foretold. Obeying instructions, Lanny said tactfully that if it ever should happen that she was disposed to consider a sale, he hoped that she would not fail to let him know, as he had friends who might be interested. The little old lady hesitated, looked troubled for a minute or so, and then said that she might be willing to consider parting with one or two of them; but the price would have to be very, very high. So Lanny knew that the trading had begun.

Zoltan had said: "Never under any circumstances make an offer, but invite the owner to set a price." He did so, and the lady told him that the price of the Greco would be at least a million and a half francs, and that of the Velásquez at least two million—for the duquesa took no stock whatever in the del Mazo theory, she declared. No, no, it was a genuine Velásquez, one of the best, and was reproduced in various books of art. Then Lanny asked about the Goya, and was told that the old lady couldn't part with that for one franc less than a million. That too was famous. Lanny noted down the names of the books in which reproductions of these paintings were to be found; he was sure that these would be in the British Museum, so he wouldn't have to get photographs. He thanked his hostess over and over again and took his departure.

III

Lanny posted a letter to his client, telling her the details of his interview, the prices asked for the pictures, and where the reproductions could be seen. His advice was that she choose the Goya and authorize him to pay a million francs for it, but of course he would try to get it for less. According to the advice of Zoltan, the actual cash should be sent to Lanny's bank in Cannes, for a bank draft or express order would be of feeble effect compared with the physical presence of a large bundle of crisp new banknotes. Lanny sent this letter by the new airmail system, and waited in no little trepidation.

Marvelous people, these Pittsburghers! Two days later came a telegram: "Will take your advice forwarding money thanks good luck. Adella Murchison." Just as simple as that; she tossed him a million francs as if it had been the price of two theater tickets! Lanny had never seen so much cash in his life, but Zoltan had assured him that any bank could obtain it if you gave notice. Lanny called his old friend Jerry Pendleton and arranged to take him as a bodyguard, Beauty having insisted upon that precaution. She made Lanny load up one of the Budd automatics and made Jerry promise to keep it right on the seat of the car.

When the money was at the bank Lanny phoned the duquesa, asking permission to see her about a matter of business. He drove Jerry to the bank, where they were escorted into a private room, and no less than three officials came in to witness the sensational transaction. The highest denomination of note which the French government printed was a thousand francs, and the money was banded up in packages of fifty each; if Lanny had been a really careful business person he would have counted every one of the notes, but he was satisfied to count the packages and the contents of one. He signed the receipt in triplicate, and put the precious bundles into a satchel, and he and Jerry went out to their car, feeling decidedly self-conscious, and looking about for anyone bearing a resemblance to the gangsters of the American movies.

They drove to the heights above San Raphael, where the duquesa's château was situated. Lanny left five of those valuable packages in Jerry's care, and carried the remaining fifteen in the satchel into the presence of the little old lady. Seated in her drawing-room, he made a carefully studied speech: "Duquesa, I have interested a friend in the purchase of your Goya, and am authorized to offer you the sum of seven hundred and fifty thousand francs in cash for it. That is the very best that I can do. It is a large sum of money, and I believe that if you think it over you will realize that it would be wise to accept it." To assist the thinking process, Lanny opened the satchel, and proceeded to count the packages of virginal banknotes onto the table in front of his hostess. The last of the fifteen he placed in her hands, so that she might feel the weight of it, and make certain that it was actually composed of notes having the guarantee of the Banque de France.

It was not a pretty spectacle that Lanny watched during the next half-hour. The old woman's mouth had come open simultaneously with the satchel; her black eyes shone with an unholy light, and her fingers trembled as she clutched this extraordinary dynamic package. It appeared as if she tried to put it down, but couldn't manage to do so. She started to bargain for more; the painting was one of the most beautiful in the world—actually, she attempted to talk about beauty! It was a family heritage—she even tried to talk about whether she had a moral right to part with it! But all the time her eyes kept wandering to the other packages, and her hand could hardly be kept from stretching out to them.

Lanny felt sure from various signs that she was not going to let that money go out of the house. So he took a firm tone; he had tried his best to get more from his friend, but that was absolutely the maximum obtainable. He was intending to get up and prepare to take his departure, if necessary, but he didn't have to. "*Bien!*" exclaimed the Spanish lady, suddenly; and Lanny produced the receipts for her to sign—two copies, for he meant to have one as a souvenir of an adventure which might never happen to him again! He had left a blank space for the amount, and he now filled it in, and placed the documents and his fountain pen in front of the duquesa.

But it couldn't be settled so quickly as that. The elderly aristocrat wasn't going to be content with counting packages; she was going to count seven hundred and fifty notes, and make sure that each had one thousand francs printed on it. With her skinny old fingers shaking she broke the bands around one package, and with her quavering old voice she counted aloud from one to fifty, occasionally stopping to wet her fingers on her tongue. One package counted, she set it aside, and went to work on the next; Lanny sat and waited patiently while this performance was repeated fifteen times. Fortunately the bank had made no mistakes, and at last the job was completed. There being no other excuse for delay, the duquesa looked at the pile of packages, she looked at the two receipts, and from them to Lanny. Was she at the last moment trying to get up the nerve for a fight?

She was trembling, and Lanny was trembling—it is always hard upon the nerves, dealing in large sums of money. But at last she took up the fountain pen, and with slow uncertain fingers wrote her name on one piece of paper, then on the other, and permitted Lanny to pick them up and put them into his pocket, together with his pen. He thanked her and shook hands with her, and her final act was to summon a man-servant to carry the heavy picture down to the car. She might have claimed the frame, and Lanny was prepared to have her do so; but she had probably never seen the picture out of the frame, and may have thought they were one. It was so big that it would barely go into the car.

They drove to the bank, where Lanny put the rest of the money on deposit. They drove to a carpenter shop and had the precious object securely crated, and then saw a truck carry it to the express office, where it was shipped to Mrs. Murchison in London, insured for its full purchase price. Lanny sent the new owner a telegram, telling her what he had done, and sent her by registered mail her receipt and a bank draft for the rest of the money, less his commission and the various expenditures. Only as time passed did he realize the impression he had made upon the plateglass couple by the return of approximately a hundred and seventy-three thousand francs. The story would be told in Pittsburgh, and the fame of it would radiate in many directions; years later someone would introduce himself as a friend of the Murchisons, and say: "I understand that you buy paintings and return part of the money if you don't have to spend it all."

IV

So Lanny had made some real money, easy money; it grew on trees for him. He found that he had grown a foot in the estimation of his family and friends. He did the "Alphonse and Gaston act" with Zoltan, and the result was that the expert consented to take one-third the commission; also Lanny gave one of the smooth virginal notes to his bodyguard, surely the largest sum that that redhead from Kansas had ever earned in so short a time. This left the budding art dealer a net of forty-nine thousand francs, or, at the prevailing rate of exchange, somewhat less than twenty-five hundred dollars; but it wasn't going to be exchanged, it was going to be spent in France, and forty-nine has a much more exciting sound than two and a half.

Lanny looked back upon a time, only four years distant, when he had been so pleased at receiving two hundred dollars a month from the disbursing officer of the State Department of the United States government. By five months of assiduous day-and-night labor he had then earned one thousand dollars. But now he had worked only a few hours, not more than one good day altogether, and see what he had! From that time on it would be difficult for Lanny to contemplate the system known as "individualism" without a certain amount of indulgence; also he would be disposed to look upon all kinds of public officials, from postmen up to premiers, as ill-rewarded drudges, the most pathetic of wage-slaves.

And what he had got was only the beginning, he found. The Murchisons received their valuable shipment and had it uncrated in their hotel room and hung up on the wall, opposite a sofa where they could sit and study it. So they discovered for the first time what art was, and is, for it remains what it is, *semper eadem. Ars longa, vita brevis!* Adella saw that gorgeous if evil old warrior occupying the position of honor in her drawing-room, and she got books about the time and its court painter, and began to prepare and rehearse her "spiel." Before long it occurred to her that there was space at the top of the broad staircase of her home where something splendid seemed to be called for. She got a photograph of the dubious Velásquez, and learned from the books that this painter's works were almost unobtainable; she decided that nobody in Pittsburgh would ever have heard of del Mazo, surely none of her friends, at least. She went to work and persuaded her husband, and then sent a wire to Juan-les-Pins, asking what the double portrait could be had for.

Lanny answered that he thought Zoltan should come and look at the work, and give his expert opinion whether it was a Velásquez; if it wasn't, that would help to shatter the old duquesa's nerve. His guess was that a million francs would do the trick, but it might be well to send a million and a half. How easily Lanny now tossed off such figures!

The program was carried out according to schedule. The expert came, and gave his shattering opinion, and the elderly aristocrat flew into a rage and considered herself personally insulted. Zoltan said that was something he had learned to expect; these people were used to having their own way, and truth and reality were not vital concepts to them. But a million francs was; so let the old creature have a while to think about them. Lanny brought his friend to Bienvenu, where the ladies all treated him as if he were an archangel sent down from the skies to set a golden crown on Lanny's head. Zoltan had his fiddle, and for two days Lanny and Kurt played sonatas with him, and they had a grand holiday, no less enjoyable because of the thought of the duquesa in her château—which they had converted into a hot griddle for her to be toasted on!

V

The money arrived at the bank, and on the third morning Lanny and Jerry went and got it. Zoltan insisted that his pupil must handle the matter, while the teacher amused himself with a more humble role. Since the picture was too big to be got into Lanny's car, Zoltan would hire a small truck and park at an inn near the château, where Lanny could telephone in case of victory. Lanny left ten of the bundles of banknotes in Jerry's care, and took in twenty and laid them out on the table. He sat and listened to scolding, whining, almost weeping; he thought: How odd that a duchess should not be a "lady"; that *noblesse* should manifest so little desire to *oblige!* It was like pulling all the old woman's teeth all over again to make her take a million francs for that dubious Velásquez. Lanny had to pretend that his dignity was affronted, and put the money back into the satchel and start to take his leave; when he was almost at the front door the châtelaine called to him *"Eh bien! Revenez!"*

It was a game, and he had won. She composed her face, and went at the serious business of counting one thousand banknotes. Everything must wait until she had accepted the money and signed the receipts and Lanny had them in his pocket. Then he telephoned, and the duquesa rang for her servant; she was quite cheerful now—it wasn't so hard to make the best of being a millionaire. The great picture was so heavy that Lanny had to help the servant carry it down the steps; and here came Zoltan, the truck-driver, with a lot of blankets, one of them waterproof, for wrapping the precious treasure. Off they drove in triumph, Lanny following the truck, and Jerry with the automatic on the seat beside him.

This time they came to Bienvenu, for it had been decided that Jerry should drive that precious freight all the way to London, Lanny following with Marie in his car. It was June, and time for their trip to Seine-et-Oise; they would take a little excursion to London, where Marie would meet that ex-secretary who was scattering her husband's money like a drunken sailor—that straightforward American type in whom she still found it impossible to believe. But she had to admit that if Adella Murchison was setting a trap for Lanny, she was certainly baiting it generously!

An odd sort of holiday! The truck broke down and had to be repaired, and meanwhile the treasure was carried into a bedroom of an inn, where either Lanny or Jerry stayed with it every moment. On their overnight stop they saw to it that Jerry got a room with a good stout bolt, and he slept with the gun under his pillow. They took both truck and car across on the ferry and delivered their consignment to its owners—also a bank draft for half a million francs less expenses. Adella met Marie, and behaved like a woman of the world, giving no sign of being shocked to discover that this exemplary young lover of the arts was also the lover of another man's wife. She spent most of the time hearing Lanny's story of the purchases, and asking him questions about the paintings; she made no signs with her eyelashes or anything else, and so Lanny's *amie* had to give up and admit that there really was an "American type."

VI

The two dealers went fifty-fifty on this second transaction, so Lanny had almost a hundred thousand francs. That was news to take to the Château de Bruyne, to lend glamour to *la vie à trois*. Impossible for a businessman not to respect a youth who had performed such a feat! From that time on Lanny Budd would be no playboy but a serious man of affairs. When he entered a home of wealth, he wouldn't be thinking, as formerly: "Am I going to be bored here?" He would be thinking: "I wonder if they buy paintings, or if they have any they'd like to sell." When he saw a beautiful work, he would enjoy its beauty, but his mind would go on to the thought: "I wonder what that would bring," and then: "I wonder who would be interested in it." He would run over in his mind the different persons he knew, and the art collections he had seen or heard of—not those in museums and galleries, but paintings in private homes, where they had been for a long time, so that the owner had had a chance to get tired of them.

A similar transformation took place in the minds of the ladies who played a part in Lanny's life. To them art had been an expensive form of pleasure—conspicuous waste, to use Veblen's phrase; but now it became a source of income, it was game to be hunted. Beauty Budd began thinking of all the persons she knew in or near Paris; all the rich homes to which she might arrange for Lanny to have access, and work up schemes of plunder. It was the thing that Beauty had done for Robbie for some twenty years, and there wasn't a device that she hadn't put to use. Now, of course, it was a double pleasure, for Lanny was young, and her maternal impulses came into play. Sophie, the ex-baroness, a childless woman, shared these feelings; also Emily, the *salonnière*, who had taken Lanny as a sort of foster-son. She even began to think of certain of her own paintings which it might be fun to replace with others having somewhat more lively colors.

But the most eager and most active friend was Marie de Bruyne. Here was the way to make her lover into something substantial and useful! Marie didn't want his money, but she wanted him to have money; her mind, at once unselfish and materialistic, wanted him to take hold of life and make himself a place in it. Above all, here was the way to get him out of the clutches of those dangerous Reds! When he had to earn money, he would learn the value of it; he would become a man among men, competing with them, winning their respect, and bringing all his faculties into play. Marie loved art herself, and wanted Lanny to love it, and wouldn't have turned him into a manager of taxicab companies like Denis or an oil operator like his father. No, she understood his fine gifts and wanted to cultivate them, and it seemed to her a most happy development that he should be able to combine his love of art with the easy acquisition of the money he would need for the gratifying of all his tastes.

After consulting with Denis she invited Zoltan Kertezsi to their home, and for a week they played music and talked art, and it was wonderful for Marie's two boys as well as for her lover. The woman herself listened and learned, for she must know all the phrases, all the cues, so that she could guide a conversation into proper channels and help to start a deal or to put one through. Zoltan knew a thousand stories about painters and paintings, and there was hardly a subject you could mention that he couldn't connect with the buying or selling of art. And one thing leads to another, as we all know.

Yes, Zoltan was a wonderful fellow, and wouldn't have been different if he had really been that archangel sent down from the skies to tear Lanny Budd out of the hands of the dangerous and disreputable Reds, and make him into an art authority. Marie devoted a full week to cultivating this Hungarian gentleman, making him comfortable, praising him, drinking in his stories—always, of course, with Lanny present, Lanny kindling with delight, warming both hands before the fire of life. Also two lads budding into manhood, who had hardly been aware of art before, listened to stories about enormous sums paid for paintings by the richest and most famous persons; they too began to kindle, and wanted Lanny to take them to the Louvre and the Luxembourg and let them see such wonderful creations, and try to understand what it was about Jan van Eyck's little painting of a madonna and child which caused it to be worthy sixty-four thousand francs per square inch!

When Zoltan was gone, Marie began taking Lanny about to the rich homes in the neighborhood, to show him the treasures they contained and give him a chance to mention that he knew many Americans who were on the hunt for such things. Most of Marie's acquaintances would be sellers, not buyers, so when she told what her young magician had been able to do for a Spanish duquesa, she shaded the story in favor of the seller's side; the American millionaires were represented as infatuated persons scattering their money like Millet's *Sower* with his bag of seed. On the other hand, when

Denis brought out a great banker over the week-end, a man who might be a customer, the unnamed duquesa was transformed into a slightly ridiculous person whom Lanny by extraordinary cleverness had managed to hold down to very low prices. *Mutatis mutandis*, is the Latin phrase; and Zoltan said that Latin is a wonderful language, well suited to apothegms and inscriptions, since it says so much in a few words.

VII

This development came at a fortunate moment in the life of Lanny and Marie. Three years had passed since their intimacy had begun, and that is time enough for lovers to discover what is wrong with each other. Their physical happiness was as complete as ever, but intellectually there were large tracts where they would never meet. Marie wasn't a political-minded person, and would have been content to avoid the subject; but Lanny couldn't or wouldn't do so; he kept meeting persons who stirred him up, persons whom his *amie* hated and feared. He knew it, and refrained from mentioning those persons; but somehow it always came out where he had been, and even if he didn't say what he was thinking, Marie guessed it, and it made her unhappy and him impatient.

They might have let each other's ideas alone; but the world and its events wouldn't let either of them alone, it kept forcing itself upon their attention. That dreadful strangling process was going on in the Ruhr, and the cries of it penetrated the ears of every thinking person in Europe. Germany was down and France was at her throat, and either you sympathized with France, or else you were a friend of the Boches, and therefore a suspect. Denis de Bruyne would come home from conferences with members of his party and would tell what he had seen and heard, what Poincaré was doing and what his supporters expected to get out of it, and to Lanny it seemed repulsive, almost crazy; he would know that his beloved one agreed with these ideas, and Marie would know that Lanny hated them. The only way they could avoid quarreling was to wall off portions of their minds completely from each other.

Robbie came to Paris after the close of the Lausanne conference in midsummer, and spent a Sunday at the château. He listened to everything Denis said, and they talked as two businessmen who understand each other's point of view; but Lanny knew that his father wasn't saying all that he thought, and when they were alone Robbie remarked that France was in one hell of a mess, and that men like Denis were blinding themselves to her plight. He said that Poincaré was really a very timid and incompetent bureaucrat, a slave to routine and red tape; he had promised the French people things that he couldn't deliver, and now he was scared to death by what he had started and didn't know how to finish.

"France can starve Germany into bankruptcy," said Robbie, "but France will get nothing out of it, and will only cripple both countries. The plain truth is that France hasn't the economic resources to support the military role that her pride forces her to play. The part of wisdom would be to accept her position as a second-class power and tie her fortunes to those of the British Empire; but she may put off doing this until it's too late, and the British offer of an alliance may not be renewed."

If that was the situation, it was obvious that an ardent Nationalist and his wife were not going to be very happy people in the years to come. Their country would suffer, and they would look around for somebody to blame. They would blame the Germans for failing to pay indemnities. They would blame the British for encouraging the Germans. They would blame the Americans for not ratifying President Wilson's treaty of alliance and for trying to collect debts which France couldn't pay and pretty soon wouldn't want to pay. Altogether it was going to be a mess; and how was Lanny going to be happy in a home where people were bitter against the Americans, how was Marie going to be happy in a home where people out of the kindness of their hearts felt sorry for the French?

At this critical moment came the picture business; something new, something exciting to both lovers, something they could do in harmony. It provided excuses for traveling and seeing new places, for meeting important people; it provided abundance, even luxury, for both of them—and it is a sad fact about most humans that if we have abundance and luxury for ourselves, it is easier to put off doing something about the troubles of other people. This new activity of Lanny's brought applause from nearly everybody he knew; even his Red uncle smiled indulgently and called it a harmless way for a playboy to pass his time. "It surely makes no difference which of two bloated parasites owns a painting, and if in the process of exchanging you collect some of their cash—well and good!" Uncle Jesse didn't add that he and his friends would come around and try to get a share, to pay the perpetual deficits of their party press.

Robbie Budd, of course, was tickled to death by the development. It didn't make any difference to him how his first-born made money; any way would serve to establish sound habits and teach a youngster to take care of himself. Robbie promised to spread the word in Newcastle that Lanny had become one of the leading art experts of the Continent; he would talk up old masters as a form of investment second only to oil. He would be sending over a string of customers and orders—perhaps Lanny's stepmother would be the first! Could Lanny suggest any paintings that would relieve the austerity of Esther's walls?

Also there was Johannes Robin—had Lanny written the boys about his good fortune? Yes, Lanny had done so, and they had replied, begging him to come to Berlin and set up in business. Many of the aristocracy and other depressed classes were selling their art-works; many of the *Schieber* were buying. "Let me know if you have anything good," the Jewish trader had scrawled on the bottom of a letter.

"He'll buy anything you offer, just to please you," was Robbie's opinion. But Lanny didn't care to do business on that basis.

VIII

The budding expert decided to take his new profession seriously and make a success of it. He would study the books on art and make elaborate notes. He would drive into Paris and see what the dealers were offering, and familiarize himself with the prices current. He would keep a little notebook in his pocket and jot down the various items. Following the suggestion of his businesslike father, he started a cardfile on the various painters, where their works could be found, and the prices; also a cardfile of the persons he met who might become purchasers or sellers; their names and addresses, interests and tastes—anything about them that might be of use at some particular moment. In course of time these files would acquire a considerable size, and be worth their weight in diamonds to their owner.

Both dealers and painters were glad to meet Lanny Budd and to talk shop with him. He looked like money, and it was obvious that he knew moneyed people; word spread that he was the stepson of Marcel Detaze, a pre-war painter in whose work there appeared to be quite a boom. Critics were mentioning it, and dealers had inquiries and didn't know what to say. They would ask Lanny, and he would say that Detaze was being handled by Zoltan Kertezsi. Lanny and his mother had decided that this was the wise way to deal with their problem. Zoltan really understood Marcel's work, he had started the boom, and his steady pressure to keep it going would be worth more than the commission they would pay him. All would-be customers who wrote or came to Bienvenu were told that Zoltan Kertezsi was the sole authorized agent.

The Hungarian came often to the Château de Bruyne that summer, and the happy sounds of his fiddle were heard in its drawing-room. He adopted Lanny as his pupil, filled him up with information and wise counsel, and threw several opportunities his way. In one of the aristocratic French homes to which Marie took Lanny was a Drouais, a perfect gem of a Drouais, a portrait of a gaily dressed, exquisite little noble lady with a round face, and dimples in her rose-pink cheeks, and the funniest little twinkle in her bright brown eyes—a picture so full of life that you felt you were sitting in the room with her, and might kiss the tips of her little pink fingers. Zoltan had sold several works of the French master, and didn't even have to see this one; Lanny's delight was enough, and Zoltan wrote to a client in Boston who was making a great collection, and in due course came a cablegram saying that six hundred thousand francs were at his disposal at Morgan, Harjes et Cie.

So Lanny and Zoltan went together and bought the picture for five hundred and fifty thousand francs, and divided the commission.

Lanny had another small fortune, and the two pals came home and played the *Kreutzer Sonata* to tell the world how cheerful they felt. Lanny began to figure what he was going to do with all this money. Said he to Zoltan: "I'll come on an old master that's really a bargain, and I'll buy it for myself, with no commission!" Said Zoltan: "Find some new painter, a coming genius, and buy him up and put him in the storeroom along with Marcel, and you can live on him the rest of your days."

"And grow fat like M. Faure!" added Lanny—referring to an importer of wines and olive oil who came to look at a picture, and would sit in a chair and study the work for a long while, and gradually his eyelids would droop and he would have a little nap, and wake up with a start. You mustn't notice what had happened, for he would sometimes buy the picture to make it all right. He was a very kindly old gentleman and a pleasant customer to deal with; he liked drinking scenes and nude ladies, and that made it easy to please him.

Zoltan said he had several customers with peculiarities of one sort or another; one old Jewish lady, a friend of his mother, had raised half a dozen children and now had a dozen or more grandchildren, and would buy paintings of babies—nothing else. Zoltan had sold her a handsome Scotchman by Raeburn, thinking to seduce her imagination; but no, some other dealer had come along with a couple of Romney babies, and had persuaded her to trade a picture worth thousands of pounds for one worth half as many. Lanny had never heard so many funny stories as Zoltan told.

IX

That summer was the climax of the agony of Germany. In the effort to maintain the passive resistance of the Ruhr she printed and spent some three and a half trillions of marks; and it is a strange law of the process of inflation that the effect exceeds the cause many times over. By the end of May of that year one American cent would buy fifteen hundred marks, and by the end of July it would buy ten thousand. Abroad, this process was called "the mark swindle," and it was estimated that Germany had taken more than a billion dollars out of America alone; but the speculators had got a great part of it, and the firm of "R and R" was among the successful.

In September Germany gave up. Impossible to feed her population any longer. The miners and steelworkers of the Ruhr would go back to work under French supervision. It was a time of triumph for Poincaré and his supporters; they proclaimed it as a vindication of their policy and an assurance of peace at last. Lanny wasn't sure, but he was glad of any chance of reconcilement, and accepted politely the assurances of Marie's husband. When he drove her to the Riviera he believed that their happiness was again secure.

But right away in Bienvenu there began to appear one of those little clouds no bigger than a man's hand. Beauty had written to her son that Kurt was in a terrible state of agitation over what was happening in his Fatherland, and that she again was in dread about him. Lanny hoped that the surrender would settle this trouble, but he discovered that Kurt was one of those Germans who weren't going to surrender. Terrible letters had come from Kurt's home; he didn't want to show them to his friend, he didn't want to talk about the subject, but just to lock it up in his heart and brood over it; his music became more and more somber, and in Beauty's heart a worm of fear gnawed unceasingly. Some day her lover would decide that music wasn't enough, and would go back to fight for his country's liberation!

Five years and a half had passed since the forces of nature and the accidents of man had thrown Beauty and Kurt into each other's arms. Assuredly it was one of the oddest of couplings, yet it had worked out unexpectedly well. So long as Kurt wanted nothing but to go off by himself and invent new combinations of musical sounds, Bienvenu and its mistress offered a wellnigh perfect solution of life's problems. Beauty had her home to run, and her baby to bring up, and when her social impulses became overwhelming, she could dress herself and go to parties with no worse penalty than some playful teasing by her lover. It had become the accepted practice that once during each winter Emily Chattersworth would get up a recital and invite the most distinguished persons, who would be duly impressed, and thus the respectability of the *liaison* would be maintained:

Beauty Budd's lover was a great artist, a future celebrity mewing his mighty youth. Visitors who came to the home rarely saw him; he would be busy with his work, and they had to make the best of that. When they did see him he was clean, his hair was trimmed, and his manners were impeccable. Many a rich woman wished she might have such a handsome and serviceable male, who would stay at home and "behave himself"—that is, would have no eyes for any younger woman.

X

But time passes, and all things change, and apparently no happiness is without its enemies. After three years of living in the same house for months at a time, Beauty's lover and Lanny's *amie* had come to the point where they could manage it only by never opening their mouths in each other's presence. They respected each other, and didn't want to quarrel; but they were France and Germany, and one was at the other's throat. At the table it became the rule that no political subject was ever touched on, even remotely; nothing that anybody had read in the paper, nothing that Robbie or Rick had written. Several intimate friends understood this, and helped to keep the rule; then they would go away and speculate as to how long this strange tension could continue. Little by little they began to notice that when Marie was at table Kurt was apt to be absent, and vice versa. Marie was finding more excuses to be with her aunt, and Lanny would go there to visit her.

Then came another serpent creeping into this Eden. The thing that Beauty and Marie and all Lanny's friends were so happy about, the wonderful new easy-money profession that he had discovered—that failed to satisfy the ethical sense of his mother's beloved; it was the commercializing of art, which to the austere German artist was the profanation of a sanctuary. Very certainly Kurt wasn't commercializing *his* art; he couldn't, if he wanted to—for how could any music publisher continue to put a price on musical works and, when he had sold them, discover that the proceeds wouldn't buy food for his employees, to say nothing of buying more paper? The fact that Kurt, who was producing original work, stood no chance of getting any reward for it, while Lanny, who produced nothing, was having fantastic sums of money dumped into his lap—that situation mirrored the economic and moral decay of Europe at the end of the year 1923.

Nor was the trouble remedied by the fact that Lanny, out of the kindness of his heart, kept clamoring to be allowed to put up money for the publishing of his friend's work. That was charity, and Kurt was thinking about justice. To him the situation was a symbol of the oppression of the Fatherland, the crushing of the spiritual impulses of a great people by the three plutocratic empires which called themselves democracies and which had obtained the mastery of the modern world. Lanny and his mother and father represented one of these empires, Rick represented another, and Marie the third, and Kurt didn't want to live by the charity of any of them; he didn't want to talk about it with any of them, and did so only when Lanny questioned him, and tried to console him or to argue with him. Lanny insisted that this was only a temporary condition, and that time would remedy it; but Kurt didn't believe in time, he believed in human effort, and he said: "If the German soul is ever set free, it will be because Germans set it free."

Lanny had to go and explain all this to his mother, and they had to make new rules for keeping the peace in their safe warm nest. They mustn't talk too much about making money out of art; they mustn't exult about "deals," or about the price that a new Detaze had brought. Also, they must not force Zoltan Kertezsi upon Kurt, because Kurt said he didn't care for merchants of beauty. Only after he had said this did Kurt realize that it wouldn't sound very kind to his patron and friend, Lanny Budd.

18

Into This Wild Abyss

I

THE two Robin boys were always trying to devise ways to be of use to their Lanny Budd in his new profession. They didn't see him often, because during the time when he was at Bienvenu they were busy with their studies, and during the holidays he was at the Château de Bruyne, where he couldn't invite them, they being at that susceptible age where they were not supposed to know about sexual irregularities. But now had come this new development—Lanny was a businessman, and so was Papa Robin, and in the course of his activities as money-lender Papa acquired a great deal of information as to the affairs of important persons. He was glad to help such persons, because he was a good-hearted fellow; but he charged them ten percent interest, the prevailing rate in Germany, and of course he made them give adequate security.

As it happened, they sometimes owned valuable paintings, and offered these as security. And how was a businessman to be sure what they were really worth? Papa Robin needed expert advice, he said. Did he really need it, or did he just pretend to need it, in order to do a favor for the handsome and socially prominent son of Robbie Budd, who played accompaniments so delightfully for Papa's darling boys? Lanny would never be sure about that; it was more easy money that would be laid in his lap.

At first he said he was too busy to come to Berlin, which looked like a dignified way of saying that the offer was too small for his attention; Papa had made a cheap bid, and had been properly rebuked. So naturally he was called upon to do better; the two boys wrote again, saying that one of the deposed noblemen of Germany

361

was in serious financial straits; he had a palace near Berlin and another in Munich, and both were filled with art treasures, of which many had to be sold; of course it had to be done in strict privacy, for such people don't let their troubles be advertised. Papa had lent this gentleman a lot of money, so Papa had something to say about the sales, and if Lanny and his friend Mr. Kertezsi would come and give their time to the matter, it would be a great favor to Papa, and there would be really large sums of money for all concerned.

Lanny forwarded this letter to Zoltan, who was then in London, and Zoltan wrote a business letter to Johannes Robin, laying down very stiff terms; he and Lanny would have to be put in exclusive charge of the selling, and would receive a ten-percent commission on all sales they might arrange. The offer was accepted, and an agreement was signed by Johannes Robin, and by Prince Hohenstauffen zu Zinzenburg, who couldn't help himself, for it was a polite and refined sort of foreclosure. Zoltan wired Lanny to meet him in Munich, to help pluck the fine feathers out of the German goose on its way down the staircase of history. He actually wired that, and wasn't arrested for *lèse-majesté!*

It was the beginning of November, a delightful time of the year in Bavaria; why not have a family holiday? If we're going to make so much money, let's get some fun out of it! Beauty hadn't had a trip for a long time, and Marie hadn't been anywhere except back and forth between the Riviera and Seine-et-Oise. If two pairs of lovers went, they couldn't get into each other's way; Kurt could attend the concerts and opera, and interview music publishers, while Beauty and Marie could have tea with the deposed Princess Hohenstauffen zu Zinzenburg. They would go on to Berlin and see the sights—doubtless it wasn't altogether pleasant in Germany just now, but it was surely educational, something that you could tell your children and your grandchildren about; it might never happen again that a great nation would have its currency entirely devalued, and you could exchange one French franc for the price of a diamond ring. Lanny said this for the benefit of Marie—and when Kurt wasn't in the room.

All during that year Kurt had been receiving literature of the

National Socialist German Workingmen's Party, sent by Heinrich Jung, son of the Oberförster of Schloss Stubendorf. This young enthusiast had the dream of making a convert out of one who was looked upon in his home community as a future musical genius. And right at this juncture Heinrich wrote a letter full of portentous hints: "Great events are due in a few days. I am not allowed to tell about it, but history will be made. You will learn from your newspapers that our labors have not been in vain."

Of course both Lanny and Kurt could guess what that meant—the Nazis were going to attempt their long-planned uprising. Could they succeed, as Mussolini had done, or would they fail, like Kapp? Kurt decided that he would like to be on hand; and Beauty decided at once that she would go along to keep him out of mischief. Marie came to the same decision. Was it just to watch Lanny, or was she making a genuine effort to be interested in his ideas? Could she endure the sight of Germans? Could she feel sorry for them in their dreadful plight? The human heart is a complex of motives, and Marie de Bruyne, torn between passionate love and passionate hatred, could perhaps not have sorted out the different forces which took her to the land of her hereditary foe.

II

Lanny sent an airmail letter to Rick, telling him of the program and inviting him to help spend some of the money that grew so abundantly on trees. Lanny quoted the words of Heinrich, and interpreted them; surely if a *coup d'état* was going to be attempted, it ought to be good for an article. The one which Rick had written, "Upper Silesia after the Settlement," had made a good impression, especially at Stubendorf, where it had been translated and published locally. Lanny wrote: "Come and help us to hold Kurt down. Those Nazis will be swarming about him, and Beauty will want to scalp every last one of them."

The family purchased tickets and made test of that slogan which was spreading the fame of Fascism throughout Europe and America: "In Italy the trains now run on time!" But this was equally true in the people's republic of Germany, at least so far as concerned the fast international expresses; these were for the rich, who must be served and made comfortable, for they brought foreign exchange, the most precious thing in the Fatherland. At this moment it was increasing in value at a rate which suggested Jack's beanstalk in the fairy-tale. If you owned so much as one round red copper cent with the head of an American Indian on it, you could lie down to sleep with the knowledge that you were a millionaire, and that you would wake up a multi-millionaire. The figures were fantastic, seeming to belong in the realm of nightmare. On the day that Lanny and his friend arrived in Munich one dollar would buy 625,000,000 marks, and the next day it would buy a billion and a half. On no day did it go backward, and when they left, a dollar was worth seven trillion marks.

Impossible not to pity the distracted people who had to live in the midst of such a cyclone. Employers paid their workers for a half-day at noon, so that they could rush out and buy some food before it was out of their reach. People bought whatever they could find in the shops, regardless of whether they had any use for it; so long as it had value it could be sold later on. In the midst of such confusion a foreigner moved like an enchanted being; his status was that upon which the fancy of all races and times has been exercised —he had the lamp of Aladdin, the purse of Fortunatus, the touch of Midas, the Tarnhelm which rendered him invisible so that he could walk into any shop and take whatever he wanted. Omnipotence places a heavy strain upon human character, and not all visitors to the Fatherland made wise use of their magic. To put it briefly, many proved themselves to be the vultures which the Germans called them behind their backs.

III

Zoltan Kertezsi arrived the same day as Lanny, and the two men of business proceeded at once to the palace of their aristocratic client. There wasn't going to be any social intercourse, they discovered; Seine Durchlaucht's steward received them, and escorted them to a large *salon* where all the paintings had been hung, and left them to make such examination as they wished. They would have the freedom of the *salon* at reasonable hours, and might bring clients to inspect the offerings. But this, as it happened, was no part of their program, for Robin had made the loan in pounds sterling, and it had to be repaid in the same currency, which meant that sales must of necessity be made to foreigners.

An odd and miscellaneous collection, with a great deal of commonplace German stuff which Zoltan said would have to be auctioned off in Germany later on. But it might be that the amount of the loan could be realized from the "good stuff" alone. There were some Holbein drawings, and one small portrait; there were two Hobbemas, and a very luxurious Rubens, besides large and less valuable canvases by his pupils. Modern France was represented by two bright lilyponds at Giverny by Monet, in that pointilliste style which he had developed, and which had caused Sargent to remark that the old man had become color blind—he could see nothing but color. Modern Germany was represented by a superlative Menzel, a romantic Feuerbach, a head of a peasant by Munkacsy, and a group of mythological subjects by Arnold Böcklin, whose patron Seine Durchlaucht's father had been, so the steward told them.

They made a list of the paintings which Zoltan thought could be sold without delay, and then he put his young assistant through what amounted to an examination. Let each take a copy of the list, and set down what he considered a proper price for each item. This proposal made cold chills run up and down Lanny's spine, but he admitted that it would be educational, and when they compared lists, Zoltan was kind enough to say that Lanny hadn't done so badly. They discussed each painting, and gave their reasons, and Lanny thought the Böcklins ought to be higher because the painter was well known to Americans; they appreciated what Lanny called "philosophic content." But Zoltan said that that was something rarely recognized in sales; the pictures were *démodés*.

The proposed prices had to be approved by both creditor and debtor, so a schedule was prepared, and two copies placed in the hands of the steward. Seine Durchlaucht couldn't have done much more than glance over it, for a copy with his signed approval was returned within an hour, and Robin's O.K. came by telegraph next day. Zoltan sent off several cablegrams to clients in America; all he had to do was to describe one item in a few words, with the name of the painter and the price, and in the next three days he had sold the Holbein, one of the Hobbemas, and one of the Monets. It was all in the knowing how, he said, with a happy smile.

IV

Lanny decided to try the same method. He cabled his father about two Böcklins whose "philosophic content" he thought would appeal to Esther Budd; also he cabled the Murchisons about the Rubens, a female nude which he thought might give a jolt to Pittsburgh. He had had a couple of jolly letters from Adella, enclosing a bunch of newspaper clippings in which the Goya and the Velásquez were reproduced and the full story told. Said the plateglass lady: "My dreams of cultural prestige have been fully realized!" Lanny now told her that Zoltan expected the Rubens would be sold within a week, and Adella's reply came within twenty-four hours: they had put Lanny's message in the hands of a well-known steel man of advanced age who collected fair ladies in the name of art, and his money was in the Munich bank two days later.

Lanny's stepmother would be more cautious, naturally; she might travel to the New York or Boston public library to find out all she could about Böcklin. When her reply came, it was a request that the sale be held up until she could receive photographs of the paintings; but Lanny had to answer that it was first come first served, and Zoltan was pretty sure one of his British clients would cable acceptance on receipt of a letter. Lanny smiled, realizing the mental stress of his cautious Puritan stepmother, invited to pay eleven thousand dollars apiece for two paintings that she had never seen. Probably it was Robbie who decided the matter; anyhow, he cabled the cash, and included a commission for Lanny, even though Lanny had said he wouldn't accept one.

A list and description of all the paintings was prepared, with photographs of some of them, and sent with a letter to a number of persons, including names which Lanny had accumulated. Zoltan expected that most of the collection would be sold in that way, and he would take the remainder to London under bond. Wherever and however they were sold, Lanny would receive half the commission; he couldn't raise any question this time, for Johannes Robin was assuredly his client. So Lanny could afford to have a splurge in Germany; if he wanted any paintings he could buy them, and the same would apply to any of the girls he saw on the streets or in the cafés. Zoltan said this sadly, for he was a tender-hearted fellow, and was sorry for these pathetic creatures, with their painted hollow cheeks and eyes feverishly bright, who would go with any foreigner for the price of a piece of bread.

V

Meanwhile Rick had arrived, and he and Kurt set forth to investigate the activities of the National Socialist German Workingmen's Party. They found quickly that Heinrich Jung hadn't exaggerated the situation, for all Bavaria was in turmoil. The surrender to France hadn't had the expected effect of stopping the flight from the mark; "runaway inflation" ran over everything which tried to stop it, governments included. The distracted people were ready to hear any agitator with a plausible program, and the dingy headquarters of the Nazis were like a beehive at swarming time. Hundreds of young ex-soldiers with their swastika armbands were pouring in from near-by towns, saluting all over the place and being marched here and there.

It was the same odd combination of conspiracy and propaganda which the visitors had noted nearly a year ago. Nobody had the slightest hesitation about telling what they were all going to do: first take Munich, then march on Berlin. There was the same unwillingness to admit any imitation of Mussolini, but if you had read about the March on Rome you would hardly fail to recognize the pattern. The great war-leader General Ludendorff had publicly declared his adherence to the party's cause, so the success of its coming coup was assured. The extraordinarily bright blue eyes of Heinrich Jung shone with excitement as he whispered the most holy of secrets to a future musical genius and a representative of an English newspaper.

Heinrich's particular "hundred," as the Hitler groups were called, was going to march at seven o'clock the following morning. Heinrich couldn't tell where, because only the leaders knew, but Kurt and Rick might come along and see—it would be real history, said the youth. He used that phrase often, and it was evident that this thought had inspired him—he was going to be in history! In one nation after another, first Russia, then Hungary and Greece and Turkey and Italy, it had been shown that vigorous, determined men might seize power, and the followers of these men might become officials, persons of importance and of fame. It had been shown right here in Munich by the Reds; and now a new group was going to try it, with the newest of slogans, the most timely and potent: *Deutschland erwache!* Germany awake!

That was how it appeared to the visiting British journalist; but of course to twenty-year-old Heinrich Jung it meant the deliverance of Germany from the heel of the oppressor, the casting out of the money-changers from the temple, the setting free of honest German labor—the young Nazi's doctrines seemed as pink as his cheeks, and Rick laughed and said that the longer he talked the redder both became.

That evening there was a mass meeting in the same Bürgerbräukeller where they had heard Adi speak in January. This time it was a meeting of the Bavarian monarchists, who were also planning a revolt against Berlin. Heinrich Jung was very insistent that the visitors should attend this meeting—he practically told them that the Nazis meant to attempt some sort of coup; so the four friends went, and they saw plenty of history. Promptly on the second of eighty-thirty, Adolf Hitler burst into the hall, followed by steel-helmeted men, some of them pushing Maxim guns. Hitler rushed to the platform and took possession of it, delivering one of his wild tirades and telling the audience that the National Socialist regime had begun. At the point of his revolver he forced the monarchist leaders to pledge their allegiance to *his* kind of revolution, and to order their troops to obey him.

The meeting broke up in the wildest confusion. Apparently "history" consisted of parties of men rushing this way and that about the streets, so the visiting strangers went back to their hotel. They were out again before dawn, an ungodly procedure for two society ladies, but Beauty wouldn't let Kurt go without her, and Marie didn't think it "sporting" not to accompany Lanny's mother. When Kurt decided to walk alongside the "hundred," Beauty insisted upon walking with him; a fashionably gowned lady holding onto his arm would keep a sight-seeing stroll from becoming a military expedition. It appeared that other women of Munich had the very same idea, for many a young Nazi had a sweetheart hanging onto his swastika armband. Rick, being unable to march, followed the troop in a taxi, and Marie rode with him, glad of the protection of his journalist's credentials. Lanny and Zoltan were busy with their picture job.

VI

There wasn't much cheering, for apparently the working people on the streets at that hour didn't know what it was all about. The troop marched to the Capuchin convent, under whose five-foot walls great stores of rifles had been buried. All night the monks had held torches while the arms were being carried out and distributed to the storm troopers. Ammunition had been stored in the vaults of one of the city's great banks; a peculiar circumstance, in view of the party program concerning the money-changers. But nobody stopped to think about that, save only the skeptical Britisher; the eager young Nazis were busy getting their share of cartridges from the truck which suddenly put in appearance. Their guns were loaded, and then it was real war.

Off they marched, singing *Deutschland über Alles*, until they came to one of the city's bridges, where they halted, and there was an interminable wait. Nobody knew what it was for; presumably they were to hold the bridge against the enemy, but no enemy appeared, and making history was gradually discovered to be as tedious as making motion pictures. The four visiting strangers finally decided to repair to a near-by café for breakfast, and they gave a few marks to a street urchin to keep watch for them, promising him a still larger fortune if he would run to the café and advise them whenever the *Sturmabteilung* started to advance. One of the advantages of making history in a great city is that you can take a taxi and catch up with events.

They had an excellent meal, and sat for a long time over their cigarettes and coffee, agreeing that Lanny and Zoltan had been more sensible to stick to their picture job. But Kurt and Rick wouldn't quit and go home, and Beauty wouldn't desert Kurt, and Marie wouldn't desert Beauty. Presently Kurt and Rick got into an argument as to whether this Nazi movement was a plain "racket," or whether it had any ideas that might be fruitful for the Fatherland's future. Was Adolf Hitler Schicklgruber just a plain "nut," or was he an expression of the *Volk* spirit? Kurt insisted that for a people beaten and depressed as the Germans were it was important to have their courage and hopes restored, to be made to believe that they were a race with a world destiny. Rick replied that all this talk about racial superiority was "the bunk"; a half-cracked Englishman by the name of H. S. Chamberlain had put that bug into the Kaiser's ear—the Kaiser, half cracked himself, had circulated the book all over Germany, and it had spawned a whole library of rubbish, some of which this poor Schicklgruber creature had picked up.

Rick insisted that he knew just the type: you could hear a score of them ranting in Hyde Park any Sunday afternoon. One shouted that Britain was being bankrupted by the upkeep of the royal family, the next clamored that it was belief in God which was wrecking civilization; one would tell you that money must be abolished, and the next that Esperanto offered the only way of understanding among the peoples. Many of these poor devils slept in flophouses and old men's homes, exactly as Adi had done, wearing out their own vocal cords and the eardrums of their fellow inmates.

Kurt and Rick might have started a small civil war right there, but the urchin came rushing in to report that the *Sturmabteilung* was on the march. They paid him the promised fortune and took their taxi and followed. Kurt wanted to walk, perhaps to revive his enthusiasm for the Nazi cause; but Beauty wouldn't let him take a step without her hand in the crook of his arm. He couldn't raise the question of etiquette, for other women and girls were marching, each with her man. Would this become one of the war customs of the new Hitler Germany?

They were joined by thousands of other troopers, and with the *Hakenkreuz* banner at their head they marched out into the Marien-platz. Farther on was the Ludwigstrasse, and there, apparently to the surprise of the marchers, some forces of the *Reichswehr*, the regular army, were lined up. Then from behind the Feldherrnhalle came a body of the Bavarian state police; it looked as if the swastika bearers had been led into an ambush. As they continued to advance, orders rang out and shots were fired; a dozen or more of the Nazis fell, and the women began to scream and to scatter. Be sure there was no louder screamer, no quicker scatterer than Beauty Budd! She dragged Kurt with her, willy-nilly, dignity or no dignity; the taxi came speeding up, and in they hopped, and around one of the corners they went, the troops letting them pass unchallenged. And that was all they saw of the "Beerhall Putsch," the derisive name for the history that was made on those two days of November 1923. General Ludendorff was a prisoner, Adolf Hitler Schicklgruber was a fugitive with a dislocated shoulder, and Eric Vivian Pomeroy-Nielson was shut up in a room of the Vier Jahreszeiten Hotel, pounding out the story on his portable typewriter, to be cabled to a London newspaper.

VII

The visitors finished with their business and pleasure in Munich, and meanwhile they read that Herr Schicklgruber was in prison, and his movement outlawed under heavy penalties; they were glad to know that they would never again have to think about that danger-ous and most unpleasant "nut." Rick, explaining history to his Brit-ish public, wrote that people did not starve gladly, and that these events served notice that humane and rational elements in Britain and France must get together with those in Germany and find a way of reconcilement. The twenty-five-year-old social philosopher was planning a play in which these issues would be fought out among a group of characters. It was the "note" of the time, and even the French Nationalists were beginning to admit that the Ruhr technique hadn't proved a success.

Lanny celebrated his twenty-fourth birthday during this Munich visit. Zoltan asked Beauty's permission to give him a surprise party and invite several lovers of music and art whom he knew in the city. These were the "good Europeans," the sort of people whom the three musketeers of the arts had met in Hellerau before the war, when it had been possible to believe that the golden age of peace had come to Europe, that Orpheus with his lute was charming the furies of greed and hate so that they would no more torment mankind. What a change in ten years! Now many of the art lovers were dead, and others in mourning, or broken in health and spirits. If you invited them to a dinner party in a de luxe hotel, they would take out some ancient finery from a trunk and brush it and mend the mothholes; they would come timidly, as if no longer sure how to behave. For a couple of those fabulous American dollars the most distinguished artists in Munich would be happy to sing and play for the gratification of a young Croesus, a young Fortunatus, a young Harun-al-Rashid.

The party moved on to Berlin, where there was another picture job to be done. This time Lanny guessed the values more closely; he was learning fast and gaining assurance. A portion of his mind would be set aside for a catalogue of art-works; in it would be several thousand names of painters, and the instant he heard a name and the date of a picture he would be able to say: "One thousand dollars," or "ten thousand," or "a hundred thousand." With lower figures it wasn't worth while to bother; but here was one of the temptations to which he would never be entirely immune—some poor devil of ability would be brought to his attention and he would have an urge to promote him, even though the commission on the sales wouldn't pay for the gasoline he used in traveling about.

But that didn't apply to the palace of a deposed nobleman in the suburbs of Berlin. Here were a dozen old masters, and Zoltan Kertezsi would decide their destiny in the manner of a hostess writing the place-cards for a dinner party. This Frans Hals should be in the Taft collection in Cincinnati, and that Sir Joshua belonged in the Huntington collection in southern California. Zoltan would "shoot a wire" and the sale would be made—those American millionaires like to do business in that swift yes-or-no way. Apparently they put a price on every minute of their time, and Lanny wondered what they did with any which they had left over. It must seem unbearably extravagant to go for a stroll or to look at anything so cheap as a flower. Zoltan said that that was the reason they had orchids.

Johannes Robin was delighted with what had been done. He was getting his money back in short order, and without earning the enmity of an aristocrat who had many powerful friends. He began to sing the praises of this Budd and Kertezsi outfit, and the pair received inquiries from other *Schieber* who wanted to put a part of their gains into something that could be rolled up into a small package and carried out of Germany quickly. One thing led to another, and Lanny could have spent all his time at this exciting new business.

But they must have some fun, too. Zoltan had brought his fiddle, and with two of these, a clarinet, and a piano they could play most any chamber music; they did so for hours on end. They even tackled the later quartets of Beethoven, and became lost in their mazes, and had to admit that they didn't know what the great master was driving at. Could it be that there was truth in what the critics of the time had said, that, being deaf, Beethoven no longer knew what he was writing? Or was he trying to say things so subtle that only a metaphysical mind could follow him? Lanny didn't know, and would have liked to ask Kurt; but the former artillery officer was firm in his refusal to visit the home of a Jewish speculator in marks, one who had so large a share in responsibility for the misfortunes of the Fatherland.

VIII

Kurt was staying with his brother; and Lanny was invited to a dinner party given by a group of young officers, Emil's friends. Lanny had met British army people and French, but this was his first acquaintance with Germans. He got the impression of men who took their profession much more seriously; they were highly trained technical men, like engineers. But that didn't make their conversation very interesting at a dinner party. All men "talk shop," but when your "shop" is killing other men, it is depressing to a lover of humanity. These officers were young in years, but old in tragic experience, and they had to drink too much wine before their tongues were loosened. They were interested in what Lanny and Kurt had to tell about events in Munich, and from their comments it was clear that they had little tolerance for Nazi lunacies; they were supporting the present republic as a stop-gap, but to a man they were convinced that the only permanent government for Germany must be a monarchy, and when the time came they meant to strike toward that goal.

During the Berlin visit Lanny and his mother laid siege to Kurt to persuade him to let them advance money for the publishing of his musical compositions. Here was the extraordinary situation, that for what Beauty would spend and did spend for a pair of dancing-slippers, all Kurt's compositions might be put into type by faithful German workmen who would be glad of a chance to earn their daily bread. Lanny's commission on the sale of a single mediocre painting would pay for paper and printing, and all Kurt's friends might have copies of half a dozen opera in first editions.

It was too great a temptation for any man who believed that his work had merit. Kurt gave way, upon the understanding that the money was to be a loan, to constitute a mortgage upon receipts for the rendition rights of the works. Lanny went with him to one of the old-established music houses, and a contract was signed, and Lanny wrote a check for a few of those pounds sterling which he had in one of the Berlin banks. Nothing he had ever done with money gave him more pleasure; and Beauty was even happier, for she knew that Kurt was at a serious crisis just then, and that attention paid to his music would be a powerful force to keep him at work. Beauty loved Kurt's music for one solid and practical reason —that it kept him shut up in her sanctuary, away from Schicklgrubers and Maxim guns!

IX

Christmas was near, so the party broke up. Beauty and Marie took the night train for Paris, the latter to return to her home, the former to spend a couple of days with Emily Chattersworth at Les Forêts and then to motor with her to the Riviera. Zoltan would have to travel between Berlin and Munich to oversee the selling and shipping of pictures—no simple matter in these times of disorder, when people did not starve gladly and any servant or employee might steal a painting and substitute an inferior one. Rick was returning to The Reaches, to write an article about inflation and its effects upon everyday life. After Christmas he was planning to bring his family to Bienvenu.

Lanny and Kurt traveled to Stubendorf, which had now become a sort of third home for a wandering young American. Once more the elderly horses toiled up the slope to the castle on the height; once more the sleighbells jingled and the family came running out; once more the hearts of two blond young Aryan widows went pit-a-pat at the sight of a super-eligible young American whose dark love secret would never be told to them. They sang the old Christmas songs, and some new ones which Lanny had picked up at the publishers'. They rejoiced at the news of Kurt's good fortune, and did their pathetic best to reward his benefactor and pupil—as they still thought of their guest. Once more the wise Herr Meissner discussed the affairs of Germany, and Lanny set down some of his opinions for Rick to use in his article.

In Upper Silesia were once prosperous families having art treasures they would gladly exchange for foreign money; Lanny traveled about and looked at them, and made notes as to prices expected. He learned that the Graf Stubendorf had a cousin in Vienna with a famous collection, and that this gentleman shared the hardships of his dismembered land. So, on their way home, Lanny and Kurt stopped for a couple of days in a city which had been famed as the home of wine, woman, and song, and which now had been sentenced to slow misery and decay. The beautiful blue Danube had turned a muddy yellow, the skies above it were gray and the people depressed, and pitiful in their faded finery.

The two friends looked at more pictures, and Lanny imparted some of the knowledge he had gained—but nothing about prices! He sent Kurt off to a concert while he discussed that delicate subject with an elderly aristocrat who seemed too tired to care what happened to his fortunes. Lanny made notes, and promised to do the best he could. He sent a complete schedule to Zoltan, and when he got to Bienvenu called in a stenographer and wrote letters to his growing list of prospective customers. Lanny figured that after deducting all the costs of the trip for himself and his friends he had cleared more than twenty thousand dollars—and he was only twenty-four years old!

So for the rest of his days he would have the comforting certainty of being able to have whatever he needed, and without asking any man's permission or being told what to do or say. The only thing that would make trouble for him was the trouble of all the people around him, of a world in torment whose cries came to him as if in a delirium. It seemed irrational to heed these cries, for there was nothing you could do about them; yet how could you help wishing that you could, and wondering if you couldn't? A strange plight for art lovers, who trained themselves to be receptive and then didn't dare use their faculties except upon imaginary things! Divide your mind in half, and build an emotion-tight compartment between the two; be sensitive to art and insensitive to life; learn to follow the example of that Russian countess who wept for the woes of the tenor in the opera while her coachman froze to death on the box outside!

19

Broad Is the Way

I

IT WAS to a greatly depressed France that the travelers came back. The franc had been going down all through the Ruhr invasion; reparations appeared to be mythical, and bonds that had been issued on them were losing value. Exaggerated amounts had been paid as restitution, for war-damaged properties—it was a way of rewarding political supporters, not so different from what is called "graft" in the States. All the losses came back on those who had fixed incomes and salaries; the only gainers were speculators, and those fortunate few whose incomes were in dollars.

A delightful thing to find that you could get fifty percent more francs for your remittances from home! American visitors wrote or cabled about it, and steamers were crowded with refugees from Prohibition and Puritanism. Each year the boom on the Riviera became bigger and noisier; hotels and pensions were crowded, jazz-bands thumped all night, casinos were crowded with gamblers and dancers. The bathing-suits worn on the beaches became more and more scanty, until it seemed that nothing more could be spared. There was no longer any limit to anything; you did what you pleased, provided you had the price or could get it away from somebody else.

All the familiar figures came back every season: the kings playing tennis and baccarat, the maharajas playing polo or "chemmy," the Russian aristocrats running tearooms as a cover for pandering; the "beauty queens," the "lounge lizards," the "sugar daddies" with their "warm babies," the "hot mammas" with their "dancing boys" —the types were old, but the language was fresh from New York or Hollywood. The movie stars came, and walked like gods among an adoring population which had seen them magnified and transfigured upon the screen, and now stood to watch them, sleek and supple in tight bathing-suits, diving from the springboards below the great Hotel du Cap, or strolling on the Boulevard de la Croisette in costumes fit for a million-dollar superfeature.

Pick any famous name from the headlines of the newspapers, and it was a safe bet that you would meet him or her on the Côte d'Azur some time between January and March. The money they spent filled the purses of food and wine merchants, and the money they owned made the subject of awe-stricken gossip. If a giant hand could have come down on the Riviera and swept up a few hundred of them and put them through a financial squeezer, it would have collected most of the treasures of the earth. Cattle kings from the Argentine, wool kings from Australia, diamond kings from South Africa, copper kings from Montana—you had only to list the places where wealth was produced, and here were the owners of it.

Sir Basil Zaharoff, wearying of *la haute politique* and the financing of wars, had found himself a friendly little business, a toy to play with in his old age, a means of recouping his losses in Turkey; he had purchased for a round million pounds the stocks of the "Société Anonyme des Bains de Mer et du Cercle des Étrangers de Monaco," and was now its president and manager. The Knight Commander of the Bath had become yet another kind of bathing-master—but don't imagine that he went into the sea himself, or that he rented the privilege to others; no, the name of this company was a sixty-year-old camouflage for the most sumptuous and ornate gambling-palace in the world, so important that its locale was a separate nation all by itself, its owner a prince by right of purchase. The Monte Carlo casino had been done over and made more fashionable than ever. Previously you had been admitted free, but that was not according to the moral code of an old Greek trader; you now paid to get in, and paid still more before you got out—despite the fact that thousands of brains in Europe and America were concentrated on the devising of a "system" whereby they might beat the bank. Sir Basil himself might be observed taking his constitutional every afternoon, just as Lanny and his father had observed him ten years before; but he had a fixed rule never to go into the casino, and there was a story of a lady who had lost money and appealed to the great man to tell her how to avoid losing more. "Certainly, madame," he replied. "Do not gamble."

II

Ever more varied and strange were the forms which life took in this world of pleasure; and few were in better position to observe them than a young man with an agreeable smile, a well-filled purse, and a reputation for being able to dispose of works of art. It was astounding how many persons had inherited such works from their forefathers and cherished them as treasures without price; also how many schemes they devised to get introductions to Lanny Budd so that they might show him these possessions and sell them to him at almost any price. A Coromandel screen, a Japanese golden Kwannon—what means did Lanny have to know whether such things were genuine or not? He would never forget a sight which he had been taken to as a boy—a workshop in an obscure quarter of Florence where replicas of marble sculptures were made wholesale. The device, invented in America, consisted of half a dozen steel drills attached at intervals to a long rod, and caused to revolve by machinery. In front of each of these whirling drills a block of marble was fastened, and at one end of the rod an operator sat in front of the statue which was to be reproduced, a steel point attached to his end of the rod was passed over the model, and the other six drills moved in unison, eating away the marble from the other six blocks and gradually bringing into existence six replicas of the original. In other parts of this workshop the products were sprayed with chemicals and otherwise treated to make them "genuine old masters" for the American trade. *Garde à vous*, Lanny Budd —this art business is not all beer and skittles!

There was a young and dashing Rumanian countess who had fled from her country at the height of the war, bringing an old mother and a few art treasures in her automobile. She was pathetic, almost tearful over the plundering of her castle—she really had had one, and Lanny had been taught to respect genuine titles. The lady took him to her apartment and showed him an invaluable cloisonné vase —at least she called it that, and only with difficulty was she persuaded to suggest a value of a hundred thousand francs. Lanny said he didn't know anyone who bought vases, and he himself was not a dealer, he acted only as an agent for customers. The upshot was that the countess broke down and wept, admitting that she was in desperate financial straits. Perhaps Lanny might have been moved if she hadn't tried to spill the tears on him; he kept politely out of reach, and said that he would try to interest someone in the vase— with the result that the price came down ten thousand francs at a time, and in the end he paid two thousand for it, just to get away from a painful scene.

He packed the object carefully and shipped it to Zoltan, who was in Paris at the time, and in due course came a letter from his friend saying that it was a very lovely vase for anyone who wanted something to put flowers in, and if Lanny needed another to match it, Zoltan knew the shop in Paris where it could be bought for a hundred francs. Two thousand being then less than ninety dollars, it was a not too expensive lesson; but when the story was told to the family it was suggested that in future Lanny should take Jerry Pendleton or someone else when he inspected *objets d'art* in the apartments of strange ladies. Beauty made this suggestion, but Lanny had an idea that Marie had been taken into consultation!

III

Artists, also, began to take an interest in this well-connected youth. They all knew him because he was the stepson of Detaze and the nephew of Blackless—to say nothing of being the son of a pink-and-gold butterfly who had emerged from the chrysalis of an artists' model in Paris. Several who had painted her and fallen in love with her now lived on the Riviera or came there to paint, and when they heard about Lanny's good fortune they all brought their works and invited him to make such fortunes for them. It got so that the servants were told that whenever anybody came to the gates of Bienvenu with a portfolio, Lanny was absent for an indefinite time. That didn't fit very well with a name meaning "Welcome"; but how often it happens in this world that people are not able to carry out their good intentions!

American painters came often to the Côte d'Azur; among them the great John Sargent—a hard man to know, but Zoltan knew him and gave Lanny a letter. Sargent was old, but still erect, a broad-shouldered, handsome man with ruddy face and a small white beard; he had painted portraits of the wealthy and great, and made them noble-looking as they wished to be, but now he was weary of them and desired no more of their wealth. One of the last had been old John D. Rockefeller, who had paid him fifty thousand dollars for a portrait, and the painter had given the money to the Red Cross. Lanny brought him an offer from one of the richest ladies in Cannes; he was free to name his own price, but he looked at a photograph of her and remarked that he would as soon paint a bar of soap.

Instead he said: "Come sketching with me." So Lanny, who had loved this coast from childhood, took him to some little-known beauty spots, and sat and observed Sargent making watercolor sketches. One of the most interesting things in the world, to watch a man of genius working in a frenzy of concentration and something lovely growing under his hands. Lanny kept as still as a mouse, answering only when he was spoken to, and after several such expeditions the artist gave him sketches which might have been sold for a thousand dollars.

All kinds of people on this lovely shore, and all kinds of art-works coming into being! One day Lanny went with his mother to lunch at the home of a divorcee from New York who had brought a considerable fortune with her. On the walls of her dining-room he saw four panels which hit him between the eyes. They were painted on silk backed with wood, and he thought he had never seen such a glory of color; peacocks and other great tropical birds, magnificent stylized designs in purple and gold and scarlet and black. Lanny couldn't eat for looking at them, and the hostess said: "Oh, don't you know Dick Oxnard? He's spending the winter here."

Lanny listened to the story of a genius who came of one of the oldest and proudest New York families, and had inherited a fortune in his own right. He was divinely handsome, gay, a darling of the ladies; he was living here because of some scrape he had got into at home. "He's a bit wild," admitted the hostess, "but the most delightful company. You really ought to know him." Beauty, who watched over her darling so carefully where Reds and Rumanian countesses were concerned, saw nothing to worry about in a society painter, and later on the hostess went to the telephone and told Dick Oxnard about her friend. The answer was: "Send him to lunch tomorrow."

So, promptly at the appointed hour of one, Lanny's sport-car drove up in front of an elegant villa in one of the Riviera valleys. There didn't seem to be anybody around, and perhaps the bell was out of order; but the door was wide open, which seemed hospitable. Looking in, Lanny saw some of those gorgeous decorative panels and screens in the entrance hall, and as they were what he had come for, he ventured in. Presently along came an elderly Chinese servant in a white duck suit, grinning amiably. "Mornin'. You come blekfas'?"

"Lunch," replied the guest.

"Blekfas', lunch, allee same, maybe blunch. You go up, all light, allee same home." Nothing could have been more cordial; so Lanny went up the wide stairway, stopping half-way to look at a breath-taking design of a market girl of Tehuantepec wearing an elaborately embroidered dress and seated under a tree with an array of fruits piled up in great painted gourds. In the hallway above were several doors, all open, and Lanny didn't know which to go to; but he was in no hurry, for on the wall was a black Chinese dragon against a background of gold and scarlet flames. Lanny would have been just as well content if there hadn't been anybody at home in Dick Oxnard's villa.

IV

But the house was full, as it turned out. Through the open door of a large room the guest saw an enormous canopied bed with four posts of carved ebony and draperies of cloth of gold. It was such a bed as Marie Antoinette might have slept in; Lanny had never seen one so big in any castle. But even so, it was hardly big enough for the assortment of girls who were sleeping in it, and some of their arms and feet hung over the sides. They were in miscellaneous scanty costumes of as many hues as an Oxnard wall panel, and appeared to have draped themselves with unconscious art around the central figure of a man.

Lanny thought he might as well inspect this art along with all the rest. It was of the genre known as "still life," for the whole group were sound asleep, and their combined breathing was like the sound of a summer zephyr through a grove of pine trees. But suddenly Lanny gave a jump, for behind him the air was shattered by the most astounding racket. On the stair-landing was a great Chinese gong, and somebody must have been hitting it sideswipes with a hammer, for the crashes came rolling through the hall like breakers on a beach; they sped up and down and clashed with one another until it seemed there was nothing in the house but sound.

It caused one or two of the girls to open their eyes and stretch their arms. Finally the half-buried man came to life and, when he saw Lanny, sat up. "Hello!" he said, with no surprise. "You company?"

"Lanny Budd," said the visitor.

"Oh, good! Make yourself at home, Budd." The speaker deftly extricated himself from the tangle of girls, and slid over them to the floor. His costume consisted of a loincloth of green and silver, which had come from Ceylon, or Siam, or some such tropical land. He was a grand figure of a man, thirty or so, built like a statue of Hermes, with wavy golden hair and mustache of the same. Apparently this was the way he lived, and he made no apologies. He caught one of the girls by the toe and gave a firm pull, and she let out a shriek of pain; it must have been a familiar procedure, for all the others leaped into life and tumbled out of bed as if they had had an electric shock.

Some of them wore the costumes of Bali and some of Hawaii; others wore bathing-suits or birthday suits. They came streaming from other rooms—there were more than a score of beautiful young girls in the house, fair and stately ones from the north, and dark, languorous ones from the south. Lanny never did find out about them all, but he learned that several had followed the young god from America, and others had just drifted in and stayed. The doors of the villa were never locked, and coming and going were equally free and easy. The host who was so gay and hospitable would become angry upon the slightest whim, and then he was incredibly brutal to his attendant nymphs; he would address them in language which could not be indicated in print, and one who gave him displeasure would be propelled through the front door by the agency of the beautiful white foot of Hermes, messenger of the gods.

That came later. For the present all was gaiety. "These are the girls," said the painter; "help yourself." That was all the introduction required; apparently the girls liked the visitor's looks, for several attached themselves to him, told him their first names, and tried to sit in his lap at the first occasion.

The guest had come to lunch, but the host revealed that they had finished supper not long ago. Lanny said he would just as soon look at paintings, but the other declared that they were always ready to eat. The troop of nymphs came dancing and chattering into the dining-room, which had more of the vivid panels, this time of tropical fishes and long, waving sea-growths. The old Chinese brought in platters of scrambled eggs and buttered toast, and when he had distributed these he brought in half a dozen bottles of champagne and proceeded to open and fill glasses around the table. Fortunately it was a day of warm sunshine, and when you are young you can sit half naked and drink iced champagne for your morning pick-me-up.

There was another man present, an Englishman who was introduced as "Captain Abernethy, call him Neethy." It was he who had pounded on the gong in honor of Lanny's arrival. He too was fair, with brick-red, apoplectic cheeks; he was somewhat older than Oxnard, and apparently acted as his guardian, providing what little sanity there was in the establishment. But he hadn't always been like that, for presently Dick was telling with laughter how Neethy had been in the cavalry, in the days when there was real cavalry, and while his brother officers were having a party in the mess-room he had ridden his horse through the door and sprung him over the table. Neethy and Dick had been all over the world together, and in Mexico the cavalryman on a wager had leaped into the bullring and onto the back of the bull. He had stuck there, too. "But you know," said the host, "those greasers mobbed us; they took it as an insult to their bull!"

In one of the few moments of rationality during this visit Lanny expressed his admiration for the American's work, and asked him if he ever sold anything. Oxnard said that he hated to do so because it was such a bother; but if Lanny admired the things, he'd be happy to present him with one, for they cluttered up the place. Lanny said that he couldn't think of accepting such a favor. He said the same thing to a beautiful blond nymph who offered to accompany him to one of the bedrooms, and the result in both cases was the same. When he took his departure he found that a large black-and-gold tiger in a green-and-scarlet jungle had been deposited in his car; also he found a nymph—no painting, but a flesh-and-blood one dressed in a sports costume of knitted pink silk, waiting in the seat beside the driver's. She was determined to stay, and since Lanny was unwilling to use his foot, it took a lot of argument. He explained with all gentleness that he was devoted to a French lady and by no possibility to be won away from her. The blond darling, who couldn't have been more than eighteen years of age, wept gently on his shoulder, declaring that it was the dream of her life to find a man to be true to. Lanny said that he would have been delighted to be that man, had she not unfortunately waited so long before presenting herself.

V

Rick brought his family to Bienvenu, and he was in a more hopeful state of mind than Lanny could recall since the war. There had been a general election in Britain, the dreadful Tories were out, and the Empire had its first labor government. The Prime Minister was a

Socialist, a former schoolteacher from Scotland; a tall handsome man and an elegant orator. Ramsay MacDonald had taken a courageous stand against the war, and all forward-looking men now predicted a regime of peace and reconcilement. The German Foreign Minister, Stresemann, was also a reconciler, and all that was needed now was to get rid of the dull Poincaré. The French elections were due in May, and everybody agreed that the tide was running against the party which was responsible for the Ruhr fiasco and the *dégringolade* of the franc. The left forces were working out an agreement not to oppose one another's candidates, and Rick was as keen about it as if he had been a Frenchman. Lanny agreed with him, as he always did—but never a word about it in the presence of Marie!

The problem of reparations was at last being dealt with on a rational basis. A commission of experts was named to determine what Germany could actually pay—this after five years of efforts to compel her to pay what she couldn't. A Chicago banker was at the head of it, and this so-called Dawes Commission worked out an arrangement; by dint of scaling down the claims every few months—always amid cries of anguish from the French—they would gradually accomplish the purpose of letting Germany get on her feet.

When the Easter holidays drew near, Robbie was in London and intending to come to Paris; so Lanny drove Marie up, and once more in the drawing-room of the Château de Bruyne he listened to Denis and his father discussing the affairs of Europe; once more in his uncomfortable way he would begin wondering whether all the conclusions to which his English friend had brought him could be trusted after all. Was it really safe to let Germany get on her feet? Could you trust that thing in Berlin which called itself a "republic"? How long would it be before Hindenburg or somebody like him would come into power, and the old dreadful menace would be hanging over France?

Denis de Bruyne pointed out something which Lanny had heard in Germany, but of which the significance had not been made clear to him. All during the "mark swindle" the great German industries had been required to keep their workers employed and had received government credits for that purpose. They had set the workers to rebuilding and expanding plants; so now, having wiped out her debts both internal and external, the Germans were starting afresh with the most modern productive machinery in the world. What chance would the French stand in international trade, with their still-ruined factories, mills, and mines? It really seemed that the Germans were more capable than their foes. You could say, as Denis did, that it was because they were without moral or business scruples; that made you hate them more—but it didn't make your peril any less!

Denis had the idea that the United States ought to recognize this situation and put her moral and financial power behind France. But Robbie had to tell him the painful fact that this was out of the question; any American statesman who advocated it would be quickly retired to private life. This was a world in which you had to look out for yourself, and the very word "idealism" now gave Americans what they crudely called "a pain in the neck." Europe would have to find a method of paying her debts to America before she asked for any more favors.

VI

Fate had given Robbie Budd a new executive of his country. Poor old Harding had died, perhaps of a broken heart—anyhow, just in time to escape an avalanche of scandal which had been sliding down onto his head. The man who ruled in his stead was even more satisfactory to Robbie and his friends; the father described him as the oddest figure, the son of a country storekeeper, with exactly that sort of mind. Vermont, his home state, is a cold, mountainous country, where people work hard to wrest a living from a stony soil; they save every penny and hold onto it tightly, and keep their mouths shut concerning their own affairs. "Cautious Cal" was the name of the new President, and by the easy method of saying nothing he made it possible for the newspapers to build him into a "strong silent statesman." In reality, Robbie said, he liked to go down into the basement of the White House and keep track of the groceries that were being used. This suited Robbie and his big business friends, for he let them run the country and didn't meddle with what he didn't understand.

The master of money smiled when his son, the gentle idealist, talked about Ramsay MacDonald and the French Socialists with their dream of peace in Europe. Robbie revealed the one really significant fact: the munitions industry was coming back! All through the post-war depression Robbie had argued with his father against the entire making over of the Budd plants; Robbie's oldest brother, Lawford, had wanted to drop arms-making, but now, as usual, Robbie was proved to be right! Already he was picking up small orders for various sorts of arms; Dutch traders were buying them and smuggling them into Germany by the network of canals which ran into that country. Also France was making new armament loans to Poland, and to the Little Entente, a new coalition to hold off the Russians on the east and to attack Germany if she should attack France. "Just as soon as business picks up there's bound to be a boom," said Robbie; "and we shall get our share, believe me."

"But," argued the son, "what about those huge stocks that were left over after the war?"

The father smiled. "We have had engineers and technicians at work for five years, and so have Vickers, Schneider, everybody. We have a new machine gun that fires two hundred more rounds per minute than the old one, and reaches a thousand yards farther. The old guns will be all right for South America or China, but not for a modern war. The same thing will apply to grenades, fuses, bombsights; everything that America is going to use in the next war will have to be made new—and not far ahead of the war, either!"

VII

Lanny would absorb this information, direct from the fountainhead, and would be impressed by the authority of his masterful progenitor. Robbie Budd was acquiring weight, along with money, and it would be a long time before the sensitive and affectionate son would have courage to face him in a mental showdown. Lanny would drive the busy man of affairs into Paris, and then go wandering to look at new paintings at the dealers'; a temptation would assail him, and somehow he would be powerless to resist it—he had to go calling on that Red uncle of his! He would fool himself with the idea that it was to pick up gossip about painters and what they were doing, the boom in Detaze and what the dealers were saying about it—all that "shop" for which artists have just as much weakness as munitions men. But sooner or later one of Jesse's left-wing friends would drop in, or perhaps Jesse's *amie* to arrange lunch; the talk would turn to politics, and the forbidden "dangerous thoughts" would be flying about the room, hitting Lanny Budd in vital parts of his mental anatomy.

Again he would be struck by the curious point: how completely his revolutionary uncle and his reactionary father agreed as to the facts of the modern world. Both would say that it was money that made the mare go, and they would agree as to the road on which the mare was traveling and her rate of progress; they would even agree as to what lay over the next hill; their dispute began only beyond the far horizon's rim. Really, two such surveyors ought to have been able to combine forces and make their maps in common; Lanny, the great reconciler, had been able to bring Britain and France and Germany together in the same household, so why shouldn't he dream of bringing capitalism and Communism together?

Jesse Blackless was a man who had channeled his feelings in accordance with a set of social theories. According to his formula, the exploited workers were going to overthrow their oppressors and take control of the world and make it over into something much more rational. This being so, Jesse looked for all merit in the workers, and found it; he would sit all day in a barely furnished little room and paint a picture of some poor waif of the Paris streets, making a touching and pathetic portrait, and when the dealers weren't interested in it, he would understand that it was because their customers wanted pictures of rich and elegant things. When the painter went for a stroll in the parks and saw the children of the rich with their pretty clothes and their *bonnes* watching over them, he would have no use for these children, because what they had was taken from the poor child whom he had painted.

All problems that arose in conversation were disposed of by Uncle Jesse in the same way. All capitalists, all capitalist groups and nations, were seeking profits; they were like hogs rushing to a feeding-trough, trampling down everything that stood in their way. By the same formula, all Socialist politicians were "labor fakers," making promises to the people and selling them out to the big business interests. That included Ramsay MacDonald, in whom Rick placed such high hopes; it included Léon Blum and Jean Longuet, and the others who were now carrying on such a vigorous election campaign in France. Jesse Blackless described them as "yellow Socialists," and hated them for luring the workers away from their true goal of revolution. Lanny said: "Uncle Jesse, your mind is like a phonograph; I put the needle down, I push the lever, and I know exactly what you're going to say."

The painter was a good sport, and willing to take cracks as hard as he gave. "Maybe so," he replied; "but if a record is right, why change it?"

Lanny would go off and think about that. If it was true, as both Robbie and Jesse agreed, that competition for raw materials and markets was getting the world ready for another great war, it was certainly desirable that the common people of all nations should know about it and try to stop it. But what could they do? Uncle Jesse said that the capitalists would never give up to mere ballots. Was that true, or wasn't it? If they would, then obviously the wise thing was to use ballots; but if they wouldn't, you had to prepare other means. But it was possible to argue that the threat of using other means—that is to say, violence—would frighten the propertied classes, and lead them to use the violence first.

They had so used Mussolini and his blackshirts in Italy—that was one of the points on which Robbie Budd and his Red near brother-in-law were in their curious state of agreement. Fascism was capitalism's answer to the threat of Communism! But why make the threat, if you couldn't get any farther with it than that? A complicated world that Lanny Budd had been born into, and one must not blame him too much if he took a long time to decide by what road he wished to get out of it!

VIII

Zoltan Kertezsi came to Paris. He had sold more of the Berlin and Munich paintings, also he had been to Vienna and inspected those which Lanny had found, and had done some business with them. He presented an accounting and a large check, and said there would be more. If what he wanted was social life with Lanny and his friends, he had taken the right way to get it, for Marie invited him out to the château, and she and the boys listened for hours while he and Lanny played music and while they talked about art. Marie approved of "old masters" in the same way that Beauty Budd approved of Bach and Beethoven and Brahms; not knowing very much about them, but observing that they kept her *ami* out of mischief. Day after day she went with the two men to the *salon* in Paris, and to the Vente Drouot, and the various exhibitions of the dealers; she listened to their highly technical conversation, and when it dealt with prices, she considered it not a profanation but something very much to the point.

Zoltan was going to London to attend some of the sales. Why not come along? Marie had heard about London sales, and they sounded interesting. So Lanny put his two friends into his comfortable car—Zoltan in the back seat, leaning forward and talking away the whole time. He never got tired of telling stories about pictures and their painters and their prices. Lanny listened, and Marie never interrupted; it was education, as good as going to college—two kinds, in fact, an art school, and one of commerce and finance. When they stopped to eat, or to buy *essence*, Lanny would make note of things he wanted to remember. In this school one never knew at what moment the examinations might be held. Zoltan would say: "What do you think I should have got for an especially beautiful Ingres?"

London was always delightful in the spring; everybody and everything happy to come out of the fog and cold, and to discover that the sun still existed. It was the first time Marie had been there since love had awakened her heart; they walked on air together, and did those delightful things which people can do when they have money, and a bit of culture to help them enjoy it. They went through the

Tate Gallery, reveling in the Turners, and Lanny explained what his stepfather had taught him about "atmosphere." Zoltan told stories about various famous works. If one had been retouched, he knew it, and showed exactly how he knew it. He was bitter against leading dealers such as "Joe" Duveen, who would buy some old master that had become dim and proceed to "freshen it up"; this would double the price for the American trade, but the result was no longer an old master, and the fact that "Joe" had become "Sir Joseph" for his services to art didn't decrease the disapprobation of a Hungarian commoner.

Rick had brought his family back to The Reaches, and invited all three of the visitors for a week-end. Marie was shy about going to the home of a respectable English family in company with her lover, but Lanny assured her that these were "mod'n" people and proud of it; this *liaison* was now four years old, and surely that was enough for respectability. All three of them had an enjoyable time, and Sir Alfred told them about paintings in the neighborhood that might be bought. But Marie had to listen to plain talk on the subject of the French election results, for that was the English custom; you said what you thought, and if the other person didn't agree, he said what he thought. Strange how people could hold such opposite opinions; to Marie and her husband the victory of the left coalition threatened the end of France, while to everyone at The Reaches it was the beginning of a new and better era.

After the middle of May Zoltan had to return to Germany for more business; and just then he received a letter from one of his American clients who had taken up the notion that he must have cinquecento Italians for his collection. It happened that Sophie Timmons, ex-baroness, had just been visiting in Rome, and Lanny said she knew everybody, and he would get her to introduce Zoltan to some of the old Roman families. The dealer said it would be wise to act quickly, because there was talk of a tariff on art-works imported into the United States. There was already a law in Italy forbidding the exportation of art-works, but one got around this by the payment of what was called a *regalo*, a polite word for a bribe.

The upshot was that Zoltan asked Lanny if he would like to take a run into Italy when he got home, and if he could find anything worth while, Zoltan would come and look at it, and Lanny would get half of whatever he helped to earn. The prices would doubtless be high, and the reward according. Lanny asked Marie, and she said she would enjoy such a trip—but on one essential condition, that her escort wouldn't get himself mixed up in any more political affairs. Lanny had no hesitation in promising that, for he was in one of those moods which seized him whenever he had been listening to his reactionary father and his revolutionary uncle, and having his mind pulled and hauled between them. Away from all that!

IX

They went back to Paris and stayed for a day, because Marie wanted to leave some of her clothes and get others. Lanny went into the city, and in the Café de la Rotonde he ran into an American journalist whom he had come to know at some of the various conferences—there had been so many of them by now that they made rather a blur in one's mind. Lanny mentioned that he was going to Rome, and why, and the other suggested the names of persons who might know where old masters were hidden. Lanny in return passed on some of the funny stories his father had told him about "Cautious Cal," also some inside stuff about how the French Nationalists were taking their defeat at the polls.

Persons who possessed such information were very useful, so presently this journalist remarked: "By the way, I'm giving a dinner party for some of the French leftists this evening. I thought it would be a good thing to get them together informally, and let them iron out their differences while their stomachs are full and they feel good. Wouldn't you like to join us?" Lanny understood what would be the position of a young man of fashion at such a gathering; he would put on his glad rags and provide a couple of receptive ears into which each person of importance might pour whatever he pleased. Lanny had served acceptably at such affairs, and said he would be happy to come to this one.

In the far-off days before the war Lanny had met at one of Mrs.

Emily's lawn parties a tall and slender middle-aged Jew who was then the dramatic critic of one of the Paris dailies; an art lover and friend of poets, a lawyer who didn't practice very much, a rich man's son who could afford to play, and did so in refined and delicate ways like Lanny himself. The American had forgotten him, and if anyone had asked him if he had ever met Léon Blum he would have said no. But here he was; impossible not to recognize the rather full brown mustache, the high-pitched voice and manner of an aesthete. Blum had traveled far in the past ten years; after the assassination of Jaurès he had become editor of the Socialist party's newspaper and leader of its group in the Chamber of Deputies. Lanny had been reading his scholarly and vigorous editorials, and being convinced by them—up to the moment when he heard the other side presented with equal cogency. Now Blum gave an eloquent talk, referring to the tragic years through which Europe had passed and the hope that the new regimes of France and Britain would get together *pour changer tout cela.*

Next to Lanny sat another lawyer-editor, a younger man, kind and gracious. He had delicate, sharp features, a thin nose with pince-nez, a light brown mustache, and rather unruly hair. This was Jean Longuet, a grandson of Karl Marx; during the war he had had the same kind of trouble as Ramsay MacDonald, for he was one of those who stood by the program of the Socialist International. Lanny, who had lived through all this in his mind, would have liked to talk it out with this man, but a dinner party was hardly the place.

He mentioned that he was on his way to Italy, and they discussed the tragedy which had befallen that country. As it happened, Longuet had written an article on the recent Italian elections, which the Fascists had carried by a reign of terror; this was to appear in *Le Populaire* next morning, and Lanny promised to read it. The Socialist deputies of Italy were in a desperate struggle against the increasing tyranny, and Longuet said that Daniel in the lions' den was nothing for courage compared to them, because Daniel had the Lord to trust in, while Matteotti and his comrades had only the moral sentiments of their half-strangled people. Said the lawyer-editor: "There is something in each of us which makes us willing to die rather than consent to evil. Whatever that is, it lifts us above the brutes and makes it possible to have hope for the human race." Lanny said that if that was Socialism, he was ready to enroll his name.

After which he went back to the Château de Bruyne, and didn't say much about the matter, knowing that, when it came to distinguishing among the various shades of Reds, Marie's eyesight was not very keen. Driving to Juan, they talked about pictures and the business in Rome; about the play Rick was writing and the music Kurt was publishing; about Marie's two boys and what they were doing and thinking; about their own love—in short, about anything in the world except the fact that Lanny liked to meet Socialist agitators and let them persuade him that the business system of France was all wrong, and that Marie's father and brothers and husband and their relatives and friends were collectively responsible for the drop of the franc and the piling up of debts and dangers for *la patrie!*

20

Roma Beata

I

LANNY and Marie stayed at Bienvenu for a couple of days, to rest and tell Beauty the gossip and hear what she had collected. Lanny had letters to read and to write; he had become quite a businessman, and would summon a secretary and say: "Take a letter," just as if he were the European representative of Budd Gunmakers. Sophie gave him letters to friends in Rome, and so did Emily Chattersworth and M. Rochambeau. These preparations made, they set out on the four- or five-hundred-mile journey to the Eternal City;

taking it in leisurely fashion and looking at both nature and art on the way.

The last time Lanny had made that journey had been ten years earlier, in company with old Mr. Hackabury, creator and proprietor of Bluebird Soap. So now this highly original character traveled along with them, and his amusing remarks were repeated to Marie. At San Remo they stopped off for a call on Lincoln Steffens, who now had a young wife and a baby, and was very proud of both. Stef had retired from politics for a while, in somewhat the same mood as Lanny. He had tried to change the world, and couldn't, so let's wait and see what the stubborn critter was going to do for itself!

When they came to the valley of the river Arno, they traveled up it to Florence and paid another call—this time on George D. Herron. He had moved to Italy because he couldn't endure to meet all the people who came to see him in Geneva—especially Germans—to ask how he had come to be so cruelly deceived about Woodrow Wilson! The father of the League of Nations had just died, broken in both body and spirit, and poor Herron was in much the same state; the two visitors agreed that he couldn't last much longer. A saddening thing to see what the world did to those idealistic souls who tried to improve it. A warning to Lanny, which his companion hinted at tactfully.

In Rome the "season" was just coming to its end, and hotels were still crowded; but there was always a "royal suite" or an "ambassador's suite" or something like that, which you could have if you were willing to pay; and of course it would pay to pay when you were there to make an impression upon the aristocracy. In such exclusive homes you didn't talk about money, but you had a secret code of a thousand small details whereby you made plain that you had it, and had always had it. Marie understood this code, but she didn't know how the old families of Rome would receive a French *amie;* since this was a business trip, she was quite willing to go and look at churches and tombs and paintings while her companion groped cautiously in the mazes of a world which had as many "circles" as it had periods in its architecture.

It wasn't going to be an easy matter finding four-hundred-year-old paintings and persuading their owners to sell at anything like reasonable prices. Lanny ought to have presented his various letters at once, before people went away to the seashore or the mountain lakes. But he had been deeply impressed by his talk with Longuet and the article he had read about the Italian Socialists; he knew that the new Parliament had just opened, and he could read enough Italian to learn from the newspapers that the country was in a political fever at the moment. Ever since the days of the Paris Peace Conference, Lanny had had a hankering to observe history from the inside, and he bethought himself who there was in Rome that might take him behind the scenes of this political show. The first thing he did after getting himself and his friend settled comfortably was to telephone to a newspaperman; taking the precaution to do this from the lobby of the hotel, so as not to worry his *amie*—so he told himself. She wanted to rest after the trip, and would wait until the cool of the evening before going out.

II

The man was Pietro Corsatti, American-born Italian correspondent of one of the New York newspapers; Lanny had met him at San Remo, and again at Genoa, and knew that he was open-minded and free-spoken. Lanny himself had something to offer, for he had just come from London and Paris, where he had talked with persons "in the know." He mentioned that he had recently dined with Blum and Longuet, and asked the journalist to have lunch with him. Corsatti said: "Sure thing. We'll have a fine time chewing the rag."

Corsatti had an olive complexion, sparkling black eyes, and wavy black hair; he was a Neapolitan, but also he was a New York boy. Funny thing, how one culture could be superposed upon another, and the stronger and more recent would prevail. Corsatti spoke English with an East Side accent and the latest slang; he was completely American in his point of view, and looked upon this dead old town with pitying condescension. He revealed this to Lanny, but of course he kept it down in his contacts with the Italians, and mustn't let it show in his dispatches, because the censorship watched him like a hawk. Just recently they had "raised hell" with him for mentioning that Prime Minister Mussolini had appeared at some public function "in need of a second shave."

Lanny was a friend of Rick, of Stef, of Bill Bullitt, so he was an insider, a "right guy." He could be introduced to "the gang," he could be trusted with "the dope," and if in the course of his picture-hunting he should stumble upon any political "leads," he would not forget his friend. Seated over a bottle of good chianti in a little *trattoria* frequented by the foreign newspapermen, Corsatti proceeded to "spill the beans" about Italy and its upstart political movement. It appeared that the American newspapermen were divided about fifty-fifty on the subject of Mussolini; some thought he was a man of destiny, and others were equally sure that he was a "four-flusher," a "flat tire." Discussing him in a public place like this, you didn't use either his name or title; he was "Mr. Smith"—perhaps because that had been his father's occupation. Lanny's companion warned him that in this aged town there were as many spies as there were statues of saints, and one did not speak freely even in bed with one's mistress.

There had been a general election for members of Parliament in the previous month, and Mr. Smith's followers had won a majority. They had got it, Corsatti declared, by the most vicious repression; the opposition leaders had been beaten, and many of their followers killed; the police and the Fascist Militia, some of whom called themselves "Savages," had turned the election campaign into a farce. Mr. Smith had just made his appearance before the new Parliament, clad in a costume which the journalist said was suited to "a Gilbert and Sullivan Admiral of the Queen's Navee." In his speech he had remarked: "You of the opposition complain that you were restrained from holding free electoral meetings. What of that? Such meetings are of no avail, anyway."

The program was to have the Parliament validate these frauds, three hundred and twenty of them all in one lump. The "Verification Committee on Mandates" had put such a proposal before the Chamber, and it was to be debated that afternoon. "Longuet urged me to hear Matteotti," said the visitor. "Do you suppose he will speak?"

"He will unless they prevent him," replied the journalist, and Lanny asked: "Do you suppose I could get in?"

"I'll see if I can take you into the press gallery with me. Can you call yourself the correspondent of any paper?"

"I imagine Longuet would be glad if I'd send him a story."

"That wouldn't be so good—a Socialist paper. You don't want to put a label on yourself. But five lire will do a lot in Rome."

"Whatever you have to pay, it's on me," said the son of Budd Gunmakers.

"Too much would be no good," explained the other. "You'd frighten the attendant and excite suspicion."

III

They took a taxi to the Palazzo di Montecitorio with the obelisk in front of it, where the Chamber of Deputies meets. At the door the correspondent took his young friend by the arm, and said to the doorman: *"Il mio assistente."* At the same time he slipped him five lire, and they went in, as Corsatti phrased it, "on a greased skidway." Lanny had a front seat to watch the making of history in a scene of bitter and furious strife.

Giacomo Matteotti was the Socialist party secretary and leader of its forces in the Parliament. He was then close to forty, but slender and youthful in appearance, with a sensitive, rather mournful face. Corsatti said that frequently he wore a frank, boyish smile, but he had no chance to show it that day. Lanny agreed with Longuet's remark that Daniel's stunt in the lions' den was easy compared to what this Italian idealist was doing. He didn't rave, or call names, but spoke in a quiet, firm voice, giving his people the facts as to what had been happening in their country during the past two years. Every promise to labor had been broken, while the inheritance taxes had been abolished at the behest of the rich. The financial statements of the nation had been deliberately falsified; there had been no reduction of expenditures, but on the contrary an orgy of stealing.

The intimate associates of the head of the state were smuggling arms into Yugoslavia, they were oil corruptionists, they were terrorists who had stolen an election by vicious cruelty and now presented themselves in the Chamber to have their crimes officially sanctified.

Such was the substance of Matteotti's speech. He was not content with vague charges; every time he made an assertion he went into details as to places, dates, and sums of money. Evidently he had been delving deeply, and he had a mass of papers before him, indicating that he was in position to go on for hours. The alleged criminals sat before him, and their reaction was the most appalling demonstration of mass fury that Lanny had ever heard. The Fascist deputies, about two-thirds of the Chamber, would leap to their feet, shake their clenched fists, and literally shriek with rage. Murder was in their aspect and murder in their cries; the frail orator blanched before this blast, but he did not yield, and as soon as he could be heard he went on with his implacable arraignment. What was spoken in this Chamber would become a matter of record, and sooner or later could be got to the people.

This continued for two hours—until it seemed that the Fascist regime was crumbling there before everyone's eyes. Mussolini's followers shouted insults and imprecations, and one of their orators rushed to the opposition side and bellowed into their faces: "*Masnada!*"—that is, band of scoundrels. Somehow—Lanny's eye wasn't quick enough to follow the events—a fight started, and in a twinkling it was a free-for-all, in which everybody jumped on anybody of whom he disapproved. That was the last that Lanny saw of the Italian *Parlamento*, for his friend whispered: "I have to get this story off!" and he went, his *assistente* following.

IV

Lanny mailed his letters of introduction and awaited replies. There were one or two which he might have presented informally, thus saving time, but the truth was, he had something else on his mind: he wanted to shake hands with Matteotti. He was on fire with admiration for a deed of splendid courage, and he wanted to say so. One doesn't meet a hero face to face every day of one's life.

"Sure, you can meet him," said Corsatti. "Just walk into his office. He's the party drudge, and everybody brings him their troubles and quarrels. He'll be there—if the *militi* haven't raided him in the meantime." So Lanny went to the Socialist headquarters, which weren't so different from those of the Nazis which he had visited in Munich.

Lanny had to learn the important lesson that heroes rarely look heroic, especially behind the scenes. The new Prime Minister of Italy had practiced thrusting out his jaw and swelling up his chest, and had created for himself the costume of an Admiral of the Queen's Navee, but this friend of the working classes had had no time or thought for histrionics. He sat at his desk with papers piled around him, looking like the overworked city editor of a newspaper close to the "deadline." People came and went, the telephone rang, and in a few minutes there was to be a conference of party leaders to determine whether they were to withdraw from the Chamber. But meanwhile the secretary could find time for a young American who had just come from Jean Longuet, and brought a copy of Longuet's recent article. Matteotti glanced at it, and asked if he could have a copy made, so that it could be reprinted in the party paper.

Lanny poured out what was in his heart. Behind his fervor of admiration was a feeling of guilt, because he too ought to have been a man of iron determination, instead of wobbling this way and that and changing his mind whenever he heard new arguments. This lion-hearted Italian had every excuse that Lanny had, for he was the son of a well-to-do landowner, he was a lawyer and a man of culture; doubtless he too loved music and art, and might have enjoyed time off for play. Heroes sound grand in the history books, but it's damned uncomfortable being one, and Lanny would be one in his fancy, but when it came to reality he just couldn't stand it.

Giacomo Matteotti of course didn't know all that. He saw a handsome, ardent youth, with the signs of money on him, and the flush of enthusiasm on his cheeks, the light of admiration in his eyes. Every now and then it happens that some generous soul among the privileged classes becomes touched in his conscience, and you have a convert, and a pair of purse-strings will be loosened to help a party which is always in debt, always facing some emergency. So the secretary took time off to explain the Italian situation to this scion of Budd Gunmakers.

Yes, it was a tragic crisis which the organized workers faced; they were completely unarmed, except for moral and intellectual weapons, and were confronted by enemies who had given themselves such names as "the Savages," "the Damned," and "the Desperadoes." With all their control of the government, they had been able to get a circulation of only 400,000 for their newspapers, while the opposition had ten times that. How long would men of violence permit that state of affairs to continue? How long would criminals allow the public exposure of their crimes? What might happen was terrible to contemplate; one woke in the small hours of the morning facing it, and could find no way of escape during the day.

Lanny mentioned his experience with Barbara Pugliese. "Poor soul!" exclaimed the Socialist. "I knew her well; we had many a conflict in party gatherings. One cannot help sympathizing with people who are driven to desperation by their sufferings, but it is a tragic blunder to brandish an empty gun. Now we face the consequences of the unwise tactics of these extremists; I have the agonizing task of urging our people to keep their hands down, to take their beatings, to die without resistance, if and whenever it pleases our foes to kill them. Such has been the destiny of the wage-slaves throughout the centuries, and the roll of our martyrs is far from complete."

Someone came to remind the secretary of the important conference. He shook hands with his visitor and said: "A little later, when this emergency has passed, will you do me the honor to come to my home and meet my devoted wife and children?" Lanny said that nothing would give him more pleasure.

"You understand," continued the other, "in the next few days I have to complete my unfinished speech. If they prevent my doing so, we must try to find some other way to get the facts to the outside world." He put into the visitor's hands a book which he had published, *A Year of Fascist Domination*, in which he had listed more than two thousand murders and other crimes of violence which Mussolini's partisans had committed. "We shall be glad of any help which you can give us in making these things known," said Matteotti, and Lanny promised to do what he could.

"Remember this, whatever happens," continued the other; "they cannot kill our cause. The workers will learn what we have tried to teach them, and there will be a new generation with more wisdom and courage than ours."

"Surely not more courage!" exclaimed Lanny, and added: "God help you!" He hadn't been able to make up his mind on the subject of God, but he had to say some word to this sorely tried soul.

V

The visitor went about his business of looking for sixteenth-century art. He studied the psychology of members of old Roman families, who had had these things in their palaces until they had grown tired of the sight of them; they didn't believe in the symbolism of the religious ones, and as for the worldly ones, they preferred flesh-and-blood beauties to painted; they preferred modern costumes, and thought how pleasant it would be to have a new motor-car and to pay their gambling debts. The lira was down to four cents, and the very word "dollar" had the power of magic. The only question was, how many could you get? Be wary, don't show too much interest, and try to figure out this good-looking, easy-going young aesthete. Was he a millionaire, or just bluffing, like the Americans in their well-known card game? Why wouldn't he come out and say what he was willing to pay, instead of insisting that you set a price—something which tore your soul in half, because no matter how much you got, you would think you should have asked twice as much.

Jerry Pendleton had told about a walking-trip which he and a friend had taken through Italy before the war. They had picked up

half a dozen words of the language, among them *Quanta costa?*—
how much? They would go into a country inn and eat, and when
they were through they would spread out small coins on the table
and say their phrase. The innkeeper would set aside what he thought
he should have, and they would divide this into three parts and give
him one of them. This was the normal difference between the price
to an American and the price to a native, and the proprietor would
grin and accept what was offered. Lanny had told this story to
Zoltan, who said they would try it in their trading. Lanny would
get a price on a painting, Zoltan would come and look at it, and, if
it was genuine, he would bring one-third the amount in cash—always
in lire, because they looked and sounded so much more!

Lanny put his mind on these affairs, because he had come to Rome
for them, and he couldn't keep evading and deceiving Marie. But
he had only half his mind on the work, while with the other half
he read the newspapers and kept in touch with his friend Corsatti.
In Mussolini's paper, the *Popolo d'Italia*, which Mussolini couldn't
get the people of Italy to read in spite of being their Prime Minister,
Lanny observed pretty broad hints of violence against the opposition.
Said the head of the state: "Matteotti made a speech of an out-
rageously provocative nature which should deserve some more
concrete reply than the epithet of *masnada* which Signor Giunta
flung at him." Corsatti said that this was Mussolini's way. He would
call for violence, he would give secret instructions for violence, and
then when violence resulted, he would be shocked, and would say
that he couldn't control the ardor of his followers.

The Socialist secretary spoke again in the Chamber, and came
into direct conflict with the Prime Minister. Day after day this went
on. Said the Socialist Gennari: "We are just out of prison, and we
are ready to go back there for the sake of what we believe." Said
Mussolini, amid shouts and uproar: "You would have got a charge
of lead in your backs. We do not lack courage, as we will show
you. There is still time and we shall show you sooner than you
think."

Such debates provided exciting copy for foreign newspapermen,
and Lanny would drop in at the little *trattoria* where they gathered;

Corsatti introduced him to "the bunch," and they would tell him the latest rumors and gossip. They were making wagers on the subject of the life-span of Giacomo Matteotti, and this seemed rather cold-blooded—but newspapermen have to live, and they are no good if they let themselves take sides on the issues which they have to report. The few Socialist papers in the United States couldn't afford the luxury of correspondents in Rome.

VI

For the afternoon of the tenth of June Lanny had an important engagement with the head of one of the leading princely houses of the Italian kingdom. He had already inspected several of this nobleman's valuable paintings, and now there was an intimation that prices might be discussed. If a deal was made it would be the biggest stroke of Lanny's art career, now in the second year. He was just finishing lunch with his *amie* when he was called to the telephone, and heard a voice, trembling, broken with anguished sobbing. It was the young wife of Giacomo Matteotti, and she was trying to say, in uncertain English, that her husband had been kidnaped from the Via Antonio Scialoja a few minutes ago and carried off by men in an automobile, and wouldn't Mr. Budd do what he could to save him? The horrified Lanny asked what he could do, and the distracted wife said to tell the newspapermen, to tell the outside world, there was nothing else that could restrain the cruel enemy but the opinion of Europe and America. "It is Dumini!" she cried, and repeated the name. "Dumini who was staying at the Hotel Dragoni—Giacomo knew that he had orders to do away with him. Oh, for the love of God!—" the voice broke off, the woman couldn't control her sobs.

Lanny hung up and rushed back into the dining-room to tell the dreadful news. "But, my dear Lanny!" cried Marie. "What have *you* to do with it?"

"I met him, and I must try to help him."

"But how, Lanny—for the love of God?" The same appeal as the wife had made. God would have to choose between them!

"I can't stop now!" Lanny exclaimed. "I must see the newspapermen, and find out what can be done."

"But your engagement!"

"I can't keep it. Phone the Prince for me and make my excuses—tell him I'm sick—anything."

"Lanny—I will go with you."

"No, please—stay here, and I'll phone you." He didn't wait for her consent, but darted out of the room. He didn't wait to get his car out of the garage, but hopped into a taxi and drove to the *trattoria* where he knew that Corsatti and the others would be, unless they had already got the news.

There were three of them, peacefully sipping their *vino rosso* and discussing the young American playboy who dabbled in art and politics, and did he really mean either? When he burst in among them they forgot both their wine and their ideas. "Jesus Christ, I've lost my bet!" exclaimed one, who had been betting on Matteotti's life-span.

They asked him a score of questions, most of which he couldn't answer; but one thing they got: Dumini! Oh, yes, they knew about him; one of the most notorious of Mussolini's associates. In the days before the March on Rome he had boxed the ears of a girl who wore a red carnation, the Socialist symbol, and when her mother and brother protested he had shot them both dead. "And it was he who kidnaped Mazzolani!" exclaimed Corsatti. "Carried him off in a car and forced him to drink castor oil."

"And Forni!" put in the others. That was a crime of the recent electoral campaign, the victim being a candidate for Parliament. It was what Mussolini had meant when he admitted that free electoral meetings had been prevented.

"What can we do?" asked Lanny, in anguish.

"Not much," replied Corsatti. "I'm afraid it's all up with your friend."

"What *we* have to do is to get the story," said one of the others. "If we let the outside world know, there will be repercussions, and that may do some good."

"But then it will be too late!"

"Probably so. It doesn't take long to club a man to death—especially if you shoot him first."

The correspondents had to hurry; it was all in a day's work for them, no matter what their private feelings. Lanny rode with Corsatti to the government office, where he would get the official handout on the story; the government would be in complete ignorance, of course, and would deplore the crime. Corsatti told his friend that, on the chance that Matteotti was still alive, Lanny might do some good by communicating with persons outside who enjoyed means of publicity. "Longuet, for example," he said. "Tell him what Matteotti said to you—the personal touches that will make a human interest story about a Socialist martyr."

VII

Lanny followed this course, because he couldn't think of anything else to do. After some delay he got Longuet on the long-distance phone, and poured out his grief and indignation. Then he went to the telegraph office and wrote a long dispatch to Rick; he was sure that Rick would attend to getting publicity for it. But the message was never sent, for as Lanny was about to hand it to the clerk, two men in the uniform of the Fascist Militia entered the office, looked at Lanny, asked his name, took the telegram away from him, and informed him that it would be necessary for him to accompany them to "headquarters."

It was the second time that this had happened to the son of Robbie Budd in his young life. During the Peace Conference in Paris it had been the *flics;* but French police agents were gentlemen and scholars compared to these self-styled *Disperati*, and Lanny had to think quickly. Was this a kidnaping, and was he to share the fate of Matteotti? If so, would it be better to make a fight for it here, in public? They were hard-looking guys, and had automatics in holsters at their waists; but at least he might attract attention, let people know what was happening.

"Where do you propose to take me?" he demanded, in his best Italian, which wasn't so good.

"To headquarters," was the reply.

"I am an American citizen." Technically it may not have been so, but they couldn't prove it.

"Tell that to the Generalissimo," was the answer.

"I demand the right to telephone to the American ambassador."

"You are to come without delay."

"I am a personal friend of the American ambassador." That too was a slight exaggeration, but he might get away with it. He was trying to get time to think.

"We have nothing to do with any of that."

"And if I refuse to go?"

"You won't refuse very long." The speaker moved his hand toward his holster, and Lanny decided that it would be useless to argue. He went to the street, with one of the men at either side, and he saw that they had an automobile, with a chauffeur in uniform. That reassured him slightly, and he got in and was driven quickly to the general headquarters of the National Militia. He had heard dreadful stories of things that went on in these places; his knees were weak and he had a hard time to keep his teeth from chattering. Inside him he didn't feel the tiniest bit of heroism, but he knew that he ought to behave as if he did. He tried to keep his face set and his head erect, as he had seen heroes do on the stage and screen.

They didn't take him to a cell, but directly to the office of the Generalissimo, whose name was Italo Balbo. Lanny, who had learned a lot about Fascist affairs in twelve days, knew that he was one of Mussolini's intimates, and had led the armed *squadre* in the March on Rome. He was the Ras of Ferrara—Ras was a word which they had taken from their Abyssinian foes, and meant a chieftain. Among the stories which Corsatti had told was of a letter this Balbo had written to the secretary of his home *fascio*, ordering that certain Socialists should be "bludgeoned, not to excess, but in style." The journalist had explained that *bastonatura in stile* was a technical Fascist phrase—let no one say they had not enriched the Italian language—meaning not to hit the victim over the skull, which might kill him, but to beat the lower part of the face and break the jaw-bone, which would lay him up for months. There was a special kind of blackjack, known as the *manganello*, made for this purpose.

VIII

Generalissimo Balbo was a stoutish, military-looking man with sharp black mustaches and a black beard trimmed to a point. In the room with him was another man in Fascist uniform, and a secretary with a notebook—all the apparatus of the *procès verbal*. The two *militi* gave the Fascist salute, and Lanny was marched up in front of the official's desk. The telegram was presented, and Balbo read it; then, fixing a pair of angry dark eyes upon the offender, he proceeded to shoot questions at him: his name, residence, and nationality; his father's name, residence, and occupation. Manufacturer of munitions might help, Lanny thought; but there was no change in the aggressive tone of the questioning.

"What is your business in Rome?" Lanny replied that he had come to arrange for the purchase of cinquecento art-works for an American collection.

"You called at the office of the Socialist party on May 31?"

"Ah!" thought the prisoner. That explained much! He answered, without hesitation: "I went to call on Signor Matteotti."

"What did you want to see him about?"

"I wanted to tell him that I had heard his speech in the Chamber, and how greatly I admired his courage."

"You are a Socialist?"

"I am not."

"Then why do you have so much admiration for a Socialist speech?"

"I admired a brave man speaking the truth."

"You feel quite sure that what Matteotti said was the truth?"

"Quite."

"What sources of information do you have about Italian affairs that you feel able to judge on such a subject?"

It was the sort of question for which Lanny's experience in Paris had prepared him, and his answer was prompt. "I shall make no statement regarding any source of information I may have."

"Oh, so that is your line!"

"That is my line."

"You may perhaps know that we have ways of persuading people to talk when we very much want to."

"You have no way of persuading me to talk about anyone but myself." Something strange was happening to the scion of Budd Gunmakers at that moment, something which surprised himself; a rush of feeling came up in him, telling him that he would stand anything these brutes might do to him—just for the satisfaction of not letting them have their way! Of course he couldn't know whether the inquisitor actually meant these threats or was just trying to frighten him; the need for determination was great in either case.

"You have consorted with certain newspapermen in Rome?"

"I have told you that I will answer no such questions."

"You know Pietro Corsatti?"

"Pardon me. I shall not speak again while you follow that line." There was a pause.

"You say you admire courage, young man. You think you have enough to go through with what we shall do to you?"

"I make formal demand as an American citizen to be permitted to communicate with my ambassador."

"You will not be permitted to communicate with anyone until you have answered my questions; and I warn you that if you don't answer them, you may never do any more communicating anywhere."

Lanny knew that Ambassador Child had recently returned to America; but he might serve in this crisis, even so. "I warn you that the former ambassador knows me personally, and it won't be very long before he will be inquiring as to my welfare."

"How do you come to know the former ambassador?"

"He was a guest of my father and myself at luncheon during the Genoa conference two years ago. It happens that my father was a personal friend of the late President Harding, who appointed Mr. Child to his post." Lanny thought he might as well pile it on; because, while you can endure torture, there's no use doing it unnecessarily. "It happens that my father is a leading backer of the Republican party in the United States, and when the newspapermen learn that his son is in the hands of the Italian authorities there will certainly be vigorous action on the part of the Embassy."

Lanny had shot his bolt, and could only wait to find out if it had come anywhere near the target. "Take this man out into the corridor and wait," said Balbo. "Watch him carefully."

IX

Lanny was seated on a bench with a stone wall to lean against, and one of his captors on either side of him, not speaking. He thought as hard as he could, and decided that the Generalissimo had been trying to frighten him and that, having failed, he would now do some telephoning. Having an abundance of time on his hands, Lanny tried to imagine those telephone conversations. Would the new ambassador know about Budd's? And what would he do? Lanny knew that Mr. Child had been filling American magazines with enraptured praise of Mussolini and his regime. Was the new ambassador of the same opinion? Would he throw Lanny to the Roman wolves? A far from pleasant thought!

For the second time Lanny was making use of his father's name and influence to get himself out of a serious predicament. It was humiliating, but how much chance would he have stood if he had given his name as Blackless, nephew of a notorious Red agitator? No, certainly Robbie would wish him to be a Budd in this crisis, and to use the Budd name to the limit!

What was actually happening Lanny found out later on. Marie hadn't stopped to telephone to the Prince, but had taken a taxi to the American Embassy. The ambassador wasn't in, but she had talked with the chargé d'affaires, who didn't need to be told that there was a munitions firm known as Budd Gunmakers in Connecticut, or that Robert Budd was a backer of the Republican party. Being a woman of the world, Marie knew how to present the case of an overemotional young art lover who had listened to an eloquent orator and been moved by an impulse of hero-worship. The chargé smiled and said that once upon a time he had been young himself. He promised that if Lanny got into any trouble owing to his too sympathetic nature, the Embassy would assure the Italian government that he was both well connected and harmless. The chargé hadn't heard the news about Matteotti; he said that it was unfortunate, but of course as a diplomatic official he was compelled to preserve an attitude of aloofness from Italian affairs.

So when Lanny was brought back into the office of Generalissimo Balbo there was no more "rough stuff." The official contented himself with saying: "Mr. Budd, the Italian government is under the necessity of requesting you to remove yourself from this country at once."

Said Lanny: "I am entirely willing to comply with that request."

"Where do you wish to go?"

"To my home on the French Riviera."

"There is a train this evening, and you will take it."

"You have perhaps overlooked the fact that I am motoring."

"Oh, you have a car?"

"I have. Also I have a friend with me."

"A lady friend, I believe?"

"*Si.*" Lanny wondered if he was going to have to refuse to answer questions about Marie; but he didn't.

Said the Generalissimo of the National Militia: "You and your lady friend will start this afternoon. What is the size of your car?"

"It carries five passengers."

"These two *militi* will ride in the rear seat and see you over the border. You will not be permitted out of their sight until you are across."

"It is going to be rather crowded, because we have considerable luggage."

"You will have to find some way to strap the luggage on, or else have it forwarded. The men will ride with you."

"It wouldn't be possible for them to follow in a separate car?"

"I see no reason why the Italian government should be put to that expense."

"If that is the difficulty, you might permit me to pay the cost of an extra car."

The Generalissimo thought for a moment. Was he afraid that a fast driver might leave the *militi* behind? Anyhow, he answered, coldly: "The arrangement would not be satisfactory. You will take the men to the border in your car. And you will leave at once."

X

A third man in uniform drove Lanny and his two escorts to the garage where his car was stored. Lanny got it out and drove the two to the hotel, where they accompanied him upstairs. Marie was pacing the floor in an agony of fear, and when she saw him enter the room she had to sink into a chair to keep from fainting. When he explained the situation, she wasn't so much reassured; the sight of two dark and grim-faced men in uniform made it seem to her another Matteotti affair, and without saying what she was doing she rushed to the telephone to call the Embassy and explain the situation to the chargé. The latter told her that he had talked with the Generalissimo and received his assurance that no harm was intended to an indiscreet young American—they just wanted to get him out of the country before he made any more trouble for himself.

The hotel attendants carried the luggage down and it was stowed in one way or another. A great sensation in this de luxe establishment, a scandal that would be talked about under cover; but no one ventured to reveal curiosity in the presence of the two *militi*. This, Lanny came to understand, is a phenomenon of dictatorships; nobody stops to ask questions or even to stare; everybody has only one thought, to be somewhere else but where power is being manifested.

There were still two or three hours of daylight when the four set out on their strange drive. All the Embassy officials in the world couldn't give Marie complete assurance, and so long as those two partisans of despotism were in the car her heart would never beat a steady stroke. In Rome itself there was a certain amount of restraint upon the Fascists, there being embassies and newspaper correspondents from all over the world; but in the villages, in remote country districts, armed power had its ferocious way. The highway north which the two travelers had to take crossed many lonely wastes, and wound through mountain passes where an occasional peasant's hut or a shepherd watching his flock was all they saw. And soon it would be night!

XI

Fascismo had won its way as a revolutionary movement; it had sounded the slogans of the poor and dispossessed, promising them dominance over their oppressors. To be sure, it had been vague as to who these oppressors were, and still vaguer as to what was to be done to them; but the emotional content of the movement was subversive, its followers had marched and sung and shouted their joyful thirst for vengeance. These two soldiers were peasant lads who had been half starved and frozen in the trenches of the Adige, and had fled ignominiously from Caporetto; they had been forced to subservience all their lives—and now for the first time they enjoyed power over the most hated of all types, the idle rich foreigners who had helped to cheat Italy out of her war gains, and who dressed themselves in splendor and came into the country to lord it over the poor and live on the fat of the land.

Had anyone told this pair that they were at liberty to frighten these *stranieri* and teach them respect for the Blessed Virgin and the Pope, the ancient Roman *fasces* and the new Roman Empire? Or was it their own inspiration, their native folk humor, a spontaneous contribution to the evolution of *Fascismo?* No sooner had the car got beyond the suburbs of Roma Beata—blessed Rome—than they started telling each other what they thought of these two bloodsucking leeches, and what was going to happen to them before they escaped from the soil of *la patria*. They employed the most pungent words in their native dialect, and neither Marie nor Lanny understood them all, but the tone of venom was enough for the purpose.

The foreigners knew that they were being deliberately tormented; but how could they be sure whether words were to be translated into deeds? The safe-conduct they had received was purely oral, and there would be little possibility of appeal to authorities on the way.

Just one thing they could do, and that was to drive. Marie didn't know how, so it was up to Lanny. He would sit with his hands on the steering-wheel and his eyes fixed on the right-hand edge of the tortuous highway, guiding his car through all the different kinds of scenery there are in Italy, seeing nothing of it, but keeping his mind on the one essential task of putting five or six hundred kilometers behind him, one after another. Try not to listen to the "Savages," the "Damned," or the "Desperadoes," whichever they happened to be. Try to understand the poor devils, pity them as the victims of a perverted culture, products of forces which were forever beyond their capacity to comprehend. Apply the wise ancient maxim, to hate the sin and love the sinner!

Marie couldn't cling to his arm, for fear of interfering with his driving; she could only hold his coat edge, and whisper words of love and comfort. It would be all right; the ride would have its end, they would be safe at home. These poor fools had no real power over them, they could do nothing but talk. Marie whispered in English, on the chance that the poor fools might know some French, and of course she must do nothing to provoke them.

Not being able to get any reaction from the *stranieri*, the ingenious peasants bethought themselves of a new line of conversation. Those who live close to the soil, in intimate contact with animals, are well-informed concerning the processes of nature; they do not believe that babies are brought by storks, and when they discuss the facts of life they do not talk about the bees and the flowers. They knew that this insolent young *americano* was traveling with a beautiful *francese* who was not his wife, and they guessed what they did when they were alone in a bedroom; it entertained their imaginations, and they went into full details about it. Again Lanny and Marie did not know all the words, but they got the gist of it. The *francese* have a world-wide reputation for being sexually passionate; and perhaps it would be fun to stop the car in the course of the night and show her what real Italian *virilità* was like. Perhaps the *favorita francese* might like it so well that she would decide to return to Rome with them. What a joke upon the American millionaire—and surely the Generalissimo would promote them for such a feat!

Marie felt her escort trembling, and that made her tremble. She began a swift whispering, close to his ear, to keep him from hearing what the beasts were saying. "Lanny, don't speak to them! They are poor country louts. What they say means nothing. They dare not do me any harm, or you. It will soon be over, and we will be safe. Promise me that you won't answer them, no matter what they say! You broke one promise to me—don't break another! They want to provoke you, they would like a chance to beat you, perhaps to kill you. Promise me that you will not speak!"

"I promise," muttered Lanny. He knew that she was right. He would be the young philosopher, and observe human nature in the exercise of suddenly acquired power. He would reflect upon the state of a nation which trained its youth to hold such ideas as this pair revealed. It was something worth learning, it would help one to understand the future. These men were worse than the "Savages" they called themselves; they were barbarians armed with modern weapons, with science and its techniques, not merely industrial, but political and psychological. What would Italy be like if a generation of such men grew up and took possession of its affairs? What would become of history, of music and literature and art? What would they do to the rest of Europe?

XII

Lanny had one way to punish this pair; he discovered it with a sudden thrill of amusement. As the sun sank behind the hills and twilight settled upon the landscape, the spicy conversation gradually lost its charms. They came to a village, and there was an inn with lights, and an odor of roasting meats coming forth; but they drove by it without stopping; they passed through the village at the precisely lawful speed of fifteen kilometers per hour, so that no one could have any excuse for stopping them. When they were well outside, Lanny heard the first civil words he had heard from the lips of *Fascismo*. It was the Italian version of the familiar American slogan: "When do we eat?"

The deportee answered promptly, in the best Italian he could muster: "We do not eat; we drive."

Consternation in the back seat. "But, signor, it is necessary to eat!"

"The Generalissimo said nothing about eating. His order was that I should get out of Italy as quickly as possible. Shall I dare to disobey him?"

A long consultation on the part of *Fascismo*. It was carried on in low whispers, and Lanny could only try to imagine it. Would they consider putting a gun between his shoulders and ordering him to stop at the next *taverna?* Or would they reflect that on this basis they would have to pay for their own supper? Could it happen that a government sorely straitened for funds would fail to reimburse its servants for their meals? Would they reflect upon the reputation for lavishness enjoyed by American millionaires? And did they have in their language any equivalent of the American saying that molasses catches more flies than vinegar?

Perhaps so; for when the corporal of the guard raised his voice again, it had a sweetness equal to that of the thickest New Orleans "blackstrap." "Signor, if you will be so kind as to stop and let us eat, we will be *puliti* for the rest of the journey."

"Are the *militi* permitted to be *puliti?*" inquired Lanny, coldly.

"We will be *puliti, Signor. Onestamente!*"

So it was time for an American millionaire to show his better nature. "When we come to the next *taverna*, you may eat and I will pay." The whole atmosphere of the journey was changed by that one magical sentence.

They went into a little *albergo*, and the two "Savages" who had promised to be "polite" seated themselves at a separate table from the *damigella*. She wouldn't eat anything, just a cup of what was called coffee; Lanny ate a little, because he didn't want to feel weak; not too much, because he didn't want to feel sleepy. He told the *militi* to have what they pleased, including a bottle of wine, and he raised no question when the *conto* was presented. Lanny got a fresh load of gasoline, and as soon as they were in the country the two peasants fell asleep; they snored the whole night through, and Marie had nothing to worry about but the possibility that Lanny might doze at the steering-wheel.

He was determined to drive straight through. Soldiers had done such feats in wartime, and he would do one now; he felt safer in the car with these men than he would in any hotel room with a bed in it. He bade his *amie* to sleep, and she did so for a while, her head resting on his shoulder. But most of the time she watched the road, winding through the unending mountains of Italy, and if she saw the slightest sign of wandering of the car, she would whisper to Lanny to be sure he was awake.

XIII

They came out to the Riviera di Levante, and there was the familiar blue sea; also there was breakfast, with another bottle of wine for the *militi*. Still Lanny drove, haggard and in need of a shave, but silent and determined; the two Italians respected him now, a man of capacity as well as of millions. They had made a great mistake; if they had been *puliti* from the beginning he might have made them a fabulous present.

Here was familiar scenery; tunnels through the hills and glimpses of bright blue bays with little boats having red sails; cypress-covered promontories, gardens gay with flowers. But Lanny saw nothing of all that; he kept his eye on the right-hand edge of a winding highway—fortunately the inside track, not the one close to the cliffs! Pretty soon it was Rapallo, and he thought of the Russians, two of whom had been shot to death in the interim. Then it was the crowded streets of Genoa, and the dark medieval building where the conference had been held, and the hotel which he had last seen while the body of the dying Barbara Pugliese lay in the car. After that it was not two *militi*, but one *sindicalista* who was being carried in great haste toward the French border.

Perhaps Lanny was growing a bit delirious, having sat for twenty-four hours at the steering-wheel of a car, with only two intermissions for food. His shoulders and arms ached, and a spot just above the first spinal process, where the motions of the car caused his head to sway, felt as if one of the Italians had put his Fascist dagger-point there and was pressing. But it was all right; they would soon be in France, and he wouldn't have to sit up any longer. He found himself repeating the *Mower's Song* of Andrew Lang: "Hush and be silent, for all things pass!"

At San Remo the party stopped for lunch, in the same little *trattoria* where Lanny and Rick had watched an obscure Italian editor, known as the Blessed Little Pouter Pigeon, devouring his *pasta*, and had seen his eyeballs nearly pop out with rage at the insults of a one-time Red crony. It amused Lanny to put his *amie* in that same seat, and then tell her about it—using, of course, the name of "Mr. Smith." What a sensation he could have caused if he had told the two guards! But he would speak no unnecessary word until he was out of the Fascist domain.

He drove to the border, and when the two men stepped out of the car, he thanked them for having been *puliti*, but offered them no tip, and turned his attention to the formalities of the French customs. The pair stood on their side of the line, watching mournfully; after the luggage and the passports had been inspected and the car was about to start on its way into France, the spokesman of the pair remarked, humbly: "We are poor men, Signor."

Lanny smiled his most amiable smile. "Your Signor Mussolini is going to remedy all that. Very soon you will be richer than we!"

21

The Course of True Love

WHAT had happened to Giacomo Matteotti? Lanny got all the newspapers he could find, and read their accounts of the affair. The Italian government had given out a statement to the effect that a passport to Austria had been issued to the Socialist deputy, and that he was probably on his way secretly to Vienna. Also the papers of that morning had a story about the son of a well-known American manufacturer of munitions who had been expelled from Rome for activities considered inimical to the government, and was believed to be motoring toward France, together with a woman companion, a Madame de Bruyne.

Of course that made it necessary for Lanny to phone at once to Beauty, to let her know that he was all right; also to send a cablegram to his father. The story had one unpleasant aspect, which he didn't realize until Marie called his attention to it—she had to be taken to a different hotel from the one at which he was planning to stop. He had involved her in a "scandal." Their love affair, which so far had been discreet and in all ways charming, was now a subject of publicity and gossip; therefore it had become something painful, dangerous, and morally wrong. If Marie had been a Red, or even a Pink, as Lanny appeared to have become, she might have been willing to brazen it out, to say that she was his lover and had been for the past four years—so what? But Marie was a conventional French lady; her friends would be shocked, her husband's family would be inexpressibly shocked, and therefore Marie herself was shocked.

In short, it was a sort of volcanic eruption in their love-life. When Lanny tried to argue with her about the matter, she exclaimed:

"There will be newspaper reporters looking for you. And what will you say?"

"I'll tell them about Matteotti, of course."

"But—are they to find me in the same hotel?"

There was nothing he could do to change the world's code of propriety, so he took her to one hotel in Menton and himself to another. It was a measure of the upheaval in his own soul that, instead of grieving over the grief he had caused his *amie*, the first thing he did in his room was to write out again the long telegram to Rick; then he wrote one to Zoltan, and after filing these he phoned to Longuet in Paris, telling him to pay no attention to the stories about Matteotti having fled to Vienna, there was not the slightest doubt that he had been abducted.

By that time the reporters had found the American deportee; they were supposed to be watching the border, but they hadn't thought he could arrive so quickly. He stopped only long enough to wash his face and shave off a two days' growth of beard before he invited them to his room. He talked to them about the dignity of soul of Giacomo Matteotti and the hideousness of the regime which Benito Mussolini had established in Italy. No, he was not a Socialist, he didn't know enough to say what he was, but he knew human decency when he met it, and he had learned what it was for a modern state to be seized by gangsters and used by them to pervert the mind and moral sense of mankind.

In short, it was a declaration of war against Italy; and this was a serious matter for Lanny, if not for Italy. It meant that he permanently removed from his list one of the great art repositories of Europe; also it meant that he branded himself with numbers of persons who might be or might have been his future customers. Many of these persons were like Marie de Bruyne: their eyesight wasn't good when it came to distinguishing among the various shades of red and pink. They had heard two things about Mussolini—that he had put down the labor agitators and was causing the trains in Italy to run on time; over their *apéritifs* or their teacups they would say: "We shall have to be finding someone like that in France before long."

II

Lanny took the long sleep which he had earned; and when he opened his eyes it was morning. His first thought was of Matteotti, and he rang for the newspapers; the boy who brought them to his room brought also a note from Marie. He tore it open and read:

CHÉRIE:

My heart is wrung by the decision which I have to take. I know that you have your ideas, and that you must and will follow them, and it is impossible for me to put chains upon you. Men have to choose their own lives, and it has been made plain to me what your choice is going to be. I am not blaming you in my heart; I am bowing my head to a blow of fate. It would be fatuous to hope that our love might continue under the circumstances. In any case it is impossible for me to travel with you now, so I am taking the night train for Paris. I am trusting to my husband's kindness not to deny me access to his home.

Be assured of my undying gratitude for the devotion you have shown me, and that my heart will always be with you. May God make it possible for you to find happiness in the course which you have chosen.

Your devoted

MARIE.

Lanny was shocked; but not so shocked that he could keep from turning to the newspapers to see what they reported from Rome. Matteotti was still missing, and the government still maintaining that he must have fled to Vienna; there was great excitement in Italy, rumors of uprisings against the regime and so on. The local papers reported the safe arrival of Lanny Budd in France, together with his companion Madame de Bruyne. They quoted the picturesque details regarding his expulsion and long drive, but they gave nothing of his denunciation of the government of a neighboring and friendly state. That sort of thing was left for *Le Populaire* and *L'Humanité* and the rest of the left-wing rabble; and of course anybody who was quoted by them was branded Red.

It was a sad and chastened playboy who drove home to his mother. She was prepared to supply him with a warm soft bosom to weep on, but he didn't make use of it; he was too busy getting the newspapers which came to Cannes on various trains from Paris and London and Rome, and writing long letters to Rick and Longuet and his Uncle Jesse. Lanny was haunted by the thought that Matteotti might still be alive, and that if there was enough clamor in the outside world the gangsters might be frightened into sparing his life. Hadn't Lanny promised the Socialist deputy to do what he could to make the truth known? It was very nearly a death-bed promise, not to be forgotten. He had a mass of facts which he had picked up from the conversation of the newspapermen, and he considered himself morally bound to get these facts published wherever possible. Of course, the more he did this, the more deeply he smeared his name and that of his father.

He had to write a long letter to Robbie, explaining and apologizing. He wrote to Zoltan, in the hope of excusing his bad conduct. He wrote a letter of apology to the noble gentleman in Rome with whom he had broken an engagement. To Zoltan he sent a list of the pictures he had found, with descriptions of them and his guess as to prices. Zoltan, a politically untainted person, could go to Rome at his convenience and take up the negotiations where Lanny had dropped them. To punish himself, Lanny said he wouldn't take any of the commission on these Roman sales. So would start another series of "Alphonse and Gaston acts" between the partners.

To his *amie* the young recreant wrote a love letter. He didn't try to justify his conduct, nor did he say any more regarding Matteotti. During the latter part of their long drive he had told her about the case, and had hoped that she was being sympathetic; now he realized that she had kept her thoughts to herself, in order not to excite or worry him while he was under such heavy strain. Whether she would ever forgive him for his broken promises he couldn't guess, but he wrote that he loved her, and pretty soon he would come and tell her so. "Meanwhile," he said, "remember that scandals have a way of blowing over. There are so many fresh ones for people to talk about."

III

The story of Giacomo Matteotti proved to be a long-drawn-out serial. The unfortunate deputy was never seen alive, and cries were heard in the Parlamento: "The government is an accomplice!" Mussolini had to drop his tale that his opponent had fled to Vienna, and stated in the Chamber that Matteotti had evidently been abducted, but that no one knew where he was. However, the car was traced by its license number, and the names of Dumini and four other criminals became known. Public clamor forced their arrest, and they were supposed to take their punishment like gentlemen, but they weren't that; three confessed that they had committed the crime at the order of Mussolini. Shivers of terror ran through the regime, and the uproar in the Chamber was such that for a few days it seemed possible that *Fascismo* might fall.

The five ruffians had taken their victim to a dense wood a few miles from Rome. They said that they might have spared his life if he had pleaded for it, but he had been "fresh." What he had said was: "You cannot kill my cause. My children will be proud of their father. The proletariat will bless my cause." So they had beaten him to death, mutilated his corpse, and left it unburied. His dying words had been: "Long live Socialism!"

Such were the stories which came out of Rome during the next couple of weeks. Later on the murderers escaped, except Dumini, who was sentenced to seven years' imprisonment. He served about two years and then they let him out. He was heard to remark: "If they gave me seven years they ought to have given the President thirty." So they arrested him again. He denied that by "the President" he had meant Mussolini, but the judges wouldn't believe him, and sentenced his bold tongue to fourteen months and twenty days additional.

All that took time; and Lanny had to manage somehow to go on living, and realize that he couldn't overthrow Fascism, but could only make life uncomfortable for himself and those who loved him. Ambassador Child, alias "Cradle," having resigned his post and returned to the United States, was using his prestige to tell the people of his country that Mussolini was about the greatest man of modern times. He wrote article after article in praise of the "empire builder's" achievements, and these were featured in a weekly magazine having two or three million circulation. What could the feeble voice of one obscure playboy accomplish in the face of such publicity? Lanny was spitting to windward.

"Take it easy, son!" wrote Robbie, patiently. "The world is a tough old nut, and uncounted millions of men have broken their teeth upon it." The father went on to point out that despotisms had existed upon the continent of Europe farther back than any archaeologist had been able to trace; and doubtless there had never yet been a tyrant who hadn't been able to provide moral sanctions satisfactory to himself. "They have built fortresses with thick walls," wrote the salesman of munitions; "and doubtless there have always been idealists butting their heads against those walls—but history hasn't found time to make up the roll of their names."

IV

Beauty had been very considerate of Marie de Bruyne during the past four years; they had made a tacit treaty of alliance; but all the same, there was treason in the mother's heart, and right now seemed to be her opportunity. Very subtly she began to hint to her darling that perhaps it wasn't such a bad thing that Marie had returned to her husband's home; that was where a woman of forty really belonged. Lanny had arrived at an age where he ought to begin to think seriously about his duties to society; it was time for him to look around and find some suitable girl whom he could marry. To save him as much trouble as possible, Beauty herself took up the search.

The Coast of Pleasure had not hitherto been a summer resort, but the "discovery" was being made, and there were a number of young females of property now sojourning in the neighborhood. Beauty put on her gladdest rags and went to parties, and asked such questions as mothers ask, for reasons which all mothers understand. In a few days she had the necessary information, and she gave a tennis party, inviting several darlings of fortune, who all came; for Lanny belonged to the sex which is not harmed by scandals, but on the contrary acquires a certain piquancy, a flavor of romance. Watching her son with hawk's eyes, Beauty saw that his attention seemed to be caught by one young thing of a delicious debutante age; one who enjoyed excellent financial prospects—not a great fortune, but a reasonable one—plus exceptional good looks and a lively disposition. With some encouragement from both mothers, Lanny invited her to go sailing the next day, and when Beauty saw them off across the Golfe Juan, she looked upon it as a major diplomatic triumph.

The young people knew what was being done to them, and took it gaily, playing with the idea of love in harmless delicate ways; making jokes, teasing each other, feeling each other out. It is one of the delights of being young; one of the ways of making a pleasure out of a duty. This girl wanted to fall in love, yet she didn't want to fall too much in love; she wanted to keep her pride, and the independence which her fortune gave her. But at the same time she wanted a thrilling and passionate lover; in short, she wanted a great deal for her money. She was conscious of the money, yet she knew that she mustn't be, because that would be vulgar. She wanted to be loved for herself alone; but it had been pointed out to her that this might be difficult to arrange in France. She had the idea that a youth who was able to make large sums of money by anything so easy as selling pictures wouldn't stoop to fortune-hunting; on the other hand she was frightened by the idea that maybe this would make him too independent, and too desirable to other women. She made little coquettish approaches, and then shrank away; she brought the conversation to a basis of intimacy, then with a quick turn changed it into a joke, and they were laughing at each other.

She was good company, and Lanny wouldn't have minded making love to her if circumstances had been different. What she did was to awaken in him vivid feelings which politics had driven from his mind for a while. He found himself thinking about Marie and wondering what she was doing. It was Marie he wanted in his arms, not any fluttering young thing who didn't understand him and perhaps might never trouble to. The upshot of the afternoon's sail was that he sent a telegram, saying: "*Je viens*," and packed a couple of bags, and kissed Beauty on each of her still-dimpled cheeks, and also in the soft warm neck which he told her was accumulating *embonpoint* once more. This outcome was a disappointment to the mother, but there was nothing she could do about it except beg him to drive carefully.

V

When he arrived in Paris he took the precaution to telephone Marie, who said she would rather come to the city to meet him. He named the hotel, and she came to his suite. She would never fail to be happy when she entered his presence. However, he saw that she was paler and thinner than when he had seen her last, and he had a pang of remorse. He had been cruel to her, he had hurt her more deeply than he could ever realize.

She said: "No, dear; you did nothing that you could help. It is fate that has put a hand between us. The gods are jealous, and they won't let such happiness as ours endure too long."

She didn't want to talk about the "scandal," the unhappiness of her family and her husband's; she knew that was all nonsense to him, and would be a bore. She said: "I am yours whenever you ask for me; but I can't travel with you any more. You must realize that."

"I realize it if you say so, dear. You don't want me to come to the château?"

"I don't think it fair to the boys, Lanny. They are bound to know about it."

"They have probably known for years. Why not be sensible and have it out with them?"

"I can't do it, Lanny. They are Denis's sons, and he has a right to say. After all, it is his home; and he has been very patient and tolerant."

It seemed to Lanny that nothing in the world could be more silly. Here were these big gangling fellows—Denis, *fils*, was now eighteen and Charlot seventeen; they were nearly as tall as Lanny, and their school companions had without doubt told them all there was to know about sex, and perhaps had taken them to those places which Paris has provided for youth to try experiments. But they were being brought up as good Catholic boys, and must believe that what they did was wicked; also that their mother was pure and good, and never did anything like that.

There was no use arguing about it. Marie settled the matter when she said that the home was not hers but her husband's. Lanny would have this hotel suite, and she would come there whenever he invited her. But their love would have to be "clandestine." Marie didn't want to meet any of Lanny's friends, because that would remind them—and her—of the fact that she was the woman who had been named in the newspapers as his traveling-companion. Anyhow, she didn't care for his friends, because they talked politics of the wrong kind, and she was an embarrassment, a wet blanket on the conversation. The only exception she made was Zoltan Kertezsi; he wasn't interested in politics, and he was discreet, a kind friend to Marie as well as a useful influence for her lover.

All right; Lanny would adjust himself to this new life. It had been pleasant sitting in the garden at the château reading a book; it would be equally pleasant sitting in the chairs in the Bois, at the price of a few sous which you paid to an old woman collector. There were any number of sidewalk cafés where you could find all the good things to eat that your fancy might suggest. There were theaters, concerts, and no end of pictures; Lanny could go on studying prices and carrying on his business correspondence. He could have a piano in his rooms, and get a fresh supply of music—yes, Paris could be delightful in summer.

Marie would stay with him two or three days, and then go home and stay with the boys. While the cat was away, the mouse would play—that is, the Lanny mouse would go off on a debauch of politics. He would pay a call on Longuet or Blum, and perhaps hear one of them make a speech. He would call on his Red uncle, whose "free" domestic arrangement was turning out successfully. He would meet Albert Rhys Williams, just back from Russia—the Soviet Union, they preferred to have you call it—with truly marvelous tales about progress in that vast land; they were actually managing to drill some oil wells without any help from Robbie Budd or Henri Deterding or Basil Zaharoff! Lanny would have lunch or dinner with George Slocombe or John Gunther, just returned from one of the capitals of Europe, and hear the latest developments in the world-wide struggle for oil and steel. Doing these things gave Lanny a tremendous sense of adventure; he would get quite drunk on dangerous thoughts—and when he had slept it off he would phone to his beloved and she would come to his arms again. She would guess that he had been misconducting himself, but she would ask him no questions and he would tell her no lies.

VI

Poincaré was out, and there was a new Premier of France, named Herriot. He was a "radical," a word which had its special meaning in that land. It didn't mean an enemy of the property system, as in the States; Uncle Jesse said it meant that France was no longer governed by the Comité des Forges, but by whatever miscellaneous capitalists had chosen to buy the politicians. Of course you couldn't take Uncle Jesse literally; he was just trying to find the worst things to say about the capitalist system. But Robbie Budd would come along and say practically the same things, and it was harder to disbelieve them both.

Anyhow, Herriot was a peace man; he wanted to get out of the Ruhr, and he wanted some way to make sure that Germany would pay her debts and stay disarmed as she had promised. He went over to London with his staff, and they had a series of discussions with the Ramsay MacDonald outfit; the statesmen were hurrying back and forth between London and Paris and Berlin, and it was in the air that big things were being planned. Rick wrote about it, and had high hopes of results. For the first time since the war there were statesmen thinking about the welfare of Europe as a whole; for the first time there was a prospect of real reconstruction for the tormented Continent. Once there was assurance of peace, it would be possible to think about a gradual evolution from the system of private industry to one in which the public welfare would be the end and goal. Rick wrote an article to this effect, and it sounded quite "radical," in the American, not the French, sense. Lanny thought it would please his Red uncle; but, alas, it appeared that no one could please that uncle except the uncle himself. When he read the article he said: "The tiger will agree to have his teeth extracted, one every year, and the extracting will be done by the lambs."

The London conference decided to refer the whole complex of problems to the League of Nations. Everybody had come to realize that the individual nations couldn't handle these matters, and the Entente Cordiale couldn't stand the strain of trying. Let all the nations agree to respect one another's territory, let all unite to punish any transgressor. The fifth meeting of the League Assembly was to take place in September, and Rick was going there to report developments. As soon as he heard this, Lanny began remembering what a pleasant time he and Marie had had in Geneva three years ago. Why couldn't they do it again? Alas for that dreadful, irretrievable thing called a "scandal"! Marie couldn't enjoy being in Geneva; she wasn't even sure that she could return to Bienvenu; not even under the chaperonage of Lanny's mother could the pair of besmirched lovers be made respectable again. Lanny tried to argue about it, but it did no good; he was butting his head against the social code of France.

VII

Every now and then the pair of lovers would have another threshing-out of their problems. Marie kept fearing that she was neglecting her boys—even though the boys themselves preferred to be away from home with their boy companions. Also, she was well aware that Beauty didn't want her at Bienvenu. Beauty had been an angel, but in her heart she must hate the interloper. A devoted mother desired to find a proper wife for her son; and Marie, also a mother of sons, felt that Beauty was right, and even went so far as to say to Lanny that if her love for him were deep enough and strong enough, she would renounce him and help to find a proper wife for him.

The playboy never let himself be annoyed by the determination of all the ladies of his acquaintance to see him permanently paired off. He took it as a compliment, and amused himself exploring their ideas about his requirements. What did Marie think would be the proper sort of life-partner for him? She answered that it had become clear to her that Lanny would never be satisfied with a wife who wasn't interested in public questions, and who wouldn't travel with him to conferences and agree with what he thought about them.

"But I never can agree with myself!" objected the young social philosopher. "Don't you think I ought to make up my own mind before I make up my wife's?"

"I think I know pretty well what you believe," persisted the other. She wouldn't tell him what it was, because that might turn into an argument. "I think it's Englishwomen who take the sort of attitude that appeals to you."

"Well, I might go back to Rosemary," he said. He had told her all about that early love affair. But now Rosemary was the Countess of Sandhaven, and had three children—one worse than Marie!

She wouldn't let him turn it off with jokes. It was a real problem, which sooner or later they would have to face. If she had been a selfish woman she would have taken what she could get and let matters ride; but she was good—and that was why Lanny loved her, so the complication grew, and the more they struggled in the net the more they entangled themselves.

"What you are proposing is that I marry a Pink girl," said the wanton trifler. "I have met some of them, and they have indicated that they are willing."

He went into details. Recently he had attended a Socialist *réunion*, and had been introduced to the daughter of one of the speakers. "She isn't a bold new woman, as you might expect from a Pink, but a very simple old-fashioned girl, and I got the impression that she thought I was a romantic personality—on account of what happened in Italy, you know. It might be that she could easily be won. Do you think that would appeal to Beauty?"

Marie couldn't be sure whether he was spoofing or not, but she saw that he was determined to have her return to Bienvenu, whereas she wanted to stay with her aunt. Of course Beauty would have the last word to say about it, and Lanny had asked her to invite Marie, and Beauty hadn't yet done so. Now, smiling to himself, the rascal decided that he would use this old-fashioned Pink girl to settle the matter. He wrote his mother a long and quite serious letter about her, and of course threw Beauty into a panic. She was clinging to the hope that this stage of her son's development was a form of intellectual measles, which he would soon get over. But if he married into the Red movement, that would fix him forever; the designing creature would get him deeper into her toils—Beauty couldn't have said exactly what "toils" were, but they sounded terrible, and even a forty-year-old *amie* would be better. The anxious mother wrote Marie that she was the best influence Lanny had ever had in his life, and please to come and be their guest during the coming winter.

VIII

Marie wouldn't drive with Lanny to Geneva, but urged him to go by himself, and he decided to do so. He stopped off at the Château Les Forêts overnight and had a long talk with his wise friend Mrs. Emily, one of those talks which always left him clearer in his mind as to every subject they discussed. The châtelaine had many friends but few intimates; she said that she understood human nature too well, and it made one rather lonely. This woman of too great wealth presented to the world an aspect of proud serenity, but in the deeps of her heart she craved affection, and for the many years that she had known Lanny Budd she had watched him with maternal tenderness. She had never revealed this, other than by being always glad to see him and doing him any favor that she could. With the deftness of a woman of several worlds she would guide the conversation so as to bring into it anything that she thought he ought to know.

Either through Beauty or through Lanny himself she had shared the secrets of his love affairs, and had no fault to find with them. She thought that Lanny's present *amie* was doing him no harm, but much good. She had told Beauty that, and had something to do with the peace which had prevailed in the singular ménage on the Cap d'Antibes. She considered it much better for Lanny to earn money than to marry it; she could recall few cases where the latter process had done a man any good—and especially a young man. Many had wanted to marry Emily Chattersworth's money, but she hadn't thought it would do them any good!

Lanny told about his misadventure in Italy. Emily didn't think that men could change the world's economic system, which arose out of the excessive greed in their hearts; but that was an old-fashioned idea, perhaps, and she didn't urge it. She recognized it as something natural that a generous-minded young man should try to combat injustice; but she warned him as to the sad discovery he would make, that many of the people who pretended to be combating it were merely seeking advancement for themselves; they would use you all they could, and when they got power they would have no use for their old ideals or for those who had helped them to rise.

Lanny said: "I have observed that. Its name is Mussolini."

"I am sorry to say its name is legion," replied the other.

She talked about Isadora, who had gone to Russia with such high hopes three years ago. Doubtless she had expected too much; she always did. Russia was a place of starvation and dreadful suffering; a little handful of fanatics were finding that they had tried too much. "I don't know whether they are idealists or devils," said the châtelaine; "probably they are half and half."

Lanny cited what his Uncle Jesse kept insisting, that they were rebuilding the country out of their own flesh and blood; they were industrializing a modern state out of its own resources, the first time that had ever been done in history. All the other states had done it with foreign loans.

"That may be true," admitted the other. "But you can't expect that those who have money to lend will lend it for the abolishing of money-lending."

"Uncle Jesse calls that the class struggle," said Lanny, smiling. "He would say that you are a good economic determinist." Emily had never met Beauty's Red brother, but had heard about him; she was content to get her information second hand.

Anyhow, Isadora was having a hard time. She had danced and talked revolution, and had had thrilling receptions, but she had been unable to get what she needed for a school. She had fallen under the spell of a mad Russian poet who was trying to see how quickly he could drink himself to death. Just recently she had divorced him, and the government had arrested him for "hooliganism."

Emily showed Lanny some distracted, scrawling letters from the unhappy dancer. She wanted money, of course; she always had, and would so long as she lived. Emily had sent her a little, which ought to go a long way in Russia. "You are lucky," she said to a susceptible youth, "that you didn't get yourself involved. I suppose that is one of the things you owe to Marie."

IX

The Assembly of the League of Nations was the greatest international event that Lanny had witnessed since the Paris Peace Conference. Here were the diplomats of some fifty nations, many of them stirred by the belief that now, at last, they were going to do something for the peace of the world. Here were journalists, many with the idea that something big was going to happen and they were going to write the story of their lives. Here were the propagandists, the people with ideas, who chose this gathering as a pulpit from which to address the world. Here were the people with wrongs to be righted, lured by vain hopes. Here were observers, curiosity seekers, tourists who preferred to look at live statesmen rather than at statues of dead ones. The old city of watchmakers and money-changers was crowded, and Lanny, the young prince with a private car, took his English friend to a hotel farther down the lake, and would drive him in every day to do his interviewing and drive him back again to write his stories. Lanny liked to sit in at interviews, and nothing pleased him more than to pay for the dinner of a diplomat.

The correspondents here were the "old bunch," whom the pair had met year after year. San Remo, Spa, London, Paris, Brussels,

Cannes, Genoa, Rapallo, Lausanne—it was like trying to remember the kings of England, which Rick had learned, or the presidents of the United States, which Lanny had never learned. These writing men remembered where they had been, and the statesmen they had interviewed, even the good things they had eaten; they would recall this or that event, what So-and-so had said, how Somebody had got drunk, the girl that Some Other had got mixed up with. Lanny found that his adventure in Rome had turned him into a personality; he had made the headlines, and was no longer a playboy. Men didn't have to agree with his ideas, they might tell him he was a "D.F." to imagine he could buck the Fascists, but all the same he had ideas and had stood up for them, so they respected him.

The young fellow, for his part, never tired of listening to men who traveled all over the world and had new stories every time you ran into them. He took a naïve attitude toward their wisdom; absorbed it gladly, and was puzzled when the wisdom of the next contradicted that of the former. Rick was tremendously impressed by Ramsay MacDonald; he was writing for a clientele to whom the Prime Minister of Labor was the banner-bearer of a new, revivifying force in British political life. Lanny accepted Rick's idea as a matter of course, and found it confusing to meet a correspondent for one of the Tory papers, and hear him declare that he had known Ramsay most of his life, and that there was as much substance to him as to a child's red balloon; Ramsay used fine phrases which he had no idea of relating to reality—his test for them was that they brought applause from the working-class audiences he had spent his life addressing.

The statesmen were working over a thing which was to be called the "Geneva Protocol." The real initiator of it was France, and its purpose was to enable her to back out of the Ruhr without too great admission of failure. Robbie wrote to his son that Marianne had got hold of a bull by the tail, a trying position for a lady; she wanted guarantees that the bull wouldn't turn around too quickly when she let go. According to the Protocol all the nations would agree to apply "sanctions" against any nation which attacked a neighbor; it was another effort to remedy the condition of which Clemenceau had complained, those twenty million too many Germans in Europe. The old Tiger, by the way, was still alive, in a little den he had made for himself on the Vendée coast; every now and then some journalist would travel there just for the fun of hearing him snarl at the statesmen who were throwing away the hard-won safety of *la belle France*.

The Versailles treaty had set up a row of little states between Russia and Germany, made out of territories taken from both those countries. So long as the little states endured, France was comparatively safe; but who was going to protect them? France couldn't do it alone, and the British navy couldn't get there. But British money could arm them, and Zaharoff had the plants to make the arms. Of course Robbie Budd didn't fail to point that out to his son, and Lanny showed the letter to Rick. Was that what Herriot meant when he clamored for "security" as well as "arbitration"? MacDonald insisted that arbitration was enough, and he drew a picture of "the League of Nations looked up to, not because its arm is great but because its mind is calm and its nature just." Were those samples of the phrases which the Prime Minister of Labor used because they brought applause, but which he didn't know how to relate to reality? Suppose somebody came along who wasn't either calm or just, and didn't respect those qualities?

X

Zoltan Kertezsi had been to Rome, and stopped to see Lanny on his way to London. He skipped about the world like that, and always had something to report. He had sold a Moroni which Lanny had found, and expected to sell a Lorenzo Lotto when he went to New York later on. He had done more business in Berlin and Munich, and had deposited to Lanny's bank account close to fifteen thousand dollars. It was not merely having money grow on trees, it was having it drop off into your pocket; in fact, this lively and intelligent money opened your pocketbook and forced its way in. Zoltan wouldn't listen to the nonsensical idea that Lanny hadn't earned his share in Rome; if they started splitting hairs like that, they would have no firm basis for co-operation. Lanny didn't know what he would do with all that money, but hoped that somebody would come along to suggest uses for it.

He and Zoltan were two men who knew how to enjoy life as they went along. Lanny took him driving along the shores of that incredibly blue lake. The tang of autumn was in the air and the leaves were falling from the plane trees which line the streets of the towns and villages; the sun shone dazzling bright, and the tops of the mountains glittered like scenes in a fairy-tale. Long after the sun had disappeared the snow-caps were changing from pale pink to lilac and then deep purple. Stop and watch them—for it's no good being so wrapped up in pictures that you can't enjoy the realities which the pictures attempt to portray!

They climbed to the Old Town of Geneva and looked at the ancient gray buildings and monuments; they went through the Musée d'Art together, and Zoltan said: "Why don't you hunt up some pictures here?"

"The Swiss made too much money out of the war," replied Lanny; but his friend said he'd find many German Swiss who had speculated in marks, and would be glad to get some cash.

So when Lanny was tired of hearing statesmen argue about the details of "sanctions" and who was to decide what an aggressor was, he would amuse himself looking for private art collections. Among his friends in Geneva was that Sidney Armstrong who had introduced him and Rick to the League more than three years ago. The young American had been promoted, and now was an important official, tremendously proud of his work in this crisis of history. He knew a lawyer in the city who was a lover of paintings, and for the cost of a luncheon Lanny got from this gentleman the names of several possessors of valuable works. Almost always a courteous note would gain permission to view one of these collections, and after that the tactful sounding out was a matter of routine. Before Lanny left Geneva he was able to send Zoltan a list, and when he got home he would add to his cardfile and send more descriptions and photographs to possible customers.

XI

Also, the day before Lanny took his departure he had an adventure. His *amie* had been talking about his finding a young woman who was sympathetic to his ideas, so Lanny could hardly be blamed for adding that idea to his others. It chanced that Armstrong had a secretary, an American woman a year or two older than Lanny—which wasn't as bad as being forty. She was quiet and unobtrusive, extremely well informed, refined in her manners—in short, everything that a secretary ought to be. Besides, she had qualities not so necessary to her profession—she was slender and graceful, had soft brown eyes and fluffy brown hair, and wore a cream-colored sweater of soft knitted stuff which set off her figure. When Lanny asked questions about people in Geneva who knew about art, it was Miss Sloane who looked up their addresses, and Armstrong remarked that Miss Sloane knew more about everything than he did, and what would he do without her? Which of course made Miss Sloane blush and made Lanny decide that she was an attractive young woman. He was always deciding about some one of them.

When he was ready to leave, he called on Armstrong to thank him and say good-by. The official was expected back shortly, so Lanny sat in his office, and as Miss Sloane happened to be there, he told her about the satisfactory outcome of his art researches. He discovered that she knew the Musée d'Art very well, but she had the impression that all great paintings were in such public places, and hadn't realized that great numbers were privately owned. She was disposed to find the buying and selling of them a highly romantic occupation.

She was going out to lunch. Of course it was accidental, their leaving the old League of Nations building at approximately the same moment. It was natural that he should ask if she was going to lunch, and then if he might invite her; it was natural for her to be taken aback, and to ask if she ought to let him. Lanny said: "Why not?" and she didn't seem to know any reason, so he took her. Because he was fastidious about his meals he drove to a good place, where they would be waited on in style. This would take time, and

'em and leave 'em might be a good motto for callous hearts, but Lanny was kind, and really cared about the women he met, and so it was the very devil.

Right now was an especially distressing situation. He had labored for months to persuade Marie to come to Bienvenu. Now he had told her that he was coming for her, and she would be packing for the journey south. He had planned to drive all the next day and reach Paris late in the evening; Marie would be waiting at his hotel, and the blood would be in her throat and cheeks also, her arms would be warm for him. Now her image rose between him and Janet Sloane and made a blur between them.

No, he mustn't do it! He went on talking about the problems of war and peace, and when they went back to the car he wrapped her warmly, without adding the warmth of his arm. But it was hard to keep down his curiosity concerning her. Was she one of these modern women who took what they wanted? Most of the women of all nations who came to Europe didn't come because they meant to remain virgins. While she talked about the problems of "sanctions," and the deplorable consequences of American refusal to pledge support to any boycott—"It'll be exactly like breaking a strike!" she said —Lanny's mind would wander off on these sidepaths. He would be thinking: "I wonder if Beauty is right, and if I ought to find a wife. I wonder if this girl would make me a good wife. Perhaps I ought to stay and find out about her. How will I ever know if I run away from them?"

It was late when they arrived in front of the pension where she lived. There was no moon, and the street light was some distance away. Lanny got out, and took her hand to help her out, and her hand stayed in his; that was perhaps natural, since you shake hands with a friend when you part. He said: "I'm sorry I have to go." Then he should have gone, quickly. But he felt her hand trembling, and doubtless his was trembling. Suddenly he heard a faint whisper: "I want you to know, Lanny, I think you are the nicest man I have ever met."

"Oh, no!" he exclaimed; there was pain in her voice, and he didn't want to hurt her so much.

"Oh, yes!" she answered; and then: "Would you be willing to kiss me just once?"

Of course he couldn't say no. He took her in his arms, and it was one of those long kisses that don't want to end; the kind the Japanese censors cut out of the motion pictures that come to their country, and they put the pieces together and make one huge film of a great variety of Anglo-Saxon lips clinging to lips, and they show this to their friends with hilarious glee. Lanny still didn't know whether Janet was a virgin, but he knew if he had drawn her back to the car, she would have let him take her wherever he wished.

But close as they were together, the image of Marie was still between them. So Lanny said: "I'm sorry, dear. I wish I were free." That was enough, and she whispered a quick "Good-by" and fled to the door of her pension. Lanny stood by the car with his head bowed, mentally kicking himself. He would have been kicking himself whichever way that adventure had turned out.

BOOK FIVE

The Valley of the Shadow

BOOK FIVE

The Valley of the Shadow

22

How Happy Is He Born

I

LIFE settled into its old routine for Lanny Budd. He practiced his music and danced with his little half-sister, who was now seven, a fairy creature, a wellspring of gaiety bubbling incessantly. He attended to his growing business; somebody was always telling him where there were art treasures, or introducing him to someone who loved paintings and might buy something special if it was brought to his attention. Zoltan would give him tips, and also his many lady friends were helpful; this occupation was ideal from the point of view of that buxom butterfly his mother, providing excuses for buying clothes, going to parties and receptions, and meeting the wealthiest and most elegant people. Everywhere she told the wonder-tale of her son's successes, nor did she forget her former husband and the astonishing way his fame was spreading. So Lanny promoted Detaze and Detaze promoted Lanny, and the widow and mother basked in the warm sunshine of celebrity.

It was a way of keeping Lanny entertained, and out of the hands of the dreadful Reds. Of course the tactful Beauty and Marie and Emily didn't say that; they would never find fault with their darling, never let him feel that they were putting pressure upon him; they would just surround him with other interests, flatter him, marvel at his achievements, make him feel that a big picture deal was the most exciting thing in the world. Lanny knew what they were doing; he knew that when he went off to Cannes to give some money to a pitiful Italian refugee, or to meet some friend of Lincoln Steffens just returned from Red Russia, they guessed it and were whispering their fears behind his back. Because he was kind and hated to keep them in a stew all the time, he would do what they wanted, and for the most part refrain from doing anything else. That is the way men are managed, and is one reason why the world changes so very slowly.

There was Kurt Meissner also to be guarded; and Lanny had to be taken into that conspiracy. They knew that Kurt was always brooding over the state of the Fatherland, which he said was in pawn to Britain and France, and could no longer move hand or foot without their consent. Living in the enemy's country, Kurt had to be persuaded to see Bienvenu as a little island of neutrality, a shrine set apart for the worship of the sacred nine. Beauty, who really knew very little about music, had to try to understand her lover's; she would ask Lanny about it, so as to have something to say that wouldn't sound fatuous.

She would devise elaborate intrigues to force a new *Komponist* upon the attention of a heedless public. After many delays, due partly to his meticulous care in reading proofs, the *Spanish Suite*, *Opus 1*, and the *Piano Concerto, Opus 2*, had been published; Beauty would send copies to friends, asking that they be brought to the notice of critics and conductors; if a letter was received or a comment made in print, she would bring it to Kurt without mentioning her part in the matter. She kept a mental cardfile of musical people who came to the Riviera, and if she heard that one had noticed Kurt's compositions, she would contrive to have that person come to tea and meet him. Sometimes Kurt would be bored, and then Beauty's feelings would be hurt, for that was her idea of how reputations are made and she was ready with numerous instances to prove it.

II

In December Kurt and Lanny made their annual pilgrimage. In Berlin Kurt went to see his brother, also his publisher, and buried himself in the reading of more proofs, while Lanny went to stay in the Robins' nest. Kurt still held to his determination not to go there, and of course the Robins knew the reason, and it hurt their feelings; but Johannes wasn't giving up his business and the boys weren't turning against him. They still lived quite simply in their apartment with two old servants; what Johannes enjoyed was getting things done, and he was surely doing that, for he had offices downtown that occupied a couple of floors of a large building. Nobody but himself and a couple of trusted employees knew how many properties he had acquired in Germany, but he was being mentioned in the newspapers as one of the "kings" of the new finance; like most of the "kings" Lanny had met in his life, he looked harassed and tired. The old mark had been wiped out, and there was a new currency called the "rentenmark"; it was being kept stable, which was a great relief to everybody in that harassed and tired land.

Amazing the way young people grew up! Here was Hansi, now twenty, an inch taller than Lanny. He had grown so fast that he hadn't had time to fill out; he looked frail, but really wasn't, for playing the violin is vigorous exercise. Not that Hansi was one of those performers who toss themselves around and act as if they were conducting an orchestra; he stood as still as he could, and let the music do the talking. He said that the day of the long-haired and theatrical musician was past; with his well-trimmed black hair you might have taken him for a serious young student in a rabbinical school. He had beautiful large dark eyes and a gentle voice, and more and more he seemed to embody all that was noble and inspiring in the tradition of the Jews.

Nobody was promoting Hansi Robin; he knew how it was done but didn't want it. Having the good fortune to have a rich father, he was helping several poor students at the conservatory. What he wanted for himself was to play the best music as perfectly as possible, and he said that when he could do that he would make a public appearance and wouldn't need any promotion. He was learning Joachim's great *Hungarian Concerto*, which he said would delight Zoltan. He played difficult things such as Paganini's *Moto Perpetuo*, but he didn't love technique for its own sake—he spoke with scorn of "finger gymnastics." He and Lanny played Mozart's sonatas, and he extracted loveliness from them just as diligently as if he had had several thousand people listening. Lanny couldn't be sure how much was Mozart and how much was Hansi, but he felt sure that some day audiences would throng to hear this playing; and of course he had only to say this in order to transport all the Robins into their Jewish heaven. Lanny didn't know just what they had in that heaven, but he knew that Elijah—or was it Elisha?—had been taken up there in a chariot of fire. He was sure also that the residents there would play Ravel's *Kaddisch*, and Ernest Bloch's *Schelomo*, which Hansi had transcribed for violin.

One interesting discovery for Lanny: this young virtuoso had turned into a full-fledged Socialist. He had carried out his promise to study the movement, and announced his conviction that it held the hopes of the future. He wasn't ever going to put a party label on himself, but he would play his music for the people at prices they could pay, and he would play their kind of music if he could find it. Lanny asked what Papa Robin thought of this, and Hansi said that Papa wanted his boy to believe what seemed good to him. Whether this would hold if Hansi should ever leave his studies and get into a conflict, say with Generalissimo Balbo, Lanny ventured to doubt; but he didn't suggest it, not wishing to trouble the soul of a sensitive and noble-minded youth.

III

Lanny and Kurt went on to Stubendorf, in company with Emil; the Reds had been definitely put down, so army officers could have Christmas leaves. At the Schloss things were much the same, except that one of the two young widows, Kurt's sister, had been married to a middle-aged official of the neighborhood; not a love match, but men of her own age were scarce, and this was a well-domesticated gentleman who would be kind to her children. Lanny loved German music, German cheer and *Gemütlichkeit;* how he wished there might be some way to extract and eliminate from these people those aggressive qualities which caused the rest of Europe to fear them so greatly!

Among those they met was Heinrich Jung. He too had grown several inches and was a grand and sturdy forester; he was going to school for two years more, to make himself a real expert; Germany was setting the world an example in the conservation of her forest treasures, and the blond and blue-eyed Heinrich studied with a sense of consecration to the Fatherland. He talked with fervor about the National Socialist movement, to which he was still devoted, in spite of the debacle it had sustained the year before. The leaders of that putsch had all been tried, and Adi, their favorite orator, had delivered a masterpiece of oratory in court. He and his associates had been convicted and sentenced to several years' "detention" in the fortress of Landsberg, but a few days ago they had all been let out on parole.

During the period of their incarceration Heinrich had traveled to the fortress to take gifts to the captives, and he was full of the ardors inspired by this visit. He reported that the prisoners had been well treated, it being recognized that their motives were patriotic; they had had better food than most of them had ever enjoyed previously. The young forester was a serious acolyte, with no trace of a sense of humor where his cause was concerned; he had no idea that he was amusing Lanny when he explained that Adi's oratory was adapted to audiences in large halls and not to the confinement of a cell, so his companions had suggested the writing of his memoirs as a means of keeping him occupied. Heinrich reported that he had produced a massive manuscript, and that some of the others were helping to revise it. Lanny said it ought to make an unusual book, and Heinrich promised to send him a copy when it was published.

IV

The story of these martyrdoms produced in Kurt Meissner that state of melancholy for which the German soul is celebrated; he was led to pour out his feelings to Lanny after a fashion which he had not used for a long time. It was agony to the ex-officer to see the Fatherland despoiled, dismembered, and helpless in the hands of its foes. All the country's financial affairs and most of its economic affairs were now under the control of the Reparations Commission, and Kurt said it was evident that they never intended to release their stranglehold. Germany was down; and how could the German soul develop while the German body lay bound and gagged?

Lanny thought: "Certainly not gagged, for it's making an almighty clamor." But he didn't say this. He pointed out to Kurt that reversals of fortune were no new thing in Europe. A little more than a century ago Napoleon had held the great part of Germany and Austria; a little more than a half-century ago Germany had conquered France. "You have to allow a little time for the passions of war to cool off, and the balance will right itself."

Kurt argued that balances had no such power. Whatever happened would have to be done by men. "Germans have to make an effort; they have to struggle against oppression and enslavement. The intellectual and spiritual leaders have to supply the courage and devotion to country."

In short, Kurt was in a mood of martyrdom, and Lanny knew what that meant. The ex-officer's conscience was troubling him about going back to the land of his foes to live in peace and comfort with a beautiful blond mistress. He was too polite to say this to the son of that mistress; he wouldn't even say it symbolically, by referring to Samson and Delilah, to Antony and Cleopatra. But he talked about Wordsworth's "Stern Daughter of the Voice of God," and Lanny in return reminded his friend of the fact that all through the struggle against Napoleon the serene Goethe had continued his labors as thinker and artist.

"But he was a much older man," argued the German. "He couldn't have fought."

"He could have gone into the political struggle, and have tried to inspire the Germans to resistance. But he really believed in the importance of art, and he left us products of his genius which are still working when the political problems of the time are forgotten."

"I know, I know," Kurt said—for Lanny was speaking his own language here. "But the suffering is so dreadful, it throws me into a state of despair whenever I think about it."

"I dare say that happened to Goethe also. It is your problem as an artist to find a way to embody those feelings in the art which you have chosen." Not for the first time, Lanny quoted Goethe's verses to the effect that he who had never eaten his bread with tears, who had never sat by his bed weeping, knew not the heavenly powers. Not for the first time in his struggles with his friend, Lanny thanked God for Goethe! He had even taught Beauty about the august Olympian of Weimar, and about the ladies who had comforted him—so that she might be able to present herself under a more dignified guise than that of Delilah or Cleopatra.

V

They came back to Juan, and Rick and his family arrived in a few days. Rick was planning a play, and intending to devote himself to it all winter and permit nothing to interrupt him. Exciting to the impressionable Lanny to know that a masterpiece of music was being composed in one corner of the estate and a masterpiece of drama in another. It never troubled the young lord of the manor that he had no masterpieces of his own to contribute. Perhaps one might say that he was producing masterpieces of friendship, giving two artists a place where they could work unhindered, and providing that sympathy and admiration which appear to be essential to their functioning.

There was the estate with three pairs of lovers and four assorted fruits of love—Lanny counting in both classifications. Rick and Nina had the only marriage certificate on the premises, and there were people outside who turned up their noses at Bienvenu, saying, like Kurt's aunt, the Frau Doktor Hofrat von und zu Nebenaltenberg: "*Unschicklich!*" But such persons didn't really belong on the Coast of Pleasure. Those who stayed permanently came to realize that morals are a matter of geography, and that love and kindness in the heart count for more than any legal document stuck away in the bottom of a trunk. So, at least, it seemed to Lanny, and he was content to choose his friends among those who agreed with him; in fact he hardly knew that the others existed.

February was the month for Kurt's annual recital at Sept Chênes. This was really a favor that Emily Chattersworth did him, but she insisted upon sending him a check for two thousand francs; it provided all the pocket money he needed for a year, and thus helped to preserve his self-respect. There was always a rumbling and thundering of piano practice for this event, for Kurt was the most fastidious of virtuosi, and every phrase of one of his compositions was sacred to him. A week or so before the event he would begin worrying as to whether his selection of pieces was the best. He would ask Lanny's advice, and Lanny would point out the danger that, loving his music so intensely, Kurt was apt to give his audience more than it could carry away. To most fashionable people a musicale was an occasion for displaying their finery, and for exchanging chit-chat with other prominent persons. They wanted the music to be cheerful and brief.

Kurt's certainly wasn't either of these. He was packing sorrow and revolt into his work, more of it than could be contained within the classical forms he favored. Pretty soon people would be calling him a "modernist," and that would distress him; he would go off and shut himself away more persistently than ever. Kurt wanted to tell the world that the German soul was in chains; while what the world wanted was to eat, drink, and be merry, and not be reminded that there was suffering anywhere. Dressed in his tails and fresh white tie, Kurt remarked on his way to Sept Chênes that he was Wagner producing *Tannhäuser* before the members of the Jockey Club of Paris.

He rendered a new composition of his own to which he had given the odd title *Inner Life*. Most of those present were reducing their inner lives to the minimum, and didn't like the idea of having them exposed even to themselves; but they couldn't get away from the realization that something tremendous was going on here, and a few led in vigorous applause, and made it quite an event. As a result, the conductor of the orchestra in one of the Riviera casinos invited Kurt to give his piano concerto, and actually offered to pay him five hundred francs, at the prevailing rate of exchange about twenty dollars. As the orchestra would have to have all the parts copied out for the various instruments, they were really doing an unknown man, and a German, a great honor.

Of course it wasn't a first-rate orchestra, but all the same it was a chance for Kurt to hear his own orchestration for the first time in his life. He was as much excited as Beauty could have wanted him to be; those musicians who had to play regularly for the entertainment of gamblers and dancers were asked to come overtime and rehearse with an unknown genius—and strangely enough many of them caught his enthusiasm and tried to become a good orchestra. Lanny would drive Kurt in, and sometimes Rick would go along, neglecting his own *chef-d'œuvre*. A fire came from somewhere—the Greeks said from heaven—and entered the hearts of men; it came unannounced and in unexpected places, perhaps after you had given up hope of it and had even forgotten its existence; it overcame men's jealousies and suspicions, and they began to run here and there and whisper excitedly; there was a rustling and a murmur, as of the wind stirring in the myriad leaves of a grove sacred to the Muses.

VI

Robbie Budd came along on one of his business trips. He stayed for several days with Lanny in his studio, and told Beauty to "blow herself" to the grandest possible party. She gave her vote for an *al fresco* luncheon on the lawn at Bienvenu; caterers would bring it from Cannes, and there would be an orchestra and dancing, or tennis, or bridge—whatever people wanted. The weather proved friendly and it was a delightful occasion; Beauty's friends came to meet her former husband—so he was called—and speculate as to whether she was taking up with him again. Since the alleged "music-teacher" from Germany was on hand, they supposed not, but hoped for the worst.

Robbie always brought something from America, usually some new gadget of the sort for which the Yankees were famous: electrical irons for curling ladies' hair, or a device that you could put on the breakfast table to make your own toast—what wouldn't they think of next? Last year he had brought a thing called a radio-set; an extraordinary invention—the air or whatever it was all around you was full of music, and there was a tube with two prongs which you stuck into your ears and you could plainly hear a whole orchestra. This time the traveler brought a bigger and better one, having a horn like a phonograph, so that you could hear the music anywhere in the room, and could dance to it. You could even listen to a man making a speech in Paris! Robbie said this invention might provide a new method of controlling public opinion; you could tell the people whatever you pleased and they had no way to answer back! He had bought a patent and launched a company to manufacture a set that didn't have to have batteries, but could be plugged into an electric light circuit, and you could make it as loud as you pleased. Imagine thousands of people sitting in a hall, and a great voice roaring to them about the dangers of voting for the other fellow's candidate!

Robbie appreciated this idea, for his native land had just passed through a red-hot Presidential campaign. There was what Robbie called a demagogue by the name of La Follette who had come near to ousting Robbie's prize President, the "strong silent statesman." Robbie got fun out of that phrase, for he had met "Cautious Cal" during the campaign and put up a lot of money to elect him, and might have become ambassador to France if he had been willing to give up his lucrative contract with Budd Gunmakers. Robbie said Cal was the funniest little man that had ever come out of the Green Mountains. He was so cautious that he didn't talk even to his wife. She told a story about how he went to church, and when he came home she asked him if the sermon had been good, and he said yes, and then she asked what the preacher had preached about and he said: "About sin." The wife asked: "What did he say about it?" and the answer was: "He was agin it."

The opposite of the silent Coolidge was the overtalkative Scotchman, Ramsay MacDonald; at about the same time that Cal was elected, Ramsay was ousted, and once more there was a Tory Prime Minister of Britain. Robbie said that was all to the good, for now the two countries could get their affairs on a business basis. Robbie listened politely to the "liberal" ideas of Lanny's English chum and didn't argue with him, but when he was alone with his son he said that the British "liberals" and all others were in for a sad disillusioning as to the conduct of the United States. The first thing Britain had to do, if she expected any sort of co-operation in future, was to get busy and pay the debts she owed. Robbie had spoken to the President on this subject, and the country storekeeper's son summed up his attitude in six plain Yankee words: "They hired the money, didn't they?"

Lanny had been hearing a lot about those war debts in Geneva, and he asked by what means they could be paid. Robbie was ready with an answer—he always was. He said that British citizens owned billions of dollars' worth of American stocks and bonds, and if Britain wished to she could tax those citizens and buy those securities to be turned over to the United States government. The reason the British wouldn't do it was plain enough—they were afraid for their world position in the face of intensified competition, and if they kept their claims upon American industrial plants they were sure of having some income anyhow!

VII

One of the purposes for which Robbie had come south was to see Zaharoff, so Lanny drove him to "Monty" and sat in at one of their sessions. The munitions king of Europe had at last obtained that prize which all his wealth had been unable to buy him—the wife for whom he had had to wait thirty-four years. The madman in the Spanish asylum had passed away, and just before Lanny had set out for Geneva the seventy-five-year-old Knight Commander of the Bath had escorted his lady-love, the Duquesa María del Pilar Antonia Angela Patrocino Simón de Muguiro y Berute, Duquesa de Marqueni y Villafranca de los Caballeros, to the *mairie* of the small town of Arronville, near the great estate of Château de Balincourt which Zaharoff owned. There the duquesa, now in her sixties, was made Lady Zaharoff in a strictly private wedding, the crowds being kept at a distance and the shutters of the *mairie* closed so that people with opera glasses couldn't see in. Lanny had read in the Paris *Temps* an account of the event, somewhat playful but still respectful, giving no hint of the fact that the elderly couple had been living together all over the continent of Europe for more than a generation.

Lanny listened while the two businessmen discussed oil company reports, bond issues, expansion plans, the personalities of executives, and of statesmen whom they considered as executives somewhat more tricky and difficult to control. Lanny was again surprised to realize how deeply his father was involved in money transactions with this man whom in former days he had described by names such as "old spider" and "lone gray wolf." *Pecunia non olet* was one of the few Latin phrases which Robbie had brought away from Yale—perhaps because it was associated with a slightly off-color story which had caught a college youth's fancy. Certainly Sir Basil's money now smelled sweet to the Connecticut Yankee, and the smear of oil which ran all through their conversation didn't offend his aesthetic sense.

Lanny listened to many things which the world would have paid a high price to know; among them the financial difficulties in which the enormous institution of Vickers was involved. The old Greek trader was withdrawing from the company, and hinted that he had unloaded a lot of his securities, but he didn't give any figures; he had been scared by all this peace talk, and had seen what was coming to the munitions industry in a world which scrapped its battleships and talked about boycotting aggressor states. He and Robbie discussed the subject in detail, and differed about it, for Robbie had got some small contracts for Budd's and hoped to get more on this trip; Zaharoff said that such contracts might help out a small concern like Budd's, but not Vickers.

Lanny never heard these two men of large affairs say that they hoped for the spreading of distrust among nations, in order that their own business might thrive; he never heard them say that they hated pacifists and pacifying statesmen because they kept Budd's and Vickers "in the red." But that was the attitude to which they were automatically driven; it was the underlying assumption of their talk. Lanny knew that many people hated them, and wrote books attacking them bitterly; he had started to read one of these, but it had made him unhappy. He knew that the "merchants of death" were the product of forces beyond their own control. It was a game they played, and they lost themselves in the excitement of it. He told himself that it wasn't so different from the thrill of selling pictures. He won thousands, while his father won hundreds of thousands and Zaharoff millions; but the feelings were the same.

VIII

Robbie told his son that Esther was going to bring the family to Europe for the coming summer. This was a part of every young person's cultural equipment—that is, among those who had the price. Lanny's stepmother didn't approve of Europe or of Americans who lived there, but she knew that Europe was history, Europe was art, and she couldn't deny her children their share. So they were coming, along with a million other tourists, as soon as school closed; reservations had been made and tickets paid for.

Also Zoltan happened to be passing, and gave his opinion that the time had come to let an eager world see the work of Marcel Detaze; they would rent a first-class gallery in Paris and have a "one-man show," not letting any dealers in on it; they would put extremely high prices on all the works, not with the idea of selling many but of lending glamour to them all. The latter part of the season would be best; Zoltan suggested June, and Robbie said: "Keep it open into the first days of July, so that the family can see it, and they'll help to advertise it in America."

Soon after that came a letter from the Robins. They too were interested in culture; they too were working hard at their studies and earning a vacation. Papa had promised to let them come to Paris and learn all they could about French music. They knew that Lanny was accustomed to spending his summers in or near Paris; might they see something of him, and perhaps visit art galleries with him? Would the kind Mrs. Chattersworth care to have Hansi play music for her? And so on. These two virginal youths had never got any hint of the real reason why Lanny spent his summers in or near Paris, and could have no idea that they might embarrass him by an offer of intimacy. Lanny didn't worry about it, for the pair were old enough to know their way about; he would say to them quite simply: "Madame de Bruyne has been my *amie* for the past few years." And that would be that.

Gracyn Phillipson, alias Pillwiggle, showed up on the Cap at the height of the season. Did she come on account of the delightful Lanny Budd, or was she too seeking culture? "Pillwiggle" of course wasn't any name, just an absurdity that Robbie had invented for a high-school girl presuming to act in a play at his country club. Since then she had made herself a name that even the flippant munitions man could remember. Her show had run in London for the better part of a year, after which she had gone back to New York and starred in a "triangle" play which hadn't done very well—but everybody agreed that it wasn't the fault of Phyllis Gracyn, whose acting had been brilliant. Her producer had given her a rather repulsive play, in which she had set out to carry off another woman's husband, and the man was such a dub that nobody cared very much who got him or what they did with him.

To be sure, the star might have gone to Florida for her rest; Florida also had a "season." It had alligators and palmettos and gambling-palaces, but it didn't have culture; except for St. Augustine it had no history, no romantic-sounding names that highbrow people talked about. So the ambitious young actress took the warm Mediterranean route, which brought her via Gibraltar and Algiers and Naples and Genoa; at this last port she parted from a young man of wealth whom she had been fascinating for eleven days, and took the train to Antibes and put herself up at the expensive hotel on the Cap. From there she wrote a note to Lanny; her friends now called her "Phil," but to him she would always be "your grateful and admiring Gracyn."

Naturally, he went to call on her. He had found her good company in London, and she had helped to bid up the price of the Detaze. She had asked a lot of questions about the Côte d'Azur, and he had said: "Come and see it." Now he decided—out of the vast knowledge of the heart of woman which he had acquired at the age of twenty-five—that he would tell Marie where he was going, and all about the Broadway celebrity whom so many people adored, but not he. Gracyn might be ever so expert at creating "triangles" on the stage, but she wouldn't make Lanny a part of one, and would Marie please not worry because he was polite to her? Marie promised, and Lanny kissed her to seal the compact.

IX

There were other celebrities on the Cap; it was coming to be a rendezvous for them, and they preferred one another's company, looking down on the uncelebrated as not worth bothering with. Already there were several at the hotel who called Gracyn "Phil," but when Lanny appeared she shook them all off and strolled with him to a quiet seat in one of the nooks with which the grounds had been thoughtfully provided. She was only a year or so older than he, but she had matured with surprising speed, and was nothing of the crude small-town girl who had been so excited over playing the part of Puck in *A Midsummer-Night's Dream.* She was the same small sylph-like creature who had been dowered with charm; but now she had made a study of it, both on stage and off, and could exercise it when and where she pleased—just as Hansi Robin could pick up a fiddle and a bow and extract melancholy or rapture from it. It didn't matter what Gracyn had been in the past, any more than it mattered that the bow was strung with horsehairs, and the fiddlestrings made from the intestines of a pig.

Her way of charming Lanny was to be his old pal, with whom it was a delight to be simple and straightforward. He, the old-timer, could come into her dressing-room and see her with her grease paint off and her wig on the dressing-table. Not literally, of course, for she wore a gay spring costume of white organdy and a wide floppy hat with pink poppies, and if all that color in her cheeks was real her sea voyage had certainly done her good. She chatted about old times, and what funny young things they had been, and how little they had guessed what was coming to them. He told her about the picture business, and about his friend who composed music, and how Rick was writing an extraordinary play. "Oh, has it got a part for an *ingénue?*" she asked.

Lanny, who had learned something about worldly arts himself, had meant for her to put that question, and he answered that it surely had. "I want a good play the worst way!" exclaimed the actress. "Could I read it?"

"I don't know," said the other. "Rick has always been fussy about getting his work just right before anybody sees it. He says that first impressions are permanent."

"You know how it was with us in the old days—we worked over a play and we all helped to get it right."

"I know, but Rick has ideas about literature. He wants to write something that will be published in book form and be permanent; and then he wants it produced just the way he writes it."

"That makes it very hard," replied the actress; "but anyhow, will you bring him to see me?"

"My mother wants you to come to our home, and he'll be there. Also you'll meet my *amie*."

"Oh, have you got an *amie*?" On the stage great ladies of fashion met unexpected situations with perfect *savoir faire*, and Gracyn had learned the phrase and what it meant.

Lanny explained that he had been for many years in love with a married lady who didn't live with her husband. Gracyn found that romantic, if disappointing; she said that she would feel exactly as though she were on the stage. Lanny laughed and said: "Don't behave as you did in your last play!" He had read reviews of it, and told her that he would always follow her career. Friendship was a pleasure, memory was a pleasure, and by means of art both could be extended.

"Oh, Lanny darling, you do say such lovely things!" exclaimed the star. "Why didn't I stick by you when I had you?"

"Because you wanted to go on the stage," he replied, gravely. "Don't say you aren't satisfied!"

"Who is ever satisfied, Lanny? Are you?"

"Indeed I am!" he replied.

X

Phyllis Gracyn came to tea, and there were the three embattled ladies of Bienvenu, each prepared to guard her own. But the actress kept to her role of an unpretentious small-town girl, grateful for an opportunity to observe life in a villa on the Riviera about which she had heard so much. She wanted to know an artists' model who had married a munitions king and borne him a son; ditto a French lady who didn't love her husband but did love a shining art expert; ditto the young wife of a crippled English aviator turned playwright. The Prussian artillery officer turned musician didn't often show up at tea parties, but Gracyn had heard about him, and it was her thought that if she proved herself a perfect lady, attentive, considerate, and in no way dangerous, she might have a chance to study all these fascinating types. It was what the French called the *haut monde*, which the actress learned to her great bewilderment sounded like "Oh Maud!" It was "high life," which the French pronounced the way it looked to them—"hig leaf!"

What are the emotions of a mother who meets for the first time a woman who seduced her son at the age of eighteen years? Well, it depends upon the mother, and also upon the son. Lanny laughed at Beauty's idea of the episode, insisting that Gracyn hadn't done him any harm, but had taught him to look out for himself. Seven years had passed, and bygones were far gone, so be a woman of the world, and maybe Gracyn would get interested in Rick's play and make a fortune for both author and star. Nina was not indifferent to that argument, and was quite sure that nobody was going to run off with Rick. As for Marie, if she had any anxieties she was too proud to reveal them.

Gracyn found the lame playwright difficult to deal with. He didn't show himself sufficiently eager for the attentions of a leading lady of renown. He told her that if ever he wrote a play that he thought would please the great public, he'd be happy to let her see it, but the one on which he was working was an attempt to portray the spiritual problems of the youth of his generation, and he thought that only a few were as yet awake to them. The story had to do with a young writer who had made a success, and whose socially ambitious wife looked forward to moving on to the next one; but the writer had become troubled with the problem of poverty *versus* wealth. His questionings were embodied in a girl of the ruling class—the scenes of the play were laid in England—who didn't appreciate her high social position, but wanted to help the workers to pull down her own class.

When Rick outlined this story, Gracyn looked worried. "It sounds as if it was going to be a 'radical' play."

"Stupid people will call it that," answered the playwright; which might or might not have been impolite.

Gracyn noted that it was going to be another "triangle," a theme which has been thoroughly tried out on the stage. She begged Rick to read her the first act, and he did so, with Lanny listening, and afterward they had a discussion, Lanny still listening. It carried him back to those old days which Gracyn called "funny," when he had been driving a real *ingénue* about the roads of Connecticut, she plying him with naïve questions about the world of fashionable society to which she looked up as if it were heaven. Now she had managed to climb there, by what sacrifices she would never tell; and here was a young man to that heaven born, assuring her that the place was "phony," its scenery *papier-mâché*, its glory tinsel and gilt, its dwellers spoiled and silly children, playing on harps out-of-tune music which they had got from degraded savages in the jungles of Africa!

To Gracyn all this sounded crazy; but if it was the latest thing, of course she wanted it. Rick quoted the phrase of an American philosopher: "the worship of the bitch goddess Success." But what did that mean? Didn't everybody want to succeed? And what was wrong with succeeding? You worked hard and got on top and then somebody told you it was all nothing. But how did Rick know? If everybody and everything was bad, who was going to judge? Said the darling of Broadway: "The way it seems to me, you and Lanny have had success all your lives and you've got bored with it. But I've just got mine, and, believe you me, I like it."

The fastidious young Englishman was amused and somewhat

touched. It was a statement of the *arriviste* attitude. It seemed characteristically American—because in that "land of unlimited possibility" the classes were in a state of flux, and it was possible for a girl who had been brought up in rooms over a decorating-shop to find herself at the age of twenty-six at a de luxe hotel, diving off springboards into the same water with the sons of German barons, Rumanian *boyars*, and members of the old French *noblesse*.

Lanny, who had watched the birth of this dancing star, now listened while the baronet's son patiently explained that modern society was based on commercialism, and therefore many of its values were open to suspicion; there were a great many people trying to hold onto their money, and making whatever pretenses were necessary to that end. Lanny wondered: Is Rick going to make a "radical" out of Gracyn? Or is he just going to get his play turned down?

He guessed that the latter would be easier, and so it proved. Gracyn didn't give up her stage career and become a crusader for social justice. What she did was to tell Rick that his ideas were interesting, and that she was grateful for the explanation; she would think about his play, and do what she could to find a manager who was interested in modern ideas; but it wouldn't be easy, because managers also worshiped the bitch goddess, who was known in the theatrical world as Box-Office.

To Lanny the actress said: "Your friend is a very bright man; but he doesn't realize what an advantage he has over the rest of us. You can't look down on things until you've got above them." Lanny said that was a good "line" for Rick's play.

XI

The lady from Broadway and Forty-Second Street made herself so agreeable that Beauty decided she was a real celebrity and gave a tea in her honor. The members of the smartest sets came, and Gracyn liked that a lot better than listening to talk about the woes of the poor. These ladies and gentlemen wore such elegant costumes and had such smooth and easy manners that it was hard indeed to believe they were *papier-mâché*, tinsel and gilt, spoiled and silly. Even those who criticized these people went on playing their game; Rick's wife wore a lovely tulle frock to this tea party, and her sweet little children were dressed up and showed off their perfect manners along with Baby Marceline; Lanny wore a simple sport-suit, but somebody had seen to it that it was freshly laundered. To a poor girl from a near-slum in a New England manufacturing town it appeared that the sons and daughters of the rich had had things far too easy.

There came a cablegram from a manager in New York who had a play for Gracyn, so she went to Marseille to take a steamer. Lanny offered to drive her, and invited Marie to go along, but Marie found an excuse for letting them go alone. Maybe an old friend might have something she wanted to say to Lanny; and so it proved.

"Darling," she began—it being the stage formula—"are you sure you are happy?"

"Perfectly, dear."

"It seems a queer sort of arrangement. It can't last forever, can it?"

"Forever is a long word."

"Do you think that you and I could ever be happy again, Lanny? I mean as lovers."

"No," he answered, promptly. "I don't."

"Why not?"

"It's like two comets flying about in space. We come near each other, and then fly a long, long way apart and stay for a long, long time."

"But I could stay with you, Lanny, if you wanted me very much."

"You're an actress, old dear. You know I like you, and I'll always be interested in what you're doing. Let's be friends."

She was leaning toward him, but he kept both hands on the steering-wheel, as good driving requires. She was going to a great city where there were plenty of men; perhaps she had one waiting there. Lanny's father had seen to it that he was well informed on the subject of venereal diseases, and Lanny didn't like the thought of Gracyn's men, and had no desire to take a chance on what they might or might not have had. He had made up his mind that one woman at a time was enough—and let it be some woman who wanted one man at a time!

The great steamer lay at the *quai*, and there were a couple of hours to spare. The actress had a comfortable cabin to herself, and there was a bolt on the inside of the door, so it would have been an easy matter for them to be alone for a while—such things have happened on transatlantic steamers, even in the *première classe*. But Lanny showed her the sights of the crowded *quais*, and took her to a little place where there was sawdust on the floor and *bouillabaisse* in bowls; he told her that Thackeray had praised this seafood mixture in a poem. When she revealed that she had never heard of that novelist, he told her about *Vanity Fair;* there had been people finding fault with fashionable society long before Rick was born!

When he took her back to the steamer he kissed her hand, French fashion, which she found delightful; he told her that he wished her all the luck there was, and promised to do his best to persuade Rick not to make that play too "radical." He quoted: "To go away is to die a little." She always took any quotation as a product of his own brilliance, so she said again: "What a darling you are!" Her last words were: "If ever you want me, Lanny, I'll come!"

23

And Both Were Young

I

THE Galeries Freycinet are strategically situated on the fashionable Rue de la Paix, and with money furnished by Lanny and his mother, Zoltan hired their two largest rooms for a month. This was a long time for a one-man show, but Zoltan was planning a campaign and was sure the public would keep coming. The first thing he did was to present a copy of one of Marcel's small seascapes to the art critic of one of the great Paris newspapers; so, a few days before the opening, this gentleman published a two-column article about a painter who was taking his place as a shining light in the galaxy of French genius. Without any advertising or promotion, Marcel Detaze was forging to the front of French representationalists; in spite of all the fads and follies of a frivolous time, it was possible for sound and solid work to find recognition in the art worlds of both Paris and London. This article was illustrated by the *Poilu*, the *Sister of Mercy*, and the aforementioned seascape; before the month was over, the seascape was placed on sale at one of the near-by galleries and sold for thirty-five thousand francs.

This one article started the ball rolling, and the other critics didn't have to be paid so much; there were even a few so important that they didn't have to be "sweetened" at all. Socially prominent persons had to be visited and told about the forthcoming event. For that purpose Lanny and his mother came to Paris a week in advance and told all their friends what they were there for. At such a time one reaps the reward of having such a person as Emily Chattersworth for a friend; she would spread the word among key people, and no one doubted her judgment in a matter of art.

The fact that Marcel's face had been burned off in the war, so that he had been forced to wear a mask, and that in spite of this handicap he had gone forward and developed a new style—this didn't make him a great painter, but it surely made him a great subject for conversation about painting; it made him popular with persons who had to fill newspaper space with gossip and comment. It caused his name to stand out, and gave people a reason for attending a one-man show instead of races at Longchamps, steeplechases at Auteuil, or polo at Bagatelle.

So the opening day was a real occasion. Zoltan acted as master of ceremonies; looking as if he had been "poured out of the egg," as the Germans say, precisely correct in his "morning," his striped gray trousers, large silk tie, and boutonnière. His slightly florid light-brown mustache lent the right touch of artiness. He had hired at a fancy price the best-trained doorman in Paris, who knew everybody who might by any possibility come to an exhibition; this man was provided with a telephone in a booth, and upstairs was a messenger who would bring word to the expert, so that he might be waiting at the head of the stairs. "Oh, how do you do, Lady Piddlington? Have you quite recovered, Your Grace?" Greeting each one in his or her own language—French, English, German, Spanish, Italian, Hungarian, even Swedish—he had a bit of them all. His manners were always French, they being international and romantic. He would stroll with the important ones and tell them what to see and they would see it.

Beauty Budd was, of course, an indispensable part of the show. You might say that she had been preparing for it ever since her arrival in Paris, a seventeen-year-old virgin. Meeting painters and posing for them, learning all the patter; meeting Robbie Budd and acquiring the manners of the *beau monde;* learning to dress, learning to be gracious, to exercise charm; meeting Marcel and loving him, so that he poured his genius into glorifying her. He had painted her when he had first met her, a piece of ripe fruit with the loveliest colors that nature can produce and that paint can imitate; a woman in a light summer dress, standing in the doorway of his cabin with a little straw hat and veil in her hand. He had painted her again in the days of his deepest tragedy, when she had stood by him and he adored her as the embodiment of womanly pity.

The picture, *Sister of Mercy*, was one of those things like Whistler's *Mother*, whose merit no critic can dispute, and which at the same time are so simple that the least-taught person can understand them and share their sentiment. There would always be some people standing in front of it; and when they saw Beauty, they would stare at her, and the blood would climb into her cheeks and stay there—in fact she wouldn't need any rouge at all for a month, though of course she would put it on for safety. She was forty-five, and no flower blooms, no fruit hangs on the tree, forever.

What she had to do for a whole glorious month was what she loved most of all things in the world: to dress up and meet swarms of the right people, and be admired by them, and tell them all they wanted to know about Detaze—who could tell them better than Madame Detaze, *veuve?* Zoltan had advised her to dress very simply, and with dignity, and she played to perfection the part of a woman who had been the saving influence in the life of a genius. The fact that she really had been that made the playing much easier.

II

Lanny also had his place in this more-than-one-man show. The stepson of the painter had shared the secrets of the last five years of his life; had traveled with him to Greece and Africa, watched his work of this period, and had something to do with its moods. This was also true of the war years—no doubt whatever that he had helped to bring some of these later works into being. He really understood Marcel's technique, and could talk to critics and experts about his development. Zoltan declared that many an art critic got his job because he was a relative of the newspaper proprietor or of his mistress, or because he owned the right clothes and would work for practically no salary. You saved the life of such a man when you tactfully gave him his cues and his technical terms.

Something even more important than being an art expert was being a social expert. Lanny knew how to talk to a duchess whose

title came down from the *ancien régime*, or to a Russian princess in
exile, or to a Hollywood movie star. He could guess that the
duchess had come because she loved paintings, but that she wasn't
likely to buy one; that the Russian lady was hoping to meet somebody to whom she could peddle her fur coat; that the movie star
wanted to be looked at and mentioned among those present. He
knew how to watch Zoltan and pick up his signals, whether he
should devote his time to this one or get rid of that one. He could
meet sudden emergencies—as when Zoltan introduced him to the
widow of a great department-store proprietor from St. Louis, and
this stout bejeweled lady somehow got things mixed up and proceeded to express to Lanny her wonder that one so young should
have painted all these lovely pictures. If he had dealt with that situation crudely and affronted a dowager queen of merchandising, he
might have deprived the people of the Mississippi valley of their
chance to have a great art collection brought among them.

To a show such as this came many sorts of people. Some really
appreciated the pictures, and followed Lanny about, drinking in
every word that he said. Some were persons of wealth, who might
have to pay in cold cash for their enthusiasm. Others bore upon
their persons evidence that they were poor—but Lanny would give
time to them, regardless of the high prices which he and his mother
were paying for these rooms. Old friends of Marcel, or young
painters and students from the Left Bank, word spread among
them—"*Il faut les voir!*"—and they came in clothes that had been
patched and collars that had been trimmed with scissors. Some
looked so ill-nourished that Lanny wondered how they could stand
up for long periods; their fingers were bloodless and wax-like as
they pointed out this or that feature of a canvas, and one couldn't
be sure whether the trembling was caused by excitement or ex-
haustion. But they were living the life of art which they loved,
and wine of the spirit was here poured out for them without price.

Great numbers of Americans were in Paris seeking culture, and
they always wanted the very latest thing. Some knew what they
were seeing, and others took it on faith. A couple of wizened little
old ladies whom Lanny guessed to be schoolteachers heard him

telling an English journalist about Marcel's life and work, and they attached themselves to his coat-tails and followed him from one painting to the next. They never made a sound, and in the end faded away as quietly as they had come; but for an hour or more they were his adoring pupils, drinking in culture like two topers who have knocked out the bung from a cask of wine.

Others did less honor to their native land. Two ladies of fashion, loaded with expensive decorations, gushing in unnecessarily loud voices—they too had read the papers, or perhaps somebody had told them, but they hadn't bothered to get it quite straight. They came up to a canvas and one said: "Who painted that?" The other drew closer and peered through her lorgnette. As it happened, if Lanny knew what a land- or seascape represented, he had given it a title as well as a number. The lady read and exclaimed: "Cap Ferrat! Oh, I adore his work!" Said the other: "Yes, it is grand. But I wonder why they call him 'Cap.'" The learning of the one with the lorgnette was equal to this test. "They say he was in the French army," she explained.

III

Two friends of the Murchisons from Pittsburgh showed up; elderly, quite plain-looking people, but you couldn't always tell by that. They said they liked the pictures, and spent a lot of time studying them and discussing them quietly. Finally they came to Zoltan and asked for the prices of three—one of the Riviera, one of Norway, and one of Africa. The prices were not posted on the pictures, but kept decorously on a typewritten list in the pocket of Zoltan and of an assistant. The cheapest of all the canvases was priced at fifty thousand francs, and the three which the old couple wanted came to a quarter of a million, or about ten thousand dollars. That didn't seem to worry them a bit; the man wrote out a check on a Paris bank and asked about arrangements to have the pictures shipped. Nothing was to be taken away until the exhibition was over.

Then an English couple, identifying themselves to Lanny as

friends of Rosemary, Countess of Sandhaven. This was a swanky young pair, dressed up to the last minute, the man with a monocle and the lady with a swagger-stick. She pointed it at a weather-beaten old Greek peasant, holding under his arm that little lamb which Mr. Hackabury had purchased and caused to be served for dinner on the yacht *Bluebird*. "How much is that one?" asked the Honorable "Babs" Blesingham, and when Zoltan said: "A hundred and seventy-five thousand francs," she exclaimed indignantly: "Oh, but that is cheek!"

Zoltan, who knew the manners of the British aristocracy, replied: "Your grandchildren may sell it for five thousand pounds, my lady."

She frowned as if she were doing mental arithmetic; then she said: "Well, anyhow, I like it. Send it around to my hotel when you're ready."

Zoltan, sure of himself and not awed either by smart costumes or by insolent manners, replied: "We are not reserving anything, my lady. If you wish to be sure of it, be so good as to make it definite."

"All right, Reggie, give him a check." Just as if she were tossing a five-sou piece to a beggar!

In the midst of all these excitements came the Robins. They had seen some of the paintings at Bienvenu, and now they saw them all, and were so excited that they wrote a long letter to Papa, enclosing some of the bought-and-paid-for newspaper clippings. The result was a telegram to Lanny, directing that the boys with Lanny's advice were to select a million francs' worth of the Detazes and have them shipped to him. Papa had just bought a palace in the suburbs of Berlin, it was revealed, and they were going to move into it, and Marcel's landscapes would hang on the marble walls of a very grand entrance hall where the proudest Prussian nobility had trod. Quite a step upward for a Jew who had been raised in a hut with a mud floor; also for a painter who had lived in a cabin on the Cap d'Antibes and dressed most of the time in a workman's blouse and a pair of corduroy trousers smeared with all the colors he had put on a hundred canvases!

Lanny couldn't give much time to the boys right then, but he had told Mrs. Emily about them, and they went out to Les Forêts and played for her. She fell in love with them as Lanny knew she must; she invited musicians to hear them, and made them happy with her praise. She was one person who had no trace of prejudice against the Jews; if they had better brains that was the hard luck of the Gallic and Anglo-Saxon races! Lanny wasn't so sure about Marie; but she knew how he admired this pair, and she couldn't fail to invite them to her home and have them meet her two boys, who were of nearly the same age and whose musical tastes she wished to cultivate. Hansi was a good example for anybody's sons, for all could see how hard he had worked and what a reward of happiness he had won in his mastery of a great musical instrument. The boys made friends gladly and when the *Schieber* heard how his dear ones had been received in two *châteaux*, he could consider that he had got double value for his million francs.

IV

The Budd family arrived on schedule. They had reservations at the Crillon, Lanny's place of memories; he went there to see them as soon as the boat-train arrived. Six years and a half had passed since he had left their home; he had changed a lot, and wondered how it would be with them.

It seemed to him that his stepmother hadn't changed at all. She was one of those cool, quiet persons upon whom the years made little impression; tall and still slender, with no wrinkles about her eyes, no gray in her straight brown hair. She had parted from her strange stepson on friendly terms, and greeted him as if it had been last week. She had come to his world, where he would play the host and she would accept his kindnesses as he had accepted hers; she wouldn't approve of all that she saw, but she would be carefully polite, watch over her children, study the guide-books with them, learn history and art—but not manners and surely not morals.

Robert, junior, was twenty and Percy a year younger. They were handsome, upstanding fellows who had enjoyed the best possible upbringing, and had played football in prep school; both were at Yale, the target which Lanny had been aimed at but had missed.

They were still repressed, and knew that it wasn't good form to show much excitement over being in a foreign country; but they had their own ideas about Paris, which they would reveal to Lanny before long. Their main desire was to get away from mother and Miss Sutton, the gray-haired lady who had been Bess's governess and had been as it were adopted; she traveled with the party as a combination of companion and secretary, doing the telephoning, buying the tickets, running the errands. No Budd would do anything so vulgar as to enlist among the "Cookies."

Bess was the one in whom Lanny had been interested in Newcastle. They had kept their promise not to forget each other, and had exchanged letters now and then, telling the news and enclosing snapshots. So Lanny knew that his half-sister had turned into a very proper young miss of seventeen; she was going to be tall, like her mother, and now she was what the English call "leggy." She had her mother's high round forehead and rather thin nose, but her brown hair was unruly like her father's; her upper lip was a little short, which made her smile rather quaint. She had candid brown eyes, and an expression of eagerness which mother and governess combined had been unable to subdue. Bess wanted to know, and not to have somebody tell her. She wanted to see Europe so eagerly that it hurt; she had kept her face pressed to the window of the train and of the taxicab. "Oh, Mummy, look!" Mummy would say: "Yes, dear." She had learned that it didn't do much good to say "Don't."

Now her wonderful half-brother was going to show her Paris: the Louvre, Notre Dame, Versailles, the Eiffel Tower— "Is that the Obelisk over there, Lanny? And is that really the Place de la Concorde? Have they taken away all the big guns? Is the picture exhibition still going? Mummy, can't we go over and see it right now?"

Esther wasn't ready to go out yet; she wanted time to prepare for the ordeal of meeting her husband's ex-mistress, who she had to pretend was an ex-wife; that was what Paris meant to a daughter of the Puritans, and no wonder she didn't like it in her heart. But she could think of no reason why Lanny shouldn't take the children to see his stepfather's paintings; the place was only five minutes' walk, he told them. So they set out, with the arrangement that they were to bring Beauty back for lunch.

Of course the three "children" had their curiosities about this mysterious mother of Lanny, about whom they had been told so little. Had the boys picked up any hint of the truth? If so, they were too well bred to reveal it. The Detaze show was the best of all places for them to meet the dubious charmer, with everybody paying court to her and two portraits presenting her in the best possible light—but not that naked one, which was safely locked in the storeroom at home!

Anybody who met Beauty could see that she was a kind soul. Naturally, she was in a flutter over meeting Esther's children, but then she was always in something of a flutter. She was still nearly as eager as Bess, interested in everybody and everything that came along. She wanted Robbie's children to approve of her, and she even had hopes that she might win their mother's regard.

The young people looked at the pictures, and Lanny told them the stories, and it was a most interesting lecture, something that couldn't have been had in Connecticut. It took them over the Mediterranean lands, and to the fiords of the Northland; it took them through the war, and taught them about French patriotism, as well as suffering and horror. The very elegant Hungarian art expert lent his aid, explaining the fine points about Marcel's technique. When the morning was over, the young Budds could never doubt that Lanny's mother had been married to a great painter. The prices asked for his work would have convinced them of that! Moreover, Mr. Kertezsi had told them that the French government had just purchased a Detaze for the Luxembourg. (He didn't tell them that he had let the government have it for a couple of thousand francs, so that he might have something with which to impress Americans.)

V

They went back to the hotel, where Beauty and Esther came face to face. The young people didn't realize that anything special was

going on; they took divorces more as a matter of course than did
their mother and, besides, young people are rarely interested in their
elders' states of mind unless these are forced upon their attention.
Assuredly that wouldn't be done by either of these disciplined ladies.
It is one of women's duties to cover over and conceal the scars, the
defacements, the wreckage caused by the sexual divagations of the
male animal. Robbie Budd's two women kept smiling hard; Esther
asked questions about the exhibition and Beauty answered them;
both ordered something to eat and pretended to enjoy it. Meanwhile they measured each other, Beauty with tremulous concern,
Esther with steady, businesslike glances which seemed to say: "You
let me and mine alone and I'll let you and yours alone."

Really there wasn't any reason for their getting into each other's
hair. Esther didn't begrudge the thousand dollars a month which
Robbie paid to his former mistress, or the simple villa he had given
her. In order to put his wife's mind at peace concerning his frequent
visits to Bienvenu, Robbie had told her about Beauty's new lover.
That, of course, seemed disgusting to a daughter of the Puritans; but
so long as Esther didn't have to go there or to let the children go
there, it wasn't her concern. She was prepared to believe that her
husband's former mistress was no worse than most of the women
who left their own country in order to enjoy the license of France.
Esther knew how many had come in order to escape Prohibition,
and she considered it a good riddance. Now when she saw this
Madame Detaze, blooming so offensively, finding such pleasure in
having paintings of herself hung in a gallery for the public to stare
at, she was glad that the family program allowed only a week's stay
in Paris, and none at all on that dreadful "Coast of Pleasure."

Knowing how her husband loved his first-born son and was determined to protect him, Esther said how greatly all her friends had
been pleased with the Böcklins which Lanny had selected for her.
It was her intention to visit the exhibition and perhaps acquire one
or more Detazes for her home. Beauty said: "Frankly, we have put
the prices very high because we don't want to sell too many. I'll tell
Mr. Kertezsi to make them right for you." Esther replied: "Not at
all! Please let me pay what anybody else would pay." That might be

a way of making friends; or it might be a way of patronizing your husband's cast-off sweetheart. How difficult to be sure!

VI

Lanny said: "I hope you are free for tomorrow, for Mrs. Emily has asked me to bring you out to Les Forêts. Hansi and Freddi Robin are coming, and she has invited friends to hear Hansi play." Esther knew about Mrs. Chattersworth, and she had heard much about the Robin boys, their father being her husband's partner in so many profitable enterprises. She replied that they would enjoy visiting a great French château, and of course they must hear the young musician.

Lanny motored the family, Bess riding beside him and the mother and the boys in back. All the way it was history: the flight of King Louis and Marie Antoinette from Paris, and then the battle of the Marne, the first one, in which the Château Les Forêts had been so nearly wrecked, and the second one, in which Marcel Detaze had given his life to save Paris. Lanny told how the Germans had dumped the furniture of the château out of the windows, and how the old librarian had died of a broken heart. He told how Anatole France had talked on the lawn—the old gentleman had passed away just recently and had had a grand funeral in Paris. He told how Isadora had danced in the drawing-room—but not how she had tried to take her musician for a ride!

They arrived at the estate, and in the drawing-room where the best wits of modern France had exercised themselves the châtelaine received them graciously and introduced them to her guests—one of them the shepherd boy out of ancient Judea, the tall young David who had played the harp before the mad King Saul, the minstrel who had heard the voice of the Lord. At the luncheon table Hansi and Bess sat opposite, and each looked into the other's face and found something that neither had ever seen before. Bess saw fire in those large dark eyes; in the ascetic face she saw exquisite sensitiveness, as of someone who had come from a world where things were better.

Hansi saw what seemed to him the face of all his dreams, that would live in all the music he played from that hour forth. Each of them saw eager intelligence, asking a thousand questions of life and rarely satisfied with the answers it got.

In due course Hansi took his violin and stood by Mrs. Emily's grand piano, with Lanny sitting before it. On the rack was the piano part of Beethoven's violin concerto, a composition born of the master's deep stress. When Hansi sounded the opening theme it was as if the gates of heaven swung suddenly open before Bessie Budd; this strange-looking, tall young Jew took on the aspect of an archangel descending from the skies. She had never known that such sounds could be produced on earth. She needed nobody to explain this music, nobody to point out first and second themes, working out portions, modulations, harmonic intervals, or other technicalities; the music took her into its arms and carried her along through the many moods of which the human soul is capable. When Hansi came to the slow movement, the tears streamed down the maiden's cheeks; no use trying to stop them, she didn't even know they were there. Her mother, who never forgot the proprieties, not even for Beethoven, gazed at her in dismay. Bess's eyes were fixed as if she were in a trance; her jaw hung loose, as if she were trying to absorb the music through her mouth; she looked silly, and her mother wanted to nudge her—but unfortunately she was out of reach.

Esther was fond of music, or so she would have said; but she liked it to have dignity and restraint. She had been made uncomfortable by watching the seventeen-year-old Lanny in her home, pounding the piano as he did, losing himself so completely in it that he wouldn't know when his stepmother entered the room. Now here were two of them in that state, and no doubt it represented a lot of study and hard work, it was considered to be "classical," and all that; but the daughter of the Puritans disliked it, just as she would have disliked Beethoven if she had seen him composing it—roaming through the fields, waving his arms and shouting, or pacing up and down in his room, muttering to himself, rolling his eyeballs, carrying on like a crazy person.

VII

That stormy composition came to its end; and Esther was fully prepared to find that all the other persons in this drawing-room considered it a great work, or would pretend to. She was used to the idea that she was fighting against the current of her time, and wasn't succeeding in stopping it. Only the little bit around her, the members of her own family! Seeing her daughter sitting as if she thought the music was still being played, the mother arose and went to her and whispered: "Please, dear, try not to carry on so!" Bess started from her trance, and the mother went back to her seat and listened to excitable foreigners expressing their admiration for rare musical technique. Of course this dark-eyed Jewish youth loved his music, and maybe it was all right for him, it kept him busy and happy—but what did it do to people who let themselves get worked up to such frenzies?

They wanted him to play more, and the hostess said: "Some of your Jewish music." Her wish was a command, and Hansi, with his brother accompanying, played a new work called *Nigun*, from the *Baal Shem* suite of Ernest Bloch. This music of grief and despair Esther could understand better; she knew a great deal about the Jews, their ancient literature having been taught to her as Holy Writ. God in His dealings with His chosen people had of course been God, and you couldn't criticize Him; but the Jews in their dealings with God had been another matter, and Esther had got the feeling that they had been noisy, presumptuous, and disobedient, and had deserved most of the troubles that He had sent to them.

Their modern descendants in Newcastle, Connecticut, kept clothing-stores and drove shrewd bargains—to put it mildly. When Esther had learned from her husband that he had gone into business deals with one of them in Europe, mainly in order to please Lanny, she had been prepared for the worst, and when it didn't happen, she explained it by saying that of course a Jewish speculator had much to gain by keeping Robert Budd for a friend; he and his family aspired to rise in the world by attaching their fortunes to those of a prominent New England family. When Robbie came back and reported that the two sons of his partner were fine musicians and that one might be a genius, that was part of the same thing to Robbie's wife; now she saw the outcome—they had gained access to an elegant French château, and the musical genius was casting his net over Esther Budd's susceptible young daughter!

Esther couldn't find any fault with Hansi personally; she couldn't deny that he was of refined appearance and excellent manners; but that only made matters worse, it deprived the mother of any pretext for interfering with the operations of destiny. When she saw her daughter listening to Ravel's *Kaddisch* in that uncomfortable state of semi-hypnosis, she couldn't scold her publicly or drag her off privately. When Bess told Hansi how much she had enjoyed his playing, and when he told her that he would be delighted to come and play for her again, what could the mother do to break it up?

She learned to her dismay that the two Jewish youths were staying in Paris, and that Lanny was taking it for granted that they would be a part of the various sight-seeing expeditions. He had arranged for one to Versailles; he was telling now about the Île de la Cité and the sights to be seen there—Notre Dame, the Conciergerie where Marie Antoinette had been a prisoner, an old barracks occupied by the Sûreté Générale, where Lanny himself had been a prisoner on the day the treaty of Versailles was signed. He was telling the young people how he had been suspected of being a Red agent; he said it was a mistake of the police, but Esther knew about Lanny's Red uncle and wished very much that he wouldn't mention such unpleasant subjects to her carefully guarded children.

VIII

Whatever sins Esther Budd might have committed during her life she paid for during that unhappy week in Paris. She couldn't bring herself to break up their long-planned schedule. What excuse could she give for dragging the children away without seeing those sights about which they had been talking for months—yes, for years, ever since Lanny had brought his dubious glamour into their home? She couldn't say to her stepson: "We would rather see Paris by ourselves." Nor could she say: "We prefer not to have your young friends with us." Rack her brains as she might, she failed to find any reason why the Robin boys shouldn't stroll about the grounds and the palaces of Versailles with her children. Being Jews, they were bound to be on the lookout for slights, and Robbie had said: "If you meet those young Robins in Paris, be polite to them, because I've made a pile of money through their father." When Robbie used such a phrase, it meant a pile!

So there was nothing Esther could do but keep watch; and that didn't seem to do any good at all, for what was happening was like a river flood, it went on regardless of spectators. It was plainly a case of the distressing phenomenon known as "love at first sight," but it took forms to which the most exacting chaperon could make no objection. All that Bess wanted, apparently, was to listen to Hansi and her half-brother play duets. She wanted to hear everything they knew, and then hear it all over again, while she sat in her ridiculous pose, looking like St. Cecilia at the organ as painted by the German Naujok, a print of which Esther had hanging in her bedroom— never dreaming that it would come to life and plague her like this!

As for Hansi, he made matters more difficult by being so respectful that the mother couldn't find the slightest flaw in his conduct. Apparently he was so stricken with admiration for Bess that he couldn't bear so much as to touch her hand, hardly even to look at her continuously. Of course that was the right attitude for a Jewish lad of no family to take to a daughter of the Brahmin Budds, and if it hadn't been for Bess's temperament it might have been all right; but was Bess going to be content to sit on a throne the rest of her days and have this young genius kneel before her and bow his head in adoration? Not if Esther knew anything about her daughter—and she thought she did!

This torment went on during the excursion to Versailles and the one to Saint-Cloud. It went on amid the architectural glories of Notre Dame, the historial associations of the Hôtel de Ville, and even on top of the Eiffel Tower. It went on when Lanny purchased tickets and took them all to see Sacha Guitry. It went on in all the interims between excursions—for Lanny, in his role of young prince, had

had a piano brought up to the family suite, and lugged over a stack
of music which he had in his rooms, and at Bess's suggestion Hansi
kept his violin in the suite, so that every shining hour might be im-
proved by the master-spirits of the past two centuries. Respect for
"culture" required Esther to sit there and pretend to enjoy what was
really an indecent spectacle, this open and public mating of two
souls.

IX

The mother had had the fond idea that her little family of four,
plus Miss Sutton, would "do" Europe as a group. But now it developed that the boys didn't want to sit in a hotel room, however
elegant, and listen to violin sonatas, however well played. They
wanted to see Paris. Lanny knew what this meant, for "Junior" had
approached him rather timidly and asked for help in getting away
from his mother and the rest, so that they might visit some of the
"hot spots." These two youths had heard talk among the younger
brothers of returned soldiers about the sights that were to be seen in
such places; naked women dancing on the stage, and even more
startling things. To come all the way across the ocean and miss them
would mean being cheated badly.

Lanny didn't show surprise, for he had met other Americans in
Paris, and not all of them young. He surprised his half-brothers by
telling them that, though he had lived here most of his life, he hadn't
ever been to those places. He said that they were run mostly for
tourists, and that the French themselves didn't go. He talked with the
pair frankly and learned that their father had done for them what he
had done for Lanny in his time—that is, warned them about venereal
diseases and the predatory nature of prostitutes, but he hadn't tried
to teach them anything about idealism in sex. It was rather late now,
because both boys had had experiences with girls in their factory
town. Lanny told them that they really wouldn't find naked women
so interesting; it was just a question of what one was used to—and
why not try the Rubenses in the Louvre? It was cheaper and a lot
safer.

Esther didn't know any of this, but she had her fears, and wasn't going to turn those boys loose on the streets of this most wicked of cities. She realized that it would seem rather absurd to send a gray-haired governess with them, so she found excuses to go herself. She thought that it was safe to leave Bess and Hansi together, so long as Lanny played accompaniments; but that was only because Esther didn't understand the many kinds of love-making which modern music has made possible. Hansi played Rubinstein's *Sphärenmusik* and Bess fell in love with him one way, and then he played Schumann's *Widmung* and she fell in love with him another way. He played the César Franck *Sonata*, which they had once played for Barbara; that set them to talking about an Italian syndicalist martyr—which caused Bess to fall in love in the most dangerous way of all!

She said she wanted to understand these ideas, but nobody would talk to her; either they didn't know or they didn't want her to know. Were the Socialists and Communists as bad as they were painted? What did Hansi believe about them and what did Lanny believe?—please tell her, and of course they did. Hansi expounded his beautiful dream of a world in which no man would exploit any other man's labor, but in which the great machines would be used to produce abundance, so that all might have a share; no child would know hunger, no old person would be homeless, no man would shed his brother's blood. It was an ancient Hebrew dream—Hansi quoted the prophet Isaiah: "And they shall build houses, and inhabit them; and they shall plant vineyards, and eat the fruit of them. They shall not build, and another inhabit; they shall not plant, and another eat; for as the days of a tree are the days of my people, and mine elect shall long enjoy the work of their hands."

A wonderful Hebrew dream, twenty-five centuries old, but it hadn't come true yet, and wasn't apt to during the lifetime of Bess's grandfather, the president of Budd Gunmakers, or of her other grandfather, the president of the First National Bank of Newcastle, Connecticut. The latter's daughter came in during this conversation, and it didn't stop when she appeared, for the reason that Bess had become kindled with the ancient Hebrew fire. Said she: "I always knew that it was wicked for some people to have so much and others to have nothing! . . . Oh, Mummy, you must hear what Hansi says about how machinery can make all the things we need now, so that nobody has to be poor!"

Lanny could understand everything that his half-sister felt, having been through it all when he was younger than she was. The sparks from the divine flame had leaped from Barbara's soul to his; they had leaped to the souls of the two Jewish lads, and so had been carried from Juan to Rotterdam and to Berlin; now apparently they were going to be carried from Paris to New England! What fuel would they find on that stern and rockbound coast? Lanny knew that the fire of social justice changes those whom it touches; it fills them with fervor and consecration, or else with irritation and rage. Impossible for Esther to conceal what was in her mind as she said: "Yes, dear. It is time for you to get ready for dinner."

X

At home in Bienvenu, before coming on this expedition, Lanny and his mother and Marie had discussed the entertainment of these guests from the land of the Pilgrims' pride. Lanny had thought of the Château de Bruyne as a delightful place for them to visit, for tea at least; and of Denis, *fils*, and Charlot, as French boys who would interest three young Americans. But Marie had said it was impossible; no woman could see her with Lanny and not become suspicious; Robbie's wife would think that he had committed an indecency in bringing her children to the scene of his offense against morality. "But how can she find out?" he argued; and his *amie* replied: "Women have a thousand ways of finding out. Suppose one of my boys makes a remark about your having stayed in our home, helped them with their piano lessons, gone fishing with them, played tennis—anything at all? Wouldn't your stepmother take notice?"

This discussion occurred in the intervals of a bridge game, and the fourth hand was M. Rochambeau, old friend of the family. A retired diplomat had time for reading, and he told Lanny about a novel by an American expatriate named Henry James; it was called *The Ambassadors*, and Lanny borrowed it. He was bewildered at first, but he put his mind upon the disentangling of those tremendous sentences, carrying a heavier burden of qualifications, reservations, modifications, stipulations, circumstantiations, elucidations, and other assorted subtleties than had ever before been crowded between two small black dots on a printed page. But finally he got into the story, and of course saw himself in that expatriate Bostonian, and watched the uncovering of his deadly sin in Paris. He finished the book before he left Juan, fully decided in his mind not to take the chance of bringing Marie's and Esther's progeny together.

What happened was that Marie chanced to visit the exposition at a time when Esther and her brood were there, and Lanny hardly dared speak a civil word to his *amie* in his stepmother's presence. After the ordeal was over and he met Marie at their rendezvous, she gave him proof of the strange intuitive powers of the experienced woman of society. Said she: "Your sister and Hansi have fallen in love."

"Oh, surely not!" exclaimed the stupid male creature.

"They are so much in love that their eyes cannot meet without a flutter."

"I thought she was moved by his music."

"Women aren't moved by music," declared Marie. "Women are moved by musicians."

XI

A day or two later Hansi came to Lanny and confessed. Bess was leaving in a couple of days, and he might never see her again. What should he do? He couldn't keep the tears from his eyes.

Lanny talked it out with him. He said that, so far as he personally was concerned, he thought it would be a grand match, and he would try to make it. Doubtless it would win him the everlasting enmity of his stepmother, who was bound to have some high state enterprise in mind—it would be the Empress Maria Theresa of Austria and her daughter Marie Antoinette.

"How will your father feel about it?" Hansi wanted to know.

"Robbie's a pretty good sport," replied Lanny. "He has some of the fashionable prejudices—we've got to face the facts, you know, Hansi."

"Of course. I know I'm a Jew."

"Robbie likes your father, and he admires you. He doesn't know much about music, but if you make a success he will hear about it."

"I *must* make a success, Lanny! I have waited too long!" Poor Hansi's proud aloofness had been knocked into a cocked hat.

"You're both young yet."

"Listen, Lanny—this is important. I have an old teacher who has moved to New York. He was in Berlin this spring and heard me play, and said he might get me a chance to make my debut with the New York Symphony there."

"Oh, grand! That would be a wallop!"

"You think Bess would come to hear me?"

"Of course she'd come. Maybe I could pull wires and arrange for you to give a concert in Newcastle. After the New York appearance, of course!"

Lanny advised Hansi to speak to Bess, but said he couldn't do it; his teeth chattered when he even thought of it. And, besides, what chance did he have? They wouldn't leave him alone with her for a minute. He could only speak with his music, and hope that she would get its meaning. Lanny replied that while program music was supposed to portray all sorts of natural phenomena, he didn't know any that would set a date for a wedding.

XII

They were going to the Louvre that afternoon. Lanny spent some time explaining the *Mona Lisa* to his half-sister, pointing out its qualities and telling her about Leonardo. When the others moved on he said: "Let's stroll the other way. I want to show you something."

They strolled; and perhaps Esther noticed it, but she couldn't very well object, for she had Hansi by her side, and it was of him that she was afraid. Lanny took Bess to a seat and got her firmly settled so that she wouldn't keel over; then he said: "Look here, kid; Hansi's in love with you."

She caught her hands together. "Oh, Lanny!" and then again: "Oh, Lanny!" Lovers are rarely original, and what seems eloquence to them doesn't impress a third party, the sober man at the feast. "Lanny, are you *sure?*"

"He has chills and fever whenever he speaks your name."

"Oh, dear, I'm so happy!"

"Did you think you weren't good enough for him?"

"I thought I didn't have anything he'd care for. I'm just a stupid child."

"Well, he assumes that you'll grow up."

"Will he wait for me?"

"I'm sure he will, if you ask him to."

"But he ought to ask *me*, Lanny!"

"He's too frightened of our god-awful family."

"But Hansi is a wonderful person! He has more than all of us put together."

"In his heart I dare say he knows it; but he doesn't think that we know it. It'll make the devil of a row, you know, for you to marry a Jew."

"Tell me, Lanny, do you think there's anything wrong with the Jews?"

"Bless your heart, old dear, there are so many things wrong with all of us—thee and me included."

"But I mean—so many people look down on them. What is the reason?"

"Well, Mrs. Emily thinks they have better brains than we have; or maybe they work them harder."

"Jesus was a Jew, Lanny!"

"I know; but the rest of them treated him badly, and they've been paying for it ever since."

"Lanny, I ought to tell Mummy, don't you think?"

"Indeed, I think it's the last thing on earth you should do!"

"But I want to be fair to her and Father!"

"If you tell her, you'll just keep her in misery, and she'll do the same for you. If you part friends with Hansi, she'll hope that you'll forget him, and you can go on with your school work without any fuss."

"But Hansi and I will have to write to each other."

"Write nice friendly letters—'All well, and hope to see you soon.' Tell him the news, and let your mother see his letters. Sign them all, 'yours truly'—that's enough."

"Are you sure it'll be enough for Hansi?"

"He'll be walking on the clouds until the day comes."

"And then what, Lanny?"

"Wait until you're eighteen; then, if you haven't changed your mind, tell your mother that you're going to get married."

"How will she take it?"

"Pretty hard, I imagine; you'll have to be ready for the worst. But have your mind made up, and don't give way. It's your affair; it means more to you than it can mean to anybody else." He thought for a space and then added: "Perhaps it might be wiser to go to Robbie first and get him on your side. You'll have a hold on him, because Grandfather broke up his love affair when he was young, and he knows how it feels. He told me all about it, and he took it terribly hard. Remind him of it, and that will break him down!"

24

To Madness Near Allied

I

THE new Tory government of England rejected the Geneva Protocol, which had been planned to bring peace to Europe by the method of boycotting aggressor states. The British gave several reasons, the most important being that the United States refused to pledge its support to the program. If the aggressor could buy all he needed from one great country, the other countries would be depriving their businessmen of profitable trade to no purpose. That statement set everybody in the States to debating; the Wilsonites, of whom there were many, insisted that their country was betraying the hopes of mankind. The crippled champion of internationalism had been in his grave more than a year, but his arguments lived on, and Lanny listened and as usual saw both sides of a complicated question.

Robbie Budd came over on some of his many affairs. He was the plumed knight of isolationism, riding at the head of the procession with a pennon on his lance. He said that both Britain and France were stumbling in the march of history, and might soon fall out. They were adhering to antiquated methods in industry and refusing to modernize their plants. America, on the other hand, renewed its machinery every decade, and could turn out goods faster and better than any other nation. All we had to do was to arm ourselves and be ready to meet all comers, but keep out of other people's quarrels. Let them destroy themselves if they wanted to; on that basis the world would be ours.

Robbie worshiped a deity known as *laissez faire*. Let manufacturers everywhere produce what goods they pleased and offer them in whatever market they could find; let government keep its hands off, and the intelligent men of the United States would make prosperity permanent. In the old days there had been crises and panics, but Robbie said that modern technology had solved that problem; mass production of goods at ever-cheapening prices was the answer to everything. Employers could afford to pay high wages, money would buy more and more, the workers would attain an ever-higher standard of living. The solution of this problem was America's; no other nation could approach her, and the one thing she had to fear was political demagogues throwing monkeywrenches into the machinery. Robbie said he didn't know why that name had been given to a useful tool, but it fitted the politicians who presumed to meddle with the production and distribution of goods.

Fortunately, the country had that most admirable of presidents, that strong silent statesman who never interfered with anything, but was happy to stroll through the power-plant and listen to the rich humming of the dynamos. Nobody was going to get Cautious Cal into any sort of foreign entanglement, no one was going to get him to stop any American oil man or munitions man from selling his products wherever in the world he could find a customer with the cash. The Vermont country storekeeper's son was going to sit tight in the comfortable mansion which the government provided him and save all he could of the $6125 per month which would fall due to him, up to and including the fourth day of March 1929. To Robbie Budd that was equivalent to saying that God was in His heaven and all was right with the world.

Robbie himself was "sitting pretty," but of course in a much more highly priced seat. He never told his son just how much his services to his country were bringing him, but from one sign and another Lanny knew that it was a very large sum. When Lanny said that he no longer needed the three hundred a month that his father was sending him, Robbie smiled and said it would be too much of an effort remembering to tell his secretary to stop it. When Bub Smith presented a bill for salary and expenses incurred in certain confidential work having to do with Standard Oil in the Near East, Robbie glanced at the account and read: "Eight thousand one hundred and seventy-five dollars and twenty-eight cents." He wrote a check for ten thousand, and remarked: "I couldn't manage to get all those figures straight."

II

A delightful thing to have such a father—and a temptation to agree with him on matters of business and finance. Very certainly the system of *laissez faire* was vindicating itself so far as it concerned Lanny Budd's own affairs. That system was pouring thousands of rich people into the playground of Europe, their pockets bulging with more money than they knew how to spend; quite literally bulging, for Lanny met men who thought nothing of carrying a hundred thousand-franc notes in a billfold, and when he asked one of them why he did it, the answer was: "Well, I might want to invite you to lunch." If these people had any culture at all—and many of them did—it was the easiest thing in the world to seduce them with the prestige of great paintings. Lanny's position became that of the fishermen on the rivers of Oregon during the latter part of the month of July; catching salmon becomes a labor, not a sport, and one never wants to see or smell or taste another fish.

People came every day and begged to look at Detazes, until that too became a nuisance; you had heard everything said that could be said, and you suspected the motives of people who posed as your friends and hoped to get a lower figure. "Boost the prices," Robbie said—that being the businessman's way of reducing an excessive demand. But it didn't seem to work in the case of art, for there was no way to determine the cost of a canvas; it was worth what you could get, and the more you asked, the more the customer seemed to value it. The dealers would come, and when you showed reluctance to sell they would assume that it was a business maneuver, and would go on making offers until it became fantastic. Lanny thought this couldn't last, but Zoltan was in command, and he said there might be a break in the case of work that was faddish, but not for solid merit like Marcel's. Ask a high price, pay some of the money as a tip to get the high price talked about in the papers—and then you could ask still higher prices!

Lanny had so much money that he didn't know what to do with it, and had to ask his father's advice. To Robbie that was a delightful experience; to have this playboy, of whose future on its practical side he had begun to despair, come of his own free will and ask how to invest a hundred thousand dollars that he had earned without a stroke of help from his father—well, that was something to go home and tell to the old man of the Budd tribe! Robbie sat down and made out a schedule of what he called a "portfolio," a list of gilt-edged stocks and bonds which his son was to acquire. Robbie took as much interest in it as if it had been one of those crossword puzzles which had become the rage. He wanted to explain it to Lanny item by item—A. & P., A. T. & T., A. T. & S. F.—as if Lanny could ever remember all those initials! The son wrote a check on his bank in Cannes, the father sent a cablegram, and, by the magic which American businessmen had contrived, all those valuable pieces of paper were in a vault in Lanny's name before he had gone to sleep that evening. Robbie estimated that his son would enjoy an income of more than seven hundred dollars a month for the rest of his days, and without ever doing anything but signing his name. How could anybody question the soundness of a world in which such a miracle could be wrought?

Yet Lanny couldn't keep himself from performing that unreasonable mental action. No longer an innocent child, he looked about him at the idlers of this Côte d'Azur and they had ceased to appear glamorous. He saw gambling and drinking and assorted vice, and what seemed to him an orgy of foolish and profitless activity. He saw swarms of parasites preying upon the rich, getting their money by a thousand devices, few of them so harmless as persuading them to purchase old masters. He saw, too, the signs of poverty and strain; when he went into the great cities he was made sick by the spectacle of human degradation, and he had too much brains to be able to salve his conscience by giving a coin to a beggar now and then, as some of his kind-hearted friends would do.

The spacious drawing-room of Bienvenu was cool on hot days, and a generous open fire kept it warm on cold nights. In it were courtesy, kindness, love, and every kind of beauty that the skills of men had been able to create: oriental rugs of rich harmonious colors on the floor, inspired paintings on the walls, long shelves full of masterpieces of literature old and new, the music of a piano, a phonograph, and the newly devised radio at command. But outside, waves of human misery beat against the foundations and winds of social rage howled about the eaves. The ladies of this house cried to Lanny: "Why have we worked so hard to make safety and comfort for you, only to see you go out into the midst of storm and danger? Is it because we haven't done our duty? Is it lack of devotion or of charm on our part that you wish to throw yourself into a chaos of clamoring greeds and hates?"

III

In Cannes lived a Spanish youth by the name of Raoul Palma. He was an ardent Socialist, and had brought a letter of introduction from Jean Longuet; "a faithful party worker," was the editor's phrase. Physically Raoul was a study for a painter; slender yet active, with delicately chiseled features and an expression of sweetness almost feminine—Lanny wished that Marcel had been there to immortalize him. The young man spoke all the languages of the Latin tribes, and had a good education, but worked in a shoe-store because that appeared to be the only employment available to one who wished to spend his evenings agitating for Socialism among the workers.

Cannes was thought of as a playground for the rich; a city of lovely villas and gardens, a paradise of fashionable elegance. Few stopped to realize what a mass of labor was required to maintain that cleanliness and charm: not merely the servants who dwelt on the estates, but porters and truckdrivers, scrubwomen and chambermaids, kitchen-workers, food-handlers, and scores of obscure occupations which the rich never heard about. These people were housed in slum warrens, that "cabbage patch" where Lanny's Red uncle had taken him to meet Barbara Pugliese. The ladies and gentlemen of fashion didn't know that such places existed; they could hardly believe you when you told them—and they wouldn't thank you for having told them.

If the slums of the Riviera were ever to be razed and decent housing provided, it could only be through the action of the workers themselves; the rich wouldn't make any move unless they were forced. The question was whether it was to be done by the method which the world had seen in Russia and didn't like so well, or whether it could be carried out by orderly democratic process, such as the workers of Vienna and other Socialist cities were proceeding to apply. Which way you chose determined whether you called yourself a Communist or a Socialist; whether your opponents named you Red or Pink. Raoul Palma, idealist and something of a saint, persisted in advocating the patient and peaceful way. His hobby was what he called "workers' education"; he wanted to get the tired laborers to come to school at night and learn the rudiments of modern economic theory: just how their labor was exploited and just what they could do about it. He wanted a Socialist Sunday school, to which the workers' children might come and learn those facts which were not taught in schools conducted by their masters.

Raoul had got a little group together, and they had raised a few francs from their earnings and bought pencils and paper and set to work, at first in an open shed in summer, then in an unused store-room. They needed more money; and how could Lanny, believing what he did, fail to help them? He rented a proper room with a stove to heat it when the mistral blew; when he saw how pathetically grateful they were, and how fast the enterprise expanded, he offered the young leader a pension of fifty francs a week, about two dollars, so that he might retire from the business of fitting shoes on ladies' feet and devote all his time to workers' education. Lanny would go now and then to the Sunday school, and thereby he acquired a number of what the ladies of his family considered undesirable acquaintances; he learned the names of a swarm of little brats who of course didn't know that they were brats, and would come running up to greet him when he was on his way into a fashionable hotel or restaurant, throwing their arms about him and calling him "Comrade Lanny"; which was hardly *en règle*, to say the least.

Lanny had entertained his little half-sister with Beethoven's *Contra-Dances:* delightful tunes with pronounced rhythms, to which she and Nina's children would caper about the room like incipient Isadoras. Why not have an entertainment for the children of the workers, and give them a chance to develop their latent talents? If Lanny could have had his way he would have brought the whole troop to Bienvenu and let them dance on the loggia, and Marceline with them; but the bare idea frightened Beauty out of a night's sleep. To her the very word "workers" spelt Red revolution and bloodshed; she had White Russian friends in Cannes and elsewhere who told her terrible stories of the outrages from which they had escaped. Out of the kindness of her heart, Beauty gave these people money, and a part of it went to maintain White Russian papers and propaganda in Paris. So Beauty's money worked against Lanny's money, and perhaps neutralized it. Lanny went and rented for one evening a sort of beer-garden in a workers' district, and there he had a party and played Beethoven's *Country Dances* for his little Red and Pink *gamins*.

IV

In October of that year 1925 the governing statesmen of the great nations of Europe gathered for an important conference at Locarno, a town on one of the Alpine lakes which are divided between Switzerland and Italy. Rick didn't attend this affair, because his new play had been accepted by one of the little theaters, and he was rewriting part of it, in spite of his literary *hauteur*. Lanny didn't go, because Marie wouldn't keep him company and it wasn't so much fun alone. He read accounts in the papers and magazines, some of them signed by men he knew. Everybody considered it the most important conference since the war; Lanny, who had seen so many of them, tried not to feel cynical about it.

Aristide Briand, the innkeeper's son, was Premier of France again, and had taken up the job which he had been forced to abandon at Cannes nearly four years earlier. This time he didn't need any fashionable ladies to get him together with the Germans; for now France had the Ruhr and was getting so little out of it that peace and disarmament were the *mots d'ordre*. The German Chancellor was still Stresemann, the pacifier, while the British Foreign Secretary was Sir Austen Chamberlain, a proper Conservative with a monocle, so whatever he did would be ratified by Parliament. For the first time since the war the great nations of Europe met as equals, and the word Allies was not spoken at a conference.

Of course the diplomats had been working behind the scenes for months, and had planned exactly what they were going to do. They adopted a series of treaties, renouncing war as an instrument of foreign policy. Germany pledged herself to arbitrate all disputes with her neighbors. All these proud nations abandoned a portion of their sovereignty, and the glad tidings went out over the earth that a new spirit had been born. Germany was to be admitted to the League of Nations, and hopes were held out that before long France would consent to withdraw from the Ruhr. The word Locarno became one of magic, from which all good things were expected. Currencies would become stable, trade and industry would revive, the unemployed would be put to work. Even disarmament agreements were being discussed.

All this, of course, struck a sour note with Robbie Budd and Zaharoff. Robbie had promised his father and brothers fresh trouble in Europe and all over the world, and so his prestige was at stake. It was expecting too much of human nature that he should credit the fine promises of statesmen looking for votes. Robbie wrote to his son that the Germans were buying arms through Dutch and Italian agents, and doubtless some of these arms were going through Locarno while the statesmen were in session. He said also that there was another famine in Russia, and that when the inevitable collapse in that chaotic land occurred, all the bordering nations would grab what they could and the fat would be in the fire. "I have a chance to buy some Budd stock," wrote the father. "Shall I add it to your portfolio? It will give you weight with the family."

V

An Italian refugee by the name of Angelotti came to the gate of Bienvenu, having a letter of introduction to Lanny. A servant admitted him, saying that Lanny was expected, and the man sat on the front veranda for an hour or more. Beauty saw him and considered him a sinister-looking person—many Italians have dark hair and eyes, and are reputed to be vengeful, and to carry stilettos and the like. Beauty's distrust of the Reds was of long standing—she having a brother among them. This visitor wanted money, of course; it was a kind of polite blackmail to which Lanny exposed himself, and what would they do if he refused their requests? A thankless thing, for such people rarely repaid, even with gratitude; according to their theories, all your money ought to belong to them, and in giving them a part you were doing less than justice. Beauty would have liked to give orders that all such strangers should be sent packing, but she couldn't very well, for the prosperous Lanny was now paying half the expenses of the place so that his mother might be able to pay her dressmakers and hairdressers and the rest.

It happened that there was a murder committed in Paris shortly afterward, and the police were reported to consider it political and to be looking for an Italian anarchist by the name of Angelotti. It may not have been the same man, but Lanny said that even if it had been he would have refused to worry, because such cases often represented police frame-ups, or perhaps newspaper efforts to discredit what they chose to call "subversive movements." Naturally, this statement caused Beauty distress of mind, and they had an argument, and afterward the mother was uneasy, because Lanny might feel that his rights in the home were being denied him, and he might take up the notion to go off and get a place where he could see his friends when he pleased.

Beauty and Marie shared this problem, consulting each other and worrying together. And of course Lanny knew about it; people can't keep things from each other when they are living in the same house. He would go out and spend his time with alarming-looking strangers; then he would find his *amie* looking hurt; he would ask her about it, and all her tact would be needed to keep a controversy from getting started.

VI

Beauty had other worries, more and more of them, and all centering on Kurt. A sense of doom hung over her, knowing that she had had no business to take a lover so much younger than herself, and that some day fate would present the bill and she would pay with her happiness. Day and night she watched her German idealist and studied him, trying to please him, making herself a slave to this strange being. Kurt was a man of conscience, and she could hold him only by being good; but it must be his peculiar kind of goodness. She would lose favor with him whenever she revealed an excess of worldly vanity; he would let her have a fling now and then, just as if she were a drunkard going off on a spree, but it mustn't last too long or cost too much, and then he would expect her to come home and be a good German *Hausfrau*, managing her servants and taking care of her child according to his ideas of discipline.

With the passing of the years Beauty had grown more and more pro-German in her feeling. Not publicly, for she couldn't expect her friends to agree, and the best she could achieve would be to keep them away from the subject. She wasn't a political person, and couldn't understand all the forces and factors involved in the struggle for the mastery of Europe. What she wanted was peace in her time, and she would not haggle about the price. The news that came from Locarno rejoiced her soul; at last Germany was going to be allowed to take her place in the sisterhood of nations, and to build up her foreign trade and be able to import food for her hungry children. Germany did really feed her children, and care for her aged, and build decent homes for the workers, all of which practices Beauty praised ardently—never dreaming that they had anything to do with the dreaded Socialism. When her brother Jesse came along and uttered one of his familiar cynicisms, that all capitalist states must have things which they could get only by war, Beauty gave him a scolding so severe that it both startled and amused him.

During the period of Beauty's "spree" in Paris, Kurt had stayed at the villa, working on one of his compositions. When he wanted company he would play music for Marceline, and teach her German folk songs; she had already begun piano practice under his direction—and it wasn't going to be any haphazard, hit-or-miss technique such as Lanny had acquired. Then a cousin of Kurt's came with his young bride to Nice to spend a part of the summer, and Kurt would get on the tram and ride to visit them. When the cool weather came, his aunt, the Frau Doktor Hofrat von und zu Nebenaltenberg, returned to the apartment in Cannes from which she had been rudely removed during the war; she had vowed that she would never come back, but her health was troubling her, and now the Locarno settlement decided her to give the French another trial. She had told her nephew that Lanny Budd's mother was *unschicklich*, so she could hardly be deceived by the pretense that Kurt was Lanny's music-teacher; but men have been known to do worse things than succumb to the wiles of a fashionable widow, and any arrangement which survives over a period of six or seven years acquires a certain sort of respectability. Kurt came to visit his aunt and was not rebuked; he played his compositions for her and they were appreciated.

Thus in one way or another Kurt was meeting Germans. They had been coming back to the Riviera, and now with the new spirit of peace there arrived German steamers, brand-new and beautiful models of what a steamer should be, full of large and well-fed passengers desiring to put on bathing-suits and expose their fat ruddy necks and shaven bullet-heads to the semi-tropical sun. They brought with them rolls of money which had mysteriously become more stable and desirable than the franc; with it they could eat French food and drink French wines and put up at the best hotels; French waiters would serve them, and French *couturiers* would labor diligently but for the most part vainly to make their women *chic*.

Many of these Teutons were what Kurt in old days had described as "hottentots," crude persons without culture, and he had no more interest in them than in Americans or Argentinians of the same sort. But now and then he would meet some music lover or scholar, someone who had heard his music, or, hearing reports about it, wished to hear it. Beauty was always glad to have Kurt's friends come to the villa, any who were willing to keep up the polite fiction under which he lived with her. Once more the dream of the "good European" was spreading, and Bienvenu would become a center of international culture. This was the thing for which Lanny had been working and struggling ever since the happy days when the three musketeers of the arts had danced Gluck's *Orpheus* at Hellerau and had been certain that they were helping to tame the furies of greed and hatred. Lanny felt that the war was at last really over, and that Britain, France, and Germany were reconciled in his American home.

VII

At Christmas time the two friends made their customary journey north. This had now become for Lanny a business as well as a pleasure trip. He was learning more and more about the art world;

it happened almost automatically—a person from whom he bought a picture would tell his friends about an agreeable young American who had his suits of clothing made with a large pocket inside the vest, having a flap and a button, with a safety-pin as an extra precaution; from this secret hiding-place he would produce a flat packet containing an incredible number of immaculate new banknotes, and would count them out on the table and let them lie there until one could no longer withstand the temptation and would say: "All right, the picture is yours." Lanny and Zoltan between them had found so many persons who wanted to buy old masters that it was continually a problem with the playboy whether to do the things he wanted to do, such as listening to Hansi's music and to symphony concerts, or to go out and work up another deal.

Visiting Hansi was now quite a new experience. It appeared that the pressure upon a rich man to live according to his wealth was irresistible, and here were these Robins in this new and sumptuous nest, with servants in livery and everything perfectly appointed. Johannes was a man of action, and when he wanted something done he went and got experts and had it done right. In this palace he had been confronted by gaping rows of shelves in the library, and he had promptly had the shelves measured, and had summoned the manager of the oldest-established bookstore in Berlin and astounded that personage by saying that he wanted one hundred and seventeen meters of books. There they were, all sizes to fit the varying height of the shelves, and all subjects to fit the varying minds of readers. Johannes didn't have time for them just now, but his children and his children's children were going to enjoy culture.

The Detazes pleased the trader greatly, but they looked lonely on those vast walls, and he said that he wished to place an order for paintings by the square meter, or perhaps the square kilometer. Impossible to leave the place bare, because what was the use of having it if you didn't have it right? "Isn't it better to hang your money on the walls than to hide it in a bank vault?" asked Lanny's old friend. "Here I am getting twelve and fifteen percent for my money, and what am I going to do with so much?"

"You mean that's the interest rate?" asked the younger man, somewhat shocked.

"Our new rentenmarks are scarce," smiled Johannes. "They must be kept that way to be sure there's no more inflation!"

He went on to say that he knew one person whose taste in art he trusted wholly and that was the wonderful Lanny Budd. If he trusted Zoltan Kertezsi, it was because Lanny told him to. His idea was that Lanny and Zoltan should make a study of the palace and turn every room into a small art gallery—not too much, but the right number of pictures with the right atmosphere; they would go scouting over Europe with *carte blanche* to buy whatever they considered proper. Lanny was staggered, and said, well, really, he didn't feel equal to it, he hadn't intended to get so deeply into business as all that. "Take your time," insisted the money-master. "It'll be all right if I tell people that I'm looking for the best."

For a while the younger man wondered whether all this was part of the price of his half-sister, tactfully offered. But Hansi told him that he hadn't mentioned the love affair to either of his parents. Only Freddi knew—having been there and seen. They had decided that maybe they didn't have a right to speak of the matter; maybe nothing would come of it, and, furthermore, Papa might prefer not to know, because if he knew he might feel in honor bound to tell Lanny's father. Lanny said they had been wise.

Hansi took him to his room, where he had devised a hiding-place to keep Bess's letters. They were written in that expansive handwriting which is taught to young ladies of fashion, perhaps because it uses a great deal of stationery without requiring them to have many thoughts. Hansi let Lanny read the letters, and they affected the brother deeply; they might have been written by a fourteen-year-old Juliet to her Romeo; they were naïve, genuine—and comforting to a heart-smitten musician not yet of age. The pair had devised a code for the reciprocation of their sentiments; when Hansi wrote about the weather it was to mean the state of his heart toward the granddaughter of the Puritans, and Hansi said he would declare that the weather was heavenly in Berlin, even when the iciest blizzard was raging.

While Lanny was there a cablegram arrived from New York with thrilling tidings: Hansi was engaged to make an appearance in Carnegie Hall during the month of April; they would pay him five hundred dollars, the first money he had ever earned in his life. When they were alone, Hansi looked at his friend with a frightened expression and said: "Bess will be eighteen!"

"All right," smiled the other; "why not?"

"What shall I do, Lanny?"

"Stand up to them. Get it clear in your head that they're just human beings like yourself; they're only great because they think they are."

"How I wish you'd come with me!" exclaimed the young virtuoso.

"Don't let them bluff you, Hansi. You'll find their bark is a lot worse than their bite!"

VIII

The morning before Christmas Lanny and Kurt arrived in Stubendorf. Emil couldn't come that year; it was some other officer's turn. Also the two Aryan widows were missing, Kurt's sister-in-law being with her parents and his sister with her husband's family. Thus it was a quiet Christmas, but happy, on account of the spirit of Locarno; Poland had signed those treaties, and the two peoples were doing what they could to get along with each other. Trade was picking up and life was becoming easier.

Lanny had serious talks with Herr Meissner. The old gentleman was beginning to show his age, but his mind was no less vigorous, and what he had to say about the problems of the Fatherland always interested Lanny; it troubled him also, for it seemed to reinforce the idea of his conservative father and his revolutionary uncle, that the basic demands of Germany and her neighbors were irreconcilable. Lanny still met no one in Stubendorf who had any other idea than to get back into the German fold, or who would think of the present arrangement as anything but a breathing-spell. But imagine saying that to a Pole or a Frenchman!

Heinrich Jung was there, and he was the lad that could tell you how the getting back into the fold was to be done. Adolf Hitler Schicklgruber, having had a whole year out of prison, had reorganized his movement and was carrying on his propaganda without rest. Had Lanny read that book which Heinrich had sent him? Yes, Lanny had read it. And what did he think of it? Lanny answered as politely as he could that it seemed to him to convey Herr Hitler's ideas successfully; it was unusual for a public man to outline in such detail a series of events which he intended to bring about. That satisfied the young forester, who couldn't imagine anybody's failing to honor the inspired leader of the coming new Germany. His sky-blue eyes shone as he informed Lanny that the great man was now in retirement, writing the second part of his masterwork. That too would be sent to Juan when it was published.

The truth was that Lanny had found the first portion of Adi's book extremely hard reading. It was called *Mein Kampf*—that is to say, *My Fight*, or if you wished to take it symbolically, *My Struggle*. But its author had no idea of taking it that way; his book was a declaration of implacable and unceasing war upon the world as at present organized and run. *Mein Hass* would have been a better title, it seemed to Lanny, or perhaps *Meine Hassen*, for Hitler had so many hates that if you read off the list of them it became a joke. Lanny saw him as Rick had explained him: the poor odd-jobs man, the artist *manqué*, the dweller in flophouses who craved ideas and read all sorts of stuff; it was jumbled up in his head, the true and the false hopelessly confused, but everything believed with a fury of passion that came close to the borderline of insanity. Lanny was no psychiatrist, but it seemed to him that here was an indivisible combination of genius and crackpot. Lanny had never before encountered such a mind, but he accepted Rick's statement that you could find them in every refuge for the derelict, or hear them by the dozens in Hyde Park, London, on any Sunday afternoon.

The author of *Mein Kampf* had a dream of a tall, long-headed, long-limbed, vigorous man with blond hair and blue eyes whom he called "the Aryan." This seemed funny, because Hitler himself was an average-sized dark man of the round-headed Alpine type. His dream Aryans didn't exist in Europe; for the Germans, like all the other tribes, were mixed as thoroughly as a broth which has been stewing on a hot fire for a thousand years. Hitler had got his emotions out of Wagner's Siegfried mythology, plus a bit of Nietzsche, who had gone insane, and of Houston Stewart Chamberlain, who didn't have to go. This provided him with reasons for hating all the other varieties of mankind. He hated the yellow ones as a kind of evil gnomes; he hated the Russians, calling them sub-human; he hated the French because they were lewd and decadent; he hated the British because they ruled the seas and blockaded Germany; he hated the Americans because they believed in democracy. Most of all he reviled the Jews, obscene caricatures of human beings who had crept into Germany and corrupted her heart and brain, and had got so much of her property away from her, and filled so large a share of the professions, crowding out the noble blond Aryans.

The Jews must be driven from the Fatherland and ultimately from the world. The Jews were the international bankers who had a stranglehold upon the poor; the Jews were Marxist revolutionists who wanted to destroy all Aryan institutions. That they could be both these things at the same time didn't surprise Adi because he himself could believe and be all sorts of opposite and incompatible things. He loathed the Marxists because they laughed at his Aryan myth and all others. He hated the people with money because he had never had any. He hated the department stores because they took the trade away from the little merchants, his kind of people. He hated the Catholics because they were internationalists and not German; he hated the Protestants because they taught the Christian ideals of brotherhood and mercy instead of the noble Aryan ideals of racial supremacy and world domination.

Lanny could picture this frustrated genius-psychopath, this great wit to madness near allied, shut up in a fortress because he had caused the deaths of sixteen of his noble Aryans in an effort to overthrow the republic which he hated because it had accepted the treaty of Versailles. His twenty comrades in confinement couldn't stand his oratory, so he had sat off in another room, dictating his frenzies to one patient and devoted disciple. Because he was a patriot in spite of being cracked, the prison authorities permitted him to keep a light until midnight, and there he sat, pouring out such venom as should have caused the pen to curl up and the paper to burst into flames. From April Fools' Day to a week before Christmas he spouted, and then he had a book, and one of his friends, a Catholic priest, straightened out the sentences and made what sense he could of them, after which an edition of five hundred copies was printed. Lanny Budd had honestly tried to read it, all the time thinking: "My God, what would the world be like if *this* fellow should break loose!"

IX

The strangest thing was the effect of *Mein Kampf* upon the person who for a matter of twelve years had stood in Lanny's mind as the representative of all that was best and noblest in Germany. Lanny had passed the book on to Kurt because Heinrich had asked him to, and because he thought that Kurt would be interested in it as a sample of mental aberration. But he found that the former artillery officer read the work with absorbed interest. While he agreed with many of Lanny's criticisms, he agreed only half-way and made so many qualifications that it amounted to a defense of both Hitler and his ideas. The man might be abnormal, but he was a German, and it appeared that German abnormality was only for Germans to understand. Kurt didn't say that, and Lanny didn't say it either, for he dreaded to wound his friend; but that was the impression he carried away from their discussions of the National Socialist movement and its newly printed bible.

Hitler hated the Poles, and Lanny could understand that Kurt should be especially aware of their defects, since they had taken his chunk of homeland and were governing it incompetently. Lanny could understand that Kurt should distrust the French, at whom he had shot many thousands of artillery shells, and against whom he had carried on a deadly secret intrigue. He could understand Kurt's being humiliated by the arrogance of the British ruling class —Lanny had learned that from his father in boyhood, and was now acquiring from his Socialist friends a new dislike of "brass hats" and "stuffed shirts" of whatever nation. But these feelings were inter- nationalist, based upon a dream of a humanity to be helped and perfected. Adi, on the other hand, abhorred internationalism as a betrayal of the German spirit; he was for his Aryans and none others, and his words were incitements to all Germans to get to- gether and compel the other races to submit to German domination.

This book provided a kind of litmus paper with which to test Germans and find out how German they were. "You can't deny that it is a forceful book," asserted Kurt, and Lanny answered: "Yes, but one can say that about a maniac who hurls half a dozen men about until they get him into a straitjacket. Force has to be combined with judgment if it's to be of any use in the world." That sounded reasonable, but Lanny saw that it hurt his friend, and they couldn't go on arguing in that manner. No use to quarrel with people; they were what they were, and would remain that; all you could do was to observe them, and understand what made them so.

Lanny retired into himself and faced some painful facts. Kurt hated Jews; no use trying to deny that any longer. Lanny had ob- served that Kurt always found some other reason for disapproving of Jews, but it was always about Jews that he gave these reasons. Year after year Kurt had refused to go to the home of a *Schieber* who was profiting out of the sufferings of the German people. All right, Lanny could understand that feeling; but what about this cousin of the Meissners who showed up for the *Weihnachtsfest* and mentioned casually in the course of the meal that he had had the forethought to sell marks all through the inflation? "Foreigners were losing money," he said, "and why shouldn't a German get some?" Kurt didn't leave the table or show any diminution of cor- diality to this blond Nordic *Schieber*. Lanny said nothing; he was a guest and not a censor of Nordic morality.

X

Kurt talked about the new party and its affairs with the young forester, and Lanny sat by and absorbed information. Heinrich was the incarnation of the Aryan dream, and Lanny could understand his enthusiasm for a movement made to his order. Heinrich reported that the leader, the Führer, had been released from arrest upon a pledge to conduct his party as a legal one; the leader had adjusted himself to this idea, but it had greatly displeased some of his followers, for it meant going into democratic politics, which they had been taught to despise. There had been a lot of dissension, and some schisms, but all Adi had to do was to get them together and orate to them, and he could sweep all opposition before him; none of them could withstand the fervor of his eloquence, the contagion of his faith in the Fatherland.

Making all allowances for Heinrich's optimism, it was plain that this dangerous movement was growing, and that imprisonment had only served to increase the prestige of its founder. You could see this right here in Stubendorf, a German-owned estate governed by Polish officials and worked in large part by Polish peasants. The blond student of forestry had come home for vacations and distributed Nazi tracts among his German friends, especially the younger ones; he had invited them to his home and taught them the formulas, and now Stubendorf was a vigorous and active *Gau*, with Heinrich as proud and exultant *Gauleiter*, or district captain.

"Aren't you afraid of the government officials?" asked Lanny.

"What can they do?" challenged Heinrich. "We aren't breaking any laws."

"You're getting ready to break them, aren't you?"

The other smiled. "How are they going to prove that?"

"But it's all here in the book," argued Lanny, pointing to Heinrich's copy.

"They don't read books; and anyhow they wouldn't believe it."

"You expect the movement to grow, and if it does, people will certainly read the book. Does Hitler expect to convert the masses with a book in which he explains his contempt for them and shows how easy it is to fool them? He says it's all right to tell them a lie if it's a big enough one, for they will think you wouldn't have nerve enough for that. To me it just doesn't make sense."

"That's because you're intelligent," replied Heinrich. "You're an

Aryan, and you ought to join our movement and become one of our leaders."

Lanny said no more, for he had made up his mind that it would be poor taste for him to get into a dispute with Kurt or his friends while on a Christmas visit to his home. He would wait until they were in Lanny's home, and perhaps they would take a walk up to the heights of Notre-Dame-de-Bon-Port, which had so much meaning for them both, and then Lanny would ask his friend how he, a disciple of Beethoven and Goethe, could make excuses for a political movement which repudiated every notion of honor and fair dealing, both among individuals and among nations.

XI

Lanny had learned of some pictures in Dresden, and more in Munich, so they would take in these cities on their way home. Kurt was glad to do this, because it gave him a chance to become acquainted with the musical life of Germany. Zoltan met them in Dresden, and while Kurt went to a symphony concert, Lanny brought out the photos of the new Robins' nest, the plan of the rooms, and the ideas he had jotted down. Because Johannes had begun his career in Rotterdam and his children had been born there, Lanny had suggested that he put Dutch masters in the principal downstairs rooms, and Johannes had been pleased with this. He wanted no imitations of anything; he was prepared to invest several million marks in old masters, and then he would feel safe against any blows of fate. "Funny thing, how much it takes," commented Zoltan. "Doubtless he used to feel safe on his mud floor, and was glad if he had one ragged shirt."

They made purchases, and then went on to Munich. The distressed nobleman there had had time to incur new debts, and so they bought more paintings from him, and went scouting for others. Meanwhile Kurt went to the headquarters of the National Socialist party and talked with men whom he had met previously. Adi was scheduled to speak at a public meeting, and Kurt wanted to hear him: did Lanny care to come along? Lanny said he had too much work on hand; Kurt could tell him about it. Lanny had thought it over and realized that he was in a delicate position, for Kurt was not merely his friend, but his mother's lover, and if they got to disagreeing about politics it might have an effect on both relationships. Let Kurt believe what he pleased and let Lanny keep out of it!

The former officer came home late, with a moderate amount of good Munich beer in him and a large amount of bad Nazi eloquence. He said that he didn't like the type of men whom Hitler had got around him; they were adventurers, some of them no better than American gangsters. But the Führer himself was another matter; a complex and bewildering man. Almost impossible to resist him when he became inspired; he was simple and unaffected, but then something would rise up and take possession of him and he would become the very soul of the Fatherland. "At least that's the way it seems to a German," Kurt added, in an effort to be fair.

Lanny said: "Yes; but we're all trying to get peace right now, and surely Hitler isn't going to make it any easier."

"It's no good fooling ourselves," replied his friend. "If they really want peace with Germany, they'll have to make it possible for our people outside the Fatherland to get back in."

It made Lanny a little sick to hear that. He knew the answers, having heard every possible point of view threshed out during six months of the Peace Conference. If you returned Stubendorf to Germany, what about the Poles who lived in that district? For the most part these were poor, so they didn't count for very much, at least not in the estimation of the Germans. But if you made the transfer, then right away the Polish agitators would start working among them, and you would have the same old fight in reverse; it would be Hitler *versus* Korfanty to the end of time.

Lanny had definitely made up his mind not to argue. He said: "I don't know the solution, Kurt. But let's try to approach it in the spirit of open-mindedness, not of fanaticism." He wanted to add "like Adi," but he withheld the words.

In his heart Lanny was thinking: "Kurt is turning into a Nazi! And what is that going to mean?" The American remembered how vigorously his father had warned him, after their misadventure in Paris, that Kurt couldn't stay in Bienvenu and go on with his activities as a German agent. For years Kurt hadn't met any of his countrymen in France, but now he was beginning again, and would they be trying to use him as they had done before? Maybe it was snobbery on Lanny's part, but it seemed to him that agents of Hitler would be far worse than agents of the Kaiser! Lanny had seen enough troubles by now so that he was able to foresee them; and that has its advantages, yet also disadvantages, for one may take to seeing more troubles than ever eventuate. But Lanny couldn't help thinking: "Poor Beauty! What sort of Nazi is she going to make!"

25

Backward into Shadow

I

ANOTHER season on the Riviera. People piling in from all over the world, until the hotels and pensions were stuffed, and you couldn't get so much as a cot. It was fantastic, the prices which were offered for the rent of the tiniest cottage; some owners couldn't stand the temptation, they leased and went elsewhere. And still the trains and steamers came with fresh loads of passengers; they slept in the chairs in lobbies, or rented rooms in workingmen's quarters or the homes of peasants.

There was a building boom, and the soul of Beauty Budd was kept in torment by real estate agents who called and begged the privilege of seeing her; they had figured out a scheme whereby a little corner could be spared from her property without doing the slightest harm; they wanted to cut this up into *lotissements*, and they offered such sums as made Beauty turn pale. When she said no, they would come back with a doubled offer. For an acre they would pay ten times what Robbie Budd had paid for the entire estate twenty years ago! They argued that it was cruel to keep all that land idle when it might be having a dozen cottages on it, filled with happy people who would come to the village to shop and thus build up prosperity for everybody. The agents put it before Madame Detaze as a public duty.

To Madame it became a cause of distress to be so wealthy and yet unable to touch the wealth. The villa and the lodge and the two studios seemed to shrink to smaller proportions, and became unworthy of the immensely valuable tract which they occupied. Why, it was almost as if you were living in a garage! But it made no difference how many millions or tens of millions of francs were offered, nobody could buy a square millimeter of this estate; Robbie had fixed it so, declaring that Bienvenu was Beauty's home, and the home of her children and her grandchildren if and when. Accordingly Beauty had to get her happiness out of telling her friends how rich she might become if she didn't love this old home so greatly.

Rick and his family came for their customary sojourn. Nobody mentioned to them the prices which had been offered for the rental of the lodge, but they could guess, and were embarrassed to be taking so much from their friends. Rick's play had been produced in London, and had done the same as the first one; that is, it had won esteem but practically no money. And of course what a journalist could earn by miscellaneous writing wasn't enough for a family which had rich friends. Nina was game, and stuck by her husband in his determination to write, but that didn't keep her from having regrets. Beauty tried tactfully to help her without seeming to do so. Whenever the Pomeroy-Nielsons had visitors who could be entertained, Beauty would beg to do it; if they needed a car, Lanny would offer to drive them. "Friendship is more than money," he would say, and of course it is, but the fashionable world isn't always run on that basis.

Kurt gave his annual recital at Sept Chênes, and played with three orchestras that season, with no little *éclat*. Lanny encouraged him and Beauty intrigued to push him to the fore. Lanny hadn't told his mother about his fear of the Nazis, for Beauty couldn't get political movements straight, and her son's antagonism to Hitler and Mussolini was to her merely an aspect of his friendship for the Reds. The Germans whom Kurt met seemed to be musical people, and all that Beauty wanted was for them to tell Kurt that he was a great *Komponist*, so as to keep him happy in his work. She would do any entertaining, pay any sums to that end; she would have been willing to pay orchestra directors to hire Kurt, if it had been possible to arrange this without its becoming known.

Lanny made trips to look at paintings, and Zoltan came to report on others. They had detailed plans of the Berlin palace, with red lines marking where pictures were to go and blue lines around them when the spaces had been filled. Gradually the blue was encompassing the red, and both men were making themselves multimillionaires—that is, of course, French multimillionaires, with the franc approaching forty to the dollar. The franc continued to decline incomprehensibly, regardless of Dawes Commission and Locarno treaties and all the rest. The cost of living kept rising, and in spite of the boom on the Riviera there were unemployment and very little increase in wages. A lovely world to be rich in, but not so good to be poor in.

II

There was a subdued but incessant strife going on between Lanny Budd and his mother over this issue of riches *versus* poverty, Whites *versus* Reds. From Beauty's point of view, everything was marvelous right now; everybody told her that it was "prosperity," and that it was spreading all over the world. Why couldn't they all be happy, after so many years of suffering? But Lanny had gone out and got himself mixed up with these malcontents, these agitators, people who were always in trouble, and kept coming to him with hard-luck stories and disturbing his peace of mind and that of his family. Really, Lanny couldn't get any pleasure out of his financial success because of the crazy notion he had adopted that this success was responsible for other people's failures; the profits he had made had been wrung out of the sweated labor of the poor.

Beauty couldn't keep from trying to set him straight about it; she would point out to him how, when she went to M. Claire and ordered a new party dress, several women were immediately set to work at good wages——

"How do you know they're good wages?" broke in the exasperating Pink. "Did you ever make inquiry?"

Beauty knew that a great establishment, the leading *couturier* of Nice, wouldn't have anything but the most skilled workers and pay them handsomely. Anything else was unthinkable. And couldn't you see how these employees would take the money and spend it in the stores, and it would keep circulating and make prosperity all over the Riviera? Some of Beauty's business friends had explained that to her and she had got it fixed in her mind. The people who came to Lanny with stories of unemployment and misery were moved by jealousy of the more fortunate classes, and naturally, if they spent their time agitating and making trouble, nobody would want to hire them. Lanny encouraged them in their notion that they had a grievance against society, and thus made them into permanent parasites who would never have any way to live except on his bounty.

"I suppose you're not doing anything to make parasites out of your White Russians!" the son would remark, not without irritation.

"But that's different, Lanny. Those people have been delicately reared and they've never learned how to work. What can they do?"

"No use to argue with a bourgeois mind!" Lanny would exclaim.

Beauty never got clear just what this meant, but she knew it was a term of reproach and it hurt her feelings. She was annoying her son, whom all his life she had tried to make happy. How could she help worrying about him and trying to keep him out of trouble? Twice he had been in grave danger and might have lost his life; but he wouldn't see it, he didn't care, he was willing to throw himself away on a sudden whim. How could his mother have any peace, knowing that every time he left the house he might be walking into some mishap of this sort? Oh, how Beauty hated those Reds! But she had to choke down her feelings and keep from exposing her "bourgeois mind" to the dialectical materialism of her too highly educated son.

III

Marie de Bruyne also was unhappy. She spent the winter in this lovely home, to which so many people would have paid highly to be invited; she smiled and played the social game according to the rules, but the verve, the *élan*, had gone out of her. Lanny assumed that it must be because of his misconduct: his interest in Socialist Sunday schools, his meeting with various Reds who came along, and giving them money for their propaganda. He didn't think it quite fair of Marie to take it so hard, and he tried to justify his ideas to her; she would listen politely and rarely argue, but he knew that she, too, believed in the property system of the world in which she lived. He felt that he was being punished rather heavily for having sought what seemed to him the truth; but he loved her, and wanted very much to see her happy as in the old days, so he made many concessions, gave up engagements and avoided expressing ideas which he knew were disturbing to the bourgeois mind.

But it didn't seem to do any good. He would see her sitting alone when she didn't know he was watching, and there would be an expression on her face of the *mater dolorosa*, the look which he had noticed the first time he had met her and had thought one of the saddest he had ever seen. He began to wonder if there wasn't something else upon her mind. Nearly two years had passed since the "scandal," and she had begun traveling about with him again; surely she couldn't still be brooding over that! Lanny had read that persons who had been brought up under the dark shadow of Catholicism rarely got over it entirely; they always had guilty feelings lurking in some part of their minds. Could it be that she was turning back to her husband and the family institutions of France?

He began to inquire, very gently, tactfully. Six full years since that luncheon at Sept Chênes, when it had been planned for him to fall in love with an heiress off a yacht, and he had chosen the wrong woman. Had he succeeded in making her happy? Or did she regret her choice? Smiles came back to her face. Now, as always, she responded to his advances of affection. He decided that his guess must be wrong.

Was it that she was troubled about her boys? They were good, sturdy fellows, both of them now doing their military service—something which Lanny had escaped because everybody took him for an American, and he hadn't ever had to show that he was born in Switzerland. Just what that made him he would never know to the end of his days, but it didn't bother him; he wanted to play the piano and he didn't want to shoot people. As for the young de Bruynes, they seemed to have a mechanical bent and were planning to study at the École Polytechnique; they weren't running wild so far as anybody knew, and there was no war in sight. Lanny asked casual questions about them, and made certain that they were not the cause of the mother's state of mind.

Could it be her deeply rooted idea that she ought to retire from his life? He redoubled his attentions to her, and his evidences of contentment; he became ostentatious in his lack of interest in the damsels who displayed their shapely limbs on the bathing-beaches and their virginal backs on the dancing-floors. But all in vain; Marie remained depressed whenever she was not playing a part. Her lover began to think of unlikely, even melodramatic reasons. Could there be some blackmailer preying upon her? That impecunious cousin who had come more than once to the Côte d'Azur and had shown a weakness for *boule*, the least expensive of the gambling-games?

He decided to force the issue. He brought her over to the studio alone, and sat by her and put his arms about her. "What is it, darling? You must tell me!"

"What do you mean, Lanny?"

"Something is troubling your mind. You are not yourself."

"No, dear, it isn't so."

"I have been watching you for months, a year. Something is seriously wrong."

"No, I assure you!" She fought hard and lied valiantly. It was nothing; she was the happiest of women. But he would not take no; she must tell. At last she broke down and began to weep. It was better for him not to know, not to ask—please, please!

But he didn't please, he wouldn't stop; he kept saying: "Whatever it is, I have a right to know it. I insist."

I V

In the end she had to give up. She revealed to him that for more than a year she had had a gnawing pain in the abdomen. At first it had been slight, and she had thought it was some digestive disturbance. But it had grown worse, and she was in terror of it.

"But, Marie!" he cried, amazed. "Why don't you have an examination?"

"I can't bear to hear about it. I am a coward. You see, my mother died—" She stopped. There was a word of dread which he could guess.

"And you've been keeping it from me all this time?"

"You have been happy, Lanny, and I wanted you to stay so."

"Darling!" he cried. "You have let it get worse, and it may be too late."

"Something told me it was too late from the beginning."

"That is nonsense!" he exclaimed. "Nobody can say that. I am going to take you to a surgeon."

"I knew you would insist. That is why I couldn't bring myself to tell you, or anyone."

A strange thing. Her resistance was gone. She couldn't bear to be examined, but she had known that he would make her go, and that she couldn't stand out against him. She was like a child in his hands. She didn't say yes, she didn't say no; she let him go ahead, as if she were on a train that she couldn't stop. She sat staring in front of her, her hands clasped, her face white, a picture of dread.

He rushed to his mother. He called up Emily Chattersworth,

who had lived in this part of the world so long, and knew everybody and everything. She gave him the name of the best surgeon in Cannes, and Lanny phoned and made an appointment. Marie had delayed a year, but Lanny couldn't bear to delay an hour.

He was ready to take her. Another strange thing, the fixed attitudes of women. She was numb with dread, facing the thought which had paralyzed her brain for a year—but she couldn't go to a surgeon's without being properly dressed. Lanny helped her, he took the part of a maid, of a nurse; from that time on he would be everything. All trace of their disharmony was gone, his irritation swept away in a moment. What a fool he had been, what a cruel, blind person, to be arguing with her about politics, to be finding fault with her in his heart, never guessing this dreadful secret!

To the doctor he said: "*C'est mon amie.*" It was a recognized status, and no apologies called for; he went through the ordeal with her, stood by and held her hand while the surgeon asked her questions and examined her. The man shook his head and said he would give no opinion until they had X-rays.

Poor Marie let herself be led like a lamb to the slaughter. Her lips trembled, and she pressed them together. Her hands trembled, and Lanny held them tightly. He would have liked to hold her soul, but there was no way to reach it. She awaited the word of doom, and it was delayed. The pictures had to be taken and developed and studied. Somehow she would have to live through the night. She would take a sleeping-powder, something with which Lanny was to become familiar. Driving her home from Cannes he whispered consolation, or tried to. "I love you," was the only sentence that seemed to have any effect. She would answer: "Oh, Lanny, what will become of you?"

In those days the art of photographing the human interior was not so well developed as it has become. The surgeon pointed out shadows which were suspicious. He said that there was probably a growth, but there was no reason to assume that it was malignant. The fact that Marie's mother had died of cancer might mean something, or might not—in short, there was no way to say except to perform an exploratory operation. There was certainly some pathological condition—the surgeon used long words which were not familiar to a youth whose reading had been mostly in the field of *belles-lettres*. The surgeon tried to comfort them both. If all the women who dreaded cancer died of it, the human race would be rapidly depleted.

Marie felt that it was her duty to write to Denis, and next day came a telegram from him, begging her to come to Paris, where he knew a surgeon in whom he had confidence. He telegraphed Lanny also, urging him to bring her to the château. It was an overture. In the presence of danger the members of any group get together; kindnesses are remembered, enmities forgotten. Marie said that might be better; she would be near the boys in case of emergency. Lanny said: "All right; let's start at once." He would take her by train if she didn't feel equal to motoring; he could have the car shipped to Paris, where he would need it if he were to be of use to her. She was shocked by the extravagance of shipping a car; she could stand the drive. "Then let's get going." That was his way, the American way.

V

In Paris there was the husband; anxious, kind, repenting of his sins, no doubt, and not reminding the truant pair of theirs. These two men, the old and the young, would walk together down a long road of sorrow which fate had paved for them. Hat in hand, they would wait in medical offices; they would walk through corridors of hospitals; they would go side by side to the bitter end. They had few things in common, but these they would talk about—for to sit without a word suggests hostility, and France is the land of *politesse*. The weather, political developments—facts, but never opinions; the international situation, the state of business, the decline of the franc; the pictures Lanny had seen or bought, the charms of a new actress, the voice of a new singer—with such matters they would seek to maintain sympathetic relations while they motored, waited in an office, dined in a restaurant—whatever circumstances compelled them to do.

The surgeon in Paris was no stranger to the customs of the land. It had happened before that two anxious gentlemen appeared, escorting one lady; it had even happened that two ladies brought one gentleman. That one of the men should be elderly and the other young was not incredible; that both should be rich, elegant in their manners, sorrowful in their souls—all that was nearly as familiar in medical offices as in *romans*. The surgeon made his "palpations," asked his questions, studied the X-ray photographs. His verdict was the same as the other's: an exploratory operation was called for, and ought not be delayed.

Marie let herself be handled as if she were a piece of merchandise; valuable merchandise, to be carefully packed and kept covered by insurance. Three men decided her fate; they fixed the time and the place; she had known that they would do it, and for that reason had kept the painful secret for so long, perhaps too long. The surgeon said nothing discouraging to her, but to the men he called it a great misfortune that she had waited so long. She knew he would say that; she seemed to know all things that were going to happen; it had been just so with her mother, and Marie had been old enough to watch it and remember it. Cancer is not hereditary, but the susceptibility to cancer is; she had that firmly fixed in her mind, and it was enough.

She was going to the hospital in the morning, and wanted to have a talk with each of her men separately; a sort of ceremony, a last will and testament orally delivered. What she said to Denis would never be known to her lover; what she said to her lover would never be forgotten by him—the words, the tones, the whole impress of a personality. No use trying to say that she wasn't going to die; she might not die on the morrow, but she would die soon, and the only way to help her was to assume it, and let her say her say.

She didn't know where human souls went when they died. Her childhood religion didn't return to life in this crisis. Denis wanted her to receive extreme unction according to the rites of their church, and she said that would be a small matter to make him happy, and perhaps the boys. Pascal had argued, with French common sense, that if it wasn't true it could do no harm, whereas if it was true it would be of great importance; so take your free chance of getting into heaven.

But Marie's thoughts were all on this earth; she was walking backward into the shadows. She wanted to know what was going to become of the two young soldiers whom she was contributing to the defense of *la patrie*. Lanny had been right, she should have told them the truth long ago; she wanted him to promise to talk to them, to be their friend, a *parrain* to them. Denis had consented to this; they were going to be tied together for the rest of their lives. No simple affair, *la vie à trois*, but a subtle and intricate product of an old, perhaps too old, civilization!

She wanted to talk to Lanny about marriage. She should have followed her better judgment and done it some time before. No one could appraise a woman but another woman; no one knew a man's needs but the woman who lived with him and loved him. "Look for a woman with a wise mind and an honest soul, Lanny. Pretty faces fade, as you can see by looking at me; but the best things endure longer." Tears came into her eyes; alas, the best things do not endure long enough! That, too, he could see by looking at her.

That was all she had to tell him; except to help poor Denis in case of need. He was a much better man than anybody guessed; perhaps that was true of all men. Her four men—husband, lover, and two sons—were going on in a cold and strange world; Marie herself was going into one perhaps colder and stranger, but she did not think about herself. Lanny must help the boys to choose their helpmates; that was a mother's duty in France, and they would miss her. Lanny would miss her, too; the tears were running down his cheeks as he promised to comply with her various requests. She said that if there were spirits, and if they could return, she would be present when he chose his bride. He tried to say that he would never marry, but she stopped his lips with her fingers. That was silly, that was no way to console her, and certainly was a poor compliment for the woman who for six years had sought so earnestly to make him happy.

VI

They took her to the operating-table, and the two men sat side by side in a waiting-room and tried to talk about other things, but found it difficult. She did not die, but perhaps it would have been better if she had. The surgeon reported that it was a cancer, and that it already involved the liver and was impossible to remove. Nothing to do but sew her up, and make life as easy as possible during the time that was left to her. It might be half a year, but probably less. She would have a great deal of pain, but they would ease her with opiates. The surgeon would leave it to them to tell her what they thought best.

The two men took their hats and walked down the corridor of the hospital. *Exeunt duo;* a melancholy stage direction. They had feared the worst and they had got something almost as bad. They got into Lanny's car, and he said: "We shall have to be friends, Denis. We must do the best we can for her sake." The other pressed his hand, and they sat for a while in silence before Lanny started the car.

When she was recovered enough, they brought her home and got a nurse to attend her. The two boys got leave and came to hear the tragic news, and to hear the messages of love and wisdom which she had for them. Each day was harder for her; the pain of the surgical wound was replaced by the pain of the gnawing demon. The local doctor agreed that she should not be allowed to suffer; there was nothing to be gained by denying her drugs. The law did not permit them to put her out of her misery all at once, but it permitted them to accomplish the same result by stages.

Lanny was young and rebellious, and did not submit readily to these hammer-blows of fate. Once more he was in rebellion against a universe, a Creator, whatever one chose to call it, which decreed the snuffing out of his happiness. Even after having passed through the horrors of a world war and an abortive peace he could not become reconciled to the idea that Marie de Bruyne, a bubble on the surface of the stream of life, was about to break, and lose all her rainbow colors, and return to the substance of the stream. He wouldn't give her up; when he had worn himself out cursing the universe, he cursed the doctors who didn't know their business, who couldn't stop large wild carcinoma cells from eating up the normal, well-behaved cells in a female abdomen.

He went to an American surgeon, to see if he knew any more. This man called up the French surgeon and heard his account of the conditions in the interior of Madame de Bruyne, and then confirmed the diagnosis of doom. No, there was nothing new in the treatment of cancer; at least nothing that could affect such a case. Some day, perhaps, the world would know more; it might know it now if men had not expended so great a part of their energies upon the destruction of their fellows instead of upon the conquest of nature's hostile forces. The American surgeon had almost Pink tendencies, it appeared.

Still Lanny would not give up. He took to reading the medical books, and acquired a mass of information, most of it far from cheering; he went to the libraries and read the latest periodicals in French, English, and German which reported on the vast field of cancer research; he learned a great deal about the chemistry of cancer cells, their biology and habits, but he didn't find any hint as to how to stop their invasion of a woman's liver. There were left only the quacks, whose advertisements were prominent in the newspapers; also the various kinds of cultists, who were ready to tell him that cancer could be cured by a change of diet, the omission of meat, the use of whole grains, raw foods, or what not; also the faith healers, who would assure him that God could stop the growth of cancer cells, and would do it if the patient believed it. That mental changes in a human being might also change his body chemistry was a not altogether absurd idea, but Lanny had never heard of it, and if Marie had she did not mention it. The religion which she had been taught concentrated upon her sins and left her diseases to the doctors.

VII

Lanny went back to live at the château and devoted himself to nursing his beloved. When the sun shone he would help her into the garden by the south wall where the pear and apricot trees were trained like vines; there amid the colors and the scents of tulips and fleurs-de-lis, hyacinths and crocuses and narcissi, he would read her sad stories of the death of kings, and of the course of true love which never did run smooth. It had been springtime when he had first carried her away from this land of gentle streams and well-tended gardens; it would be springtime when an angel of mercy would come and perform the same service for her. When the weather was inclement, he would play music for her, gentle music which turned sorrow into beauty, gay dances to remind her of old days, brave marches to escort her into eternity. When her pains became too great for endurance, he would put her to bed and give her some of the sleeping-tablets which had been entrusted to him. Always he took pains to hide the bottle, lest she be tempted to take more than her due allowance.

He didn't want to do anything but stay with her. Business became a profanation, and meeting the Reds seemed like breaking faith with her. Pretty soon she would be gone, and then he would have no more of her time, so make the most of what was left. They talked long and deeply, probing the mysterious thing that is called life. They were in a state of ignorance very trying, but apparently not to be remedied in their time. If there was any plausible theory as to what life was, or why it was, that theory had not been brought to their attention. Marcel Detaze had speculated about these matters, but his ideas hadn't meant as much to a happy boy as they would have meant to an unhappy man. Apparently unhappiness had something to do with the teaching of wisdom, but that was another thing that didn't make sense to Lanny; he couldn't get up any interest in anything that he was learning or gaining just then. What he wanted was for Marie to get well; instead of which she was subjected to torture and destined to blind annihilation, and no philosophy or religion was anything but empty wind in the face of that cruelty.

They had been happy, and it pleased her to go back and remember the perfect days. Pain became endurable when they recalled the scenes of their honeymoon trip through northwestern France, and of their sojourn in Geneva; she saw with her mind's eye the cold blue waters of Lac Léman, the old city with the plane trees, the snow-capped mountains turning pink in the twilight. He recalled his later visit to that city, and told her about the American secretary who had fallen pathetically in love with him. She said: "That sounds like a very sweet woman, Lanny. Tell me more about her." When he did so, she said: "Why don't you go back there and meet her again?" When he said that no woman would ever be able to take the place of Marie de Bruyne, he brought down upon himself a gentle scolding.

"Dear," she said, "I cannot go and leave you to grief. I grieved for my mother, and then for my brother. It is the most futile of all emotions; it gets you nowhere, brings you no growth, no help. You have to promise me to put it out of your heart, and do something constructive, something that will be of help to other people."

She came back to this again and again, forcing it upon his attention; he must take it as a psychological exercise, to think of the good things he had got from her, and to lift himself out of grief. As a part of that, he must face the idea that he would fall in love again, and would marry; he must talk about it sensibly, and let her give him the advice which she would be unable to give later. She knew about women, and she knew about him; he would not be an easy person to mate. She voiced again the thought that she should have performed an act of renunciation some time ago. She saw herself going to some suitable damsel and saying: "I am growing too old for the man I love; will you consider taking my place?"

Lanny couldn't keep from smiling. He couldn't imagine any of the American misses he had met relishing that method of wooing. She answered: "You Americans leave engagements to chance, and you have many divorces."

"In America they have divorces, and in France they have *liaisons.*"

"But there are *liaisons* in America, too." He couldn't answer that, statistics being difficult to obtain. He subdued himself to listen to her monitions, and promised to profit by them if ever the time came.

VIII

The pains increased, and the drugs she was taking reduced her strength; she could no longer walk alone and pretty soon she could not walk at all. It was evident that the final agony was approaching, and she didn't want him to see it. She begged him to go, so that his memories of her might not be defaced by these hideous things. But he wouldn't listen to her. He had loved her in happiness and would prove that he could love her in sorrow. He would drink the cup to the dregs.

Poor Denis didn't know what kind of friend he was, or what he could do. He loved pleasure and he hated pain; when she begged him to go she provided him with a good excuse; he could say that he was *de trop*, that she wanted to be with her lover. But his conscience tormented him; he would come back, and sit by her, and listen to her gasping out a few words, begging him not to grieve. She was determined to spare her sons this futile suffering. They had their military duties; let them stay and learn to serve their country.

Late one night she talked to Lanny with infinite tenderness, with all the yearning of her soul. There wasn't anything new she could say; there cannot be, when you have had so many years together. But she told him again of her devotion, and the bliss that he had given her; she left him her blessings, and then begged him to get some sleep. He counted out her tablets for her, a dose which increased almost daily; she told him to put them on her table; she wanted to write a letter to her boys before she took the drug. He went into the next room and lay down.

He slept deeply; he had made the discovery that painful emotions can be as exhausting as physical toil. When he opened his eyes, daylight had come, and he went to her room to see how she was, and found her lying still, her eyes closed. Something told him; he touched her and found her cold. On the table beside her was the bottle in which the tablets had been kept; she had got up in the night and crawled or dragged herself into his room, and slipped her hand under his pillow and found the bottle. It must have been an agony to her to get back into bed, but in the interest of decency she had achieved it; she had taken all the tablets, and her troubles were over. In past days she had said to him more than once: "Whatever may be the truth about the hereafter, I shall have got rid of the cancer, and you of the knowledge that I am suffering. Count that blessing—count it over and over."

So he obeyed her. He put the empty bottle into his pocket, and would take that secret to his grave. No need to shock a Catholic husband and sons. The surgeon who had opened her abdomen would have no difficulty in certifying that she had died of cancer.

She left a letter to the sons; and a little note for Denis: "*Je pardonne tout, et dieu le pardonnera.*" Another note, perhaps the last, very feebly written. "*Adieu, chéri.*" Underneath it, as if an afterthought: "*Ange de dieu.*" She meant that to apply to him, but he could take it as a signature; she had surely been an angel to him, and would accompany him wherever he might travel, here or hereafter. He put the note into his pocket, along with the bottle.

IX

The sons were summoned, also the relatives of Marie, and they had a proper French funeral in the village church which had been built five hundred years ago, and from which the husband's family had been buried. The elderly priest who had been their genial guest on occasions asked no questions about sleeping-tablets, and what he did not know could not hurt him with his heavenly powers. The neighbors came, in decorous black; they had gossiped about her in life, but in death they knew that she had been a good woman. The servants came, and tradespeople of the village who had known and esteemed her. In the family pew of the de Bruynes sat four men in mourning, and when they walked out two by two, the older pair leading, everybody bowed respectfully, and nobody considered it a scandal any more. These things happen, and it is well if there is only one extra mourner, male or female.

Marie was laid to rest in the family crypt, and the living members drove back to the château. Lanny had promised to talk to the boys, and he waited for a chance. He found that they had known the secret for years, and had no bitter feelings about it. They looked up to their mother's lover as a young man with many kinds of prestige; he was good-looking, he had traveled widely, he had conversation, and he made large sums of money; they would model themselves upon him as far as possible. He told them what their mother had requested him to do, and the kind of wives she had hoped that they would choose; he told them that, contrary to widespread belief, it was possible for a young man to wait until he had found a woman who was worthy of his love. He invited them to Bienvenu, and offered his mother's help with their matrimonial problems. Being French boys, they did not find anything strange in this offer.

Marie left a will. She had little property, but had bequeathed to Lanny a couple of paintings and some books that he loved, and smaller pieces of jewelry that would remind him of her. Denis told him to take these things without awaiting formalities. Lanny said his farewells to the weeping servants, and to Marie's relatives; he embraced the three de Bruynes in French fashion, and remembered once more the saying of their poet: "To go away is to die a little." He had lived in this château a great deal, and had died there still more. When he stepped into his car and drove out of its gates, it was the closing of a large and heavy volume of the life of Lanny Budd.

BOOK SIX

Some Sweet Oblivious Antidote

26

Pride and Prejudice

I

HANSI went to New York and made his debut at Carnegie Hall. This was shortly before Marie's death, and the news of it helped to divert her mind in the intervals of her pain. Since Lanny had attended a concert in that auditorium, he could picture the scene to her; since they had both heard Hansi play Tchaikowsky's concerto with Lanny's piano accompaniment, she could hear the music in their minds at the very hour it was being played. The concert was given on Friday afternoon, and then repeated on Saturday evening; the first performance, allowing for the difference in time, was at the dinner hour in the Château de Bruyne, and Lanny could hardly eat for his excitement. He wanted to hold his breath while he imagined Hansi playing the long and difficult *cadenza*. He felt better during the *canzonetta*, which every violinist tries to play, for he knew what lovely tones would come floating forth from Hansi's bow. He wanted to sit with his hands clenched tensely while he knew that his friend would be rushing through the frenzies of the *finale;* ecstasy alternating with depression, after the fashion of the old Russian soul. The Bolsheviks were laboring mightily to change that natural phenomenon, but whether they were succeeding was a subject for controversy.

Informed well in advance, Bess had extracted a promise from her parents to take her to this recital. How could they refuse, considering the nature of that institution known to Europe and America as "R and R"? Freddi was coming with his brother, and there was nothing that Esther could do but swallow her pride and prejudice and greet the sons of a man so important to her husband. The three

Budds sat well up in front, where they could watch the bowing of the young violinist and every expression of his face. Whatever these things meant to them, they couldn't fail to realize that he was making a success, for at the end of the stormy composition the audience rose to its feet and shouted approval, calling him back again and again; they wouldn't take the conductor's no, but forced Hansi to play an encore. He stood there alone, a tall, slender figure, and played the *andante* movement from one of Bach's solo sonatas, very dignified, austere, and reverent.

What happened after that Lanny learned in letters from Hansi and Bess, and later by word of mouth; also from Robbie—for it was an important story to them all, and had elements of both drama and comedy. Returning with her parents to their hotel suite, with the plaudits of the multitude still ringing in their ears, Bess revealed that she was going to marry that young Jew. As Robbie admitted to his son, neither he nor his wife was taken by surprise, for Esther had told about their daughter's extravagant behavior in Paris, and they had discussed the painful possibilities. Having watched the two Robin boys developing, the father admired them, and thought that Bess might go a long way and do worse; but out of consideration for his wife he had agreed to let her try to restrain the girl if it could be done.

To the mother it was a dreadful humiliation, and the more so because she dared not express all that she felt. Her prejudice against Jews was deep, but it was based upon the snobbery of the country club set, and she knew that this wouldn't get her very far in controversy with an idealistic child. "You will have children with kinky hair and short legs! They will be dumpy and fat when they are thirty!" Of course Bess didn't fail to point out that Hansi had long, thin legs, and hair that was only slightly wavy.

There wasn't a thing to be said against the young violinist, except that his father had been born in a hut with a dirt floor in a Russian ghetto; and you wouldn't have known that if he hadn't been honest enough to tell it. Mama Robin was said to be without equipment for a career in society—but then she lived in Berlin, and would probably never cross the ocean. When Esther protested against losing her daughter to a foreigner, Bess replied that Hansi would probably be coming on a concert tour every year; playing the violin was as international an occupation as selling munitions.

The one real objection was the youth of both lovers; they couldn't know their own minds at such an age. Hadn't it always been Bess's plan to go through college before she married? She answered that she was going to a different kind of college, one that she had learned about from Lanny; you could read books and teach yourself whatever you wanted to know. Bess was going to work at piano practice, so as to be able to accompany Hansi. She wasn't going to have any babies, whether long-legged or short—it was amazing what young women knew nowadays, and would talk about even in the presence of their fathers! Bess said that when Hansi went on tour she was going with him, to keep the other women away from him. Mummy had always said that travel was educational, and so were languages, and meeting distinguished people all over the world. Look at what Lanny had got during the Peace Conference in Paris; the girl had heard her father expatiate on this and had treasured it in her mind.

II

The most alarming fact was that Bessie Budd was of legal age and knew it; she had been making inquiries—in the Newcastle public library, of all places!—and had ascertained that she and her young genius could take a ferry-boat across the Hudson River and without any preliminaries whatever be married in a few minutes. That was what she proposed as a method of sparing her parents' feelings: to be united to her lover by some judge in a dirty police-court in Hoboken, or in the front parlor of a Weehawken preacher wearing a frayed frock coat and a greasy tie!

Bess was proposing to go back to Germany with Hansi, and the family need have no contact with the despised Jews. Newcastle would soon get over the shock—"Out of sight, out of mind," said the granddaughter of the Puritans. She had taken up the notion that fashionable weddings were "ostentatious," and much preferred to start her married career without any rice in her hair. With the self-confidence of extreme youth she never doubted that Hansi was going to make great sums of money; but they weren't going to spend it on themselves, they were going to use it to uplift the "workers." They used that Red word instead of saying "the poor," as Esther would have done. They were a couple of young Pinks, it appeared!

Amazing what had been going on in the mind of an eighteen-year-old girl; appalling to a mother to wake up and discover how little she knew her own daughter! The proud Esther couldn't keep the tears from her cheeks. "I don't see how you could do such a thing to me!"

The girl answered: "But you see, Mummy, you make it impossible for anybody to be frank."

"What do I do?"—for soul-searching, the conscientious examination of one's self, is a feature of life among the Puritans.

"You are so rigid," explained the girl. "You know exactly what is good for people, and it's no use trying to make you see that they don't want it. When I heard Hansi play the violin, I knew right away what I wanted; but I knew that if I told you about it, you would make yourself miserable and me too, because when I have made up my mind it's just as fixed as yours, and why should I make you suffer when it couldn't help either of us?" Bess rushed on, because she had a lot pent up in her.

"You don't even know the man!" exclaimed her mother.

"If you understood music, Mummy, you'd know that I know him very well indeed."

"But that is romantic nonsense!"

"Mummy, you're like a person on the witness stand who gives himself away without realizing what he's saying. You are telling me that you don't believe in music as a means of communicating. You might just as well refuse to believe that two people who are talking Chinese are communicating. Because you don't understand doesn't mean that they don't understand."

Said the daughter of the Puritans: "I suppose there were several hundred women in that audience who imagined they were in love with the violinist."

"Of course," replied the daughter of the daughter, "and they were. But only one of them is going to get him, and I'm the lucky one!"

III

It wasn't the first time in Robbie's life that he had sat by and watched members of the Budd family slug it out between them. He admired his daughter's suddenly developed sparring power, and made up his mind that she was coming out on top; but he wanted to keep out of it—for Bess was going to Europe, whereas he had to stay! When she appealed to him for his opinion, he said that he hoped she would find a way to avoid causing unnecessary unhappiness to her mother.

"It seems that one of us has to be unhappy," argued the girl. "And I surely think it means more to me who is my husband than it does to anybody else."

"It certainly makes some difference to me who my grandchildren are," replied the mother.

So they were back at the question of the Jews. Esther, who had been brought up to accept their ancient literature as the inspired word of God, couldn't plausibly deny that they were a great people. Somehow the opinions of the Newcastle Country Club shrank in importance when you quoted the Psalms of David or the Epistles of Paul; or even when you called the roll of the great musicians who had been Jews. Bess, who had been getting ready for this argument, named a list of names which Esther had heard all her life, but without knowing that they had been of the objectionable race. Hardly a fair debate, when one side has had time to prepare and the other has to speak extempore!

The outcome was a compromise. Esther would pay any price for delay; she would hope against hope that the child might change her mind. She begged her to agree to wait four years and go through college; then she whittled down her demand to one year. Finally she agreed to take six months—and she had to pay high for even that much.

Said Bess: "You complain that I don't know Hansi; but during our week in Paris you watched me as if I had done something wicked. Now if I give up my happiness for six months to oblige my mother, I surely have a right to be free to meet my fiancé as I would any other decent young man. If there's anything wrong with him, give me a chance to find it out! Here are these boys in a strange city, and Lanny accepted their parents' hospitality in Germany, and Father did it, too; but you seem to think you've done your full duty when you invite the boys to dinner in a hotel and take them to a show!"

Not easy to answer that argument. Obviously, it was Esther's social duty to invite the young Robins to Newcastle; Robbie wanted it, and had a right to ask it for business reasons. Yet, the moment Esther made this concession, other consequences would begin to follow. When a great lady of society invites anyone to her home, the guest becomes a person of importance, and her prestige requires her to insist upon it. Esther would have to take up the cause of the two strangers; she would have to remember that Hansi was a celebrity, with the glamour of a New York appearance. If the matter was handled properly, his newspaper notices would be reprinted in the Newcastle *Chronicle*, and the town would be on edge with curiosity. He would give a recital there, and the Budds would shine as patrons of culture. Make a virtue of necessity!

The young Robins were touchingly happy to visit the Budd home, but also a little scared; while they themselves lived in a very fine mansion, it wasn't real to them, and they wouldn't have been surprised to wake up some morning and find themselves back in the apartment with the steel door. But where Bess was, there was heaven, and to have her take you driving and show you the lovely New England country in early springtime was enough to inspire several new musical compositions.

Hansi consented gladly to give a recital for charity in the large reception hall of the Newcastle Country Club. The place was packed to the doors, and people paid to sit on campchairs outside, or just to stand and listen. It was the room in which Gracyn Phillipson, alias Pillwiggle, had first met Lanny Budd, and had danced with him with scandalous vivacity. Now it echoed the strains of Kreisler's *Caprice Viennois*, and Chopin's *E-flat Nocturne* as transcribed by Sarasate, and finally, as a compliment to New England, a transcription which Hansi had made of three of MacDowell's *Woodland Sketches*. He made his concert short and sweet, because Lanny had told him that that was what fashionable audiences appreciated—they would much rather talk about music than listen to it. Freddi played his brother's accompaniments—extraordinarily talented people, these Jews, and, gad, how they do work! All the Yiddishers of the Newcastle valley were there that night—a warm one, fortunately, so the windows were left open and everybody could hear, and according to Robbie's report the enthusiasm outside made one think of the "peanut gallery," sometimes known as "nigger heaven." The crowd applauded and wouldn't stop, and made Hansi play several encores. There had been no such triumph of the Hebraic race since the days of Solomon in all his glory!

IV

The outcome of that debut was highly amusing; Lanny collected the details from various sources and pieced them together. His stepmother fell victim to her own social campaign—or perhaps to the sovereign power of genius which she had set out to exploit. In the first place, just to have a genius in the house is a startling experience. Very timidly Hansi asked if it would be all right for him to practice; the most considerate of human creatures, he wouldn't dream of doing it if it would disturb the family—but Esther said no, not at all, go right ahead. It transpired that he was accustomed to practice six or eight hours every day, and he had no conception of vacations. He offered to retire to his room and shut the door; but obviously that was no way to treat a genius; Esther said to use the drawing-room, where Freddi or others could accompany him.

So there was that uproar and clamor, that banging, wailing, shrieking, grinding, going on all morning and most of the afternoon, setting the house a-tremble with clashing billows of sound. It was like living in a lighthouse on a rock over a stormy ocean; only it was an ocean which changed to a new kind of storm every few minutes—in other words, the human soul. Impossible not to be affected by it; impressed by the amount of labor, if nothing else— physical labor, mental labor, emotional labor! Impossible to resist the impact of it, to grow accustomed to it, to be dull in the presence of it—for at the moment when you had done so it devised a new method of attack upon your consciousness, it leaped at you, seized you, shook you. All the angels of heaven were in it—or the demons of hell, whichever way you chose to take it; but either way they wouldn't let you alone.

And then the social consequences of having a genius in the house; unforeseeable, and in many ways embarrassing to a person trained to reticence and decorum. The weather was warm and the windows stayed open, which meant that the billows of sound flooded the driveway, and people would stop and just stay there. Word spread that there was a free concert at the Robbie Budds' every day, and crowds gathered as if for a patent-medicine vendor or a puppet-show. They seemed to consider that the presence of genius rescinded the ordinary rules of privacy. Esther would find people on her front porch; not doing any harm, just standing or sitting: a boy who had delivered a package and forgotten to go away; an old friend who had come and hesitated to ring the bell. A schoolteacher of Bess's humbly sought permission to come and sit on the steps; she would steal up on tiptoe as if it were a shrine, sit with her head bowed, and steal away again without a sound. The servants forgot their work, and friends of the servants sat in the kitchen. The house was besieged—and every one of these persons administering a silent admonition to the daughter of the Puritans who considered herself the apex of culture; each one saying: "Do you appreciate the extraordinary honor which has come to you?"

All sorts of people wanted to meet the young genius; curiosity-seekers, lion-hunters, obviously not persons who had any right to enter the Budd home, and who had to be turned away. Others, more surprising to Esther, persons of her own circle who actually considered that she was exalted to have a Jewish boy as her guest! She was forced to give a reception in his honor, and let the socially acceptable ones come and praise his playing and express the hope to hear more of it.

V

Robbie Budd had a keen sense of humor, and knew the people of his town and the members of his own tribe. Very funny to hear him describe the social war that was waged over those two migratory birds, those Russian Robins, those Semitic songbirds—so he would call them according to his whim. The elders of the Budd tribe coming to look them over, and to warn Esther and himself about the alarming possibility of short-legged and kinky-haired babies appearing in this old and proud New England family. Grandfather Samuel, now nearly eighty, sending for his son and having to be mollified by the assurance that this shepherd boy out of ancient Judea was no upstart adventurer, but the son of one of the richest men in Germany—far richer than any of the Budds!

Esther had fondly imagined that she could keep her daughter's secret for six months; but in three days the whole town was talking about it. Most distressing, but impossible to prevent! Anybody who looked at the girl while she was with her young genius could see the status of the affair; and there were Bess's girl friends, keen-eyed as so many young hawks, and her boy friends, in whom she had formerly been interested and to whom she was now indifferent. Newcastle was quite a town, but its country club set was a small village like any other, and Lanny knew from his own experience how fast it could spread rumor and gossip by telephone.

Esther's friends began coming in to question her about this love affair. By all the social conventions she had the right to lie brazenly about it; also they had the right to know that she was lying, and to say so, provided they used the polite word "fibbing." They told her that if she didn't know what was happening she had better; then they went away to take sides on the issue and fight it out all over town. Robbie said it was what the diplomats call "sending up a trial balloon"; they were able to ascertain Newcastle's reaction to the proposed nuptials, without having to admit that any such proposal had been made. A staggering surprise for Esther Budd: there actually were some among the "best people" of her town who didn't think it would be a disgrace to the Budds to take a young Jewish genius into the fold! Members of the younger set mostly, the free-thinking, free-spending crowd, who sought their amusements in New York or Palm Beach, and were looked upon with silent disapproval by Robbie's strict wife; but there were more and more of them, and they made a lot of noise in the community.

It happened that Bess drove her friend to the country club for tea; and all the women came crowding around to pay their tributes to the "lion." Mrs. "Chris" Jessup, that maker of scandal—she who had got Lanny into the mess with the young actress—came up to Bess and exclaimed: "Congratulations, my dear!" Then, seeing the maidenly blushes, the flashy young matron had the nerve to add, in the presence of quite a crowd: "Newcastle needs a celebrity to put it on the map. The Chamber of Commerce ought to vote you a resolution of thanks!"

VI

Lanny knew his stepmother very well, and could put these episodes into their proper place in the story. She considered herself a person of wide interests, but in reality she was quite provincial. Hearing Hansi play in Paris had meant something to her, hearing him play in Carnegie Hall had meant more, but seeing the people on her front porch meant more than everything else. What broke her down was watching her own daughter; for now that the child didn't have to act a part, the state of her emotions was painfully apparent. While Hansi was practicing she couldn't be induced to go anywhere; all she wanted was to sit in a corner of the drawing-room and not miss a single note. She had promised to wait six months, and now she announced what she meant to do with those months—hire the best piano teacher she could find and spend all her time practicing. She had set herself the goal which Lanny had put into her head—to be able to pick up any music score and play it at sight. When she had perfected herself she would be her husband's accompanist and go with him on all his tours.

Impossible not to know that she meant it; and so for six months the mother would have to go on living in this lighthouse on a rock over a stormy ocean; either that, or have her eighteen-year-old daughter rent an office downtown and put a piano in it! The majestic and powerful Muses called to Bess like the Erlking to the child in Goethe's ballad. Said Robbie Budd to his wife: "It looks to me as if we're licked!"

The matter hung in the air until the night before the young Robins were scheduled to fly away to Germany. Bess came to her mother's room and sank on her knees before her and burst into tears. "Mummy, what right have you to steal my life from me?"

"Is that the way you feel about it, dear?"

"Don't you see what a responsibility you are taking? You lock me up, and send my lover away as if he were a criminal! Can't you realize that if anything should happen to Hansi, I could never forgive you? Never, never, so long as I lived!"

"Are you afraid that some other girl will get him?"

"Such an idea couldn't cross my mind. I think he might be ill, or hurt in an automobile wreck, or if the ship were to go down!"

"Your mind is really quite made up, my daughter?"

"The thought of changing it would seem like murder to me."

"Just what do you want to do?"

"You know what I want, Mummy—I want to marry Hansi tomorrow."

The mother sat for a while with her lips pressed tightly, her hands trembling on her daughter's shoulders. At last she said: "Would Hansi wait here for a week or two longer?"

"Oh, Mummy, of course—if you asked him."

"Very well, I'll ask him, and we'll arrange it in a decent way—not a church wedding, since you object, but here at home with a few friends and members of the family."

Bess dashed away her tears, and the music of the violin and piano which had been in the mood of *Il Penseroso*—"of Cerberus and blackest midnight born"—was changed as by magic to that of Milton's companion piece. A whole train of nymphs came dancing through the rooms and up and down the stairways of the Budd home, distributing freely their happy gifts—jest, and youthful jollity, quips and cranks and wanton wiles, nods and becks and wreathèd smiles, such as hang on Hebe's cheek and love to live in dimples sleek!

VII

A cablegram telling Lanny of this arrangement came just a couple of days before Marie died; he told her the news, and it brought a smile to her pain-haunted face. That was a lovely young couple, she said; life would renew itself, in spite of all suffering and defeat. After the funeral Lanny cabled that he was going back to Juan, and inviting Hansi and Bess to come there on their honeymoon travels. He didn't say anything about Marie; no use complicating the family relationships by letting Esther hear about her. He wrote the news about her death to his father, and also to Hansi in Berlin; Hansi could tell Bess about it in his own way.

The violinist had revealed the engagement to his parents prior to his leaving for the States, and Mama Robin had cried all over the palace. She had seen pictures of Bess, for these young people all had cameras, and whatever happened to them was preserved in innumerable little snapshots which became a nuisance in bureau drawers. A sweet-looking girl—but Mama would have liked it so much better if she had been Jewish. If it made Hansi happy, all right, but he was so young, and what would she do without him? She had thought of braving a sea voyage with him, but of course she would ruin his chances with those fashionable *goyim*. Mama had stopped wearing a wig and keeping the *shabbas*, but in her heart she was troubled, and was ready to fly back into the shelter of her ancient Judaism at the smallest sign of danger.

Papa Robin wanted to load his new daughter-in-law with more gifts than the Queen of Sheba had received from Solomon; but first he had to find out if she would take them. He began with a fancy sport-car made in Germany; surely that would be useful and sensible! Hansi would never drive, for a violin virtuoso does nothing with his hands that he can avoid. Cautious Mama wanted to wait and make sure that Bess knew how to drive, but Papa said: "*Gewiss*, all those rich young *goyim* have cars, in America they are driving all over the place." Indeed they were, and sometimes over bridges and embankments and things like that.

So this honeymoon couple showed up at Juan, radiating happiness like one of the new high-powered broadcasting-stations. It was the best of all possible things for Lanny, who was deeply depressed, and for a month had been playing the saddest music, such as the tone poem of Sibelius called *Kuolema*, which is *Death*, and the one called *The Swan of Tuonela*, which is *River of Death*. He had dug out a lot of old books from his great-great-uncle's library: books like Mackail's *Greek Anthology*, containing the sorrowful things which the ancients had carved on tombstones and mausoleums; also Amiel's *Journal*, full of discouraging reflections; a tome by a three-hundred-year-old Englishman, called *The Anatomy of Melancholy*, and another by an equally venerable scholar, entitled *Urn Burial*.

Beauty had been unable to get him to meet a single one of the many fair misses who would have been so glad to heal his broken heart. But now came Bess, his half-sister and the bride of his friend, and she was different from other young females. Marie had loved Hansi, and had put the seal of her approval upon these nuptials; so Lanny could enjoy vicarious happiness. Hansi knew what to do, and went right to it; he brought out his fiddle, and told Lanny how the Tchaikowsky concerto had been received in Carnegie Hall, and how differently the orchestra conductor had interpreted various passages; Lanny must try this and that, and he did, and naturally they could spend many hours getting that great work right. It would always be cherished by Lanny as his young friend's debut music.

And then those little MacDowell pieces which Lanny had transcribed, and which the audience at the country club had appeared to like. They were full of romantic feeling, and playing them and hearing about them carried Lanny back to his year and a half in Newcastle, now far enough away to appear glamorous. He was eager to hear the adventures of the young Jewish Lochinvarsky who had come out of the East. Hansi told his version, and later on, when Bess was alone with her brother, she added the intimate family details which Lanny had a right to know.

Beauty had never been to Newcastle, but she had been born in New England, and of course had had Robbie's family in her thoughts ever since she had met him; so Lanny couldn't withhold this delicious and exciting gossip from her. When you stopped to think of it, the story was not without elements of triumph for the mistress of Bienvenu; she the cast-off one, the almost *demimondaine*. Esther had raised a lovely young daughter, and tried her best to keep her, but now this pearl without price was in Beauty's hands! Beauty wasn't malicious, and didn't want to harm the woman who had supplanted her; but nobody could blame her if she was kind to Bess, and tried to gain and hold her affection.

At the first opportunity Lanny's mother would tell Lanny's half-sister the whole sad story of Marie de Bruyne; being now a wife and no prude, Bess would become familiar with the customs of France. Beauty would ask for her help in lifting Lanny out of his depression, and in finding some suitable wife for him. That would be among Bess's duties as a member of the family. There was a firm known as "R and R," and now let there be another known as "B and B."

Esther Budd's daughter was gaining her first knowledge of illicit love; also she was being initiated into the secret society of the matchmakers! A most noble, benevolent, and protective order—for how could Bess, drinking deep drafts of happiness herself, fail to wish the same for her adored Lanny, the center of her admiration since childhood? She would enter an alliance with this wise mother, and together they would search the Côte d'Azur, and pick the very likeliest among all the international damsels, and contrive plausible schemes to have her meet Lanny by pure chance. They would get the pair in a corner of the bowered summer house in the garden of Bienvenu, with the moon shining overhead, the scent of star jasmines loading the air, and Hansi on the loggia playing, say, the *Angel's Serenade*.

VIII

There was the empty lodge, Nina and Rick having returned to England in May. It would be at the disposal of the young Robins every summer, if they found Juan tolerable in the hot season. A great many people had discovered that they liked it, and more and more were coming. If you dressed lightly and followed the southern practice of the siesta, you would find it not so bad. Beauty urged Bess to think of this place as her home; for Lanny loved and admired her, and felt that her blissful marriage was partly of his making. There was a piano in the lodge, and Bess could practice as long as Hansi could stand it, and then she could come over to the villa and practice, for it made no difference to Beauty, who had lived in the lighthouse over a stormy ocean ever since Lanny had taken up the piano in earnest.

Of course Hansi wanted to pay rent for the lodge, but Beauty said that was nonsense; Lanny was making so much money out of Hansi's father that it was really embarrassing. He had those plans of the Robin palace with the red and blue marks on them; Bess had seen the paintings which were already installed, and now she and Hansi encouraged Lanny to show them the plans and explain what was to go here and what there. Prior to Marie's illness Lanny had "lined up" several paintings on the Riviera, and now came Zoltan, and Lanny had to take him to inspect these works. They took the bridal couple along, to continue their education in the graphic arts; this was a service to Zoltan, for in due course the sons and daughters of art collectors become collectors on their own. Incidentally it was another stage in the process of luring Lanny from his grief.

Kurt Meissner did his part, contributing dignity and prestige to the life at Bienvenu. Being a man of the world as well as a *Komponist*, he wouldn't fail to realize how important it was to Beauty to gain and keep the esteem of Robbie's daughter. Kurt's prejudice against Jewish *Schieber* could be modified to exclude their sons, especially one who was an artist. Since Hansi had been "finished" in Berlin, there was no basis for refusing to recognize him as a distinguished musician; Kurt, who aspired to compose for all instruments, could make good use of a violin virtuoso on the place. He brought out his orchestral works, both published and in process, and played them with Hansi, and discussed the technicalities of bowings and fingerings of the whole stringed choir; he was properly pleased by Hansi's praise of his work, and practiced piano accompaniments for the young artist's repertoire.

To cap the climax, Kurt said that if Bess really wanted to work at the piano, he would help her; but only if she meant it, and no nonsense. The granddaughter of the Puritans was in awe of this grave Prussian ex-officer, about whom she had been hearing ever since Lanny had read her his letters while he was serving a battery of heavy guns on the Russian front, and then lying in hospital with pieces torn out of his ribs. Bess was honored by his offer, and accepted it gladly, which meant that the young couple would stay at Bienvenu for a considerable time.

There was no use trying to hide from Bess the truth about Kurt and Lanny's mother, and Beauty told her the whole story, even the part about Kurt's having been a secret agent of the German government; seven years having passed, that could be classified with old, unhappy, far-off things. Bess was in a mood to believe in all love affairs; she felt that she was being initiated into *la vie intime* of Europe, and never stopped to realize how she was weakening the ties with her mother and her mother's world, and forming new ties with a world which had been a menace on the horizon of her mother's life for a quarter of a century. It was a sort of war; and it would go on and on, for it was not merely between two individuals, but between two civilizations.

IX

In this sheltered nest were all the makings of a happy family and a happy life; if only the outside world had been willing to let it alone! But in that world were misery and anguish, and they came knocking on the gates of the estate, and on the hearts and consciences of the persons who dwelt within. Impossible to build an ivory tower which was entirely soundproof; impossible to play music loudly enough to drown out the cries of one's suffering fellow-beings!

Less than forty miles from Juan was the Italian border, and within it a new form of society was being brought to birth. You might love it or you might hate it, but you couldn't be indifferent to it. Benito Mussolini, that Blessed Little Pouter Pigeon, had been proclaimed *il Duce di Fascismo*, and was making it necessary that you either adored him or wanted to overthrow him. His government was following in the path which all one-man governments are forced by their nature to tread. Having procured the murder of Matteotti, he was threatened by the vengeance of Matteotti's friends and followers, so he had to put these out of the way. He could not permit the agitation, the discussion of this notorious case in his realm, so he was driven to outlaw the opposition, and have its leaders slugged and shot, or seized and immured on barren sunbaked islands of the Mediterranean.

There was one continuous reign of terror, with thousands of people seeking safety in flight, trying to get into France by climbing through wild mountain passes or by rowing in little boats at night. They would arrive destitute, having had to flee with no more than the clothes they had on their backs, and sometimes these would have been torn to rags; many refugees had been beaten bloody, or mutilated, or wounded by bullets. They were pitiable objects, pleading for help in the name of that cause to which they had consecrated their lives: the cause of justice, of truth, of human decency. They appealed to Lanny Budd because he had been the friend of Barbara Pugliese and a public defender of Matteotti; they appealed to Raoul Palma as a leader of Socialist workers' groups, a conspicuous comrade; and of course Raoul would call up Lanny and tell him—for what could a few poverty-stricken toilers do in the face of such mass need? Lanny lived in a rich home, he was known to be making large sums of money, and how could he shut his ears to the cries of these heroes and martyrs, saints of the new religion of humanity? "For I was an hungered, and ye gave me no meat: I was thirsty, and ye gave me no drink: I was a stranger, and ye took me not in: naked, and ye clothed me not: sick, and in prison, and ye visited me not!"

The balance of opinion in Bienvenu had shifted on this issue; Marie, who had been Beauty's chief ally, was heard no more; instead there were Hansi and Bess, who were worse even than Lanny. Two sensitive, emotional young things, without any discretion whatever, without knowledge of the world, of the devices whereby charlatans and parasites prey upon the rich. If Hansi and Bess could have had their way they would have thrown open the gates of the villa and turned it into a refugee camp for the victims of Fascism; they would have had former Socialist editors and members of the Parlamento sleeping on cots in the drawing-room, and a continuous breadline at the kitchen door. Being guests, they couldn't do those things; but they gave away all their money, and wrote or telegraphed their parents for more, telling the most dreadful stories about the deeds of this black reaction. Such stories were hard for the parents to believe or understand, for the newspapers and magazines which they read were portraying Mussolini as a great modern statesman, builder of magnificent new morale in Italy, the man who was showing the whole world the way of deliverance from the dreadful Red Menace.

The worst of the matter was the moral support which the young idealists gave to the always pliable Lanny. They dinned their convictions into his ears, they swept him away with their fervor. To these exalted souls the thing called "social justice" was axiomatic, something beyond dispute; they took it for granted that all good people must agree with them about the wickedness of what was going on in Italy. Bess had come from a new land, where cruelty wasn't practiced; at any rate, if it was, nobody had ever let her know about it. Beauty saw that she had to step carefully in her opposition, lest she forfeit all that regard which she had been so happy to gain.

Nor could she expect much help from Kurt. To be sure, he disliked and distrusted the Reds and Pinks; the movement of National Socialism which he favored was pledged to exterminate them just as ruthlessly as Fascism was doing. But the Nazis were Germans, and Kurt was interested in German problems; he took no part in French politics, and concerning Italian politics he followed the advice of a distinguished personality by the name of Dante Alighieri —to do his work and let the people talk. Kurt and Lanny had an old understanding, that the Idea precedes the Thing, and now Kurt would remind his friend of it. He would say to Bess: "You remember that you weren't going to let anything interfere with your piano practice." He would say to Hansi: "The violin is an extremely complicated instrument, and if you expect to master it you will have to keep not merely your fingers but also your mind on it."

Quiet rebukes such as these would bring the young people to their senses for a time; but they did not diminish the disturbances in the world outside or the knocking at the gates of Bienvenu. Poor Beauty found herself back in the position of the early settlers of her New England homeland, with hordes of a new and more dangerous kind of Red Indian lurking outside her little fort and shooting arrows of poisoned propaganda into the minds and souls of her loved ones.

27

Neue Liebe, Neues Leben

I

IN OCTOBER Hansi and Bess motored to Berlin; Hansi was still a pupil—he said that the artist's path was without an end. It happened to be a time when the Red siege of Bienvenu was especially hot, and the worried mother thought that a change of scene might be of benefit to her too compliant son. She wrote a letter to Emily Chattersworth, explaining the situation, and by return mail came a letter to Lanny: wouldn't he come for a visit to Les Forêts, and visit the autumn *salon*, and perhaps take his hostess along and explain the new tendencies in painting?

Very flattering; and Lanny began to think of pleasant things in Paris at this pleasant time of the year. When you have stayed several months in one place, you develop an itch for adventure; distant fields begin to look green. Lanny reflected that Zoltan would be there, and they would have business deals to work out. He would meet painters, writers, journalists, and hear inside stories of events; he would pay a duty call upon the de Bruynes; he would see Blum and Longuet, and his Uncle Jesse, and, as usual, listen to conflicting views. Lanny had youth, he had health, he had a car, and he had all Europe for his entertainment. How pleasant it is to have money, heigh-ho!

He wired Emily, and packed up and set out with some eagerness; but he couldn't drive far without being assailed by melancholy. There was that empty seat beside him, and Marie would come and sit in it; he would comment on the scenery and remind her of the inns where they had stopped, the food they had eaten, the little incidents; he would tell her his plans for the future. A wave of grief would sweep over him, an ache of loneliness, and he would want to stop the car and put his head down on the steering-wheel and weep. Sentimental, and quite irrational, for France was full of lovely young women, her native product as well as visitors from hundreds of nations and tribes of the earth; how many of them would have been happy to fill that empty seat, and stop at the inns, and eat the delicious foods, and share in all the incidents! The number of young men in France had been abnormally reduced, and the same was true of most other countries of Europe.

Lanny knew that he could count upon the help of his hostess at Les Forêts. She would know the state of his heart without any explaining, and it would give her pleasure to assist him in finding a traveling-companion. The proprieties required you to wait a year after the death of a wife—but what was the rule regarding an *amie?* Lanny didn't know, yet he knew that he had waited longer than Marie would have wished, and that the empty seat was not of her making. Everything was pushing Lanny in one direction: his mother, Bess, Nina, Sophie, Mrs. Emily—every woman he knew, to say nothing of many who wanted to know him.

II

The day after his arrival at Les Forêts, Lanny drove the châtelaine into Paris and they wandered through the rooms of the *salon*, examining hundreds of pictures and discussing them. Then they had lunch; and because Emily wasn't as young as she had been, and tired easily, she went to a hotel room and lay down for a rest, while Lanny went back to the *salon*, to give more time to paintings which interested him especially. A matter of business as well as of pleasure; those paintings were for sale, and he had money in the bank. It was his form of gambling; he rarely went into the casinos and risked his cash on the turn of a wheel or a card, but he would risk it now and then on his judgment that this or that painter would some day win the prize of fame. Zoltan liked to play this game, and they would put their heads together, discussing details of technique and subject and feeling. It was one of the most fascinating speculations in the world; more so than the "woman game," which so many played with similar ardor.

Zoltan had many times as much knowledge and experience as his pupil; but Lanny was young, and bold, as becomes youth; many times he had bought paintings and put them away in the storeroom at home. Of course, having banked on a certain painter, he set out to make good on his guess; he would tell others about the man, and they would listen, because Lanny was getting a reputation as a connoisseur. He would mention him to critics and news-writers, and these would take his hints, for they were looking for things to write, and why bother to think for themselves when it was so much easier to pick up conversation? Of course Lanny wouldn't sound eager, or give any hint that he was backing So-and-so. It was a common practice to corner the work of some unknown painter and then have him boosted to sudden celebrity. The only trouble was that the painter might get busy and break your market; the ungrateful wretch would dig up his old works, or rush out new ones in a few days and sell them through some scoundrelly dealer!

Anyhow, the pictures were beautiful, and if you enjoyed looking at them, the rest didn't matter. What you lost on half a dozen bad guesses you would make up on one good one, and meanwhile you had the fun. You could have many kinds of fun in Paris, and if you chose wisely you could live to enjoy spring and autumn *salons* for many a year. It might have seemed strange that a young man who was to be twenty-seven next month, and who had grown a little brown mustache, English fashion, to make himself look more dignified, should choose to attend a *salon* with a white-haired lady who might be taken for his grandmother. To be sure, she was a very rich lady, and childless, and many a young man would have squired her about town on the chance that she would remember him in her will; but Lanny wasn't interested in that aspect of friendship, and Emily knew it, which was why she liked to be with him.

III

Reclining on a chaise-longue in her sitting-room in a very grand château, Emily listened to the tale of what had happened to him during a sorrowful year; also the story of Hansi and Bess, and an account of the great unhappiness in Italy and its repercussion upon the dwellers in Bienvenu. Emily didn't mention that Beauty had written about this; she heard Lanny's side of the story, and it was a means of checking on his mother, something which is just as well in dealing with fashionable ladies. They don't tell lies, but they frequently "fib," and if you wish to live wisely you watch people and understand their frailties—not blaming them too much, for we are none of us perfect, but knowing exactly how far you can trust each one.

"Do you want to marry, Lanny? Or do you want to go on drifting around?"

Lanny was prepared for that question and it didn't trouble him. He said that marrying seemed a serious matter, and maybe he expected too much, but he didn't want to tie himself until he had met a woman he really loved.

"Just what do you expect in a wife?"

He was prepared for that also; he had been forced to give thought to it by both his mother and Marie. He told her what his *amie* had said to him, the death-bed promises he had given her, and Emily knew that that had been real love, and wouldn't be easy to replace. Lanny said that he wanted a woman who was interested in the same things that he was, and when she opened her mouth he wanted her to say something. "Most of the time they're just trying to make conversation, and it gets to be a bore."

"If they're young," said the woman, "they don't know what they believe, or what to say; they're apt to be nervous, meeting an attractive young man, and they fall into a panic."

"What I find is, it's darned uncomfortable, because your emotions get in the way of your mind; everybody else is thinking, are you going to fall in love? The girl is thinking it, and you don't have any chance to find out what you really think about her or what she really thinks about anything."

"Sex is much too urgent," assented Emily; "but what can you do about it?"

"I often wonder if they've solved the problem in those co-educational colleges in the States. Do the young people get used to each other and go on with their work in a sensible way?"

"I hear a lot of talk about what they call 'petting-parties,'" replied the other. "When they are supposed to be reading Plato or Spinoza they are parked out somewhere in an automobile."

"I suppose so," he responded. There appeared to be more problems in the world than he or anyone could solve.

His friend mentioned a problem of her own. She had two nieces, one in New York and the other in the West; one the daughter of a sister and the other of a brother. They were both of marriageable age, and it was their aunt's obvious duty to invite them for a visit in Paris. "I haven't seen either since they were children," she said. "They have both been to finishing-schools and no doubt are perfect young ladies, and probably virtuous; their pictures are attractive, and their letters intelligent, but of course they can't say much because they don't know me at all. I can't recommend them beyond that, but it won't do any harm for you to meet them when they come."

"Of course, Mrs. Emily," he replied, "I'll be glad to meet relatives of yours; but it'll be a little awkward—" He stopped.

"I'll have them at different times," she smiled.

"I don't mean that; I was thinking—if it didn't happen——"

She began to laugh. "I absolve you in advance, Lanny. I have very little pride of family, and if neither of them happens to strike a spark in your soul, I won't have my feelings hurt."

"It's something you never can tell," continued the cautious young man. "They mightn't see anything in me; but if they did, and I didn't happen to—then I'd feel embarrassed."

"I could tease you," said his friend, banishing the twinkle from her eyes; "I won't, because I know you are kind. I have listened to women talking about you, and it appears that you are attractive to them. Do you know why it is?"

"I've guessed that it's because I have learned to do things by myself; I mean, I like to play music, and read, and look at pictures. I suppose that makes me seem aloof and mysterious to them."

"They are used to being pursued by men, and the men want only one thing, it seems. But they feel that you want more."

"I want love, of course," said Lanny.

"That's what the woman wants; but it's hard to find, and seems to be getting harder."

"They do appear more anxious," admitted the young philosopher. "It's getting so that it's dangerous to go about."

"I suppose it's the effect of the war."

"You show the least little bit of interest in one, even look at her a few seconds too long, and you see the color begin to mount in her throat—whatever places she hasn't taken to painting yet; you see her eyes get sort of misty, and you know you'd better cut the conversation off and get somewhere else. Don't even stop to shake hands, or you may find that you've got a girl in your arms, and you don't know what the devil to do with her."

The châtelaine of Les Forêts was laughing heartily. "I see I'll have to get busy and get you some protection," she said.

IV

Lanny called up Denis de Bruyne, and arranged to spend a night at the château. Charlot was still at his military camp, but Denis, *fils*, had finished his eighteen months' training, and he and his father would be at home. A widowed sister of Denis had taken charge of their household, and they all gave Lanny a warm welcome. A strange thing to return to that house where every object spoke of Marie; to sit in the chair where she had sat, to rest his head against a cushion which she had sewed, to touch the keys of a piano which she had played. He went into the garden, where the leaves that she had seen burgeoning had fallen and been swept up like herself; the flowers that would spring from her plants would never meet her eyes, and the fruits of her trees would never touch her lips.

They put Lanny in the room which had been his in the old days; there was a connecting door to her boudoir, in which she had died and which had not been used since her body had been carried from it. A clamoring multitude of memories, the intensest pleasures and pains that Lanny had experienced. On the table under his night-lamp lay the copy of *Eugénie Grandet* which he had been reading to her on the last day; a bookmark showed where he had stopped, and now, seeking to compose his mind, he lay reading the part which she would miss forever. Whatever they have in that land of shades, the *Comédie Humaine* of Honoré de Balzac would hardly be included.

In the library of Eli Budd the bereaved lover had found a two-volume work called *Phantasms of the Living*, a study bearing on that strange experience which he had had in his youth, when his English aviator friend had crashed and been near to death, and Lanny had seen, or had thought he saw, an image of him standing at the foot of the bed. That happening had been unique in his life, but from Gurney's volumes he learned that it was not uncommon, and that hundreds of persons had taken the trouble to write out detailed accounts of similar experiences.

More than once in her last days Marie had promised that if it was possible, she would come back to him; that was one of the reasons why he had come to visit the Château de Bruyne, and why he lay in this familiar bed in a room so haunted with memories. Late at night, when the house was still, he turned the light out and lay staring for a long time into the darkness; the door to her room was open, and he watched it, and trembled at the thought of what he might see, but he did not see it. Later he got up and lay on her bed; he was there when the first trace of dawn began to outline the windows of the room. This was the hour when the image of the wounded Rick had appeared to him in Connecticut, seeming to gather all the coming dawn into an image of light. Lanny could see an image of the wounded Marie in his imagination, but he knew that it wasn't the real thing.

Perhaps she couldn't come; perhaps she had decided that it was better not to; perhaps she just wasn't, and couldn't know or decide anything. Lanny fell asleep at last, and when he opened his eyes it was a bright and bracing autumn day, and he knew that he would have only the memory of his beloved, and would have to make some new love and new life for himself.

V

He came to Paris. That beautiful city was shining in bright sunlight, and seething with an infinitude of activity. A delight to walk its streets, so full of his own memories and those of the world for a thousand years. Full also of promises of delight for a young man of good health and inquiring mind. Gaily dressed and *chic* women and girls tapped the pavements with their sharp little heels and smiled their carmine-painted smiles at one who obviously had money in his pockets. Lanny wished that he could have believed about them some of the wonderful things which were necessary to his temperament. He strolled up the slopes of Montmartre, through crooked old streets which sometimes had only a couple of feet of sidewalk, and again had sidewalks raised high above the street, with a railing. Queer shops and odd sights—paintings for sale in many of the windows, and out in the open, set up against railings, or hanging from lamp-posts or trees. He would stop and look at them, but again he did not find the genius which his soul craved.

Isadora Duncan was dancing in Paris, and Lanny attended an exciting performance. Always now she included revolutionary themes and waved a long red scarf; when a part of the audience applauded, she came to the footlights and spoke in praise of Russia. After the performance, Lanny went behind the scenes and greeted her, lying on a couch with a heavy robe over her. She welcomed him cordially, and he told her that she was the world's wonder. She answered that Russia had conferred a great boon upon her by depriving her of twenty pounds of flesh; to a dancer it was a renewal of youth.

"Oh, Lanny, you should go!" she exclaimed, and he said it was one of the hopes he was cherishing. She told him of her adventures there, and in Berlin and New York, where she had made a tour—and many scandals. She had taken along the half-crazy and half-drunken Russian poet; a "divine child," this Essenin whom she had pitied and tried to help. "But evidently I wasn't the right person to do it," she remarked, sadly. "I had to divorce him, and now I'm desolate, as usual."

Isadora was as irresponsible as a child, and told with laughter things about herself which anybody else would have tried hard to conceal. In Berlin she had been stranded, unable to pay her hotel bills, and an American newspaperman had learned that she possessed a trunkful of letters from her old-time admirers, many of whom had admired extravagantly. The story had been cabled to America that she was writing the story of her love life, and meant to publish a selection of the letters. This had brought a cablegram from "Lohengrin," the American millionaire who had been the father of her second child. This gentleman's real name was almost as famous as the play-name which she gave him, for he had inherited a great company which made sewing-machines, and in remote villages of Paraguay and Iceland and Ceylon peasant women honored and blessed him. "Lohengrin" had come by the first steamer, and had provided for Isadora's needs so that she could discontinue writing and continue dancing.

But not even the wealth of a sewing-machine company could keep this daughter of the Muses in funds, for she spent everything as soon as she got it. She had found herself stranded in Paris, and her studio in Neuilly was sold for her debts, and she didn't even know about it because she had thrown the legal papers into the wastepaper basket. The news of her plight was published in the press, and the artists of Paris rushed to her assistance; funds were raised and the studio was saved, but unfortunately nobody thought to provide money for Isadora's food and lodgings, and she inquired sadly what good it would do to save her studio while she herself starved to death.

She asked what Lanny was doing, and he told her about his Socialist Sunday school. She had apparently not heard that his *amie* was dead; he refrained from mentioning it, out of fear that she might again propose to go motoring. He did promise to visit her studio and play for her when he had transacted certain business which he had in hand; but, thinking it over, he decided to stay busy for the present.

VI

He went to call on his Socialist friends and hear stories about the sufferings of the workers, the franc still going down and the cost of necessities rising. Great bitterness among the masses, and a plague of strikes. Paris was living by the tourists who came thronging to spend their money where it would buy the most; that was good for the merchants, but it took food out of the workers' mouths. When Lanny learned that they were printing a pamphlet to tell of the Fascist terror in Italy he gave them a thousand-franc note to help in the distribution. It was a fortune for them, but it represented only twenty dollars to him; less than a day's proceeds from the contents of his safe-deposit box in New York.

He went next to call on his Red uncle. Here, too, he heard about strikes and discontent; but here it seemed that the capitalists were less to blame than the yellow Socialists, who misled the workers into politics. It seemed to Lanny that the Communists were in politics also; but they called it revolutionary agitation, it was only for propaganda—using the institutions of the republic as a fulcrum by which to overthrow it. Lanny had described his uncle's discourse as a phonograph record, and now he put the record on and started it.

He found that the older man was informed as to what was going on in Italy, and hated the Fascists, but there was a subtle difference in his feeling—he had adopted the theory that *Fascismo* was a stage toward the social revolution; Mussolini was destroying the bourgeois state, and in due course the Communists would take it over. Lanny said: "When he gets through, there won't be enough of you left to take over a village." But the bald-headed and wrinkled old painter replied that hunger would make more; it was a process, like the grinding of a machine; capitalism put the workers through a hopper and ground the profits out of them, and the residue came out Red.

The nephew told about two young converts who hadn't had to be poor. A delightful story, even if it wasn't according to the Marxist-Leninist formula. Jesse's *amie* came in in the middle of it, with an armful of things which she planned to make into a supper; but she became interested in hearing about romance in a munitions town in far-off New England. With her was her younger sister, and the two of them, in spite of their revolutionary convictions, swallowed the details of life among the bloated rich as eagerly as any reader of a "confessions" magazine. Seeing how he had delayed their meal, Lanny said: "Let's go out and see what we can find."

He took them to a near-by café, full of tobacco smoke and a clatter of conversation about art, music, books, politics, and the events of the day. Artists with spike beards and flowing ties proclaimed the glories of surrealism, or pounded the tables and denounced it. A poet with a spade beard would be called upon by his followers and would stand up on a chair and recite. A singer with a von Tirpitz bifurcation would be shouted for, and he would chant a ballad denouncing the latest crimes of the government or praising the white limbs of the lady-love who sat by his side and did not blush. It was the *vrai ton* of Montmartre, but Jesse Blackless said that half the people in the place were tourists, and the old crowd was moving out and finding new haunts.

VII

Paris was a beautiful city, but, if you could believe a revolutionist and his companion, it was a city very near to collapsing of its own rottenness. Sitting at a crowded little table in this noisy room, being served a dinner which cost about fifteen cents per plate in United States money, *vin compris*, Lanny spent a couple of hours listening to a picture of corruption—moral, social, political, financial—that would have appalled him if he had not been taught from childhood that that was the way of all the world. The newspapers and every department of them were for sale to the highest bidder; and that went not merely for the scandal sheets, but for the most august and conservative, whose names were famous all over the world; they took British money, Turkish money, Polish money, even German money—as Lanny knew, because Kurt had been one of the paymasters; they took the money of Zaharoff, and Deterding, and the Comité des Forges—the son of Robbie Budd didn't have to be told about that. The same thing was true of the politicians, the members of the Cabinet and of the Chamber—their campaign expenses were put up by special interests, and they faithfully served these until some more generous paymaster put in his appearance. From top to bottom this condition prevailed, so Jesse Blackless declared; the services of government were for sale to those who bid highest, and the laws were enforced sternly against the poor alone.

Paris was the world's center of fashion and luxury, and this included every form of vice that had been devised by mankind. No use to say that this was all for the tourists, for that didn't change the fact that it was Parisians, both men and women, who performed the services, and they were molded by the work they did. In the same block with the café where Lanny sat you could find a place where women dressed themselves as men and danced with women, and another place where men curled their hair, powdered and painted themselves, put on frills and flounces, and danced with other men. Upstairs were rooms where unnatural vices were practiced, and if you had a curiosity to witness them, the price would be within any means; benevolent *laissez faire* favored the customer in the field of depravity as in all others. For a few francs you could get a ticket to the Quatz-Arts ball, conducted by the art students, and there you could see naked orgies conducted on an open dance floor; you strolled about the great hall and observed raised platforms against the walls, with men and women giving demonstrations of every sort of abnormal procedure.

Such things had always been a part of the meaning of the word Paris, but they were far more open and more widespread since the war, so Jesse declared. This to him was a part of the breakdown of capitalism. As far back as one could peer into the mists of the past were civilizations arising, always based upon some form of slavery, the exploitation of man by his fellows; and always these great empires had been undermined by luxury at the top and misery at the bottom. To Lanny's Red uncle the spectacle of decadence was gratifying, because it proved his thesis that a parasitic society could not survive. Upon the walls of every splendid building of Paris he saw the handwriting of the ancient legend: Thou art weighed in the balance, and art found wanting!

VIII

Lanny had girls on his mind, and was thinking: "How would it be if I should find a Red one?" He looked at Françoise, the older of the sisters; she was somewhere between twenty-five and thirty-five, one couldn't be sure because she sacrificed her appearance for the cause. It had become the fashion for women to have their hair "shingled," but Françoise had done it for years, because it saved time and trouble. She wore cotton stockings, low-heeled shoes, and a brown dress with no aesthetic properties. She worked all day as a stenographer in the party office; she came home and prepared supper and cleaned up the rooms, and often they went out to a meeting, where she would sell "literature." Her talk was of party problems and personalities; Lanny knew that if he chose one like that he would have to follow the party line, and he couldn't depend upon himself.

Suzette was different; she was only twenty or so, her sister's *mignonne*. She had a thin, eager little face, decorated with purple rouge; the fashion of knee-length skirts suited her, both because it was economical and because she had shapely legs. She was a *midinette*, earning nine francs a day, which was little more than the price of the dinner to which the princely American was treating her. He asked questions about her life and that of her fellow-workers, collecting data which he could use the next time he got into an argument with his mother. He realized that Red doctrines wouldn't mean so much to this *petite;* she wanted a man, and her state of mind was such that it was the part of wisdom not to study her features or to smile at her with too great friendliness. He felt certain that if he crooked his elbow she would slip her little hand into it and go along with him to any place in Paris that he chose.

Parting from his three guests, Lanny set out to walk to his hotel. But it was difficult for a man to walk alone in Paris; he was favored with the companionship of a succession of brightly decorated ladies, each of whom would insist upon taking his arm. Lanny had been told that the easiest formula was: "*Je couche seulement avec des hommes.*" He couldn't bring himself to say that, but he would say: "I have *une amie*, and am on my way to her." He was always polite, because he had come to understand the economic basis of the oldest profession in the world. He knew that rich women deliberately starved themselves because they were commanded to be svelte; but these poor creatures of the *trottoirs* stayed in fashion whether they wished to or not.

There came one with a soft, murmuring voice which reminded him tragically of Marie's. He looked into her face, and saw anxiety and nothing worse, so he said: "*Vous avez faim?*" She answered promptly, and he took her into the first café and ordered a *plat du jour* and sat and watched her devour it; meanwhile he asked questions about her life and state of mind. So Jesus had done, and brought censure upon himself in ancient Judea, but it attracted no attention in modern France. When she had finished he gave her a ten-franc note, and the waiter a five-franc note, and went his way, leaving the two to speculate about him. "*Hélas,*" exclaimed the woman, "it is always the best fish that gets away!"

IX

Mrs. Emily had been fishing also. Lanny found a telegram at his hotel summoning him to lunch next day. "I have a catch for you," it read, and Lanny replied that he would be on hand. At Christie's, and at the Vente Drouot in Paris, they set up pictures on an easel; at an auction of horses they trotted them out into the ring; while in the marriage market, the practice was that they came to lunch and you looked at them across the table and sampled their conversation. Always with decorum, pretending that it was a casual affair and that your mind was entirely absorbed in the conversation. Lanny was appreciative of the kindness of an old friend, and would do anything he could to oblige her—except marry some girl whom he didn't especially care about!

Emily had caught a whale this time; the young lady whose arrival was awaited bore the name of Hellstein, one of the most widely known Jewish banking-houses in Europe. Lanny didn't need to ask if it was the real thing, for the châtelaine of Les Forêts did not deal in imitation goods. He understood that she must have taken some trouble, for the daughters of such houses do not go out unguarded, and do not meet strange men except after careful inquiry.

Lanny had met not a few daughters of the rich, and had got the general impression that they needed only money, and so they had very little but money. But now from a limousine with a chauffeur and a footman in livery there descended a vision straight out of the Old Testament pages. What shall I liken to thee, O daughter of Jerusalem? What shall I equal to thee, that I may comfort thee, O virgin daughter of Zion? She had all those charms which had inspired the fervor of the Song of Songs. Turn away thine eyes from me, for they have overcome me! They were large dark eyes, very gentle, such as poets are wont to compare to a gazelle's; they were shaded by dusky lashes, which dropped modestly when a young man gazed. She was soft, tender, and well rounded, not more than eighteen, Lanny judged; the color which came and went in her cheeks and throat was not to be purchased in any cosmetic establishment.

Her mother, it transpired, was an old friend of Emily's, and her father had attended Emily's *salon* in years long past. He was a connoisseur of the arts, so his daughter had heard about them. Also, she had that which King Lear described as an excellent thing in woman, a soft voice. Had the hostess given her any hint that Lanny liked to talk? Anyhow, she listened, and interrupted rarely. She was greatly intrigued by the business of finding and purchasing old masters, and he told her enough, but not too much, for by no chance must it appear that he might be thinking of Olivie's family as possible customers. When they finished lunch they went into the drawing-room, and Lanny sat at the piano and made the discovery that she had a pleasing voice which she did not try to force beyond its capacity. In fact she seemed to be content to be what she was in all things.

Lanny found that he could think of her only in Old Testament language. How beautiful are thy feet with shoes, O prince's daughter! the joints of thy thighs are like jewels, the work of the hands of a cunning workman. Thy neck is a tower of ivory; thine eyes like the fishpools of Heshbon, by the gate of Bath-rabbim. How fair and how pleasant art thou, O love, for delights! Lanny remembered these phrases from the King James version, because he had been so amused by the efforts of the pious church scholars to interpret a torrent of sensuality into conformity with their doctrinal proprieties. They had put at the head of this chapter the heading: "A further description of the church's graces. The church professeth her faith and desire." Truly there was no way to keep men from believing that which they were determined to believe! Three hundred years ago the Anglicans had set out to prove that all sexuality was religion, and now came the Freudians to prove that all religion was sexuality!

"Well, how would it be if I chose this one?" he asked himself. Fate had given poor Beauty one Jewish near-relative, and if now it gave her a Jewish daughter-in-law she would be like the people of Jericho surrounded by armies of the Israelites. But the family was among the richest, and they would undoubtedly make a settlement that would smother any mother's objections. The girl would be devoted and submissive—or would she? That was the devil of it, you couldn't guess what any eighteen-year-old might turn into later on!

X

Lanny's destiny might have been on the way to being decided. He offered to call upon Olivie Hellstein, and she was pleased. He guessed that he would meet the great banking lady, her mother, and he would ask permission to escort the daughter of Zion to the *salon*, and there display the knowledge of the art of painting which he had acquired. Who could say what might have come of it? But chance was not planning for this playboy to chant the Song of Songs for the rest of his days; there came next morning a cablegram from his father, saying that he was sailing for London; also a letter forwarded from Juan, in a familiar square handwriting which he saw on the average about twice a year, and then not much of it.

"Dear Old Lannie," this missive began, and continued: "How are things with you these days? It is mean of you never to write"—not exactly to the point, since it was not Lanny who owed a letter. "There isn't much news here, I stay at home and am bored being domestic. Nina told me of your loss, and I meant to write, but you know how it is, every bally old thing has been said so many times. Cheerio! Come over and let me find a rich girl for you. We have brewers and South African diamond princesses and all sorts. I hear that you have got putrid rich selling old pictures. Do come and get rid of some of poor Bertie's, for the government are taxing us visciously." (She had never been quite sound on spelling.) "He is working hard for them and has to stay in town most of the time, but they don't remit our taxes for that. About the pictures, I am serious, because we have a lot of old things which people make a fuss about but to me are a ghastly bore. *Au revoir*. Yours as always, Rosemary."

It was a casual enough note, and the casual reader might have found nothing special in it; but Lanny was a different sort of reader, and knew what to look for between the lines. Rosemary, Countess of Sandhaven, was bored, and her thoughts had turned to that agreeable youth whom she had initiated into the arts of love more than ten years ago. All she had to do was to lift one finger and move it ever so slightly; if he was the same kind and understanding playmate, that would suffice. She conveyed the information that "poor Bertie" was in town; and when a woman precedes her husband's name with that adjective, and continues the practice after eight years of marriage, it tells everything necessary to a one-time lover. She provided a proper business excuse for his coming—was that in the interest of propriety, or because of some doubt in her heart as to his present attitude? If so, it was a new Rosemary! The casual "*au revoir*" was more like her; to Lanny it meant: "I told you that the wheel would make a full turn, and here it is."

The last time he had seen her was toward the close of the Peace Conference, after he had resigned in disgust. He had not offered to see her from then on, the reason being his preoccupation with Marie. Rosemary had known about the affair, for Rick's sister had been a schoolmate of hers—it was at The Reaches that Lanny had met her and sat in the moonlight holding her in his arms, listening to Rick playing Mozart's D-minor piano concerto. Lanny had been only fourteen then, and how wonderful she had seemed to him! Now he discovered that she hadn't changed; at least, not to his mind.

She had been not only his first love but his second mother; so kind, gentle, quiet—she had held him spellbound. She had always been a mystery to him, a combination of seemingly incompatible qualities; she was warm in love, but cool in the approach to love; cool in everything else, serene, matter-of-fact, sensible. He supposed it was the English temperament, which never loses self-control, never surrenders its integrity. "All right," it seemed to say, "I love you, and you may have me, but never forget that I am myself, and can withdraw into myself and stay there to the end of time."

Or was it the effect of the ideas of her age, that feminist movement for which she stood to him? Now she and her suffragette friends had got the vote they had fought so hard for; and what did it mean to them, what had they done with it? Lanny wanted to hear it from her own lips. He could think of a hundred things he would like to ask her, and to tell her. What a good time they would have, sitting in front of an open fire these chilly autumn days! He didn't have to hesitate or debate with himself; he knew that he was going to England to meet Rosemary Codwilliger, pronounced Culliver, granddaughter of an English earl, wife of another, and mother of one to be.

XI

What was he going to do about the daughter of Jerusalem? He couldn't be rude to her, if only for Emily's sake. He must keep that engagement, but of course his attitude would be different; he would present himself as a candidate for friendship, not as a *parti*—at least not right now! He drove to the town house of the famous banker on the Parc Monceau; he passed Zaharoff's, not far away, and was reminded of the aging Greek trader. Poor old man—he had waited thirty-four years for the thing he wanted most, and then had been able to keep it only eighteen months! His duquesa had died that spring, and left him without heart for anything, so people said; but Robbie Budd had written to his son: "He still knows where his money is kept!" Lanny, on his way to be inspected as a possible heir-in-law for another rich man, found his thoughts on the duquesa of the many names and on Zaharoff's two nieces, either of whom he might have had for a very small price—just selling out the American Commission to Negotiate Peace and becoming a spy for the armament king of Europe!

What would he have to pay for the daughter of a banking-house with branches in all the capitals? Doubtless he could have found out, but he didn't want to; he was resolved to be as reserved as any member of the English nobility. He met the daughter of Jerusalem, and her large-bosomed mama, wearing an Empire robe of purple velvet, with pearls on her neck and diamonds on her fingers in the afternoon. His sense of humor was too much for him; he couldn't resist the temptation to mention number 53 Avenue Hoche and his visits to that mansion so difficult of access. He told what a sweet and gentle person the duquesa had been, and how she had shown him her *bybloemen* and *bizarres;* also how she had been buried in a lonely funeral on the estate of the Château de Balincourt, favorite property of that embittered old man who had discovered too late the limitations of his money.

Madame Hellstein could not help being greatly impressed by these philosophic profundities. One must indeed have a great deal of money, and have had it for a long time, in order to regard it so patronizingly! Also, one must have lived among highly cultured people to be able to speak of all the arts with such intimacy as was revealed by this young man of fashion. He praised the voice of Mademoiselle Olivie, and hoped that he might be able some day to bring to her home his brother-in-law, who had recently made his debut with the New York Philharmonic; Hansi, a son of Johannes Robin, perhaps known to Madame. Yes, indeed, she knew about this active man of affairs, and was still more impressed.

Lanny said that, after all, Europe was a small continent, and they probably had many friends in common. Had Madame by any chance known Walther Rathenau? Oh, yes, they were old friends of that Jewish family; Madame told about the broken-hearted mother of a dutiful son who had never married. Lanny narrated how his mother and Mrs. Emily had hoped to solve the problems of Europe, and how Rathenau and Briand had been scheduled to meet in Bienvenu, but the Poincaré opposition in the Chamber had knocked the scheme on the head, and Europe had had to wait four years longer for Locarno. Lanny told the story with humor, and went on to mention funny things he had seen at the Peace Conference—Colonel House carrying his silk hat in a paper bag because he hated so to wear it, and so on, until the large lady with the pearls and diamonds found herself entertained in spite of herself.

Olivie Hellstein obliged her visitor with simple melodies such as a maiden will sing in the presence of her mother: Schubert's *Die Forelle* and *Hark, Hark, the Lark,* then *Florian's Song* in French. Lanny enjoyed these, and expressed regret that he couldn't call again soon; his father was on the way to London and must be met, and after that he had promised to visit the Robins in Berlin, and he always spent Christmas at Schloss Stubendorf—did Madame know the place? It was in that part of Upper Silesia which had been turned over to Poland, and so was not very happy. Lanny didn't know the politics of his hostess, but assumed that international bankers would have international sympathies, and this was a good guess. *Nie mehr Krieg* struck a warm note in the soul of this mother of several sons, and she invited the young man of brilliant conversation to repeat his visit whenever his multifarious social duties brought him to Paris.

XII

Lanny reported to Mrs. Emily, and thanked her for her great kindness. He had already shown her the cablegram from his father, so he had a valid excuse for hastening away. Impatience possessed him; "O that I had wings like a dove! for then would I fly away, and be at rest." He might have taken a plane, but he would need his car in England, so he faced a stiff crossing of the Channel and lost his appetite for a few hours. The last time when he had gone to meet Rosemary the submarines had been hunting him in those waters, so now he counted seasickness as a small matter.

November is a raw and rainy month in this exposed island, and the landscape is depressing; before Lanny's car the leaves dead were driven like ghosts from an enchanter fleeing. But his thoughts were on the problem of himself and his lady who awaited him. Ethical problems, social problems, practical problems! Rosemary at the age of eighteen had explained to him the marital customs of the British ruling class. To oblige her family she would marry a man whom she would possibly not love and who would possibly not love her; she would bear this man two or three children, and when that duty was done, she would be free. That was what "feminism" meant to her; body, mind, and soul, she would belong to herself, and her husband would belong to himself, and neither would ask questions of the other.

This code had been presented to Lanny as something which the banded "wild women" of the suffrage movement had created and were willing to die for—and some of them did. Take it or leave us, they said, and Lanny took it, and so apparently had the young grandson and heir of the old Earl of Sandhaven. How had the program worked out? Rosemary's brief notes hadn't told Lanny, and he hadn't felt free to ask. But now he was going to learn!

Driving along the winding roads of England, he was saying to himself: "Take it easy, and don't lose your head. Maybe she just wants to talk to you. Maybe it's a business matter, as she says. Maybe she's getting along with her husband, and do you want to break them up?" That surely was not according to his code; he had never intentionally made unhappiness for any human soul.

But he would surely be making it for poor Beauty if he resumed this affair! After getting providentially free from one married woman, to go and tie himself to another! As he drove he had imaginary arguments with his mother. What was it that made it impossible for him to fall in love with some pure and innocent girl? Couldn't he manage to have his love and his conversation separate? Couldn't he be satisfied to talk with men? If he required a woman to know as much as himself, no wonder he had to choose old ones! Replying, Lanny pointed out that Rosemary was only a year older than himself, and really that didn't count at their age. "But I want you to have children!" cried the mother. "Not to go about adopting other men's children!"

Also he carried on one of his imaginary conversations with Marie. During her life he had told her all about Rosemary, and had said that he preferred not to see her again. But now that Marie was absent, it was all right. Rosemary was the sort of woman who would neither do him harm nor let him do harm to her. Receiving these assurances, Marie promised not to worry about it in the realm of the shades.

Thus Lanny Budd, completely surrounded by women; they traveled with him, talked to him, helped to decide his fate. It had always been that way, he had been a lady's man from childhood. Perhaps it was because he had had no father, except sporadically. Perhaps if he had been sent off to a boarding-school, English fashion, he might have learned to be a grand superior male, to shake the women off and go his lordly contemptuous way. But he had sat in his mother's boudoir and listened to the ladies discussing their clothes and parties and love affairs, using esoteric words which they imagined a little boy wouldn't understand—but he had worked it out after a fashion.

So here he was, no great shakes from the masculine point of view; he had never knocked anybody down with his fist, never fired a gun at anybody, didn't especially enjoy killing anything warmer than a fish. But he liked to be with women; he liked to listen to them and to tell them about himself; he set store by their opinions, and lived a good part of his life in and through them. Now he was on his way to one of the loveliest; and while his car sped past this chilly and very wet landscape, keeping carefully on the wrong side of the road, there raced through his head the glowing words of English poets and the tripping steps of Purcell's melodies, having so many notes to one syllable. A jewel is my lady fair, a queen of grace and beauty; and where she treads, each blossom rare bows down in humble duty!

XIII

Sandhaven Manor is a Georgian house of red brick, ample but not too much so; it has had bathrooms put in, but still requires maids to carry coalscuttles all day. When Lanny had visited it in the spring of 1919, Rosemary had been living in the "Lodge," but now she was the mistress of all she surveyed. He caught his breath when she came to greet him, for she was everything pleasant that he had remembered. She was the mother of three children, and had gained a little in weight, but that was becoming to her role of Minerva, goddess of wisdom. Feminist and rebel though she was, she still had her heavy straw-colored hair, and had made no attempt to "wave" it. She held out welcoming hands to him, and there was friendship in her hazel eyes and her serene, gentle smile—never anything to excess, everything exactly right for Lanny. Mother Nature had armored her against *malaise* of body, mind, and soul. Neurasthenia, restlessness, discontent—such modern ills were banished from her person and her presence.

"Oh, Lanny, this is the duckiest thing that has happened to me in a long time!" She took him into the library, where there was a great log fire, very welcome after a cold ride. She seated him in a massive ancestral chair, ordered him a whisky and soda, turned the beam of her smile upon him, and said: "Now, tell me about yourself!"

She had always been a tireless questioner, childlike in her curiosity about people. Her interest in affairs of the human heart made her sister under the skin to Uncle Jesse's Red Françoise and the little Suzette. "Tell me about Marie de Bruyne, Lanny! What a dreadful thing to happen to you! Is your poor heart entirely broken?"

She took him back over the happy years. Where had he met this French lady, and how had she behaved? Had she had to propose to him, as Rosemary had done? "Such a funny, shy little chap you were, Lanny! Do you remember how we sat on the bank of the Thames? Do you know what it was that Rick was playing up at the house? You must play it for me!"

He assured her that he had summoned his courage and fought hard for his right to Marie de Bruyne. He described their honeymoon trip—even to the too ancient inn with the built-in bed that had been a habitation of *Cimex lectularius*. He told her about the château, and the garden with the apricot trees that grew like vines, and about Denis who had to have virgins, and how well he had behaved. "Oh, the poor fellow!" exclaimed Rosemary. "I have an uncle like that, and nobody can do anything with him."

Then she wanted to know about Lanny's mother and that strange affair with a German. How was it turning out? What on earth did they talk about? These things were not gossip, they were psychology, the study of human nature, and it was the custom of all "advanced" people to tell everything about themselves and their friends, and the more painful the facts, the more credit you got for providing people with scientific data. Robbie Budd had said that the young people nowadays would talk about anything, and they wouldn't talk about anything else!

And then that story of Bess and Hansi, so delightfully romantic. Seven years ago Rosemary hadn't been much interested in Connecticut, she had thought of it as a remote provincial place; but now she wanted to know all about Robbie and Esther, and how they got along together, and every word they had said to their love-stricken daughter. Lanny said he was expecting his father in a couple of days, and Rosemary could ask him herself. She answered that he probably wouldn't tell her anything—these New England people seemed to be exactly like the English, only a generation or so behind. "I suppose they took everything over in those little ships, Bibles and bad manners and all."

"Even spinning-wheels and children's cradles," replied Lanny. "My stepmother has a cradle that was made in England before the Spanish Armada sailed."

XIV

Now Lanny had a right to know all about the life of an English countess. He had to draw it out of her, for she wasn't naturally prodigal of details. Was she happy? Oh, yes, of course; what was the use of being unhappy? She didn't mention this great house and the servants and tenants—all that was taken for granted, she being to the manner born. She mentioned her three lovely youngsters: the oldest the future earl, the second what Hollywood called a "stand-in," a precaution against accidents. Both were sturdy and sound, and then there was a girl, a quiet, gentle little soul; Lanny would see them soon and he would love them, they were darlings.

And Bertie? Oh, Bertie was in the Foreign Office, getting to be important, or so he thought; he was so-so.

"And do you get along?"

"Oh, well, you know how it is; we manage. He has a lot of friends, and I have mine."

"You know what I want to find out, Rosemary. Do you live together?"

"Oh, no. He has a woman in London, and they seem to be quite happy. I don't think so much of her, but then that's not necessary."

"And you, Rosemary?"

"Well, I get along. I don't have everything I want, of course."

"Have you a lover?"

"I did have, but they took him away from me."

"How do you mean?"

"A man has to marry. He was a dear fellow, but he was older than I, and his parents kept nagging him. No good telling you his name—it's rather important, and the family wants it carried on; they found him a wife, and of course I had to be a good sport."

"You don't see him any more?"

"We have an empire, darling, and it's rather hard on love. They've sent him to Singapore, no less."

"How long ago was that, Rosemary?"

"I've been a widow about as long as you've been a widower."

"And so you wrote me a note! It wasn't entirely on account of the pictures?"

"Lanny, don't be horrid! I wanted to see you after all these years."

"I'm not such a shy little chap now, dear. I know what I want, and I ask for it. Do you think you and I could be happy again?"

"I don't know, exactly. Do you want to try?"

"Indeed I do—the worst way."

"You still think I'm a good sort?"

"The best in the world!"

"You always were extravagant in your language, Lanny; but you were sweet and kind, and I don't suppose anything has spoiled you."

"If it had I wouldn't be the one to know it. But I know I still love you; I knew it the moment I read your note."

"You won't be thinking about Marie all the time? It's rather horrid, you know, to be making love to one person and thinking about another. That was the way it was with poor Bertie, so you see I didn't stand much chance as a wife."

"If there'd been anything like that, Rosemary, it would have been the other way around. You came first, you know."

"I suppose Marie didn't do you any harm."

"She taught me a lot, and it will all be of use to you."

"Probably that's the sensible way to look at it. I really think we might make a go of it, Lanny. Let's try."

Never had her smile seemed more lovely. He started to rise from the massive ancestral chair, but she stopped him with a little gesture of the hand. "Not here, darling. There are so many servants, and there'd be such a mess of gossip. You go up to town tonight and I'll come in the morning. Nobody pays any attention to you there."

He swallowed hard, and said: "All right."

"Before you go, do look at our horrid old paintings and see what you can do with them. I'm serious about that, too."

28

Fire Burn and Cauldron Bubble

I

ROBBIE BUDD arrived in London to find his son and the Countess of Sandhaven installed in adjoining suites in a second-class hotel where no questions were asked. Robbie was not disturbed by the information; he had thought that Rosemary was the right sort ten years ago and he found her even better now. He was not among those who were trying to get Lanny married in a hurry; let him have his fling, and he'd know better the sort of woman who suited him. It was the first time that father and son hadn't stayed together, but Robbie was very busy and had no time to miss him. He had lunch with the young couple, and, accepting Rosemary as a member of the family, he recounted news from home, including his observations of the Hansi-and-Bess adventure.

He spoke only in general terms about his many business affairs. When he was alone with his son he cautioned him that the less women knew about one's business the better for both sides; their heads were easily turned by the proximity of money, and they had as a rule no judgment where large affairs were concerned. Lanny replied that Rosemary had little interest in the subject, even where it concerned herself. In the manor they had some fine paintings which she disregarded just because they needed cleaning, and because she was tired of the sight of them. Lanny thought he could get at least fifty thousand pounds for them, and she would accept that as manna from the skies.

Robbie's purpose was to get information about the international situation. The domestic market for armaments had fallen off to almost nothing, owing to the spread of pacifist sentiment; even Robbie's ideal President, the strong silent statesman, was being influenced by it, and the State Department behind the scenes was mixing itself up with Geneva and taking part in silly schemes for disarmament. "All that is a snare for our feet," repeated the father—it was his theme-song. "The nations over here won't keep their promises, but we will, and get ourselves in a hell of a mess."

Lanny was pleased to serve as informant for this solid and vigorous father, reporting on the various capitals which he visited. What did Denis de Bruyne think about the prospects in France? Lanny reported that Denis was greatly distressed over the situation. Poincaré had been brought back, in an effort to save the franc, but Denis said that the prestige of the country was greatly impaired. Here too the ideas of disarmament had made inroads; they took the form of a line of defensive works all the way from the Swiss to the Belgian borders, in the hope of keeping the Germans out. That would be cheaper than a first-class army; but it wouldn't get France any coking coal for the Lorraine iron ore!

Then Robbie asked what Kurt's friends were saying. He didn't want Kurt using Bienvenu as a center of espionage, but he didn't mind if Lanny used it as a center of counter-espionage! Robbie reported that the Nazis were smuggling in more and more small arms to be used in their street-fighting against the Communists. The significant fact was that these fellows had so much money. Cash on the barrelhead! Bub Smith was directly in touch with their agents in Holland and had made several deals, which helped to keep up the courage of Budd's at home.

II

This gave the watchful father an opportunity for a little sermon, likely to be of use to a young man playing about with Reds and Pinks. Obviously, these National Socialists were taking somebody's money; and what did it mean? The situation was the same with each and every one of the demagogues and agitators: no matter what fancy labels they gave themselves, no matter how freely their hearts bled for the poor, the time arrived when they couldn't pay the rent for their headquarters, and they came cap in hand to some great industrialist, banker, or politician having access to the public till, and said: "I have some power; what's it worth to you?" They made a deal, and from that time on the movement became a trap for the millions of poor boobs who came to meetings, shouted and sang, put on uniforms and marched, and let themselves be used to bring a new set of rascals into power.

A discouraging view of modern society; but Lanny didn't want to get into any argument with his father. He had regretfully decided that Robbie was just another phonograph; or perhaps the same phonograph with a different record. The one labeled Jesse Blackless produced Red formulas, and the one labeled Robbie Budd produced anti-Red formulas; once you knew them, you wanted to leave them both on the shelf—or on different shelves, so they wouldn't scratch each other!

Robbie was to fly from London all the way to Aden below the Red Sea. He was going to have a look at that oil property which had been doing so well, but now wasn't. He and his associates suspected that some of his rivals might be interfering with production; no end to the tricks in this highly competitive game! He wanted to meet some of the desert sheiks who were the neighbors of his property, and make up his mind how best to deal with them; their prices for "protection" were going rather high. Robbie said it was like Chicago, where a fellow named Al Capone had to be seen if you wanted to do any sort of business.

All this promised to be interesting, and Lanny was invited to go along. Ten years ago he would have jumped at the chance; now he was tied up with Rosemary, and had engagements in Berlin and other places. He wasn't a playboy any more, but a man with affairs of his own, and Robbie was glad for that to be so, and didn't urge him. Lanny said he'd go if his father really needed him—but Robbie answered no, Bub Smith was going and he would be well protected. Lanny eased his conscience by promising to ask questions while in Germany, and report all he could learn about the Nazis.

Robbie said: "What I'd like to know is whose money they are spending for Budd automatics and daggers."

"Daggers?" echoed Lanny, much surprised.

"Yes," replied the other. "They tell us they are most useful in street-fighting."

III

Lanny and Rosemary were in love. Nothing had changed since a decade ago. Their passion was intense, yet peaceful and secure; it burned like the English soft coal in a grate, steadily and dependably, lending a glow to everything in the room. Magically they took it with them wherever they went or whatever they did: walking, talking, listening to music, meeting friends.

These friends came with eager curiosity. Rosemary, Countess of Sandhaven, had a new lover—what was he like?—*buzz, buzz!* An American, but half Frenchified, perhaps a bit of a bounder, good-looking and all that—but what a funny idea! Childhood playmates, and they thought they could pull it off again—*buzz, buzz!* Winnie and Patsy and Edie and Cissy, Creapy and Aggie and Jippy—all ultra-smart young men and matrons with nothing to do but play around all day and most of the night, and love was their most exciting form of play. When any pair of them tried a new combination, the rest came running like spectators outside the monkey-cage in a zoo, to watch and gossip and speculate. If one of them brought in a stranger, some welcomed a novelty, others resented it, but all chattered like the simians when a leopard appears under their trees. None of them took much stock in childhood sweethearts, but it was a chance to exercise one's wit, to show one's sophistication, ultra beyond all other ultras.

Rosemary and Lanny made a mystery of it and wouldn't give their address; it was a honeymoon. They went to theaters and picture exhibitions, they walked in Hyde Park, and when the fog was too thick to grope through they stayed in their rooms and he played for her—he always got a piano wherever he stayed for even a few days. Bringing it made exercise for four sturdy men who appeared glad to get the tips. Also he read to her. Nothing old, nothing foreign; she liked English scenes and people that she knew about. She found Galsworthy right, so he read *The Dark Flower*, and it caused her distress. A warning against letting passion run away with you! Keep your head, don't expect too much, or make extravagant promises! Sufficient to the day is the pleasure thereof, and tomorrow will be another day, and perhaps entirely different.

IV

Lanny telegraphed Zoltan, who was in Amsterdam, and he came at once. Lanny drove him and Rosemary out to the manor to inspect the paintings. Rosemary wasn't interested in the details; she went to play with her children and hear what had happened since Mumsy had gone up to town. Later, after the experts had finished their inspecting and discussing, she came to get the results. She was no trader, and made no effort to conceal her astonishment when this agreeable Hungarian gentleman confirmed Lanny's idea that they should be able to get at least fifty thousand pounds for those dingy and tiresome old family heirlooms. Absolutely incredible! Why, Bertie would be able to pay all his debts and be on easy street the rest of his life! The money-lenders had been riding him hard, and he couldn't sell any part of the estate because it was entailed. The Honorable Little Bertie, now seven, would have everything it might produce after his accession; but he needn't have any old paintings!

Rosemary said she would leave everything to Lanny. Make out a contract or authorization or whatever they needed, and she would take it to Bertie and have him sign it right away. She thought that Lanny ought to get more than five percent, but she waited until she was alone with him to say that. When he told her that they planned to put several of these English masters in the palace of the new German money-lord, Johannes Robin, and that they wouldn't charge her and Bertie a commission on these, because Johannes was paying them and they never took commissions from both parties, Rosemary had the bright idea that she would get that commission for pocket money! "I've done the work, haven't I?" she asked, and he assured her that he himself had received large sums for doing no more.

The three of them went to the shop of an expert in London who attended to the cleaning of old pictures. Rosemary was interested now, since she had learned how much money was at stake. She witnessed the excitement of the bespectacled old man who did this delicate work when Zoltan told him that they had an undoubtedly genuine Gainsborough of his best period, and two Richard Wilsons— "poor red-nosed Dick!" the man called him; also a full-length Raeburn, a Hoppner, and two characteristic portraits by Opie, that sarcastic and unpopular painter who had told a patron that he "mixed his paints with brains." Zoltan was minute in his instructions as to how each of these masterpieces was to be treated, and said that he would submit his orders in writing for safety. None of the "Joe Duveen monkey-shines" this time! Lanny listened attentively and learned how to handle such matters, what prices to pay and how to speak with authority, courteously and yet firmly. "This is what I want"—and if you knew what you wanted you could get it.

V

Rosemary went home for a week-end, and Lanny drove to The Reaches, home of the Pomeroy-Nielsons. Everybody so kind, and glad to see him, in the quiet, undemonstrative English way. Rick's sister, married for several years, gentle, refined young mother with two babies, had come for a visit. A sense of peace and security prevailed in this home; everybody did or said what he or she pleased, but no one did any harm, because they had lived that way for generations and learned to combine liberty with order. If only everybody, all over the world, would do the same! They set the example, and hoped others would follow.

Among the week-end guests was a member of Parliament; large sort of country-squire Englishman wearing a snuff-colored golf suit. His complexion worried you because you thought his blood vessels were breaking; but it didn't worry him. He smoked a pipe and listened to the others, and only when they got on the subject of "shootin'" did he have much to contribute. Later, after a game of billiards, he and Sir Alfred discussed foreign affairs and Lanny discovered that he was very well informed. They talked about France, which had done herself so much harm because she couldn't make up her mind whether to let Germany get up or not; she kept scolding at Britain like a bad-tempered woman, because Britain wanted to trade with everybody, including her former foes. There was trade enough to go round, and you could always make more. Why couldn't people do business instead of "fightin'"?

Mr. Cunnyngham learned that Lanny had come from France, and so took him into the conversation. What was the matter with those Nationalists? Lanny explained their neurosis on the subject of Germany. And did the plain people of France feel like that? Lanny said no, but they felt that they had been let down by the war. The average Frenchman had an urgent desire to re-establish the *foyer*. Also he wanted real disarmament—a peace that could be trusted. He was provoked by the idea that the English used the Germans as a counter-weight against the French. He felt contempt for the Americans, who had come into the war so late, yet thought that they had won it; who wanted their money back—as if it hadn't been America's war, too!

The talk moved on to Germany. Lanny told his new friend about the Nazis, but found that no member of the British governing class could be persuaded to concern himself with people of that sort. There would always be fanatics, and they would always be yellin' and makin' speeches; let the blighters blow their heads off. Mr. Cunnyngham told of troubles he had experienced in India. Cows were sacred, even though they blocked the streets and made them filthy; crocodiles were sacred, even though they ate the babies. The Hindu fanatics insisted on breakin' up the sacred processions of the Mohammedans, and vice versa—they were always havin' shindies

in the streets, and the British had to bring up native soldiers armed
with long sticks called lathis and beat them over the heads. In India
these things were centuries old and you couldn't change them; but
this fellow Hitler with his notions couldn't get anywhere in a country as enlightened as Germany. Let him fight the Reds—that was all
to the good.

Lanny had expected to tell Nina and Rick about his new adventure
in the garden of love, but he found that it had already reached them
by the gossip grapevine which flourishes so luxuriantly in that garden. They thought the affair was "rippin' " and wished him happiness, and why hadn't he brought Rosemary with him? Rick had a
new play, but hadn't been able to get it produced because it was too
grim. People wanted to be happy, and tried so pathetically hard.
Rick was writing articles in which he predicted new troubles for
Europe, and nobody would publish them but the Labor papers. Rick
didn't know whether they could afford to come south that winter,
and Lanny had to argue with him; he stood to make more than half
a million francs out of those pictures of Rosemary's, and what would
be the good of it if he couldn't be allowed to buy a bunch of railroad tickets for his best friends?

They promised to come; and so did Rosemary. She hadn't had a
holiday for many months, and this would be her time. She didn't
care anything about Berlin, that cold, forbidding city, and, moreover, couldn't be away from the children at Christmas; but after that
the youngsters would get along with a competent governess and
maids, and Rosemary would come to the heights above Cannes,
where one of her friends had a villa that stayed empty most of the
time. If the friend came, Rosemary would be her guest, and otherwise the caretakers would take care of Rosemary, and in either case
Lanny would visit her and everything would be "ducky." With
Rosemary everything pleasant was that, and everything unpleasant
was "horrid," and so one could get along with a comparatively small
vocabulary.

But this was a minor defect in an otherwise almost perfect mistress. Lanny had everything that a man could crave; he would have
said that he was completely happy—and yet always that worm within

the bud, that doubt which gnawed in his soul: the spectacle of misery amid luxury in all the great capitals of Europe! The knowledge that you couldn't step a hundred yards off the main thoroughfares without finding yourself in some hideous and depressing slum! Here on one of the fashionable shopping-streets of this fabulously rich capital—on Regent Street, where the great ladies descended from their limousines to enter jewelers' and *couturiers'*—here you saw war veterans still grinding hand-organs or rattling collection boxes. England had just had a coal strike that had become a general strike and had looked desperately menacing; it had been starved out, and so bitterness and hate were in the faces of the people, and misery and depression could not be hid. All that a rich man needed to be happy was to have no heart. If he had one, then all the gifts which fortune showered upon him might turn to dust and ashes in his hands.

VI

In the middle of December Lanny set out for Berlin. He had a heating device in his car, and enjoyed seeing the German countryside in its winter garb, and watching the people at the places where he stopped. His mother was due to be waiting at the Robins', for she was coming with Kurt. She too had earned a holiday, and had found a reliable governess to take care of her child. An English maiden lady, very stiff and strict High Church, had been coming every day to give Marceline lessons, and twice a week took her to town for dancing-lessons. The proper soul must have been shocked by what she found going on in Bienvenu, but she wasn't asked to take part in it, and had become fond of her eager and lovely charge. Now she was staying at the villa while the mother was traveling. Beauty said that religious principles didn't make very good company, but were indispensable in the persons you employed to wait on you; she was always particular in her inquiries on the subject.

The blond Beauty was gorgeous in her autumnal blooming, and never more so than in this cold weather which seemed to bring a glow to her whole personality. The German palace provided just the sort of background she was made for; she was as completely in place in it as the owners seemed out of place, and they were aware of it, and proud and happy to have such elegant interior decoration. Beauty knew rich and important people in every part of Europe, and she brought some to tea and showed them the lovely paintings which her son had collected, and was as proud of them as she was of her son. It was the thing she had done through so many years for Robbie Budd, meeting the right people and making the right impression, so that they would buy machine guns and hand-grenades and automatic pistols; now she would cause them to buy Halses and Dürers, Marises and Israelses and Menzels—she could have drummed up enough business to keep Lanny occupied for a year, if the eccentric fellow hadn't preferred to sit and play piano accompaniments for Hansi and Freddi!

Only one fly in this Beauty cream—the painful news which Lanny imparted about his evil behavior in London. There wasn't anything the mother could do about it, of course; the tears ran down her cheeks and she said: "I am being punished for my sins!" Lanny wanted to know: "Am I such a bad sin? And are you really so sorry about me?" He petted her, and presently was able to get her to reflect that a genuine English countess wasn't such a heavy social handicap; she had only to look at the photos of Rosemary which Lanny had brought in order to see that she wouldn't really be embarrassed to present her son's lady-love in the drawing-room of her home. Beauty made a *moue* and exclaimed: "Oh, dear, what will poor Miss Addington say now?" Lanny burst out laughing and answered: "She'll say that Rosemary belongs to the aristocracy and that only God can deal with her."

VII

Hansi had made his first public appearance in Berlin with success, and Lanny thought he had never seen two human beings so happy as his half-sister and her bridegroom. Apparently Bess was never going to tire of listening to the music of the violin, clarinet, and piano, and had been working loyally at her own job—she had a teacher who came every day, and a study of her own in which to pound away to her heart's content. She wished that Kurt might see how much progress she had made. Lanny didn't tell her the true reason, but said that when Kurt came to Berlin he was occupied with his business affairs and with his brother and friends.

For how long would it be possible to keep hidden from a keen-eyed girl the painful facts about this Europe which she had adopted as her home? Not long, Lanny feared, for she was determined to know all about it; she read the incendiary pamphlets of which her husband had a supply, and Lanny saw Socialist and Communist magazines and newspapers in her study. It couldn't have escaped her attention that the Jews were the objects of bitter dislike among large sections of German people. Would she discover how the fashionable ones whom Beauty brought to the house despised the *Schieber*, their host, and resented the fact that he was able to live in a palace and to decorate it with masterpieces of art? Sooner or later Bess would have to learn that Lanny's friend and Beauty's lover tolerated Hansi only because he was a genius, and refused to tolerate Hansi's father on any terms.

Kurt's attitude was a source of increasing uneasiness to Lanny. He had difficulty in understanding it, and had started more than once to press inquiries, but had been forced to realize that they were not welcome. The Kurt Meissner who had come out of the trenches and entered France with forged passports and money to buy Paris news-paper publishers, was a different human being from the consecrated lad with whom Lanny had pledged everlasting friendship on the heights of Notre-Dame-de-Bon-Port. Kurt was a man who no longer told what he thought, at any rate not to foreigners. He had built a shell around him like a tortoise, and he drew into it and shut it tight when he was approached.

Kurt never said in so many words that he didn't like the Jews as Jews; but he must have known in his heart that it was so. Lanny asked, had any Jews ever done him any wrong, and Kurt replied that this was a ridiculous question; he didn't let himself be influenced by personal prejudices. His attitude to the Jewish race was a scientific one, he declared, based upon observation of the part they played in German society. Doubtless they had been a great race in their own Palestine, and it might be well if they went back there, as the British were endeavoring to arrange. But in Germany they were a source of many sorts of corruption. Perhaps they were too shrewd traders for the honest, straightforward, kind-hearted Aryan folk.

VIII

Lanny tried also to argue with Kurt about the National Socialists. They seemed to him terrible men; harsh and violent, their doctrine a kind of madness. Incomprehensible how a generous, idealistic philosopher could tolerate either their ideas or their company! Kurt would answer that Lanny didn't understand the position of Germany, a nation able to exist only upon the sufferance of Britain and France. Kurt would cite facts about the orders which the Reparations Commission was issuing to his country. They had even taken the national railways and turned them over to private foreign ownership! The Fatherland was to become a sort of serfdom, a nation of robots which toiled to produce wealth for their conquerors. The German people didn't think of themselves thus and wouldn't stay thus; they were a proud people, and had a future.

"All right," Lanny argued; "but can't we by orderly and peaceful methods——"

"We have tried them, and it's not that sort of world. It's a world in which you only get what you can take! We have to awaken the consciousness of the German people, inspire them with courage and hope, and that takes a leader, a prophet. If there's any other man in German life who can do it except Adolf Hitler he has not been shown to me."

"But look at the men he's got around him, Kurt!"

"He has to take what he can find. Our politicians are corrupt or cowardly, our intellectuals are infected with skepticism and dilettantism—this job calls for men of action, willing to go out and give their lives in the streets, fighting the Communists with their own weapons—and you can't get that sort of work done by saints and idealists."

Yes, Kurt Meissner was a different man! No longer rigid in his uprightness, but what the world called "practical," willing to compromise, to make concessions; he wanted to get something done so badly that he would seize whatever tools were at hand. He would excuse lying and cheating, and the smuggling in of Budd automatics and daggers! Nor was he any longer satisfied to live in an ivory tower and produce music which mankind might discover and appreciate after he was dead; he wanted to write something which would stir the German soul now—a rallying song for the people, a cantata which patriots could sing at meetings, and which would inspire masses of men to battle for the Fatherland. It was significant that Kurt didn't tell Lanny about this idea, which had been suggested to him by some of the leaders of the new movement. Lanny found out about it only from a chance remark of Kurt's brother.

So it was plain that Kurt was no longer trusting his friend. Here in Berlin he was going about with these Nazis, attending their meetings and conferences, not saying a word about it to either Lanny or Beauty. Kurt had chosen his way and didn't want any arguments about it. He was no longer interested in Lanny's opinions, because Lanny wasn't a German, and only Germans could understand German ways and German needs. Lanny realized that it would be better for him to follow this example and keep his thoughts to himself. For Kurt was not only his friend, he was Beauty's lover, and it would be a tragedy indeed if Lanny should force himself between them, and make Bienvenu a place where Kurt no longer felt at home.

IX

Lanny walked or drove about the streets of Berlin, another city with the double spectacle of wealth deliberately flaunted and poverty that could not be concealed. The number of undernourished and overpainted women roaming the streets was no less than in Paris; the males who strolled and bargained for them were larger and stouter, but their clothing had apparently been cut from the same cloth and by the same pattern. The night life of Berlin was said to be worse than that of any other city; it lacked the touch of *chic* which the French gave to everything, and was merely brutal and hideous. Germany was a republic, and had a constitution that was fine on paper, but it didn't seem to be living up to its language. The Social-Democrats, who had been preaching economic justice for half a century, appeared to be paralyzed by their notions of legality, and the bureaucrats were running the country in their ancient established way.

In the working-class districts, if you troubled to go there, you would see the swarming millions who existed just over the borderline of hunger. Better not pursue your researches in these streets at night, and better not wear jewels or fine raiment—some Communist might spit on them. Better not attend Communist meetings, because the Nazis made a practice of raiding them—the technique which had been known as "cutting out" during the war; an armed party would swoop down in motor-cars, seize several men and carry them off, beat them and throw them into one of the canals. You were safer at the Nazi meetings, because they had armed men on guard all the time; but don't express any disagreement with the speaker, and it would be safer to give the salute at the proper time.

The Hitler movement was a different thing from what it had been four years ago. Then it had been poor and rather pitiable, its followers wearing old war uniforms, often turned inside out for double use; an armband with a swastika on it and a home-made banner at the head of the troop were the only insignia they could afford. But now the storm troopers, as they were called, wore brown shirts, trousers with black stripes, and shiny leather boots; they had banners and standards, and, what was more important, side-arms in abundance. Where had they got the money for all this? If you asked them, they would say that the German people were contributing their pfennigs, out of devotion to the Fatherland and the Führer; but Johannes Robin said that it was well known in financial circles that Thyssen and his associates of the steel cartel had taken over the financing of the movement.

The attitude of the *Schieber* to this phenomenon was a singular one. He was a man of peace, and wanted to be let alone; he was afraid of the Communists, considering them wreckers and killers; he wanted them put down, and knew that the government then ruling Germany had put them down sternly, but he was afraid that it might let them get up again, because they had four million votes, and politicians can hardly be indifferent to such power. These Nazis really meant to finish the Communists once for all; they said also that they were going to finish the Jews, but Johannes didn't think they meant that, for some of their representatives had come to him privately and told him so; they had asked him for money and he had given it, so he felt that he had friends at court. His feelings as a Jew and his feelings as a rich man were in conflict, and he advanced contradictory opinions. If you called his attention to this fact, he would smile rather feebly and ask you, what could a man do in a world as crazy as this one?

The pattern seemed even crazier when you considered the fact that the two sons whom Johannes adored and the daughter-in-law whom he had so eagerly embraced all declared themselves determined Reds. Johannes didn't smile when you spoke of that; he said it was because they were so young, and didn't really understand the world. They took party platforms and doctrines at their face value—whereas it was clear that such things were merely bait to draw young birds into the snare. Johannes said you had only to look at Russia to see the difference between Red profession and practice; the wonderful fine language about brotherhood and solidarity of the toilers, and the starvation and slavery which prevailed. Those things would become apparent to the young people in due course, and they would be sadder but wiser. Johannes said that the remedy for poverty was for people to stop fighting, and give trained executives like himself a chance to show what modern machinery could do to produce quantities of goods.

"Yes," said Lanny, "but what's the use of producing so much, if the people haven't money to buy it?"

"They'll have money if we pay them higher wages, as we can all afford to do in prosperous times."

"But suppose the manufacturers in other countries pay low wages and undersell you, what then?"

The *Schieber* answered: "You know I never had much education, Lanny; I've just had to puzzle it out as I went along. I don't pretend to know all the answers—maybe you smart people will have to get the governments together and agree on a schedule of wages, and divide up the markets. Maybe those League people in Geneva are on the right track. All I'm sure of is that it won't do any good for either side to use force, because that doesn't convince anybody or run any machines."

X

Johannes Robin thought that he was putting money into circulation when he bought old masters; he thought also to win favor with the intelligentsia of Berlin by showing himself a man of taste. He was delighted with the pictures which Lanny and Zoltan had hung on his walls; many distinguished persons came to look at them, and the *Schieber* saw himself in the role of one of the old merchant princes, many of whom had been of his race. Being a person of expansive nature, happy to be seen and admired, Johannes turned his home into a sort of art gallery, to which any person with credentials would be welcome. He had engaged a man whom he called a "steward" to run his household, and one of his duties was to answer letters and make appointments, and then a footman in uniform would escort the visitors about.

In accordance with Lanny's suggestion of a collection of Dutch masters for the principal downstairs rooms of the house, a grave and impressive Rembrandt now confronted you in the entrance hall, while over the mantel of the dining-room was a fine van Huysum, and in the library a Bol, a Frans Hals, and a de Keyser. The great drawing-room was given over to various modern Dutchmen, Mauve, Israels, and Bosboom, Weissenbruch and the Maris brothers. A breakfast-room had been specially decorated according to Zoltan's idea, harmonizing with the moderns, Jongkind and van Gogh—in one painting the latter had put three suns in the sky to make it brighter! Johannes didn't own this particular work, but many people wanted to see anything by so original an artist.

The visitors might be taken even to the bedrooms when these were not in use; for there were French masters delightfully adapted to bedrooms: drawings by Watteau and Fragonard, Lancret and

Boucher. It had been hard for Johannes Robin to face the idea of paying forty thousand gold marks for a red-chalk drawing by the first-named of these painters; he had taken the precaution to bring in an independent expert and make certain that Lanny hadn't committed a folly in that case. The man offered him fifty thousand, and Johannes felt vastly relieved.

Visitors could stop in the hallway outside a door where Hansi was practicing furious arpeggios or difficult double stopping, or where Bess was running piano scales in octaves. Only one door was never opened, and that was where the Mama Robin had her nest; no pictures there, but all the old things from which she would never part, because they reminded her of the days when she and an ambitious young salesman had lived in one tenement room and had been lucky when they could have *gefüllte fisch* and *blintzes* for supper. Now they had dinner at eight in the evening, sat at opposite ends of a long mahogany table with silver service and hand-embroidered napery and two men servants to wait on them, and it wasn't comfortable because you couldn't talk about any of the intimate things you wanted to. You had to live that way because fashionable people like Mrs. Budd expected it; also the important business people whom Jascha—so she still called her husband—brought home with him. It was grand to know that her man had become so successful, but in her heart Mama would have been glad to take her little brood back to some poor street among the sort of people she could understand and be fond of.

Lanny told Johannes a lot about the English masters which he had been purchasing for him and which were in process of being cleaned. The *Schieber* said he would be proud to own heirlooms of the Earl of Sandhaven; it would be something to tell visitors about. Lanny didn't go into details about the countess, just said that she had been a girlhood friend, and that was how he had learned about the paintings. He knew that Johannes would be amused by the story of a noble English lady collecting a commission from her husband; incidentally this was a way of letting a man of business understand that Lanny and Zoltan meant what they said about never taking commissions from both parties. There was a lot of rascality in the world, and having elegant manners and even a title was no guarantee against it. Lanny took a haughty attitude about himself; he told his clients exactly what he would do, and then he did it, and if anyone so much as hinted at distrust of his word, he took up his hat and told that person that he would prefer to have him or her find some representative in whom he had confidence.

XI

Beauty of course couldn't go to Stubendorf, for the Meissners were people with fixed notions of propriety and, while they had doubtless guessed the truth about Kurt's stay on the Riviera, they couldn't be asked to receive the woman in their home. That didn't worry Beauty, because she had been used to such things all her mature life and was well content with her own world, somewhat more than *demi*. Kurt and Lanny would go to the Schloss, while Beauty continued to meet the smart set of Berlin and be made dizzy by the "social whirl." So many fascinating men—and she was still at an age where she might have made a brilliant match, if it had not been for her sense of loyalty to a penniless genius.

At Stubendorf life was quiet and happy. Locarno was having its effect; industry was reviving throughout Upper Silesia, both German and Polish, which meant that there was a ready market for country produce, and it was possible to get needles and thread and clothing and shoes as in old days. There was a member of the family whom Lanny had never met before—that shell-shocked brother whom Kurt had visited in the Polish town. A somber, sad-eyed man with prematurely gray hair, he was dealt with gently, a little fearfully, as if people weren't sure what he might do next. Lanny didn't know what to talk to him about, but found that he was fond of music, and after that it was easy.

Heinrich Jung was there, having completed his studies in forestry; but he wasn't going to work at it because he had become a party leader and gave all his time to that. He was the same ardent propagandist, but no longer naïve, and Lanny didn't like him so well. Was it just Lanny's distrust of the Nazis, or was it the fact that Heinrich had become harsher and more cynical? Lanny listened to the conversation of the two friends about the details of party affairs, which appeared to be intrigues and treacheries, gossip concerning personalities, their weaknesses and inadequacies, and the methods of driving them to do what you wanted. It appeared that two wings had developed in the Nazi movement: in the north the party was under the control of one Gregor Strasser, and was "radical," that is, it took seriously the party's promises of economic change; whereas Hitler and his Munich group were now "conservative," possibly because of the large sums they were getting from Thyssen and his steel cartel.

Would it have been the same if Lanny had been listening to the talk of Social-Democratic, or Centrist or Communist party organizers? He told himself that it was probably so, for human nature remained much the same, regardless of what theories or programs men adopted; those who acquired power in any field found themselves in conflict with others who coveted that power and who had to be held in subjection by fear or greed. Lanny wanted to go back to his ivory tower, but his heart was sore because he wouldn't be able to take his old friend with him. Kurt was going to compose music for the Hitler movement, and was to be paid for it out of party funds; so there would be people intriguing for and against him, and the lofty serenity of Johann Wolfgang von Goethe would no longer be his prized possession!

They had motored to Stubendorf, and as Heinrich wanted to attend some party affair in Berlin, Lanny brought them both back with him. Kurt and Heinrich sat in the back seat and talked all the way, and by the time they arrived there wasn't much that Lanny didn't know about the National Socialist movement. The Führer, it appeared, was an ascetic who neither smoked nor drank nor ate meat; but he had on his hands a group of men who were far from saintly, and he had to rave and storm at them; sometimes he had to overlook their abnormal conduct because of their great ability, with which he could not dispense. Lanny heard about an ace aviator by the name of Göring who had fled to Sweden because he would not live under a Socialist government; now he had come back to help put the Reds of all sorts out of the Fatherland. He heard about a little club-footed dwarf named Goebbels who was the most marvelous propagandist in all Germany. He heard about others who had been police agents and still might be; some who had been criminals, but had fallen under the spell of the leader's patriotic fervor. The war had deprived Germany of many things, but it had provided her with a super-abundance of ex-soldiers, especially officers, some eight or nine hundred thousand of them—from the Führer, who had been a corporal, up to the great General Ludendorff, commander of them all. From lowest to highest, all were discontented, and formed material from which this movement of patriotic resurgence had recruited both leaders and followers.

XII

Lanny delivered the pair safely at their destination, in spite of a snowstorm. He did not go to their party affair, saying that he had picture business to attend to. Later, Kurt told him that he wanted to go to Munich to make arrangements for the publication of the music he proposed to write; Beauty wanted to go with him, but didn't want Lanny to motor through the high mountains in winter, so she and Kurt would return to Juan by train, and Lanny would drive to Holland and so into France. At Flushing he would be met by Rosemary; and what a blissful thing to be with an Englishwoman, after all the large beefy bodies, the loud guttural voices, the storm and stress and conflict of Germany! Lanny decided that except for Hansi and Bess and Freddi he didn't care for anybody in Germany any more, and wouldn't go there. He loved the English people, who were quiet and restrained and easy-going; practicing pacifists, safely tucked away on their foggy island; blundering and bungling, but managing to improve things little by little, and hating hatred and violence and unreason.

So when he saw his sweetheart coming off the packet-boat, with only a few of her blond hairs ruffled by the January gale, he behaved just like a proper Englishman; that is to say, he shook hands with her and inquired: "Passage too beastly?" When she said: "No, not bad," he knew that there would always be an England.

29

Let Joy Be Unconfined

I

A NEW stage began in Lanny Budd's career. Living with the Countess of Sandhaven was a different thing from living with Marie de Bruyne. The latter had been a mature woman of quiet tastes; she had been content to stay at home and read or listen to Lanny's music. But Rosemary was young and beautiful, popular and *très snob;* she liked to go about, see the gay world, and meet other young people. Be assured, if Lanny didn't take her, plenty of others were eager to do so! Marie had been like a wife, upon whom he had claims; but Rosemary was a sweetheart, having to be perpetually courted. She didn't ever make him jealous, but just took it for granted that he would look out for her, and, valuing his treasure highly, he did so.

Never had the Riviera been so gay. Each season surpassed the last. By the beginning of 1927 prosperity had returned; industry was booming to make up for wartime destruction, and everybody who had money counted upon having more. Americans, escaping Prohibition, came pouring into France; with the franc at two cents, one-tenth its pre-war value, champagne was practically free. In the cold weather most Paris visitors came to Cannes or Nice, Menton or "Monty," and the bands thumped, there was dancing all night, and insane gambling in the casinos—it was done mostly with thousand-franc notes, the highest the French government printed, and the devotees of roulette, baccarat, and "chemmy" brought great wads of the stuff into the gambling-rooms. Wild parties and every sort of excess became familiar, and suicides were decorously hushed up.

In the daytime the outdoor sports flourished: golf and tennis tournaments, polo, and all sorts of water games, including the new device of water-planing; a sort of sled was towed by a fast motor-boat and you stood on it and had a wild time keeping your balance. The young people with nothing else to do sought thrills of danger and found them. The bathing-suits they wore or failed to wear became scandals which lasted for a week or two, until people found something else to be shocked by. Novelty was craved above all things; love-making took exotic forms, and at the afternoon parties and *thés dansants* the ladies were not content to have shoes and stockings and jewels and handkerchiefs to match their costumes, they now sought rouge to match, and daubed their faces with green or purple, like realizations of those futurist and surrealist paintings which had seemed to be nightmares but turned out to be prophecies.

The granddaughter of an English earl and wife of another didn't take part in silliness like this, but she liked to watch the crazy ones and make amused comments; she and Lanny went about with the smart set, and many times it would be daylight before they returned to that villa in the hills where Rosemary was a guest. You slept by day if you slept at all, and it soon destroyed a woman's health and complexion. Lanny as a boy had seen Marcel protesting against it with his mother, and now he would protest to Rosemary, and she would promise to reform, and do so—until the telephone rang and it was another invitation.

Amusing to see the effect of all this upon Beauty Budd, that old war-horse, who would smell the battle afar off, the thunder of the captains and the shouting. She would start to run up bills at dress-makers' and *marchands de modes*'. The real estate men had convinced her that she was worth tens of millions of francs, so why not get some good out of them? Eat, drink, and be merry, for tomorrow you will be offered twice as much for your property! The ex-baroness Sophie, being an heiress, always had a superfluity of beaux, and she would tell one of these to take Beauty to a dinner-dance, or something that meant late hours, and brought the mother into conflict with Kurt's rigid notions. She too would have to promise to reform.

If she stayed at home she would play bridge, a game which had been something of a nuisance in Lanny's young life. It seemed forever needing a fourth hand—and how very unkind of anyone to want to go off by himself and read a book! It transpired that Rosemary liked to play, and also that she was used to having men be "attentive." What was the use of a title of nobility if you couldn't command the services of a commoner—a foreigner, too—upon whom you conferred your favors? Lanny played cards many times when he would have preferred to examine the contents of a weekly which had just arrived from England; he played and liked it, because his sweetheart said it was "ducky" of him—also his mother said it was "darling." Seeing him so obliging, Beauty became reconciled to the fact that he didn't interest himself in this or that heiress who was the toast of the Côte d'Azur and who might have been persuaded to furnish grandchildren. Very soon Beauty adopted Rosemary as a member of the family, and urged her to move to Bienvenu, which she did, and it was more convenient for all purposes.

II

Kurt Meissner looked upon these activities with thoughts which he kept to himself, but Lanny knew him well enough to hear the unspoken words. Lanny was a weakling; he had always been led around at women's apron-strings, and would never amount to anything because he couldn't choose and follow a consistent course. Kurt wasn't being led around by anybody—at least not by anybody in this land of wasters and parasites! Kurt solved the bridge problem by the simple method of refusing to know one card from another. He was working at his music, and produced a cantata for four voices and chorus, designed to inspire the youth of the Fatherland with new vision and resolve. Kurt showed his attitude to the playboys and girls of Bienvenu by not offering to perform this work for them, hardly even bothering to tell them about it. The culture of the Fatherland was becoming revolutionary and sublime, and was wholly beyond the grasp of slack and pleasure-loving foreigners.

Kurt sent the score to Munich, where the Nazis had a publishing-house and were pouring out a stream of literature. No delays, no inefficiency here; proofs came promptly, and Kurt read them, and very soon had copies of his finished opus. Then it would have been rude not to offer one to Lanny and Rick, and he did so. Lanny played as much of it as could be played with two hands, and saw that it was a glorification of young people as the builders of the future, a call to them to take up the sacred duty of making themselves the torch-bearers of a new civilization. *Deutscher Jugend*, naturally; *unser Jugend* meant National Socialist Party youth.

But why limit it that way? Lanny said that all the youth of the world ought to help to build that future, and he felt sure that Kurt's words could be translated and his opus published in Britain and the United States, possibly also in France. He was saddened to find that Kurt wasn't interested in this proposal; Kurt didn't think those nations could understand the spirit of his work, and didn't even care to find out. Apparently he wanted the new German culture to be kept a German secret!

Lanny knew that *Fascismo* had been devoting its attention to its youth from the very outset; their song was called *Giovinezza*, and its spirit was identical with that of Kurt's new work. But it would be tactless to hint at this, for Kurt regarded the Italians as a thoroughly decadent race, and would be indignant at the idea that the Führer had taken the smallest hint from the Duce. The fact that one word was a translation of the other was not mentioned in Nazi circles. Truth was German, virtue was German, and power was going to be German. *Kraft durch Freude* was a German phrase, and the idea of cultivating youth, glorifying it, feeding it well so that it would be sound and vigorous, teaching it to march and drill and chant about solidarity and devotion to *lieb' Vaterland*—assuredly all this had come not from Mussolini, but rather from Bismarck, if you must go back of the present Nazi movement. It was a part of the German system of social security. Call it paternalism if you wished —it meant that the *Volk* was one, its sentiments one, and those who had the gift of genius and the technique of art would inspire the rest with hope and courage, a new ideal of service.

"Of course," assented Lanny; "that is what we have talked about since we were boys. But what kind of service is it to be? For what purpose are the young people marching? We used to dream that it was to help all mankind."

"The rest of the nations don't want any help from Germany," replied the ex-artillery officer; "neither do they want to give us help. We social outcasts have to do our own job."

III

Rick and Nina came, according to their promise. Nina was a devoted wife and mother, and didn't go about much. Rick was working hard, making a book out of his various magazine articles; weaving them into a picture of Europe during the eight years since the Armistice. He read, wrote, and studied most of the time, and was rather pallid and harassed looking. Nina tried her best to divert his mind and to get him out of doors. She and Rosemary, being English, understood each other and were good friends. Lanny would take them sailing, or drive them whenever Rick could be pried loose. The children played happily with Marceline, under the watchful eye of the most proper of governesses, who was glad to see one respectably married English couple installed on the estate.

Lanny took a great interest in Rick's output; read his manuscript day by day and discussed the different points with him. It was Rick's thesis that nature had intended Europe to be a unity; economics and geography made it necessary, and the splitting of the continent into a number of little warring states meant poverty for them all. Lanny considered that an unanswerable proposition, but when he took it to Kurt he got the reply that Europe would have been a unity half a century ago if it had not been for England, whose fixed policy it was never to permit one people to gain hegemony, but always to raise up a rival. Divide and rule, the ancient formula. What Rick wanted was a Socialist Europe; but when that proposal had passed through Kurt's mind it emerged as a Europe disciplined and organized by the genius of the blond and blue-eyed Aryans.

While the Englishman was in the midst of his work there arrived from Heinrich Jung the second volume of Hitler's *Mein Kampf*.

Kurt read it, but didn't offer to talk about it with either of his friends. However, to a visiting German professor he declared that with all its obvious faults it was the work of a genius, a revelation of the insurgent German *Geist;* all kinds of mystical things like that, and so Rick decided that perhaps the book had a place in what he was writing, and he borrowed and read it. He judged it important enough to write a review and offer it to newspapers and weeklies, but in vain —for nobody in civilized and rational England could be interested in such stuff. Rick's favorite editor wrote him that there were hundreds of eccentric movements all over Europe and thousands in America, and why single out an author who was so clearly pathological?

Rick didn't mention the subject to Kurt, or to any other German; but to Lanny he pointed out the passages in which the Nazi Führer proclaimed it the destiny of the German race to rule the world. That was what the blue-eyed young Aryans were being marched and drilled for, that was what the fair Aryan maidens were taught to have babies for! "It's nothing but old-style chauvinism, with a German label instead of French," said the Englishman, who knew his history. "Not a new feature in it from cover to cover."

"Isn't the anti-Jew business new?" asked the American.

"Have you forgotten the Dreyfus case? It's the same thing all over Europe. Demagogues who don't know how to solve the problems of their time find it cheap and easy to throw the blame on the Jews, who made use of the scapegoat and now have to play the role."

Lanny was sad over these developments. His private Locarno wasn't succeeding so well as he had hoped. Rick and Nina stayed more and more in the lodge, and Kurt stayed in his studio; both worked hard, and their products would go forth into the world to wage ideological war upon one another! How long would it be before that kind of war became a deadlier kind?

IV

Robbie Budd came back from his journey to the land of desert sheiks. Lanny and Rosemary drove to meet him at Marseille, and found him browned by the sun and fattened by the life on shipboard. With him was Bub Smith, ex-cowboy and handy man in all emergencies. Bub was taking the first train for Paris on important business, but the father was coming to Juan for a few days' visit with his ex-family, or whatever you chose to call it. Robbie was good company, as always; he had funny stories to tell about the primitive world into which he had plunged, and was proud of Lanny and the tiptop young female he had picked for himself. He showed it in just the right jolly way, and Rosemary, who didn't as a rule take to Americans, found this a pleasant breeze out of what was to her the Far West. Connecticut was an Indian name, wasn't it? Did they still have them there?

When Robbie and his son were alone in the sailboat, the father had a lot of news. He had found things very bad at the property of the New England-Arabian Oil Company. None of the various kinds of trouble had been accidental. Robbie had fired one man, and had cabled to New York for an engineer to meet him in Paris. Robbie had made friends with some of the desert sheiks, and Bub Smith had awed them by a demonstration of pistol-shooting the like of which had never before been seen in Arabia. Robbie had learned that the sheiks' increased demand for money hadn't originated in their own brown skulls, but had been suggested from outside—in short, money had been paid in this desert land to make trouble for Robbie Budd and his associates.

"Who's doing it?" Lanny asked, and Robbie said: "That's one of the things Bub and I have to find out. I've had a notion in the back of my head for quite a while that Zaharoff may have something to do with it."

"Oh, my God!" exclaimed the son.

"Don't put it beyond him. It's an old trick, and he knows them all."

"But why should he be sabotaging himself?"

"He owns many oil properties, and mightn't object to shutting one of them down and waiting. If he could get us well 'softened,' as the military men phrase it, he might buy us out at his own figure."

"He's supposed to be broken-hearted over the duquesa," remarked the unmilitary Lanny.

"Doubtless he misses her; but it only leaves him more time to think about his money."

"What do you expect to do about it?"

"I haven't made up my mind yet. I'm going to see him, and I'll be able to judge better when I note his attitude."

V

The old munitions king now spent his winters regularly at Monte Carlo, and was a familiar sight strolling on its wide parkway, or sitting in the sunshine alone, staring ahead into vacancy. If some stranger approached and ventured to disturb him he would bite, and the severity of his bite had become something of a legend. He stayed at that same hotel where the young Lanny had had his amusing adventure with him; thirteen years had passed, but the richest man in Europe had never forgotten it, and there was always a twinkle in his blue eyes whenever he saw the son of Budd's.

Lanny and his father came by appointment, and were ushered to the same drawing-room by the munitions king's secretary, a retired British army officer. They were struck by the change in their host. Both his face and figure seemed to have shrunk, with the result that there were wrinkles in his skin, and his green satin smoking-jacket was a size too big for him; it covered half his hands, and Lanny wondered if it was because of the fact that the duquesa wasn't there to get him properly fitted. The snow-white mustache and imperial which he wore seemed longer and more straggly, and perhaps he needed someone to remind him to have it trimmed. A forlorn old figure he seemed to the sensitive younger man.

He was glad to see this pair, because they had known the wife whom he so adored. He spoke of his bitter loss, and they talked for a while about her; Lanny would have talked the same way about Marie de Bruyne, and it seemed to him that the genuineness of the old trader's feeling was obvious. Was it possible that a man could speak such words of sorrow, and accept words of sympathy in return, and then go off and stab the speaker in the back? Robbie said that he could and would, and to Lanny it was a type to study and a problem to meditate upon. In spite of having lived in a very bad world, the younger man hadn't had much personal acquaintance with villains, and was inclined to think of them as sick men, objects of pity. Had this master of money spent so many years tricking people that he couldn't help doing it, even when he could no longer use his gains?

"Well, young man," said Zaharoff, "I hear that you have become a captain of industry since we last met." Lanny was struck by the remark, which seemed to suggest that the old spider was getting reports on him. Surely Lanny's doings weren't important enough to be a subject of investigation by the munitions king of Europe!

"It wouldn't seem much to you, Sir Basil," he replied politely. "But it's enough to keep me contented."

"In that case, you might take me into partnership," remarked the other. "You have a secret worth more than money."

"Well, if you have any pictures that bore you, I will help you to get rid of them."

"I have a great many, and they all bore me."

"Perhaps you have learned too much about your fellow-men, Sir Basil," suggested the young philosopher; and the other replied sadly that there was no way to unlearn such lessons.

He always talked like that to Lanny. Was it because of the odd set of circumstances which had begun their acquaintance? Or was it because he thought that was the way to please a young idealist? Robbie had remarked to his son that a rascal was the last thing in the world that a successful rascal would appear to be. If he wished to win your favor he would find out what you admired and then be that. So don't take any of Zaharoff's remarks too seriously; don't be surprised if he was a scholar and an art lover—or even a moralist and a pacifist!

VI

The two oil men got down to business. Robbie reported on his visit to the Gulf of Aden; he gave no hint of his suspicions of sabotage, but laid the blame upon the native turbulence of Arab sheiks. He reminded Zaharoff that his reason for taking British investors into this undertaking had been the hope that British power could be assured for their protection.

"Yes," agreed the other; "but you know that these are disturbed times, and governments are less willing to incur risk and expense for us investors than they used to be."

"It is an awkward position for Americans to be caught in, Sir Basil. We had every hope that your influence could be counted upon."

"My influence is not what it was, Mr. Budd; I am an old man, and have retired from all activities."

"But you have many friends in the government."

"Governments change rapidly, and so, I am sorry to say, do friendships. When you sever business ties, you find that you are left pretty much alone."

The old Greek talked along that line for quite a while; he was extremely pessimistic concerning both himself and his world. The Reds were hanging on in Russia, and this was having the worst possible effect in other countries; the propagandists of sedition were spending fortunes in all of them, including Britain and France, to undermine the morale of the workers. "That Zinoviev letter wasn't the only one, Mr. Budd."

Robbie knew about that document, which had been given out a few days before the general elections in Britain and had enabled the Tories to sweep the country. Lanny's Uncle Jesse was sure the letter was a forgery, but Lanny knew that this idea could have no place in the discussion of two masters of money. He listened in silence while his father felt out the old trader's position on the subject of oil markets, prices, prospects, and what might or might not be done to persuade the British government to give naval support in places under British mandate from the League of Nations. Robbie suggested that Zaharoff might go to London and see if he could not get the necessary assurances; but the reply was that he was seventy-six years of age and his physician would not permit him to take such a trip in winter.

Finally Robbie dropped a hint to the effect that certain of his associates were discouraged about the prospects for New England-Arabian Oil, and were inclined to dispose of their holdings. Both father and son watched with interest to see what would be the reaction. Zaharoff said that such persons would be ill-advised, because there were many signs of trouble in various parts of the world, and if war broke out, oil shares were sure to rise. Lanny decided then that Robbie must be mistaken as to Zaharoff's purposes; but later, when the pair were leaving, the old man put in a casual remark that if any of the Americans were determined to part with their holdings, he might be willing to consider making an offer. Lanny changed his mind hurriedly; and when they were out in the car the father said: "You see, the old spider spinning his web!"

Zaharoff's last words had been addressed to Lanny: "Come to the Château de Balincourt some time during the summer and let me show you my paintings." So Lanny asked his father: "What does he mean by that?"

"He'll try to find out things from you, as usual. He'll ask you how I am and what I'm doing, and maybe he can get some hints—just as I got some from him. He guesses that we're in trouble; but you see how shrewd and cautious he is—he doesn't want to make any enemies, and if he takes our shares, it will be as a favor. But somebody has made more than one attempt to burn that oil field."

"But, Robbie, wouldn't that hurt Zaharoff, too?"

"The greater part of the wealth of an oil field is underground, where fire can't get at it. But if your derricks and your tanks burn, you have to raise a lot of new working capital, and that's where he figures he'd have us."

Lanny was silent for a while; then he said: "It's hard for me to look into a man's face and imagine him plotting devilish things like that!"

The father gave a little snort. "He has been doing things like that for fifty years. My guess is he has a dozen men in his employ, to any one of whom he can hand a hundred thousand francs and say: 'There'll be a million for you if that field should burn.' After that he can forget the matter and not let it worry him."

Lanny thought: "Thank God I didn't go into the oil game!" He didn't say it, of course; there wasn't a soul on earth to whom he could say it. He had been born in the crater of a volcano, and he still played about its slopes, catching pretty butterflies and making garlands out of flowers; but he heard the rumble and smelled the sulphur, and knew what was going on below.

VII

Kurt gave his annual recital at Sept Chênes. Each year he made a deeper impression, and this year he was asked to conduct a program of his symphonic works with an orchestra at Nice; it was the nearest thing to a *rapprochement* between France and Germany that Lanny had been able to achieve, and he was happy about it, and proud of the man whom he had encouraged and promoted. For Beauty Budd it was a personal triumph, a vindication of her career. The gossips might say what they pleased about her, but how many women had helped two geniuses to flower? Whenever Zoltan came with a dealer to buy a Detaze, or whenever a critic referred to the classic dignity of Germany's newest *Komponist*, Beauty's sins were turned to glories, and she went out and bought herself a new evening gown.

More Germans were coming to the Riviera, and Kurt was beginning to have some social life; he was more willing to meet people since he had found a new hope for the Fatherland. He talked a great deal about Adolf Hitler and his movement, and to Lanny it sounded like propaganda, but nobody objected, because it was of a respectable kind. Lanny observed that whenever the Nazis talked among themselves it was of the glorious destiny of the Aryan race to rule Europe; but when they talked to foreigners it was of the Nazi purpose to put down the Reds. Practically all people of property and social position wanted that done; they looked with favor upon Mussolini for that reason, and never got tired of hearing how all the labor unions had been put down in Italy. Now they were glad to hear that Germany had a capable and determined man who hated Marxism and wasn't afraid to fight it with its own weapons. One and all they said: "We need something like that here."

Lanny was amused to see how under Kurt's influence his own darling mother was evolving into a Nazi. She tried not to show it to her son, but she got the formulas in her head, and the emotional attitudes, and every once in a while something would pop out of her mouth. Lanny knew his mother pretty well and understood that she had to believe what her man believed; the son tried not to make it hard for her, and kept out of arguments with both of them. He didn't have much time for his Red friends these days, but he salved his conscience by giving them money to help them out of trouble. He learned to say: "Don't come to the house, please. You understand how it is with one's family."

He was interested to observe the attitude of his new sweetheart to his eccentricity. To Rosemary politics was a personal affair; that is, it meant that her friends got interesting assignments to do things for the Empire—in Africa, or India, or the South Seas, or whatever remote place. This was important for the younger sons of good families, who had to earn their livings; Rosemary knew a lot of them, and got word from one or about one every now and then, and would tell Lanny: "You remember that redheaded chap who danced so well at The Reaches? He's been made secretary to the Commandant of the Port of Halifax"—or it might be Hong Kong. The idea of worrying about anything that could happen in political affairs just didn't occur to the granddaughter of Lord Dewthorpe; she knew that there would always be a British ruling class and that she and her friends would belong to it. In her easy-going way she was amused by her lover's notion of knowing Red agitators, calling them by their Christian names, and helping to support a Socialist Sunday school; she looked upon it as rather a lark to go to such a place and let grimy little *gamins* adore her. *Noblesse oblige* was the formula; and so long as Lanny's hobby didn't interfere with his putting on the right clothes and taking her out to dance, she was willing to have him called a Pinko and to pass it off with a joke. Why shouldn't he be what he jolly well wanted to be?

VIII

Isadora Duncan came to the Riviera that season. In the outskirts of Nice she found a large studio, almost a cathedral, and hung her blue velvet curtains on the walls, laid a huge green carpet on the floor, and put couches around the walls, covered with old-rose velvet and great numbers of pillows made of the same stuff. Alabaster lamps in the ceiling shed their light upon immense vases filled with Easter lilies, producing a very gorgeous effect. The art lovers of the Coast of Pleasure were invited to pay a hundred francs to see Isadora dance, and as this was only a couple of dollars in American money they came in great numbers. She had grown heavy again, and didn't dance very actively, but made as it were motions symbolic of dancing, and, strange as it may seem, she conveyed her charm by this means.

Lanny and his countess were among the visitors. After the dancing there was a reception, and Isadora welcomed her old friend. She invited him to come and call on her, and he did so, taking his *amie* by way of precaution. The dancer talked about her adventures in Russia, and mentioned the sad fate of her ex-husband, the poet Essenin, who had sunk into the gutter and recently had hanged himself.

Isadora herself was unhappy because her tours in Germany and America had not been a financial success. The newspapers made a scandal of her dancing with red scarves and delivering Red speeches. Isadora mentioned this with plaintive bewilderment; she never could understand the bourgeois world, or why it wouldn't accept the love and kindness of her heart. She was childlike, and still charming, in spite of evidences of drink.

Here on the Côte d'Azur were many friends who had helped her, but they seemed to have grown tired of it. She told Lanny how she had gone to Sept Chênes, and the châtelaine had received her kindly, but had refused to give her any more money because she disapproved of her way of life. Such things threw a genius *égarée* into a state of melancholy which lasted for days. She always had some marvelous dream, and just now it was to send for the children she had trained in Russia and have them dance in Paris and London and New York. Or she might set up a school in Nice and train the children of the residents! Here was this lovely studio, a true temple of art—but unfortunately there was neither water nor gas in it, and where could she live? Didn't Lanny know some rich person who would help her? Couldn't Rosemary appeal to some of her English friends?

"Oh, Lanny darling, please, please!" she begged, and turned to the woman, saying: "Don't think that I'll try to seduce him again." (Lanny hadn't told Rosemary about the first time!) "I have a perfectly lovely Russian boy—he's a divine pianist, and stays by me and never gets drunk but plays for all my practice, and I couldn't get along without him. But you know that I can't make my art pay—" and so on. It was embarrassing, because Lanny had no such sums of money as Isadora would spend.

He gave her a little, so that she could eat if she would, but the empty champagne bottles scattered about the place suggested that she mightn't be hungry. He gave no more, because Beauty started making a fuss as soon as she heard about it. "The woman is crazy!" she declared, and begged Rosemary to keep him from going near her again. A day or two later the papers were full of a story about a drinking-party at the dancer's home, in which a young American girl painter refused to drink, so Isadora's feelings were wounded; she decided that her days of usefulness were over, and wrapped her green velvet mantle about her and stalked into the Mediterranean at midnight. She got in as far as her mouth when a one-legged British army officer came plunging after her and managed to drag her out unconscious. Assuredly a piteous story, and not a very good advertisement for a school for dancing children! Lanny was forced reluctantly to give up his idea of having Marceline sent to this school. The teacher went back to Paris, where she still had her empty house and her swarms of artists to appeal to.

IX

Robbie Budd had been to London to see what he could do with the British officials; he had got promises, he wrote, but the language of bureaucracy was vague. He was at home again, but might be returning soon; there was to be a conference on naval limitation at Geneva. America had let herself be drawn into it, and some of the armament people, the boatbuilders and armorplate manufacturers, were going to have representatives at this conference, so threatening to their common interests. "Let the rest of the world do the disarming," said the father. "They have nothing to fear from us if they let us alone, and they know it. So why should they concern themselves whether we are armed or not?"

In the month of April Herr Meissner was down with the flu, and Kurt was worried about him and wanted to visit him. It would be the first time in eight years that he had seen his family except for the Christmas week. Beauty would have been glad to go with him, but of course he couldn't ask her; Lanny couldn't go on account of Rosemary, and also Zoltan coming with an important customer. Sorrowfully Beauty saw her lover depart; the years were passing, and she couldn't hope to hold him forever. She tried hard to persuade herself that she had a right to try. He was producing worthwhile art, wasn't he? And wasn't that as important to the Fatherland as producing babies with blue eyes and straw-colored hair? If you argued that Kurt might produce both, Beauty was able to make out a good case, for he was earning very little money, certainly not enough to support a family, and if he had to earn it he would sacrifice that leisure to compose which he enjoyed at Bienvenu.

The mother talked about it with her son, and he said: "There's nothing you can do, old dear, but leave it to fate and take what comes. You know how much you wanted to get me away from Marie, and you can't blame Kurt's parents if they behave the same way. A grandbaby is bound to count for more with them than any number of musical compositions."

Lanny said this with bluntness, because he guessed what was in Kurt's mind. For how many years could a German live outside his own country and associate almost entirely with foreigners without losing touch with the soul of his own people? Great events were preparing in Germany, or at any rate so Kurt believed, and he wanted to be the interpreter of them, perhaps their spiritual guide. If the day came when he made up his mind that he had to live in the Fatherland, what would Beauty do? Apart from the question of Aryan babies, which she, alas, was no longer able to provide, would she be willing to break up the home in Bienvenu? Would she expect to take Marcel's daughter to Germany? Would she expect Lanny to come? Quite a complication of questions!

X

The son of Budd's had a problem of somewhat the same sort. Rosemary had been away from her children for four months, and that was long enough; also, springtime was coming, and "Oh, to be in England!" It was Lanny's turn to visit her, and it certainly would not be gallant of him to refuse. But he had invited Bess and Hansi to spend the summer at Bienvenu, and had been looking forward to that with joy. He kept quiet about the problem, because he didn't know the answer.

A solution presented itself, quite beyond guessing; a rising financier, Johannes Robin, appeared in the role of *deus ex machina*, cutter of Gordian knots, stander of eggs upon end, performer of all magical feats. It happened that during Lanny's pre-Christmas visit he had talked to his friend about the array of Detazes which he had acquired. It was supposed to be Lanny's duty to explain them. There being two of the Norwegian pictures, he had told about the cruise of the yacht *Bluebird* to those lovely fiords; there being a Greek picture and an African one, he had described the Mediterranean voyage, going into details of its delights: how Mr. Hackabury had bought a baby lamb for the larder; how his small boy guest had caught fish in the Channel of Atalante and the host had called them "lannies"; their visits to the hanging monasteries on Mount Athos; the music and dancing on the deck of the yacht—all sorts of goings-on which sounded leisurely, romantic, and *snob*.

"How does one get a yacht?" Johannes had inquired.

"One buys it."

"But where does one buy it? Do you go to a yacht shop?"

"I guess you go to a shipbuilding concern, if you want a new one; or else you find somebody who has one to sell. Mr. Hackabury found a man who was in financial difficulties, and he bought the *Bluebird*, crew, captain, and all, even to the groceries on the storeroom shelves."

"That sounds like fun to me," said the man of great affairs. "I haven't been sleeping well of late, and I know I've been worrying. If I got away on a yacht, I'd really have to rest, wouldn't I?"

"Surest thing in the world."

"Suppose I was to get one, and take Mama and the boys and Bess, and invite you and your friends, do you suppose they'd come?"

"Some of them would, I'm sure," said Lanny, using a bit of caution. "Those who didn't happen to have engagements."

Now came a letter from Freddi, telling the news that Papa had bought a yacht called the *Drachen*, but unless Lanny objected he was going to change the name to the *Bessie Budd*. It was in the Kiel basin and was being refitted. They were planning a cruise up the Norwegian coast during the months of July and August, and of course it wouldn't be any fun unless Lanny and his friends came along. Papa hoped that the whole family would come, even Marceline and the governess. Papa would leave it for Lanny and his mother to select the guests, so as to be sure they were all congenial.

Nothing could be handsomer than that, and it suggested a solution for more than one problem. Lanny would motor Rosemary to England and she would spend part of May and June with her children, after which she and Lanny would go on the cruise. Nina and Rick would join them. As for Beauty, she said yes, but then became uneasy about Kurt, who would certainly not join such a party. Kurt's father was getting better, and the son was talking of returning to Bienvenu for the summer; but if Beauty were not there, he would probably remain in Germany, and so she might lose him.

That settled the matter, and Beauty decided to stay at home and take care of Baby Marceline, which the stern Kurt considered her first duty. She would manage to entertain herself, for Sophie was staying at the Cap this summer, and she had a beau, a retired businessman of settled habits, among which was contract bridge; old M. Rochambeau could always be depended upon for a fourth. "You young people go and enjoy yourselves," said Beauty, wistfully. It was hard to give up the idea that she too was a young person!

There was only one difficulty, a question of morals. Lanny sat down and wrote a letter to Johannes Robin, imparting a family se-

cret, the story of the Countess of Sandhaven, that lady to whose
initiative Johannes owed his Gainsborough, his full-length Raeburn,
his Hoppner, his two Richard Wilsons and two Opies. Lanny explained that this unhappily married noble lady was for all purposes
his wife, but maybe Mama Robin wouldn't think so, and mightn't
be happy on the yacht with such unconventional company; therefore he thought it best to decline the kind invitation. He put it thus,
so that the Robin family might have an easy "out" if they wanted
it; but straightway came a telegram reading: *"Das macht nichts aus.
Wir sind nicht Kinder.* Please reconsider. R.S.V.P." This international message was signed jointly: Mama, Papa, Freddi, Hansi, Bess;
so there was no more need for qualms, and Lanny, feeling gay over
the solution of a difficult problem, telegraphed his Jewish friend a
good-sized chunk out of Tennyson's *Ulysses*, writing it the way he
had seen his newspaper friends do it:

QUOTE THE LIGHTS BEGIN TO TWINKLE FROM THE ROCKS PARAGRAPH
THE LONG DAY WANES THE SLOW MOON CLIMBS THE DEEP PARAGRAPH
MOANS ROUND WITH MANY VOICES COME MY FRIENDS PARAGRAPH TIS
NOT TOO LATE TO SEEK A NEWER WORLD PARAGRAPH PUSH OFF AND SIT-
TING WELL IN ORDER SMITE PARAGRAPH THE SOUNDING FURROWS FOR
MY PURPOSE HOLDS PARAGRAPH TO SAIL BEYOND THE SUNSET AND THE
BATHS PARAGRAPH OF ALL THE WESTERN STARS UNTIL I DIE PERIOD UN-
QUOTE SIGNED LANNY BUDD.

XI

The *Bessie Budd* came to rest in the basin of Ramsgate, near the
mouth of the Thames. She wouldn't come up to London because her
master told her owner that, on account of the traffic, that was the
most dangerous stretch of water in the whole world.

The yacht was not so big as the *Bluebird*, but big enough; graceful, trim, and white as any swan, a product of the German effort to
show how much better work they could do than the British. She had
been built since the war and was Diesel-powered; the owner had
died, and Johannes had stepped in with an offer—he didn't say how

much, for he was playing the grand gentleman, showing these fashionable foreigners what a perfect host a Jew could be. Lanny and Rosemary, Rick and Nina, came on board with their belongings, and the proud owner was about to give the order to cast off when there came a telegram from Juan-les-Pins: "Will you wait for me if I fly? Beauty."

Of course he answered yes, and they waited. Lanny, who had just put his car in storage, hired one, and drove to the Croydon airport. He knew how carefully Beauty had thought out her plans, and he knew how she hated the idea of flying and had never done it; he guessed that this sudden change meant serious trouble. When she stepped out of the plane he saw her face was set grimly. "What is it, dear?" he asked, and she answered: "Kurt is going to be married."

He was so sorry for her, he caught her in his arms right there; but she said: "I've had it out with myself, and it's all over. Forget it."

There were passports and customs formalities to be arranged, and he knew she wouldn't want the officials to see tears in her eyes. "Business as usual," was the plucky English formula, so he squeezed her hand and went ahead helping her with the practical affairs. After they were in the car, and before he started it, she took a letter from her handbag and gave it to him. He sat and read:

DEAR BEAUTY:

This is the letter which you have so many times told me I would some day write to you. It is hard to do, but your kindness and common sense have made it possible.

I have been told by my father's physician that he is not likely to live many years longer, and so I have to consider his happiness, if ever. Hitherto he has made little objection to our relationship, but of course it is not what he has hoped for, and now he has put it up to me in a way which I have not felt able to refuse. In short, dear Beauty, I am planning to be married, so it will not be possible for me to return to Bienvenu.

Knowing your goodness, I am sure you will be glad to hear that the young woman whom my parents have chosen is one with whom I can be happy. She is nineteen, and while she has not your beauty, over which the world has raved, she is of the type which I admire; her family are old friends of ours, so my parents know her character and qualifications for wifehood. She is gentle and good, and I have made certain of her feelings toward me before writing you this news. I count upon your friendship, so many times manifested, to appreciate my position and understand that I could not refuse the duty which has been forced upon me here.

As you know, you have saved my life, and you must believe that my gratitude will never cease. I did what I could in my inadequate way to repay you. The happiness which you gave me for eight years I shall never forget, nor the wisdom and loyalty. If I possessed the magic to make you twenty years younger—and if you were not a rich woman—I would take you to my parents and they would love you also. But they feel about me as you feel about Lanny—they want me to have a family, and good sense as well as tradition is on their side. I write this with tears in my eyes and I know you will read it in the same way. Show this letter to Lanny and ask him to forgive me and permit me to think of him always as a dearly loved brother. Explain matters as you think best to little Marceline, and let her remain my adopted daughter as well as pupil. I hope that in the years to come we need not always be strangers, and I hope that you may find the happiness for which you were made and which you have deserved.

Adieu, dear Beauty. From now on, your half-brother and half-son,

KURT.

"Don't say anything about it to the others," Beauty commanded, with hands clenched tightly. "I don't want to be a wet blanket. I came because I felt I must have a change of scene."

"Of course!" he exclaimed. "I am glad, and the others will be, too."

"This thing has been hanging over me, and I suppose it's better to have it over with." She only half meant it, but it was good propaganda.

He started talking about the people he had met in London, the plays he had seen and the exhibition. The "season" had been a gay one; the country was recovering from the great strike, and everybody was making money again. Now and then he would see out of the corner of his eye that his mother was wiping away a tear, but he pretended not to notice. There were eight kind friends waiting for her, and the stimulus of companionship was what she lived by. "What shall I tell them, Lanny? I mean—why I came."

"Just say you couldn't miss the fun. That will please them all. But don't have your eyes red."

"Are they?" She got the little mirror out of her vanity bag; so he knew she was going to survive.

XII

The *Bessie Budd* put to sea, with her namesake and the other guests all determined to be happy, and succeeding as well as possible in an unhappy world. It was really too much to expect that Beauty wouldn't mention her secret; first she told Nina, who in turn told Rick; Lanny told Rosemary, and presently Beauty was tempted to unburden her soul to a kind Jewish mother who had no social pretensions and therefore made it unnecessary for other people to have any. These two female elders enjoyed exchanging wisdom, mostly in the form of personalities, as is the female way.

The marriage arrangements of this strictly brought-up mother of Jerusalem had been made by her parents through the agency of a *schadchen*, or marriage broker. To Beauty it seemed romantic to have been married in a tenement room, to have stuck to one poverty-burdened man and seen him become the owner of a palace and a private yacht, and seen your first-born make his debut in Carnegie Hall. Mama Robin didn't say that to her it seemed romantic to have run away from home, and to have been the adored of three remarkable men and the mother of a fourth; but she listened with eagerness to Beauty's tales about high life, and if she felt moral reprobation she kept it locked in her own bosom. She had known about Kurt Meissner for a long time, and had foreseen the grief that was coming; she was interested to be present at the *dénouement*, and to provide a receptacle for all the tears her fair but frail guest might desire to shed.

The little yacht slid over the still blue waters to Oslo. The munificent host hadn't been content with the piano which was fixed in the saloon; he had got an extra one on little rubber-tired wheels, so that it could be rolled onto the deck and made fast there. Hansi did his practicing in his cabin, but if you requested it he would bring his fiddle on deck, and Lanny or Freddi would play his accompaniments, and the cruise of the *Bessie Budd* resembled Rubinstein's *Ocean Symphony*. Johannes had been to his bookseller's again, and ordered eleven meters of books for the saloon of a gentleman's yacht, and there they were, safely shut up in glass cases to keep them from spilling. There was something for every taste, and their owner, who had never had time for reading, now proceeded to acquire culture with the same speed and efficiency he had displayed in acquiring ownership of industrial establishments throughout Germany.

He was interested in talking to all these people, who had come from social groups so far removed from his own; he was not frightened by any of their unusual ideas, not even those of a baronet's son. As for a countess, Johannes had the idea that she would prove not so very different from Mama Robin under the skin. They got along quite amiably; for Rosemary, Countess of Sandhaven, had that comfortable sense of superiority which is so very superior that it never has to assert itself, but takes it for granted. To her the owner of a yacht and the steward of a yacht each had his separate functions; the owner put everything on board at her disposal, while the steward performed the physical labor of bringing things to her, and each had his proper place and knew it. Lanny also had his duties, and performed them without too great reluctance; he was the only male on board who played bridge acceptably, and when Beauty, Nina, and Rosemary united their demands there was no escape for him.

XIII

The *Bessie Budd* followed in the long-vanished track of the *Bluebird* up the Norwegian coast. Beauty remembered the places, and noted the changes—there weren't many. She told about this place and that; she knew where the great waterfalls were, and the *saeters* to which you could be driven in a car. Up on that mountain slope was one of the very old farmhouses with a hole in the roof for a chimney; beyond that village was a house that had a tree growing in the roof to hold the turf—perhaps it had grown too heavy in fourteen years. Now and then Lanny would recognize a scene from one of Marcel's paintings; a great moment when Johannes cried: "Look, Mama, there is the place that is in our upstairs hall!"

Beautiful rocky shores, dark blue waters, towering mountains! The yacht went all the way north to the Arctic Circle, where there is no night in midsummer. Lanny had read in his anthology of English poetry about "the shore where loud Lofoden whirls to death the roaring whale," but he had never learned who or what Lofoden was. Now he learned that it was a group of islands much frequented by fishermen, but he couldn't seem to find any who had ever heard a whale roar.

The yacht put in to buy supplies at the little port of Narvik, where the Swedish iron ore was brought down in long trains of dump-cars, and day and night there echoed through the narrow fiord the sound of heavy minerals sliding down chutes into the ore-ships. The visitors were plain mortals with no gift of second sight, so they heard no other sounds: no shattering crash of shells, no airplane bombs bursting among the docks and loading machinery; no sheets of white flame, no shrieks of dying men, no rush of waters closing over vessels going down into the darkness. Wait a few more summers, O trim white *Bessie Budd*, and come back to loud Lofoden once again!

30

Birds of Passage

I

ON BOARD the *Bessie Budd*, Lanny and his lady were as happy as the prince and princess in a fairy-tale; but as the cruise approached its end a tiny rift began to develop between them. "Where do we go from here?" It appeared that the circumstances of their lives were in conflict; Rosemary had her splendid manor house and her children, while Lanny had his home, his mother and his half-sister, and these various possessions were hard to fit into one pattern.

On the Riviera Lanny had learned of some pictures that might be sold, and he had promised to inspect them in September; Rosemary had promised her children to be with them after the cruise, and also she had friends whom she wanted to see. All right, Lanny would go home and attend to his job, and then he would come back to England, and stay—how long? Rosemary wanted to be with the children until after Christmas; since Lanny hadn't been at home at that season for many years, he could surely afford to miss one more!

But it wasn't so pleasant for Lanny at Rosemary's home. He had to pretend to be a guest, and there had to be other guests, to serve as informal chaperons; and whatever he and Rosemary did that was not according to the code of Queen Victoria had to be clandestine. If they went up to London they traveled separately, and stayed at an obscure hotel, and Rosemary was not registered under her own name. All this was inconvenient for a businessman, and seemed rather futile, because if anyone had wished to employ detectives, these wouldn't have had any trouble in following Lanny.

What was the reason for all this? He could never be quite sure. Didn't Rosemary trust her husband entirely? She wouldn't admit it, and perhaps protected him even in her own thoughts. Impossible that an English earl might turn out to be a cad! Lanny knew the law—if Bertie proved one act of infidelity, he could divorce her, turn her out of her home, deprive her of her rights to her children. In that case it would be up to Lanny to marry her, and he would like nothing better; but apparently the Countess of Sandhaven wasn't satisfied with that solution of her problem.

So there were many difficulties. It was England, not Provence, and the proprieties must be observed. The servants must not be allowed to know that Lanny and Rosemary were lovers. They would know really, but not officially. Robbie Budd said that change in England was like the small hand of your watch; it moved, but so very slowly that no one had ever seen the motion. Lanny could comfort himself with the reflection that a century or two earlier Bertie would have challenged him to a duel, and a century or two earlier still Bertie's henchmen would have run him through with their swords.

The young art authority became more than ever a bird of passage, flitting back and forth between the Mediterranean and the English Channel, but having no regular seasons like other birds. When he could persuade his sweetheart to stay at Juan, he provided her with every comfort and some luxuries; but it appeared to be a matter of prestige with her to make him spend half his time in or about her haunts. In order to prove that he loved her he had to be damned uncomfortable: he had to miss his music, his books, and his regular habits, to say nothing of his mother and his half-sister. Marceline acquired the place of a stepchild in Rosemary's life, and her children became stepchildren to Lanny—and it is well known that this relationship is a perilous one. Little inconveniences produce larger jangles, and Cupid goes off in a corner by himself and sulks.

II

Marceline was ten years old, a slender, graceful child, full of eager gaiety. She was at about the same age as Bess when Lanny had first known her in Connecticut, and the difference between them made a study in heredity. Marceline was less intellectual than the daughter of Esther Budd; less concerned to know how the wheels went round, and rarely plaguing you with questions that you couldn't answer. Nor did she worry about whether what she was doing was right; she acted from the impulse of her heart, and if she was fond of you that was enough. She was the daughter of an artist, and would stand for a long time watching a gaily colored butterfly, drifting from flower to flower in the patio of her home; a sunset would cause her to lose herself as her father had done. When Lanny played the piano, she didn't want to sit and listen like Bess; every pulse of the music was a call to her feet.

Lanny had taught her all about her father. She had seen his paintings until they had become a part of her life. Lanny had related them to Marcel's life; so the child was conscious of being a daughter of France; she knew its recent tragic story, and the part her father had played in it. She was her mother's daughter also, and couldn't well forget it, with the mother right there to set her an example of beauty culture, to serve as a walking encyclopedia of fashion, of colors, of fabrics, methods of cutting and arranging them, and of displaying or concealing the feminine form divine. There was a dressing-table loaded with perfumes and cosmetics, all in the prettiest jars and bottles labeled with the most seductive names. There were Beauty's smart friends coming in at all hours to make use of these allurements, keeping up a chatter about them, their uses and effects. Marceline was a little primper, a little *modiste*, a little coquette.

Also there were the servants, who exercise great influence upon children everywhere, and nowhere more than in Provence, where they consider themselves members of the family, tell you about themselves and their families, give advice about yourself and yours. Leese, the cook, had gradually promoted herself to the position of housekeeper, with the power to hire and fire; so there were two families on the estate, that of the mistress and that of the servant, and neither could have got along without the other. Leese and her nieces and cousins all had their ideas and taught them to the child. When she was kind they adored her, when she was beautiful they raved over her; she ate their foods, spoke their dialect, danced their gay and lively steps.

Also a German musician, a former foe, had played his part in the shaping of the little one's character. Kurt had taught her discipline and obedience, and it was a serious matter for her when his influence was withdrawn. When Lanny came back in September he saw that she had already made note of the change; she could now have her way with the servants and presently she was having it with her mother. Lanny had the unpleasant duty of interfering; it wasn't according to his nature, but he, too, had learned a lot from Kurt, and would plead with Beauty to realize the importance of controlling a child's whims. Beauty would agree, and do her best—but she was part child herself, and needed someone to control her.

There was a gaping cavity in Bienvenu where Kurt had been: the deserted studio, the piano from which came no more rolling thunder; his room, his bed, the empty closets. Beauty had told the servants to pack up all his things and ship them to him, and this had been done: clothes, music, books, assortment of noise-making apparatus. The studio was locked up, and Beauty couldn't bear to go near it. But the place in her heart was not so easily shut, and Lanny saw her eyes red many a time.

What was she going to do about it? She swore that she was through with men forever, but Lanny didn't have to believe this; he took it for granted that she wouldn't spend the rest of her life alone, and the question was, what sort of man would it be? If only she would pick some settled retired businessman, like this Mr. Armitage with whom Sophie was getting along so well! But Beauty was flighty, and still had romantic notions buried somewhere inside. Of course, the man who won the love of Madame Detaze, *veuve*, would step into a warm and well-padded nest, and candidates presented themselves promptly. Lanny began to worry about the sort of men who came to this playground of Europe, and he took counsel with Sophie Timmons and Emily Chattersworth as to how to find a proper beau for his too charming widowed mother. The ladies found this delightful, and the story spread up and down the Coast of Pleasure.

III

Isadora Duncan came back to the Riviera. She put up at a little inn in Juan-les-Pins, and Beauty was quite indignant about it, saying that she would be expecting Lanny to pay the bills. The dancer had a woman friend with her, an American who was supposed to have money, but said that she had spent it all getting Isadora "out of hock." Beauty said that was the way they all did, they hid their money and said they were broke, trying to put the burden off on others. Well, Beauty was broke, too; she hadn't paid her dress bills for last season, and here was a new season almost upon them, and was she to go about naked—or to stay at home and die of loneliness and grief?

Isadora and her friend put on bathing-suits of the ultra-scanty sort and lay about on the white sand of the Juan beach. Lanny joined them and listened to an account of what had happened in France one night while Lanny had been on board the yacht in the North Sea— the night of August 22, 1927, when Sacco and Vanzetti had died. Lanny recalled the first time this case had been mentioned in his hearing, by Ambassador "Cradle" during the Genoa conference. Since then it had become an international scandal, and when the Italians were executed there had been mobs marching in all the cities of Europe, and many American embassies and consulates had had their windows smashed. To Isadora the two men were martyrs and heroes, and their death had been a personal bereavement; she was going to create a dance for them, and take it to New York—yes, and to Boston!

The daughter of the Muses was still a beautiful creature; she had been dieting and was getting herself into condition so that she could dance again. She was a completely reformed woman, so she assured Lanny; the rest of her life to be consecrated to that marvelous art which she alone could embody and express. She said it, and who could deny it? She was going to be a dancing nun from this time forth; except, of course, that she had to find a pianist, some devoted soul who would play her accompaniments. The young Russian had left her.

Always when Isadora was in a mood like this she had to have a school. Children became the incarnation of her thwarted dreams; children were the future, the repository of her art, the torch-bearers who would carry it to posterity. She had been to Les Forêts and persuaded Emily Chattersworth to give her another chance; now she wanted Lanny and his mother to persuade some of the fashionable residents to send her their children as pupils. That beautiful studio near Nice was to be consecrated to this noble service.

Lanny took the problem to his mother, who didn't want to have anything to do with it. He sought to persuade her that this might be the great chance of Marceline's life. Isadora was nearly fifty, and couldn't live forever. She had something that no other woman in the world had. Lanny reminded his mother of that cruel tragedy which had wrecked the dancer's personal life; thirteen years had passed since her adored little ones had been drowned in the river Seine, and everybody knew that she had never got over it, the horror haunted her dreams and poisoned her joys. And when her third baby, that had died in her arms a few hours after it was born—had Beauty forgotten how she and Emily had wept over the event, in those tragic hours while the troops were being mobilized in Paris and marched to the trains? Surely a woman who had suffered such griefs could be forgiven many errors!

Beauty said: "She will get drunk and the child will see her."

"All right," argued Lanny, "what of it? Marceline is not going to live in this part of the world without seeing somebody drunk. We'll just have to explain to her what it is. You managed to teach me not to get drunk, and surely you and I together can teach Marceline. If she sees an example it may give her a shock, but it will disgust her and warn her, too."

"All right," said the mother at last; "but it's your responsibility!"

IV

Lanny drove to tell the dancer that they would help to find pupils for her. But he found everything changed, the studio in a turmoil, Isadora raising a ruction because a second-hand dealer had offered her such small sums for the furniture of the place; she would give everything to a hospital, rather than sell at such prices. It appeared that she had changed her program a couple of days ago, and had been too busy or too excited to let Lanny know about it. She was taking a long motor-trip; she was going to be happy again; youth and joy had come back to her. She told Lanny about it in the extravagant language which she loved.

What had happened? She forgot to explain, but presently it came out—"Lohengrin" had returned! The sewing-machine man had promised her a large check, and all her problems were solved. "You know how I always adored him, Lanny." Yes, Lanny had met this tall, blond gentleman, who looked like a middled-aged Norse god, and poured out bounty like the purse of Fortunatus. He was going to take her on a tour, and they would sample the fresh new wines of all the vineyards of France. She would still have her school, of course, but it would have to wait. "Oh, Lanny darling," she exclaimed, "I am truly grateful to you—honestly, I'll prove it!" She gave him a great hug and kiss as earnest of her intentions. Rosemary was in England.

In the studio was a young Italian, who had been an ace aviator during the war, and Isadora adored men who had defied danger. He looked as if he didn't enjoy seeing Lanny kissed, so she kissed him also; she was so happy, she had enough for everybody. "This dark-eyed Adonis is going to take me to a concert tonight," she said. "Won't you come along?"

"No, thanks," replied Lanny. "I have an engagement at home."

"Oh, my dear, don't be provoked with me! If you knew the depth of misery I have been in, you would understand my need of happiness. Look, I will dance for you and change the world."

She had a marvelous red shawl made of Chinese silk crape, heavy, and with long fringes. It was a couple of yards in length, painted with an enormous yellow bird, and in the corners were blue Chinese asters and black Chinese characters; Isadora pretended to find meaning in the latter. She adored this treasure, and had used it in many of her dances. Now she caught it up from a chair, and tossing it about began a dance of the vineyards of France in the harvest season. "Play for me, Lanny!" she cried; and he, remembering the happy hours at Les Forêts, played the ballet music from *Samson and Delilah*. Again the magic of art; a lily blossoming from the mud, a miracle repeating itself, always astonishing, the last time as the first.

Lanny wished her luck and went home. Again he had no gift of second sight, and it wasn't until the next morning that he heard the dreadful tidings. The young Italian had come with his low racing-car to take Isadora to the concert, and she had come out from the studio with that marvelous long shawl about her neck. To those who came to see her off she said: "*Adieu, mes amis; je vais à la gloire.*" She stepped into the car, leaning her head against the side, and one end of the shawl hung down outside, and the wind blew it about. As the car began slowly to move, the fringes caught in the rear wheel and were twisted round and round. By the time the car had moved a few feet the tightening fabric had become a strong rope wound about Isadora's neck; it drew her lovely face against the side of the car and crushed it, broke her neck, and severed her jugular vein.

All the world of art was grief-stricken when that story reached it next morning. The ruined body was sealed in a zinc-lined coffin and taken in a funeral train to Paris. Lanny didn't go, for Lohengrin was in charge, the man she had chosen. At the Père-Lachaise cemetery there was such a throng that it was hard to get the funeral car in. Soldiers stood with heads bowed and art students sobbed aloud. At the crematory an orchestra played Bach's *Mass in D*, which was her favorite. Thousands stood and watched the pale gray smoke rising from the chimney of the crematory, and wondered to what heaven the soul of their adored one was bound.

V

Lanny came to London in the disagreeable autumn weather, and installed himself in a little flat to which Rosemary would come when the spirit moved her. Zoltan was there, and they attended the exhibitions and sales, and the Countess of Sandhaven helped to find members of the aristocracy who had old pictures and would prefer to have cash. There were theaters to visit, and concerts to hear;

dancing with the smart young people, and supper parties, all the "social whirl." One could have a very good time if one didn't think, didn't see the signs of poverty and suffering, didn't read the sort of papers in which such things were mentioned.

Robbie came for another visit. He had been in Geneva while Lanny was on the yacht, and had helped to set up a bureau to send news back to America, opposing the naval-limitation project which was being discussed. Robbie was aggressive and determined about it, and pleased because he had won. Britain and Japan had been unable to agree with the United States regarding the limitation of cruisers. Robbie said it was preposterous to imagine that Japan would keep such agreements; Japan would keep secrets.

This time Robbie was here because of his oil business. You couldn't make large sums of money without having troubles, it appeared; all sorts of people rose up to make them for you. One of the old sheiks had died, and his nephew had ousted the son—a sort of South American revolution in Arabia. There had been a raid on the oil field, just like the gang wars in Chicago; amazing how fast civilization had spread! Robbie had pulled wires through the State Department, and had got a British destroyer sent there, but the Arabs had fled on their horses and the destroyer didn't have any. Robbie wanted a British army post established on or near the concession of the New England-Arabian Oil Company, and when he failed to get it, he served notice that he was going to have his own private army, and cabled the New York detective agency which did the underground work for the Budd plant in Newcastle to go ahead and recruit some men. A rather amusing circumstance: Robbie Budd, head of the European sales department of Budd Gunmakers, was going to sell arms to Robbie Budd, president of New England-Arabian Oil—and get his commission on the deal!

Lanny and Rosemary would go to The Reaches for a week-end, and listen to Sir Alfred and his guests discussing the state of the world. The older men had now decided that Europe was in for a long period of peace, such as it had enjoyed before the World War; they would give figures regarding the revival of trade, and since the general strike had been put down, they expected prosperity at home.

Rick, the young firebrand, had written a book opposing this comforting faith; but nobody objected—in their easy-going way they all took it for granted that a young man should wave some sort of torch. Only when you were thirty-five or forty were you expected to settle down, and when you were seventy you were ready to become an unpaid magistrate.

Rick's book was out, and getting very good notices; he had a new lot of press cuttings whenever Lanny saw him. Because of Rick's knowledge of political movements in Europe a well-known theatrical producer had invited him to do some writing on a play; it might be an important connection, so Rick and his family wouldn't come to the Riviera that winter. As it happened, one of Rosemary's children had had a severe cold; and there was that lodge at Bienvenu standing vacant. Why wait for Christmas? Have Christmas there! The decision was taken; Lanny motored down to get things ready, and Rosemary came by train with the governess and maids and three children. Marceline would have a different set of playmates that winter, but Lanny would have the same one!

VI

The beautiful estate on the Cap d'Antibes had passed through a series of stages. It had been one sort of place when Lanny Budd had been a little boy and his mother had been alone. It had been another sort when Marcel was living there, and yet another under the regime of Kurt. Now, without Kurt and without Rick, the life was without its intellectual distinction. No more discussions of politics, literature, and art; no more music, except what Lanny made for himself, plus the phonograph and a new radio-set. Kurt's big piano had been brought over to Lanny's studio, and he would play it there; he found time for that and for reading, because the bridge problem had happily solved itself. Sophie Timmons had married her retired businessman, and was now Mrs. Rodney Armitage, and they made a contented four with Beauty and Rosemary.

Mr. Armitage was older than his wife, a widower with grown children in the States. It meant that Sophie had accepted middle age, and was sad about it, or pretended to be; though, with a comfortable villa and plenty of money, her fate might have been worse. The new husband was a vigorous man in spite of his gray hair; sensible and dependable, he knew several different bridge systems, and used the one his wife preferred, which, as everybody knows, is important to marital happiness. When they weren't playing cards he told stories about the strange parts of the world which he had visited as an engineer installing electrical equipment. Rosemary liked him, and got along with the flamboyant and free-spoken Sophie because they were so different that they amused each other.

Lanny's business kept on growing. Amazing, the way people were making money! Those who came to the Riviera seemed to have unlimited drawing-accounts, and those who laid claim to culture wanted to take home something distinguished to remind them of Europe. The Murchisons showed up, after nearly five years; Harry a little stouter, Adella more sure of herself. If she was shocked to discover Lanny with a married sweetheart, she was too well bred to speak of it; after all, an English countess was not to be sneezed at. Adella reported that the Goya and the alleged Velásquez had hit the bull's eye; also, those friends whom she had sent to Lanny were well pleased with what he had done for them.

Now they had more money than ever, for Harry was shipping plateglass all over the world. They wanted to be taken about and shown old châteaux, and meet distinguished people, and be told what was what by an elegant and fashionable guide, a super-cicerone. "Give us some of your time," said the lady from Pittsburgh, in her straightforward way, "and I'll see that it's made worth your while." It cost them a total of a hundred and seventy thousand dollars, but they carried home a couple of Gobelin tapestries and a magnificent Turner landscape which Lanny had discovered in the home of an English family, residents of Cannes for half a century. Lanny pocketed his ten percent and was satisfied with the value set upon his time.

Rosemary was more contented that winter, because she had the children with her, and didn't gad about so much or miss so much sleep. The children throve in the sunshine, and Lanny said: "Why not bring them every season?" Rosemary was pleased by this evidence of his honorable intentions, but she said: "What will Rick and Nina do?" The young prince of plutocracy replied: "I'll build another lodge for you."

Why not? Money was rolling in, and there was plenty of room on the estate; a house anywhere on the Cap would never be wasted, it could always be rented in case of need. Robbie approved of buildings, even more than of stocks and bonds, and Beauty, sociable soul, was glad to have more people around her. No sooner said than settled; they amused themselves planning the sort of house that Rosemary and her children and servants ought to have. The more nursery space the better it pleased Beauty, for she had a purpose hidden in her heart; that space wouldn't always be used by other men's children!

VII

Kurt was married, and sent a picture of his bride, sweet and gentle-looking, as he had said; a bit insipid, Beauty thought—but then you couldn't expect her to be enthusiastic. No doubt the girl was what Kurt needed, and Beauty hoped he would be happy, and not remember too vividly the raptures of illicit love. Kurt sent copies of his new compositions, and press items about them. He didn't send Nazi literature, for he knew that Lanny was never going to become a convert; but Heinrich Jung still clung to his hope—impossible for him to believe that anybody could resist the pull of a movement that was spreading so rapidly over Germany. Once in a while the papers he sent would have something cut out of them, and Lanny would smile to himself and wonder just what it was that Heinrich didn't consider proper for a foreigner to read. Some too crass announcement of Aryan purpose to rule the world? Some too crude abuse of that vile and poisonous race which was conspiring with both Bolsheviks and bankers at the same time?

Lanny still kept up his interest in the Reds and the Pinks, though he didn't work very hard at it. He took several of their papers and read them now and then, and his conscience was kept uneasy. In

Italy the labor movement was completely crushed; there were no more strikes, and those who might have any thought of opposing *Fascismo* were either dead or in exile. The latter group wanted support for their paper in Paris, and Lanny could help them generously, owing to the fortunate circumstance that what was a little money for him was a great deal for them. In France nobody was getting arrested or beaten, at least not that Beauty Budd heard about, so gradually she decided that being a Pink meant nothing worse than having lunch with a visiting journalist, or giving a thousand-franc note to some poor creature with ill-fitting clothes and hair untrimmed. Since the amount was no more than she would spend for a spring hat or an embroidered handkerchief, she put it down as a form of charity, to which we all have to make contributions for the good of our souls.

The only time when Bienvenu became really Red was when Hansi and Bess came for a visit. These two young people were really quite shocking; especially Bess, who now called herself an out-and-out Bolshevik. Silly to imagine that the propertied classes would ever give up their stranglehold upon society unless they were forced to! Silly to waste your time talking to them about brotherhood—who was ever brother to a slave but another slave? The daughter of Esther Budd had conceived the most intense antagonism to the social system which had given her so many privileges. She had decided that her education was a mass of falsehoods, and was ready to prove it by illustrations taken from personal experience.

That was the way the young folks were going, and there seemed to be nothing you could do about it. Hansi, gentle and sweet-natured, was careful not to say things to hurt people's feelings, but in his convictions he was at one with his wife. He was going back to Germany to begin a concert tour and in the autumn was going to make a tour of the United States. He was to be paid a percentage of the receipts, and if the tours were successful he would make large sums of money. Everything above their traveling-expenses he was going to turn over to organizations which gave relief to the refugees of Fascism and to workers persecuted for their labor activities. That meant for the most part Communists, and both Hansi and Bess were prepared to tell the newspaper reporters what they believed—and so perhaps ruin their tours, as poor Isadora had ruined hers.

Lanny saw in the attitude of his half-sister the impatience of the very rich, who were used to having their own way; also of the young, who had never suffered and therefore knew no fear. No stopping her, and no use to argue with her. To her mind Lanny had become one of those ineffectual dreamers who proposed to cut off the claws of the tiger of capitalism one by one—and always with the tiger's kind consent. It was all right to be a noble-souled idealist, but when you let your influence be used by Social-Democratic politicians who were misleading the workers, using them to get elected to office and then to dicker and betray—that was terrible! Lanny, for his part, thought that Bess was becoming one of Uncle Jesse's phonograph disks. As always, he lamented the tragic split among the workers, which made them impotent in the grip of their exploiters. In due course, he told himself, Bess would discover the flaws in the tightly welded formulas of the Communists; also, alas, the difference between the preaching and the practice of most humans. "Take it easy, kid," he would say. "A lot of things are going to happen, and you'll have plenty of time to think about them." So old and worldly-wise he had become!

VIII

Another old friend came visiting that season: Margy Petries, Dowager Countess Eversham-Watson. Poor old "Bumbles" had died in great pain of his gout, and his son by a previous marriage was the young lord. Margy wasn't as rich as she had been, for "Petries' Peerless" had been put clean out of business by Prohibition, the most wicked act of confiscation ever perpetrated, so Margy would declare; however, her family had seen it coming and had salted money away, so she didn't have to "go on the county," as the phrase was at home. She and Beauty were old cronies, and never were there two more sprightly widows; they would put on their best duds and amuse themselves breaking the hearts of all the suitors on the Riviera—but as for letting one trap them—never, never! Wealthy widows come to look upon themselves as grouse in the shooting-season; all the men on the moors are carrying guns and looking especially for them.

Margy solved the problem of Beauty's immediate future by inviting her to London for the fashionable doings. Margy still had her town house, her own property, and it was "a barn," and hard to fill; Beauty would come and help her to entertain. She could bring Marceline and the governess if she wished, and Marceline could have music- and dancing-lessons, or could stay out in the country, where Margy had the use of the lodge on her stepson's estate. Later on, the Robins were planning a cruise in the Baltic, and would visit—of all places on earth—the city which had once been called St. Petersburg and now had a name which one apologized for pronouncing. A special concession to the young Reds in the family, Beauty explained; but Margy said it required no apology, it sounded like a lark, and Beauty thereupon wrote to Johannes, who in turn wrote inviting the Dowager Countess Eversham-Watson to join the cruise. Lanny was delighted, for it meant, among other things, that he wouldn't have to play bridge on the new trip.

Thus everything was happily arranged for the rest of the year. Toward the end of April, Rosemary took her brood home by train and Lanny drove to Paris, where he met Zoltan; they discussed their many business affairs and attended the *salon* and some of the sales. Lanny paid his duty call at the Château de Bruyne and met the two young men, now students at the École Polytechnique; Denis, *fils*, had become affianced to a young lady of the neighborhood, the match having been arranged by his aunt. It seemed one of which Marie would have approved, and, anyhow, it would have been awkward for Lanny to meddle. He slept again in the room which had so many memories, but they were growing dimmer, or at any rate the emotions they brought were less intense. He saw no apparitions.

He went also to call upon his Socialist and his Communist friends, and gave them money which they promised not to use in fighting one another. They had their rival papers and rival political candidates. The Communists sang the glories of an epoch-making event now getting under way in the Soviet Union, the Five-Year Plan for the industrializing of what had been the most backward of great nations. The Socialists charged that their rivals were subordinating the interests of France to those of a foreign land. Uncle Jesse invited Lanny to a *réunion* of the Communists, and made a speech in which he denounced the rival party for betraying the international hopes of the workers in the interest of French nationalism.

Lanny refused to argue, but took the family to supper after the event. Little Suzette had got herself married to a party member who was one of those homicidal taxidrivers of Paris; he came along, and Lanny was amused to discover that he was much too far to the left for Uncle Jesse. Suzette was expecting a baby, and also expecting the social revolution in France, and didn't seem quite sure which would arrive first. Lanny thought he could tell her—and without being an authority on obstetrics.

Robbie sailed for France in his impromptu way, and Lanny waited to meet him. Always pleasant to hear the news from the family across the seas, and to tell Robbie about Bienvenu and its visitors, and about the beaux who were dancing attendance on Beauty, and about Robbie's Red daughter and son-in-law. But when those personal details were finished, Lanny didn't have much to talk to his father about. Robbie was a rich man, and growing richer, and this brought him satisfaction, but it didn't widen his interests. Such things as *salons* and concerts weren't real to him, and the details of his battles over oil and munitions brought Lanny no happiness.

Also, he had to work so hard to avoid provocative topics! Just now the father was in a state of exasperation over the so-called Kellogg pact for the outlawry of war, which had been the subject of negotiations between France and the United States for more than a year, and was now being broadened to take in all the nations. They were going to renounce war as an instrument of national policy, and forbid all wars except those of self-defense. As if any nation ever went to war without calling it self-defense! Robbie said that all these moves were just devices to keep the United States from arming as it could and should, and he took this Kellogg pact as a personal betrayal by the strong silent statesman whom he had helped to make President of the United States. Right now he and his associates were looking for a more trustworthy candidate!

IX

Lanny drove Zoltan to The Hague, where there was a friend of
M. Rochambeau with some old Dutch masters for sale. From there
they drove to Hanover, in Germany, where Hansi was giving one
of his concerts. Bess was with him, also an accompanist—for Bess
wasn't nearly good enough yet. All three were most conscientious
about their work, and happy in its success; the audience was enthusiastic, and Hansi didn't wave any Red flags or make incendiary
speeches. If he said anything about political questions to the inter-
viewers they were considerate enough not to mention it in what
they wrote. They reported that the German musical classics had a
new and inspired interpreter; and Bess dutifully cut out the notices
and mailed a set to Papa and another to Robbie.

Lanny and Zoltan took the Hook of Holland ferry to London and
attended the sales and shows there. Another season, and everybody
rolling in money—that word "everybody" being used in a special
sense, for there were few streets so fashionable that you didn't see
men peddling matches and women peddling their bodies. That remained a part of what was called civilization, and you had your
choice of hardening your heart and refusing to think about it, or
else tormenting yourself with problems which couldn't be solved. If
you chose the former course, you became irritated with persons
who threw spokes into the wheels of your forgetting machinery.

The play on which Rick had collaborated was produced, and Lanny
and Rosemary, Zoltan and Beauty attended the opening. It was what
the critics called a "problem play," and they praised it as conscientious and well informed, but didn't think it would appeal to the
general public. Rick was choosing the hard road to success; he was
interested in ideas, and refused to write down to his audience. His
book had done fairly well, and he picked up a few pounds here and
there, but couldn't have got along if he hadn't lived with his parents,
and at Bienvenu.

Since Kurt Meissner had passed out of Beauty's life she had taken
her position as a perfectly respectable Franco-American lady, widow
of a painter whose work was winning the esteem of the most dis-

tinguished critics. There was no longer any blot upon her scutcheon; she could even be a chaperon! Rosemary invited her to visit at Sandhaven Manor, and she came for a week-end, arriving conspicuously with her son and her pretty little daughter, and being conspicuously driven away again. After that the most prudish Victorian could have cherished no doubts concerning the relationship between the mistress of the manor and the handsome young American who was conducting her education in the arts.

The season waned, and there came what was called the hot weather in London, though of course it never seemed that to visitors from the Riviera. The fashionable folk went away to the beaches, or to Switzerland, or to the Normandy coast. It was arranged that Marceline and her governess were to spend July with Rosemary's children at the seashore and August with Nina's at The Reaches. The yacht *Bessie Budd* made its second appearance at Ramsgate, bringing the Robin family and one new member, Freddi having got himself engaged, without the help of a *schadchen*, to a very intelligent Jewish girl, a fellow-student in the University of Berlin. She was an addition to any yachting party, for she had a lovely soprano voice and a boxful of music for which Lanny played accompaniments.

Also there were the ex-baroness and her new husband, and Margy with a visiting nephew who raised thoroughbred horses in the bluegrass region of Kentucky. Altogether a variegated party; a host who had sat and scratched fleas in a hut with a dirt floor in the ghetto of Lodz could figure that he had traveled a long distance in a very short time. Where had he acquired that cultivated, agreeable voice? By what model had he shaped his gracious manners? Who had taught him never to boast, never to make pretenses, never to talk about himself unless he was asked to, and then to say simply what he had been and how hard he had struggled to become better. A man can pattern himself on good models, but there has to be that in him which knows the good when he sees it. Jascha Rabinowich had learned something from every person of culture he had met in the forty years since his parents had brought him from Russian Poland to Rotterdam. And most of all he had learned from the Budd family.

X

The *Bessie Budd* sailed to Copenhagen and the party inspected that lovely city, not overlooking its art museums. Thence they proceeded across the Baltic, stopping in the harbors of those little states which had been set up by the League of Nations in the hope of keeping Germany and Russia apart. Nine years and a half had passed since Lanny had served as secretary to an expert on geography at the Peace Conference, and now another section of that geography came to life for him. He remembered the elaborate detail maps, tons of them; the filing clerks who had had to get them out and spread them on the floor, and the aged statesmen who had got down on hands and knees and crawled here and there making pencil marks to decide the destinies of millions. It had seemed rather haphazard and crazy at the time; but when Lanny told Johannes about it he said: "Was it any crazier than having armies fight battles and settle down on whatever they could take?"

The trim white yacht glided over the still blue waters, and they inspected the gracious capital city of Sweden. From there they crossed to the Gulf of Finland, and as they neared the head of it the owner and host told a story which he declared was true, he had it direct from the horse's mouth. There was, he said, a certain young graduate of the technical schools of the new Soviet Union who had been asked to fill out a questionnaire for the guidance of his superiors in placing him under the Five-Year Plan. He had received a mimeographed form and had studied the questions carefully and replied conscientiously, as follows: "Where were you born?" *Answer:* "St. Petersburg." "Where were you educated?" *Answer:* "Petrograd." "Where are you employed at present?" *Answer:* "Leningrad." "Where would you prefer to be employed?" *Answer:* "St. Petersburg."

This was a sample of the kind of anecdote which was going the rounds outside the Soviet Union. It amused all the guests on the yacht save the young ones: Hansi and Freddi and their two ladies. A curious situation, that Johannes should have toiled so hard to climb in the world, and should then discover his sons and the mothers of his future grandchildren looking with moral disapprobation upon his triumphs. He took it in a sporting spirit—too much so for some of his guests; Mr. Armitage, the retired engineer, remarked to his wife in the privacy of their cabin that it would have been better if Johannes had given the two young jackasses a good hiding.

A strange situation, and certainly not according to the alleged laws of economic determinism. If the formula had been working, you would have looked in the fo'c'sle for the Bolsheviks—and of course there may have been some there, though nobody tried to find out. The records of the Comintern contain cases of sons and daughters of the master class who have espoused the cause of the wage-slaves, but there has not yet been brought to light any case where the former have tried to incite the latter to mutiny on board their father's yacht!

The young people on the *Bessie Budd* were going to visit Leningrad with eager curiosity, while their elders were going to visit St. Petersburg if they could, and if not they were going to put flowers on its tomb. There were discussions, and when these became too animated, they had to be hastily dropped. The piano was wheeled onto the deck, the amateur orchestra struck up, and it was Flora's holiday, sacred to ease and happy love, to music, to dancing, and to poetry. Pipe and tabor gaily play, drive all sadness far away, and fitly crown with dance the day!

XI

The floating dance-hall came to rest in the harbor of the great city of palaces and churches built on a marsh. They had procured their visas at home, but discovered that there were many formalities to be gone through. Not many pleasure yachts came to "the Tsar's Window" in these days, and it was difficult for overworked and suspicious revolutionaries to realize that there were persons in the world with nothing to do but glide about from place to place on a vessel big enough for all the pupils of a school or the patients of a sanatorium. In the end the strangers were permitted to come ashore and spend their *valuta* in the new workers' state, but all baggage had to be gone through with care, and they might bring in without duty only precisely measured quantities of perfume, soap, cigars, and so on. They could not return at night to sleep on the yacht, or they would have to go through the same formalities each morning. They had to stay at the Hotel de l'Europe at twenty-five dollars a day per person, and be waited on by pathetic servitors left over from the old regime, men and women who had been born and trained in St. Petersburg and would have been glad to go back there.

The various members of the party saw what they had come to see. Several of the elders had visited this city in the days of the Tsars, and remembered the gaiety and splendor, the handsome guards, the elegant officers, the traffic, the busy shops, the scenes of luxury. Now they saw one vast slum, as drab and dull as it had been before Peter the Great had struck his staff into a marsh and said: "Build here." A tired, bedraggled population, wearing worn and patched clothing full of smells; execrable service, table linen unclean, toilets out of order, nothing in the shops, and in the markets the painful spectacle of former ladies and gentlemen peddling furtively their faded finery to peasants who brought in eggs and vegetables and stood on the embankments along the canals chewing and spitting sunflower seeds. It was enough and more, and the general cry was: "Let's get out of here!"

But to the young people there was a new world to be explored. Knowing few words of Russian, they employed the young women guides whom the regime supplied for tourists. These were ardent propagandists, inclined to patronize bourgeois visitors and, if antagonized, to argue in a manner most exasperating; but when you called them "tovarish" and convinced them of your good faith, their faces lighted up, and they would conduct you sixteen hours a day to look at nurseries and kindergartens, playgrounds and wholesale feeding establishments for factory workers, model creameries, clinics, laboratories—all the marvels of this new world which they were building with such pride and joy. It was "the future" to them, as it had been to Lincoln Steffens nine years ago, and it was still "working," as he had seen it with prophetic eyes. Huge new factories arising, former laborers learning to run them; rivers being dammed, power-houses constructed—and all these things public property in which everyone had the pride of ownership.

XII

A conflict of wills developed between the two groups of visitors. To the ladies of fashion it was as if someone had dumped them into the midst of the East End of London and left them there. The ex-baroness found a family of old friends, members of the former plutocracy, now turned out of their palace and living in one room in the utmost misery; the great slum became a jail to Sophie, a scene in a nightmare from which she struggled to escape. She and Margy and their escorts came back to the hotel for elaborate but tasteless meals, and exchanged new impressions of disgust. "Oh, let's go!" they cried, each day more loudly.

The plan had been for the yacht to visit the Finnish towns and sail up the Gulf of Bothnia. Now the young people said: "All right, but go without us! We want time to visit a co-operative farm and see all the things that interest us, and we'll rejoin you in Helsinki."

So the arrangement was made; and it suited Lanny, because Leningrad possessed one of the world's great treasure-houses of art, the Hermitage Museum, and he wanted to spend days wandering through its halls. Rosemary had no fine frenzies over paintings, but she elected to stay with him because she knew that otherwise she would have to help Beauty teach Mama Robin to play bridge.

When the reunion of the groups took place, the *Bessie Budd* had become a yacht divided against itself. There was no open warfare, for these were all polite people; but when the bourgeoisie spoke of the Soviet Union as a slum, the intelligentsia wanted to know how much time the contemptuous ones had spent in the slums of London and Berlin and Paris. When the bourgeoisie inquired what was gained by reducing everybody to the level of the lowest, the answer was that the slums of capitalist nations were a permanent part of their system, whereas the Soviet Union's prosperity, once achieved, would be shared by all. It was a debate that was going on in every part of the earth; "the future," as the Reds proposed to make it, by force if necessary, was a fighting topic wherever people talked, and on board a yacht the only solution was for the young to do their talking on one part of the deck while the middle-aged did their bridge-playing on another part.

It ruined the cruise, and made sorrow for the well-meaning host and hostess. Johannes took it without complaint, but he had to abandon his dream of using this trim white vessel as a means of cultivating the favor of the enviable classes. Otherwise he would have to leave his adored boys and their wives at home—and then, of course, it wouldn't be any fun for Mama, she would prefer to stay with her darlings, no matter what outrageous opinions they chose to voice. After all, there was something to be said for their side; it hadn't been so pleasant living in a slum, as Jascha himself ought to remember. Jascha talked about the problem with Lanny, strolling on the deck one windy night, and the best the young man could suggest was for the owner of the *Bessie Budd* to become a convert to the new cause, and use the trim white vessel for excursions of the proletariat in need of recuperation. A floating "Park of Culture and Rest"!

the earth," the tunnel," as the Reds proposed to make it, by force if necessary, was a fighting topic wherever people talked, and on board a yacht the only solution was for the young to do their talking on one part of the deck while the middle-aged did their bridge-playing on another part.

It ruined the cruise, and made sorrow for the well-meaning host and hostess. Johannes took it without complaint, but he had to abandon his dream of using this trip whitewashed as a means of cultivating the favor of the enviable classes. Otherwise he would have to leave his adored boys and their wives at home—and then, of course, it wouldn't be any fun for Mama, she would prefer to stay with her darlings, no matter what outrageous opinions they chose to voice. After all, there was something to be said for their side; it hadn't been so pleasant living in a slum, as Jascha himself ought to remember.

Jascha talked about the problem with Lanny strolling on the deck one windy night, and the best the young man could suggest was for the owner of the Bessie Budd to become a convert to the new creed, and use the trim white vessel for excursions of the proletariat in need of recuperation. A floating "Park of Culture and Rest"!

BOOK SEVEN

The Paths of Glory

BOOK SEVEN

The Paths of Glory

31

God's Opportunity

I

EX-TUTOR and ex-lieutenant Jerry Pendleton had set himself up, with Lanny's help, in a tourist bureau in Cannes and was doing well with it; in these times it would have been hard to do badly. His devoted French wife had three little ones, and the pension was thriving under the management of the hard-working mother and aunt; money was being put away, and some day it would come to Cerise and her children, so Jerry had every reason to feel content with the world as it was. He would visit Bienvenu now and then to go sailing or fishing with Lanny, or play tennis; once in a while Beauty out of the kindness of her heart would invite Cerise to a lawn party or other affair where there were many people and it wouldn't be necessary to devote much time to her. Cerise, although quiet and inoffensive, was an outsider because she couldn't talk about the fashionable people and what they were doing.

One of the steady boarders at the pension was a gentleman who had come from a small town in the American Middle West more than fifteen years ago, which was before the Budds had known Jerry or his wife. This boarder had been an insurance agent, and, having inherited a small income, had decided to see the world. He had discovered that his money would buy more in Cannes than anywhere at home, and so he had settled down in the Pension Flavin. He told a peculiar story about how he had come upon this respectable boarding-house; he had sat on a bench on the Boulevard de la Croisette and closed his eyes and asked God to send him to the proper sort of place; then he had got up and walked, and God had told him to turn off that fashionable and expensive avenue, and pres-

643

ently had told him to enter a certain house, and he had done so—
and there he was.

The board had been forty francs per week, which in those days
was eight dollars. With the rise in the cost of living the proprietors
of the establishment had been forced to raise the price again and
again, until now it was two hundred francs, which at the present rate
of exchange was only five dollars; so the American considered that
God had shown him partiality. He had occupied the same third-floor
rear room all through the World War and the peace and what had
come since. Having learned to speak French with a strong Iowa
accent, he had won the esteem of everybody in the establishment.

This exemplary boarder went by the unusual name of Parsifal
Dingle. The first half was due to the fact that an expectant mother
in an unromantic small town on the prairies had seen a picture of an
opera singer in shining armor. The French found nothing eccentric
in either name; they pronounced the last one "Dang'," with their
nasal sound. The visitor had long ago got used to this and other eccentricities. He told himself that God had made the French as well as
the Iowans; God was in them all, and God no doubt had His purposes.

Mr. Dingle did not belong to any sect, or give himself any label,
but followed along the lines of what was known at home as "New
Thought." A surprisingly great number of people believed in it;
people scattered all over the farms and villages of America, or living
obscurely in the great cities, where they listened to lectures, formed
hundreds of sects with odd names, and printed papers and magazines which often attained large circulation. Mr. Dingle subscribed
to several, and after he had read them he would pass them on to
others, and if these persons showed interest he would explain his ideas.

In brief, Mr. Dingle believed that there was a God, and that he,
Mr. Dingle, was a part of Him. This God was alive and He was real,
and He lived and worked in you; He would guide you if you asked
Him, and especially if you believed that He would. The way of
asking was to retire to some quiet place, as Jesus had directed, close
your eyes and think about God and His goodness, and believe that
He would do what you asked, if it was a good and proper thing.
Mr. Dingle had never asked God to give him a mansion on the

Boulevard de la Croisette or a beautiful blond mistress, for he did not consider such things as proper objects of desire; he asked God to give him peace of soul, kindness to his fellow-men, and contentment with his lot in life, and God had granted these modest requests.

The effect of this credo was to produce a highly desirable inmate of a pension. He never tried to force his ideas upon anyone, and it was impossible to quarrel with him about anything; if you tried it, he would retire to his room and pray, and emerge with such a beatific countenance that you could only feel ashamed of your bad disposition. He was not stout, but comfortably eupeptic; his face was round and rosy, so that he looked like a mature, slightly graying cherub in a well-laundered white linen suit. Mr. Parsifal Dingle from the state which he called Ioway, at your service.

II

Ever since the year 1914, when a runaway college student boarding at the Pension Flavin had become Lanny Budd's tutor, the family at Bienvenu had been hearing about this unusual but worthy boarder. Jerry liked him because, their hometowns being close together, they understood each other's accents and taste in foods. As the years passed, Jerry began to talk about Mr. Dingle's peculiar ideas, first in a "kidding" way, later on more seriously. It appeared that Mr. Dingle had some sort of strange gift; he would put his hands on people and give them what he called a "treatment," and their pains would disappear. Neither Lanny nor his mother had ever met this boarder, but they had seen him coming out of the pension, and he had become in the course of the years something of a legendary figure to them.

A couple of years ago it had happened that Miss Addington, Marceline's governess, had suffered an unusually severe spell of her periodic headaches. Lanny had mentioned it to Jerry, and a little later Jerry had phoned; Mr. Dingle wanted to know if he might be permitted to call and try to help the lady; if so, Jerry would be glad to drive him over. The stiff and proper member of the Church of England was startled by the proposal; but she knew that the American gentleman operated in the name of God, and there was nothing in that special charter which God had granted to the Church of King Henry the Eighth which forbade other persons to call upon Him if they so desired; besides, the headache was really very bad. So Mr. Dingle came, and asked to be alone with her, which caused a maiden lady to feel uneasy; but he seemed to be a respectable person, and presumably one could think of him as a physician. He asked her to sit in a chair, and he stood behind her and put his hands across her forehead, and then just stayed there with his eyes closed.

The result astonished everybody, especially the governess. When he got through and took his hands away, he asked: "How do you feel?" and she blinked a couple of times and exclaimed: "Why, it's gone!" It was really quite preposterous, but it was so—and it was certainly convenient. After that, whenever Miss Addington had one of these spells, she would send in haste for Mr. Parsifal Dingle. She tried to pay him, but he didn't want money. Seeing that his cuffs showed signs of wear, she argued that at least she ought to pay his carfare, and in the end he permitted her to give him twenty francs, which varied somewhere between forty and sixty cents during this period.

Any prim and easily shocked maiden lady of forty was naturally a subject of humor among Beauty's fashionable friends. They anticipated a romance, and asked eagerly how it was developing. Sophie referred to the healer as Miss Addington's Knight of the Holy Grail, and said that the only barrier to a perfect match would be that dreadful name Dingle—why didn't he change it to Bell? Wasn't there a song: "Dingle bell, dingle bell, dingle all the day"? Margy, who had read poetry, said that a dingle was a dell or a dale, and the poor man ought to take one of those names. But Mr. Dingle had heard all these jokes when he was a schoolboy, and he stayed as he was.

III

Now came Rosemary with her brood and settled them in that comfortable, spick-and-span house which they were calling "the cottage," in order to have a name for it, though it was bigger than the lodge and nearly as big as the villa. The first thing that happened was that the youngest child, little Blanche, got hold of some green fruit and had a violent attack of colic. There was great excitement, and the English doctor whom they all patronized was not in his office. They gave the little one an emetic, but perhaps that wasn't enough; she lay in a semi-coma; her skin began to assume a greenish hue, her heart seemed weak, and Rosemary· was in a panic. Miss Addington, without a word to anyone, rushed to the phone and called Mr. Dingle, telling him to take a taxi at once.

The same thing happened again; Mr. Dingle asked to be alone with the child, and put his hands on her forehead, and in a very short while her heart had revived and her color returned and she fell peacefully asleep. Of course everybody knows that children have these attacks suddenly and get over them no less suddenly, and perhaps that was all it was; but it gave the ladies a great deal to talk about, and after this crisis was over, Beauty invited the gentleman with the strange gift to come over to the villa and tell her about his ideas and how he performed his miracles. He said very modestly that it was no miracle at all, but something which God did, and would do for anyone who believed in Him and who would take the trouble to follow the plain directions which Jesus had given us.

Now Beauty Budd had managed to live her adult life without any clerical assistance. She had been taught early in life that God forbade her to do all the pleasant things, and she had just gone ahead and done them, and decided that God was the creation of a domineering Baptist preacher by the name of John Eliphalet Blackless. Here on the Riviera were a number of well-trained professional gentlemen engaged in God's service, and she had met several of them, both Catholic and Protestant, and found them agreeable men of the world, good conversationalists and judges of food and wine. It had been tacitly understood that they kept God for those special occasions when they performed His rites in church, and you were free to attend if you cared to, but no priest or clergyman had ever been heard to mention the name of God on any social occasion; everyone whom Beauty knew would have considered it something in the nature of a *faux pas*.

So this idea of a God whom you carried around with you was something entirely new and decidedly startling. The idea that God was inside Beauty Budd, and had known all that she was thinking, and all that she had done—for God's sake, why hadn't He stopped her? Mr. Dingle insisted that it was a comfortable idea when you got used to it, because it took away all fear; God loved you, in spite of your faults, and all He asked was that you should try to improve yourself and let Him help you. It was what Mr. Dingle described as a "free" religion; you didn't have to have any priest to intercede for you, but God was here all the time, at the center of your consciousness, and you could appeal to Him, and get your answer in the state of your own heart. "No," said the healer, "you don't hear any voice, you just feel different. Try it; you may be astonished to see how it works."

Beauty knew how all her fashionable friends would laugh if they heard about this. But God wouldn't laugh, Mr. Dingle assured her, and it could be a strict secret between God and herself. But very soon, if Madame Detaze found that her prayers were being answered, she would gain courage, and would wish to tell others of her discovery, just as Mr. Dingle himself had been doing since the door of faith had been opened in his heart.

Of course it wasn't within Beauty's nature to keep any such secret. When Lanny came back from a swimming-party she told him what had happened to little Blanche, and all that Mr. Dingle had explained to her. Had Lanny ever heard of such an idea? The young scholar replied that he had indeed, many times; it was a very old idea, which had appeared everywhere among the tribes of men. Socrates had talked about his *daimon*, and Jesus about his heavenly Father. People of this way of thinking were known as "mystics," and Lanny had learned about them from his study of Emerson. He got the volume which Eli Budd had given him, inscribed by the philosopher's own hand, and told Beauty to read the essay called *The Oversoul*. But Beauty couldn't make anything out of this highbrow language, and much preferred the simple, A-B-C explanations which the healer gave her.

She invited him over to tea, and had only Lanny and Miss Adding-

ton and Rosemary—for of course the latter couldn't laugh, seeing
how terrified she had been, and how kind the man had been, whether
he had really healed the child or not. They all asked questions, and
Mr. Dingle talked inspirationally. He had been thinking about these
matters ever since he was a young man, and had absorbed the formulas of all the New Thought groups; but Beauty didn't know that,
he seemed to her one of the most original and most exalted personalities she had ever encountered. No priest or clergyman she had
ever heard in a church had more noble ideas, or voiced them in more
beautiful phrases.

After that the gentleman with the odd name became an habitué of
Bienvenu. No one could have been less intrusive; he never came
unless he was asked, he rarely spoke unless he was spoken to, and if
he had the slightest reason to think that he might be in the way he
would go into the court and look at the flowers, or onto the loggia
and watch the sun set over the *golfe* behind the Estérels, and you
knew that he was praying. He was a very good influence for everybody, because they were ashamed to voice cynical or unworthy
ideas in his presence. Also, it was comforting to know that if anything serious happened to you, he would be on hand and call God
to your aid.

I V

There was never a more inveterate matchmaker than the lovely
blond mistress of Bienvenu, and having this new male on the premises, she couldn't help thinking about Miss Addington. That badly
inhibited English lady was surely in need of assistance; so Beauty
would perform the kindly service of inviting Mr. Dingle to lunch,
and then arranging that the governess should be excused from her
duties for a while. This was easy, because there were two governesses, and the children wanted to be together all the time. Miss
Addington became greatly interested in Mr. Dingle's views on religion, and he convinced her that there was nothing contrary to
Anglican etiquette in what he did. Had not Jesus after his death
returned to his disciples and given the explicit instruction: "In my

name they shall lay hands on the sick, and they shall recover"? How could words be plainer?

But in spite of their being an obviously well-matched couple, that was as far as matters proceeded between them; and after several weeks of watching and waiting, Beauty began to find it rather provoking. What would become of the future of the human race if men and women did nothing together except to search the Scriptures and practice praying? If Beauty had been a selfish soul she would have remembered that she had a good governess and had better let well enough alone; but Beauty believed in love, and she thought: "I could arrange for them to live on the place, and Miss Addington could continue her duties until Marceline is grown." She had it all worked out in her head, and she tried to put it into Miss Addington's head. The maiden lady would blush, and the next time the visitor appeared she would have some old-fashioned ruching about her somewhat shrunken neck, also a bit of ribbon in her hair. But these hints didn't appear to be caught by Mr. Dingle.

Evidently he had lived alone for so long that he had become shy; or was there something in his religion which committed him to a celibate life, the attitude which Beauty had heard referred to as "platonic"? She felt that it was her duty to straighten the matter out; so one day when she was alone in the drawing-room with the healer she sprang the question: "What is your attitude toward love?"

Mr. Parsifal Dingle blushed slightly, and showed signs of being flustered. "I had," he explained, "a very sad experience, one which altered my whole life."

"Indeed?" said Beauty. She didn't say: "Would you mind telling me about it?" but there was that in her voice. She wished earnestly to understand this gentleman's ideas and everything that had helped to shape his personality.

"When I was a young man, Madame, I became deeply attached to a young lady of excellent character, and suffered a tragic bereavement. Somehow I have never been able to think about love since then—I suppose it is because I have looked for the qualities which I found in that young lady."

Beauty felt that such a love story would touch Miss Addington's

Victorian heart. She said: "I appreciate your delicacy of feeling; but is it wise to let one's whole life be dominated by an old grief?"

"I have never felt that it was a deprivation, Madame. I have submitted to God's guidance, and He has given me other kinds of happiness."

"Yes, Mr. Dingle; but have you never reflected that you might be denying happiness to some woman?"

"I must confess that I never gave a thought to that aspect of the matter. I haven't appeared to myself as an especially desirable suitor."

"Perhaps you are too modest. May I speak to you frankly?"

"Of course, Madame, I am honored."

"Well, you must know that I have come to have a very great esteem for Miss Addington, who has been with us for several years and has won the regard of everyone in our home. Has it never occurred to you that she might be interested in you?"

The blood began to climb into the cherubic cheeks of the man of miracles, and his bright blue eyes opened wider. "Oh, Madame!" he exclaimed; and there was no mistaking the tone of dismay.

"You haven't given any thought to her?"

"I have done everything in my power to assist Miss Addington, and to guide her in her religious researches when she herself requested it. I sincerely hope there has been nothing in my conduct which has caused her to think that I—that I harbor any other thoughts of her."

"You don't feel that you could be interested in her in that way?"

"Oh, Madame, not possibly."

"Why are you so positive?"

"It is difficult to explain without sounding offensive. Miss Addington is one of the most estimable of ladies, but she is not the type which could interest my—shall I say imagination?"

There was a pause; then Beauty was moved to ask: "Just what do you think would interest your imagination, Mr. Dingle?" She wished so much to understand the platonic philosophy.

"Would you really like me to tell you, Madame?"

"I want to be your friend, and to help you, as you have helped so many others."

"You do me great honor, and your kindness touches me deeply. I have never had anything in my life that has pleased me so much as your friendship, and I wish to preserve it as I would a precious jewel, and be sure never to do anything that would tarnish it."

"Of course not, Mr. Dingle—why should you?"

"You have asked me an intimate question, Madame, and it fills me with anxiety—because, through many weeks I have said to myself: oh, if only Madame were not a rich lady, so that I might be at liberty to tell her what is in my heart!"

It was the lovely blond Beauty's turn to blush, and be sure that she did not fail. The exclamation burst forth: "Oh, *mon dieu!*" The French do not spell it with a capital letter, which perhaps keeps it from seeming so violent as it does in English.

"Madame!" exclaimed the man of God with much anxiety. "You asked me a question, and it seemed to me that courtesy required me to give an answer."

"Yes, of course, and I am obliged to you; only——"

"I shall be deeply grieved if Madame is offended."

"No, surely not. Why should I be? You do me a great honor, Mr. Dingle."

"Please, please, do not let it make any difference in your regard for me. I know that it is utterly impossible, and I do not permit it to become anything but a beautiful dream, one which may perhaps be realized in heaven, where we do not take our title deeds to property. May I be assured of your forgiveness, and remain your humble and devoted admirer?"

"Yes, surely, Mr. Dingle. Yes, yes—let us talk about God for a while!"

V

Beauty had to tell someone about that most embarrassing episode, and she chose her son. First he said: "Well, I'll be damned!" Then he thought it over and added: "But, darling, you can't blame him; it's the price you pay for being irresistible."

"It's really most painful," complained the mother. "How am I going to meet the man after this?"

"Oh, you don't need to make so much out of it. You have had plenty of broken-hearted suitors around you."

"But, Lanny, a man of that class!"

"Class?" inquired the young Pink. "He's about the same class as my maternal grandfather, I'd imagine."

"But, I mean—a man of no culture."

"He's got a lot of culture, it seems to me; only it's different from ours; not so smart, but a lot cleaner, if I'm any judge."

"I didn't know you thought so highly of him, Lanny."

"Well, I think he's earned our respect. We don't have to agree with his ideas, but we can admit that he's honest and kind—and that's more than I can say for some of the men you have been stepping out with."

This was a subject on which the son had been expressing himself emphatically as occasions arose. In London there had appeared an elegant man of fashion and of no small means; he had been most attentive, but had omitted to mention that he had a wife somewhere in the background; Margy had found it out. Here on the Riviera had been il Conte di Pistacchio; a charming personality, only he disappeared now and then for a week and reappeared rather pale except for his painted cheeks—he had the habit of taking ether. On the last trip of the *Bessie Budd* Margy's nephew had attached himself to this richly blooming beauty, suggestive of the rose at its most complete unfoldment, just before the petals begin to drop; but he was even younger than Lanny, and surely Beauty didn't have to learn that lesson over again! In short, Lanny had a problem mother; and the more he thought about it, the less disposed he was to ridicule this conscientious if somewhat boresome man of God.

VI

Nothing more was said for a while; but Lanny watched closely, and suspected that nature was getting in her subtle work. Or perhaps it was God—it is a matter of words, for what do we really know about it after all? Mr. Dingle continued to visit at Bienvenu, and to instruct "Madame" in that New Thought which is so very ancient;

Beauty listened, with no apparent diminution of interest. The difference was that she no longer invited Miss Addington to share in the instruction. Did the man of God note this difference? And did he attribute it to the fact that he had disclaimed interest in the state of Miss Addington's heart? If so, what inference was he to draw from the fact that Madame continued as his pupil?

Whatever his thoughts may have been, he was invariably proper, even saintly in his attitude, and if his eyes happened to meet those of the lovely blond rose in full blooming, he would drop them quickly. His state of adoration was apparent, and could not be without its effect upon one who lived to be admired, as Mabel Blackless, alias Beauty Budd, alias Madame Detaze, had done since childhood.

Mr. Dingle began to come more frequently, and was told that he no longer needed to wait for a special invitation. Beauty's friends got used to finding him there, and after a while they got tired of teasing her about it; they didn't come so often, because the plain truth was, they began to find Beauty's conversation boring. That religious crank must have her hypnotized, for she talked about his ideas even without knowing it; things which had formerly been fashionable were now worldly, and those which had been delicious had become frivolous; it was really pathetic.

"Lanny," said the mother one day, "what do you honestly think about Mr. Dingle's ideas?"

"Why, I don't know," said Lanny; "they may be all right. A lot of great minds have accepted them. Very largely it's a matter of how you phrase things."

"Mr. Dingle seems to phrase them remarkably well. But I don't trust my own judgment—I'm so frightfully ignorant, you know."

"We're all ignorant," said Lanny. "If I were you, I wouldn't worry about that. If the ideas work with you, they're right for you."

"Why don't you try them, Lanny?"

"I suppose it's because I've never felt the need. People seem to take up with them when they get into some sort of trouble. What is it Mr. Dingle said: 'Man's extremity is God's opportunity'?"

"He was quoting Mrs. Eddy, I believe. Do you remember old Mrs. Sibley, Emily's mother? She was a Christian Scientist, and it seemed to work very well for her. She often tried to tell me about it, but I wouldn't pay any attention. I've been a very worldly woman, Lanny."

"I know," said the other; "but you've managed to get out alive." Then, with a wicked twinkle in his eye: "Would you like me to speak to Mr. Dingle and find out if his intentions are honorable?" The way Beauty blushed made the son realize that things were getting serious.

VII

Lanny wasn't surprised when a few days later his mother brought up the subject again. She had to talk about it with somebody, and there was no one so deeply concerned as Lanny. "Do you still have such a good opinion of Mr. Dingle?" she wanted to know.

"Better than ever," he replied. "It seems to me he has been behaving very well indeed."

"Do you really mean, Lanny, that you'd be willing for me to think of marrying that poor man!"

"What has being poor got to do with it? We have much more than we need."

"I don't mean poor in that sense."

"Then in what sense? If you mean that he isn't *chic*, we have enough of that quality also."

"Everybody would think that I'd made a misalliance!"

"Well, they thought that about you and Marcel; but you lived it down."

"Lanny, I believe you really *want* me to do it!"

"I've been thinking a lot about it. If you married him, you would know exactly what you are getting. He won't have his head turned by money, and he won't go chasing after younger women; he'll worship you as a goddess out of the skies."

"Oh, you want to get rid of me!" exclaimed the errant female.

"I'll stay right here," he promised, "and lend Mr. Dingle my Swedenborg and St. Theresa's *Way of Perfection*—Great-Great-Uncle Eli was strong on the mystics, you know."

"Lanny, I just couldn't face the idea of being known as Mrs. Dingle!"

"Let it be a sort of morganatic marriage; take him as a prince consort. Your friends will go on calling you Beauty Budd, and the servants and tradespeople calling you Madame Detaze. Why should anyone change?"

"Lanny, I think it's horrid of you to urge such a thing!"

"All right, old dear; it was you who brought up the subject. All I say is, if I had to choose among the beaux in sight at this moment, this miracle man would be my stepfather."

"Do you realize that if I married him here in France, he'd own— I don't know just what, but a large share of this property?"

"In the first place I doubt if he'd touch it."

"But he may have relatives who would feel differently."

"Well, go to your lawyer and fix up a property settlement. Marceline gets along with him all right; and you surely don't have to worry about me, for I can make what I need, and all I want for you is to be happy, and safe from the buzzards I see hovering over this Coast of Pleasure."

"Lanny, I think it's perfectly awful—it's humiliating!" There were tears in the mother's eyes.

"Bless your heart, I'll never mention it again. If you want to stay a fascinating widow, you have everything it takes."

VIII

Several days passed, and Beauty said no more. It chanced that Mr. Dingle came calling, and gave her an especially beautiful discourse on the love of God as an example to our frail mortality. Beauty was deeply moved, and when it was over, she began: "Do you remember what you said about your attitude to me, Mr. Dingle?"

"Of course, Madame. How could I forget?"

"Are you still of the same opinion?"

"I could never change."

Whereupon Beauty, blushing most becomingly, set out upon a long explanation, to the effect that she had two children, and that

Marcel had wished and Robbie required that her property should go to these children. If Mr. Dingle were to marry her it would be necessary for them to make a special legal arrangement.

"Oh, Madame!" exclaimed the man of God. "I wouldn't dream of touching a sou of your money! Never would the purity of my love for you be sullied by a question of property." He fell upon one knee before the loveliest of Franco-American widows and kissed her hand in the perfect tradition of the Victorian romancers.

Beauty might have said: "Rise, Sir Parsifal." But instead she sat with tears running down her cheeks, and when he looked at her and saw them, he also wept; it was an emotional betrothal, and very soon the pair were as completely dissolved in bliss as if they had been seventeen years old. If Beauty had not been restrained by fear of her fashionable friends, she would have got a complete trousseau and a dress with a train several yards long.

There is no such thing as getting married in a hurry in the staid land of France. For one thing, both parties had to have birth certificates especially obtained from their native land—the certificates had to be no more recent in date than three months. Also Beauty's lawyer had to prepare the documents concerning the property settlement; and lawyers work carefully and methodically in France. Then there had to be ten days for the publication of the banns. When all these formalities had been arranged, Sophie and her husband came over—two friends who could be counted upon not to laugh publicly; the party traveled to the *mairie*, where they were declared man and wife under the French civil code. They did not take a honeymoon journey, for Mr. Dingle said, what was the use of going elsewhere when God was here? Marceline and her governess went over to have a holiday with Rosemary's children, and the new bridegroom brought his few belongings and installed them in the room which had never been used since Kurt had moved out of it a year and a half ago. The miracle man moved also into the heart which Kurt had vacated, and he filled it full. An odd sort of ending to the adventures of Beauty Budd, but her son sighed with relief, and crossed off in his mind a string of painful incidents which weren't going to happen.

IX

Rosemary was not present at these nuptials because she had left hurriedly for London, there being some family trouble about which her brother had written her. She came to Lanny about it, but said that it was a matter of which she hadn't the right to talk; he understood that it was the well-known English reticence. He asked if there was anything he could do—go with her, drive her, run errands —but she answered that she would have to do it alone. She would write to him.

Rosemary's letters had never been what you could call inordinate; she used a lot of paper and ink, but gave only a sketch at best. This time, "A bally mess. Cheerio!" was the extent of her communication. However, Lanny had other ways of getting news. Rick was still in England, and he had played with Rosemary's smart friends in childhood—and what one of these young people knew, all the rest knew quickly. Moreover, this set went in for the intellectual life, and the smart press people circulated among them like busy bees, gathering tiny drops of the sweet honey of gossip. On the news-stands of every town on the Continent you could buy newspapers and magazines having columns from which you might learn that Lady T*tt*nh*mpt*n was seen frequently in the fashionable clubs nowanights, but she and her lawful spouse sat at different tables; her ladyship was oft observed in the company of a bachelor captain of the Hussars. A few paragraphs later you would read that Captain So-and-so of the Hussars had changed dancing partners recently, and was teaching the newest steps to a fair young matron in Burke's *Peerage*. If you couldn't put these twos together, you must indeed be ignorant concerning the ways of ladies and gentlemen in Mayfair.

From various sources Lanny was able to gather the story. Poor Bertie had had the bad judgment to stray from the couch of the lady with whom he had been happy, and she had left him in a fury, and from somewhere in the distant background a husband had appeared, making threats of a divorce suit and scandal. Being in the Foreign Office and hoping for a career, Bertie had paid the fellow money, but he, being a gambler, was never satisfied, and the two had got into a fight, and now it wasn't just a question of money, but a vicious grudge. After Rosemary arrived in London it broke into the papers. Bertie was considered to be "ruined," and was in that state where he might retire to his manor and shoot off his head. But the Earl of Sandhaven of course had influential friends, and Rosemary's family also had them, and they insisted that something had to be done to help the poor fellow. There were conferences with important officials, and presently came to Lanny the longest letter he had ever received from his *amie:*

DEAR LANNY:

I have had a hard decision to make, and can only count upon your kindness. Do forgive me and not take it too hard. Bertie has been offered a post which will give him a future. You know what I told you about the Empire and what it does to people's private lives. The condition of this appointment is that I shall go with him to the Argentine, and that he promises to settle down and work very hard. I assume you have been told about some of the unpleasant events here, and will not expect me to put the details on paper. Believe me that life has jolly well got to be real and earnest for us; the law has been laid down. It is a question of my children's future, and the situation is such that I am morally bound. It is just one of those things that come, like the war, you know. Your many kindnesses to my family will never be forgotten, and I hope you will do one more and tell me that you understand and forgive. I have told Nina about it, and she will tell you.

Bertie and I are leaving for our new post in a few days. I am writing the governess to bring the children home at once, as we are taking them. Give my best love to your darling mother, and thank her for her hospitality. I will write her a note before I leave. You can understand that I am frightfully crowded. Everything has to be arranged in a few days. Good-by, and believe that your friendship will be one of my very best memories; nothing will take it from me.

ROSEMARY.

So there it was. When you had to cut off a love affair, you just took a pair of scissors and—snip!—there it wasn't. Lanny couldn't complain, for Rosemary had made it clear to him that that was the way with life among the governing classes of an empire. Britannia, who ruled the waves, had put an end to Rosemary's previous affair, and now had put an end to Lanny's. How many times he had heard his sweetheart say: "We mustn't fall too much in love, dear. We can't count upon it." Now he learned the lesson of how to write a letter that could never be used by any blackmailer. One can never tell into what hands a letter may fall, and when you belong to the governing classes, you are careful what you set down on any piece of paper!

X

Lanny hadn't taken Rosemary's advice, and neither had she; they had fallen too much in love, and would suffer, in spite of all resolves. There was nothing he could do about it; she preferred her social position, and the future of her children in the Empire, to what she got from him, and so she had taken herself out of his life. He didn't want to make it harder for her, so he telegraphed that he understood her position and wished her and Bertie all good luck in their new career. Everything would be done to help the governess and children get off promptly, and Beauty and Marceline joined in sending regards. A message that could do no harm in the hands of any blackmailer.

Man's extremity being God's opportunity, this might have been a time for Lanny to turn to his mother and her new husband, who was now available at all hours. But it happened that Lanny had just been reading an article about Chopin, who had been proud and passionate, and had been spurned in love and brought to despair. Lanny went down to his studio and played all the eighteen Chopin nocturnes, one after another, and imagined that Rosemary was in the room and sorrowing with him. He played other Chopin pieces, not forgetting the very somber funeral march. In the course of days and nights he played ballades and polonaises and mazurkas, fiery and tempestuous, yet freighted with a burden of bitter pain; he played études which were studies in emotionality even more than in piano technique. Before he got through he had played some two hundred compositions and got a fine lot of exercise, a workout both physical and spiritual. After it he was ready for some new kind of life.

There came a telephone call from that patient, hard-working young Socialist Raoul Palma, who was in need of help, and Lanny decided on the spur of the moment that this was the fellow who understood what was wrong with the world and what to do about it. While Lanny had been playing around, tied to the apron-strings of a shining lady of fashion, his friends the workers had been having a devil's own time with the rising cost of living, wages lagging behind, and no certainty and very little hope in their lives. Lanny decided that he had been an idler, a parasite, deserving the worst that any rabid agitator could charge against him. To the young Spaniard's delight he announced that he was ready to teach a class in the night school, and one in the Sunday school. He would tell the workers of the Riviera and their children about the great war which was already growing dim in the world's memory; he would try to explain to them the forces which had caused it, and what they could do by their collective efforts to prevent another such calamity from breaking in upon their lives.

Naturally, this interfered somewhat with Beauty Budd's honeymoon and her initiation into the contemplative life. She was greatly upset about it, but knew better than to make a frontal assault upon her son. In his *distrait* state of mind he might go off to Paris and get mixed up with Jesse and his dreadful crowd—for Beauty had managed to get into her head the distinction between Red and Pink, and which was worse. It was just before Christmas, and she wrote to Nina, begging her and Rick to come immediately after New Year's, so that Lanny might have somebody to tell his troubles to. Also she wrote to Emily, telling her what had happened, and asking about her plans. Now was the time to put an end to this business of Lanny's living with other men's wives and raising other men's children! Out of the kindness of her heart Emily had forgiven the playboy's rejection of her last effort; she wrote that she was coming, and that Irma Barnes also was coming, and what would Beauty say to her as a possible daughter-in-law?

What Beauty would say would have taken a whole mail-pouch to carry it. She started saying it *viva voce,* first to Sophie and then to Margy, who arrived to occupy the "cottage" as soon as Rosemary's children had been sent to England. These three knew that they had to move with caution, owing to Lanny's peculiar Pink attitude; the moment he heard that anyone had a great deal of money he began finding fault with that person and shying away from him or her. So there must not be the faintest hint that anybody was thinking that he might fall in love with Irma Barnes, or even that he might meet her; he must just begin hearing about her charms, about the sensation she had made in New York, about her interest in intellectual things—in short, everything except that she was the legally established possessor of twenty-three million dollars in her own right!

XI

J. Paramount Barnes had been a public utilities magnate, or, as they were now being called, a "tycoon," and had had a dizzying career in the "pyramiding" of companies. Robbie had explained this process to his son in his half-cynical, half-respectful way. There were men who controlled the investing of insurance company funds, and of industrial concerns which kept hundreds of millions of dollars in "reserves." Those who handled such funds were, of course, favorites of the big banks, and could borrow unlimited amounts of money which nowadays came pouring into Wall Street from all the rest of the banks of the United States. Using such borrowing power, these men would get options upon the stocks of utility concerns controlling the light and power of cities and states, and would organize a great "holding company" to own these enterprises. The top concern would be controlled by three "voting shares," having a par value of one dollar each; which meant that the colossal enterprise would rest permanently in the capable hands of J. Paramount Barnes, his personal secretary, and one of his office clerks. The concern would proceed to issue several hundred million dollars in common shares, give part of them to Mr. J. Paramount Barnes for his services, and sell the rest to the public. In their present mood millions of the plain people all over the country would rush to buy the shares of any concern about which they read in the papers, and they would start bidding up the price on the exchange so that everybody would be rich and continuing to grow richer every day.

Such was the Wall Street game, with which Robbie had been in conflict over a long period of years. Robbie himself was really producing things, and when he issued stock it represented real value in equipment, land, and so on; he sold the shares to people in Newcastle and elsewhere who trusted his name, and when the Wall Street slickers came and wanted to work their rackets with his company, Robbie would tell them to go to the devil. What they would do was to go to the stockholders and buy some of them out, and then the crooks would show up at a stockholders' meeting of the company and try to get control. They would prepare an elaborate campaign, hiring shrewd lawyers and publicity men, and framing a set of false charges to bewilder and confuse investors, most of whom didn't know about the business and were ready to run and sell their shares at the least rumor of something wrong.

J. Paramount Barnes had begun life as a broker's messenger boy, and had learned all the tricks and invented many new ones. He had organized a utilities holding company, and had been so successful that he had repeated the stunt again and again, until he had a holding company for holding companies, a colossal pyramid with himself sitting on the top, and so many subsidiaries and investment trusts and stock-issuing and dividend-receiving devices that it was to be doubted if any human brain knew the whole of that tangle of complications.

And then one day J. Paramount Barnes suffered a heart attack and dropped dead in his office. It was discovered that he had left a comfortable income to his wife, a small one to his son who lived in Hawaii and was rumored to be "no good," and had left the bulk of his fortune in trust for his only daughter Irma. How much it amounted to made a guessing contest for the newspapers of the metropolis; the conservative ones said fifty million dollars and the yellow ones said two hundred million or more. It transpired that the "tycoon" had got rid of his holdings in his own companies and had put most of his money into bank stocks and other gilt-edged securities. After the lawyers had been paid, and the commissions, and the state and federal inheritance taxes, and the back income taxes which were in dispute with the government, Irma Barnes, just about to emerge from finishing-school, had a net fortune of twenty-three millions, and, at the rate which the investments were earning, would have something over two million dollars to spend or invest each year.

This favorite of fortune was good to look at, and had been taught how to dress and to walk and to talk; so she became a headliner in the newspapers, and what the gossip columnists called "the toast of New York." It meant that a train of suitors attended her; whenever she entered a restaurant everybody turned to stare at her, in the night clubs the spotlight was turned upon her and the band played a song which had been composed in her honor. Pictures made her features familiar to the great public, and what she wore set the styles for shop-girls as well as debutantes from Portland, Maine, to Portland, Oregon.

And now Irma Barnes was coming to spend the winter on the Riviera! Forthwith the promotion agencies of half a dozen towns began cabling to New York and pulling wires to get her. Her social secretary, her publicity man, her business manager were besieged by representatives of noblemen who had palaces to rent, of hotels which wished to lodge her in the royal suite, of automobile manufacturers offering to put a fleet of cars at her disposal. The French newspapers took up her story, so typically American, and the smart people of the Coast of Pleasure speculated about her for hours on end

XII

In her letter Emily Chattersworth explained, among other details, that the maternal grandmother of this matrimonial prize had belonged to one of the old New York families, and had been at school with Emily; she had been a guest at Les Forêts on various occasions. So now it had been arranged that Irma was to visit Sept Chênes for a week or two, until she had a chance to look about and judge where and how she wished to live. If during that period a fastidious young art expert saw fit to call and pay his respects, he would have the inside track over the other suitors. If his sense of dignity forbade him to do so, perhaps he might condescend to be at home when Emily brought the young lady to call upon his mother.

Having read all this more than once, Beauty retired to her boudoir to pray, in the fashion which her new husband had taught her. "O Lord, grant that Irma Barnes may fall in love with Lanny!" But then a sudden fear smote her, a doubt whether this might be considered a proper subject for a petition to the Most High; whether, in fact, the desire might not be an unworthy one, what Mr. Dingle had taught her to think of as "worldly." She began to argue, saying: "No, no, God! I want Lanny to have children! I want him to have the happiness of true love, as you have given it to me!"

"Couldn't he just as well marry a poor girl?" inquired the voice inside.

Bewilderment seized the soul of the lovely blond mother. Was that really the voice of God, or was it just her own frail mortality, or the notions which Lanny had helped to fix in her head? She cried: "Please God, don't be unreasonable! This girl is all right, and the fact that she has money surely ought not to bar her from having a good husband such as Lanny would make. Think what sort of man she might get here on the Riviera! Young as she is, and ignorant of the world!"

The voice said: "My daughter, it is the money you are thinking about, not the girl."

So then Beauty became rebellious—just as had happened in the case of Lucifer, aeons ago. She exclaimed: "My God, that is ridiculous! I never agreed to give up everything. If Lanny has money, he can help people in all sorts of ways, and Lanny would know how to do it much better than any of these idlers."

The voice replied, sternly: "Be careful, Mrs. Dingle!" It had taken to calling her that when it wanted to humiliate her. Now the tears came into her eyes, and she was in a state of confusion. The "Way of Perfection" was far less simple for a worldling like Beauty Budd than it had been for the naturally pure St. Theresa in medieval Spain.

Beauty felt the need of counsel, but was determined not to take the problem to her husband. Was she afraid of what he might tell her? After all, he had had little experience in the *grand monde*, and one might be justified in distrusting his judgment. Beauty knew that, whatever she did, he would not interfere, for he never tried to impose himself, even morally; he was content to go on living his inner life, trusting that it would have its effect upon others in time. Let your light so shine before men that they may see your good works and glorify your Father which is in heaven!

32

In That Fierce Light

I

Rick and Nina showed up in due course, very curious to see what sort of man it was who had managed to crash the gates of Beauty's heart. Lanny in his letters had put the best possible face upon the affair, and Rick and Nina, as guests, would do the same. In the privacy of their chamber Rick said there was one thing you could say for Mr. Dingle, he didn't try to force his ideas upon you; too bad the same couldn't be said for his wife! It was going to be a bit trying, but of course they would have to be polite. Nina said she hoped none of the children would fall sick, because Beauty was obviously hoping for a chance for Mr. Dingle to display his powers.

The young couple told Lanny the details of the Rosemary affair, and Nina delivered the messages which had been entrusted to her. Poor Bertie had got himself into a frightful mess; he had paid the blackmailer a good part of the money he had got out of his family art treasures. He wasn't a bad fellow, but weak, and a woman could twist him around her finger. An odd aspect of life in the diplomatic service—the head of the Foreign Office had come to the manor and had put it up to Rosemary: a scandal in London could be pardoned, but the prestige of the Empire couldn't stand one abroad, therefore Bertie's future depended upon his wife's willingness to go with him and stick by him. It amounted to getting married all over again; "forsaking all others, cleave to him only." But this time it wasn't a formula that you said in church, it was a gentleman's agreement, and you had to mean it!

Rick was now thirty-one, and was recognized as one of the younger writers with a future. He was working on a new book, not just a compilation of articles, but a carefully thought-out discussion of the world as it stood at the beginning of the year 1929. It was his thesis that the improvement of communications, especially the airplane, had reduced the size of the world so that there was no longer room for separate nations with their separate sovereignties. When airplanes loaded with high explosives could appear over the capital of a nation without warning, that nation wasn't safe; since it had to arm against the same sort of attack, the other nations were no safer. Agreements such as the Kellogg pact, which had just been signed with a great fanfare, meant nothing; each nation was an agency for its big-scale businessmen, competing for markets and resources, and the coming of war didn't depend upon signatures and gold seals on pieces of vellum, it depended upon some dissatisfied group of exploiters wanting more than they had, and seeing a chance to strike and get it.

Lanny had decided that Rick was the sanest thinker he knew, and he longed for the completion of this book so that he might give copies to various persons with whom he had arguments. Lanny couldn't pretend to foresee what was coming, but he had got fixed in his mind the proposition that there would never be peace in the world so long as the sources of wealth were left to be scrambled for and seized by the biggest and strongest. Lanny's young life had been dominated by one great war, and now he saw another in preparation, and who was going to stop it? Surely not those futile old gentlemen whom he had followed about Europe and watched in action at one conference after another. Ten years had passed, and they hadn't yet succeeded in fixing the amount of German reparations!

Young people in each nation were making up their minds that the only force in modern society that might avert another catastrophe was the exploited workers, organizing themselves for resistance to the ever-increasing pressure of capitalist greed. Rick was calling for an international government based on a Socialist economic system. That had to come, he insisted, and the only question was how was it to come? There were only two ways; revolution on the Russian model, or action by democratic consent to abolish autocracy from industry, as the British and Americans had long ago abolished it from their political affairs. The trouble was that you put off gradual changes until there was a crisis, and then it was too late. Rick said it was later now than anybody realized.

The two young men would discuss those questions in abstract, theoretical terms, and then Lanny would go to his class in the workers' school and be confronted with them in concrete, personal terms: Socialists *versus* Communists! There was hardly a question of strategy or tactics in the workers' struggle that didn't end up in that. If you urged obedience to law, the Communists would point out the lawlessness of the capitalists. If you talked about acquiring possession of the means of production by democratic methods, the Communists would say: "By electing politicians?" They would point to the career of one statesman after another; Briand, for example, had been chosen as a Socialist, and after he got power the railway workers struck, and he mobilized the troops and made them run the railways. Now he was a "radical," French style, which meant that he signed peace pacts, but took no step to interfere with the stranglehold of big business and finance on the people's means of life.

II

Emily Chattersworth came and opened Sept Chênes, and naturally one of the first things she wanted to do was to come over and inspect Beauty Budd's newest acquisition. Beauty was a friend, but also she was a phenomenon of nature, and the idea of her having got religion was nearly as entertaining as her having been shut up in a hotel suite with a German secret agent. Emily had done considerable reading in her life, and she knew that the idea of the immanence of God hadn't been invented in the state of Iowa; but it was undoubtedly "new thought" so far as Beauty was concerned, and what had it done to her? Lanny, who had learned to talk to this old friend with frankness, assured her that she would be disappointed in the result; like many other kinds of respectability, it was rather humdrum.

He told Emily the news about the pictures that Zoltan was selling, and the prospects for one that she wished to get rid of; about Hansi and Bess and their tour in the United States, the fine notices they were getting, and how Esther Budd had apparently reconciled herself to having a genius in the family; about his own latest bereavement and the state of his heart. "Do you miss her very much?" asked Emily.

"To be perfectly honest, not so much as I did Marie. She never wanted love as Marie did, wouldn't accept it from any man. I knew it was bound to end sooner or later; I was up against the British Empire."

"Did you get along well with her?"

"It was like being married. I had to go a lot of places when I'd much rather have stayed at home and read a book."

"You really want a studious woman, don't you, Lanny?"

"One that wears glasses," he smiled.

"Most of them would rather go blind nowadays," replied this white-haired *grande dame*—who used a lorgnette except when she was reading. Presently she remarked, *à propos de bottes:* "Irma Barnes is coming next week."

"I know; the ladies are all ganging up on me. Even Nina has joined."

"Don't be foolish, Lanny. I have every reason to think she's a fine young woman. I haven't seen her since she was a girl, but then she was bright and intelligent. Her mother is one of the Vandringhams—an excellent family, old New Yorkers, not the flashy ones."

"Quite a change in one generation, wouldn't you say?"

"You can't blame a girl because her father grows rich. It's to be doubted if she put him up to it."

"I know, Mrs. Emily; but the fact remains that when people have so much money, it does something to them; it seems to be stronger than they are."

"That is true; I've felt it myself, even though I never had any such sums as the Barneses. But remember, she's a girl like any other, and she wants some man to love her for herself."

"She'll have the devil of a time finding him, I'm guessing."

"If so, that's a reason to be sorry for her."

"Oh, I'll do that," he laughed; "but I doubt if she'll thank me!"

"What I mean is, give her a chance, like anybody else. See what she's really like, and don't make up your mind in advance."

Lanny told her about Tennyson's *Northern Farmer: New Style*, with which he had teased his mother. "Doänt thou marry for munny, but goä wheer munny is."

"You come to lunch and meet Irma and her mother, and I'll let them know that you're one caller who isn't interested in her fortune."

"I wonder," said the young man, promptly. "I have been quite entertained, thinking what I'd do if I had a fortune like that. I've decided that I'd set up a foundation to study the effects of stock-market speculation upon wages and the cost of living!"

III

Kurt Meissner wrote now and then. He was glad to hear the news about Beauty's marriage, and sent his best wishes for her happiness. He enclosed a picture of his young wife and their first baby, a boy; also of the very modest cottage in which they were living on the Stubendorf estate, the Graf having given them the use of it for the glory of German music. Kurt told about the composition on which he was working, and about a trip he had made to Munich, where his work was being taken up by the National Socialists with ardor. Heinrich Jung had become an active party leader, and they had won successes at the last elections. They were a legal party now, but they were still carrying on street wars with the Communists.

Rick looked at the photo of the bald little Aryan, and said: "I suppose they'll be having one every year for the glory of the Fatherland." He added: "Birth control is an important discovery, but it may prove a trap for the more progressive nations if the backward ones refuse to adopt it."

"Is Germany a backward nation?" inquired Lanny, with a grin.

"It'll be one very soon if those Nazis have their way. Women become brood-mares, and babies become soldiers to march out and conquer those decadent peoples who dream of being let alone."

Rick was worried about what was going on in Germany. He insisted that the republic was growing weaker, and failing completely to deal with the nation's internal problems. Britain and France couldn't agree on any consistent policy; they wouldn't help Germany to get on her feet and they wouldn't pay the cost of holding her down. They had just lifted the arms control of the country, and Germany was busily arming—Rick agreed with Robbie Budd about the facts, and what they meant. The next war was going to be fought with airplanes, and Germany hadn't been permitted to have military planes, but had been getting a great fleet of commercial planes, and how long would it take to convert them? Moreover, what was important was not so much the planes, but the factories and the skilled workers. Given these, a fleet of war-planes could be turned out in a year or two.

Rick had been to Geneva in September and had written up the situation confronting the Ninth Assembly of the League of Nations. Germany had been admitted, and had been fighting the admission of Poland to the League Council. Anyone could see that Poles and Germans were ready to fly at each other's throats. "That's where the next war will start," said Rick; "right at Stubendorf, or perhaps in the Corridor. It would take a permanent army there to prevent it —and who's going to pay the bill?"

Rick brought another item from Geneva; greetings to Lanny from Mrs. Sidney Armstrong, wife of that young American functionary who had introduced them to the insides of the League. "You remember her? She used to be his secretary. Janet Somebody."

"Sloane," said Lanny. "A jolly girl. We had the idea of falling in love with each other, and I was thinking I might go back and ask her to marry me."

"You waited too long, old top. They have a baby."

When Lanny told his mother about this, she said, with a touch of acidity: "There, now! Another one for you to adopt!"

IV

Lanny kept thinking: "Do I want to give my time to that Barnes girl?" He knew he had to give it to some girl before long; but a girl with twenty-three million dollars—even supposing that she would look at a poor man, and that he married her—what a nuisance to be carrying a load like that, having the world make a fuss over you, everybody trying to get something out of you, nobody ever telling you the truth, newspaper reporters besieging you for interviews! What could you say? Lanny had been with Hansi Robin when newspapermen had called, and that had seemed all right, because Hansi had done things and was going to do more; he had talked about music, and it had been worth while. But to talk because you had inherited more money than any other girl! Or because you had married such a girl! Lanny felt cheap even to think about it.

He discussed the problem with Rick, who looked quizzical, and said: "You really haven't the least bit of curiosity about her?"

"Maybe a little; enough to last through one luncheon."

"Well, I'll tell you what: be interested for me. Go and find out all you can about her. Ask her straight questions: What does it feel like to be a glamour girl? Are you excited, or are you bored, or are you scared, or exactly what? And whatever you get, bring it home."

"What for?"

"Copy, you imbecile. Don't you know that's what the public would rather read about than anything else in the world? You and I will collaborate on a play called *The Glamour Girl*, and make such a hit that we'll be the glamour boys of Broadway."

Lanny grinned, but then he reflected: "I'm afraid that would be giving her a rotten sort of deal."

Said the baronet's son: "If you find that she has a noble soul and that you are falling in love with her, I won't use the stuff."

V

Irma Barnes arrived at Sept Chênes, and the reporters came hurrying, and the photographers, and they put her on the front page of the Riviera papers. Emily telephoned that Lanny was to come to lunch next day. Beauty wasn't invited, because she might talk too much; Emily didn't say that, but explained that she wanted Lanny to have the field to himself, and Beauty understood. She had managed to get matters straightened out with God, and He had agreed to allow Lanny to treat Irma Barnes as he would any other young woman, not denying her happiness just because she was rich.

The mother had worked herself into a state of excitement, and came to Lanny's room to see if his tropical worsted was without a spot or wrinkle, and that the shades of his brightly striped tie harmonized with his tan-colored shirt.

"You know, old girl," he said, "your high-up Englishman is a trifle careless in his dress."

"He has some details that look careless," responded the fashionable mother, "but they are studied."

"Which details of mine are supposed to be careless?" inquired Lanny.

"You're not English," said Beauty, and passed on to another problem. "What are you going to talk about?"

"I rather thought I'd leave it to the inspiration of the moment."

"If I were you I wouldn't talk about politics, because you don't want her to find out that you are radical."

"All right, dear."

"And I wouldn't say anything about Marcel's work, because they might think you were hinting for them to buy it."

"I'll leave all business out, I promise."

"You understand that any sums of money you have made would seem just small change to her."

"I understand."

"And better not mention Budd's, because you don't want her to think that you're bragging. Emily will have told her all that sort of thing."

"I get you," said Lanny. "I'll tell her that the sun is shining brightly outside, and that we have many such days on the Riviera, even in January."

"You used to let me give you advice," complained Beauty; "but now I've become just an old shoe."

He gave her a hug and a large fat kiss, and said: "I never did that to any of my shoes."

The mother exclaimed: "Wait! You have pushed your tie all crooked."

VI

The elaborate carvings on Emily's white stone villa in French Renaissance style were shining brilliantly in the aforementioned January sunshine when Lanny came up the broad drive. Half a dozen cars were parked there, and he wondered if there were other guests after all; but they were cars of the members of the Barnes entourage who were staying at a hotel in Cannes, also of persons who were trying to see the heiress but were seeing the secretary instead. Lanny went into the drawing-room, and, having been at home here since childhood, he seated himself at the piano. He tried to think what might appeal to a girl who had just come from the hurlyburly of the Great White Way, and he chose the very lovely andante movement of Kurt Meissner's *Spanish Suite;* a serenade having all the seductiveness that anyone had ever imagined about Valencian nights. "Come out," it seemed to say, "for the scent of the orange blossoms is heavy in the air, and my heart aches with a longing which I strive to express—it is something beautiful which torments the soul—which cannot be explained."

Lanny thought: "I will find out if she knows what music is."

The three ladies appeared in the doorway, and he stopped. The hostess entered first: kind Mrs. Emily, her white hair worn long in defiance of the fashion of the hour; her finely chiseled, intellectual face lined with wrinkles which could no longer be concealed. She had had a surgical operation last summer, and was now supposed to be getting stronger. She had spent a lifetime entertaining other people, trying to give them pleasure, and at the same time a little more wisdom than they had or seemed to want.

Next, Mother Barnes, who had been born a Vandringham, and had acquired weight and majesty through the years; she had an ample bosom, and layers of *embonpoint* which the dressmaker's best arts were powerless to suppress; her gray silk chiffon might have been a maternity dress. She had dark hair, and dark eyes set under heavy brows, looking at you through a lorgnette. She was not a talkative person—it seemed that it might be an effort to bring that deep contralto voice into action; but when she did speak it was with authority. She listened and watched attentively, and Lanny could be certain that every detail concerning himself was being noted—perhaps even things which he himself didn't know. After the meal was over, and they lighted cigarettes, he saw the butler bring Mrs. Barnes a silver tray containing a long torpedo wrapped in gold foil. She unwrapped a dark brown cigar, bit off the end like a man, and proceeded to light up and puff vigorously.

And then Irma. A brunette like her mother, and no sylph according to the modern style, rather a young Juno. Her dark hair was shingled in the current style and waved about her ears; she wore a cream-colored frock of a simple cut, with a necklace of pearls. Her features were regular and her expression rather placid; she smiled easily, but quietly. Lanny saw at once that she was not a talkative person, which was rather a relief from his home life. She didn't say: "Oh, what was that lovely music you were playing?" She wasn't going to gush about anything, but wait for the world to bring her gifts; she would examine them carefully, and if there was anything wrong with them, her mother would tell her about it afterward.

All right; Lanny could talk for a whole tableful of people. He asked the young visitor how she liked the Riviera at first glance, and she replied that it reminded her of parts of the California coast, and also of Bermuda. Lanny hadn't been to either of those places, but he said that he had lived here since he could remember, and it had been pleasanter in the old days, before the place was so much advertised and such mobs came in. He told how it was when the beach of Juan-les-Pins had been used by fishermen, and he had played with their children, and helped to haul the seine. He had seen many strange creatures come out of that water—the strangest of all a submarine. Then Lanny told about the monument inscribed to the little "Septentrion child" who had "danced and pleased in the theater" some two thousand years ago. He told about the ruins and relics which various tribes of mankind had left on this Côte d'Azur, and how it was still the custom of some of the peasants to pray against the coming of the Saracens.

VII

In short, Lanny did what he could to entertain the minds and stimulate the imaginations of two ladies whom he didn't know at all. He brought his gifts of myrrh and frankincense, and the queen mother and the royal princess accepted them graciously, but did not indicate that they found them superior to the many other gifts which had been laid before their throne. Presently Lanny told about M. Pinjon, the gigolo, who had come when Lanny was a little boy and played the piccolo flute and showed him the steps of Provençal dances; afterward the poor fellow had lost one leg in the war, and had retired to his father's farm, and every Christmas he sent Lanny a little carved dancing-man of olive tree wood. "How pathetic!" said Miss Barnes, and Lanny replied: "The Duquesa de Villafranca, who was Zaharoff's wife, was so touched by the story that she sent him a very fine flute, and I suppose he plays it every night while the flocks come in. Some day, if you and your mother would enjoy a trip into the mountains, I would take you to call on him."

It appeared that the girl was about to say yes, but she stole a glance at her mother, and then said: "Thank you. Perhaps we can arrange it some time."

Well, Lanny had done his part. He let the stately Mrs. Emily talk about the fashionable people who were on hand this season, and the interesting events which were scheduled. After the meal they strolled out to the loggia in the rear, overlooking the gardens. The best view was from the front, but they couldn't go onto the portico because of strangers coming and going. However, on the second story there was a balcony, and Lanny asked if Miss Barnes had observed it. He offered to point out the landmarks to her, and she assented.

To the west lay the Estérel mountains, of blood-red porphyry, and to the east Monaco on its rock. The city of Nice was white sprinkled on green. In front lay the blue Golfe Juan, with several gray French warships at anchor; beyond were islands, one of them Sainte-Marguerite, where you could sail and have tea; the Germans of the Riviera had been interned there during the war. Over to the left were the heights of Notre-Dame-de-Bon-Port, where the sailors came once a year, walking with bare feet and carrying the image of the Virgin down to the sea so that she might bless the waters and protect them from storms. Apparently Miss Barnes found all this interesting, and Lanny said that he would be happy to come and take her and her mother to see the sights of the coast. She thanked him, and he wondered, was she more human than her mother? Did she perchance consider that she had enough money, so that she might feel free to chat with a poor man now and then? A plausible theory, but it required more evidence.

They went downstairs and he didn't offer to play the piano, because she knew that he could do it, and it was up to her to ask the favor if she wished it. After some miscellaneous conversation he excused himself, and made no suggestion of a second meeting. If they felt any urge to see him again, they could reveal it to Mrs. Emily. He had done his duty, and at home Rick would have some pages of new manuscript ready—not a play about a glamour girl, but a book supporting the program of the Socialist International!

VIII

"Well, how did it go? What is she like? What did you talk about? What did she say?" Such are the questions which every mother asks; and every mother knows that her son makes unsatisfactory answers, and has to be cross-examined—but not crossly! It all sounded rather enigmatic as Lanny told it, and Beauty could hardly wait until she had a chance to ask Emily. They could only talk guardedly over the telephone, but Emily said that Lanny had been his usual friendly self and nobody could help but like him when they knew him. The last clause gave a dubious turn to the statement; but apparently it was all right, for the next day Emily called Lanny and asked if he would come and take them for a drive—she had assured the ladies that he could tell them more interesting things about this Coast of Pleasure than any other person she knew. "Good old scout!" said Lanny—and that was hardly being guarded!

Doubtless there had been some conversation between mother and daughter, and it must have contained an element favorable to the young art expert, for in spite of the fact that they had a chauffeur with them, and that Mrs. Emily also had one, they permitted Lanny to drive them about. Miss Barnes sat in the seat beside him, and he pointed out the places of interest and told her about the life, not all of it favorable; it would be well for her to know that the coast abounded in swindlers and pretenders, many of them highly ingenious. He mentioned the Rumanian countess, genuine, who had sold him a vase that wasn't.

They came to Monte Carlo, and had lunch at Ciro's, and strolled about, looking at the sights. Lanny said it was time for Zaharoff to be taking his constitutional, and Irma asked: "Who is he?" He told her, and thought it was interesting, but discovered that for the young the aged are but dim shadows. His offer, half playful, to take them for a call upon the munitions king did not interest a glamour girl; what she wanted was to see the gambling which people talked about all over the world. Followed by the two elders as chaperons, he escorted her into the sumptuous rococo palace; they wandered through the white and gilt rooms, overdecorated and very ill-ventilated, and explained that they no longer belonged to Zaharoff; the old trader had sold the place for three times what he paid—trust him for that!

They watched the players at the various tables, and finally Irma wanted to try roulette. Did Lanny have any idea which number was likely to win? He said that he had not the slightest idea; his father had insisted that he must never harbor any such thought, never let anyone persuade him that it was possible to know or to guess, for that was the shortest road to ruin in the whole world. Irma said she had a hunch for the number eleven, having somewhere heard some-body say "Come eleven," so she took out a ten-franc note and laid it on that number; if her hunch should prove correct, she would be paid thirty-five times the amount of her stake.

The *croupier* spun the wheel, and presently said his formula: "*Rien ne va plus.*" The little ball dropped into number twenty-eight, so the *croupier* raked in Irma's ten francs. She moved on, saying: "Perhaps it's just as well, or I might have got interested."

"It doesn't always work that way," commented the escort. "Many people try to win their money back, and that's where their troubles begin."

The party had been recognized in the restaurant, and people had turned to stare at them; several had followed at a discreet distance. Now they were known in the casino, and next day stories appeared in the papers; the American heiress had visited "Monty" and risked and lost ten francs. This seemed to amuse the newspapermen; they fig-ured that it was the one hundred-millionth part of Irma Barnes's fortune, and telegraphed this calculation all over the world. One of the gossip writers in New York compared it with the practice of another very wealthy American, old "John D.," who gave a shiny new dime to every person rich or poor whom he met. Mrs. Barnes received a cable from her brother in New York, saying that this wasn't very good publicity; he didn't make clear whether he meant gambling in general, or gambling for such a puny stake. He himself was a Wall Street operator.

The incident had its effect upon Lanny's affairs. He was named as the escort of the glamour girl, and it gave him a taste of publicity not so disagreeable to his mother and her friends as the occasion of his escape from the Fascists. Many persons called up Bienvenu asking to meet the American heiress; persons whom Beauty had well-nigh forgotten presented themselves suddenly as old friends. They had houses to rent to Irma Barnes, family heirlooms to sell to her, sons to marry to her—or they just wanted to meet her on general prin-ciples, they were moths who flew to the spotlight, hoping to have their names in the papers as Lanny had succeeded in doing. Beauty informed these persons that Miss Barnes's business manager was staying at such and such a hotel in Cannes; but of course that wasn't what they wanted.

There was a very grand reception to the heiress at Sept Chênes, and the *crème de la crème* attended; more titles than you could shake a stick at, or could keep in your memory no matter how hard you might try—and Irma didn't. To an American girl the difference between a marquess and a marqués and a marquis and a marchese was not readily apparent, and a dark brown skin meant just one thing to her, even when the bearer was an East Indian potentate. Some of these gentlemen were bachelors, and others willing to become so if Irma Barnes would smile upon them; since she smiled upon all impartially, they gathered around her like bees at swarming time. Lanny, having no title and no fortune to speak of, realized what a silly enterprise the women of his circle had pushed him into, and sat out in the sunshine with M. Rochambeau and a French diplomat of the latter's acquaintance, discussing the probable life-span of the Kellogg pact and which nation would be the first to breach it.

IX

Irma Barnes had inspected the Riviera, and had learned that Nice was "common," while Cannes was "right." She had visited and approved the château of an American copper-mining heiress up on the heights not far from Sept Chênes. There she and her entourage were installed: a business manager, or steward, his secretary and a bookkeeper, Irma's social secretary, her maid and her mother's maid and a chauffeur; that was the staff with which she traveled, and the manager would engage servants for the château locally. She herself would never have to move a finger, or use her mind longer than it took to learn the names of the butler and the housekeeper. Her function was to have beautiful clothes draped upon her, and go forth to give the world the pleasure of gazing at her. In due course she would be named as one of the best-dressed women of the Continent, an honor which one attained by purchasing the most clothes from the fashionable *couturiers* of Paris—or from their Riviera branch estab-

lishments—and permitting them to design everything and charge double or triple prices.

The story which the papers told was that the great American heiress had come to Europe in search of "culture," but of course that didn't go down with the *beau monde*. It was taken for granted that she was looking for a husband, and it would have to be a title, one of the greatest. Every mother of an eligible son was on the *qui vive*, and some came to the Riviera especially on Irma's account; who would begrudge the price of a ticket in a lottery such as this? The smart people were agog, and the smart newspapermen amused themselves and their readers by listing the eligibles, as they would have done for a race at Longchamps: the name of the entry, what stable it was from, what prizes it had won, the names of the sire and the dam. This was a convenience for both Irma and her mother, for they could cut out the list and learn the titles: Prinz zu Pumpernickel of the royal house of a German state, the Duc de Chou̶ of the old French *noblesse*, the dashing young Baron Snuff̶ Poland, the fabulously wealthy Maharaja of Gavardior.

The proper procedure was for Mrs. Barnes to have a lawyer to whom these candidates might send their lawyer, presenting their photographs and credentials, a list of their titles, castles and other possessions, and a statement of the dowry which the bride would be expected to bring. Mrs. Barnes's lawyer would convey these various proposals to her, and if the family was interested, arrangements would be made for a meeting between the bride and the prospective bridegroom. That was the dignified way to handle it, but of course with crude Americans one must be prepared for almost anything. Did they expect the business manager who hired their house and paid their servants to handle their marriage arrangements? Or did Mrs. Barnes expect to discuss such matters herself? The social secretary was asked this question, Mrs. Chattersworth was asked it, and discreet inquiries came to Mrs. Barnes by mail: "Will you kindly designate in what manner, etc."

Lanny had retired to his studio and was reading Marx's *Capital*, in order to try to understand the theory of surplus value to which Rick and others were so frequently referring. Emily came to Bienvenu, and she and Beauty had a pow-wow, after which the châtelaine of Sept Chênes strolled over to the studio and walked in on the young social scientist. "See here," she said, "do you want to or don't you?"

"Don't I what?"

"Don't waste my time. Do you or don't you?"

"Well, honestly, Mrs. Emily, I don't think that I do and I do think that I don't. It's awfully good of you, and I'd do most anything in the world to oblige you; but I just feel silly. The girl hasn't any interest in me, and I don't want anything she has, and why should I sacrifice my self-respect and make her think that I do?"

"Are you quite sure she hasn't any interest in you?"

"Well, my God, she had every chance to show it, but I might as well have been a hired guide."

"Do you expect the woman to do the wooing?"

"You're darn well right I do—when she has as much money as this ... an feels like a cad if he so much as looks at her."

"... ure you're not the one who's making too much out of her money, Lanny?"

"Well, I know a little about the world; and if that mother of hers isn't thinking about her money, then I'm a hard-boiled cynic."

"Let me tell you about them. Irma loves her mother, and respects her, but all the same there's a struggle going on between them, and it's hard on both. Fanny Barnes has had a very unhappy life; her husband kept women all over town, and she loathed him; it's affected her attitude to pretty nearly all men. She doesn't like to see them come around Irma; she can't help knowing what they want, and not liking it."

"Does she want the girl to grow up an old maid?"

"What she would like is for her to marry some mature businessman, who can handle her fortune; she has a man in mind in New York, but Irma won't have him, so here they are."

"Well, I'm no businessman, Mrs. Emily, and I wouldn't have the least idea what to do with her fortune."

"What Irma wants, Lanny, is to fall in love."

"Has she told you that?"

"Not in so many words, but it's written all over her."

"Well, if she wants to fall in love with me, the first thing would be to know something about me. She can't very well judge with her mother sitting by and making me feel that she'd like to call the police."

"No doubt she would," laughed the woman. "But she won't."

"Irma has got swarms of men around her and she's on the go all the time. I don't think she's missing me."

"Maybe she's missing something that might be of advantage to her if she knew about it."

"You were always too kind, Mrs. Emily. The way I feel is this: whether she likes it or not, she's in the position of a queen, and if she wants a man she has to say so. He can't ask her."

"That's really making it too hard for any girl."

"Well, if she wants a man who doesn't want her for her money, how else will she get him?"

The woman thought that over; then she inquired: "Is there anything you would suggest?"

"I'd suggest meeting her like any other young woman. I'd invite her for a drive, or a sail, or something, and she could see if she likes me, and I'd see if I like her."

"All right," was the reply. "It may mean a fight with Fanny, but I'll see if it can be arranged."

X

Rick said: "I'm not rotting, there's an idea in that play. If you'll get the stuff, I'll write it."

Lanny, amused, inquired: "Shall I tell her that you want to write it?"

"Tell her that you want to write it yourself."

"That would make me another kind of fortune-hunter. And a cheap one, I fear."

"Well, don't fear too much. Go right after her."

Lanny said: "I'll see." He was amused by the advice, so exactly the opposite of Rick's own manner of approach to anything or any-body. An Englishman's idea of an American man dealing with an American woman!

One bright and pleasant day right after lunch Lanny drove up to the château on the heights, and the new English butler received him and said: "I will notify Miss Barnes, sir." Lanny sat in a large recep-tion hall which had portraits, and he used such occasions for testing his professional skill. Without looking at the signature, he would ask himself: "Who painted that? What is the period? And what would I offer for it?" He would find out how near he had come on the first two points, and Zoltan would tell him about the last.

The daughter of Midas appeared, wearing what was called a sports ensemble, white with gold trim, very gay. "Take a warm wrap," he said. "You can never tell when you go sailing." They rolled gently down ˑ slope, over the boulevards of the city of Cannes, and out ˑap, where Lanny had his boat. On the way he asked what ˑ been doing, whom she had met and what she thought of ˑ the easiest kind of conversation. She was reserved in her com-ments on people, and he thought: "Is she being kind to them? Or is she not very perceptive?" A few matters he had become certain about; she would never "rave" over anything, and, on the other hand, she was not malicious, she didn't say contemptuous things. Maybe she was just slow in her mental processes. It was hard for Lanny to imagine that, for his own mind was usually behaving like fireworks inside.

He assisted her into the boat. Just enough breeze for pleasant sail-ing; but one couldn't count upon permanence in January. Emily Chattersworth had assured Mrs. Barnes that Lanny had sailed the Golfe Juan since he was a boy, and never had been upset. He would take her around the Lérin islands, and perhaps stop on Sainte-Marguerite and have tea under the soughing pine trees.

He said: "Over there close to shore is where the submarine came up. It was always my favorite spot for torch-fishing." He told her about Captain Bragescu, the Rumanian officer who had painted and powdered his face, but, even so, had speared and landed the biggest green moray that Lanny had ever seen. He told about goggle-fishing, and how for months he had watched and stalked a big *mérou*. He mentioned that his father had used this boat as a place of retreat in which to impart the weightiest secrets about munitions deals. "I'm not sure they were really so weighty," he said, "but he wanted to impress me with the importance of not letting people fish things out of me. You can see that a sailboat is a fine place for private conferences."

"I wish my father had thought of it," said Irma Barnes. Evidently she had some incident in mind, but didn't tell it.

Lanny said: "Do you find it interesting to watch people and try to understand them—what they're thinking about and what makes them tick? They don't always want you to know."

"I've been told that is sometimes the case," admitted the heiress with a smile.

"My life has been a queer one," the young man went on to explain. "I've never been great or important, and never wanted to be; but accident has thrown me among people of that sort—at least, they considered themselves that, and were able to get the world to accept them. My father being in munitions, I can't recall the time when I wasn't meeting generals and cabinet members and bigwigs like that. Then for six months I was on the American staff at the Peace Conference, and I didn't really have any influence, but a lot of people thought I might have it. So, one way or another, I'd meet this or that headliner, and I'd think: 'What is he really like? What's he thinking about right now? What does he want to get from me, or from my father, or from my chief?' It gets to be a habit—maybe a bad one."

"It sounds rather alarming," commented the girl in the sailboat. There were a few others on the *golfe*, but some distance away.

"Oh, I never did any of them any harm," said Lanny. "I just thought about them, and often I never had any chance to check up and find out if I was right."

"Are you trying to check up on me?" she smiled. It was certainly a "lead," but Lanny judged it best not to follow it too eagerly.

"I told you about Zaharoff," he said. "I saw a great deal of him during the Peace Conference in Paris. He wanted something from me—I'm not at liberty to say what it was, but it was a matter of state, and the old gentleman gave quite a fascinating demonstration of how a Levantine trader sets about getting what he's after. You understand, he was at that time the richest man in Europe; my father said he was the richest man in the world. He has two daughters who are going to be his heirs. He invited me to meet those young ladies —he was using them as bait. I was supposed to keep on coming, so that he could win me over. They were lovely girls, and their mother was a Spanish duquesa, a relative of King Alfonso. They probably had no idea what they were being used for; they met a young American connected with the Peace Commission, who told them amusing stories about what was going on; they were modest and reserved, quite romantic-looking—I was only nineteen at the time, so I was susceptible. I had read fairy stories when I was a child, and I thought: 'Here are two princesses, and I wonder what princesses really think about, and are they as interesting as the stories make them seem.' "

"What happened?" asked Irma.

"It's too bad. It's like a serial story when you miss the next issue of the magazine. My position was such that I couldn't honorably go back again."

"You were just getting to the interesting place," remarked the glamour girl.

XI

The breeze was from the west, and the little boat was close-hauled; Lanny, holding the tiller, had to keep watch ahead, so the girl, seated farther forward, was in his line of vision. She, for her part, might have been interested in the view, in which case she would have turned her back to Lanny; but she didn't. Looking into the mainsail of a boat gets rather monotonous, so now and then she would direct her glance toward the young man at her side. It was a time for confidences, if ever. "Go after her hard!" Rick had said.

"Now I meet another princess," Lanny remarked, "and I am wondering what she is really like."

"Oh, dear!" exclaimed the girl. She shot a quick look at him, and then, meeting his eyes, looked back into the mainsail. He saw the color mount in her cheeks.

"I have been thinking a lot about a princess," he said. "It is not just a title, you know; it's a state of affairs. Few kings of old days had as much power as your father wielded, and few kings' daughters have as much passed on to them as you."

"I suppose so," she admitted, in a low voice. She did not look at him again for quite a while.

"A princess is born to power; she doesn't have to do anything to get it, and, on the other hand, she has no way to escape it. She is a prisoner of her destiny. People behave to her in a certain way, and expect her to behave to them according to her station; there is a code of etiquette which has grown out of the circumstances, much the same all over the world, and it quickly becomes fixed. The courtiers and ladies-in-waiting are shocked if the princess doesn't do what they expect, and the princess, knowing this, finds it hard to break out of her role. Isn't that true?"

"That's about the way it is."

"But all the time the princess knows that she's a woman, like any other. She becomes a double personality, leading a double life. So when someone comes to me and says: 'Would you like to meet the Princess So-and-so?' I usually answer: 'Not especially.' I have learned that meeting one is usually a bore; you don't meet the real person, you only meet the role, so to speak, the figurehead. Of course if you believe in royalty, and like to stand about a throne—or if you're looking to get something by royal favor—that's another matter. But not wanting anything, I find myself thinking: 'What is Her Royal Highness really like? What is she thinking at this moment? Is she bored by her role, or does she enjoy it? Is she perhaps frightened —afraid not to play it right, because people will laugh at her if she does it wrong? Is she flattered by their praise, or is she afraid of their malice?' That malice can be a terrible thing, Miss Barnes; for the world is far from being kind."

"I know," said the young woman, her voice still low.

"Maybe I'm imagining most of this, and maybe you haven't ever thought of it, except vaguely. Maybe you've just been raised a certain way, and you go on living from day to day. Maybe you don't like to question your own soul, or to have some impertinent young upstart begin doing it!"

His companion had turned her head away, and he saw her reach hurriedly for her handkerchief and put it to her eyes. He exclaimed, in concern: "Have I offended you?"

"No," she answered, hastily. "Wait." He did so, and presently she turned her face half-way toward him, and explained: "You see, Mr. Budd, my father killed himself getting all that money; and I'd ever so much rather have had him."

XII

There was the answer to the riddle, and there was Rick's play if he cared to write it. Irma Barnes had loved her father. Had she known that he "kept women all over town"? Maybe so, maybe not —Lanny wasn't going to inquire about that. Anyhow, she had loved him, and admired him, a capable, hard-driving master of men, a gay companion when he was at home. She had known him as a little girl knows a playmate and friend, and when she learned that he had dropped dead in the middle of a hard Wall Street battle, she didn't feel compensated by his possessions. She didn't mention her mother, but that too was significant, and, with the hint that he had got from Emily, Lanny could guess that she thought her mother had set more store by the money than by the man.

Anyhow, there was the soul of a princess. After a while she smiled and said that Lanny wouldn't miss the next installment this time. He decided then that her mind wasn't slow; she just stayed withdrawn into herself, watching the world go by and doing what people asked her to do. Was it out of kindness, or lack of initiative? She was only twenty, and hadn't thought much.

What had they taught her in school? Apparently nothing very useful: good manners and deportment, some French, and a smattering of the arts. She knew how to read, but she didn't know how to enjoy reading. When you have so much money, and so many persons to attend you, it becomes your duty to let them do it; having things done to you and for you is in accord with your station in life, your social importance; but to go off into a corner by yourself and bury your nose in a book is a waste of opportunity, to say nothing of seeming churlish to all the dressmakers and hairdressers and manicurists and masseuses and dancing- and music-masters and maids and secretaries and other humble persons who get their living by serving you, and are so pathetic in their efforts to please you. "You've no idea how many people I had to disappoint in order to get this sail with you!" confessed the princess of public utilities. "But I'm glad I did."

The ice was broken, and she told him about her life, which seemed like one in a high-class jail to Lanny, who had been accustomed to do so much for himself and to spend so large a share of his time alone, dreaming his dreams, trying to express them on the piano, or to find them in books or works of art. Irma Barnes had hardly ever been alone in her life, despite the fact that she had been an only child. She had hardly ever been able to do anything for herself; there was always somebody ready to leap to do it ahead of her, and to have his or her feelings hurt if the young mistress didn't wait and submit. That she was physically vigorous was due to the fact that she had played tennis with a tennis instructor, ridden horseback with a riding master, swum with a swimming expert—and so on, one thing after another all day long. Irma Barnes had never hauled a seine with fisherboys and -girls on any beach; to her a fish was something the butler brought in steaming hot on a large dish of chased silver, and showed to the master with a flourish, and then proceeded to cut into slices on a side table.

XIII

The weather continued to favor them, and they sat at a little outdoor table by a teahouse and ate tiny biscuits with butter and honey, discussing the fact that riches accumulated automatically, and what caused them to behave in that way. Someone had told the mother and daughter about Lanny's strange eccentricity of teaching in a Red Sunday school. He was quite sure it wasn't Emily who had done this; more likely some lady with an eligible son of her own. The facts were notorious, and, despite his mother's anxious warnings, Lanny had no idea of trying to slur them over. What he believed meant much more to him than it did to Beauty, and it would have been silly to let the girl take an interest in him without knowing the pink tinge of his mind.

He told her about the children of the workers who came there; what they looked like, how they behaved, what he taught them. She imagined unruly little ragamuffins, but he assured her that they came with clothes carefully mended and that they had been washed for the occasion, at least everything that showed. They were, he said, the élite of the children of the poor; alert, eager-eyed, taking their class-consciousness as a religion; their parents had been acquainted with suffering and they knew that life was no playground. To all this a glamour girl listened as to something from another planet; things strange, rather thrilling, but also alarming.

What was it all for? What did these people expect to do? He explained in words of one syllable the idea of social ownership: the means of producing what all had to use were to be public property, publicly administered for the public benefit; something like the post-office, the army, the trams. He forgot for the moment that Irma came from a country where the trams and the railroads were privately owned, and that her father had owned some. She listened to his picture of a co-operative society, out of Bellamy, and she brought up the stock objections. Who would do the dirty work? Would people work if they didn't have to? And would you pay everybody the same?

She wanted to know how he came upon these unusual ideas. He told her about his Red uncle, not trying to prettify him. This dangerous person, so greatly disliked by Lanny's father, had taken him, half by accident, to a slum in Cannes. "Oh, do they have slums in Cannes?" exclaimed the girl, and Lanny replied: "Would you like to see them?" He told her about Barbara Pugliese and her tragic fate. He told about the Blessed Little Pouter Pigeon, and the regime of despotism which he had set up in Italy. "Oh, but they tell me the country is much better managed!" exclaimed Irma. "The trains all run on time!"

Lanny perceived that he would have a job of educating to do. He talked about the Peace Conference and what he had seen and learned there. He mentioned Lincoln Steffens, and found that she had never heard the name; in fact, her mind was pretty much a blank about current events. She knew the names of the leading screen stars, of the singers she had heard at the opera, the leaders of jazz bands who were announced over the ever more popular radio; but literary names, except for a few best-sellers, were unknown to her. The names of statesmen also were vague in her mind; she had no idea what they stood for, except that her father had approved of certain ones at home and disapproved violently of certain others. Lanny could guess that the former were men with whom the father had been able to do business.

It wasn't at all the sort of conversation that he had planned, or that Beauty would have approved; but the heiress asked questions, and he answered, and told her stories which he thought were within the range of her understanding. Perhaps he did not allow enough for the immaturity of her mind; perhaps he talked too long and wearied her; but certainly she saw that he was kind, and perfectly respectful, possibly even grandfatherly. If she was looking for a man who wasn't after her money, she had reason to believe that this was the one. She said: "I don't think my mother would approve of these ideas."

He replied: "Probably not. You don't have to tell them to her unless you wish." That was the nearest he came to sedition, or seduction, or whatever the mother would have considered it.

They went back to the boat, and it was turning chilly, so she was glad to have her wrap. The breeze held, and they sailed before it merrily. They saw the sun go down behind the open sea, and before dark they reached the little pier. Driving to her home he was smitten by doubts, and said: "I do hope I haven't been boring you with all this political stuff."

"Not at all," she answered. "I was truly interested. I hope you will come again."

"I'll be delighted to. I know that you have many engagements, and I don't want to intrude; but this is my home, you know, and I am at your service."

"Call me up," she said; and they left it there.

Driving back to his home, Lanny was thinking: "Well, she'd be all right, if I could get her out of that environment." But then he thought: "Her environment is her money, and she won't get out of it till she dies."

He found that his mother was out, so he strolled to the lodge. "Well?" asked Rick, quizzically. "Did you get me that story?"

"I got one," Lanny replied. "But I'm afraid I can't let you use it."

The lame Englishman sat up in his chair and looked at his friend. His wife was in the next room and he called: "Ho, Nina, come in here! Lanny is going to marry Irma Barnes!"

33

Uneasy Lies the Head

I

IRMA BARNES was going about with Lanny Budd. All the Riviera took note of the fact, and the million tongues of gossip were busy. He was the lucky one; favored over all the millionaires, the princes and the dukes and the marquesses. In various ways it was made apparent to him that he had become a person of importance. The spotlight swung onto Bienvenu and stayed there. Peace and privacy were gone; there were visitors calling, motor-cars in the drive, the telephone ringing; people urging Lanny and his beautiful mother to come here and there. "And bring Irma," they would add, casually.

He had the time to give to her, and she took it for granted that he would give it. She enjoyed his company; he knew everybody and everything, or so it seemed to her; he made clever remarks, and while she wasn't clever herself, she smiled appreciatively when he was. Moreover, he was kind; and while nobody was unkind to her, she had been put on guard against insincerity. It wasn't long before they were calling each other by their first names, and he had the run of the château. Irma had had it out with her mother; the older woman wasn't pleased by it, but she would be polite, because the young generation was running wild and you had to give them their head.

Lanny played tennis with Irma and beat her regularly. It was a novel experience for her; not one of her suitors had had that much originality. He escorted her to a cocktail party, *très snob*, and when she had had two drinks he told her that was one too many, she showed the effects. He wasn't sure if she'd take it from him, but she did; moreover, she told others about it, and rumor spread, he had her completely under his thumb; he was posing as a young Puritan, a moralist. Imagine, after the way they lived in Bienvenu! She'd soon find out, if the million tongues had their way. One proper English lady told Mrs. Fanny that the place had "a faintly incestuous atmosphere!"

Lanny didn't leave it for the gossips to tell about himself. He took Irma for a long drive in the mountains, to that village of Charaze where the one-legged gigolo resided. On the way they talked about love, and he told her the story of Rosemary, beginning on the banks of the river Thames when he was sixteen and she was seventeen, and ending two or three months ago, when she left for the Argentine. No use keeping back the names, for "everybody" knew about it, "everybody" knew that he had built a "cottage" for her and her children. Just now the Dowager Countess Eversham-Watson had it for the season. "You know," said the million tongues, "that whisky woman from Kentucky. Is she his latest flame? Nobody seems to be quite sure about it."

There was snow up in those mountains, and one had to drive carefully. The retired gigolo hopped up on his peg-leg and embraced Lanny; he was so happy that the tears stood in his eyes. He had a wife and several brown little ones; they sat in his stone cabin and listened while he played the marvelous silver-embossed flute which the duquesa had presented to him. The wife spread a red-and-white-checked cloth on the table, and brought a long loaf of bread, fresh butter and cheese, dried figs and new wine; before they left, Irma purchased the whole row of little dancing men which M. Pinjon was carving for the next Christmas trade.

Then, driving down in the late afternoon, Lanny told the story of Marie de Bruyne. Again no use hiding names, for it had been in the newspapers; it was a "scandal," and there were those who cherished that sort of history and would remember it till they died—and perhaps later, if they were consigned to the same place as Marie. Lanny had no shame about the story, and if it was going to shock a strictly brought-up American girl, the sooner he knew it the better. He was in his thirtieth year, and had had only three women in his life; he hadn't bought any of them, or betrayed any, and all had been happy. If Irma were to investigate the records of her many suitors, both in New York and on the Riviera, she would hardly find a better one.

II

Irma Barnes liked love stories, it appeared; especially when they were autobiographical. She asked questions, not bold or improper, but questions of a stranger in a strange land, trying to understand its customs. This very old continent of Europe had its long-established institutions, and *la vie à trois* was one of them; doubtless the practice existed also across the seas, but more carefully hidden, at least from young girls. It was a daring adventure to have a man tell her such things; a tribute to her maturity, and one more proof that he wasn't after her money—or if he was, he was taking a bold line!

He didn't say: "I tell you these things because I am thinking about asking you to marry me." But it was understood between them. Silly to pretend otherwise, when it was in the thoughts and conversation of everyone who knew them. They were feeling each other out, trying experiments, making little tentative approaches and then retreating. Lanny would go off and think: "Well, what would it be like with her?" or "What did she mean by that remark?" Irma would step out of his car, asking herself the same questions. She would go into the house, and there would be an Austrian baron or the son of a South African gold magnate waiting to take her to dinner. She would think: "Would this be better?"

Everywhere she went people were attentive to her; every man bowed, clicked heels, kissed her hand in the romantic European way. Each studied her tastes, her whims, and sought to please her by every gesture and word. The European men were ardent; with hardly an exception, they made love to her all the time. Never for a moment did they let her forget that they were men, and she an adored woman; their manners, their phrases, their tones, had all been created for that purpose. It was called "gallantry." She found it exciting; she lived in a pleasant state of surprise, for there was always a new type of man, a new sort of elegance, a new distinction of appearance, costume, gesture, intonation; a new foreign accent, with perhaps a hint of mystery, of power, something to be awed by, perhaps even to be afraid of. Hard to be sure, when you were so young, and didn't entirely trust anybody, not even your own mother. How often she missed the strong, capable father, who knew men and could have told her what she needed to know.

Lanny was different from all the others. He was casual, sometimes irritatingly so; he seemed to take too much for granted. Or was it that he thought too well of himself? Was he a bit conceited? She asked him, and he said it wasn't that he valued himself so highly, he valued some of the other men so little, and didn't care to mix up with them. Was it the remark of an honest man, or of a jealous one? She asked him about some of the other men. He answered that he didn't know these individuals, but he knew a lot about European men in general; watch their attitude toward women—other women!

Lanny was younger than many of the suitors, but he talked the oldest. Many of the things he said were over her head; she told him so, and he explained what he meant. He didn't make love to her; hadn't even tried to take her hand. She wondered why. He had made love to other women. Didn't he care for her that way? Was it because of her money? Hang the money!—so she would think, but not for long. It was pleasant having money, and if anyone failed to treat her with the deference due to her money rank, she would resent it quickly. Her mother kept her attention firmly fixed on the fact that she was the greatest "catch" on the Riviera, perhaps in Europe.

The ladies at Bienvenu and its vicinity did the same thing for Lanny. With them it was the way it had been during both battles of the Marne; everybody wanted bulletins every hour! They were, as the phrase had it, "dying with curiosity." Nina and Margy would come over to the villa to hear what Beauty had to report, and Emily and Sophie would telephone and ask questions—not going into detail, because telephone wires have leaks. Each of the ladies would give Lanny advice; Sophie, the henna blond with the henna laugh, quite differently from the gentle, reticent Nina. But even Nina prodded him. "You know, Lanny, girls don't propose to men, except in Bernard Shaw's dramas." Rick added: "Not even in *The Glamour Girl* by Pomeroy-Nielson!"

The drama of Lanny and the heiress was being produced and directed by the wise and tactful Emily Chattersworth. She would carry messages back and forth; she would investigate the wavering young hearts and report upon their condition. Irma found it amusing that a white-haired *grande dame*—everybody considered her that—should be carrying on a proud young man's romance for him; she didn't mind being questioned, though she knew that every word she said was going back to Lanny. She liked him very much, but she liked other men too; she liked the excitement of keeping them on a string and watching them dance, such very elegant and graceful dancers. In return for this confession she received the latest cardiographic reports from Bienvenu. Lanny liked her, but didn't know if she liked him enough, or if he could make her happy, or whether a poor man had a right to try. He was afraid he bored her, and also afraid she wanted to "gad" too much. The tactful ambassadress took the liberty of putting this last in more diplomatic language.

III

This went on all through the Riviera season; they had a pleasant time, and nobody was hurt, unless possibly it was Beauty, who declared that she was living "on pins and needles," a distressing state of affairs even for one so well padded as she was getting to be. She had got it fixed up with God so that He didn't object to Lanny's marrying Irma, and didn't even object to petitions ascending to His Throne soliciting aid in the matter. Beauty had even been able to make some impression upon her spiritual-minded husband, by persistently calling his attention to the many worthy works which he and she might be able to do—not with Irma's money, but with Beauty's and Lanny's, which might be released for the service of Divine Truth if Lanny were to marry a fortune. The devil is a subtle worm, and it is known that he assumes many disguises to gain access to the hearts of his victims.

Lanny, being a human ego, operating in connection with flesh and blood, was likewise exposed to these satanic wiles. It occurred to his mind that a Socialist Sunday school which was helping the workers of Cannes might be extended to bring similar benefits to the workers of Nice and Toulon and Marseille. There might arise somewhere on the Riviera a so-called People's House, an institution such as Lanny had inspected in Brussels to his great satisfaction. Also, if an Englishman of brilliant parts were to write a wise and useful book, it might be possible to have it printed in a cheap edition and made available to the sort of persons who needed it. Such thoughts, haunting the mind of Lanny Budd, were proof that the mental powers of Satan have remained unweakened during the course of nineteen hundred years.

"Lanny, for God's sake, why don't you ask her?" clamored Beauty.

"I really think that the time has come," declared Mrs. Emily. It was a special council of war, called at Sept Chênes.

"I simply can't do it," declared the scrupulous suitor. "She has too much money."

"You just don't care for her enough!"

"I care for her enough so that I would ask her if she didn't have so much money."

"Then can't you say: 'Irma, if you didn't have so much money, I would ask you to marry me'?"

"No, because she has the money. I simply won't put myself in the class with those fortune-hunters."

So there they were. Beauty said: "Lanny, you are provoking!"

Emily said: "Just what do you want to happen? Does she have to say: 'Lanny, will you marry me?'"

"I don't care what words she uses. She can say: 'Lanny, I know you're not a fortune-hunter.' That's what I want her to know, and I want to know that she knows it. She ought to understand my feelings. If she expects to be happy with me, she must never have the thought that I was after her fortune. It's a question of her self-respect as well as of mine."

Beauty broke in: "Suppose she should ask you to kiss her?"

Lanny grinned. "Oh, I'd kiss her," he said. "But that wouldn't be asking her to marry me."

"I think you're acting horrid," said that exemplar of the proprieties.

IV

Such was the point at which matters stood when the telephone rang in Emily's Renaissance villa, and it was Mrs. Fanny Barnes saying: "Emily, I want to talk with you about something urgent."

"All right," said the châtelaine. "Come on over."

So the mother of Irma had her two hundred and forty-five pounds of dignity transported down from one Riviera height and up to another, and came stalking into Emily's boudoir, holding in her hand a small rectangular piece of paper having on it the imprint of a transatlantic cable company. "Please read that," she said, holding it out. "From my brother."

Emily took it and read: "Definite reliable information party illegitimate no marriage occurred advise immediate breaking connection greatly concerned please acknowledge receipt. Horace."

"Well?" demanded the mother of Irma, frowning under her dark, heavy brows.

"Of course," replied the older woman, quietly. "You didn't have to cable inquiries. I could have told you if I had thought it would interest you."

"Interest me? Good God! You mean you knew all along that this fellow was a bastard?"

"We're in the twentieth century, Fanny, not the eighteenth. Lanny's father has acknowledged him as his son. The boy lived in his father's home in Connecticut during all the time that America was in the war."

"Emily, you introduced this man and let him make love to my daughter!"

"My dear, you're just working up an excitement. You know of many cases—I'll name names, if you want me to."

"Not among the Vandringhams."

"Maybe not—I admit that I lack the data. But let's not be childish. Robbie Budd and Beauty were for all practical purposes man and wife. He told me the story and asked me to befriend her, and I did. The only reason they never had a ceremony was that Beauty had had her portrait painted in the near nude—a very lovely painting which Lanny now has in his storeroom, and which he'll show you some day. The old grandfather is some sort of hardshell fundamentalist, a religious crank, and he threatened to disinherit Robbie if he married, and Beauty wouldn't marry him, which was something very much to her credit. I've known Lanny since he was a tiny little fellow, and right now I've been having rather amusing negotiations, because he has old-fashioned notions of honor that won't permit him to ask for a rich girl's hand."

"You don't think his old-fashioned notions of honor ought to have caused him to tell the girl that he's a bastard?"

"I'm quite sure he gave no thought to it, Fanny. He's managed to get along quite cheerfully in spite of that handicap."

"He knows about it?"

"Beauty told him when he was a small boy. He can't see that it's done him any harm, and neither can I; nor can I see how it would do Irma any."

"I must say that I am surprised by the extent to which you have adopted European attitudes toward moral questions."

"Well, my dear, there's an old saying over here: 'When you are among wolves you must howl with them.' When you talk about moral codes you raise a large issue, and I think it better to deal with the practical question. Robbie Budd told me that Lanny is to share in his estate."

"Thank you, Emily, but I don't think Irma will be much concerned about that aspect of the matter."

"Are you quite sure she will be concerned about the bad name you give her young friend?"

"I don't know, but I certainly hope so. I may be eighteenth-century, as you say, but I still have the idea that a mother ought to have something to say about her daughter's love affairs, and that she ought to be a party to whatever negotiations are being carried on." And without another word the outraged Mrs. J. Paramount Barnes lifted her two hundred and forty-five pounds of majesty out of her chair and bore them swiftly out of the room and down the stairs to her limousine.

V

Fate arranged it that this was the moment when Ettore, Duca d'Elida, showed up on the polo fields of the Riviera. He was twenty-four years of age, a cousin of the Italian royal family; handsome as a movie idol, tall, dark, romantic-looking, with regular white teeth and shiny smooth black hair. He was hard as nails and rode like the devil, and when the polo game was over he put on a brilliant uniform, being a captain in the Italian air force. He knew all about Irma Barnes, and when he was introduced to her he displayed none of the inhibitions of Lanny Budd. He didn't mind asking for the hand of a rich girl, and the presence of spectators did not deter him from being stunned by her beauty, ravished by her charm, completely carried away by her *tout ensemble* of dignity, grace, and general irresistibility. He told her all that in very nearly perfect English, and a thrill went through the spectators of the scene.

There ensued a whirlwind courtship. He followed her everywhere, and never left her side if he could help it. He said that she was a treasure—and then, minding his metaphors, he said that she was a vision out of heaven, and that he desired only to dwell in the light of her presence and never depart therefrom. He seemed to know all the beautiful phrases that had ever been written or sung in praise of woman; to Irma it was all the things she had seen portrayed on the stage, sometimes lifted to glory by operatic music. This was love, this was passion, this was romance.

Lanny Budd's nose was put completely out of joint. He was no longer invited to the château on the height, and he did not attempt to go. He gave up without a struggle; if that was what she wanted, all right, the quicker she found it out the better. The ladies of his entourage all but went into mourning; his mother scolded—but he wouldn't budge. No, indeed, she had a free choice, and if she wanted to be an Italian duchessa, that was one way to invest her money. The smart set might get what pleasure they could out of his humiliation; he would go back to his Sunday school and his music, and manage to have a very good time, as before.

"But, Lanny," cried his mother, "she doesn't know what it will mean to marry an Italian! Somebody ought to tell her what their attitude toward women is, and their marriage laws."

"Somebody else will be the one to tell her," said the haughty young intellectual.

"Oh, I was so happy in the thought that you were going to get settled down!"

"Well, don't give up, old dear. There are as good fish in the sea as in any man's net—even a duca's."

The season was drawing to its close on the Riviera; the season at Rome was just beginning, and abruptly it was announced that the Barnes family was leaving for the Eternal City. That settled it, of course; she was going straight into his arms! The business manager hired an airplane and flew to Rome, rented a suitable palace and engaged servants, and a couple of days later everything was in readiness for the queen mother and the princess. They would be taken up in aristocratic circles, received by the king and queen, surrounded by pomp and glory; Lanny Budd, notorious young anti-Fascist agitator, wouldn't even be permitted to attend her nuptials!

What he did was to stroll over to the lodge and say to Rick: "Well, old sport, you can write that play!"

VI

Robbie Budd came to London. He was having more trouble with his oil wells in Arabia; also he was in a state of exasperation because the Geneva politicians—Robbie's name for the League of Nations—were threatening to interfere with the international shipment of arms. They had been talking about it for years, and now they seemed to be at the point of taking action. If you studied the list of portions of the earth's surface to which they proposed to forbid such shipments, you would observe that they were those inhabited by dark-skinned peoples; but some of these peoples had gold that was no darker than any other gold, and Budd's could see no reason for not doing business with them.

Beauty wrote Robbie the news about Irma Barnes, and of course that touched the father deeply. He telegraphed, offering to come to the Riviera and interview Mrs. Barnes and try to straighten matters out; a day or two later, when he learned that the ladies had fled to Rome, he offered to travel there. Lanny and his mother had quite an argument about it, and settled it by agreeing that each should wire what he and she had to say. Beauty said: "Beg you to come. Your action might be decisive." Lanny said: "Always glad to see you but don't want intervention in personal matter." Receiving those conflicting messages, Robbie decided that it would be pleasant to have a swim and a sail in the Golfe Juan; also to see Beauty's new husband. He stepped into a plane for Paris, and next morning stepped out of the night express at Cannes.

After having heard all sides of the story, Robbie found it hard to decide whether his son was being quixotic or whether he didn't really care enough about the girl. Anyhow, it seemed certain that the "wop" was going to get her. There were Rome newspapers to be bought in Cannes, and Lanny had some of them, and translated for his father accounts of the "to-do" that was being made over the American heiress. "That's what they both enjoy," said Lanny, "and I'm just not equipped to play that game."

"It's possible that I might be able to make some impression on the old lady," said the father.

"You don't know her," replied the son. "She'd light up one of her cigars and blow the smoke into your face and read you a lecture on your loose ways of life. She hates men, and she'd be sure you were just another fortune-hunter."

"I used to know J. Paramount," commented Robbie, "so I can understand her distrust of men."

He decided to forget the matter and enjoy a few days' rest, which Lanny said he appeared to need. He didn't feel right until he had had a drink in the morning, and his hand trembled as he lifted the glass. "To hell with all this money!" exclaimed the son. "You're doing what J. Paramount did—killing yourself for what your heirs won't know how to make use of."

Lanny got his father out in the sailboat, but it wasn't very restful, because Robbie had a long story to tell of troubles with his oil business; he was an outsider and a little fellow, and it appeared that the big fellows resented intrusion, and were even more unscrupulous in the oil game than in munitions. Robbie was more than ever convinced that Zaharoff was maneuvering him into a position where he would have to sell out; but Robbie wouldn't give up, because it was a matter of pride with him—he had got his friends into this thing, and he didn't want to have to take a licking. He had hopes of getting his way now, because he and his friends had got a new President of the United States. This was an oil man, like Robbie himself, one who had made a fortune in the game, and so knew what it took. Hoover was his name, and he was known to his admirers as "the Great Engineer." To Robbie his inauguration meant the coming of a new era of efficiency and prosperity to his country, and perhaps to the whole world, which would learn from America how to manage large-scale business.

Yes, Robbie said, the British would have to give protection to American investors in Arabia and elsewhere under British mandate, or else the Americans would find ways to do it themselves. Robbie meant to visit Monte Carlo and tell Zaharoff about this change in the world situation; but when he phoned he learned that the old spider was up in Paris, or perhaps at the Château de Balincourt, his

estate in Seine-et-Oise. Robbie went north, saying that he would call
on him there.

VII

Lanny didn't realize how fond he had become of Irma Barnes until it was too late. He tried Chopin's nocturnes again, but they didn't
work. She had been such pleasant company, and it would have been
so easy to make love to her; he had just got himself to the point
where he was ready to begin, and to have her whisked away was
most disconcerting. He told himself that for her own good he ought
to have taken her. She was a child, and had no idea of the trap she
had walked into. Fascism represented the lowest degradation of
women that had been on the continent of Europe since the days of
old Turkey. What sort of brood-mare would she make, that high-
spirited American girl? If she tried to kick over the traces, they
would take her money away from her, and her children—they would
break her heart. When he imagined what might happen, he had an
impulse to fly to Rome and save her. But no, they wouldn't even
let him in; to say nothing of letting him out again!

Zoltan Kertezsi showed up with news and proposals about pictures; and that was a good thing. Even thinking about being engaged to a glamour girl put the "kibosh" on Lanny's little private
industry; what were the few thousands which he could earn compared with the millions he would have if he became Mr. Irma
Barnes? Mere chicken-feed, beneath his dignity to think about! But
now Zoltan said that the time had come to have an exhibition of
Marcel's work in London; he proposed to rent a gallery for the last
two weeks in June, and then in the autumn to take the pictures to
New York for a showing. As before, he said that the thing to do
was to sell a few works at very high prices, and thus confer honor
upon the rest; he said that, with business booming as it was in both
the great cities, people simply didn't know what to do with their
money; they wanted to be asked fancy prices, because that was the
only way to be sure that what they got was excellent.

The Pomeroy-Nielsons were about to leave for England, and so
was Margy; also Hansi and Bess were sailing for London after their

American tour. Lanny said: "All right, let's have a holiday." He had always had a good time in England. But right away the thought of Rosemary smote him. Wouldn't he miss her there? Would London ever seem the same again? Lanny had become like a sailor with a girl in every port—only these were ghosts of girls: Irma on the Riviera, Marie in Paris, Rosemary in England, Gracyn in Connecticut and New York. Would he find one with a spell powerful enough to exorcise four such delightful ghosts?

Everybody agreed that he must go where the girls were: the lovely young creatures, the debutantes, fresh and virginal, each so carefully groomed, like a thoroughbred for a cup race; each quivering with excitement, sniffing the air, hearing the shouting of the vast throng. One by one they would be trotted out, each representing a fortune in time, thought, and money; each in the pink of condition, at the top of her form. The marriage market! Mayfair! The London "season"! Lanny was excited by the thought of it, and would enjoy it with one half of him, the social half, that of his mother and her friends. The other half would analyze it and reduce it to economic formulas; that half would say: "What am I doing here? Is this what I really want?"

Lanny's new stepfather was going along, his first journey since before the war. He told the stepson he thought it was his duty to go because he was able to moderate Beauty's extravagant tendencies; she had expanded her requirements on the basis of Lanny's supposed conquest, and hadn't yet adjusted herself to the fact that he had been unhorsed in the fray. The travelers made a big party, almost a migration: Lady Eversham-Watson and her maid; Beauty and hers; Marceline and Miss Addington; Nina and her three children, and their governess. The Riviera was used to seeing families going out wholesale in that fashion in April and the beginning of May: English and Americans especially.

Lanny motored Rick, who wanted to stop in Paris and meet political people and journalists. Lanny always liked to have lunch with his Socialist friends, and then spend an evening with his Red uncle and family and hear their caustic comments on the Socialists. Lanny had the idea of being broad-minded, but what actually happened was that he became confused, and found human society more bewildering, more painful to contemplate. He had dreamed a Utopia in which people might be happy; but here they didn't seem to kncw what was good for them or how to get it, and intellectual life degenerated into wrangling and scolding. It was that way in politics, both domestic and international; it was that way even in the arts, where beauty, order, and serenity should have reigned. Every old master had its price, and became the object of barter, intrigue, and "bluff."

VIII

Robbie had written about Zaharoff; he had seen him in Paris, and the old man had taken up the role of the sphinx of Egypt; all that he would say was that he had laid down the burden of business forever. Lanny, knowing that a heavy part of this burden had been laid on Robbie, gave some thought to the matter, and recollected Zaharoff's invitation to call. The young man had a sudden impulse to try to help his father. It would be the second time he had made such an attempt in connection with Zaharoff, and the first had not been conspicuously successful; however, he had the entrée this time, and wouldn't have to break any laws.

He telephoned to the Avenue Hoche, and learned that Sir Basil was at home and would be pleased to receive him. Approaching the familiar mansion, he noticed that smoke was coming from one of its chimneys in front; it might have struck him as peculiar for anybody to be having a fire in his drawing-room on this particularly warm spring afternoon; but Lanny's thoughts were on his father's affairs, and what he was going to say to an old Greek trader. His imaginative mind was living a series of detective stories, in which one of the shrewdest and most devious intriguers of Europe was continually betraying himself to a very young Franco-American idealist.

Lanny might have worked his imagination for many a day without inventing anything as odd as what he actually ran into when the tottery old butler escorted him into the drawing-room. Everything stood exactly as the duquesa had arranged it, Lanny didn't know how many years ago; the only difference was that on the oriental rug in front of the large fireplace were several metal boxes and wooden chests, and in the middle of them, seated on the floor in oriental fashion with his legs crossed and drawn under him, was the Grand Officer of the Légion d'Honneur of France and Knight Commander of the Bath of Great Britain. Only he wasn't in the regalia of either of these high offices; on the contrary, he had taken off his smoking-jacket and tossed it onto a chair, and then, becoming still hotter, he had taken off his shirt, and now sat in his undershirt, facing a hot fire made of logs augmented by quantities of paper which he was tossing in.

"Well, young man," he said, with that strange smile in which his eyes never took part, "you have arrived at what the future may recognize as a historic moment." He did not offer to rise, but said: "Seat yourself over there," pointing to a chair at one side, where the heat from the fireplace would not strike directly. "Take off your coat," he added, and Lanny did so because it was surely warm in the tightly shut room.

What strange whim was it which had moved Sir Basil to receive a visitor at such a time? He had always treated Lanny differently from any other person, so far as Lanny had been able to learn from those who knew him. The son of Budd's had made his appearance as a little thief of conscience; he came now at rare intervals, an itinerant idealist, a roving philosopher, transported as it were from another planet, playing the game of life according to an odd set of rules of his own invention.

"You have perhaps read about the burning of the library of Alexandria by the Arabs?" inquired the aged trader. When his visitor answered in the affirmative, he added: "You are witnessing an event of similar import."

"I understand that historians deplore the loss, Sir Basil."

"Only blackmailers will deplore this. I am saving the reputations of most of the great personages of my time."

"I have been told that you were a fireman in your early days," ventured the younger man.

"In those days I put out fires; now I make one—a beneficial fire, a fire of hope and salvation for my enemies as well as my friends. Many tons of dynamite would not do so much damage as the contents of one of these little books." The pale blue eyes turned from Lanny to the metal boxes, and the white imperial waggled with laughter as its wearer lifted up a notebook bound in worn red leather. There was apparently a whole box of them. "These are my diaries; a history of world business and diplomacy for more than fifty years. You heard perhaps that these volumes had been stolen?"

"I read something about it in the papers."

"A scoundrelly valet sneaked off with them. Fortunately the police recovered them, and so far as I can learn nothing is missing. But I was forced to give thought to the future of European civilization, and whether it is worth saving. What would you think?"

Lanny never could be sure how much this strange old man was teasing him. He replied: "I should say, Sir Basil, it would depend upon what one had to put in its place."

"Quite so; but unfortunately I have nothing better. Perhaps some day the Ice Age will return, and a vast glacier will spread over Europe and grind our cities to powder. Or perhaps bombs will have done it already."

Lanny made no reply. He knew from before the World War that the old man's imagination was haunted by images of destruction to be made by the weapons which he himself had been producing most of his life.

"Many people think that I am not a kind man, Lanny; but you can tell them what trouble I have taken on their behalf. I would not trust any person alive to perform this labor; I am doing it with my own hands, and at a cost of considerable discomfort, as you can see. There are a thousand eminent persons who will sleep more peacefully when they learn what I have done."

"Do you intend to notify them, Sir Basil?" It occurred to Lanny that this might make a first-rate story for Rick; but the fireman turned stoker merely smiled, and took some more of the leather-bound books and tossed them skillfully into the flames, causing them to fall on edge, and no two on top of each other, so that the fire would get a good chance at them quickly.

IX

This went on for quite a while. The flames mounted merrily, and the spacious drawing-room grew hotter and hotter. Lanny watched the yellow tongues creeping round one mass of paper after another, and he felt sorry about it, for he knew that the world was losing many a good story, and he himself some personal enlightenment. What would there be among those papers concerning Budd's and its European representative? What about the New England-Arabian Oil Company?

The last scrap of paper was in, and the flames were roaring up the chimney. Lanny was about to decide that a Greek born in Turkey could stand more heat than an American born in Switzerland, when there came a banging on the front door. The aged butler came in haste, and then ran to the drawing-room door. "Master, the people say the chimney is afire!"

"Indeed," said Sir Basil, placidly. "Let it burn. This is an important cremation."

"But, master, it will set fire to the house!"

"The fire is more important than the house!"

The old servant stood, staring helplessly. "You do not wish me to summon the fire department?"

"Under no circumstances; at any rate, not until the papers are consumed. Go close the door and let no one in."

The munitions king did not move from his seat. Was he playing a role before his visitor? Or did he count upon it that some busybody outside would turn in an alarm? It seemed a safe gamble; and, sure enough, after a while the sound of the engines was heard outside. The old gentleman got up, with the servant's help and some grumbling about the state of his bones. He put on his shirt, in the interest of propriety, and, knowing the ways of firemen, he told the butler to go and open the door for them. Then he began poking up the fire, so as to observe the condition of the papers, and promote the process of incineration. When the firemen rushed in, they halted before this venerable presence, and listened in confusion of mind while the master of the house explained what he had been doing, and why he did not wish his fire disturbed.

It transpired that in a modern city a man may not let his house burn even if he wishes to. The best that he can do is to start an argument, and gain several minutes during which the flames may continue their work. Out of the technical knowledge gained in his youth Sir Basil undertook to maintain that a fire in a chimney would burn only the soot which had accumulated in the chimney; but the chief of the Paris fire company, from his more up-to-date experience, insisted that there might be cracks in the chimney; also that when it was heated up it might set fire to the joists or rafters of the mansion. Lanny stood listening with amusement to this novel debate.

The great man had made his identity known, and his wishes were difficult to disregard; the chief finally agreed not to attack the fire in the hearth, but to go after that in the chimney with extinguishers from the roof. The firemen were escorted upstairs; and presently came jets of liquid dropping down into the fireplace, splashing black soot upon a beautiful and costly rug. There stood the retired munitions king of Europe with a long-handled poker, trying to keep the sacrificial flames alive, and grumbling because of the lack of consideration of modern fire departments. Said he: "When I belonged to the *tulumbadschi*, those capable firemen of Constantinople, if someone wanted his house to burn down he could arrange it."

Lanny was tempted to add: "For a consideration?" But he decided to let the Grand Officer make his own jokes on this delicate subject.

X

Lanny did not find out anything about the affairs of the New England-Arabian Oil Company. Instead, he went for a stroll, and stopped in the famous Café de la Rotonde, and there met an English journalist, a big handsome fellow with florid blond hair and mustaches which had been conspicuous at all conferences from San Remo to Locarno. They compared notes, and found themselves in agreement as to the state of Europe. Germany wouldn't go on paying indemnities many years longer; there was a new generation, which felt that it was not to blame for the war. The Allies had gained little by their colossal effort; it was a saying that men had fought for freedom of the seas and women had got freedom of the knees. The two men now watched the women tripping by in their abbreviated skirts. "I suppose the new generation will be used to legs," remarked the journalist.

"I'm not sure," responded the grandson of the Puritans. "When they've seen all there is to see, they get bored, and want something *outré*."

They talked about the public balls of Paris, which grew more scandalous every year. They talked about the Negress from America, whose stage performances had become "the rage." Paris had formerly been celebrated as a home of elegant conversation, and now it was the home of tough dancing. It was the "cocktail era," and you ordered drinks with fantastic names—*Quetsche de la Forêt Noire, Arquebuse des Frères Maristes*. People ran from one sensation to another, until really it seemed that they were going crazy. A man gave a concert with sixteen pianos played by machinery, also a loudspeaker and a noisy fan. The audience stood up and shrieked either approval or disapproval. That was the way to fame; the surrealists had achieved it by creating riots, and now it was Dada, something even more loony. A painter had hoaxed the Salon des Indépendants by tying a paint-brush to a donkey's tail and letting him do the art work; the result was entitled *Sunset on the Adriatic*, and it was hung. When the story was told it caused a good laugh, but didn't stop the crazy art.

"Too much easy money," was the Englishman's diagnosis of the trouble; but what could you do about it? Lanny said that the wrong people got the money, and his friend agreed; but again, what could you do? Lanny said he didn't believe the workers would stand it indefinitely; which led them to Moscow—all talk about economic affairs ended up in the Red capital nowadays. Conflicting reports came out—the Five-Year Plan was a great success—the Five-Year Plan was a fiasco. You believed what you wanted to. Lanny's companion had recently been in Germany, and said that the Communists were still very strong, and apparently gaining; the republic found it hard

to avoid dealing with them. The Stahlhelm, militant organization of
the reactionaries, had a new *Hymn of Hate* against the republic,
based on that charge.

They talked about Italy for a while. The Englishman said that
Fascismo might be the next stage through which the aged and unhappy continent had to pass. He agreed that Mussolini had learned
from Lenin, and Hitler had learned from Mussolini. Lanny found
that the journalist knew about Herr Schicklgruber; the Nazi movement had forced its way into the headlines. Any movement started
by reactionaries was hated and feared by the masses, and could never
get the votes. But here was one that appeared to come from the left,
it was of the people, and promised them the peace and plenty which
they craved. "Votes from the left and cash from the right"—such
was the formula for victory at the polls.

X I

Lanny and Rick went on to London. The baronet's son had finished his book and the manuscript was in the hands of a publisher.
He went to get the verdict and came back disappointed. The publisher, a friend of his father, had sought to persuade him to modify
his too leftish views. It was a mistake to put a label on himself. Socialism? Yes, we were all Socialists now, more or less; but to espouse
a party cause was to weaken your influence, to limit yourself to an
audience of the already converted, who didn't need you. To plump
for outright socialization of basic industry—well, it sounded impressive, but it discouraged people who might be willing to consider useful reforms; it played into the hands of the Communists, whether one
meant to or not. It seemed plain that capitalism had reached a stage
of stabilization in which prosperity was spreading its benefits among
wider and wider groups of the community; mass production would
come in England as it had come in America, and mass distribution
would follow as a matter of course.

In short, the publisher didn't want the book, and he didn't think
any other commercial firm would want it. If Rick wasn't willing to
modify it, he would have to go to some out-and-out Socialist or

labor group, and injure his career by getting himself set down as that kind of writer. Said Rick to Lanny: "When I pointed out our million and a half unemployed, he said that I mustn't lose faith in Britain!"

Lanny and his mother and stepfather were staying with Margy. You might think that Mr. Dingle wouldn't have fitted very well into a Mayfair mansion, but that would be because you were out of touch with God, who is the same in marble halls as in a cotter's hut. Beauty had already taken her man to a tailor and had him made presentable, and now he was a quiet elderly cherub who addressed the servants in the same benevolent tone as he addressed their mistress, and if anything troubled him, he retired to his chamber, where his Heavenly Father comforted him with melodious words: "Well I know thy trouble, O my servant true!"

When Beauty went out to garden parties and *thés dansants*, Parsifal Dingle would wander about the streets of the smoke-stained old city, seeking his own in his own way. Presently in a poor neighborhood he came upon a chapel of some "quietist" movement, and there he learned that God was working in England much the same as in Iowa. There were all sorts of spiritual cults; American New Thought magazines were to be bought, and there were many groups of religious healers. Mr. Dingle carried home literature, and began attending meetings, and then he prayed that Divine Power would persuade his wife to accompany him, which it did. He escorted her to a Christian Science church, and to a Swedenborgian church; then, to his own great surprise, he made the discovery that the august Anglican establishment was making timid efforts along the lines of healing by prayer. "We are really quite respectable here!" exclaimed Beauty Budd's new husband.

XII

But the greatest experience of Parsifal Dingle in England's green and pleasant land took place in the rear parlor of an obscure lodging-house in Bloomsbury, to which Divine Guidance had seen fit to lead him. It wasn't the first time he had attended a spiritualist séance, but it was the first time that the gates of the future life had swung open for him personally. A few lower middles, small tradesmen and such, sat in a circle, holding one another's hands in the dark, while a stoutish lady medium went into a trance, and an illuminated trumpet flew about over their heads, and various voices came from it—those of William Ewart Gladstone, Napoleon Bonaparte, and Pocahontas, each in turn describing the state of bliss in which they lived on the other side. That they all spoke with a Cockney accent troubled nobody, because the medium had explained that the spirits of the departed would be using her vocal cords, and naturally would speak as she spoke.

Missouri wasn't far away from Mr. Dingle's place of origin, and he remained in a dubious state of mind—until suddenly the trumpet stopped close to his ear, and the same Cockney voice said: "This is your brother Josephus." The gentleman from Iowa could not help giving a start, because Josephus was certainly an unlikely name for a lady medium in Bloomsbury to think of—just as it had been an unlikely name for Parsifal's mother to think of when her second son was born. She had assumed that it was a Bible name, and had learned her mistake too late. The bearer of this odd name had "passed over" in youth, and now claimed to be hovering over his older brother, and for identification he mentioned the pump with the broken handle which had stood on the back porch of their home. This caused perspiration to stand out on the visitor's forehead; and when the spirit declared that Aunt Jane and Cousin Roger were by his side, Lanny's stepfather decided that a new stage in his mental progress had begun.

He went and told Beauty about it, and prayed that she might be well disposed toward his words; and again the prayer could not be resisted. Beauty went, and was troubled because the place was so "common," also the people; but her husband explained that it was people of much the same class whom Jesus had picked out for his disciples, and to whom he had appeared at Emmaus. So Beauty listened submissively; and when the trumpet stopped over her head and the voice said: "This is Marcel," and called her "*Chérie*" half a dozen times, she felt a stirring as if every hair of her body was moving. When the voice said: "You have put my little blue cap away on a shelf in the closet," Beauty began to sob audibly, and came near to breaking up the show.

She went out from that séance in a state of great confusion. For right away treasonable doubts began to stir within her. She was well known as the former wife of Marcel Detaze, whose forthcoming one-man exhibition was being discussed in the newspapers. That a French painter should have an old blue cap, and that his widow, getting married again, should have put it away on a closet shelf—well, it was at least conceivable that somebody might have made such guesses. She had been warned that there was a widespread circle of fraudulent mediums who gathered data and assisted one another. Such are the problems which a lady of fashion prepares for her mind when she starts investigating occult phenomena!

Beauty told her friends about it, and learned that she and her husband were not alone in carrying on such researches. The great city was full of mediums of all sorts—and not all in cheap lodging-houses, but many established in the most fashionable places. It was one of the striking results of the great war; so many wanted to hear the voices of their lost loved ones. There were hordes of soothsayers, clairvoyants, and psychometrists, seers of crystal balls, readers of palms and cards and teacups. They would tell you that you were about to receive a letter, and that a dark man was coming into your life; sometimes these things happened and sometimes they didn't, but the former cases made the greater impression on your mind. As for Mr. Dingle, how could anybody ever persuade him that a medium could have found out that there had been a pump with a broken handle on the back porch of his boyhood home in far-off Iowa?

34

To Him Who Hath

I

PARIS was called a city of women, while London was a city of men; not *chic*, but always in need of housecleaning. It made no fuss over you, but let you go your own way; it was dignified, even austere, and if you wanted anything improper, you had to know where to look for it. In this moral man's town you didn't pay the art critics to tell the public about what you had for sale; you managed it in the respectable way, which was to pay for large but conservatively worded advertisements in the papers. Seeing these, the critics would know that the work of Detaze was significant.

Zoltan understood such matters; he knew the writers, the editors, the dealers, and, more important yet, the buyers. He knew how to place the interesting facts about Detaze where they would get publicity; he knew who would be impressed by the prices which had been paid at Christie's, and who by the fact that there was a work by this painter in the Luxembourg. Beauty pulled wires shamelessly, and Margy helped, and likewise Sophie, who came with her new husband for the season. Very elegant show rooms were engaged, and Jerry Pendleton saw to the packing of the paintings at Bienvenu and drove the truck himself; it was off season for the tourist trade, and his little wife could attend to the office.

Hansi and Bess arrived from New York, with stories about the success of a concert tour, including a recital in Newcastle and a reception at Esther Budd's home. Genius had won out over Jewishness; Hansi was a lion, and his roars had shaken the town, and Mumsy had been all smiles over her daughter's happiness. Bess was really sticking to her piano, and Hansi thought that with a couple of years more she might be able to serve as his accompanist. "But, dear, aren't you going to have any babies?" Esther had asked. The daughter had wanted to say: "I am afraid they might have short legs!"—but that would have been mean.

Robbie had told the family about the Irma Barnes fiasco, and Bess thought it was a tragedy that Lanny couldn't find a proper wife. Wouldn't he let her take up the matter? "Where would you look for one?" he inquired, and she answered: "Not among the smart people of this town, or on the Riviera." That was the trouble— Lanny didn't go where there were decent, hard-working girls who would appreciate what he had to offer. These ultra ladies who drank like whales and smoked like volcanoes in eruption were just looking for new thrills, and when they were tired of Lanny it would be off again, gone again. A young Red was telling him!

Hansi had a bright idea, not for a wife, but for a holiday, to divert Lanny's mind. Hansi was always scheming to get his father away from business for the summer months. If they stayed at their summer place on the Wannsee there were always telephone calls and telegrams, putting problems and cares on Johannes's mind; but when he got off on the *Bessie Budd*, his subordinates had to do the worrying, and in the end everything came out just as well. The family had been planning a short cruise by themselves—since it was so plain that the fashionable folk didn't like the young Robin Redbreasts. But why wouldn't Lanny come, and just Beauty and her husband? If there was to be a Detaze show in New York in October, why not cruise by the northern route and down the coast of Labrador and Nova Scotia? Freddi was going to be married, and it would be a honeymoon for him. Maybe Bess could think of some nice girl to bring along, and Lanny could play duets with her even if he didn't want to make love to her. Lanny consulted Beauty, and said they would go with pleasure; but leave out the girl, he'd play the duets with Bess. Hansi sent a telegram to his father, telling this good news; then he and Bess left for Amsterdam, where Hansi was to give a recital.

II

When Lanny had been in London as a little boy, before the World War, watching his young mother dressing for parties and going off with fashionable gentlemen such as Harry Murchison, he had thought that the acme of all delights would be to grow up and put on a white tie and tails and take that lovely creature to dances. Now he had the opportunity, and used it. Margy gave a grand ball at the Savoy, and the blond Beauty, who would never cease to think that she was a debutante, went with her son in just as much excitement as if he had been her first beau; she really looked as lovely as ever, for she had been dieting and dancing off her *embonpoint*, and the real debutantes were using so much makeup that they made it easier for matrons and grandmothers.

Also Lanny took her to the sporting events: to Epsom Downs to see the great race, which was called the "Mystery Derby" that year, because nobody could guess the winner; also to Ranelagh for polo, and to the opera at Covent Garden, where Rosa Ponselle was singing. Nothing could have been more chaste and proper, and society was amused at these evidences of reform on the part of a pair who hadn't been exactly conventional in the past. There was a husband in the background, who retired to his chamber and communed with God. Was it his prayers that accounted for the transformation? Or was it that the American heiress had put Lanny's nose out of joint, by running off and getting engaged to an Italian duca? By the way, did you see the report that their engagement was shortly to be announced? Poor Lanny, what a come-down, to have to take to selling pictures again! But they say that fellow Detaze is bringing tremendous prices. Is he dead, or what?

Lanny played his part acceptably in this world of gaiety and gossip. When the bright young debs asked him sly questions about heiresses he told them that his heart was broken and would they help to heal it? "Is this a proposal, sir?" they would ask, and he would say: "Would you like it to be?" So they would spar and play, like a couple of kittens exercising their clawing apparatus. The kittens might grow up to be tigers, or fairly useful domestic cats—it took an expert to tell them apart. Lanny was something of an expert; but perhaps he was fastidious, he wanted more than nature provided in one female organism. Or was it that his imagination had been dazzled by Irma Barnes? He thought of her a great deal, and it seems to be one of the weaknesses of our humanity that we appreciate something only after we have lost it.

He didn't find the "society" game as delightful as he had imagined it fifteen years ago. For one thing, his conscience was continually troubled. Rick came to town, and talked about his rejected manuscript, so full of distressing facts about unemployment; about conditions in Wales and the Tyneside, where whole communities were without a single man who had steady employment. Ships were burning oil, so it appeared that Britain's coal trade was slowly dying. Steel was depressed, because the Americans had new "straightline" processes, and British employers couldn't be induced to reorganize the industry. Here in London, amid all the display of pomp and luxury, one saw the old sights of misery and despair, and knew that for every case exhibited in public there were a thousand hidden behind the dingy walls of Britain's ancient slums.

How could anyone be happy putting on fancy clothes and playing about like children in such a world? But they did; it was the "season," and the rout had never been so noisy. There really seemed to be some law that the more poverty there was for the poor, the more riches for the rich; and how they did spend it, what fantasticalities they contrived! Just now the ladies were wearing knee-length skirts on the street, but in the drawing-rooms they had long tails and streamers and what-not touching the floor. Margy, Dowager Countess Eversham-Watson, made her appearance in a teagown of blue-and-gold georgette with a long spreading train having bold futurist designs and completely bordered with ostrich feathers. Sophie, former Baroness de la Tourette, went to the races wearing a coat trimmed with mink-tails: three mink-tails around each cuff, a wide band of mink-tails dangling from either side of her waist, and an extraordinary collar made by laying thirty mink-tails not end to end, but side by side, as a baker might place ladyfingers in a tray. In all, sixty minks had died to make an Ascot holiday for this hardware lady from Cincinnati.

Naturally, in order to move in company such as this, Lanny Budd had to put some tailors at work in a hurry. The old things that he had brought in his car were out of the question. Gentlemen's morning coats had only one button this season, and if you had two or three, you declassed yourself at once. Gentlemen's coats had huge lapels, and they wore wide, bulgy ties, and rather voluminous trousers. Their top-hats were slightly less tall and more flaring. What would become of the tailoring trades if gentlemen failed to do themselves properly?

III

Lanny did as the ladies urged, because they insisted that somewhere in this rout he was going to find the girl of his dreams. Would he catch a glimpse of some gentle, shy young thing hovering on the outskirts and recognize her as a kindred spirit, wishing to escape? "Somewhere there must be one made for this soul to move it!" With the poet's lines in his ears he went from place to place, wherever his mother asked to be escorted. He watched and she watched; she saw some that pleased her, but he found faults.

Beauty heard a rumor about a costume party that was to take place on board a ship at one of the docks, very mysterious and *recherché*. It was called "A Voyage to the Island of Cythera," and as this island had been devoted to the worship of Aphrodite, the name was suggestive to say the least. The engraved invitations didn't say who was giving the party, but it was observed that only the most exclusive members of society had received them; therefore it must be important, and the newspapers were full of speculation. On the back of the invitations was a figure in an elaborate Watteau costume, telling you what to wear and informing you that you would be admitted only upon presentation of the card. Since you didn't know who was giving the party, you couldn't wangle permission to bring your friends. People found it provoking, and curiosity mounted to a high pitch.

Margy managed to solve the mystery, but only under solemn pledge of secrecy. She got a card for Lanny Budd and lady—and of course that lady would be his darling mother. He had himself fitted in the garb of a lute-player, while Beauty appeared as one of Marie Antoinette's dairymaids—the one who had the shortest skirt and the lowest-cut corsage. At ten in the evening Margy's limousine delivered them at Charing Cross Pier on the river Thames. The dark-eyed little whisky lady from Kentucky was a charming Columbine, and the widower gentleman from South Africa who was wooing her at the moment was appropriate as Pierrot. The four of them went on board an elaborately decorated brig, and found themselves among a troop of eighteenth-century ladies with powdered hair and gentlemen with perukes and swords, wandering about gazing at decorations which included Gobelin tapestries, and divans and chaises-longues covered with magnificent silks from China and Japan. The deck of the vessel had been turned into a series of bowers and nooks, all discreetly dark; while below was a great compartment with a bar at one end, having the contents of a champagne warehouse on top and behind and under it. At the other end was a jazz band with players in eighteenth-century costumes; this was certainly a novelty, and would have been a greater one if it could have been presented at the court of Louis le Bien-Aimé!

The Voyage to the Island of Cythera proved to be an imaginary one. The vessel stayed moored to the pier, and the guests danced, drank the free champagne, rested in the quiet nooks. As night turned into morning, they became hilarious, and the sights were not so different from those of Paris; except that nowhere else had Lanny ever seen half-drunken gentlemen climbing the masts of a ship and diving into the water from the yard-arms! The tide carried them swiftly, but they landed at other piers, walked back, and came in dripping to dance some more. In the small hours two in succession tried to lure Marie Antoinette's dairymaid to one of the divans, and judging by the way they handled her they must have thought she was the real thing. Rather than risk a fight, Lanny took his too attractive mother home. Later they learned from Margy that this affair, attended by the most prominent folk of London, had been an advertising stunt devised by an interior-decorating concern. Seeing that they had all the divans, the Gobelins and silks and satins, it had cost them only a thousand pounds, and they had had all London talking about it for two or three weeks.

I V

The Detaze exhibition opened, and the fashionable crowds came, just as they had come in Paris. Zoltan was on hand, elegant and affable as always. Lanny was there to help him, and Beauty to play the queen. The papers said all the kind things which Marcel's work deserved, and the high prices did not alarm the wealthy art patrons. A new assistant at this show was Marceline, now eleven; growing fast, and rather "leggy," but with sweet features and perfect manners, a miniature little *charmeuse*. It was her debut as her father's daughter, and she was bursting with happy pride at the attention given to his work. She had no memory of him, but his sad story was a part of her being, and she could talk about any one of the paintings with as much sophistication as Zoltan himself—in fact, his very phrases.

Nina brought her children up to town to see this show. They, too, had heard all the talk and knew the phrases—Detaze was a family affair. Little Alfy, two months older than Marceline, with dark eyes and dark wavy hair like his father's, talked with his father's sophistication about "representational art" and "symphonic color effects." These children, destined for each other by family arrangement, maintained a tension which was practice for matrimony. Alfy was the haughty, impervious male; Marceline was learning how to tease him, and this one-man show was her great opportunity. It was her father, not his, who was being glorified; and had not Rick been heard many times to say that the critic must hold himself subordinate to the creator? This controversy would be continued all summer, for Marceline was going to be a guest at The Reaches while her mother was visiting among the Eskimos.

Johannes Robin wrote that he had some business to transact in

London prior to the sailing of the *Bessie Budd;* so the yacht would arrive at Ramsgate, with the family on board, and they would come up to town and have a look at the exhibition. Maybe Johannes might decide that he wanted some more of those paintings in his home. Lanny said to his mother that he would drive down and meet them and bring some of them to town; he would rent another car for the rest of the party. Johannes had stated the day they were due to arrive, and Lanny looked up the tides.

V

On the morning of the day when the yacht was due, Beauty awakened first, and lying in bed she looked at the morning paper; then with a cry she started up, and slipping on her *peignoir*, ran into her son's room. "Lanny! Wake up! Look at this! Irma Barnes is in town!"

Lanny, having been to a dance and having had some champagne early that morning, had to rub his eyes and shake his mind to make sure that he wasn't still dancing. He looked at the London *Daily Mail*, which had made a conspicuous story out of the fact that the great international catch, having twenty-three million dollars in her own right, had arrived unannounced with her mother and had put up at one of the fashionable hotels. There was her picture to prove it—Irma, his playmate of a Riviera season, looking a bit careworn, less blooming than when a young Puritan had had charge of her drink and her dancing hours. The reporter had asked her about the Duca d'Elida, and she had replied, casually: "Oh, that was just newspaper talk."

"You are not engaged to him, Miss Barnes?"

"He's a very charming man, and we are the best of friends, but that is all." So ran the interview.

"Lanny, they've had a quarrel!" exclaimed the mother.

"It sounds like it, for a fact."

"You must call her right away!"

"Do you think I should?" A rather superfluous question—but Lanny, taken by surprise, was thinking out loud.

"Oh, my God!" exclaimed the mother. "If you don't call her I surely will!"

"We don't even know where she's staying." After the custom of newspapers in dealing with the great, the name of the hotel wasn't given. It was a favor which the press did to important persons, to spare them the importunities of the needy and the cranks.

However, there were only half a dozen places grand enough for the Barnes family to stay at, and Beauty guessed them in order of importance, and made Lanny inquire. It wasn't long before he had the social secretary on the phone, and only a few seconds more before he had the heiress herself. Beauty, waiting with bated breath, could hear only one side of that conversation: "Well, darling! What a surprise! What brings you to town? . . . Well, how nice of you! . . . Of course I want to see you, right away. . . . How about lunch? . . . All right. One o'clock? . . . It's a date. How are you? . . . Only so-so? Well, see you soon. Lots of news. Cheerio!"

And then, of course: "What did she say, Lanny?"

"She said she came to town on purpose to see me."

"Oh, thank God!" The phrase carried a different significance since Parsifal Dingle had come into Beauty's frivolous life. "Lanny, she's broken with that fellow and come to look for you!"

"It really sounds like it, doesn't it?"

"She found out about the Italians for herself!"

"About the Fascists, let us say."

"Anyhow, you have your chance. Oh, Lanny, you *must* ask her now!"

"I will unless she forbids me."

"You must do it anyway. Don't let anything stop you!"

"Take it easy," chuckled the son. "Remember, the duca tried to rush her off her feet, and apparently he didn't get away with it!"

VI

"Take me to some place where they won't know me," said Irma, in the lobby of her hotel.

"That's not so easy, with your picture in all the papers this morning."

"Couldn't we go a long way out into the country?"

"This is England, not France. You'd have a choice of cold mutton with pickles, or veal-and-ham pie, and you wouldn't like either."

"I'm not thinking about the food, Lanny. I want to have a talk with you."

"Well, we'll drive, and see what we see."

He took her to his car. She looked very lovely in another sports ensemble of a light worsted, brown trimmed with white at the neck and sleeves, and a little brown cap to match. She seemed to be saying: "This is simplicity, the way you prefer." Her manner was humble; she had had some unhappiness, and it had chastened her; she seemed more mature and, as her picture indicated, she had lost weight.

As soon as they had started, he said: "You have left that fellow?"

"Yes, Lanny."

"For good?"

"Forever and ever. Oh, why didn't you tell me the sort of man he was?"

"I didn't have much chance to tell you anything, Irma."

"You didn't try very hard."

"I had told you about the Fascists, and what I thought of their code. I told you what they did to Matteotti, and the experience I had with them in Rome. I thought: 'Well, if that doesn't mean anything to her——' "

"It did mean a lot in the end. It was what saved me. You remember you told me about the newspaperman, Mr. Corsatti? He was one of the first persons I met there—he and several other reporters came to interview me. The Americans always come, you know."

"Certainly."

"Well, he said: 'I know a friend of yours, Lanny Budd. I saw a lot of him here five years ago.' I said: 'Oh, yes, he told me about you.' So we were friendly; and when the trouble came, it seemed to me he was the one person in Rome I could trust."

"What was the trouble?"

"It's something horrid, I feel ashamed to talk about it."

"I'm no spring chicken, Irma. And, anyhow, I can guess it if you want me to. You found out that Ettore had a girl? Or was it a boy?"

"Oh, such a nasty thing, and it came in such a nasty way: an anonymous letter. At first I thought it was some vile slander, and I would be noble, and tear it up, and tell him that I had done so. But I'd heard things about European men, and I thought: 'Suppose it is true?'"

"What did it say?"

"It said he was living with the *première danseuse* of the ballet, and had told her that his marriage wouldn't make any difference. I thought: 'Ettore has some enemy, somebody who is jealous of him and wants to ruin him.' There was another man paying me attention, or trying to, and I thought: 'Maybe he has sent this, or caused it to be sent.' I took the letter to my mother, but she wasn't of much help, because she said that all men were like that, and there was no way to tell, and one shouldn't break one's heart over it. I said: 'I don't believe they are all like that.' Are you, Lanny?"

"I have my faults, but that is not one of them."

"I thought: 'I've got to know the truth.' So I called Mr. Corsatti and asked him to come to see me, and showed him the letter. He was worried at first and said: 'Miss Barnes, if I talk to you about this and it becomes known, it will be the end of my job here in Italy.' I gave my word of honor never to mention it to a soul, not even my mother. Later on he said I might tell you, because he was sure you would understand and keep it quiet."

"Of course. What did he advise you?"

"He said if I was looking for a husband who would respect me or be faithful to me, I had come to the wrong part of the world. He said that what the letter told me was true, that all the newspapermen knew it, and wondered if I knew it. He said there were decent men in Italy as everywhere else, but they weren't in power, and I would have no way to meet them. He said that when you met a Fascist you met a man without honor, one who laughed at it. He said: 'I've been here for ten years, and I've watched them from the beginning. If you take my advice you won't say a word to anybody, but take a plane and get out of Italy.' He really thought that Ettore might have me kidnaped."

"They've done much worse," said Lanny; "but not to foreigners, so far as I know."

"Well, anyhow, I was through. I told mother I was going alone unless she would go with me. We hired a plane to fly us to Cannes, and then I phoned to your home and learned that you were in London. So here I am. Are you glad to see me?"

"More glad than I can trust myself to tell you."

"Why not trust yourself just for once?"

"Well, you know how it is, Irma——"

"I didn't tell you all my conversation with Mr. Corsatti. Shall I finish? He said: 'Why the hell didn't you marry Lanny Budd?'"

Lanny couldn't help laughing. "How did he come to say that?"

"We had got to be pretty good friends. I had done some bawling in his presence—because I felt so cheap and humiliated."

"What did you answer?"

"Do you really want to hear?"

"The worst way in the world."

"I said: 'Lanny Budd didn't ask me.' He said: 'That proves he's a gentleman.' 'Maybe so,' I said; 'but it doesn't help me. Can I ask a gentleman to marry me?' He said: 'Sure you can. You'll have to. With all that money you've got, what can a fellow do?' So we talked about you. I told him that you had told me about Marie de Bruyne— he knew about her, of course."

"It was all in the papers," assented Lanny.

"Well, he said: 'That's a different sort of story. A man has a woman that he loves, and he sticks by her, and that's all anybody has a right to ask.' Then he said: 'If you really care for Lanny Budd, take my advice and go and have a straight talk with him. Tell him I told you to say: "I know I've got too much money, and it's silly, but it isn't my fault and it oughtn't to be allowed to mess up my life."' So I said: 'All right, I'll go and do it.' Now I've done it, and you can tell me whether he was right."

VII

So there it was. Driving on the Euston Road and watching out for the traffic, Lanny found time for a quick glance at his companion and saw that a mantle of blood had climbed to her throat and cheeks. He realized that she was doing something which she considered desperately bold. He managed to spare one hand from the steering-wheel long enough to lay it on hers. "It's all right, dear," he said. "It's very kind of you and I'm deeply grateful."

"Are you going to be sorry for me?"

"I'm going to do just what Pietro Corsatti said, have a straight talk with you. In the first place, there's that embarrassing fact that my father never married my mother."

"I don't care a thing about that, Lanny. The point is that you got here somehow."

"It's going to worry your mother a lot; and you saw that it worried her brother in New York."

"Well, I'd like to make them happy, but it will have to be in some way that doesn't make me so unhappy."

"I want you to face the facts about us," persisted the amiable young bastard. "I wouldn't be honest if I didn't point them out. If you marry me, the newspapers will probably be moved to dig up the painful secret. I doubt if they'll say it in plain words, because it's hard to prove a negative, and there'd always be the possibility that Robbie might have had a secret marriage, and that I might come down on them for a million dollars. But they'll have deft little touches, to the effect that your family has been making genealogical researches as to the bridegroom. All the smart people will know what they mean."

"I don't care what they know or what they say, Lanny. I'm sick of publicity and gossip, and all I want is to get away from reporters."

"You feel that way at the moment; but you have to live in the world, and your family and your money are both things that are going to stay with you."

"What I want to know is just one thing, and that is what you really feel about me."

"I'll tell you as honestly as I can: I think you're a grand girl, and if you'd come along with just a reasonable amount of money, I'd have kissed you sure and certain, and the rest would have depended on what you wanted. But you know how it is, you came like the Queen of Sheba—rings on your fingers and bells on your toes. I saw all that crowd of suitors. I knew some of them, and what was in their minds, and I just had too much respect for myself to breathe the same air with them."

"I know, it's all been hateful. But can't you manage to forget my money and think about me for a while?"

"You asked me to talk straight, and I'm doing it. We'll be fooling ourselves if we forget your money, for the world won't let you forget it, and you don't really want to forget it yourself. You've got to own it, and manage it, and spend it, and you've got to know that pretty nearly everybody you meet is thinking about it. You've got to shape your life accordingly, and if it isn't to get you down and ruin your happiness, you'll have to be a wise and careful person."

"You make it sound rather awful, Lanny!"

"Well, I want you to know that I've been thinking about your money, and just what I've been thinking. Everybody I know has been urging me to ask you to marry me. My mother has her ambitions for her son, just as your mother has for her daughter. So I had to put my mind on the problem, what would it be like to be married to a very rich woman? What would I do, and how would I keep it from getting me down? I said: 'First of all, she'll have to know that I don't want her money. It's got to be so that never as long as she lives will that thought cross her mind.' "

"So you took the chance of letting me go off and marry a Fascist!"

"I let you do what you wanted, Irma, because that is your right. It'll still be your right if you marry me. You'll do what makes you happy, and if you love me, it'll be because you want to."

"Are you sure that a woman wants so very much freedom?"

"When she's very much in love, she thinks she doesn't; but it won't do any harm for her to have it."

"What a woman wants is for a man to want her very much."

"She wants that; but she must remember that there are long years ahead, and she needs a lot of other qualities and virtues in the man who loves her. She wants him to be able to think straight, and to control himself."

"You talk like an old gentleman."

"I'm a lot older than you, and I have had experience, and made a lot of mistakes which you won't have to suffer for. I want you to understand me, and not expect any more than I can give."

"What could I expect that you haven't got, Lanny?"

"It all comes back to the problem of your money. I don't mean merely that I'm not much of a businessman; I mean that I don't have a proper respect for large sums of money. I don't believe in them. I've watched people getting them and spending them, and neither job appeals to me. I think that money does things to people, and when it gets through, I don't like them any more. I'd rather be able to sit down at the piano and play a Beethoven sonata than be able to make all the money in the Barnes fortune; and when you see me doing what I like, will you get provoked and think I'm an idler?"

"I don't know that I ever heard a Beethoven sonata," said Irma Barnes. "But if I promise to let you be happy in your own way and never, never ask you to have anything to do with my money, will that satisfy you?"

"Suppose you find that I am voicing ideas which imperil your fortune? I don't mean your particular fortune, but all great wealth, as something that oughtn't to be allowed. Suppose people tell you that I'm a dangerous Red, and keeping bad company, and being watched by the police?"

"They've already told me that. But you see I came and asked for you."

"Suppose I answer yes, just what would you want to do?"

"I think I should want to go to some place a long way off, where there wouldn't be any horrid gossips and reporters."

"That would be a long way, indeed!" But then an idea occurred to him, and he added: "You remember my telling you about my brother-in-law, Hansi Robin, who is such a fine violinist? Well, his father has a yacht, and they're begging me to go for a cruise with them. They're Jews. Does that bother you?"

"Not if they're friends of yours."

"There's Hansi and Bess, and there's his younger brother Freddi and his bride. They're all musical, and it'll be pretty noisy; but you can go off in a corner and read, or Mama Robin will teach you to knit sweaters for the poor."

"It sounds very homey and nice. Where would they go?"

"Iceland and Labrador, and all the way to New York. I doubt if we'll meet any reporters until we get to America; only whales and icebergs. The only difficulty I can see is how to get married without too much fuss, and having Ettore brought into it, and my bastardy."

"Oh, Lanny, don't use that horrid word!"

"You'll hear it a lot—no good fooling yourself. Would you be satisfied with a quiet wedding, or will your mother require a dozen bridesmaids and six flower girls and a cathedral?"

"Lanny, I'll go off and marry you before a justice of the peace, or however they do it here."

"You really mean that?"

"I've thought it all over. I'm throwing myself at your head."

"When?"

"Right now, if you say so."

"Before lunch?"

"Hang the lunch!"

So Lanny drew up by the left-hand curb of the street, and performed a little ceremony of his own devising. He took her two hands in his and said: "I will be gentle and kind. I will study your wishes, and try to oblige you. I will be your friend as well as your husband. I will try my best to see that you do not regret this step. Is that what you want to hear from me?"

"Yes, dear," she responded, and her eyes were misty. "Only one thing you forgot. You didn't say: 'I love you.'"

"I admit that was an oversight. I love you." He kissed her again, regardless of the spectators on the street. He had seen the English poor doing this on Hampstead Heath on bank holidays; and if the rich could see the poor doing it, why shouldn't the poor see the rich?

35

Whom God Hath Joined

I

SO NOW began the adventure of trying to get married in England. Lanny had only the vaguest notions about it. Was it done by a clergyman, or by some public functionary, or both? Was the consent of parents necessary? And up to what age? "Perhaps you had better say you are twenty-one," he suggested. Irma answered with a straight face that she had become twenty-one the week before.

The first idea that occurred to him was a "chapel." His new stepfather went to meetings in little buildings called by that name. It must be that the minister, or preacher, or whatever he was called, could marry members of his own flock, and maybe he could oblige two visiting strangers. Lanny turned his car off the main road and began wandering through little streets. Presently he stopped a small boy and inquired, in the best English he could muster: "Eh, laddie, where's the chapel?"

"Wot chapel?" demanded the boy.

"Any chapel."

"Don't know no chapel."

So the car rolled on. It was a peculiarity of this tight little island that its own inhabitants rarely knew where anything was if it was more than a quarter of a mile away. They must have had a difficult time with their geography lessons, because every villa had its individual name, and so did most every field, large tree, stile, pump, or other creation of nature or man. Few streets could pass more than three intersections without acquiring a new direction and a new name, and from there on you were in a foreign country.

At last they found a man who attended a chapel, and gave them

directions in language which Lanny was able to interpret. In the
living quarters adjoining the building they found a gray-bearded
gentleman who said that he was the pastor, and when Lanny asked:
"Can you marry people?" he declared with dignity: "This is a place
of worship duly registered for the solemnizing of marriage under
the Marriage Act of 1836, and I am a person duly authorized by the
governing body of the place of worship in question."

"Then we should like to be married," remarked the visitor, humbly.

"I shall be happy to accommodate you," said the man of God.
"Are you a resident of this parish?"

"I don't know. What are the boundaries of it?"

The minister outlined them, and they were not big enough to include either Irma's hotel or Margy's town-house. "However, that is
easily arranged," said the pastor. Apparently he had noted the fashionable costumes of the strangers, and now he noted their fashionable addresses, and desired to retain them as customers. "All that is
necessary for you to do is to rent a room and leave a bag in it, and
that constitutes it your legal residence."

"For how long do we have to do that?"

"The banns are published in this chapel next Sunday and for two
Sundays thereafter, and then you can be married at any time."

"Oh, but we wish to be married at once."

"Unfortunately that is not possible, sir."

"You mean that nobody can marry us at once?"

"You can obtain a special license from the Archbishop of Canterbury—but that will cost you something like sixty pounds."

"And then we can be married today?"

"Then you can be married after twenty-four hours."

"But that is extremely inconvenient. We wish to travel."

"I'm sorry, sir, but that is our English law." So Lanny and the old
gentleman expressed their mutual regrets, and Lanny and his lady
went out to their car and drove away.

II

"Maybe he wanted the fee," suggested Irma; "so he wouldn't tell us any other way."

"My father has a firm of solicitors in London," replied the would-be bridegroom. "I will consult one of them."

He found a telephone, and presently was in conversation with Mr. Harold Stafforth, of the firm of Stafforth and Worthingham. Lanny and his father had had lunch more than once with this gentleman, and now as Lanny talked he had before him the image of a tall, lean-faced person of dry temperament, precise ideas, and extraordinarily few words. Lanny knew that he couldn't fool him, and that the first duty was to satisfy him. He said:

"Mr. Stafforth, I wish to get married. The young lady in question is a great American heiress, and her mother is not entirely cordial to me. My father knows all about the match and approves it; he offered to travel to Italy in order to try to arrange matters with the young lady's mother. I know you will wish to be sure of this, and I pledge you my word. Now the young lady has come to London, and has made up her own mind, and in order to avoid discussion and publicity we decided to have a secret wedding, and have it today if possible. Is that possible?"

"Not in England," said the solicitor. Having answered the question, he waited for the next one.

"I have read somewhere about people going to Scotland to be married, and I have a car and could drive there. Can that be done?"

"You can be married in Scotland at once, by taking each other's hands and saying that you are man and wife."

"And will that be valid?"

"It will be valid in Scotland."

"But will it be valid elsewhere?"

"It will not be valid in England."

"Then that wouldn't do. How about the possibility of traveling to Belgium or Holland or some other country?"

"I do not happen to know the laws in those countries, but I shall be happy to look the matter up for you if you wish."

"Can you suggest any way in which we could be married without delay?"

"If you are prepared to take a sea voyage, you can be married on the high seas by the licensed master of any merchant or passenger vessel."

"And will that be valid anywhere?"

"Provided that you are ten miles from the English coast, it will be valid under English law, and so far as I know it will be valid under the laws of all countries."

Lanny thought quickly. "I have a friend who has a yacht. Would the master of such a vessel be in position to marry us?"

"Is the yacht of British registry?"

"German."

"I cannot tell you about the German law without looking it up; but if such a master is authorized by the German law, the marriage would be valid under our Maritime Act of 1894."

"The German master would probably know what he was empowered to do, I suppose?"

"I should say that he would be required to have a copy of the laws in which his own powers and duties are defined."

"I will make inquiries of the master. Thank you very much, Mr. Stafforth."

"You are quite welcome," said the solicitor. "I wish you success in your efforts and happiness in your marriage."

"Thank you again," replied the young man. "Kindly charge this service to my father's account." All the proprieties having thus been conformed to, he hung up.

III

As it happened, Lanny had already consulted the newspapers and made note as to the state of the tides; he believed that the *Bessie Budd* could not yet be in the basin of Ramsgate, but he took the precaution to telephone and make sure. In this little harbor the vessels lie against an embankment, so that they are right in the street, or alongside it, and the first thing which happens is that a telephone cable is run aboard; on the *Bessie Budd* they had had a telephone not merely in the saloon, but in every cabin, in the steward's office, and on the bridge. Lanny now called the town, and learned that the yacht had not yet put in appearance.

He went out and told Irma what he had learned. He proposed that they should drive to Ramsgate, and as soon as the yacht arrived it would turn around and start another voyage.

"Oh, how romantic!" exclaimed the girl. She was charmed by the idea of being taken out to sea in order to escape from the clutches of the Archbishop of Canterbury. "Do you suppose Mr. Robin will really do that for us?"

"Of course he will. If he's too busy himself he can go on to London and let Captain Moeller oblige us. The whole family will be delighted. They already have one bride and groom on board, you know."

"Let's get going!" said the girl—who came from New York.

They set out down the valley of that not very large river which is so crowded with shipping from every part of the earth, and with tugs and lighters and pleasure craft and everything that floats. The tide rushes in very fast and rushes out even faster, owing to embankments which keep it from spreading out over the marshes. Where nature had put marshes men had made great basins with piers and sheds, and behind them gigantic slums for the workers. Lanny told his bride-to-be-soon how he had got lost in those slums when he was a small boy. He told her about Charing Cross Pier and the Island of Cythera—not failing to mention what lady had shared these revels with him.

They discussed the problems of their honeymoon, and agreed that they would tell their mothers, but that nobody else was to share the secret until after the *Bessie Budd* had sailed. Irma made note of the name of the yacht. Was she the least bit inclined toward jealousy of it? "Lanny," she asked, "are you sure it wouldn't be better if we got one of our own?"

It gave him a start. He could have a yacht if he wanted it! The biggest yacht in the world—enough to carry a dozen Red Sunday schools! But he said: "Let Johannes have the troubles. He has asked for them."

"Will I like those people, do you think?"

"You'll find them the easiest in the world to get along with; and, moreover, you won't be under any obligations. Johannes considers that my father has paid him for life."

In after years Lanny would look back on a remark like that, and marvel anew at the strange fate of men, who can see when they turn their eyes toward the past, but are totally blind confronting the future. Bacon has said that he who marries and begets children gives hostages to fortune; and the saying surely applies to him who acquires friendships—especially if the year is 1929, and the place is Germany, and the friends are "non-Aryan"!

The eloping pair talked about themselves, a subject of interest and importance to young people. "Oh, Lanny, I have been so unhappy!" the girl exclaimed. "I want somebody I can trust."

"You have him, dear."

"I am so ashamed of what happened in Italy!"

"That's ancient history—leave it to the bookstores."

"I'll have to have time to get over the humiliation."

"Tell yourself that Ettore was a well-practiced lover, and carried you off your feet."

"That wasn't all. I wanted to be something great and important. But I didn't like those people. I didn't like the place."

"What place do you think you would like?"

"I think I'd like Juan the best of any I've ever been to."

"Well, that's fine, because that's the way I feel. There's a lovely house there, waiting for us. Only you'll have to get used to hearing people say that I built it for Rosemary."

"Lanny, I promise I'll never be jealous of her."

"There's nothing to worry about, because they're going to keep her in the Argentine, I'm pretty sure!"

IV

They were driving along the Kentish coast, through a succession of small watering-places looking out over the sea. Chance brought them to a country inn which had some outdoor tables, and they sat under an arbor of vines and had cold mutton and beer—something of a come-down from the caviar and champagne in which Lanny had indulged himself in the wee hours of that morning. They drove again, and were on the Strait of Dover, where it was all one town with different names, and presently the name was Ramsgate, a popular "watering place." In its little harbor, perhaps a quarter of a mile each way, the trim *Bessie Budd*, gleaming with several coats of new white paint, was in process of being laid against the side of the street.

There were all six of the Robin family, standing by the rail as in a line-up. How delightful to see Lanny come along and park his car right beside the berth of the yacht! But who was that lovely brunette Juno, wearing a sports ensemble of brown worsted trimmed with white, and a little brown cap to match? Had he at last found himself a girl whom he liked enough to take about on his drives? When the yacht was close enough so that they could chat comfortably, Lanny said: "Let me introduce Irma Barnes. Irma, meet Mama and Papa Robin, and, reading from left to right, Hansi and Bess and Freddi and Rahel." They all bowed and smiled, and politely covered their excitement at the magic name of the brunette Juno. They had a right to feel pleasure in meeting any friend of their darling Lanny. Of course, Hansi and Bess hadn't failed to tell the story of the famous heiress, and how Lanny had been too haughty and had wooed her with too little ardor. By what magic was she now at his side?

Obviously it was a story! Lanny took them into the saloon and closed the doors, and said: "Irma and I are trying to get married, and the English laws won't let us. We don't want a lot of fuss and newspaper talk, so will you let Captain Moeller take us out and marry us on the high seas?"

Well, you could have knocked that family over with a feather—so the saying runs, but Lanny didn't have any feather. Anglo-Saxon reticence was forgotten by all; Bess hugged and kissed her half-brother, she hugged and kissed Irma, and Mama began to sob with whatever it is that moves motherly souls at weddings. The young Jewish people all wrung the hands of the happy pair. Hansi was the first who had a wonderful thought, and exclaimed to the bride: "Oh, you will come with us on the cruise!" There followed a clamor of acclamation which left no doubt in the soul of an heiress that she was welcomed—and not entirely for her money, for, after all, Mr. Robin had his own, as this yacht proved.

Johannes said: "I will see Moeller." Captain Fritz Moeller was a gray-bearded officer who had commanded a great passenger liner before the war, and now was thankful for a chance to manage a pleasure yacht for a Jewish *Schieber*. Johannes had a talk with him and came back looking sorrowful. "*Ach! Er kann es nicht. Verboten!*"

"What is the matter?" asked Lanny.

"When he commanded a passenger vessel, yes. And before that, when he was captain of a merchant vessel. But for a private yacht, *nein*."

"He is sure?"

"He says that you would not be married, and he would be deprived of his license."

Grief appeared on the faces of all the company. How very provoking, to ruin their delightful adventure! "Well, it looks as if we have to go back to the Archbishop!" said Lanny.

"And all that publicity!" added Irma.

"Is that what is troubling you?" inquired the owner of the *Bessie Budd*.

"This kind of thing," said Lanny, and took from his pocket the clipping from that morning's *Daily Mail*. "There was a duca in Italy who thought that he was engaged to Irma; and now the papers bring it up, and write a lot of gossip."

"And my mother makes a fuss," added the girl. "We thought that we could get it over with, and then she would make the best of it."

"Couldn't we go to France?" inquired Bess.

"It is no better there," said Lanny. "They have the banns, and it takes ten days. Moreover, you have to have birth certificates. My mother and Mr. Dingle had to cable for them."

"How would it be in Holland?" persisted Bess.

"Worse yet," said Johannes. "It takes four weeks. Nowhere in Europe do they take getting married so lightly as in the States."

"It is very silly," opined Irma. "If it suits us, why should anybody else be concerned?"

Johannes looked at her. A very fine-looking girl, and he knew about her twenty-three million dollars. Lanny was too well bred to show it, but it seemed to Johannes that anybody who had a chance to marry her would be in a hurry. He could be sure that Lanny's father would take it as a favor if he went to some trouble to bring off this match. "Well, if you are game, I'll get you married tonight."

"How?" It was a chorus.

"There are plenty of passenger and merchant vessels out there in the Strait of Dover. The sea is smooth, and it should be an easy matter to get one to stop if we pay them enough."

Young hearts leaped and young faces lighted up. "Oh, how charming!" exclaimed the would-be bride.

"Are you game?"

"Indeed I am!"

"But," objected Lanny, "would the master have a right to marry two people who aren't passengers?"

"You can be passengers. We'll leave you on board."

"Where would we go?"

"We'll flag a vessel that is inward bound. You can be married before it enters the ten-mile zone, and the Archbishop of Canterbury can go hang."

They were young, they were rich and accustomed to having their own way; they were not too much burdened with a sense of their own dignity, or with respect for the laws and institutions of any nation. Mama Robin was the only one who was shocked by all this; the others were in a state of hilarity, so she held her peace. The bridegroom said: "Let me have a few minutes to get my car parked and send a couple of telegrams."

V

Lanny darted onto shore. He had agreed with Irma upon two identical telegrams, one signed by her to her mother, and one signed by him to his: "Everything settled have gone to visit friends will write"—something which these ladies would understand, but no one else. That attended to, and the car placed in a garage, Lanny hurried back to the yacht, and it crept through the opening in the breakwater and headed eastward into the Strait of Dover.

They stood in the stern and watched the sun set behind them, and Lanny talked about the exhibition and how it was going; the pair had collected themselves, and were Anglo-Saxon again. If they were to express their feelings, it could only be by the means of art. Presently the piano on rubber wheels was rolled onto the deck, and Hansi got his fiddle, and they listened to Scriabin's *Prelude*, gently solemn, with very beautiful double-stopping—a performance for which an audience would have paid a large sum of money. Bess played the accompaniment, and Lanny saw that she was improving all the time, and told her so; he was proud of her, and of the match which he had helped to make. Now they were repaying him!

Somewhere in that vague region where the Strait of Dover merges with the North Sea, so that you cannot tell which is which, appeared the lights of a dumpy old freighter. By her course they judged her to be London bound, and they waited for her, and when she was near laid their course alongside. There was just enough light so that the two masters could vaguely see each other's form. The sea was so smooth that they could talk without the need of a megaphone and a conversation ensued:

"Ahoy there! This is the motor yacht *Bessie Budd*, German registry, out of Bremen. Who are you?"

"British passenger freighter *Plymouth Girl*, Copenhagen to London."

"I've a couple of passengers who want to go ashore at London."

"All passenger accommodations full, I can't afford to stop."

"What do you want to heave to?"

"Ten pounds."

"We'll pay you twenty pounds. The young couple want to get married on the high seas. Will you oblige them?"

"Are they British?"

"Both Americans, of legal age. They want to avoid the delays of getting married on shore."

"Will they pay cash?"

"As soon as they come aboard."

"I'll take them."

The dark shape came to a stop and the yacht slowed up accordingly; when they lay still they weren't more than a cable's length apart. A dinghy was lowered from the *Bessie Budd*, also the gangway, and Irma and Lanny went down; when they reached the old vessel they were helped up a rope ladder, not so clean, and welcomed by a burly son of the sea whose job was transporting butter and eggs from a land of dairies to one of factories. Several members of the crew and a couple of passengers stood staring by the dim light of lanterns. What they thought of the adventure was not revealed.

Lanny presented two indubitable ten-pound notes and, after examining them, the captain said: "I never done this before, but I'll chance it. Can you tell me what I have to say?"

"Sure," said Lanny, who had attended many fashionable ceremonies. "You ask me if I take this woman for my lawful wedded wife, and you ask this woman if she takes me for her lawful wedded husband. We answer yes, and then you say that by the authority vested in you under the Maritime Act of 1894 you pronounce us man and wife. You give us a certificate that you have married us, and you enter it in the ship's log, and maybe you have to report it to the Registrar ashore—I don't know about that, but you can find out."

"Well, I hope there's nothing bogus about this that would get me into trouble."

"Not at all," said Lanny, promptly. "We are of legal age, and we wish to be properly married. We're yachting, and it seems that it takes a lot of time to get married ashore." He said nothing about the publicity, because that might have meant risking some.

VI

The freighter had started her engines, and so had the *Bessie Budd*, and they were running side by side, a safe distance apart, but not so far that you couldn't hear the music distinctly. Hansi and Bess were playing the "Wedding March" from *Lohengrin*, to which irreverent persons chant: "Here comes the bride; get onto her stride." But there was nowhere to march to. After clearing his throat several times, and repeating the names to make sure that he had them right, Captain Rugby of the *Plymouth Girl* asked the crucial questions and said the crucial formula. Then he took them to his cabin, and wrote out a certificate. He offered them the use of his cabin, for it was a long time before they would dock in London, but Lanny said no, they would sit on deck that pleasant summer evening and listen to the music.

The *Bessie Budd* was still alongside, and Hansi and Bess were playing the Queen Titania music. When it was over they had a gay long-distance chat, and Lanny introduced the new Mrs. Budd, and the crews of both vessels listened and acquired information as to the ways of the idle rich. There was more music, and presently refreshments were brought up on the yacht. They offered to send some over, but Captain Rugby wasn't willing to stop again; he produced some sherry and biscuits, which they ate with a good young appetite. The celebration went on until the freighter was at the Nore lightship, when the passengers of both vessels stood by the rail and sang: "Goodnight, ladies, we're going to leave you now."

So the two vessels parted company and faded out of hearing. It made them feel lonely, and Irma said: "Do you think we're really married?"

"Don't worry about it too much," he replied. "When we get to the States we can have it done again. I'm told they don't make so much fuss about it over there."

At the mouth of the Thames great numbers of vessels lay waiting for the tide. When it was right, a pilot came aboard, and a ghostly procession started: every kind and size of steamer that could be imagined on the high seas, great passenger liners down to tugs with barges. It resembled what you saw when a school bell rang and the children came trooping in from all the homes in the village; a few hours later another bell rang, and they came rushing out—only in the case of the Port of London it would be a different lot each time. They glided up the river under their own power, and in the dim moonlight Irma and Lanny could see great mud-flats, and then, standing up bare and stark, factories, many of them brightly lighted, working at night, and piers with ships being loaded or unloaded by arclights. Presently the river narrowed, and there were entrances to great basins, and the fleet of vessels began to dissolve to right or left, the big ones first and the smaller ones higher up the river.

When the *Plymouth Girl* came to her berth, there was a sleepy official to inspect her papers and interview her passengers. Going off on a friend's yacht and coming back on a dingy old freighter was a sufficiently unusual procedure to attract attention; but money can do a lot at any port in the world, and it quickly brought a couple of messenger boys, one to go to Lanny's hotel and one to Irma's, to fetch their passports. These being in order, the delay was brief and they stepped ashore. By the same magic of the Bank of England's notes Lanny arranged at a garage for a car to be driven to Ramsgate, and a man in the back seat to take the car back.

They found the *Bessie Budd* safely reposing against the street, but all the passengers had already left for London. Lanny got his own car, and he and his bride set out to explore England in the lovely month of brides and roses. "Mr. and Mrs. L. P. Budd" attracted no attention on the registers of country inns, so they had a quiet time. Up in London the Robin family kept the secret, and so did the mothers. The formula "gone to visit friends" left the newspapers baffled. Beauty, being so much the poorer woman, took it as her duty to call on the haughty Mrs. Fanny Barnes. Fate had thrown them together, and they would have to make friends; fortunately they both played a good game of bridge. Lanny had been anxious as to the possibility that his new mother-in-law might expect to be taken on the yachting trip, but Irma said she was an especially poor sailor and was planning to go to Deauville with friends.

So everything was "jake," as they said in America. The bride made the discovery that she had found an ardent lover; it was easier to forget Italy and the Fascists than she had expected. Also it seemed possible just then to get away from her money with all its claims and obligations. She hadn't brought much with her, and Lanny was paying the bills and making jokes about keeping her in the style to which she was accustomed. He pointed out the features of English landscapes and told stories out of English history; delightful indeed to have a combination of husband and tutor! In the parlor of an establishment called the Duck and Turtle he seated himself at a not too badly cracked piano and played Schumann's *Widmung. Ich liebe dich in Zeit und Ewigkeit!* It would have been a "give-away" if anybody in the place had known German music, but no one did.

VII

In short, they had a jolly time, and the only reason they returned to London was the exhibition. If Lanny stayed away from this event, some clever person like Sophie or Margy might connect him with the missing heiress. They came back and amused themselves playing a game of hide-and-seek with the smart world. Lanny resumed receiving guests at the show, and among them were Mrs. J. Paramount Barnes and her daughter. He greeted them casually, and introduced them to Zoltan, who, knowing how rich they were, produced his best "spiel" about a French painter who was forging so rapidly to the front. Word spread that this was the famed heiress, and people watched her discreetly, and it surely did no harm to the reputation of Detaze that she expressed lively admiration for his work.

It pleased her to return and continue her art studies, and to bring other Americans whom she knew. She introduced these friends to the charming Hungarian gentleman who presided over the show, and left it for him to present them to the widow of the painter and his gay and eager little daughter. If now and then the painter's stepson was included in the introductions, that amiable young man would give intelligent answers to questions about the paintings. Irma showed no special interest in his remarks, but told the alert Mr. Kertezsi that she had decided to have several of these paintings in her Long Island home. He helped her to make a selection, received her check with many bows, and made note of her address and shipping instructions. Once more Zoltan was vindicated in his theory that it was better to price works of art too high than too low!

Then, when the show closed for the night, Lanny would drive his car to an appointed place, and Irma would arrive in a taxicab and transfer herself, and they would do a little winding about the winding old streets to make sure they were not being followed. Irma would be "visiting friends" again, and Lanny amused her by taking her to that second-class hotel where he had kept two rendezvous with Rosemary Codwilliger, pronounced Culliver, some twelve years previously. The building was still there—all buildings always stayed in London, they were permanent as the pyramids, he declared. He told her how a shrapnel splinter had crashed through the window of their room in the night, and Irma exclaimed: "Oh, how exciting! Do you suppose that will ever happen again?"

VIII

The *Bessie Budd* set sail with her five honeymoon couples; at least, Johannes said that he and Mama had been on a honeymoon ever since their wedding day, and the same was true of Mr. and Mrs. Dingle and of Mr. and Mrs. Hansi. Nobody needed to say anything about Mr. and Mrs. Lanny, or Mr. and Mrs. Freddi; their state of bliss was written all over them, and made them very pretty to watch.

The yacht sailed north, past the Faeroe Islands, and toward the land of the midnight sun. They saw some whales, but no icebergs in July and August. They came to a great island set in a lonely sea; they nosed into fiords much like those of Norway, and found a lovely little city scattered over the hills of a good harbor. The name Iceland sounded forbidding, and they were surprised to encounter a cultivated people who managed to have books and newspapers in their strange tongue, yet to escape most of the evils from which the *Bessie Budd* had fled. Surprising too to see hot springs and geysers bursting out of ground which was frozen most of the year; to see active volcanoes surrounded by glaciers. Beauty, who had grown soft in the warmth of Provence, shuddered at the thought of winter on these barren, storm-swept hills; but Lanny thought the people fared better than the dwellers in the slums of Riviera "old towns."

They went on toward the west. The glowing sun went down into the water while they slept, and soon afterward it came up out of a near-by place in the water, and it was broad daylight most of the time; apparently the globe on which they lived had got tipped out of place and didn't behave as they were used to seeing it. Unexpectedly, when the sun shone in an unclouded sky it became quite hot on deck, and you might imagine you were off the coast of Africa. You had to learn to sleep in the light, or tie a bandage over your eyes.

Great lonely wastes of water—Beauty said, what on earth had it all been made for! Only the seabirds and the porpoises for company. The birds could sleep on the water, but you never saw them doing it, nor did the porpoises ever seem to rest. When fogs settled down, the yacht barely crept along; when storms came, she headed into them, with just enough speed for steerage way. The voyagers were in no hurry; they had an abundance of food and water and fuel, and had left all cares in Berlin and London, places which had so many that a few extra would hardly count. They did not dress for dinner, as they had done on the previous cruise, the fashionable one. They wore yachting togs and sports clothes, and were comfortable and free; they agreed with the one-eyed calender in *The Arabian Nights:* "This indeed is life; pity 'tis, 'tis fleeting!"

There were five musicians on board, not including Mr. Dingle, who could play the mouth-organ, or Beauty and Irma, who had learned a few pieces after the fashion of society ladies. They had great quantities of scores, so many that the handling of them was a problem, and Freddi's wife constituted herself librarian. Hansi, who would never stop improving while he lived, practiced every day. Following a custom which they had inaugurated on their first cruise, Hansi and Freddi went frequently into the forecastle and played for such of the crew as were not on duty. On this trip, having no snobbish folk on board, they went farther, and every Sunday evening invited the crew into the saloon and gave them a regular concert.

This, of course, in the name of the brotherhood of man. Mr. Dingle, exponent of the fatherhood of God, made an even wider breach in the class lines, which are nowhere stronger than on board ship. When one of the men fell ill he went and prayed for him; and thereafter he would go frequently into the forecastle and explain his ideas, and also play the mouth-organ with members of the crew who had mastered that humble instrument.

Mr. Dingle said that it made no difference what instrument you played, any more than it mattered where you traveled; God was with you on the loneliest ocean, the rockiest, fog-bound shore. He was the same God in whatever aspect you found Him. In His guise as Orpheus, maker of melodious sounds, He brought to the *Bessie Budd* all climes of the earth and all ages of history; He peopled her deck with mythological creatures born in the fancy of the various tribes of mankind; He made her guests acquainted with the moods which had possessed the souls of men since first they opened their eyes and discovered themselves struggling and aspiring, loving and hating, fighting and dying, on a great ball of matter whirling at unthinkable speeds through an incomprehensible universe. All that men had felt and suffered had been recorded and preserved in musical sound, a heritage for those who had ears to hear and minds to understand.

IX

Through long, peaceful days and too abbreviated nights Lanny Budd studied that private and special gift which his complicated fates had awarded him. After no end of uncertainty and many mischances, he had got himself a wife; in a hurry, and half by accident, as happens to many two-legged creatures, as to those which have four, six, eight, or a hundred legs! Now that all barriers were down and all veils dropped, what was this woman who was his?

For one thing, she had a naturally cheerful disposition, an excellent thing in crowded quarters. She had a normal enjoyment of her food, and of being made love to. It wasn't necessary to her happiness to talk all the time; she would give him a chance to think, even when she was in the same cabin with him. She liked to walk on deck, and enjoyed any sort of game; she was still very young, and seemed in no special hurry to grow up. She had married him in a fit of pique, but she was loyal, and expected to make the best of her bargain. He couldn't guess how they'd get along in the midst of that crazy world of money and fashion which sooner or later would come clamoring after her; but in this floating playground, with only a few kind friends, and little reason for dressing up—he had persuaded her to ship her maid back to New York with the rest of her staff—here things were peaceful and pleasant enough.

He investigated her mind. Ideas didn't mean much to her; she saw no special reason for getting excited about them. Perhaps she might later on, when she discovered that they affected herself and her life and fortune; meanwhile, it was all right, because Lanny had enough ideas for two. He discovered that she didn't understand music; its structure meant nothing to her, but she liked to listen to harmonious sounds, they threw her into a pleasantly excited state. Perhaps her subconscious forces were being stimulated to their task, the miracle that was beginning within her. Irma wasn't going to master the piano like Bess; she was content to be a wife and let nature have its way. That suited Lanny, and still more it suited Beauty, who was in the seventh heaven of mothers-in-law; she lavished her affection upon the girl, watching for the symptoms, telling her own varied experiences. Women, who have to nurse babies and change their wrappings, learn to employ explicit language, and the things that Irma said to Beauty about Lanny would have caused embarrassment even to that son of the warm south if he had heard them.

The other young wife was in the same state of mind and body, and she too had a future grandmother in a state of rapture not to be repressed. Presently the four of them got together, Beauty Budd and Mama Robin, Irma and Rahel, and after that a section of the yacht might have been called the maternity ward. Four females whispering to one another, and Johannes, proprietor of the vessel, fain to listen in but not allowed to! And aft on the deck, under a gay-striped awning, four musicians pounding and thumping, tootling and tinkling and scraping, trying in vain to create or imagine anything more strange and romantic, more terrifying and delightful than the possibility of having a baby!

of money and fashion, which scores of them would count a blessing after her, but in this floating playground, with only a few friends, and little reason for dressing up—he had perhaps, till he ship her maid back to New York, until the start of her start—her duties were peaceful and pleasant enough.

He investigated her mind, for as child, it may reach to fear the say no special action for seeing carried about them. Perhaps she might later on, when she discovered that they affected herself and her life and tongue diseased life, it was all other diseased faith. And enough ideas for two. He discovered that she didn't understand anything. In superior meant nothing to teach her she had to teach to them as well; about sounds, they threw her into a play and especially eager. Perhaps her mischievous forces were being stimulated to their peak, the current that was beginning within that time were going to brazened pimp like. Because she was content to labor over and for music and straight. That suited Lamp, and still more it suited Becky, who was still in the secure betters of spectacularism; she looked for refuge in upon the girl, and tried it to the imaginative mind; she was an... eyes a spanse Woman, who bore to endure wishes and absence a riot simple pious, learnt to employ explicit language; and she pupils sent time said to Becky about him, would have caused enough to meet a fine station on of the worst sort, she had the bad hand them.

The other young wives were the... the scale of mind and body, and the top had a futile gradual elimination, a waste of replace, about to be repressed. Possibly the flat of them our rulers, the sacred bloid and... Many flabby front, and taken and water bums; result... the world might have been called the underworld, and for... longue, very empty, to one another and forming opposition of the worst, for no ketch... follow not always took, fully thrust the look, turned a bit showed awn? my Noah music as something... and her paper, framing, seen shelling and scrapping, going In 1841, to forget to appreciate its own power a strange and romantic more enrapt and delighted than up fortuin bility of having a baby.

BOOK EIGHT

Lead But to the Grave

36

Prince Consort

I

EARLY in the month of September the *Bessie Budd* appeared off the mouth of the Newcastle River. Lanny had telephoned from Boston, and Robbie had a pilot waiting for them in a launch; he blew on a little tin horn, and the two draw-bridges swung open, first the road bridge and then the railroad bridge, and the trim white yacht glided slowly through and was brought neatly alongside one of the wharves of the Budd plant. Robbie was there with three cars, and all ten passengers stepped ashore: the family of his former wife—so called in the interest of public decency—and the family of his business associate, including Robbie's daughter. Also, there was his new daughter-in-law, whom he had never met, so it was an important occasion for him.

In fact, it was to be doubted if ever since the days of the slave trade such a package of excitement had arrived by sea in the little harbor of Newcastle, Connecticut. The news of Lanny's marriage to America's newest heiress had been released by Mrs. Barnes as soon as the yacht had left London, and it hadn't taken many hours to reach the home of Budd Gunmakers Corporation. Soon it had become known that the yacht was coming here, and fashionable society was sitting up in watchtowers. Several of the smartest set had met Irma Barnes in New York, and these distributed their information and helped to keep curiosity alive.

Irma was the brightest star in the constellation, but by no means the only one of the first magnitude. For more than thirty years the tongues of gossip had been busy with the personality of Beauty Budd. She had never been to Newcastle; in fact she had never visited her native land in all those years. Now she was coming, and was to be received in the Budd home—the fiction of a marriage and divorce being maintained. This had to be done, if only on account of Irma; impossible for the family to admit that there was anything wrong with the mother-in-law of their new fairy princess!

Also in this constellation was Beauty's son, whom you might call a variable star; a dark one when he had passed below Newcastle's horizon, he was now shining brightly, even though by reflected light. There is a phenomenon of the heavens known as a double star: a dark one and a bright one revolve about each other, and thousands of eyes are kept glued upon them in the hope of gleaning new items of information concerning the nature and behavior of celestial bodies.

And then the Robin family. Hansi might be likened to a shining meteor which sweeps through the night sky and sweeps away again. No one could be certain how long he would last, but meanwhile he was a portent, and Newcastle would not forget the explosion he had caused by picking up and dragging off in his train one of the brightest planets of the Newcastle Country Club system. Hansi's father also was a sun in his own right, and marked on the map of many Newcastle stargazers. To drop an overworked simile, Johannes was an important financier, and many of the town's leading businessmen held stock in his enterprises; these solid citizens didn't go in for society flubdub, but were glad to meet and converse with a man of ability and experience.

II

The party was taken to the Robbie Budd home for tea, and members of the family were on hand to welcome them. Not old Samuel, for he rarely went out now, and not even after thirty years could he be persuaded to meet the woman who had seduced his son. But others of the tribe were less stiff-necked, and the younger generation was possessed by curiosity. From this tea party the news spread quite literally with the speed of lightning, for in every home except the very poorest in Newcastle this force had been harnessed and taught to serve the public welfare. "What hath God wrought?" the inventor of the process had piously inquired, and the answer was that

God had wrought a means whereby gossip might be distributed over a small city with astonishing celerity. "What does she look like?" and "What was she wearing?" and "What did she say?" and "How did Esther greet her?" and "Is she going to keep them in her house?"

The press had fair warning, and it was a red-letter day for local correspondents; the stories they sent over the wire would not stop until they had reached Key West and San Diego and Walla Walla. Lanny Budd, who had had such a blissful time for two months in the haunts of the whale and the eider duck, now discovered suddenly what this marriage was going to mean. On the wharf were several men with square black boxes which made snapping noises when a button was pressed; already they had snapped the yacht, and now it was necessary for Irma and her husband to line up, and then Hansi and Bess with them. The local photographers wanted the whole party. Meanwhile the reporters were plying Irma and Lanny with questions: where had they been, what sort of weather had they had, what had they done, where were they going to live, what did they think about Europe and America, and which did they prefer?

You had to be polite to them, for they represented the most powerful force in the land, and could make you or break you. If you were wise you would employ a skilled publicity man to tell you what to say, and to be present at interviews and smooth over the rough places. Irma's mother had engaged one in New York, but now Irma was taken by surprise, and Lanny couldn't help her very much, his experience having been slight. Robbie had arranged for a collective interview at his home, but deadlines know no decorum, so Lanny had to try to think in a hurry what the great public might like to read about a bride with twenty-three million dollars, and also about the lucky young "socialite" who had got her. What would have pleased the public most was a bulletin to the effect that she was pregnant; but that being barred, Lanny said that they had played music on the deck most of the time, they had a piano on rubber wheels, also a violin, a clarinet, and a soprano voice. He didn't mention the mouth-organ; but, as it happened, one of the reporters dug that out of the crew, and made an amusing item about life on a German millionaire's yacht.

Somehow the word got about that the sons and daughters-in-law of Johannes Robin were Reds, and that the spouse of Irma Budd was decidedly tinged with pink. Wasn't there a story about his having been kicked out of Italy five years ago? The ordinary press associations didn't refer to this, for it was not their practice to mention dangerous thoughts unless the carriers of them had got arrested or something like that; but there were "tabs" in New York which would publish anything "spicy," and there were men who specialized in collecting personal details about celebrities and broadcasting them over the radio. Lanny found that he had become almost overnight a shining mark for these gentry. They didn't intend to be mean to him; he was just an amiable playboy who had been catapulted suddenly into the spotlight and had, at a conservative estimate, thirty million pairs of eyes fixed upon his daily and nightly doings.

III

Esther Budd considered it her duty to invite the entire party to her home, which had plenty of room. But the guests had talked the matter over in advance and decided otherwise. The young people would come, but the middle-aged, the mothers and fathers, would stay on board the yacht, where they were comfortable and wouldn't be in danger of spoiling the good times. Mama Robin didn't care for fashionable society; she knew perfectly well that these smart people would be laughing at her stumbling English, and she preferred her own little nook where she had everything the way she wanted it. As for Beauty, she knew that she was being forced upon Esther, and desired to make the strain as light as possible. Also there was the obstacle of Beauty's husband, whose private wire to heaven would please the daughter of the Puritans no more than that of Roger Williams had pleased her forefathers of three centuries earlier.

The Robbie Budds gave a reception in their home the second evening after the yacht's arrival, and all the members of the party came to that, and met the social élite of Newcastle valley. The doors of the country club were opened to the visitors, and there were dinners and festive events. Irma had telegraphed for her staff, and her chauffeur was on hand with her car, her social secretary, and her maid; her wardrobe trunks were brought out of the hold of the yacht, and without a moment's delay she fell into the routine which had been dropped when she fled from Rome. Everything was done to make smooth her path, and she would emerge from her boudoir ready for the world to gaze at her, and certain that it would. Lanny, too, might enjoy the same assurance; he had nothing to do but display himself as the winner and keeper of the most precious prize in the lottery of high life.

As usual, one half of him liked it, and the other half was skeptical. He had not forgotten how all these people had received him when he had come among them as a lad; not unkindly, but with watchful caution, and then with amusement or indignation, according to their temperaments, when they saw him following the footsteps of his mother in the primrose path of dalliance. Now he returned in glory, and his sins which had been scarlet became white as snow. Now he was the glass of fashion and the mold of form, the observed of all observers, the model for youth to follow—in short, he had "made good," and young and old hastened to lay their tributes at his feet. The girls of Newcastle who had been sub-debs during the war now had new names and were the "young matrons" of the country club; they recalled themselves to him, and noting his elegant manners and brilliant conversation, compared him sadly with the rather dull young businessmen whom fate had assigned to them. If only they had been clever enough to realize how an ugly duckling can grow into a swan!

The same thing happened to Mabel Blackless, alias Beauty Budd, alias Madame Detaze, alias Mrs. Parsifal Dingle. Shining in the reflected glory of her son and daughter-in-law, she was really phenomenal. Her years were almost fifty, but she had devoted a great part of them to keeping herself beautiful, and had acquired no little skill. Had she set out to punish Esther by making a conquest of the town? She treated Robbie as an old friend, and in fact treated all Newcastle that way; her manner seemed to say: "Yes, we have lived together in our thoughts for a long time, and I know that you have not appreciated me, but I don't hold it against you, for there were three thousand miles of ocean between us and you couldn't be expected to understand me and my ways. But I have always known about yours, and you are being so kind to me and my darling boy and his lovely young bride, and we all hope you will love us and see that the evil gossip about us was not true." It was a symptom of the change in the times that Beauty Budd could "get away with" all that, and that a town with so many Protestant churches presented her with the keys of its country club.

IV

One of Lanny's first duties was to take his bride to call upon his grandfather. The president of Budd Gunmakers was now eighty-two, and failing; his cheeks hung in pouches, and there were folds of loose skin under his chin; his hand trembled so that he had a hard time drinking a glass of water. But he still hung onto his power; those shaking hands held a great business, and no important decision was made without his knowledge. His sons tried to spare him, but he wouldn't let them. His old home was unchanged, and his old servants; his Sunday morning Bible class for men was now conducted by an assistant, but the old gentleman came and listened to make sure that there was no departure from the principles set forth in that *Brief Digest of the Boston Confession of Faith* which he had handed to his grandson at their first encounter.

The old man lifted himself carefully from his chair in honor of the lovely young woman who was escorted into his study. He had heard all about her, looked her over carefully, and made sure that she was well formed and healthy. "Welcome, my dear," he said; and then to Lanny: "You waited quite a while, young man!"

"I only just met her at the beginning of this year," said Lanny, with a grin. "She was worth waiting for."

The head of the Budd tribe couldn't dispute that statement. His vast plant had to work several years to gain the profits this young whippersnapper had picked up by walking off with a girl. It seemed preposterous, but it was a fact and had to be faced. "We are happy to welcome you into the Budd tribe," said the old Puritan; it was a

meant new office buildings going up in Bolivian cities, it meant Bolivian citizens ascending in Budd elevators, and when these got out of order they would be repaired with Budd wrenches.

More than that, if the Bolivians got to fighting with the Paraguayans, both sides would come to Budd's; for the munitions part of the business hadn't been abolished. They kept it going on faith, or perhaps lack of faith in human nature, which couldn't go on indefinitely without wars. It was a patriotic service to make the jigs and dies for a new and better machine gun which might be needed by the American government; the public didn't appreciate that service now, but it would when the time came. Lanny remembered a remark of Bub Smith, the ex-cowboy, that a gun was like a certain toilet necessity, you didn't need it often but when you did you needed it bad. Lanny didn't pass this Texas humor on to his wife, but he told her in a general way about the patriotic principles of the Budd tribe which had been taught to him all his life.

The old gentleman had suggested that Irma should see the plant; he wanted her to know that there were real things in the world, and how they were made. So Lanny took her through and showed her the sights which had so thrilled him as a youth. The girls who sat by the assembly lines were putting different gadgets together, and probably they were different girls, but their behavior was the same. Somehow or other they knew that the elegant pair strolling down the aisle and staring at them were the young lord and lady about whom they had read in the papers; but their job gave them little chance to observe costumes and manners. They would sit for hour after hour, day after day, year after year, making precisely ordained motions; millions of products would slide off the lines, and Lanny's and Irma's "seed" had just been promised a share of the profits in the name of the Lord. If there was anything wrong with all that, what could Lanny do about it? How could he even explain it to his wife?

She was immensely impressed by what she saw. The business of forming holding companies was purely a paper one, so all that Irma had seen at her father's office was rows of clerks sitting at typewriters and adding-machines and cardfiles. But here was something tangible, and it made the Budd family important and aristocratic, and made Lanny much less of a "come-down." She had seen him adopted into this old family, and she too had been adopted, and her seed had been blessed; it had been embarrassing, but she knew that it was out of the Bible and therefore respectable. Irma was happy in the thought of telling her uncles and aunts about it, and they would realize that this was no misalliance. After all, J. Paramount Barnes had begun life as an errand boy, but Lanny's forefathers had been building this great plant for generations. To be sure, they didn't make so much money as her father had done, but money wasn't everything, no matter what you might say.

VI

The firm of "R and R" hadn't had a consultation for some time, and they took this occasion to go into details about all their affairs and to plan what they would do in the future. Some of the concerns which Johannes had purchased in Germany were turning out the same sort of goods as Budd's, which brought them into rivalry in various markets; but that didn't trouble them, for the world was big, and there was no limit to the expansion of production. Lanny didn't sit in at these conferences, but he heard some of the casual talk and gathered that the German capitalist was much less optimistic than the American. Johannes had had to work for his money, and knew what it was to face adversity; he wouldn't expect to have summer weather during his entire cruise on the ocean of big business.

Robbie, on the other hand, was sure that for America, at least, the problem of permanent prosperity had been solved. He had got the ideal President of the United States this time; the Great Engineer, who didn't have to be told what to do, because he understood the business machine in every part and knew exactly how to help American industry and finance to conquer the world. Just look at the way things were booming, orders piling in from every land! Budd's had such a backlog that it could be sure of dividends for a couple of years if it never booked another order. Robbie said that the choicest stocks were now acquiring a scarcity value; people were putting them in safe-deposit boxes, and they no longer came on the market. "Don't sell America short!" said one half of "R and R" to the other half.

There was only one cloud in Robbie's sky, and that was his personal trouble with the business in Arabia. They talked about that at much length. Johannes advised Robbie to take his loss and get out; the place was too far away, and the factors beyond control. They had more than got back their investment, so why not call it a day? But Robbie was stubborn; it was a matter of principle. Johannes smiled and said: "I cannot afford to have principles. I am a businessman!"

All his life Lanny had sat and listened to such conversations, and learned how the world was run and how the wires were pulled. What firm of lawyers one had to employ in Washington if one wanted the American State Department to get busy with the British government and demand protection for an American oil property! What detective agency one employed if one wanted to be sure of keeping labor organizers out of a great manufacturing-plant! Or, if it was Germany, what Cabinet member one dealt with in order to get promptly the supply of rationed raw materials that one needed for export products! How to put one's earnings back into new plant in such a way as to avoid income taxes! There were no laws that shrewd businessmen couldn't find some way of getting round—and it was a good thing, because what was going to become of industry if governments kept on encroaching on all opportunities of profit?

The firm of "R and R" talked frankly in the presence of Lanny, because they didn't take any of his "radical" ideas seriously; and maybe they were right about it. Johannes looked upon the Redness in his own family as a sort of measles, German measles, perhaps, which young people had, and the earlier they had them the quicker they got over them. Robbie told how Budd's had put the Communists out of business in Connecticut, and Robin told how they were still doing it in Germany. They were using those Nazis—a dangerous weapon, but there appeared to be no other at hand. The steel and allied interests of the Fatherland were now paying a regular tribute of one-half of one percent of all their earnings into the treasury of

Adolf Hitler's party, and Johannes was paying his share; not that he liked to do it, but the emergency was extreme and a man couldn't separate himself from all his associates.

A part of that money had to be spent for arms, and Johannes had used his influence to have the Nazis purchase several thousand submachine guns which Budd's had made for the United States government during the war and which Johannes had bought at a great bargain, using cash put up by Robbie. That was the way capable businessmen took in money with both hands! Those little guns were marvels—they could be carried in one hand and fired from the shoulder like a rifle; they had been brought in through Holland canals, marked as agricultural implements, and unquestionably they had been the means of turning the tide of battle for the streets of Munich and Berlin.

VII

Esther asked Lanny to come to her room; she wanted to have a chat with him. Quite a change since he had last been in this home; then she had been relieved to see him go, but now she wanted his help. Esther wasn't the kind to be impressed by a rich marriage, but she had come to realize that while Lanny's moral code was different from hers, he had one and he lived by it. He had been right about Bess, and as a result had won Bess in a way that Esther had failed to do. Life was puzzling, and no matter how hard one tried to do right, one often blundered.

Esther was worried about her husband. She had always thought that he drank more than he should, and now he drank more and more. No one ever saw him drunk, but he depended upon liquor to sustain him, and it couldn't fail to harm him in the end. Lanny said he had seen a great deal of the same thing among the French people; they rarely got drunk, but many kept themselves mildly pickled all the time; their systems seemed to get used to it. Lanny said that Robbie drank because he was under too great a strain; he worried about his business affairs, some of which hadn't gone so well. Esther said he undertook too much, and what was the sense of it? They didn't need so much money; she saw to it that they lived within their means, and the boys had learned to do the same.

Lanny replied: "It's a kind of a game with Robbie, and he plays it too hard. It's too bad that he hasn't got some hobby."

"You don't know how hard I've tried to interest him and to help him; but there must be some lack in me. I really believe that you have more influence over him than I have."

"I don't think so, Esther." He had decided to address her thus; he couldn't very well call her "Mother" while Beauty was in town! "I have never heard Robbie speak of you except with affection and respect."

"He doesn't give me his confidence, and he resents being criticized."

"Most of us do, Esther. Robbie is proud, and he doesn't like to admit mistakes. If he takes an extra drink it's always a special case, and he wouldn't admit to himself that it's become a habit."

"That's the way men drift into it, and why I hate it so. I've tried my best to impress it upon the boys, but I don't know if I've succeeded—drinking at Yale is simply frightful."

"The boys look all right." Lanny sought to console her. They had both left for Yale a day or two ago—Junior for the law school. "The Prohibition experiment doesn't seem to have turned out very well," the stepson added.

"I hoped so much from it. Millions of women thought it was going to be the saving of our happiness; but nobody seems to pay any attention to the law."

"How does Robbie get his liquor?"

"It's the old story; 'right off the boat.' You hear the men all talking about it; each one is quite sure that his has come direct from Canada, and they swap references of their bootleggers—but how far can you trust men whose business is breaking the law?"

"Not very far, I should think."

"Robbie is careful enough when he deals with a banker, or somebody who is trying to sell him a few carloads of metal; but some plausible young fellow turns up with a tale of having just run a bargeload of Scotch into the river last night, and all the businessmen in town swallow the tale and the liquor; they bring the stuff into their homes and serve it to their families and their guests, and no one ever thinks of having a chemist analyze it!"

"They're afraid of what they might find," smiled Lanny.

"It's made the most frightful corruption in our city affairs. The bootleggers seem to have more money to spend than anybody else in town."

VIII

Esther talked for a while about Lanny and his bride, and asked about their plans. But it wasn't long before she brought back the subject of her husband. Another thing was worrying her—Robbie's playing the stock market.

"He's always done that, hasn't he?" asked the son.

"He would do what he called taking a flier; but now he plunges. He doesn't tell me about it, but I pick up hints—the way he looks at the paper, things I hear him saying over the phone. He's made a great deal of money, apparently, but at the expense of his peace of mind. And why, Lanny, why? We don't need it, and what are we going to do with it?"

"We can't stop men from taking risks, or from challenging one another. If they haven't got a real war they make an imitation one. I try to think what Robbie would be like if he wasn't playing some money game. What would he do with himself?"

Esther answered, out of her troubled soul: "There's something wrong with our education. We try to give our young people culture, and it doesn't take."

Lanny saw the traces which anxiety had left in his stepmother's features, so smooth and serene when he had first become acquainted with them. Her straight brown hair was now showing signs of gray, and there were lines about her eyes and mouth. She was a conscientious woman, and tried to play the game of life fairly; had others been unfair, or was it that the spirit of her time was too strong for her? Certainly she wasn't happy, and Robbie wasn't happy.

Had she been too strict with him? Had she resented his youthful error and punished him in her heart for it, and in so doing punished herself? She had this beautiful home, managed it efficiently, played the part of a perfect hostess, a great lady of society, a benefactor to the poor, a leader of useful civic movements; but she wasn't happy. Lanny wondered how many of these elegant homes in what were known as "exclusive residential sections" held tragedies of this slow-burning, secret kind. Lanny would have liked to ask some intimate questions: "What is your love-life with Robbie? How much trouble do you take to hold his interest? How much do you know about how to hold his interest if you want to?" Alas, he could talk about such matters with his irregular mother, but never with his tight-laced and rigid stepmother!

IX

The guests of the yacht *Bessie Budd* packed up their belongings and prepared to be transported up Long Island Sound to the richest city in the world. Her owner had business there, and Zoltan Kertezsi had arrived and was expecting Beauty's help in promoting the Detaze show. Of course, Zoltan hadn't failed to hear that the stepson of his painter had got married, nor did he overlook the advertising value of that event. He telephoned, suggesting a larger appropriation for grander show rooms, to accommodate the crowd which he felt sure would come, if only in the hope of catching a glimpse of the stepson's bride. He chuckled over Irma's having bought some of the paintings. "Tell her she wouldn't have got them so cheaply if I had known!"

Lanny bade farewell to his old Connecticut family, and prepared to meet his new Long Island one. Mrs. Barnes had returned from Europe and was waiting at their country place; to delay too long to pay his respects would have been a failure in tact. Mr. and Mrs. Dingle were also invited, but Beauty pleaded the pressure of duties in connection with the exhibition. She had lived a long while in the fashionable world, and knew when people wanted her to accept an invitation and when they hoped she'd have sense enough to decline.

She and her husband would stay in a hotel, and while he looked up the meeting-places of the God-seekers, she would renew acquaintance with the many New Yorkers whom she had met on the Riviera in the course of the years. The yacht was returning to Germany with the Robin family, where Johannes had his business and the young people their various tasks to resume. They had all had an enjoyable holiday, and promised themselves others of the sort.

Lanny and Irma were met at an East River pier and motored out to a South Shore estate for whose grandeur the bridegroom had been inadequately prepared. At last he was going to learn how really rich people lived! "Shore Acres" the place was playfully named, but it might have been called "Shore Miles." The whole great expanse had a steel fence around it, twelve feet high, with inhospitable spikes pointing outward. The buildings stood on a bluff looking out over the sea; they were of red sandstone, an adaptation of the Château de Chambord which had been built four hundred years ago for King Francis I. They had a great number of turrets, gables, and carved chimneys; in the American replica these latter had no openings, the house having a central heating system. The fastidious Lanny didn't like buildings that were too big for comfort, and he thought more of the people who had created a type of architecture than of those who "adapted" it.

The place was only about ten years old, but already the interior had been redecorated—just a few weeks before its owner had dropped dead. The entrance hall was finished in white Vermont marble, and would have served any moderate-sized city for a railroad waiting-room. The flunkies didn't line up to receive the bride and groom as they would have done at Stubendorf, but perhaps that was because Lanny's new mother-in-law hadn't heard of the practice. Over this royal domain the large stout widow of the electricity king presided with admirable energy. The place now belonged to her daughter, but she ran it, and strode through the echoing corridors smoking her large dark cigars and keeping track of everything that went on.

Lanny had heard about living *en prince*, and now he had to do it and like it. He had a suite of apartments, with a four-poster bed in which several princes had been born. (Its pedigree was on the headboard.) His upholstery was of such exquisite silk that he was embarrassed to sit on it, and certainly he would never put his feet on the sofa. His bathtub was sunk in the floor and he descended into it by three wide steps, having ruby-red lights set into the rises so that he could see where he was going. The walls, floor, and tub were of the most wonderful green marble he had ever beheld, and all the fixtures of the tub and the plumbing, at least to the point where they disappeared into the floor, were of silver, and it wasn't plated. When you turned the faucets, the water shot into the tub as if from a fire-hose. Irma's apartment, which adjoined his, had similar equipment, but her marble had the pale pink tinge of la France roses and the fixtures were of fourteen-carat gold. You might refuse to believe it, and if you had done so during the life of the owner, he would have given you the name of the concern which made them. This particular suite had belonged to J. Paramount himself, and he had been a gay dog; the first time Lanny sat on the toilet seat he was startled by pretty little chimes ringing behind his back, and they didn't stop until he got up.

A more than life-sized portrait of the financial genius confronted you in the entrance hall, and the young art expert studied it attentively. It was the work of a popular painter, who had made an honest effort to report what he saw. "J.P.," as he was still referred to, had been a robust man and a fighter; he had that sort of jaw and eye. Hair and eyes had been black, and if he had grown a mustache and beard he might have made a pirate of the Jolly Roger epoch. His look was grim, but you could imagine the eyes lighting up, and you had to imagine a persuasive tongue, which had convinced the guardians of treasure that he was the wizard who could take one dollar and put it together with another dollar, and cause a brood of baby dollars to come into existence in a few days or weeks. He had performed that biologico-financial miracle over and over—he had never failed a single time. The huge corporation pyramids which he had constructed still stood, and "the Street" was convinced that they would stand forever as monuments to this master manipulator.

Another monument was this palace; and confronting the lifelike portrait Lanny wondered, was this hard-driving spirit watching him somewhere in limbo? Challenging him, perhaps: "By what right do you sleep in my bed and splash in my bathtub and listen to my chimes?" Would he consider Lanny Budd a proper successor, fitted to wear his heavy armor and draw his mighty bow? Certainly the young master didn't fancy himself in the role. Lanny hadn't yet found out just where Wall Street was situated!

X

Irma, having spent half her life in this palace, took it as a matter of course; so Lanny must try to think of it as home. Talking to him in London, the majestic Mrs. Barnes had urged him to do this; she had made it plain that she was prepared to accept him and do her best to make him happy. Not an easy speech for a domineering woman to make; but she was the dowager, and had to humble herself. Never again would Lanny hear that dreadful word "bastard." He had won the fight; he might take charge of the mansion, or he might carry Irma away. It was the mother's hope that the pride and glory of the great domain would capture the young man's fancy and win him away from the insane idea of taking Irma to inhabit a "cottage" in that pathetic little property on the Riviera.

This conflict of purposes became more plain as soon as Fanny Barnes made certain that her daughter was pregnant. Then it developed into a struggle over a grandchild, and it was going to be waged not merely between Lanny and his mother-in-law, but between two mothers-in-law. Each had a home which she wished to offer to the heir-apparent; and who was going to decide which was the better? Who was going to find any fault with the manner of Lanny's upbringing? Let that rash one keep out of Beauty's way! On the other hand, what would be said to that depraved person who might hint that Irma was anything short of perfect? Look at her! Ask the world about her!

Lanny's intention was to wait until after the exhibition, and then take his bride by the first steamer that was properly equipped for the transporting of a princess. Take no chance of delaying until someone could argue that her condition made travel unsafe! She had told him that she would prefer Juan over any other place to live, and so Juan it was to be. Meanwhile he would be the soul of politeness, and accept with gratitude whatever courtesies might be offered. But he wouldn't change his plans.

On this huge estate there was no useful thing that a young master could do without trespassing; but there were innumerable forms of play. He and Irma might ride horseback, something which he had enjoyed in England now and then. They might play tennis on beautifully kept clay courts, or, when it rained, on an indoor court with a wood floor. They might swim in a well-warmed indoor pool. There were a "game room" with pool and billiards, a bowling-alley, a squash court—also a man in attendance who apparently had nothing to do until someone came along to play. There was a music room with a magnificent piano, and a smaller one had been installed in Lanny's apartment. All these cabinets full of scores—had they been here in J.P.'s day, or had Mrs. Fanny instructed some music-store to send out one thousand of the world's masterpieces for the pianoforte?

The only trouble was that Lanny had no time to make use of these treasures. The establishment was built for company, and Irma's young friends came pouring in to welcome her and to satisfy their curiosity about the lucky man. Lanny had to be on hand, have on the right clothes, and take his part in whatever was proposed: riding or motoring, tennis or squash parties, a sail if the day happened to be warm and the breeze right. There were teas and dinners and dances in honor of the bridal pair; and always reporters hanging onto the skirts of these events, seeking interviews and writing up the gossip from which tens of thousands of debutantes would learn how to do the right thing in the right way, and millions of salesladies and stenographers would have their imaginations fed with dreams of luxury. The time was past when Lanny Budd could amuse himself by talking to any stranger who came along. From now on he must remember that the stranger might be a newspaperman or a spy—for any item about what the husband of Irma Barnes was doing or saying might be sold to one of the "tabs" for five or ten dollars.

XI

Lanny's position was that of a prince consort, such as the husband of Queen Victoria. He had performed his first and principal duty, he had planted the seed, and now he had to watch and tend it carefully. He would escort his bride wherever she wished to go; unthinkable that he should refuse to do so—it would have started a scandal in no time. He was a member of the "younger set" of Long Island, and would learn to know a large group of handsome and fashionably clad playboys and girls, most of whom would never grow up. He would listen to their eager chatter, having to do for the most part with themselves and their playmates. He would learn to know the various personalities, and be able to understand the jokes having to do with Aggie's recent motor mishap or Tubby's excess of *embonpoint*. They drank a great deal, but rarely lost their ability to get out of the cabaret and tell the chauffeur where to take them. They had built a play world, and were gay in it, persistently and conscientiously. There was nothing they resisted with such determination as the impulse to take anything seriously.

Also Lanny had the duty of meeting two new families, that of his mother-in-law and that of his deceased father-in-law. He had to be polite to them all, and try to satisfy them as to Irma's future. J.P.'s younger brother Joseph was important, because he was one of three trustees who under the terms of the will had the handling of Irma's estate. She got the income, but couldn't spend any of the principal without their consent. The other two trustees had been confidential employees of the father, and all three of them had full-time duties. Just to keep track of twenty-three million dollars and its earnings was quite a business, and the estate had a large suite of offices. The duties of the trustees consisted of clipping coupons and depositing dividend checks, keeping books and rendering elaborate quarterly statements, which Irma turned over to her mother unopened.

Mr. Horace Vandringham was the gentleman who had sent the cablegram to his sister in Cannes. Thanks to Emily Chattersworth, Lanny knew the text of that message; but not a word was said about it now, and Uncle Horace would do his best to atone for his excruciating error. He was older than his sister, and was an "operator" in Wall Street; that is, he not merely bought stocks and waited for them to go up, but he got other people interested with him, they formed a "syndicate," and Uncle Horace caused the stocks to move in the direction he desired. If he was "long" on the stock, he would circulate rumors of mergers, stock dividends, and "split-ups"; if he was "short," he would cause the public to hear that the company was in trouble and that the next dividend was to be passed. If his judgment was good he made a "killing"; and apparently it had been, for he lived lavishly and talked money in large quantities. Robbie knew about him and said he was a "shark," which wasn't necessarily a term of reprobation in Wall Street.

To Lanny this new uncle presented himself as a "character." He was big and burly, bald on top, and the top was as rosy as his face. He was full of energy which could not be repressed. When he walked you got the same sort of surprise that you would from watching an elephant in the forest; you wouldn't have imagined that such a bulky body could move so fast. He swung his arms vehemently, and rocked from side to side even as he strode across a room. He ate violently, laughed loudly, talked a great deal, and was positive in his opinions. He was evidently trying to be agreeable to this new nephew, who might be in position to turn his sister out of her home; he would ask what Lanny thought about some matter, but it was no good trying to reply, because Uncle Horace couldn't help interrupting and telling him. Lanny gathered that these big Wall Street men were used to having their own way.

Gradually the bridegroom discovered the situation between the two families which he had acquired. The Vandringhams were real aristocrats; that is to say, they belonged to the old Dutch New Yorkers who had had money for generations. But they had lost most of their money, and Fanny had married the upstart Barnes and been unhappy. Now she looked down upon all the Barneses, and favored her brother, who was the real gentleman. She wanted Irma to be a Vandringham and not a Barnes; if ever Irma manifested any tendency of which her mother disapproved—which happened not infrequently—that was the evil Barnes blood showing itself. The mother resented the indignity of the estate's having to be handled by the Barneses and not by the Vandringhams. How much more money Horace would have made for them!

Also Lanny had to meet the dependents, a matter calling for tact. J.P. had been charitable, and his widow carried on the tradition. Irma's former governess and the master's former confidential secretary enjoyed a sort of demi-status; they dined with the family except when there was company, and then they whisked themselves out of sight without having to be told. An older maiden sister of Fanny and two aunts had what you might call a three-quarter status; they disappeared only when there was important company.

Also there lived in various quarters on the estate a number of what you might call half-servants, elderly retired attendants who performed light services when occasion arose. One of Mrs. Fanny's many tasks was to find things for them to do—for she said she hated to see people idle or things going to waste. She would set them to performing offices for one another; if one man had to be taken to the dentist, another drove him; if one woman fell ill, another nursed her. It might be that the pair hated each other's guts, but they would do what they were told. One and all, these persons desired to be of service to Lanny, and their humility, their gratitude for being alive, seemed pitiable to him. They didn't fall on their knees and put their foreheads in the dust when he passed, but it seemed to him that spiritually they did this, and it was one of the reasons why he found being a prince consort so dubious a satisfaction. But he was in for it. He couldn't change the world, or the fact that he was Mr. Irma Barnes!

37

Café Society

I

THE Detaze show opened in the second week of October, and Lanny owed it to Zoltan and his mother to be on hand. Irma was pleased to accompany him, for she had found the London show amusing, and had met a number of distinguished persons. It is the pleasantest time of the year in New York; the weather is at its best, the theaters are opening, "everybody" is back from the country or from abroad.

The business manager engaged the most expensive suite in the most expensive hotel. Impossible to live any other way, and it would have been unkind of Lanny to suggest it. Was his wife to change her system of living just because he was a poor man? Here was a smooth-running machine ready to carry him through life, and all he had to do was not to interfere with the experts who were running it. The rooms were engaged and the bill sent to Shore Acres, and Irma wouldn't even know what was being paid.

She had learned to do things in a certain way, and he was expected to do the same and forget it. She carried little money in her handbag, just enough for tips and such small items. For the rest she said: "Charge it." In restaurants and hotels she signed slips, and bills were mailed to the estate and the manager attended to them. Now it was Lanny's duty to sign slips, because it took one more burden off his wife's hands, and incidentally it looked better. Under this arrangement he would never spend any money of his own unless he was away from her—and she didn't want him ever to be away.

How silly to bother about such matters, or to try to discuss them! She had told him that she cared nothing about money, and she

775

meant it; why couldn't he mean it? She had got the money by accident, and she had to spend it, because there was nothing else to do with it. His happiness was hers, they had promised to be one in all things, and didn't that include money? Let things "ride," and talk about something worth while!

At home it had been one of Lanny's pleasures to drive his own car; and that was all right at the estate, there were plenty of cars, and one of the best was called his. But in the city you had to have a chauffeur to drive, or where would you park? If you drew up in front of a hotel and it was raining, you and your wife wanted to step out under the porte-cochere and forget the car until it was time to leave. Lanny had to learn to sit in the back seat and make himself agreeable to the ladies.

So, in one way after another, Irma's money functioned as a steamroller, making a path for itself and flattening out everything that stood in its way. Did Lanny have any idea about privacy? Did he want to be let alone? When their manager engaged rooms in a hotel, the hotel manager at once notified the press, because it would mean advertising for the hotel; so when the princely pair arrived, the photographers were waiting. Would they kindly oblige just for a minute? It would have been ungracious to say no.

And then the reporters, wishing to know what were their plans, why had they come to town? As it happened, Lanny had come to promote a showing of his late stepfather's art. That was a worthy and dignified purpose, so he told for perhaps the thousandth time the story of a French painter who had had his face burned off in the first year of the war, and had sat in his studio and painted his greatest pictures wearing a silk mask. That was a good story, and the papers would use it; but also their readers wanted to know, what was Irma wearing, how did Lanny find it in America, and how did he enjoy being the husband of a glamour girl? He said that he enjoyed it greatly, and forbore to mention being a Pink, or to record any objections to living in the royal suite of the Ritzy-Waldorf.

II

The show opened, and it was what New York called a "knock-out," or, if you wanted to be elegant, a "wow." It had everything that New York required; real art, which was in the Luxembourg and had received the *cachet* of the leading critics in Paris and London. The melodramatic story attached thereto served for the journalists to write about and for people to tell to one another as they looked at the pictures; it was like having an exciting program for a musical composition. Also, there was the painter's fashionable but slightly risqué widow, with two portraits hanging on the walls; his stepson and the latter's bride—they weren't hanging on the walls, but were an important part of the show nonetheless. Back of all this was the shrewd and skillful Zoltan, working to make the utmost of each of these various features.

The crowds on the opening day included a great part of the distinguished names in the worlds of both art and fashion. The press treated it like the opening night of the opera, when they publish two articles, one telling about the music and the singers, and the other about those present, their diamond corsages and ruby tiaras and double ropes of pearls. The critics said that the landscapes of Detaze represented a conventional but solid talent, while his later work, the product of the stresses of the war, could fairly be described as revelations of the human spirit. They called *Fear* a masterpiece, and said that *Sister of Mercy* contained real nobility combined with those elements of popularity which had caused it to be likened to Whistler's painting of his mother.

The result was that on the second day of the show Zoltan reported to Beauty an offer of fifteen thousand dollars for this picture, and a few days later the bidder, a great copper magnate, doubled his offer. It was a sore temptation for Beauty, but Lanny said no, he would never part with any of the paintings of his mother. Beauty didn't overlook the fact that they constituted an inexhaustible source of social prestige; she had had such a good time showing them and being shown in Paris and London, and she looked forward to Berlin and Munich and Vienna, Boston and Chicago and Los Angeles—perhaps even Newcastle, Connecticut, who could say?

They had greatly increased the prices of the paintings since the success in London; but it made no apparent difference to the public. New York was full of people who had money, and who felt about it as Irma did—what was it good for but to spend? It was the theory upon which the whole economic system was based; the more you spent, the more you made. It worked for the community, in that it kept money in circulation and goods pouring off the transmission belts of the factories. It worked for the individual, in that it brought him to the front, made friends for him, showed that he was on top of the wave, that his business was flourishing and his credit good. The maxim that nothing succeeds like success was old, but it never seemed so true as on the island of Manhattan in October of the year 1929.

The paintings were selling. Pretty soon there wouldn't be any left, and there couldn't be any more exhibitions! Zoltan raised the prices all the way down the line; presently he raised them again; but still they sold. People wanted to pay high prices; it was something to brag about. "You see that Detaze? I paid ninety-five hundred for it at the one-man show last year. Widener offered me twelve thousand a few days later, but I said no." The bank president or cement magnate would puff on his fat cigar and expatiate: "There's no better investment than a great painting. I keep it insured, and it's as good as cash in the bank. It may be worth more than my whole business some day. You know about that fellow—very tragic story—he had his face burned off in the war, and he used to sit on the Cap d'Antibes, wearing a mask, and paint the sea and the rocks." It wasn't quite so, but that didn't matter.

Irma's rich and fashionable friends—she had no others; how could she?—all came to see the pictures. All wanted to hear Lanny tell about them, and all said pretty much the same things. When Irma got bored, the pair would go out and have tea at one of the smart hotels, and dance for a while, and perhaps give a dinner party, and afterward return to the show rooms, because Zoltan had mentioned some important person who was coming. Irma might bring her dinner guests, for it was very "smart" indeed to be associated with paintings which caused the whole town to be talking about her husband and his mother. The glamour girl enjoyed being admired, and had sense enough to know that it was better to be admired for something else than her father's money. The town was "lousy" with rich people—such was the language of the younger set—but not many of the lice had a genius in the family. Also it was a good way to meet the whispers about "bastardy"; what was a social disgrace in America became romantic when associated with the art life of Paris.

III

After the show the happy young couple would repair to one of the night clubs. These had become elaborate establishments, decorated in gay modernistic style and serving every kind of liquor, just as if there was no such thing as Prohibition. In some you couldn't get a table unless you were considered a person of consequence, and you paid a "cover charge" as high as twenty dollars. There was a band of jazz musicians, and a clever and sophisticated master of ceremonies conducted what was called a "floor show," with singers and dancers who received high prices. From time to time the patrons danced; the saxophone moaned, the trumpets squealed, the drums thumped in desperate efforts to wake them up, but they danced monotonously like people walking in their sleep. Lanny had a feeling of pity for the entertainers, who worked so frantically to keep things going, to produce what was called "pep." The jaded patrons must continually have a new stimulus, otherwise they might stop to think—and what would they think?

When Lanny and Irma entered one of these places it was by appointment, and the moment they appeared the spotlight would be turned upon them, telling everybody in the place that celebrities were arriving. When they were seated, the master of ceremonies would make a little speech about them, and they would be expected to arise in the white glare and "take a bow." If they had been actors or people of that sort they would have made a little speech; but haughty society people, not knowing what to say, stood upon their dignity. After that the singers would sing to them, the comedians would interpolate a kidding remark or two, the Mexican guitar players would come and serenade them, the Gypsy dancers would ogle Lanny and display their seductive curves; the darlings of fashion would remain the center of proceedings until a movie star or a champion pugilist appeared.

The best of the show was reserved until after the theaters let out, when the place became crowded. Many people ate their principal meal of the day then, and paid the highest prices for the fanciest foods. There would be a great deal of drinking and excitement, and now and then a row, which was handled swiftly and efficiently by experts. Shootings were rare, and if you thought otherwise it was just because they got the headlines. Mostly it was what New York called fun, and it went on until the small hours of morning; free and easy, promiscuous, and democratic in the sense that if you had the "mazuma" you were as good as anybody who had no more. It was "café society," and in the public eye and in public esteem it had entirely replaced the old, dignified, and exclusive "Four Hundred" of pre-war days. The latter kind still existed, but no one paid any heed to it; its members might as well have been so many mummies in the Metropolitan Museum of Art.

Lanny, who knew life in France, now observed it in the land of unlimited possibilities. He remembered how he had met Olivie Hellstein, daughter of a great Jewish banking-house; what formalities had been necessary, what careful inquiries had been made. But in New York he might have been introduced to the heiress of the Barnes fortune by almost anybody in a night club. If he had had the nerve he might have come up to her and said: "Hello, Irma, I'm Lanny Budd—don't you remember me?" She couldn't be sure whether she remembered him or not, for she met so many young men, and if one was handsome and presentable it would be too bad to hurt his feelings. Any young man who had the right clothes and could make witty remarks might become a café celebrity, and have no trouble in finding some lady who had money to burn and would be glad to have him tend the fire. And it wasn't only in New York;

it was said that there wasn't a town of ten thousand inhabitants in the United States that didn't have a night club.

Lanny's duty as the guardian of the seed was to see that Irma ate the proper food and didn't drink too much. Also it was advisable for him to be right there at her side, leaving no space for any other male to slip in between. If he danced with some other girl, right away some agreeable youth would take his seat and begin what was called "making a pass" at Irma. Unless he was drunk, he wouldn't say anything offensive; on the contrary, he would be as charming as possible. He would make joking remarks about marriage, notoriously a tiresome and trying affair, a theme for banter on stage and screen; he would try to find out whether Irma was in love with her husband, or whether she was disposed to play with the idea of an adventure. If she showed herself reserved, all right, he would move on to the next young matron. Nobody took offense, for it was a game that all were playing. What was your money worth, if you couldn't have any fun?

IV

Lanny and his bride would return to their royal suite at two or three in the morning, and sleep until ten or eleven. Then they would have their baths, and have breakfast brought to them, also the morning papers. They would look first to see if there was anything about the show, and themselves as part of it; after that they would read about their friends in the society columns, and about the figures of stage and screen whom they had met or were planning to meet. Irma would want to know about the line-up for several of the football games in which friends were playing; and that would be all for her. Lanny would have liked to know about the war in China or the senatorial election in France, but it would be hard to find out without being rude, because Irma wanted to talk about the people they had met the night before, especially the dashing young man of fashion who had made a "pass" at her. If Lanny didn't listen, she would begin to think that the jokes about marriage had some basis in reality.

"Feathers" would come—that was Miss Featherstone, the social secretary—bringing a list of appointments made and requested. Then it would be time for the dressmakers and the *marchands de modes*—an urgent matter, since Irma had fallen behind on account of having eloped, and being on a yacht, and visiting at Newcastle. The urgency was the more extreme because the changes in style were so drastic. There was a great deal of complaint about them in the newspapers, and among the so-called intellectuals, who had fought hard for the emancipation of women and now saw them slipping backward. Some were saying they wouldn't stand for such absurdities; but the makers of fashion smiled, knowing that women would wear what they were told to, because there wouldn't be anything else in the stores.

But could you imagine that, ten years after women had got the ballot, after they had established their right to smoke in public places, to have their hair cut in men's barber shops, and to drink in men's bars—they would be going back to wearing skirts that touched the filthy sidewalks? And a thing called a "bertha," a deep lace collar, almost a cape, sewed to the neck of one's dress and hanging down to one's elbows! And "stays," a polite name for corsets, tight at the waist and restricting one's breathing! Up to recently a woman's whole summer costume might weigh as little as twenty-two ounces; but now there were going to be bows and ruffles and "princess slips," and eleven yards of material to a gown instead of four. Hats were going to be large, gloves long—and hair also. Back to Queen Victoria!

Most women went to their dressmaker, but not the heiress of the Barnes fortune. The "creator" whom she favored had a living model as much like Irma as possible, and fitted the "creations" on her. The work had begun as soon as Irma reached home, and now *couturier* and model would come to her hotel, and the finished product would be put on the model, and Irma would recline on a chaise-longue and survey the effect. It cost money to get your clothes that way, but it saved time and it got you the best. Each costume had a name of its own: Antoinette, Glorieuse, l'Arlésienne, and so on; each was sold with a guarantee that it would be unique. Of course others would steal the idea as soon as Irma appeared in it, but that wouldn't matter, for by the time that duplicates could be made, Irma would be done with hers and have passed it on to her subordinates.

It would have been unkind if Lanny had failed to assist in these habilitating ceremonials. He had such good taste, and so much experience at that kind of thing, ever since he was a small boy. He didn't approve of the new styles, but it was no good trying to fight them; if you didn't wear them it meant that you hadn't been able to afford new things—that was what "styles" were for. The steamroller passed over Lanny Budd again, and in the evening he escorted to the Detaze show room a lady with an elaborate lace train which compelled all the picture lovers to stop looking at pictures and look at her—if only in order to keep from treading on her train!

Such was the life; and Lanny was settled in his own mind that they were going to get out of it. He had the excuse of her pregnancy; surely she couldn't expect to wear "stays" after this fourth month! Later on, he would try to get her to nurse the baby, as Beauty had done with Marceline. But what after that? She wouldn't go on having babies indefinitely, not even to oblige the president of Budd Gunmakers. Would this crazy cabaret world continue to draw her like a moth to a candle-flame? He saw how excited she was over it, what pleasure she got from the spotlight, from seeing people turn their heads to stare when she entered a hotel lobby or any public place. She enjoyed giving interviews, and he saw that she was toying with the idea of having ideas; she would ask her husband: "Do you think I ought to say that people attach too much importance to money?" He advised her to go further and say that people were drinking too much, and that she herself was ordering mineral water. In her innocence she mentioned a certain brand, and Uncle Horace was amused, and told her that the manufacturers would pay her several thousand dollars for permission to publish that statement. A funny world to be in!

V

Lanny Budd, desiring to be known as a proper and dignified husband, satisfactory to Budds, Barneses, and Vandringhams, guarded his words and actions carefully. But he was living in a pitiless glare, and in spite of his best efforts he was drawn into a disagreeable bit of publicity. He escorted Irma into her favorite night haunt, and when they entered, a man sprang up from a table and came to them, calling Lanny's name, and then Irma's. At first Lanny didn't know him, but then realized that it was Dick Oxnard, the society painter whose villa he had visited on the Riviera and found inhabited by so many fair ladies. Nearly six years had passed since then, and it was hard to imagine such a change in a man; the fair blond giant no longer looked young and godlike, he looked middle-aged and decayed; half his curly hair was gone, and his face was bloated—he evidently had been drinking heavily.

But he still had the charm of manner, the gay laugh, and the prestige as a member of one of New York's old families. Everybody loved him, because he had been so generous and kind. "Well, well, Irma!" he exclaimed. "So this is the lucky fellow!" He caught her by the hand—evidently he knew her well, perhaps since her childhood. He caught Lanny with his other hand. "You lucky young devil, I spotted you for a winner, and now you've drawn the *grand prix!* Come over to my table and meet my friends!"

It was a public scene; the spotlight was on them. Lanny might have withdrawn his hand and said: "Excuse us, but we have other guests." It happened, however, that they didn't, and Irma appeared quite ready to go with her friend, drunk or sober. The husband followed, and came to a table well supplied with liquor, though it was decorously poured from a teapot into cups. There were three young ladies seated at the table, refined in appearance and elegantly dressed—but that didn't mean much. Was this free-and-easy painter intending to introduce Irma to some of his tarts? If he had said "Mary, and Jane," and so on, in his offhand manner, Lanny was prepared to lead his wife away. But no, all three had proper names. There was a vacant chair alongside the host's, but when Irma started to slip into it he exclaimed: "No, don't sit in that. Gertie has wetted it, the little bitch!"

Such was conversation among the smart set in their teacups. Lanny flushed with annoyance; but evidently Irma was used to the vagaries of the boys when they were "well lit up"; she laughed with the others, and a waiter hurriedly pulled the chair away and put another in its place.

"Why haven't you been to my studio?" demanded the painter, of Lanny.

"Have you a studio in New York?"

"A fine way to treat your friends! Tell him, Irma, have I a studio in New York?"

"Indeed you have, Dick; a grand one."

"I have painted some screens that will put your eyes out."

"I'll come," said Lanny, "as soon as the Detaze show is over."

"I've been meaning to get around to it. But there's so much they call art in this damned town. Irma, have you heard about the new bathroom I've painted for Betty Barbecue?"

"No, tell me."

"I've made her the finest sunken bath in the modern world. You're in a grotto at the bottom of the sea that seems made of precious enamel, all turquoise-blue and Nile green. Brilliant sea anemones grow up from the floor, and the crimson starfish and spiny sea creatures swim or crawl on the walls—by God, when the hidden lights are turned on it takes your breath away!"

"Well, I surely want to see it if she'll let me in."

"She's got to let you in! It's part of the bargain; she has to let anybody see it at any time."

"Even when she's in the bath?"

"She doesn't get in the bath. Would she take the risk of splashing the finest piece of interior decoration in New York?"

Oxnard was all right while he talked about art, and all right while he talked about Lanny. He made a joke of the fact that Irma's husband had come to his home and been so shocked that he never returned. He told Irma that if a good moral boy was what she wanted she had got him; the prettiest little blondine you ever saw had tried to ride off in his car and he had turned her down cold. Irma looked at Lanny affectionately and was glad to have this excellent report.

But then matters became less pleasant. The unfortunate female creature who went by the name of Gertie showed up at the table, which apparently she had left in a hurry. Dick Oxnard was in the midst of quaffing a cup of champagne when he espied her, and he set down the cup with a bang. "You dirty little bitch, get out of here!" he shouted. "Go on home to your kennel and don't come out till you're house-broke!" The poor child—she was little more than that—flushed in an agony of humiliation; tears came into her eyes, and she fled, followed by a stream of the foulest language that Lanny had ever heard in English. He knew a lot of it in Provençal from having played with the fisherboys; but he assumed that Irma didn't know it in any language, and being a good moral boy he didn't care to have her learn it.

He rose from the table and said: "Come on," and took her by the hand and led her to a remote part of the room. It meant that he had to summon the head-waiter and ask for a table; a conspicuous action, and a blow in the face of his host.

"Disgusting!" he exclaimed, when they were alone.

"Poor fellow!" said Irma. "He doesn't know what he's doing. He's drinking himself crazy, and nobody can do anything for him."

"Well, we couldn't stay there and let him drag us through such scenes."

"I suppose not; but it's too bad we have to do it in such an open way. He's furious about it."

"In the morning he won't know it happened," said the husband.

VI

They were seated, and ordered their supper, and Lanny was prepared to put the alcoholic unfortunate out of his mind. But Irma was so placed that she could watch him, and she said: "He's just sitting there glowering at you."

"Don't let him see you looking."

Their supper came, and they were supposed to eat it, but Irma had lost her appetite. "He's still not doing a thing but just sitting there."

"Pretend you don't see him, please."

"I'm afraid of him."

"I don't think he could do much damage in his condition."

A minute later the girl exclaimed: "He's getting up, Lanny! He's coming over here!"

"Don't pay any attention to him."

It took some nerve to sit with one's back turned and pretend to be eating supper, but that was what Lanny thought the situation called for. When the glowering blond giant was within a few feet of him, Irma stood up and put herself between them. Of course that made it necessary for Lanny to rise, too.

"So you think you're too good for me!" exclaimed the painter.

"Please, Dick, please!" pleaded the woman. "Don't make a scene."

"Who made a scene? Haven't I got a right to send a little bitch away from my table if I want to?"

"Please don't shout, Dick. We're old family friends and we don't want to quarrel."

"You were my friend before you ever met that damned little sissy. You come back to my table and let him stay here."

"Please, Dick, he's my husband."

"A hell of a husband!"

"Please be a gentleman and do what I ask. Go back to your own table and let us alone."

A critical moment. Some men would have pushed a wife aside and let the fellow have one on the point of the chin; but Lanny was sorry for this wreck of a man, and didn't wish to forget that he was or had been a genius, and had given Lanny a beautiful and valuable painting which was hanging in Bienvenu.

The drunken man raised his arm as if to push Irma away; and of course if he did that Lanny would have to stop him somehow. But at that moment Providence intervened in the shape of two husky gentlemen, one on either side of the belligerent painter. Some such form of *deus ex machina* has to be at hand in places where liquor is sold; in fashionable night spots they are immaculately clad, and never do any more damage than necessary, but they are capable, and the bulges of their shoulders are not cotton stuffing.

Lanny was relieved, and said: "Will you kindly ask this gentleman to leave our table and stay away?"

"Please, Mr. Oxnard, come back to your own table," said one of the "bouncers."

"So the little skunk has to holler for help!" exclaimed Oxnard. The men began to impel him, gently but firmly; apparently he had sense enough to know that he had to do what they told him—doubtless he had had experiences of the sort before. He made just enough noise to let the diners know what he thought of Lanny Budd, but not enough to cause the bouncers to "give him the works." They escorted him to his table, and one seated himself alongside and continued to speak soothing words. That was better than throwing him out, because he had many influential friends—and also he owed a considerable bill.

It was the thing known as a "scene." The spotlight had not been turned on it, but many people had watched it. The general opinion was that Lanny hadn't played a very glorious part, and so it appeared in the tabloids and the radio gossip. He tried not to let it worry him, and was satisfied that Irma appreciated his self-restraint. His comment was: "I wish we didn't have to go to those places." Furthermore he said: "I'll sure be glad when we return to Bienvenu and can get to bed before morning."

VII

Letters came to Lanny, reminding him of the life which he had lived, and which now seemed far away. Bess wrote, telling him of their rather stormy voyage and enclosing the program and press notices of a concert at which Hansi had played the Mendelssohn concerto with great *éclat*. "Hansi says he was playing it at Juan when Uncle Jesse came in and made a Red out of him!" How many ages ago had that been?

Rick wrote to say that he had found a small publishing-house that was willing to bring out his unorthodox book. He reported that Marceline was thriving, and enclosed a few lines from the child. Rick and Nina promised to come to Juan after Christmas as usual. Continuing, Rick referred to an event of the date on which he was writing: Ramsay MacDonald, for the second time Prime Minister of

Britain, was sitting on a log in a camp at Rapidan, Virginia, discussing peace and disarmament with President Hoover. Rick said he hoped they were getting somewhere, but he was losing faith in politicians. Even if Ramsay knew what to do, would Herbert let him?

Then a letter from Kurt in Stubendorf. He had a second son, and enclosed a snapshot. He was working hard on his first symphony, and sketched the opening theme, resolute and bold, *alla marcia*. He congratulated Lanny on his marriage, and hoped it would bring him happiness; he added that such great amounts of money put a heavy strain on the strongest character. Kurt might have said: "I know that yours will be equal to the test." But Lanny knew that Kurt didn't think that. Lanny himself wasn't sure about it, and he hoped that German newspapers didn't report the doings of café society in New York.

Kurt wrote: "I have just come back from Munich, where I met our Führer and heard him deliver a most inspiring speech. I have no hope that it will do any good to tell you about it, but mark my word that we have the movement of the future, and the man to lead Europe out of its present mess. If you don't find what you are looking for among the New York plutocracy, bring your wife and spend Christmas with us, and give Heinrich a chance to tell you about the youth movement he is helping to build." Lanny thought about that in the brief intervals when he had time to think about anything; he certainly wasn't satisfied with what he was finding among the aforesaid "plutocracy."

Also a letter from Lincoln Steffens, who was in San Francisco, writing his autobiography. Stef wrote notes to his friends in a tight little script that was as good as a crossword puzzle; if you once got going you might have quite a run of luck, but if you stopped for any single word you were lost. Stef said he had just met his little boy after quite an interval and found it exciting. He advised Lanny to have a boy as soon as possible. He said that he had known J.P. very well in the old days, and was indebted to him for taking him on the inside of the "merger racket." He concluded by saying: "If you are in the market, take my advice and get out, for the tower is now so high and leaning so far that one more stone may send it toppling.

You are too young to remember the panic of 1907, but after it was over a friend of mine explained it by saying: 'Somebody asked for a dollar.' Wall Street is in a condition now where it would break if somebody asked for a dime."

Lanny wasn't "in the market"; he was in pictures and matrimony, and that was enough. He forwarded this letter to his father, with a transcription written on the back. Robbie's reply was: "Just to show how much I think of your Red friend's judgment, I have purchased another thousand shares of telephone stock. It was up to 304 and I got it at 287½, which looks mighty good to me!"

That was the way they all felt, and the way they were acting; it was a phenomenon currently known as the "Great Bull Market," and people laughed at you if you tried to restrain them. Everywhere you went they were talking about stocks; everywhere they told about profits they had made, or were going to make next week. There was a "Translux," a device by which the ticker figures were shown on a translucent screen, in nearly every branch broker's office; such an office was to be found in most of the hotels where the rich gathered, and you would see crowds of men and women watching the figures. If it was during market hours, one after another would hurry off to a telephone to give an order to his broker. It was the same in every city and town; hardly one without a broker's office, and market quotations were given over the radio at frequent intervals. Farmers and ranchers were phoning their buying and selling orders; doctors and lawyers and merchants, their secretaries and errand boys, their chauffeurs and bootblacks—all were following the market reports, reading what the newsapers told them, eavesdropping for "tips" or following their "hunches." The country had got used to hearing about "five-million-share days" on the stock exchange, and took that for "prosperity."

VIII

Irma had become rather tired of listening to people saying the same things about the paintings of Marcel Detaze; and so, to tell the truth, had Lanny. One morning Irma said: "Mother's on the way to town and we're going to see what's in the shops. Would you like to go with us?" Lanny replied: "What I want is to take a long walk and look at New York. I don't see enough from the window of a limousine."

He set out from that temple *de luxe*, the Ritzy-Waldorf, in the direction where he knew the sun rose, though he couldn't see it from the bottom of these artificial canyons. He had learned how one half lived, and now he would observe the other half. In London it was the East End, here it was the East Side. What tropism guided the poor toward the rising sun? Was it because they got up early and saw it, while the rich didn't begin life till afternoon?

Anyhow, here were swarms of people; in O. Henry's day the Four Million, now the Seven Million. What was the limit to their crowding onto this narrow island? What was the force that would stop them? Fire, or earthquake, or bombs, perhaps? Or just plain suffocation? Some wit had said that the aim of every country boy was to get enough money to go and live in New York so that he could get enough money to go and live in the country.

Baghdad on the Subway! Lanny had read stories about it when he was young, and now he looked for the types, and it seemed to him that all were types. Nearly everybody walked fast; to stroll meant either a down-and-out or a policeman. Everybody was intent upon his own affairs, and stared straight ahead out of a thin, pale, intense face. If anybody bumped into you he didn't have time to excuse himself, he just dodged and went on. If you were in trouble, and stopped somebody to ask the way, he would come out of his trance of money-making, and tell you in a friendly enough manner where you were and how to get to the place of your desire; but as a rule it was understood that nobody had time for politeness.

Lanny came to the river, which he had seen from the deck of the *Bessie Budd*. The frontage had been given up to dingy tenements and sheds, but now the rich were taking sections for their penthouses. It made an immediate and rather startling juxtaposition of riches and poverty. Not so wise of the rich, Lanny thought—but doubtless they would get the poor cleared out very soon. If they wanted anything, they took it. What else did it mean to be rich?

He turned back into the interior and strolled south. Block after block, and they all seemed alike; mile after mile of dingy houses with brownstone fronts; if it hadn't been for the sun, and the signs at each corner, he might have thought he was walking in circles—or, rather, in rectangles. Everywhere streets crowded with traffic, sidewalks swarming with humans. How did they live? How could they bear to live? Why should they want to live? Indubitably they did all these things. You saw few faces that indicated happiness, but nearly all revealed an intense determination to live. It was the miracle of nature, repeated over and over, in antheaps, in beehives, in the slums of great cities.

So mused the young philosopher; an elegantly dressed philosopher, wearing the proper morning clothes, with only one button to his coat, and a small gardenia on the large lapel—it was one of the duties of the hotel valet to provide it. In the old days the saunterer would have been jeered at as a "dude," and some small boy might have shied a stale turnip at him; but now the boys were all in school, and anyone who had ten cents could see people like Lanny in a near-by motion-picture theater. No longer was there anything strange or annoying about a slender, erect figure with regular features, a little brown mustache, and clothes from Savile Row, London.

There was an Italian section, and stout brown women chaffering for dried garlic and strings of red peppers in front of tiny shops. Then it became a Jewish city, with signs in strange oriental characters. The tenements were obviously of the oldest, covered with rusty iron fire-escapes having bedding and wash hanging on them. The streets were filthy with litter—what taxpayers would consent to keep such streets clean? Old men with long coats and long black beards stood in the doorways of the shops, and the curbs were lined with little pushcarts having neckties and suspenders, hats and slippers, cabbages, apples, and dried fish. Women with baskets poked into the merchandise, examining it and bargaining in Yiddish, a kind of comical German of which Lanny had learned many words from his friends the Robins. Certainly everybody here was determined to live. How they did hang on! With what ferocity they asserted their right not to go under!

IX

Lanny knew that somewhere in front of him was the City Hall district, now at the height of a hot election campaign; also the Wall Street district, where for days the market had been in a state of instability. Lanny had started out with the idea of seeing these places, but they were farther away than he thought. He knew that there were subways by which, for a nickel, he could be whirled back to the hotel district in a few minutes; so he was in no hurry. He thought it might be interesting to talk to some of these people, to find out what they thought about the state of the world, and of their confused and bewildering city. People who didn't know that he was Mr. Irma Barnes!

A vague discontent had been in Lanny's mind; he was missing something in New York, and now, wandering among these dingy tenements, he realized what it was; he had no Uncle Jesse here, no Longuet or Blum, no Reds or Pinks of any shade. Nobody to point out to him the evils of the capitalist system and insist that it was nearing its collapse! Not even a Rick or other intellectual to tell him in highbrow language how wasteful was the system of competitive commercialism, and how diligently it was digging the foundations from under itself! Lanny had learned to require this mental stimulus, as much so as his glass of orange juice in the morning and his glass of wine at lunch.

There were bound to be some Reds in New York; where would one look for them? Lanny's thoughts turned to his old friend Herron, who had died a couple of years ago in Italy—one might say of a broken heart, because he could no longer bear the aspect which Europe presented to him. But his spirit lived on in a Socialist school which he had started in New York, with money left by the mother of that wife with whom he had fled from America. This had happened more than twenty-five years ago, while Lanny had been a toddler on the beach at Juan. Herron had told him about the school, but the young visitor racked his brains and couldn't remember its name.

It occurred to him that there must be a Socialist paper of some sort in this great metropolis, and a neighborhood like this would be the place to look for it. He stopped at a stand and inquired, and a copy of the *New Leader*, price five cents, was thrust into his hands. In format it was different from *Vorwärts*, *Le Populaire*, and the London *Daily Herald*, but its soul was the same, and Lanny, strolling along and looking at the headlines, was comforted at once. An editorial on the front page denounced Mayor Walker, Tammany candidate for re-election, as a waster and corruptionist, a frivolous playboy, a night-club habitué. Large headlines described a mass meeting at which Norman Thomas, the Socialist candidate, had promised to reduce the price of milk.

Lanny examined the few advertisements, and, sure enough, there was a box reporting the activities of the Rand School of Social Science. He recalled the name at once; Carrie Rand had been the name of Herron's wife. They were having lectures, courses, meetings of various sorts. Lanny walked to the nearest north and south avenue, hailed a taxicab, and got in, saying: "Seven East Fifteenth."

The driver gave him a second look, and grinned. "You a comrade?"

"Not good enough for that," was the modest reply; "but I know some of them."

"Fellow-traveler, eh?"

"I believe that's a Communist term, isn't it?"

"That's what I am, buddy."

So the ice was broken, and all the way up Third Avenue the driver would turn and explode his ideas at his fare. There is nobody more free-spoken than a New York taxidriver, and he doesn't have to be a Red, though of course that helps. His license on the dashboard has his photograph on it, so that you can look and make sure that he is the licensee; it is supposed to help control his driving, if not his tongue. This driver told Lanny about Tammany, and the crookedness of its politicians; also of the labor-skates and others who rode on the backs of the workers. "Incidentally, between you and me," said he, "that bunch at the Rand School are yellow labor-fakers. You don't have to believe what I tell you, but look out for yourself."

Lanny didn't object to these opinions; quite the contrary, they made him feel at home. It was the old phonograph record scratching away! "I've an uncle in Paris who's a Communist," he said. "His girl has a younger sister who is married to a Paris taxidriver, and he talks just like you."

"Naturally," responded the other.

"The party line," smiled Lanny. He would have enjoyed an argument with this lively chap—but only if he would stop the car somewhere. Weaving in and out among the iron pillars of the Third Avenue El, whizzing past a street car, missing another taxi by six inches, or maybe only one—Lanny found it difficult to concentrate his mind upon the problem of expropriating the expropriators. However, this was New York, and you lived dangerously if you lived at all.

X

Seven East Fifteenth Street proved to be a moderate-sized building with a brownstone front, having a proletarian drabness; it had once been the Young Women's Christian Association. Lanny gave his driver half a dollar for the cause, and received the reply: "Thanks, Tovarish." He entered and strolled into a bookstore provided with the familiar literature, including some from abroad, of which he bought a few specimens, smiling to himself at the thought of how they would look in the royal suite of the Ritzy-Waldorf. Then he asked for someone who could tell him about school courses, and was introduced to a young intellectual with fair hair and alert sensitive features.

"I'm an American who's been living abroad," said Lanny. "I'm not a party member, but I knew George D. Herron in Paris and Geneva, so I'm interested in the school."

There couldn't have been a better introduction. The two sat down, and Lanny gave his name as Budd, shivering a little inside, hoping the young comrade didn't read the capitalist press. The comrade gave no sign of having done so. Lanny knew enough about Socialist affairs by now to realize that there was one invariable rule, whether it was in Paris, London, or Berlin, in Rome, Cannes, or New York; all Socialist enterprises were running on a shoestring, and a party official who met anybody who might have money was driven automatically to think: "I wonder if he will help us!" Lanny preferred to get that part over with quickly, so he said: "I'll be glad to make a small contribution to the work of the school, if I may." Comrade Anderson graciously said that he might.

Seeing that the young official was well informed and companionable, Lanny remarked: "I've been taking a walk and I've got up an appetite. Would you have lunch with me?"

"We have a cafeteria in the building," replied the other; so they went into the basement, and Lanny chose from some dishes on a counter, and had a whole meal for less than he would have paid for his small glass of iced tomato juice at the Ritzy-Waldorf. "Comrade Budd" was introduced to several young people, and they all talked about the state of the world, and presently Lanny observed that a bright-faced Jewish girl was staring at him rather hard, and his skin began to crawl and the blood to climb into his face, for he knew that he was being recognized, or at any rate suspected. They would put it in the *New Leader*, and from there it would break into the "tabs." Unquestionably the prince consort was committing a major indiscretion!

But he stayed on, because Comrade Anderson was talking about the state of the market. There had been a slump in prices of late, and he said that stocks had been selling at from thirty to fifty times the amount of their normal earnings, whereas the proper ratio was less than half that. Anderson was giving a course of lectures on the present business and money situation, and had all the figures at his fingertips. "Do you realize, Comrade Budd, what the practice of installment buying has done to the country's finances?"

"I never thought about it," Lanny admitted.

"The American people owe seven billion dollars in the form of installment payments at the present time; and see how that has mortgaged the buying power of the country! It means that the manufacturers have got several years' business in one year; and where are they going to find new customers? It's the same as a man's spending several years' income in one year; what's he going to do the rest of the time?"

This gave Lanny a warm feeling. It had become an intellectual necessity for him to hear someone damn the capitalist system. He had fared so well under it himself that the world considered his attitude a perversity, but to Lanny it was a moral action, a tribute to the common humanity. Was he, living in the royal suite, to forget the existence of the millions in the tenements? His reason told him that the modern business structure was a house builded upon quicksand; he lacked the courage to start tearing it down—even if he had had the power—but he liked to hear some young intellectual start condemnation proceedings in the name of the working masses.

XI

After the lunch had been eaten and paid for, Lanny took his companion aside and gave him a hundred-dollar bill, perhaps the first such document that Tom Anderson had ever seen. "No, I won't give you my address," Lanny added. "I'll stop in some day when I'm in town." He made his escape quickly, because he saw the bright young Jewish girl whispering to one of her fellow-pupils, and he was pretty sure she was saying: "That must be the husband of Irma Barnes! Didn't you see his picture in the papers?"

Lanny strolled to Fourth Avenue and stepped into a taxi, saying: "Ritzy-Waldorf," and this time the driver didn't call him "Tovarish." He went into the hotel and found his wife and mother-in-law in the tea-room, having avocado salad and a fruit cup. "Where on earth have you been?" said Irma.

"Oh, I had a long walk. I saw the town."

"Where did you go?"

"All over the East Side, and away downtown."

"What on earth made you do that? There's nothing over there."

"I saw a lot of people, and they interested me."

"Don't you want some lunch?"

"I ate in a cafeteria. I wanted to see what it was like."

"What funny things you do think of!" exclaimed the wife; and then: "Oh, Lanny, Mother and I saw the loveliest diamond brooch!"

"Are you hinting for your husband to buy it?"

"I know you don't like diamonds, but I've never understood why."

"It's an out-of-date way of showing one's wealth," explained the bridegroom. "One has so much nowadays that one couldn't put it on, so it's more *chic* to look down upon the practice. Don't you think so, Mother?"

Mother was wearing a small diamond brooch and a large solitaire ring. She wasn't sure whether this strange new son-in-law was spoofing or scolding her, so she changed the subject. She had been looking at the market figures, and said that the break had become serious. She hoped Horace wasn't in the market too deeply. Was Lanny's father in?

Lanny said he was afraid so. He added that a break was to be expected, because stocks were selling at from thirty to fifty times their normal earnings, and that was twice too high.

"My brother has a different opinion," remarked Mrs. Barnes.

"Has he considered the effect of installment buying on our business situation?" inquired the son-in-law. "We have seven billion dollars of such obligations outstanding, and that is bound to cut down consumer power in the near future."

"Where on earth do you find out about such things, Lanny?" said his wife, with admiration in her tone.

38

Humpty Dumpty Sat on a Wall

I

THE day after Lanny's slumming expedition was Saturday, the nineteenth of October. The Detaze exhibition had been running for ten days, and was such a success that they were continuing it for another full week. Saturday being an important day, Lanny had promised to come over early; but first he stopped to look at the Translux —a habit more easy to acquire than to drop. It was not quite eleven o'clock, and he saw that the slump of the previous afternoon was continuing. He became worried about his father, and went to a telephone booth and called his office in Newcastle. "Robbie, have you seen the ticker?"

"Oh, sure," replied the father. There was one in the Budd office, and Lanny had observed that the carpet in front of it was well worn.

"Aren't you worried about it?"

"Not a bit, Son."

"Are you long or short?"

"I'm long on everything in the good old U.S.A. Believe me, I know what I'm doing. We had several bear markets like this last year; we had them this spring, and they were fine times to pick up bargains. The market drops ten points, and then it goes up twenty."

"Yes, Robbie, but suppose it changes about, and goes up ten and down twenty?"

"It can't, because of the underlying business conditions. Look at the orders piling up!"

"But orders can stop coming, Robbie; they can even be canceled. Do you realize that the American people owe seven billion dollars on installment-buying contracts? How can they go on ordering more things?"

Robbie wasn't so easily impressed as Irma. "Have you been talking to some of your Reds again?" He proceeded to turn the conversation around, urging his son against getting mixed up with such people in New York. Lanny was married now, and had responsibilities; he couldn't afford to make any more scandals!

"The Reds have got nothing to do with the question," insisted the younger man. "Anybody can look at prices and see they are too high —thirty to fifty times normal earnings of the stocks! How can that go on?"

"Because everybody knows that their normal earnings are bound to increase. Because we've got an administration that has sense enough to let businessmen alone and give them a chance to increase production, employment, and wages, all at one lick. Because nobody is listening to the croakers and soreheads—the people who tell us to sell America short!"

Lanny saw that he was wasting his time. He said: "Well, I wish you luck. If you run short of cash let me know, for we're banking some every day."

"Take my advice and buy Telephone this morning," chuckled Robbie. "My brokers have an office in your hotel."

II

Lanny and Irma went over to the show rooms. Phyllis Gracyn was coming; she was about to open a new show—it had just come in from a "tryout" in Atlantic City, and they had run into her at a night club. Lanny had told Irma about this adventure, now so far in the past, and Irma, who had curiosity about love affairs past or present, had been interested to meet the actress. Gracyn came, splendid in new silver-fox furs and the certainty of having another "hit" in the offing. But it turned out that she wasn't interested in Detaze that morning—she spoke of the market, and when she heard that Lanny had just been telephoning to his father, she wanted to know what that solid man of affairs thought about the situation. She had let a friend talk her into buying a thousand shares of Radio, and it was a lot of money for a poor working girl!

So it went, one person after another. Zoltan and Lanny were the only two of their acquaintance who were content to buy good stocks and put them away, and so didn't have to worry about the fluctuations of the market. Lanny was having to do a lot of arguing to keep his mother from being drawn into the whirlpool of speculation; everywhere she turned, people were telling her such marvelous stories—and offering her tips free of charge! One gentleman's butler had made three hundred and fifty thousand dollars by playing the information he had picked up at his master's dinner table; another's office boy had retired, having cleared forty thousand by following his own hunches. How could you lose, when everything was on the up and up?

Irma and Mrs. Fanny were going to a musical comedy matinee, so

Lanny had a "bite" with his mother and Mr. Dingle, who dropped in now and then at the show, but carefully kept out of everybody's way. If the man of God knew that a stock market existed, he never let on; he told them that he had found what he believed was an extraordinary medium: another of the poor and lowly, a Polish woman who sat in a dingy little parlor upstairs over a Sixth Avenue delicatessen shop, and charged you only two dollars for a séance, no matter how long it lasted. She wore a dingy Mother Hubbard wrapper, and her voice was frequently made inaudible by elevated trains roaring madly past the window; but her "control," an Iroquois Indian speaking with a powerful man's voice, declared that all the spirits of Parsifal Dingle's deceased relatives and friends were standing by, and Parsifal declared that they told him things which he himself had forgotten. If spirits were really there, it was important; possibly even more so than the question of whether the agent representing the Taft family would purchase two of the highest-priced Detaze seascapes.

The exchange closed at noon on Saturday, and after luncheon Lanny got an afternoon paper and read that the closing prices had "revealed great weakness." He went back to the show room and made himself agreeable to visitors, and later met his ladies at the hotel. Irma was giving a dinner party, and he had to advise her whether to wear the old Antoinette, which had made such a sensation, or the new Cerulean, which had been delivered that morning. Already there were imitations of Antoinette in the night clubs, but still it was lovely.

At the dinner party all the young people talked about the sensational market. Apparently there wasn't a single man or woman who wasn't "in"; some told what they had lost and some what they had gained, and all said what they thought was coming. It seemed to Lanny that they didn't really know anything, but were repeating what they had picked up here and there. The same thing was true of himself—the only difference was that they got their ideas from the New York *Herald Tribune*, while he got his from the Rand School of Social Science. To believe that prices were going up was patriotic, while to believe that they were coming down appeared slightly disreputable; so for the most part Lanny permitted his wife's guests to express themselves, which they gladly did, especially after the champagne had started flowing into the teacups.

III

Sunday was bright and warm, so they motored out to Shore Acres to play golf on their private course with friends who came in. At luncheon there was more discussion of the everlasting "market." Uncle Horace was there, bursting with energy and talking exactly like Robbie Budd; when stocks went down was the time to buy; don't lose your nerve, don't sell America short. Mr. Vandringham named the best of the "blue chips," from American Telephone and Telegraph down to Western Union and Westinghouse. There were more than twelve hundred stock issues listed on the Exchange, and as many more on the Curb, and no matter which one you mentioned, this vigorous operator knew all about it, the number of shares, common and preferred, the various classes of issues, A and B and so on, the number of shares outstanding, the prices and fluctuations as far back as had any meaning. Really, he was a walking *Moody's Manual;* he would say: "General Lawnmowers? Oh, yes, that's old Peter Proudpurse's merger, but the Fourth National crowd have got hold of it now, they've put Smith and Jones and Brown on the board, and they're taking in Amalgamated Carpettacks."

Lanny had spent his life learning the names of music composers and their opera, of authors and their books, of painters and their pictures. In the course of seven or eight years he had acquired a truly extensive knowledge of paintings and what they were worth. But now he saw that, if he was going to live with his wife's relatives and friends, he would have to learn about American corporations and their securities; if you had ears and a memory you just couldn't help it; and certainly you didn't want to be a dub, and cause chuckles as Lanny did when he assumed that Seaboard Air Line was an aviation concern, instead of a railroad to Florida. After all, there was a snobbery of the intellect as well as one of the purse, and it was no use overlooking the fact that these giant corporations were remarkable creations, dominating the age in which Lanny had to live.

So he questioned this large and voluble gentleman about what was going on, and received copious replies. He decided that his new relative wasn't such a bad fellow, in spite of being a "shark." Uncle Horace reported that three and a half million shares had been sold on the exchange in the two hours of Saturday, which was very nearly an all-time record. He said it was the result of the activities of a group of bear operators who had been pounding the market for weeks. As a result of such treatment it had revealed itself to be "spongy"; when the specialist at a certain trading-booth offered, say, one thousand Allied Chemical, he discovered that there was nobody wanting to buy Allied Chemical, there was just a blank space where there ought to have been customers. The order might be to sell "at the market," but there wasn't any market, and the broker had to go on offering at lower and lower prices, which was very bad indeed for morale.

Among those at the luncheon were two very wealthy ladies who had been invited to discuss possible operations for the morrow. Uncle Horace was proposing to form a "pool"; he explained that if stocks continued to decline, the bear interests would start to realize on their victory, and a shrewd operator, watching the signs and possibly having inside information, would step in and pick up some bargains. The market would undoubtedly rally, and he would make a "cleanup," all in a few hours.

Lanny learned from this conversation that his mother-in-law invited people to her daughter's home in order that her brother might get their money for his gambling operations. But that was all right, it was the way the game was played; they were all friends—at any rate so long as they made money. Lanny had been brought up in a home to which generals and cabinet ministers were invited so that they might order machine guns for their countries; in which a countess or other great lady would accept presents for acting as a "puller-in" for the munitions industry. For that matter, wasn't he using his wife's prestige to help sell his former stepfather's paintings? Perhaps when the Great Bull Market started its next upswing, he might be selling paintings to the ladies who had dipped some money out of Uncle Horace's pool.

It was a system of "you scratch my back and I'll scratch yours." Mr. Vandringham suggested that Lanny might put a little money into the pool; the prospects looked exactly right for a "killing." Perhaps it would have been good business for Lanny to do so, for his new relative might have been of use to him in various ways. But he excused himself by saying that he knew only one thing, pictures, and thought it wiser to stick to that. Uncle Horace said he respected Lanny's caution; certainly there was nobody more foolish than the untaught amateur trying to outguess the big fellows who devoted their lives to the Wall Street game. Having spoken, this particular big fellow bade farewell and hustled his bulky but vigorous self out to his car, to see some other persons who were going to fish in his pool next morning.

IV

Lanny and Irma drove back to the city. Lanny had got interested now, and watched the market from time to time on Monday. The same brokers who had a branch office in Newcastle had one in the Ritzy-Waldorf, and here on a translucent screen figures were continually appearing, from which you would learn what had happened on the trading-floor of the New York Stock Exchange a few seconds earlier: one thousand shares of Telephone stock had been sold at 276¼ per share, then two hundred shares of General Motors had brought 67⅝. On one side of the offices was a large blackboard with many small squares, and boys hung up cards having figures on them, while well-dressed ladies and gentlemen sitting in rows of chairs studied them attentively. Many customers remained through the five hours that the Stock Exchange was open; they had nothing to do but study these figures, and then go off and talk about them, and try to guess how they would move on the morrow.

The figures behaved exactly as Mr. Vandringham and Robbie had foretold. There was heavy selling early in the day, and prices dropped several more points; but after lunch there was what was called "strong support," and the market rallied. Lanny took this to mean that the shorts were covering, as Uncle Horace had said they would; Lanny assumed that Uncle Horace would be among the buyers, and later on he learned that it was so. The shrewd operator had bought at the moment when his chosen stocks were lowest. His pool, representing a million dollars in cash, had helped to check the drop; others had rushed in, sensing the turn of the market, and had forced the price up in the closing hour. In the last few minutes Uncle Horace had sold out, and had the pleasure of reporting gains of more than four hundred thousand dollars. Good news indeed for ladies who had come to Sunday luncheon at Shore Acres, and they hoped that Fanny Barnes would invite them soon again.

Profits in this nationwide gambling game were made several times as fast for the reason that you didn't have to put up the whole price of the stock; the buying was done "on margin." You put up twenty percent, and your broker deposited the stock at a bank which lent the rest of the money. The colossal scale on which these operations were being carried on was indicated by the fact that brokers' loans for that day were well over six billions of dollars. The thing called "Wall Street" was a machine of marvelous intricacy through which many millions of shares could be bought and sold between ten o'clock in the morning and three in the afternoon; the machine would arrange for the recording of all these transactions, the transfer of shares, the payment of the money, the deduction of commissions. Memberships in the New York Stock Exchange, which carried the right to operate on that trading-floor, represented a cash value of more than half a billion dollars. Lanny, introduced suddenly into the midst of this cosmic machinery, was quite awe-stricken by the spectacle. Events had happened so precisely according to the prediction of his relatives that he conceived a new respect for their judgment. The stocks of the Rand School of Social Science went down many points, and Lanny was sorry that he hadn't put a few thousand dollars into his new uncle's pool. Perhaps he'd come into the next one!

After his fashion, he tried to understand the meaning of the events he was watching. Uncle Horace and his friends had gained a lot of money which they hadn't earned. Who had lost that money? Lanny took it for granted that what one person gained another must lose; but the operator insisted that this wasn't so; the long-range trend of the market was upward, and thus millions were enriched without anyone's losing. Lanny wished he had had Stef here, so that he might ask him about that. After a while he decided that it was stupid not to think things out for himself, and so he went about with brow furrowed, resolutely trying to penetrate the mysteries of his country's financial system.

The greater part of the country's business was carried on by means of credit. People trusted you because they believed you had the money. So long as they believed, you could spend, and in this way a huge structure of speculation was built up; everybody counted upon having more, and so everybody spent more, and in such a world it was no longer possible to tell the difference between what was imaginary and what was real. But suddenly one man began to doubt, and he asked for a dollar; the other fellow didn't have the dollar, so he rushed off to get it, but he couldn't find anybody who had one; the demand for the dollar spread through the community, and was called a "panic." Thinking thoughts such as these was like walking on what you took for dry land, but suddenly you began to feel it heaving and shuddering, and you realized that it was a field of ice, and the hot sun was shining on it, and it was growing "spongy."

V

Parsifal Dingle had his own ideas of the difference between what was imaginary and what was real in this world. Mr. Dingle had made up his mind that his spirit was eternal, and on that basis the importance of what happened to it here and now could be mathematically determined. What was the relation of twenty-four hours to eternity? Or of threescore years and ten to eternity? This arithmetical problem has haunted the souls of mystics since the dawn of thought; for what shall it profit a man, if he shall gain the whole world, and lose his own soul?

Beauty's husband had become interested in certain souls which had "passed over" into that realm of eternity. He heard his wife and his stepson talking about who were buying Detaze pictures and what prices they were paying, but the sounds passed in one ear and out the other. Mr. Dingle was on the verge of making discoveries so important that he could think about them anywhere, whether he was in the Detaze show rooms, or in a hotel restaurant, or in a motor-car stalled in Fifth Avenue traffic.

To his wife he said gently: "I have learned through Madame Zyszynski that Marcel is waiting for you." So Beauty had to tear herself away from the elegant and famous persons who wanted to look at her and compare her with the two portraits on the walls— and allow her man of God to take her in a taxicab over to a dingy Sixth Avenue neighborhood, where poor down-and-outs stood in front of blackboards telling them that a cook was wanted in a lumber camp in Maine, or a dishwasher in a Bowery eating-joint at twelve dollars per week and two meals. The most elegant of ladies alighted in front of a delicatessen shop which had a cold turkey and half a boiled ham in the window, entered a narrow hallway lit by a dim gas-jet, climbed some creaking stairs, and entered by a door having the sign, "Madame Zyszynski: Medium."

The Polish woman had apparently got a new and clean gown in Beauty's honor; it was black, and had gold stars sewn on it. The medium herself was elderly, stout, and pudgy, with a kindly face, but entirely devoid of color, so that it looked like soft dough; her straight black hair was tied in a knot on top of her head and she was wholly devoid of charm. She said, in uncertain English, that the visitor would oblige her by sitting quietly while she went into a trance, and afterward until she came out. The name of her "control" was "Tecumseh," and the visitor might ask him questions, but please be polite to him and not excite him. After which she seated herself in an armchair, laid her head back, and presently began to moan and snort and jerk in a most disconcerting way.

Then she became still, and began to speak in a voice that was much deeper than her own, but still foreign. The voice said that a man was there, and he gave the name of Marceau, and he was happy, and he made pictures here also, and he still loved her—he said things that possibly might have been embarrassing to the new husband, had he not known that in the other world there is no marrying or giving in marriage, and no sense of possession. The messages went on and on, and Beauty began to shiver, for it seemed to her that Marcel was really speaking, and it was the same as in the old days. She was such a worldling that it had really never occurred to her that death might not be the end, and now she was so excited that the tears ran down unchecked and stained the front of the very lovely crape dress that she wore.

VI

Of course Lanny had to hear all about that experience. He had to consider every sentence that Beauty could remember, and say whether that didn't sound like Marcel. Lanny couldn't be sure, because his mother had been asking questions, and how many hints had she given? The Polish woman claimed not to know a word of what she was saying in her trance; that might be so and again it might not. But Beauty wanted it to be so, and was a little provoked that Lanny wasn't as enthusiastic as herself. She wanted him to go and have a try, and he promised that he would go after the show was over—they really owed it to Zoltan to stick by him in these crowded closing days.

But Mr. Dingle had time for God, and for all God's children in God's heaven; he had standing appointments with the medium twice every day, morning and afternoon; and right while the stock market was throwing all New York into convulsions—going down twenty points and going up ten—the very day after Uncle Horace had made his "killing," Lanny's stepfather came to him, saying: "There is a message for you, my son."

"Indeed?" said the son. "Who from?"

"The name wasn't given. But your name was."

"Have you ever mentioned me to Madame Zyszynski?"

"I have been very careful not to. I thought something might come through for you."

"Did you receive the message yourself?"

"No, a manicurist got it."

"A manicurist!" Really, that seemed too funny.

"A young woman had a séance early this morning, before she went to her work, and she wrote the message down. Madame kept it by her and asked all her clients if it meant anything to them. It is supposed to be in French, and neither Madame nor Tecumseh nor the manicurist knows any French. Tecumseh repeated it three times, and the girl wrote it the way it sounded." Mr. Dingle handed his stepson a scribbled piece of brown paper.

There was a trick sentence which Lanny had learned as a boy, and which he used to write out for his American and English friends to puzzle them. It is a sentence made of French words, *"Pas de leur Rhône que nous,"* and people would say it over and over, thinking French, trying to make it mean French, and failing to realize that they were speaking an English sentence. Now the trick was reversed; an uneducated girl had written something in American, and it was supposed to be read as French: "Brig addy ay voo zavvy rays on."

Lanny read it two or three times. He said it fast, the way you are supposed to say French; and suddenly he began to turn cold, and the strangest feeling ran over him—no, it wasn't entirely strange—he had had it once before in his life. Twelve years ago, but it was like yesterday in his memory; the hour just before dawn, when he had lain in his bed in his father's home, and had seen the first faint traces of light gather together and form an image of Rick, standing at the foot of his bed, mournful, silent, with a red gash across his forehead. Rick still bore the scar of that wound, which he had got when his plane crashed in France and left him at death's door, a cripple for the rest of his life. That had been Lanny's first contact with the supernatural—or at least what appeared to be the supernatural. Now here it was again; and here was that same creepy, crawly, cold feeling!

"Brigadier, vous avez raison!" It is the refrain of a humorous French ballad about a cavalryman who always agrees with what his riding companion says, no matter what may be the nature of it. It had

been in some book of Denis, *fils*, or Charlot, in that first happy summer when Lanny had gone to the Château de Bruyne, trembling a little over the strangeness of *la vie à trois* and wondering how he was going to make out in it. Such a good time they had all had—and that refrain had been one of the jokes with which they had amused themselves. All families develop such passwords to intimacy; and Lanny thought, suppose that Marie had wished to say to him: "I am here, waiting for you"—what could she have contrived that would tell him more certainly than the foolish little verse, which had not crossed his mind in so many years? *"Brigadier, vous avez raison!"*

VII

Lanny dropped the picture business and the stock market, and took his stepfather's appointment for the next morning. He sat and watched the pudgy old woman go into her trance, and listened with strained attention to every word that was spoken by the alleged Tecumseh. The visitor came away in that state of tormented uncertainty which dogs the lives of so many truth-seekers in those dim regions of the subconscious. "Marie" had given her name; but then it was a common name, and how could he be sure that his mother or his stepfather had not spoken it in some unguarded moment? And what about the stories of spiritualist mediums making elaborate notes and exchanging data about likely prospects? What Marie said to him through the voice of Tecumseh was what she would have said; but then it was what any woman would have said to the man she had loved and left behind. She wished him happiness in his new love; but wouldn't any woman in the spirit world do that?

Also there was the possibility of what people called telepathy; "mental telepathy," they said, meaning to distinguish it from American Telephone and Telegraph! Of course nobody knew what telepathy might be or how it would work; it was just a word, but it helped you, because it seemed easier to believe that somebody might dip into your subconscious mind and pick out something—than that the universe was full of spirits, whispering messages to an Indian, to be spoken by the vocal cords of an old Polish woman for a price of two dollars. If the spirit of Marie had wanted to talk to Lanny, wouldn't it have been easier for her to do it that night when he had come back to her home and lain in her bed?

Lanny voiced this idea to Parsifal Dingle, who replied: "Suppose that a hundred years ago somebody had told you that it might be possible to send messages under the ocean, would you have believed him?"

"I suppose I'd have been dubious," admitted the other.

"Suppose someone had said: 'It will not be possible to send the message through the water, but only through a copper wire wrapped in the extract of a tropical tree'—that would have sounded rather odd, too."

Lanny admitted that it was all rather odd; in fact, he had been finding life that way ever since he had begun to think about it instead of just living it. Now he had a new oddity to put with the many others. *"Brigadier, vous avez raison!"*

VIII

Lanny's mother-in-law resented the trustees of her late husband's estate, but she had to manage to get along with them. Mr. Joseph Barnes had come out to Shore Acres to call on the bridal pair; but the other two trustees, Mr. Marston and Mr. Keedle, having been employees of J.P. most of their lives, were not sure of their social status and were awaiting an invitation. Irma had promised to take Lanny to the office to meet them; but it was such a dull duty that she kept putting it off. Now the mother telephoned, saying: "Really, dear, it's a great discourtesy." So Irma said to Lanny: "Let's go this afternoon and get it over with."

Accordingly, Lanny phoned to Uncle Joseph and made an appointment. The office of the estate was in one of the great office buildings on lower Broadway, and they motored down through heavy traffic; the pressure was such that the chauffeur would have to go a considerable distance to park, and when he came for them he would have to drive round and round the block until they appeared. A car had become more of a nuisance than a convenience on this jam-packed island of Manhattan—which had been bought from the Indians for twenty-four dollars, but now you would pay that price for as much space as the tip of your finger would cover. Now upon this soil had arisen the most amazing of the works of man: a congeries of buildings, from fifty to a hundred stories high, turning the streets into narrow canyons or clefts of granite. If all the people who worked in these warrens had come out of them at once, they would have filled the streets several layers deep. You entered an express elevator, a little silent cell; when it started you felt your entrails sink, and when it stopped they surged up against your heart and lungs.

Uncle Joseph was a tall, distinguished-looking gentleman, like his deceased brother; always well dressed, rather pompous in manner, but friendly enough when you knew him. He had an odd hobby of collecting specimens of the old-time American dime-novels upon which he had been brought up; since Lanny was also a lover of literature, this was a bond of fellowship between them. Uncle Joseph had been a sort of chief clerk for the more brilliant and daring elder brother, and now it was a religion with him to see that Irma's capital was properly guarded. What she did with the income was none of his business—unless she would permit him to reinvest it in "blue chips." He hoped that Lanny would be on his side in controversies over this subject, therefore he cultivated the young man with extreme politeness. His suavity was that of the head-waiter in the main dining-room of the Ritzy-Waldorf, and both of them appeared to Lanny as priests who worshiped with the utmost devotion a wooden idol with no brains in its head.

Irma's father had bequeathed an annuity to Mr. Marston and Mr. Keedle, the other trustees, in order that they might devote their time to watching each other. They were, if possible, even more anxious to please than was the uncle; they bowed and beamed, and told how honored they were, and escorted the young couple through the rooms and showed them typewriters and adding-machines and filing-systems, and introduced them to the head clerk by name, and to the other clerks by a wave of the hand. To Lanny it would always be embarrassing to be mistaken for divinity, but he had to learn to look as if he didn't mind it. He and his wife sat down in Uncle Joseph's private office and permitted the three gentlemen to explain upon what principles and by what methods they managed the property. Now and then the bridal pair would nod gravely, expressing their satisfaction.

IX

Lanny, really trying to understand the great metropolis and the things that went on in it, perceived that these three conscientious gentlemen lived and operated in a world entirely controlled by pieces of paper. Not motor-cars and jewels, not even palaces and land were the basis of the Barnes fortune, but a few pieces of paper called "securities," which were worth more than their weight in anything in the world, even radium. In the estate office were other pieces of paper, a cardfile which listed all the facts about each of the precious ones. Yet other pieces called dividend checks came at regular intervals, and Uncle Joseph signed some more called receipts—and so it went on, day after day, and would go on, world without end. Uncle Joseph knew that it would, because he had the right to name his successor, and was training his oldest son in the office, and had named him in proper legal form—on a piece of paper.

For the keeping of the securities, Irma's father had found a place where surely neither moth nor rust would corrupt nor thieves break through and steal. It was a private compartment in the vault of one of the three biggest Wall Street banks, where all the resources of modern science had been utilized to contrive a really secure hiding-place for treasures of this sort. Uncle Joseph invited them to inspect it, and Lanny thought it would be interesting, or pretended to. Irma's father had shown it to her, but she went along for politeness. The great bank was only a few doors away. Their coming was announced by telephone, and they were escorted to the office of the great financier who presided over the institution and who assigned one of the thirty-seven vice-presidents to conduct the distinguished visitors to the vaults.

You descended in an elevator, for they were a hundred feet or more below the surface, cut into the solid rock of Manhattan Island. They were, in effect, a steel box as big as a good-sized house; or rather, a series of boxes, such as the Chinese make, each fitting inside the next. The outermost box was of concrete, and the others of steel. Into the space between two of the steel walls one could, by pressing a lever, introduce hydrocyanic gas, which would instantly kill any living thing. Into the layer next to the concrete a heavy stream of water could be poured, filling it entirely, and flooding any hole or passage which might be dug. In the innermost of the surrounding spaces was a walk, and a man paced round and around it, and there was an arrangement of mirrors whereby he could see all four walls of the vault, and under it and over it. The man was locked in at closing time with a time-lock and could not get out until his time was up; he paced around and around looking into the mirrors, and each time he completed a round he pressed a button, and if he failed to press it within a certain time an alarm bell rang in the nearest police station.

Thus Uncle Joseph thought that the Barnes fortune was safe from mobs and marauders. He wasn't worried when the price of stocks went down, for what the estate owned it owned outright; the stocks were a share in the producing power of America, which couldn't fail for long. However, the conscientious Mr. Joseph Barnes had worried a great deal over the fact that the heiress of this tremendous fortune went out so freely into a world consisting largely of night clubs, where she met handsome young men, a percentage of whom were scoundrels and an even larger percentage wasters. Uncle Joseph's heart had been in his mouth when he received word about the elopement; but now he was relieved, for this seemed to be a fairly decent sort of young fellow; rather airy, one might say flighty, but well meaning and apparently open to instruction. The keeper of the treasure was watchful and attentive, and took every occasion to impress upon Lanny the gravity of his responsibilities as bearer of the seed and maker of the future.

X

The next day was Wednesday, the twenty-third of October, and Lanny went over to the show room, where he heard the good news that the Taft family had purchased the two seascapes. At lunchtime, when Lanny looked at the Translux, he found that the market was beginning to slump again. Mrs. Barnes had come to town; she had had a call from her brother, who was getting up another pool, and she was putting in her "pin-money," a matter of ten thousand dollars. Irma was tempted, but she had given her father a solemn promise that never in her life would she buy a share of stock on margin, and when she heard about the Dingle family's experience with the spirits, she was more than ever afraid to break her word. Lanny saved her from temptation by inviting her to come to the show rooms and meet the Honorable Winston Churchill, who was reported to be coming.

When they came out, in the latter part of the afternoon, the newsboys were shouting: "Panic in Wall Street!" Lanny read more talk about sponginess, avalanche of selling orders, Niagara of liquidation, complete absence of support. The ticker was two hours behind the market. The bond ticker was giving selected prices for some of the "blue chips," and showed losses around twenty points, most alarming. Lanny stopped at the hotel for a look at the Translux, and found that he couldn't get into the room; it was packed with men and women, and on the edges he noticed the worried faces and heard the anxious talk. The closing hour had been terrible, and nobody knew yet what had happened.

Irma's smart friends talked about nothing else at teatime, or at dinner, or in the evening. Nobody cared what the Right Honorable Winston Churchill had said about Detaze, nobody cared whether Lanny had had a message from his *amie* in the spirit world. A six-million-share day—think of it! And what was coming tomorrow?

Mrs. Fanny had been trying to get in touch with her brother, but his line was constantly busy. She knew that her money had been put in; had it been got out again? Lanny phoned to his father at dinnertime, and learned that he was still at the office, which in itself meant that he was worried. Yes, he admitted he was in the market rather heavily; but it was all right, he was sure that prices would rally. Low prices always brought out the people who bought for investment. Don't sell America short! However, Robbie added that he was arranging to have cash in hand in case of need. Lanny said: "If you get in a jam, let me know."

Mrs. Fanny heard from her brother at last. He hadn't been able to close out his pool; the bears had had everything their own way. But prices were sure to rally in the morning. Uncle Horace had invested a couple of million dollars on a twenty-point margin; that is, he had bought ten million dollars' worth of stocks. If the price continued to drop, his brokers would call for another ten percent, so he would have to have a million dollars in a hurry; better be on the safe side and have it ready. Would Fanny get her share to him the first thing in the morning?

Fanny didn't have it, and came to Irma, who said: "Of course," and wrote a check for five thousand dollars. Irma didn't often write checks, it was too much trouble. She had promised Mr. Slemmer, her business manager, that she would never write a check of any size without letting him know; he kept no large balance, because the banks paid only two percent on checking-accounts, whereas good investments paid six or more. Mr. Slemmer was a very careful man, and insisted on saving money for Irma, whether she wished him to or not. The girl said to Lanny: "It's a nuisance, but I promised him, so you'd better phone him."

Lanny called the manager's home, on the Shore Acres estate, and was told that he had gone to the city and hadn't returned. Lanny left the message, and Irma remarked: "I wonder if he's in the market, too." She said it casually, rather taking it for granted that he would be. Everybody was.

They talked about little else but stocks. Irma couldn't understand panics, and Lanny had to explain them. It was hard for the Barnes heiress to comprehend why everybody didn't have plenty of money, and why, if more was needed, the government didn't print it. Absurd for people to be in want! Lanny tried to explain that if it were not for the poverty of the poor, the riches of the rich wouldn't be of much use to them. Irma said: "Lanny, you're just trying to make me a Pink like yourself!"

Anyhow, she didn't approve of panics; everybody worrying and rushing about, trying to get money in a hurry. She refused to have anything to do with them, even as a spectacle, like a storm on the ocean, to be watched. Uncle Joseph had suggested that Lanny might be interested to come down some day and see the Stock Exchange in action, and now Lanny said: "Tomorrow would be a good day. Wouldn't you like to be there at ten o'clock, to see what happens when the gong sounds? It ought to be a show."

"For heaven's sake!" exclaimed Irma. "Get up and go downtown at that hour, just to see a lot of brokers buying and selling stocks?" She was being fitted with her winter wraps, and that was important. However, she said, obligingly: "You go, if you really want to see it, and I'll have them wait until you get back. You won't stay long, I'm sure."

"I'll take the subway," he replied. "They tell me it's a lot quicker."

Irma declared that he'd have the breath crushed out of him; but Mrs. Barnes said no, the laboring classes traveled at seven, the clerks at eight, the businessmen at nine, and by nine-thirty the subway was quite comfortable. Many impatient people rode down for a nickel instead of using their cars. She had done it herself.

Thus reassured, Lanny called Uncle Joseph at his home, and that obliging gentleman agreed to meet him in front of the Exchange building promptly at five minutes to ten. Incidentally he said: "I hope that Horace isn't in the market too deep, for things look very serious." Then he added: "Irma and Fanny will be glad that the estate is not involved."

Lanny answered: "They ought to be!" He had to be careful not to reveal any secret from one clan to the other.

Uncle Joseph said: "Be sure to be on time. I'll have the admission cards ready."

Lanny hung up the receiver, smiling. More pieces of paper! What would they do when they got to the pearly gates, and St. Peter asked them for their admission cards?

39

Humpty Dumpty Had a Great Fall

I

THE large and splendid building of the New York Stock Exchange on Broad Street had a great crowd in front of it that Thursday morning: persons who had no way to get cards of admission, but must be content to stand in the street and try to imagine what was going on inside. The visitors' gallery was large, and crowded by several hundred selected persons. One of the first whom Lanny saw was the Honorable Winston Churchill, a pudgy but energetic gentleman whom he had first come to know at the Peace Conference, where he had labored to persuade the Allies to make an end of Bolshevism and the Bolsheviks.

The gallery looked down into a vast hall, having on one side so many tall windows that it was practically a wall of glass. The north and south walls had giant blackboards divided into squares, one for each of more than twelve hundred brokers; each broker kept one eye on his square, and when his number showed up he knew that his office wanted him on the phone. Under the board behind brass rails was an enormous telephone exchange with a row of operators; it was not supposed ever to happen that a broker would not be able to reach his office at once. Fortunes were at stake, and the fraction of a second might mean the difference between success and failure.

The obliging Mr. Joseph Barnes explained the mechanism of this great institution. On the trading-floor had once stood what were called "posts," at which certain stocks were dealt in. In those days a broker had made his memoranda in a notebook; but now the business had grown so that each broker had to have a clerk, and trading-posts had been replaced by horseshoe-shaped booths, with a shelf inside at which clerks could work recording orders. These clerks were required to wear uniforms, so that by no possibility could any one of them ever impersonate a broker. There were great numbers of boys serving as messengers, but they weren't big enough to impersonate anything except monkeys, said Uncle Joseph.

Nowadays the greater part of the trading was in the hands of so-called "specialists," men who stayed at one trading-booth and dealt in one particular stock. That made it easier for everybody, because you knew where to make a bid or to look for one. You could tell the specialists because each carried under his arm a peculiar sort of book, eighteen inches long and only three inches wide. Its pages were numbered according to the prices of the stock in which he traded; if U.S. Steel moved to 205, the specialist would turn to that page and see instantly what customers had ordered him to buy or to sell at that price. Steel might stay there for only a second or two, but that was longer than it took to act: the calling of an offer by one man and a sign of acceptance from another.

Ordinarily the elderly and more important brokers sent their subordinates to the trading-floor, but now everybody sensed a crisis, and the big men were on hand. The floor was crowded; every eye was on the great clock; you could see the hand slowly moving, and when it neared the moment, people seemed to hold their breath. Suddenly there was the crash of a gong; then—Lanny had read many times about "pandemonium breaking loose," but the first time he ever saw it was at ten o'clock on the morning of the twenty-fourth of October in the year 1929. More than twelve hundred men leaped into action at the same instant, all yelling at the top of their lungs. The sound of it shot up to the visitors' gallery, hit the high ceiling and bounced back, and from that time on there were millions of sound waves, clashing, mingling, beating one another to pieces. It was like no other volume of sound in the world; it couldn't be compared to a stormy ocean, because there are different waves and you hear each one, but you never heard any particular shout, no matter how loud it might be. The medley did not diminish while Lanny stayed in the gallery, and when he went out into the street he heard it there, though all doors and windows of the building were closed, the ventilation being from the roof.

Swarms of men jammed around each of the trading-booths, all raising their hands and waving them, dancing about. They were offering either to buy or to sell stocks; and of course whenever one bought, another had to sell, and vice versa. If buyers and sellers were equal in number, sales could be made quickly, and without excitement or strain. The frenzy meant a great excess of buyers over sellers, or the converse. Which was it? Not merely those in the visitors' gallery but all America waited for the answer.

At five places on the floor sat men at a sort of overgrown typewriter, and the moment a sale was made the clerk carried a record of it to one of these men, who typed it on his machine, and by an ingenious mechanism the results of all five of these typings were combined in one stream of figures on a ticker tape. Three underground floors of this great building were full of electrical apparatus of unbelievable complexity, whereby this precious stream of figures was sent out with the speed of lightning to three thousand places in the financial district, and by Western Union to four thousand other places scattered over the United States. Above the call board in the trading-hall was a big translucent screen, and the figures appeared here, so that both brokers and visitors could see them. The first sales were big, and the first prices were down; somebody was dumping blocks of ten and twenty thousand shares onto the market.

Twenty thousand shares of some "blue-chip" stock which is selling at 400 is eight million dollars, and that is big business on any trading-floor in the world. It couldn't be the bootblacks and messenger boys, the maidservants and farmers' wives who traded through the "odd lot" houses; it could only be the great banks seeking to protect their position, the operators who had got a fright, the investment trusts, of which there were five hundred, grown overnight like mushrooms, all assuring the public that their function was to "stabilize the market" and protect investors by spreading their holdings among the best stocks. Now they were dumping their stocks, and it was a panic.

II

The specialist in U.S. Steel who had orders to sell "at the market" had no choice; he had to go on offering. He shouted 200, and if no one answered he had to shout 199, and then 198; it seemed like the end of the world to him, but presently he would be shouting 190, and no takers. The specialist would hardly dare to open his book, for he knew that he had "stop loss" orders by the score and perhaps by the hundreds at those different prices, and what was he going to do with them all? When he made a sale, he could see that it didn't appear on the Translux; he saw there sales that he had made ten minutes ago, half an hour ago, so he knew that the ticker was overwhelmed by the rush of selling. He no longer knew where he was or what was happening; it was like having the earth drop out from under his feet.

The ticker designated the different stocks by key letters: X for U.S. Steel, R for Radio, GM for General Motors, WX for Westinghouse, and so on. The sales recorded showed that Radio had lost one-sixth of its value in the first hour; General Electric, which had been over 400 a few weeks ago, was dropping under 300. Uncle Joseph shouted into Lanny's ear: "I never saw anything like this in my life." Lanny shouted back: "What is going to happen?" The answer was: "I can't imagine."

Irma had said that it would be monotonous, listening to brokers shouting; and so it was after a while. There was no change, except that the clamor grew even louder, the signs of confusion greater. There was no way to find out the prices actually prevailing on the floor. Lanny began thinking: "What is happening to Robbie?" He shouted: "Let's go," and they went out, and right away there was a mob around them, crying for news of what was going on. They answered as well as they could, and pushed their way onward.

"The worst panic in Wall Street's history," said Joseph Barnes; "at any rate, the most sudden."

"I must call my father," said the younger man. "Shall we go to the office?"

The street was so packed that it was a job getting through, even in the middle. Lanny, being more active, said: "Excuse me if I run." Others were doing the same, without making any excuses. He arrived breathless at the estate office, where everybody fell upon him. "What is happening?" They were all excited, whether they were "in" or not.

Lanny put in a phone call for his father's office, and got the reply: "The line is busy." It was that way everywhere, Mr. Keedle said; you couldn't get anything in Wall Street, you could hardly get a broker's office anywhere in the United States.

It was easy to imagine what was happening. Wall Street had built the most perfect machine in the world to enable the American people to buy stocks, and now the American people were turning the machine around and using it to sell stocks—or to try to. The opening prices had appeared on many thousands of ticker tapes and illuminated screens; they had gone out over scores of radios. There were three hundred million shares of stock held on margin, and most of the owners had the same impulse at the same instant—to pick up the phone or rush to the telegraph office and put in an order: "Sell at the market!"

Uncle Joseph arrived, breathless. He had just learned from a friend that Telephone was below 270—the stock which Robbie Budd had been so happy to get for 287½. Lanny tried again, and was told that the trunk lines to Newcastle were all busy. He decided that there was no use sitting there waiting, what was needed was action; his father might be wiped out in the next few minutes. The brokers called on you for more margin, and if you didn't put it down on the counter, they sold you out. In a time such as this, influence, even friendship, counted for nothing; either you went down or your broker did, and no brokers were going to fail in this panic.

Lanny wrote out a message for his father. "I have three hundred thousand dollars in the bank and I am going to get a certified check and take it to your brokers' office in the Ritzy-Waldorf and have them notify your Newcastle office that they have it. Also take my stocks which you have. Borrow on them or sell them if you need to." Uncle Joseph promised to deliver this message as soon as the call came through.

III

Lanny made a dash for the subway, glad enough of this plebeian, five-cent form of transportation. The money he had was what Zoltan had deposited from the picture sales, after deducting his own commission. By right only one-third of it was Lanny's, but he had the handling of it, and he would act first and justify afterward. When the subway train came to Grand Central station he darted out, and into a taxi which took him to the bank. He gave the driver a dollar, and said: "Wait for me," ran into the bank, wrote the check payable to the brokers, and presented it to be certified. It was a world in which you wrote three hundred thousand dollars or three million as casually as you wrote three; the bank officer would step to the books to make sure you had it, and then write the bank's certification on it, and it was as good as U.S. currency. "Pretty wild times, Mr. Budd," the man remarked, sympathetically. Lanny, having been in New York for three weeks, replied: "You said it!" and was gone.

"Ritzy-Waldorf," he ordered the taximan, and gave him another dollar and dashed to the brokers' office. The place was packed to the doors; if he had been an acrobat he could have gone all the way to his goal on the shoulders or the heads of other men and a good many women. Prices were being shouted in horrified tones. The market level was down twenty points and some stocks had lost thirty to forty. Radio had lost a full third of its value. It occurred to Lanny that there might be a private entrance to the brokers' office—he was used to being taken in at such places. He found it and banged and kicked until it was opened; then he put his foot in it and waved his check—another piece of paper, and a good one. He asked for the manager, and went right after him without waiting for permission. Easy to recognize him by the fact that he sat at a desk with five telephones, trying to use them all at once.

Lanny slapped the check in front of the man and said: "I am Robert Budd's son and this is for my father's account. All I want is for you to notify your Newcastle branch that you have this money."

"I'll do my best, Mr. Budd," replied the man, who had beads of perspiration dropping from his brow.

"That isn't enough," declared Lanny. "You've got to do it."

"Here," replied the man, in between sentences of another conversation. He shoved Lanny a phone which didn't happen to be ringing. Lanny took it and put in a call for Newcastle, and for at least half an hour he sat there, worrying the operator, and between times learning about the life of a branch manager of a brokers' office. It consisted of saying: "I am sorry, we had to sell you out," or else: "I am sorry, we will have to sell you out unless you produce more margin before noon."

The telephone operator kept saying: "All trunk lines busy, sir." Apparently she wasn't allowed to say anything but a formula, no matter how mad you got or what you said. Whatever panics might do to Telephone stock, they were not permitted to affect telephone service.

Finally she said: "I'll give you the supervisor," and Lanny fussed at this official, who promised to try for him. So finally he got the brokers' office in Newcastle, and Lanny demanded the manager, and told his story, wondering if this man also was talking through five phones at once. He got the two managers together, and heard the New York one state that he had three hundred thousand dollars for the account of Robert Budd. That was all; they didn't tell him anything about the state of Robbie's account. "I hope everything is all right," said the New York man, and then started saying into the telephone: "I am terribly sorry, Mrs. Archibald. You will have to have a twenty-percent margin here in the next half-hour, and be prepared to put up another twenty percent if the market continues to drop. We may be demanding seventy-five-percent margins before closing time. This is the worst in my experience and we can make no exceptions."

IV

Lanny went upstairs to his rooms. How funny to find his wife reclining in a chaise-longue looking at the art creations of Bernice, *robes et manteaux,* and waiting for Lanny to come and tell her whether black furs or brown were more becoming to her warm brunette coloring! "There's a frightful panic in the Street," he said. "Everybody we know may be wiped out." That scattered them. Madame Bernice and her two assistants rushed off to find a telephone and put in their "stop loss" orders; meanwhile Lanny sat at his own phone and put in a call for Newcastle. The same reply: "All trunk lines are busy. We will call you."

He did what he had done before, made a fuss; of course he was gumming up the telephone service, and thousands of others were doing the same; it was *sauve qui peut.* Finally he managed to get his father's office, only to learn that Robbie was out; the secretary said he had gone to see Mr. Samuel Budd. Lanny could guess what that meant: Robbie was trying to scrape up some cash. The secretary said, very discreetly, that Mr. Robert had not told him anything about his position in the market. Lanny told what he had done, and asked the secretary to get the brokers' office and get a confirmation of the receipt of the money. He added: "Tell my father to call me at my hotel. I'll wait here in my room."

Then Lanny telephoned his mother at the show rooms, and asked her to come to him. She had heard that there was a panic; one could have told that by the way the crowd had melted away from the show. She said: "Is anything wrong with us, Lanny?" He wouldn't talk over the phone. "Take a taxi and come at once."

It was between twelve and one, the worst hour of the panic. The blue chips were tumbling, several points at a time, and one time right after another. The worst of it was that the ticker was an hour and a half behind the market, and there was a spread of thirty points between the prices quoted and those actually prevailing. So no one knew what to believe or to expect. Everybody you knew was in, and every last one of them might be ruined. Irma's large and majestic mother was pacing the floor in an agony of dread because she couldn't get into touch with her brother. "Feathers," the elegant secretary, was pale, but silent, not telling anybody what her losses were. Parsons, Irma's maid, was weeping silently in a corner because she

had put all her savings into Montgomery Ward and the chamber-
maid had just told her that it had gone from 83 to 50.

Beauty came in, and Lanny took her into his own room and shut
the door, and told her what he had done. She went dead white, except for her war-paint. "Oh, Lanny, how *could* you!"

"Think it over, old girl," he suggested. "You and I have lived off
Robbie for thirty years. You have had a thousand a month, which
makes three hundred and sixty thousand."

"But a third of that money belongs to Marceline!"

"Marceline has lived off Robbie since long before she was born.
Maybe Marcel never lived off him, but his *amie* and his wife did,
which is the same thing. We simply had to save Robbie if we could."

"What will we live on, Lanny? I have only a few hundred in the
bank."

"I have some money in Cannes; and we still have a lot of pictures."

"Will anybody ever buy any more pictures? There'll be nobody
in the rooms except poor artists and others who just want to look."

"I'll find a way to make money, Beauty, and I won't let you suffer. Also, Robbie will come back, no matter what happens; the family won't let him go down. I'm sorry to have acted without your
consent, but I knew that it might be a matter of minutes. Fortunes
are being wiped out wholesale."

"I don't understand it, Lanny. How can such things happen?"

"That's a long story, and we'll know more about it later. The
point is, I had to do what I could for Robbie, and I want you to tell
me that I did right."

"I suppose you had to; but, oh, how perfectly horrible! Why, nobody can ever be sure of anything again! Do you think you saved
him?"

"Our money may be only a drop in the bucket to him. The
brokers can demand any margin they think necessary. If you have
bought on a twenty-percent margin and the stocks drop that amount,
your margin is wiped out, and you have to put up another bunch of
money; and so on, as long as prices go down. Any time you aren't
there with the cash, they sell the stocks for what they will bring, and
you start life over again."

"Lanny, it's like a buzz-saw!"

"Well, thank me for keeping you out of it. And as for Robbie, from now on we can consider that we've done our duty; if he gets in again, it's his own funeral."

V

Beauty went off to her hotel to weep alone. No use going to the show rooms, ever again—there was nobody there who mattered, nobody worth exhibiting yourself to! Lanny stayed by the telephone, which rang frequently; various friends of the family calling, to impart dreadful news and exchange futile words.

The young man's thoughts were on the situation in Newcastle. Grandfather Samuel, the stern old Puritan, had never gambled in his life; would he forgive his son for gambling, and put up money to save him? Or would he say: "Whatsoever a man soweth, that shall he also reap"? Would Robbie's brothers help him—or were they too in the market? All the country club set was in, Lanny knew, and many of the businessmen, for he had heard them talking. Now they would all be scurrying, trying to beg or borrow cash. Esther's father was president of the First National, a Budd bank, and doubtless he would do all he could, but he wasn't allowed to lend money without security. Lanny thought: "Of course I might ask money from Irma." But he said to himself: "No, if that's the only way, Robbie will have to take the count."

There were plenty of other people whose thoughts turned to Irma, and who had not the same scruples. Lanny discovered her at the phone in her room, saying to one of her intimates: "But, my dear, I have no such sums in cash; my own mother is in difficulties, and maybe my uncle, and I have to help them first." Most embarrassing to have your best friends crying over the telephone, and thinking that you were stingy and selfish, you with all that fortune salted away—how could you? It wouldn't be long before they would be coming in person, weeping and having hysterics. Yes, Irma Budd was going to know there was a panic, and she couldn't keep it from making a difference in her life!

Horace Vandringham burst in at a little after one. The bright red color which he usually wore had faded to yellow, and he looked as if he had been put through a clothes-wringer. He had put up every share of stock he owned, and unless his sister and his niece would save him he was absolutely cleaned out. He didn't know what the market was doing, or what it was going to do; he had to have cash and more cash, they must go downtown to the vault with him and take out a bundle of their stocks and let him take them to the bank. They must do it now, instantly!

Fanny said: "But, Horace, you know the trustees won't allow that. It is expressly forbidden in the will."

"Well, you must make them consent. This is an emergency. For God's sake, Fanny!"

The mother called the estate office, and ordered Mr. Joseph Barnes to take the subway express and come to the hotel at once. Apparently he had been expecting the call, for he argued. The others couldn't hear what he said, but evidently he was laying down the law, for Fanny flushed as red as her brother no longer was. "Come up, Joseph; we can't discuss these matters over the phone."

Uncle Horace wanted to know how much cash Irma had. The mother produced the last statement of Slemmer, which showed only a couple of hundred thousand dollars on hand. "I can't tell what checks he has drawn," said Fanny.

"Well, get him and find out!" fumed the brother.

Slemmer still hadn't returned to Shore Acres. They got the name of his hotel, and phoned him there. He said that the bank balance was about seventy-five thousand dollars; the rest of Irma's money was in the hands of the trustees, who had reinvested it.

"Well, surely *that* money belongs to Irma!" insisted Horace to his sister. "All the income is her property, and is not subject to the provisions of the will. She has a right to sell such stocks, or hypothecate them—whatever she pleases. Let Joseph keep his nose out of it!"

VI

Lanny perceived that there was going to be a jolly row between the two families. His own attitude was that of the pioneer settler who came home to his cabin and discovered his wife in conflict with a bear, and who stood his gun by the fence and said: "Go it, woman; go it, bear!" Lanny had a ringside seat and he stayed, and learned more about the manners and morals of the rich. Money is supposed to improve the former if not the latter; but Mr. Horace Vandringham, of one of the old New York families, hurled his great bulk back and forth across the room and called his brother-in-law a yellow skunk and a dirty double-crosser, and the brother-in-law replied that he was a damned fool and crazy as a bedbug. Incidentally Mr. Joseph Barnes said something which interested Lanny: "My brother always knew that this thing was going to crash; he said it was jerry-built, and he wrote his will to provide for this very day."

They tried to get Lanny into it. Uncle Horace turned to him and inquired: "What do you say?" But Lanny just wasn't going to get in. He replied: "I notice that it hasn't occurred to any of you to ask what Irma thinks."

"Well, Irma?" demanded Uncle Horace. "Are you going to let me go to the wall?"

Lanny was learning about his wife as he went along. She was just twenty-one, and she was learning in the same way as her husband. She said: "Uncle Horace, I have been thinking it over, and I've decided that I don't like the business of gambling in stocks."

Uncle Horace gave a gulp. His face showed his surprise, and so, perhaps, did Lanny's. The new husband had been doing a great deal of talking to his wife and in her presence, but she hadn't given much sign that she was paying attention; however, the word "gambling" was Lanny's word, and certainly not Mr. Vandringham's.

"Uncle Horace," continued the girl, "I am sorry about this trouble you are in, and I'd like to help you, but it's no good if you're going back in, because it'll be the same thing all over again. So it's up to you to say whether you're willing to get out and stay out."

"But, Irma, it's my business!"

"I know, and you're free to go on with it, but not to come to me when you get caught. If I help you, it will have to be on condition that you'll find some other business but buying and selling stocks on margin."

She said it quietly, and having said it, she stopped. She was no longer the princess but the queen. "My lords and gentlemen, it has pleased us to decree," and so on. Lord Horace gulped again, and looked helplessly at his sister, who appeared as much taken aback as he was. He began arguing and pleading, and talked for quite a while, but Irma only said: "I'm not going to change, Uncle Horace."

So finally he gave up. "All right, Irma. I have no choice."

She turned to the other uncle. "How much stock have you invested from my income?"

"A little over three millions, at yesterday's prices."

"Well, let him have enough of it to protect his margins. But when the panic stops, he's going to sell and get out."

"I may not have anything left!" exclaimed Uncle Horace, with agony in his face.

"I'll stand part of the loss. Anything so long as we don't have this kind of thing again. You must get your affairs on the same basis as the estate—what stocks you own you own outright, and you can put them in our vault and forget them."

VII

When this Homeric battle was over and the two warring gentlemen had hurried out to obey their orders, Lanny said: "I've got to drive down to Newcastle and see my father. Would you like to go along?"

"Indeed I would," replied the young wife. "Anything to get out of this madhouse."

"I'm afraid we'll find another one there, only smaller," he remarked.

"Feathers" was instructed that, if the call came through, she was to tell Mr. Budd that the pair were on their way. They gave the chauffeur a chance to go and watch the ticker, and set out with

Lanny driving. He had told her what he had done for his father, and it had impressed her tremendously. He really didn't care for money after all! So now, while they were speeding up Park Avenue, she said: "You know, of course, I mean to help your father if he needs it."

"Thank you for the offer, Irma; but it's up to the Budds to look after their own."

"But maybe they can't. Maybe they're in, too."

"Maybe so; but I told you I wasn't going to have anything to do with your money——"

"That's all ancient history, Lanny. You're my husband, and your father means something to me, just as my uncle does." When he started to argue, she said: "Let's forget it. We'll see what position he's in, and what he has to say. If he needs help, I mean to give it." Again, the queen speaking!

Out on the highway that follows the shore of the Sound, Lanny said: "You know, Irma, it's odd; what you said to Uncle Horace is just what I've been getting up steam to say to Robbie."

"I never gave much thought to it before," she responded, "but this day has opened my eyes. I see what my father meant, and how wise he was. How I wish he were here now!"

She started asking questions about the stock market, and about business and finance; it was a primary-grade course which she should have had in school. "Where on earth does all the money go?" she asked, and he explained to her the nature of credit; the money didn't go anywhere, it just ceased to be. She tried earnestly to understand the strange idea, and the conversation was so different from her usual gossip, her boy and girl friends, their clothes and their games and their love affairs, that Lanny thought, perhaps this "shakedown" mightn't be such a bad thing for the idle rich after all!

She made the suggestion: "You might tell your father that you can't get help from me on any other terms than those I laid down for Uncle Horace." Lanny wondered, was she finding the exercise of power a pleasant thing? She could hardly be the daughter of her mother and her father and not find it so.

The drive to Newcastle was a matter of two or three hours

Lanny made it as fast as the law allowed, and now and then a bit faster. Passing through the towns you could tell where brokers' offices or newspaper bulletin boards were by the crowds in front. It was a little before six when they reached Newcastle, and there, too, were crowds on the main street, one in front of the brokers' and another in front of the *Chronicle* building. Lanny stopped at the former, for there was a chance that his father might be inside, and if not, he wished to phone and find out whether he was at the office or at home.

Impossible to get into the brokers'; but from the crowd outside he learned that the closing prices had still not come in. The ticker had fallen more than four hours behind, and it would be after seven when anxious customers all over the country could know what had happened to their holdings. Lanny felt pretty sure that his father wouldn't be at home under such circumstances, so he called the office, and at last, to his relief, he heard the familiar voice.

"How are you, Robbie?"

"I'm still alive—that's about all."

"You're not wiped out?"

"I have a call for more margin in the morning."

"You got word about the money I deposited?"

"I did, and I don't know how to thank you. It saved me for the moment."

"You're going to be at the office for a while? Irma and I will come right over."

VIII

How different the world had been when Lanny had driven his wife through those gates just a month ago! Now the genial and self-confident Robbie looked ten years older; he was so harassed that he couldn't make any pretense, even before the daughter of the Barneses. He told in a few brief sentences what his position was. His father had refused to lend him a dollar. All his life Robbie had insisted upon having his own way, and now he must pay the bill. There would always be a position in the firm for him and a good salary on which he could live; but oil ventures and stock gambling were equally sinful in Grandfather Samuel's eyes, and what had happened was the promised judgment of the Lord.

Robbie's brother Lawford was in the market too and, anyhow, he wouldn't have helped Robbie. The other two brothers didn't have much money, and they too were "in," but concealing the fact. Robbie had got a hundred thousand from one of his uncles, but that was a mere drop in the bucket. He had pledged all his own securities, even his Budd stock; also he had put up Lanny's securities, as Lanny had authorized. The father started to make apologies for this, but Lanny cut him short. "Forget it; we want to see you through, and we want to know what we're up against. Don't hide anything from us."

"No use trying to. I admit it's got my nerve. You and your Red friends can have your way from now on."

Robbie went to the ticker, which wasn't tired in spite of working so long overtime. The prices of the last hour were now coming in. "Things seem to be holding better," he said. The tape was giving only the final figure of the stock price. So you read: "R 6½ 6¼ 6⅜ 6½"; from this you understood that Radio was now holding its own, but you wouldn't know whether it was at 46 or 36. Robbie had been keeping track, and had notes of the various prices in which he was interested.

He showed a memorandum which his secretary had got by telephone from the *Chronicle* office some time ago. In the course of the afternoon a group of leading bankers had met in the House of Morgan and agreed to put up a fund of two hundred and forty million dollars to stabilize the market. Such was the story which would be in the afternoon papers throughout the country, and it was hoped that it would check the rush to unload. "If I, can only have a little time," said Robbie, "I can make arrangements and save the situation." Lanny must have heard a score of people saying those same words in the course of the day.

Irma spoke up: "I have promised to help Uncle Horace out of his trouble, and I want to do the same for you, Father Budd."

"I can't let you do it, Irma!" The once-proud father-in-law started to protest, but her majesty cut him short.

"Lanny heard me tell my uncle what I was willing to do, and he will explain it to you. But hadn't we better go home where we can be comfortable? There's nothing more can happen tonight, is there?"

"I was waiting to get the closing prices," said the exhausted man; "but I'll have my secretary phone them to the house."

IX

There was a duel coming, and Lanny had been bracing himself for it. He wanted to be kind, but also he wanted to have his way. He guessed that his father wouldn't have any interest in dinner—better get it over and done with, get the load off both their minds. So he left Irma and Esther to exchange notes on the sufferings of womankind in panics, and took his father into the latter's study.

"First, Robbie, I want to tell you, Beauty approves of your having that money. She agrees with me that you've done everything for us, and we owe you all we have."

"You're both going to get it back, Son, if I live."

"All I say is, forget it for the present. We love you, we want you to be happy; we both think you haven't been for a long time. What I ask you is, have I earned the right to talk to you straight?"

"Yes, Son—go ahead!"

"Neither Beauty nor I can see what you are trying to accomplish in this scramble for money. You're wrecking your health and your happiness; you're making us miserable, and Esther—the whole family. Nobody needs the money, nobody wants it; there isn't a single one of us who wouldn't vote against your plunging in the stock market, now or any time. You know that Bess would back me up if she were here. Do you think the boys would like it if they could see the state you're in tonight?"

"You've got me licked, Son. I have to take it."

"It's not a question of taking anything. It's a question of getting our lives on a sane basis, so that we can get some happiness out of life. Do you think the boys are so keen to be millionaires? Ask them which would they rather have, their father or his money? They are able-bodied, and why shouldn't they work and make their own way in the world? Do you admire the idlers at the country club so much that you want to add two more?"

"Just what is it you want of me, Son?"

"I want of you what Irma asked and got from her uncle. I want you to promise never again to buy or sell a share of stock on margin. It's the damnedest trap for human happiness that I've ever seen, and you know I've watched a lot of them up and down the Riviera. I want you to get out, and do it tomorrow morning."

"But at these prices it would mean the loss of practically everything I have."

"All right, take the loss; there isn't one of us that won't gladly pay his share, just to know that you're out, and to be able to breathe freely again, and not think maybe you're getting ready to shoot your head off."

"I'm not going to do that, Lanny."

"How could I know what you'd do—stuck down there in New York and not able to get you on the telephone? There'll be lots of businessmen jumping out of their office windows tonight, or into the river—and I'd just like to be sure that my father isn't one of them."

"You have my word as to that."

"I want more. I can't see you go down without going down too, and why should you drag me into a gambling-game that I despise? Beauty, Marceline, Esther, Bess—all of us have to be in it with you. I'll send telegrams and get up a round robin of protest if you want me to."

"I'll do what you ask, Son; you have a mortgage on me. But I can't possibly get out tomorrow; if I can hold on for a few days, until the market rallies——"

"There you go! It's what every gambler says—my luck is bound to change!"

"But, Lanny, you see what has happened—the big fellows are coming in to stabilize prices."

"Oh, my God, Robbie Budd, you tell me that—you swallow that bait for suckers! You're actually believing that a bunch of Wall Street bankers are worrying about the public? They're going to do something to help humanity for the first time in their sharks' lives?"

"But they have to save the market in order to save themselves."

"So they tell the suckers. They're in, and of course they have to stop the panic long enough to make a market in which to sell out. After they've done that, the market can go to hell and the investors along with it. For God's sake, Robbie, have as much sense as they have! Put in your selling orders for tomorrow morning, and take your losses, whatever they are. I'll gladly chip in everything I own to help you; I'll start life over again, and you do the same. We don't any of us need so much money. You go take a long rest—go hunting, the way you used to, or come over to Juan and go sailing with me. You used to be such good company when you had time to think about something else but the rascals who were trying to get the better of you. And yet you go on putting yourself in their clutches. You're just as helpless in that market as any hayseed being taken in by a shell-game at a county fair. Turn your back on it and walk away!"

"That's what you want, Son?"

"As sure as there's ground under your feet! Let Irma and me go back tonight with peace in our souls! Let Esther get some sleep, instead of pacing the floor all night in an agony of dread. If I've ever done anything in my life to earn your respect, do that favor for me! Sell at the market, and wash your hands of Wall Street!"

"All right, Son, it's a deal."

X

Driving back to the city late at night, Lanny described that scene to his wife, and remarked: "You and I are the gamblers now. If the market takes a turn upward, our elders will blame us all the rest of their lives!"

"Do you think it'll do that?"

"You might as well ask me what will happen if you toss a coin. That's just the hell of it. All we can do is hold our breath."

"Well, I'd rather put up a lot of money than go through things like this," declared Irma.

It was the opening Lanny had been waiting for. "I think we've both had enough," he said. "Let's get out of it—right away. I think about Bienvenu, with the sun shining in the patio—and not so many telephone calls. Surely this New York life can't be very good for a baby, born or unborn."

"I'll go any time you say, Lanny."

"There's a steamer for Marseille next Wednesday."

"All right. I'll tell Slemmer to get the tickets."

"And tell him we don't have to have the most expensive suite. Let's do a little economizing—at least until we know what's happened to our families and friends."

"All right." She was a well-tamed heiress at that moment. All the rich of New York were in the same mood. Wouldn't it be nice to go off on a farm somewhere, and grow our own vegetables, and have fresh milk, eggs, and butter, and live the simple life!

Lanny continued: "Robbie argues that this panic won't hurt business. He says it's just paper profits that have been lost, and that business is still sound. But that seems nonsense to me. The crowd that came up from Wall Street every night, flushed with victory and thinking it owned the world—it may have had only paper profits, but it bought real goods with them; and now it's going to stop spending, and that's bound to cause a slump."

"It's wonderful the way you understand these things," said Irma. Lanny felt a glow of pride, and didn't consider it necessary to mention that he had heard Stef and his Uncle Jesse saying these things, or that he had been reading them in *Le Populaire* and *L'Humanité*, in the *Daily Herald* of London and the *New Leader* of New York. He had been hearing them for so long that they were his own ideas now!

40

Tomorrow We'll Be Sober

I

THE next morning was Friday, and Lanny read the papers, each of which gave three or four pages to the panic and its ramifications. They reported that there had never been a day in the history of the Exchange when so many accounts had been dumped overboard; they estimated that, including the Curb market, thirty million shares of stock had changed hands in the United States and Canada. But, one and all, the editors and writers did their best to sound courageous and hopeful; they made all they could of the heroism of the House of Morgan and other banking heads who had stepped forward to save the financial structure of the country. President Hoover, Great Engineer by whom Robbie swore, issued a statement that the business of the country was fundamentally sound. The chairman of the powerful National City Bank, who had come from Europe a few days before and told the country that the market situation was healthy, now repeated his assurances, and nobody reminded him of his previous slip. Not merely the speculators, but the great substantial financial houses, the insurance companies, the investment trusts, were coming into the market this Friday morning to pick up the bargains which had been scattered along the roadway during the rout.

Lanny went downstairs to the brokers' office to get the opening prices, and it appeared that the writers were justified: the panic was over. If you wanted to sell stocks at reduced prices, you could do so, and if you had any margin left your brokers would pay it to you. Also, it was possible to communicate promptly by telephone. Robbie was at the office of his brokers in Newcastle, and Lanny called him there, and learned that he was carrying out his promise and selling; there was a tone of anguish in his voice, and once or twice he hinted for Lanny to let him off for just a day or two more, so that he might recoup some of his terrific losses. "I'm going to be out several million dollars, Son."

"Will you have a couple of hundred thousand left, do you think?"

"Yes, I'll have that."

"All right, that's fine. We can all get along."

"I'll have to ask you and Beauty to wait a while for what I owe you."

"So far as I am concerned, you can consider that I've paid for a part of what you've done for me. As for Beauty, she can learn to wear last season's dresses. Forget it, Robbie, and go and play golf before the weather gets too bad." So he talked, as cheerful as any financial writer on the New York *Times* or *Herald Tribune*. But inside him he was shivering. "Good Lord, suppose it *does* go up again!"

Irma was in the same state. Uncle Horace was begging almost on his knees for three days—only two days and a half, counting Saturday but not Sunday—in which to rehabilitate his affairs. The market was absolutely certain to rebound; all the authorities agreed about it, and to sell now was suicide, it was a crime. The head of the Vandringham clan sat before his niece with tears running down his sagging cheeks—he had lost ten or twenty pounds in the last couple of days, for he had been running about, perspiring, and had forgotten to eat and perhaps even to drink. "Irma, for God's sake!" He cursed Joseph Barnes because he was daring to misinterpret Irma's orders and not give him enough stocks to keep him safe for the two and a half days that were really necessary to the selling-out process.

Lanny tried to keep out of the fight; but when Irma asked him, he repeated what he had said. "It's a toss-up. You can be sure of this: if the market does come back, and Uncle Horace makes money, he'll be right where he was before; he'll say he was right and you were wrong, and he'll be independent of you, and he'll be in the market again, and the next time there's a smash, you'll have to go through the same scenes."

"I'll have given him fair warning, at any rate."

"No, you'll have taught him that you don't stick by what you say."

In spite of this advice Irma gave way. It was really hard for her; she was young, and didn't know the world, and her mother was putting pressure on her to save the dignity and credit of the great family whose blood she shared. It might have been different if Lanny had said: "I am sure." But how could Lanny say that? If he said it and turned out to be wrong, what would become of his standing as a husband? By God, you were in the market whether you wanted to be or not! A fish might as well talk about refusing to have anything to do with the ocean!

II

More and more clearly every hour Lanny realized this truth. When he came up at noon from watching the market, he found the family in a state of excitement. A check which Irma had written for her uncle had "bounced"; the bank had called up to inform her that she had no funds. The check had been written right after Slemmer had told her that she had seventy-five thousand dollars to her account; but Mr. Slemmer had been mistaken, said the seventeenth vice-president of the Seventh National Bank; on that date there had been only about one hundred dollars in the Irma Barnes account. (She still kept her maiden name in business affairs, it being one of power.)

So Irma had to phone Uncle Joseph and tell him to sell some of her stocks and put the money to her account; after which began a search for Slemmer. He had checked out of his hotel in the city, and he hadn't showed up at Shore Acres, and he didn't show up at either place or any other. Very soon there was a scandal, the police having to be notified, the district attorney's office sending a man up, and newspaper reporters and photographers coming to the hotel.

The most conscientious and efficient of business managers had been playing the market, like everybody else; and he had got caught, as the saying was, with his pants down. He had drawn out Irma's money in an effort to save himself, and when she had called him, he had realized that the jig was up and had disappeared. Had he tied a stone around his neck and jumped off one of the piers? It was a considerate way of behaving, but not all were considerate—they shot themselves in hotel-rooms, which was bad for business, or they jumped from windows and messed up the sidewalks. Or had Slemmer taken a train for Mexico or Canada? No one would ever know. He left behind him a wife and two children, who never heard from him—or if they did, they kept the secret. There they were, weeping hysterically, and what could Mrs. Fanny do—order them out of the estate with cold weather coming on?

That was one story out of thousands. If you were in a prominent position, like the Barneses, you couldn't help hearing many such. Your friends came in and wrung their hands and harrowed your soul —sometimes they actually didn't have money for food. You just had to give them small checks to tide them over. No matter what your resources were, you could be sure that the demands would exceed them. New York had become a torture house, and you couldn't bear to look at the faces of people in the streets. All sorts, rich and poor, had suffered, and would go on suffering for a long time. Lucky indeed you were if you had the price of steamer tickets for the warm Mediterranean route! Lucky if you could afford to have a baby, and not have to get rid of it by the abortion route—a well-traveled highway at all times.

III

Trading was gigantic in volume that Friday, but the market was orderly from bell to bell. The red-eyed and exhausted brokers could catch their breath, and let their hoarse throats heal, and eat a little food; their clerks and office workers could dig out from under the avalanche of paper which had overwhelmed them. There was a story of a broker who remembered a waste-basket under his desk, into which he had been stuffing bundles of orders which he was unable to handle. Now the storm was over, and everybody was saying: "Don't sell yet; wait for the rise; it's sure to come." There were signs of it all day Friday; the market had what the papers called "strong support," and the names of the great bankers were freely used to convince everybody that securities were as secure as ever.

But Robbie Budd was a man of his word; he had said that he would get out, and in the afternoon he reported to his son that he did not own a share of stock on margin. He had many pawned at the First National Bank of Newcastle, including Lanny's; now the only danger was that the bank might have to have more collateral for its loans. Lanny said: "Sell some of them now, Robbie—sell at market, and pay the bank off. Get yourself in the clear." Robbie said again: "Is that what you want, Son?" and the answer was flat: "It is."

There might have been sons who would have got pleasure out of giving such orders to their fathers, but Lanny was surely not among them. He had the right to do it, because part of the money was his and his mother's; but he hated the responsibility—the more so because he had so little assurance of being right. But he had acquired a sort of phobia on the subject of this stock market, dating from the hour when he had watched the frenzied brokers down in the trading-pit; they had seemed to him like the damned souls in Dante's inferno. It made no difference whether Satan had sentenced them to behave like that or whether they were slaves of their own greed—they were just as pitiable human victims.

So Robbie sold; and when he got through he said that he had re-deemed Lanny's stocks and put them back in the vault where they belonged; now he had just about enough money to repay the three hundred thousand which Lanny had handed him. Lanny said: "Give us three notes, one for Beauty, one for Marceline, and one for me, and we'll put them away. If you can ever pay them off comfortably, all right, and if not, we'll forget them. Now take my advice and go home and sleep twelve hours. And you and Esther make your plans to come and visit us at Juan after Christmas."

A funny thing, which Lanny had been gradually coming to realize. Bienvenu would now be a completely respectable place! Mr. and Mrs. Parsifal Dingle, Mr. and Mrs. Eric Vivian Pomeroy-Nielson, and Mr. and Mrs. Irma Barnes! Three sinless couples, each with a marriage certificate! And four children, and another on the way! The "faintly incestuous atmosphere" would be dissipated entirely, the strict Miss Addington would be happy, and any daughter of the Puritans could be invited for a visit! Surely the last trace of suspicion that Esther might have harbored concerning Mabel Blackless, alias Beauty Budd, must have been dispelled by her behavior during the last couple of days!

IV

One thing the panic had done: it had knocked the picture business flat. Plenty of people came to the show rooms to look at Detazes and talk about them, but not one bought anything, and few even asked the prices. Zoltan continued to play the perfect host; loving good art as he did, he was able and willing to forget the commercial side; the rooms had been paid for in advance, so those last three days might be taken as a gift to the public, a solace to those in trouble, a reminder of higher and better things than stock prices.

Lanny realized with a pang that in the turmoil of these days he had completely forgotten the existence, or whatever you might call it, of Marie de Bruyne. Suppose—just suppose—that she had been trying to communicate with him, and that he had failed to give her a chance, what would she think? Did they know about Wall Street in the spirit world? Seeing that the market held steady on Saturday, and knowing that his father was safe, Lanny decided to take another of his stepfather's appointments with the Polish medium. He went to the apartment and watched her go into the trance, and sat and waited for Tecumseh to tell him what else his *amie* might have to communicate.

But it wasn't Marie who "came through" this time; it was a strange creature who said that her name was "Roberta," and that she had gone very, very young into the spirit world, but that now she was happy here with "Madeleine." Lanny couldn't think of any Madeleine, and said so, but Roberta refused to be disconcerted, she said that she knew Lanny well, and watched him with love, and that her life-span had been short; also that Madeleine wore a white uniform here also, and that her hands were very gentle, and that she no longer felt any of the pain of the accident—a whole lot of stuff like that, and Lanny was bored, because Tecumseh was off the track, but you couldn't tell him so because Madame Zyszynski had said you must be polite to him, because if he got angry it made her ill.

So Lanny paid his two dollars, and went home and told his mother about this futile business; but to his great astonishment Beauty began to tremble, and turned pale, and exclaimed: "Oh, my God, Lanny, my God!" When he asked her what it was, she hid her face in her hands and began to weep, and said she couldn't tell him, she couldn't bear to think of it. Finally, when he insisted, she blurted out: "Lanny, you might have had a little sister! It was when you were only two years old, and I wanted her so much, and I thought it would be a little girl."

"What happened?" he kept asking, and finally she said: "I didn't dare to have her. I thought that two accidents were too much for one *amie*, and I was afraid Robbie would stop loving me. I never told him about it, but while he was in the States I went and had an abortion. You know, Lanny, you can't blame me—women do it."

"I know."

"I never knew if it would be a little girl—I don't know if it's possible to tell, the doctor never said. But I had imagined a little girl, and I was going to call her Roberta, after Robbie. And maybe it was a girl—and, oh, God, do they have souls when they aren't anything?"

"I don't know," Lanny answered. "Was there a Madeleine?"

"Madeleine was the nurse who attended me in the hospital. She was so kind, and I used to say that her hands were gentle. I brought her to Bienvenu for a while."

"And what became of her?"

"She was killed in a motor-car accident a year or two later."

"Really, that's extraordinary!" Lanny was quite awe-stricken for a while, and pictured the air around him filled almost solid with spirits. But then again came the idea of that thing called telepathy. Had the medium been dipping into Beauty's subconscious mind, pulling out memories that she would have been glad to banish? In any case, it was something to think about.

"Lanny," said the mother, "it really seems too bad to go off and leave that woman and not find out what else she can tell us."

"It does," he agreed. "I wonder if we couldn't take her with us."

"Oh, do you suppose we could afford to?"

"It oughtn't to cost so much. She can't be making a fortune at two dollars a sitting."

"Parsifal and I have been talking about it; but I feel so terrified over this panic, and Robbie losing all his money."

"Robbie's a businessman, and he'll make more. Go have a talk with Madame and find out if she'd like to come. We can put her up at the Pension Flavin, and pay her a little in addition. Offer it to her in francs—a thousand a month will sound like a fortune to her."

Lanny went away thinking: "Bienvenu will be a queer place after all!" He wondered which would be worse—sexual irregularity or the presence of disembodied spirits?

V

It was most inconvenient for Irma, not having any business manager; and just while she was getting ready for a voyage. She had to make all sorts of decisions, and Lanny had to help; so he learned a lot about the burdens of royalty. Uncle Joseph, that penurious person, had to be forced to sell more stocks on a very depressed market, in order that Irma might be able to sign checks for the many friends who were about to be turned out of their homes. Feathers had to write the checks and keep account of them—for the disagreeable experience of having one "bounce" must surely not recur.

Feathers would have to assume a lot of new duties; but she was so well terrified by her financial losses that she had dropped every trace of that great lady attitude which "social" secretaries are supposed to wear. She begged Irma not to leave her behind, and Irma agreed to take her on condition that she would become a plain ordinary secretary and do whatever she was told. There wouldn't be much social life for Irma, on account of her advancing pregnancy. The haughty Miss Featherstone, who was a college graduate and daughter of a decayed "old family," promised to make herself useful, even if she had to "mind the baby." That became one of the jokes in the establishment; any time there was something unusual for Feathers to do, it was called "minding the baby."

BETWEEN TWO WORLDS

Irma and her mother drove out to Shore Acres on Sunday. Irma wanted to say good-by to her family and friends. Lanny wasn't needed, so he went by train to Newcastle. Esther was happy, smiling through her tears; her gratitude to Lanny was touching. Robbie said nothing about the market, but Lanny knew what was in his thoughts. If he had waited until Saturday morning he might have got more than he got on Friday! If there was another rise on Monday, he would be wishing he had waited until that day. Uncle Horace had been allowed to wait—why not Robbie? But he would be a good sport and not say it to his son. That book was closed, and Robbie would forget his dream of becoming a really rich man; at least, he would forget it for a while.

Lanny went to say good-by to his grandfather, who was failing, and who said: "My boy, you will probably not see me again in this world." Lanny would have liked to tell him about his research into the next one, but he knew that it wasn't entirely orthodox, and so wouldn't please the president of Budd Gunmakers. And anyhow, it might be only telepathy! But Lanny thought, what a funny thing; the good Christians were all taught to believe that your soul survived, and yet they ridiculed the suggestion that after a soul had got settled in the beyond, it might have a desire to get in touch with those whom it had left behind. Didn't they really believe what their church taught them? Or did they think that the souls would forget everything? If a soul did forget, what would be left of it?

Lanny's steamer was making one of those midnight sailings; and it happened that Phyllis Gracyn's new play was to open on that evening. Lanny said to his father: "You remember the last time we sailed—how we went to see Gracyn?" December of 1918, nearly eleven years ago; right after the actress had jilted Lanny, and he was feeling that he had made a mess of his life. Now he was supposed to be sitting on the top of the world, and if it turned out to be the top of a volcano, he was still expected to enjoy it. Irma was intensely curious about Gracyn, and wanted to see how she made love—which of course she would have to do in any play. Did Irma expect to get points from her? Anyhow, they were going to the opening; and Lanny said, wouldn't Robbie and Esther drive down and join them?

They'd have dinner at the hotel, and go to the show, and thence to the steamer, and Robbie and Esther could spend the night in New York and drive home in the morning.

Esther had always refused to see the actress whom she considered the seductress of her stepson. But now she had decided that she mustn't be so strait-laced, she must try to get along with the people in her world; show her gratitude to her stepson, and do what she could to divert her husband's mind from his troubles. She agreed to come, and Lanny, knowing it was an effort, gave her a kiss and called her a good sport.

VI

So many interesting and important things in New York, and Lanny had missed them, on account of the Detaze show, and Irma and her smart friends, and the panic, and the spirits! But he didn't want to leave without seeing the great art collection at the Metropolitan. Zoltan said it was an "old fogy sort of place," but it had a few new things—and Lanny hadn't seen the old ones for eleven years. Zoltan couldn't go because he had the job of getting all the pictures packed—they were going on the same steamer to Marseille. Irma couldn't go to the museum, because she had ordered some dresses which she had to pay for, and they had to be fitted. Lanny went alone, and spent a happy morning looking at Egyptian mummies, Greek sculpture, and early American painting. He could never get through such a place as this, because he would run into something that held him too long.

Having promised Irma to be back for lunch, he rode down on a Fifth Avenue bus. He passed one of the great hotels which had a brokers' office on the ground floor, and there was a crowd of the sort which had become familiar. He thought: "Good Lord, what is happening now?" Lanny was a natural-born optimist, but he had to be a "bear" on this market for the sake of his reputation with all three of his families. On the other hand, if it was another slump, that too was serious, for this was the day when Uncle Joseph was scheduled to be selling out.

Lanny couldn't wait to reach his own hotel, but hopped off the bus and joined the crowd. One glance was enough—he knew by the faces that it was another panic! The excited people on the edge of the crowd were saying that this time was worse than Thursday; the bottom had dropped clean out from under the market. Every figure on the Translux showed a drop, and the ticker was again way behind.

Lanny took a taxi to his hotel, and there were Fanny and her brother; tears streaming down Uncle Horace's flabby cheeks, and his hands shaking as if he had the palsy. "Irma, for God's sake, it means everything I have in this world!"

"I gave you your chance," the girl was saying. "I begged you to get out. Father Budd did so, and he's all right; but you had to hold on, you were the one that knew all about it—and how could I fight you?"

"But, Irma, if I can only hold on through today——"

"I know—one day, and then one more day. But I'm not going to dump any more stocks at panic prices."

"You don't have to sell them, Irma; it's enough if you deposit them with the brokers."

"I know; and when the market drops again, I deposit more."

Lanny wanted to say: "Stand firm, Irma." But he saw that he didn't have to; she was remembering the things he had explained to her on the drive to Newcastle. She'd be quite a businesswoman before she got through.

Uncle Horace's pleading was in vain. "You had your chance; you had what you asked for." Such was her majesty's decision.

The burly and once so energetic man sank into a chair with his bald head in his hands. "What is going to become of me?"

"You don't have to worry, Uncle Horace. You know I'll always take care of you. I'll set you up in some other business; but stock-gambling is out, so far as my money is concerned."

So that was the end of one "market operator." Lanny had learned enough about New York to imagine the rest. Horace Vandringham would become an insurance broker, and peddle policies to Irma's friends; if he failed at that, he would become one of those querulous old folks at Shore Acres. Already there were too many of them, and this panic, or series of panics, would increase the number; Lanny remarked that the place would become another Hampton Court—and when Irma asked what that was, he told her about the aged servants of the British royal family, who lived out their appointed days looking out upon beautiful formal gardens.

Lanny hadn't been there, and couldn't say what they talked about, but he knew how it would be with the pensioners at Shore Acres. Thursday's panic had filled New York with people who had formerly boasted of how much they had gained, and were now almost as proud of their heavy losses. "Cleaned me out!" you would hear one exclaim. "Gutted me like a fish! I lost half a million that first day!" Now there would be a new lot, ready to chime in: "It was Monday that finished me. I played the market for a comeback, and I saw three million blow away in an hour!" As with fish stories, the biggest fortunes got away; and contrary to the laws of perspective, the farther they receded into the distance the bigger they grew.

VII

All that day the tormented city was in an uproar. It had been as Lanny had foretold—the "big fellows" had "protected the market" just long enough to get out from under. They had done their unloading on Friday and Saturday, and now, on Monday, there was nobody to buy anything. It was like the collapse of a house of cards. General Electric, the greatest electrical manufacturing concern in the country, lost 47 points that day; Western Union lost 39; Telephone, which Robbie had bought at 287½, closed the day at 232. The exhausted brokers and clerks and messengers and secretaries and bookkeepers, who had been working day and night over the weekend, now faced a sixteen-million-share day, breaking all records, surpassing all nightmares. It was estimated that the value of securities in the United States shrank fourteen billions of dollars in five hours; and it wasn't the end.

There was nothing that Irma or Lanny could do about it. A dreadful world to be in, but they hadn't made it and couldn't change it. Lanny had no more money to give, and Irma had to choose between giving away all she had or hardening her heart and closing her purse. Her friends didn't show up very well in this crisis; they wanted all they could get, and it was more than Irma owned. No use blaming them too much; they were people who had never learned to do any useful thing in their lives, and the prospect of being without money broke their nerve. Lanny, whose money had come too easily, was harsh in his thoughts of them; he remembered the conversations he had been forced to listen to, the derision with which his words of caution had been greeted. Also he remembered the unborn baby, and he said: "Let's take a drive and get away from the telephone."

Feathers assumed the duty of answering calls, and Lanny took the car and drove his wife up the valley of the Croton River to the great dam. In the lowlands the autumn foliage was still on the trees, and it was a sight you didn't see on the Riviera. Lanny tried to interest her in nature, but it wasn't an easy feat of the mind. What was she going to do about that huge country place? Would she be able to keep it up if her stocks went on tumbling to nothing? Would there continue to be dividends? Lanny wasn't sure.

They came to a swanky roadhouse, and went inside and had dinner. In between the numbers of the floor-show there were bulletins about the end of the world. Reports came over the radio; the ticker was hopelessly behind, but the bond ticker gave samples of the closing prices, and some people listened and went out without dining, because what they had in their pockets was all they had in the world.

Lanny said: "Let's not go back to the hotel tonight. You'll just get yourself in for a lot of grief."

"Oh, I have so many things to attend to before we sail!"

"Attend to them by mail after you get to Juan. Most of them will have settled themselves before that."

She gave way, and they drove over to the Hudson, and up to one of the towns where there was a good hotel. "They'll think we're not married, because we have no baggage, Lanny." He answered that they wouldn't send them to jail. He wrote "Mr. and Mrs. L. P. Budd," and was glad that the name was obscure.

Irma phoned to her secretary and learned that her mother had taken Uncle Horace to Shore Acres. "I suppose she's afraid he'll shoot his head off," Irma said to her husband. "I fear she'll never forgive me for having let him down. Do you think I could have saved him, Lanny?"

"Look at the market," he answered. "One might as well try to guess about a bolt of lightning."

He called Robbie at his home—and this time Robbie was there. "Well, what do you think of it?"

"You win," was the father's answer.

"What are you doing?"

"Esther and I are playing bridge with Jane and Tony—" that was Esther's sister and her husband. "We have lost a couple of dollars and are worried."

Lanny didn't say: "Aren't you glad you're out?" He said: "Well, see you Wednesday. I'm going to keep Irma on the road till then."

VIII

The New York papers leave the city soon after midnight and you can have them on your breakfast table if you are anywhere within a couple of hundred miles. So Lanny and Irma sat up in bed and read three or four pages of details about the dreadful events of the day before. Pleasant indeed to be comfortable while you learn about other people's misery—provided, of course, that you are without heart. Lanny, carrying that handicap, felt all his Red impulses reviving; he put on the old phonograph record, and heard his Uncle Jesse declaring that it was the downfall of the capitalist world. Very monotonous, the scratching of that old record; one had to remind oneself that a statement didn't cease to be true when it became trite.

The papers agreed that this was a "rich man's panic." The big investors, the speculators, had been hit, and many of them knocked flat. Lanny could believe it; but he knew also that millions of little people had been in that market, and had been the first to be swept away. Anyhow, when the big fellows were suffering, it didn't take them long to pass it on to others. Lanny knew that when the rich stopped buying luxuries the salesclerks would lose their jobs, and before long the workers who made the goods would be turned off also.

If Irma's income dropped, wouldn't the pensioners at Shore Acres suffer? Wouldn't some of the servants have to be turned out? It was clear to his mind that a great business recession must be on the way, and he decided to warn his father about it. This time Robbie would listen!

Lanny persuaded his wife to go on driving. What could they do in New York? Stand outside the brokers' offices and watch the tortured faces? He had seen enough of them to last him the rest of his life. Or go up to their rooms in the Ritzy-Waldorf and hear their friends crying over the telephone? Tell them for the hundredth time that Irma had very little cash, that her business manager had absconded, that her estate was tied up, that she had to help her mother and her uncle and many others? Here was New York state, which Lanny had never seen, and the sun was shining on it, the tang of autumn in the air and every turn of the winding roads a picture for a lover of art and nature. Lanny poured out his treasures of understanding and love, and beguiled his young bride farther from the great massacre of human hopes.

IX

More than once during the cruise of the *Bessie Budd* Irma had said: "I wonder if we are really married." Each time Lanny had answered: "We'll do it again some day." It might be that if it ever came to a test some stern English judge would decide that they had not been bona fide passengers of the *Plymouth Girl*, but had been perpetrating a fraud upon the Archbishop of Canterbury. More than once during their sojourn in New York Lanny had thought of suggesting another marriage; but the trouble lay with Irma's so notorious name. If they were to have another ceremony, who would believe that they had been married before? And what a juicy morsel for the "tabs" and the radio scandal-mongers!

But now the people they knew were so busy with the panic that they wouldn't pay any attention to a hundred marriages. Lanny said: "I hear it's very easy to get married in Jersey. How about crossing over there and hunting up a preacher?"

"Oh, Lanny, should we dare?"

"We can find some small village where there wouldn't be reporters. Anyhow, let's have a look."

They crossed the Hudson by the Poughkeepsie bridge and drove
south. When the road signs told them that it was the state of New
Jersey, they turned back into the well-wooded hills and began looking for a village of sufficiently humble appearance. The first one
had no church, and when they found one with a church it had no
preacher. At last, however, they found an aged Methodist minister
about whom it seemed a safe guess that he had never been in a night
club or listened to radio gossip; he was a bit tottery and his voice
quavered, but his white-haired wife was spry, and she hurried next
door for a neighbor to serve as the second witness. The three of
them were so kind and sweet that the young people were embarrassed, as if they were perpetrating another fraud.

However, it was all right; this was the sweet land of liberty, and
if you wanted to get married in every state of the Union, it was your
privilege. In this particular state there were no banns and no bars;
you weren't asked anything about your parents' consent, your religious faith, the state of your health, or even whether you were sane.
All you had to give was your name, which might be fictitious, and
your address, which might be the same, and your age, which frequently was. These were duly noted in a record book, and signed by
the preacher and the witnesses, who could see that this was a rich
young couple, but gave no sign of ever having heard the name Irma
Barnes.

The old gentleman went to a clothes closet and got out his best
frock-coat, badly in need of brushing, and put it on. He took up the
printed word of God, which he held as a sort of fetish, though he
didn't need to consult it. He took his stand in front of them, coughed
once or twice, and proceeded in a very solemn tone to invoke the
blessings of Almighty God upon what he was about to do; then he
did it, and after he had done it he wrote a certificate and gave it to
Irma for her future protection. She took the document quickly and
stepped back, because she had heard somewhere that it was the custom for the preacher to kiss the bride and she didn't want it. Lanny

provided a diversion in the shape of a ten-dollar bill, probably the largest sum the man had ever received for such a service during his long pastoral career. The two young people gave their thanks, said their hurried farewells, and made their escape. "What a funny thing that that should make us husband and wife!" mused Irma.

X

When lunchtime came they stopped in a town, and in front of a newspaper office was a bulletin board, from which they got reports of the morning's events in Wall Street. This Tuesday, the twenty-ninth, proved to be the worst of all. Apparently the entire stock-owning population of the United States was telegraphing or telephoning orders to sell at the market, and Europe and the rest of the world were joining in. The slaughter of prices affected the bond market, the grain market, even real estate; bankrupted people had to have cash, no matter at what price. The horrified brokers on the trading-floor could hardly credit what they heard. There was a story of one who was trying to dispose of a block of sewing-machine stock which had been selling at more than 40; he was calling for a bid, and a messenger boy had the bright idea to offer one dollar, and he got the stock. It had been sold "at the market."

That afternoon Lanny was driving his wife through the lovely scenery of the Catskill mountains. The air was exhilarating; they got out and walked in the sunshine, and sat for a while listening to the babble of a mountain stream. Irma developed a real appetite, and that was a good thing for the expected baby, which she was beginning to feel.

At dusk they drove into a town, and in the lobby of the hotel sat and listened to a radio telling of the wreckage of men's fortunes that day. Another record-breaker—seventeen million shares on one exchange. The ticker was again hopelessly behind, but the radio gave sample prices, from which it appeared that the entire list of United States stocks had lost nearly half their value. After dinner, they listened again, along with a miscellaneous crowd—traveling-salesmen, hunters, farmers, small-town merchants—who talked freely about their troubles. Misery loves company, and men took a perverted kind of pride in telling of their ruin. They had swallowed the bait which Wall Street had fed to them through newspapers and radios and "market reports"; they had refused to "sell America short," and now it was they who had been "sold down the river."

This was the real America, of which Lanny hadn't seen very much. Nobody shed tears—they preferred making "wisecracks." Lanny was interested to note that every last man took it for granted that stocks would come back; what fortunes would be made by the lucky ones who were able to hold on for a few days!

Presently one of the "newscasters" came on the air: a pert, aggressive gentleman, speaking with a swift staccato style; everything was "Flash," and there was a clicking of a telegraph key to suggest that he was getting it right off the wire. He told about the market crash, the prices, and who was said to be down and out, and what bears had managed to coast on top of the avalanche. Then came news of café society, the gossip of personalities which had made the man famous. "Flash! Your reporter is informed that Mr. and Mrs. Lanny Budd are expecting a little bundle from heaven some time next March. They were married in June—no time wasted. She is Irma Barnes, the glamour girl of Broadway last season. It is possible that the glamour will need polishing up after the events of the past five days. Irma's father, the great J. Paramount Barnes, took no chances with his holding companies, but put his money into blue chips. Hold onto them, Irma, they'll be worth something some day!"

There sat the glamour girl and her glamour boy, blushing and stealing uneasy glances at the people in the crowded lobby. But nobody looked at them; nobody had looked at the hotel register; nobody was thinking about anything but the closing prices—and, besides, it couldn't have occurred to them as a possibility that the greatest of café celebrities might be sitting alongside them in this remote hotel.

XI

In the morning the young couple had the papers, and read the details of that desolating day. American Telephone and Telegraph, the security upon which Robbie Budd had staked his fortunes, was down eighty-three points from the price that he had paid. Lanny, who had cast in his lot with the bears, need never again worry about his standing as a Wall Street authority! "I believe I've lost half my money," said Irma. He told her to cheer up; they would survive.

She wanted to see her mother before sailing, so they drove back to the city and out to Shore Acres. They found Uncle Horace pretty well calmed down. He no longer interrupted Lanny when he spoke, but listened politely. He had to admit that he was glad he hadn't been in that market; but, oh, if only Irma would let him get in *now*, what a killing he and she could make! Poor derelict, he would sit in the brokers' offices and watch the prices, read the gossip of the "Street," make his predictions, and see himself fail over and over again; for that Great Bull Market went on sinking, sinking —like one of those Spanish bulls when the matador has pierced him through the heart, and he stands rocking unsteadily, his great head drooping inch by inch.

Fanny Barnes wept, and agreed to forgive her daughter, and the daughter promised to come home before too long. All the dependents shed dutiful tears as the fortunate young couple drove away. Their belongings were packed for them, and a truckload of baggage was taken to the steamer. Robbie and Esther arrived, and father and son went down to the brokers' office and joined the customers, sitting with their hats tilted back on their heads and watching the Translux, far behind after another day of turmoil. But prices were firmer, and once more the market authorities were emerging from their cyclone cellars; once more leading bankers and statesmen were assuring the American people that business conditions were fundamentally all right. The Great Engineer said it, and "John D." and his son told the world that they were buying sound securities. The rest of the people would have felt better if they had had any means of knowing which securities these were; also if they had had the Rockefellers' money to buy with.

Mr. Dingle, being uninterested in worldly shows, had assumed the duty of getting Madame Zyszynski to the steamer. She had been booked in the second cabin, where she would feel more comfortable, along with Irma's maid. Lanny hoped that the spirits would take note and not be left behind. He had to stop and remind his materialistic self that spirits do not exist in space—and, anyhow, maybe they are just telepathy! Funny thing, if the subconscious mind was playing games like that, creating imaginary beings, fictional or historical, or a combination of both! The lover of art reminded himself that that was what all great artists did, and it was called genius. Maybe Madame was some kind of genius; or maybe it was Lanny's own mind which was doing the tricks. For some reason it hadn't got properly harnessed up for creative labor, like Kurt's and Rick's. Why that was, Lanny didn't know; but Zoltan said: "You are too comfortable, my boy!"

They had dinner at the hotel, a party of six: Lanny and his wife, Robbie and his, and Zoltan escorting Beauty. Robbie and the three ladies were driven to the theater in Irma's car, and after that the chauffeur would go to the hotel and take the secretary and the maid to the steamer, and then return to the theater for the party, and afterward drive the car back to Shore Acres. Lanny and Zoltan chose to stroll to the theater, and have a chance for a good-by chat. Zoltan was sailing for England in a few days, to see if anybody there would buy pictures; he had had word from two of his patrons in New York that they would be glad to sell the old masters which they had purchased. Art prices were on the way down, and Lanny would have to learn a new schedule!

XII

Phyllis Gracyn, alias Pillwiggle, was starring in *The Golden Lure*, a drama in three acts. It might have been the story of Irma Barnes when she was seventeen, a girl in school, naïve and trusting—if Irma ever had been that. Her father was a traction magnate, playing the political game in the large-scale crooked style. He was a widower and had a mistress, a golden blonde, and both magnate and mistress were tied in a net of intrigue, with a corrupt district attorney trying to get the magnate on a charge that would have sent him to Sing Sing. The stage Irma learned about the mistress, Gracyn, and went to her, asking her help in saving the father. The stage Irma thought that the stage Gracyn really loved the father, but she didn't, she had been planted there to get evidence on him. But of course she had a heart of gold, and was so touched by the daughter's plea that she told the stage Irma a secret which would save the father, and helped the stage Irma to foil the crooked district attorney in a sensational third act.

Of course it was "hokum" of the crudest sort. But Broadway had a technique for dressing up what it knew was hokum in modern costume, flavoring it with a dash of cynicism, sprinkling it liberally with wisecracks, and building it up to what was called "the big punch." There was a large and fashionable audience; some people still had money for theater tickets—or was the house mostly "paper"? There were some references to the stock market, doubtless put in at the last moment, and these got a great "hand." Gracyn carried off the honors; she wasn't the old-style slinky vamp, but the gay and smart kind that you met in the night clubs nowadays. Evidently the play was a "hit," and she would have a chance to recoup her financial losses. The real Irma didn't recognize her stage self or her father, but she thought that Gracyn was "a darling," and whispered to Lanny that she didn't mind his having been in love with her—but a long time ago, and there must be no more of it!

They were driven to the Hudson River pier and boarded the great steamer. There was music and laughter and singing—people were always a little "high" at that hour of the evening. Several of Irma's young friends had come, and they were higher. When the time came for the partings, those who were sailing threw down rolls of colored paper tape, holding one end, so that they made lines connecting them with the friends on shore. When the steamer was warped from the pier these lines were broken, and all felt sad. You stood waving and shouting, but mostly you couldn't make the right person hear you. The Budds all had tears in their eyes, for they had been through strenuous hours. Beauty had rarely been so happy, for at the last moment Esther had pressed her hand and said: "I have misunderstood you all my life, and I am sorry." Another blond mistress with a heart of gold!

Out in the river you could tell what had been happening in the Wall Street district, for at that late hour every window in every building was ablaze with light, and the same was true for many of the midtown office buildings. If you didn't know what was going on inside, it was a lovely spectacle, a dream city rising from the sea. Lanny and Irma watched it fade into the distance. Behind them, in the saloon, a party of young people were pounding the piano and singing college songs, hurling defiance at all panics:

> "For tonight we'll merry, merry be,
> For tonight we'll merry, merry be,
> For tonight we'll merry, merry be;
> Tomorrow we'll be sober."

Lanny and Irma moved over to the starboard side. There was Bedloe's Island with the Statue of Liberty. Lanny remembered how he had stood by the rail of the ship eleven years ago and watched the great tall lady at this same late hour. She had come from France, and he had been going home, and she had waved her bright torch as a sign of greeting. Now he was going again, and she waved it still more vigorously; she was singing: "I've been drunk for a long, long time—tomorrow I'll be sober!"

BOOKS BY UPTON SINCLAIR

WORLD'S END

THE JOURNAL OF ARTHUR STIRLING

MANASSAS, A NOVEL OF THE CIVIL WAR

THE JUNGLE

THE OVERMAN

THE MILLENNIUM

THE METROPOLIS

THE MONEYCHANGERS

SAMUEL, THE SEEKER

THE FASTING CURE

LOVE'S PILGRIMAGE

SYLVIA

SYLVIA'S MARRIAGE

DAMAGED GOODS

THE CRY FOR JUSTICE

THE PROFITS OF RELIGION

KING COAL, A NOVEL OF THE COLORADO
    STRIKE

JIMMIE HIGGINS

THE BRASS CHECK

100%—THE STORY OF A PATRIOT

THEY CALL ME CARPENTER

THE BOOK OF LIFE

THE GOOSE-STEP—A STUDY OF AMERICAN
    EDUCATION

THE GOSLINGS—A STUDY OF THE AMERI-
    CAN SCHOOLS

MAMMONART

LETTERS TO JUDD

THE SPOKESMAN'S SECRETARY

OIL!

MONEY WRITES!

BOSTON

MOUNTAIN CITY

MENTAL RADIO

ROMAN HOLIDAY

THE WET PARADE

AMERICAN OUTPOST

UPTON SINCLAIR PRESENTS WILLIAM FOX

THE WAY OUT: WHAT LIES AHEAD FOR
    AMERICA

I, GOVERNOR OF CALIFORNIA

THE EPIC PLAN FOR CALIFORNIA

I, CANDIDATE FOR GOVERNOR AND HOW
    I GOT LICKED

WHAT GOD MEANS TO ME: AN ATTEMPT
    AT A WORKING RELIGION

PLAYS OF PROTEST

CO-OP: A NOVEL OF LIVING TOGETHER

THE GNOMOBILE

NO PASARAN!

THE FLIVVER KING

OUR LADY

LITTLE STEEL

YOUR MILLION DOLLARS

EXPECT NO PEACE

Plays

PRINCE HAGEN

THE NATUREWOMAN

THE SECOND STORY MAN

THE MACHINE

THE POT-BOILER

HELL

SINGING JAILBIRDS

BILL PORTER

OIL! (DRAMATIZATION)

MARIE ANTOINETTE